The courtroom cast includes:

Jessica Roux: A vixen who lived off the benefits from her relationships with prominent men. She became Lew Hagerman's nemesis.

Lew Hagerman: An ex-senator and multimillionaire "King of the Comstock" mine. He was a formidable adversary, even for the wily "devil's daughter."

Mark Trumbull: An attorney and former judge, he yielded to an attraction he could neither comprehend nor withstand in defending Jessica Roux.

Malvinia Lawes: A Negro seamstress, the confidante of many women in San Francisco society and a power in the city's underworld. She would become Jessica's friend and protector.

"This is the perfect book to put into the hands of the patron heard to complain, 'They just don't write novels like they used to.' Mr. Lipsky does, and we recommend his book." —*Library Journal*

THE DEVIL'S DAUGHTER was originally published by Meredith Press.

Eleazar Lipsky

The Devil's Daughter

PUBLISHED BY POCKET BOOKS NEW YORK

THE DEVIL'S DAUGHTER

Meredith Press edition published August, 1969

Pocket Book edition published August, 1970

This *Pocket Book* edition includes every word
contained in the original, higher-priced edition. It is printed
from brand-new plates made from completely reset, clear, easy-to-read
type. *Pocket Book* editions are published by Pocket Books, a division
of Simon & Schuster, Inc., 630 Fifth Avenue, New York, N.Y. 10020.
Trademarks registered in the United States and other countries.

L

To Suzanne and Jeanne

The
Devil's
Daughter

status. "Is that fool girl Jessie here?", she boomed.

Finch glanced at a pair of empty seats. "No, Auntie," he replied.

Part One

Chapter One

On a clear day in September, the Honorable Lew Hagerman, formerly United States Senator of Nevada, stepped out of the great cool hall of the Bank of the Anglo-Pacific Company into the confusion of Sansome Street.

A stout, florid man crossed the street with an air of determination. He planted himself in Hagerman's path and raised his hat. He said, "My card."

Hagerman made an impatient gesture. "Not now, sir!" He saw an obstinate expression and yielded ungraciously. The card said that Mr. Horatio Pettibone resided at the Kimball Hotel in Eddy Street. He was associated with the San Francisco *Crusader* and took General Commissions. "Well, Mr. Pettibone," Hagerman said, "I do all my business in the bank. If you'll excuse me?" He set off with quick small steps. The stranger kept pace. "Might we talk a moment?"

Hagerman stopped. "What about, sir?"

"Miss Roux."

"You're the feller who's giving her ideas?" Hagerman recognized the accent of Australia. It was familiar enough. Thirty years earlier, San Francisco had been the Mecca for escapees from that British penal colony. "What's on her mind now?"

"She asked me to present an order." Pettibone took a paper from a billfold with exquisite care. "I think you might like to honor this, sir?"

"No, no, no, no! Damn it! I've got this blood pressure. Bring it around tomorrow and I'll look it over." The staid, squat banker scurried on. An elegant Prince Albert flapped over a small behind. Pettibone followed.

"Might I call on you tonight?"

"I'm at the opera with my family. See me tomorrow."

"But tomorrow you're off to New York."

Hagerman paused and glared. "How do you know? What

3

business is that of yours? Keep your snout out of my affairs. And tell that vexatious bitch to mind her step."

"Look here, sir!" Pettibone raised his voice. "You're attracting attention. I sent three telegrams to Virginia City. Four to Beaufort. You've ignored every attempt I've made for a quiet conversation. If you won't see me one place, you may see me another, but see me you shall, for I will be heard. This situation isn't my idea, or Miss Roux's, sir, it's entirely yours. Kindly examine the order, and give me your answer. I shall know what to do."

Clouds of sand and dust were blowing from the surrounding hills. Hagerman mastered his irritation with an effort. "Let's see it," he agreed. "But I'm in a rush. Come on." He hurried along the crowded street, squinting at the paper. The crush of traffic, the bawling of hansom cab drivers, the din and shoving made concentration difficult. He paused abruptly. "Is this your idea?" he shouted, brandishing the paper.

The stout man stood his ground. "It's no use putting it on me, Senator. I'm acting on instructions. I cannot understand such shabby behavior from a man of your standing. It's not quality."

Hagerman did a little jig of rage. "Miss Roux is a damn bitch! A filthy-skirted trollop. Five hundred dollars! Outrageous! Why should I pay her another nickel? For what?"

"I think you know," Pettibone retorted, taken aback by the outburst. "Come, Senator. Will you honor the order?"

"Not this, nor any other. You send the woman around," Hagerman said, "and I'll tell her that myself. She knows where I am."

"She's afraid of you," Pettibone said. "You've threatened her life."

"Is that what she says?"

"Isn't it true?"

Hagerman threw back his head and laughed derisively. "That woman's not afraid of the devil. Certainly not me. I'm a good Johnny, a real softy. Here!" He thrust back the paper which called on him to pay a sum of money to the account of Miss Jessica Roux of 18 Wisteria Place, City of San Francisco, State of California. It was an imitation of a banker's draft written in a familiar stilted script in green ink. "I'm going east tomorrow," he said. "Let her come around this evening before I leave the hotel. Now, excuse me, sir."

Pettibone blocked the way. "But you cannot go east tomor-

4

row, Senator. You really cannot until you have settled with Miss Roux. Not if you are wise."

"What's that you say? Eh? Eh?"

"I'm trying to avoid a scandal! Really, sir! I do not know how long I can control the situation. It won't wash, Senator."

A glint of red appeared in the sandy-lidded eyes. "I don't know what she thinks she's doing," Hagerman said in a cold voice, "but if there's any idea I'll stand for a shakedown—"

Pettibone blustered, "If you think I can be intimidated—"

Hagerman's mood of anger collapsed as quickly as it had flared. "Pennington, or whatever your name is, Pennington . . . Pendleton . . ."

"Pettibone!"

"Pettibone, then!" Hagerman went on more reasonably, "I'm being badgered by more damn emissaries than I can count. I'm not a well man and I sometimes lose my patience. What's your interest in Jessie Roux?"

"I'm determined to see that she gets justice!" Pettibone said. "I think she's being treated shabbily. Very shabbily, sir!"

"Justice?" Hagerman said incredulously. "What's your rate for justice? Half? Or something else?" Grinning coarsely, he made an obscene suggestion.

"If Jessie Roux thinks she can gouge the old man," the banker said with hard humor, "let her try. She could always get around me in her own fair person. She don't need a go-between. Try picking your clients in Pacific Street."

"Really, Senator! That's hardly becoming. If I were you, I'd think twice. Good day, sir! I shall convey your message!" Pettibone raised his hat and strode off. Hagerman waited at the curb to let a brewery cart pass, and then anxiety settled.

"Oh, damn this prostate!" he exclaimed. He hurried on toward Market Street. Men raised their hats. Women bowed and smiled. He saw no one, paid attention to nothing, until finally he stood at Market Street, facing one of his many business enterprises—the Imperial House.

The establishment was the wonder of San Francisco. It was a gorgeous eight-story structure, topped by copper roofing of verdigris green. Hundreds of bay windows, designed in that foggy city to catch the sun, soared high over the fortress walls of brick and stone. It had gone up extravagantly long before the population could support so costly an enterprise.

Its designer, a celebrated eastern architect, had borrowed liberally from motifs of the Imperial Palace in Vienna—cornices, balconies, gargoyles, and majestic ornamentation—hence its name, Imperial House. It towered over the surrounding wood structures—warehouses, stores, office buildings, restaurants, dwellings. A clanging of bells rang out. Streetcars hitched in series rumbled through a concourse of carriages and wagons of every sort—gigs and four-wheelers, victorias, broughams, landaus, full-bodied double wagons, sociables and charabancs, wagonettes, and even a governess' cart. Hagerman's expert eye caught scores of models manufactured in his own carriage works. Chinese in blue jackets crossed the street carrying shoulder yokes. Two women rode past sidesaddle toward a riding academy on Mission Street. Nestling beside the vast Imperial House was an older but still elegant hotel, the Camden, connected by a bridge that vaulted Aldus Street.

He crossed through the heavy traffic, and entered the lobby of the Imperial House.

"Oh, Lew? Can I see you inside?" Captain Philip Webster, a portly man who wore dundrearies like a badge of high office, had been waiting at the entrance.

Moments later, Hagerman found himself in his manager's office. He started a cigar with the resentful thought that everything was going wrong that day. He should have taken the familiar evasive path through the Camden across the enclosed bridge to the Imperial. Ordinarily he enjoyed this rite of accustomed passage. He loved Imperial House with its Byzantine splendor and amusing daily problems. Everything sybaritic and luxury-loving, infantile, and self-indulgent in him responded to its princely demands. But not this day, he thought irritably. Captain Webster was not only his manager. He was his brother-in-law and this was an added vexation.

"Get on with it!" he exclaimed, conscious of discomfort. "Before I piss down my leg!"

Webster winced at the coarse expression. He began a litany of complaints that ranged from the dishonesty of plumbers to mounting deficits and presented confidential records. Hagerman looked up in shock. "Five cents a pound for beef?" he squealed. He was reminded that these prices were charged by his own company—Pacific Meat Packing Houses. A suggestion to let other houses bid for the business of the hotel was rejected. "That abattoir's a good proposition. I'm not writing anything off! Anything else?"

Webster opened his mouth, then changed his mind and raised another topic. "If you'd do something about these personal accounts, Lew!" he grumbled. "I wouldn't mind letting 'em use the rooms on the top floor. Business is terrible and those suites are empty in any case. But those free-loaders are running up bills I can't stand. Liquor, food, services. I'm even cashing worthless checks. Why must I carry those deadbeats?"

Hagerman frowned at the list. Joe Kirby was a good friend, a reporter of the old Territorial *Enterprise* down on his luck. Miss Babs Littleton had been a charming soubrette; still gallant but penniless. Luke Cotrell had run through three fortunes before he hit bad luck and old age. Irene and Florrie—well, those were sweet memories. They all went back, he thought helplessly, they were the old bunch. How could this nail-paring bookkeeper be made to understand these obligations? All had been there in those first glorious times when the city was young, when they all were in it together. "These people can't pay," he said. "I don't want 'em hounded."

"That last item can pay!" Webster said warmly. "I can't stand a man who won't pay his bills."

The item was months old. "Justice Sickels? You didn't send him a demand letter?" Hagerman asked sharply.

Webster had indeed written off to Washington for settlement of the account. "I must say," he added, aggrieved, "I got back a high-handed reply. Terribly unbecoming language for a judge."

"Shouldn't wonder," Hagerman said. "You're questioning an arbitrary man. He takes a poor view of that."

"What can I do?" Webster asked helplessly.

"I wouldn't press the man," Hagerman decided. "If he's not handled with tact, he can be vindictive. And besides"—a splintery grin was suddenly attractive—"I'll take it away. The man will draw to inside straights. Let me have that statement."

"It's no way to run a hotel," Webster protested. "I don't get it, Lew! I just don't understand!"

"Then don't meddle!" Hagerman said impatiently, reflecting that the complexities were beyond explanation. John Haddam Sickels was not only an Associate Justice of the Supreme Court in Washington, he was also Presiding Justice of the United States Circuit Court for the Ninth Circuit and visited California to sit and decide cases in the Circuit Court annually. It was a seasonal rite which went back to his appointment to the high court in Washington by President Abraham Lincoln. An apartment on the third floor reserved for Mr. and Mrs. Justice Sickels and their listing as permanent guests in Langley's San Francisco Directory shed luster on the Imperial House which meant more than mere revenues. All this was an understood fact of management, he had thought. "I will not have Judge Sickels vexed. Or any of my friends. D'ye hear?" he demanded with a hard stare.

"Darn it, Lew, I can't seem to talk to you anymore." Webster went on with sly malice, "There's a man been trying to get you, process server, or something. I put a watch out for him. Calls himself . . ."

"Pettibone?"

"Why, yes!"

"Nothing to it," Hagerman said confidently. "I'm talking to the man myself. He won't trouble you."

Webster drew a pendulous lip. "Oh, good," he murmured smoothly. "Elsie and the girls will be that relieved if you can end that business with Jessie Roux."

Hagerman stared. "Jessie Roux?" he said ominously. "What brings that up now?"

Webster was taken aback. "Oh, nothing. Only that it's getting embarrassing for 'em. Lew, there are lots of fresh rumors out about you and that woman."

"Rumors? What rumors?"

"Oh, you know."

Hagerman arose and brandished his stick excitedly. "No, I don't know!" he cried. "And I will not face this constant harassment from my own family. Not from Elsie! Tell 'em nothing! Oh, Jesus! Where's that elevator?" He darted out and across the lobby, whimpering.

A smiling elevator man held open the cage. As the hydraulic lift rose slowly behind bronze grillwork, Hagerman stared at the palm-shrouded lobby below in a wave of gloom. Imperial House was a fistula in the Hagerman fortune, a flowing drain he had no business to keep up. It was getting too much, he thought glumly. Just too much. The accountants were taking over the world.

"Your floor, Senator!"

Porters and chambermaids sprang to attention, bowing and smiling as he called them by name. He asked after their

8

health, joked, and flipped silver dollars fresh from the Mint and struck from bullion smelted in his own plants from ore taken from his own mines. An affectionate chorus followed the shower of silver

"Oh, de King ob de Comstock am now passing BY;
De King ob de Comstock am NOW passing by. . . ."

An expert eye capable of discriminating between pyrites and argentum in the gloomiest depths of earth noted the polish of brass, the dust of corners. A keen nose detected plumbing smells. Try as hard as one might, modern science could not abolish the special smells that clung to hotels. A spark of electricity crackled as he seized the knob to his private apartment. A smiling little Chinese was waiting in the foyer.

"Hello, Li," Hagerman said, exhausted. He handed over his hat and strode into the bathroom. On his return to the darkened ornate living room, he paused at a sideboard. An envelope addressed to him in brilliant green ink rested on a silver tray. He would deal with it later, he thought, annoyed.

Li rubbed steadily and gently. "You not feeling good, Senator?"

"It's been a hell of a day. Why?"

"Bones you' feet. Li can tell difference. Bones tired—man tired," Li said, turning his r's to l's.

"Is that an old Chinese proverb?"

"Oh, no!" Li said happily. "I make up."

Hagerman laughed and pulled out a set of dentures. "These damn mercury pills," he complained. "Cure's worse'n the disease. I h'ain't got a tooth left in my head. Put these in water." Instantly it was done. Li asked, "How was Comstock?"

Hagerman turned an indulgent glance. Li was a paradigm of Oriental excellence. He was small and crook-backed, bowing to his task in the tunic and long sleeves of China. His queue was oiled and black and lustrous. In the street that queue would be tucked inside for safety against ruffians who at night still ruled the alleys along Grant Street. Now that symbol of piety hung loose, bouncing with the vigor of his motions. "Li, boy," Hagerman drawled, "you'd just tell it all over Grant Street. Who pays you for tips?"

Li shook his head, smiling. "No one pays this fella, Senator. I keep quiet."

"You swear by honorable ancestors?"

"Oh, Senator!" Li said reproachfully. "I Christian. I not swear by ancestor. I swear by God. Missy Hagerman, bless her soul, convert me long, long time now to Jesus Christ, our Lord."

Hagerman glanced skeptically at the queue. "Well, Li! We're drawing more water at fifteen hundred feet than the new pumps can handle. It's a serious business."

"I sell?"

Hagerman shook his head. It was in fact one of many problems left at the bank. "I'll let you know. How many shares are you holding?"

Li hesitated. "Fifty," he said reluctantly.

Hagerman turned a sharp look at the modest downcast face. He knew Li's holding precisely. "I'll guarantee 'em at one hundred." He shifted to a comfortable position, enjoying the sensual pleasure of warm, dry hands pressing tired bones. "Now tell me the news."

Li looked up with a grin. "Missy Shanahan waiting for call."

A look of suffering appeared. "No, Li. I'd rather not."

"You promised," Li reminded.

"I know, but even so."

"Oh, oh," Li said, shaking his head comically. "Missy Shanahan so nice. She past blood period now. Sorry she not be ready last time you in city. Cramps. Terrible cramps!" He held his belly, wrinkling his face hopefully. "You send?"

Hagerman felt every taut muscle ache with the tensions of a difficult week. Still, the conversation tickled him. He asked lazily, "How much does that girl pay?"

"Five dollar," Li said blandly. "You not mind squeeze?"

"I not mind." Hagerman grinned. "Anything you can get out of Rosie Shanahan, grab for your old age in China. Can't tell how long I'll be around."

"Oh, Senator! You live forever." Li's hands were gentle, soothing. "Missy Kitty Machonichee instead, maybe?" he urged hopefully. "You likee Missy Machonichee?"

"Not any more."

"Too bad." Li clucked with regret. "Missy Kitty good girl. She sad. Cry, cry all-a time you go away to Comstock." He wriggled like a voluptuous girl. "She ready now to do anything you ask."

Hagerman laughed. "Anything?"

"Oh-a, yes!" Li said vigorously, sticking out a wet tongue. "She lonesome you."

"They all lonesome me," Hagerman said skeptically, yet sourly pleased. "All right, Miss Machonichee," he decided, against better judgment. "Let her come around later and I'll see if I'm up to it." He paused.

There was that gala benefit at the MacMillan Theatre and he owed the soprano, old Congressman Miles Hooper's daughter, a visit to her dressing room. "Get the bags packed for morning. I'll be taking the early train for the East. Tell Miss Machonichee to get here early. Now I'd like to doze."

Li drew a blanket about the tired man and began to bow out in a posture of intense respect. A sandy eye opened with suspicion. "Has that woman been in these rooms lately?"

Li jumped. "Missy Jess?"

"Missy Jess," Hagerman mimicked. "Well?"

"Oh, no, Senator! You give orders. I never let her in rooms."

"Never?"

A lemon-colored hand was raised to Heaven. "I never, never, never." Li hesitated. "Not in long time."

Hagerman closed his eyes. "If she shows up, notify Captain Webster. I've had enough troubles for one day. Now git!"

The door closed. Li waited a moment and then, thrusting his hands inside long sleeves, trotted off to Miss Kitty Machonichee's.

The suite was quiet but for the breathing of a tired man. Hagerman through drowsy eyes could see the dark, ornate room. It was busy with pieces manufactured by his factory in Mission Street. A walnut wardrobe large enough to house a Shetland pony, dominated the room. The piece had been installed at Jessie Roux's bidding not his own. But then her touch was still everywhere, from the four-poster bed to an extravagant assortment of silver-backed brushes, combs, tortoiseshell disposal boxes, and nightgowns in the bedroom. He grimaced with displeasure. He had been mush in her hands, he thought venomously. Simply mush! He drowsed and suddenly a lascivious thought licked up from the depths.

A light musical laugh, climbing the scales of mirth, came seemingly from the next room.

"Sen! Oh, Sen, sweetie," the woman's voice said, drolly amused. "That's a real indecent thing to think!"

He rose on his elbow. "Jess?" There was no answer. He waited, undecided, gnawing a moustache and turned on the pillow, but he felt an uncanny presence. "Oh, damn that woman!" He arose and searched the rooms. "This is stupid, stupid!" He looked under the bed, then stared at the large walnut closet in the corner. "No, confound it! I will not look in there!" he exclaimed. But of course there was no help for it. The voice had been real—a nasal drawl straight out of Missouri. With an exclamation, he threw open the wardrobe. It was, as he had known, empty.

"Jess?"

There was an echo of silence. He closed the wardrobe and returned to the bed. The hallucination mystified him. It had been utterly real—a clear voice as distinct as the bells of street trolleys outside the window. A musky body smell suffused his mouth. "I swear I'm getting softening of the brain," he muttered. He drew the comforter over his head and thought back. A dark moist hollow went convulsive at his touch. A spider-web kiss of fine-spun hair was on his face.

The comforter went asprawl on the carpet and he sat up, restless and panting and recalling the moment it had all begun.

Three years earlier on a day in June, Miss Jessica Roux had entered the Hagerman bank at Pine and Sansome with an air of decision and sought to draw a sum of money from her account. She was dismayed at her balance. "Is that all I've got?"

The cashier looked at a lovely and baffled face. "I'm that sorry," he said with regret.

"Oh, sorry!" She turned on her heel and strode into the street. "I've simply got to get out of this darn pickle," she exclaimed. "Now where in the world?" She waited in a fury of frustration. A jaunty voice attracted her attention.

"Miss Jessica? I declare, were you about to patronize my bank?" Hagerman asked. He lifted a pearl-gray topper. "Are you getting satisfaction?"

"Oh, yes, Senator!" A black mood rolled away. Jessie

laughed infectiously, a bit more than called for. For the moment, without her glasses, she had not, she vowed, recognized him. "I reckon you're out of money in there. At least so the man told me when I asked for some."

"Do you need money?" Hagerman asked pleasantly. He examined a billfold.

"Not that kind of money," Jessica said. "I'm having a darn old time scraping some money together to close on this parcel of real estate. It's a corner location but with this cloud on the title it's bound to go for nothing. I'm short the deposit. Everybody's out of town, or I'd ask my uncle. But sho! I thought I had more in there," she said prettily. She was the picture of feminine indignation and distress.

"Well, well! Cashiers can be unfeeling, but banks do need watchdogs, don't they?" Hagerman laughed. He snapped his fingers and looked up from Jessica's swelling bosom, almost level with his eyes. "I had no idea you were in real estate, Miss Jessica. As I recall, you were a shark at mining shares. Why not come upstairs and talk things over? We just might be able to scrape up some credit for a good proposition."

Jessica tilted her head. "I'm just not sure what you intend to propose at your office, Senator."

Hagerman arched his brows. "Why, all sorts of things. Are you afraid of me, young lady?" he said gaily.

"You are kind of scary. I think you're a lamb—but your reputation? Lands!" She rolled her eyes. "I really should know your intentions."

"Purely business." He put a hand to his heart and bowed. "And perhaps sherry and the poetry of Lord Byron?"

"Byron? Oh, my! Sounds racy."

Hagerman said solemnly, "No woman was ever undone by poetry. You have my word as a banker on that."

Jessica laughed and cast a quick glance about, but saw no one she knew. "I am intrigued," she confessed. "Oh, my! The tales we heard. . . ." She halted suddenly. "Oh, say! How do you remember me so well?"

"We shared an ice at Dora's wedding," Hagerman said pleasantly. "It stands out yet in my mind's eye."

"Oh, Senator! You had two thousand guests that night. I'll bet you ate two hundred ices. One with each of us girls. We had a bet on that you would bust."

"I'll tell you something, Miss Jessica," Hagerman said archly, "I knew about that bet, and I was determined to take advantage of the occasion. I wanted something from that wedding reception besides a sharp lawyer in the family. Wonder is, you remembered an old dog like me with all those young men buzzing around the honey pot."

Dora Hagerman's wedding to the brilliant and rising lawyer, Tony Galindez, had been the sensation of San Francisco. It had been in the grand style of Bonanza days—already turning legendary. Nothing like it had ever been seen before. It had been a lavish affair on a prodigious scale. Archbishop Juan Tosefa had performed the rites in a private chapel, but thereafter carpets had been rolled out and the grounds illuminated. Experts from Chinatown had worked prodigies with fireworks at the Embarcadero. Hundreds of carriages had struggled up to the Sutter Street mansion. Three bands led by Ballenberg's had played till dawn while caterers poured vineyards of champagne and served wagonloads of delicacies from all parts of the world. Jessica had danced her shoes off that night. The affair would be remembered forever among the great social and historic occasions of San Francisco. That Senator Lew Hagerman, King of the Comstock, had recalled her among thousands. Lands! "Young men?" She shrugged with contempt. "They make me sick! Takes experience to make a man interesting."

A fixed smile did not change, but the Senator's eyes showed a quick dilation. The sunny creature holding a wide-brimmed flowered hat against the wind seemed intent on her thoughts, unaware of any effect on him. Hagerman thought he had never seen a more superb figure, nor more delicate features. "Won't you honor my counting house?" he asked gallantly. He held out an arm. A drunken voice interrupted.

"Oh, Jay-sus!" the voice cried. "Will yez git on?" A brewery truck halted at the curb. A pair of Percherons, straining against their collars, slipped on the cobblestones, stumbling and whinnying. A lash went out, again and again.

"Oh, lands!" Jessica's eyes flashed. "I cannot watch this. Senator, stop that man!"

"I don't think I should," Hagerman said doubtfully. "He knows what he's doing. He's a drayman."

The lash cracked. Foam dropped from the leader's bit. Iron shoes backed in a clumsy dance, striking sparks from cobblestones as the beasts with terrified rolling eyes strove for footing.

"If you don't do something," Jessica panted, "I will. He'll

hurt those animals." She grasped a parasol and strode, white-faced with fury, onto the cobblestones, beside herself. "I'll kill that man, I swear. Come down, you! You, there! I say, come down!" she shouted.

A hairy mask of innocence peered from the perch. "Who the hell says so?"

"I do," Jessica cried. "Come down at once! I want to talk to you!"

Hagerman made a signal and the uniformed bank guard went forward. "Well, now," the drayman said thickly when the matter was explained. "A shot to the fundament never hurt horseflesh, but that ain't for me to say. Sorry, Senator," he said humbly. "I hope this ain't a bad mark against me. Had no idea 'twas against the rules." He went off, leading the team on foot.

"I could kill him!" Jessica said viciously. She caught an amused glance and laughed uncertainly. "Oh, I reckon I get carried away," she confessed ruefully, "but I just love horses and I cannot endure to have 'em abused. Back home, we had this stable boy . . ." She paused and her eyes were narrowed slits. "Well, it was lucky I got pulled off or I'd have killed him sure. Not that it wouldn't have been worth it. That was a blooded mare." She paused and her mood changed. "But, lands! It was wonderful how you stopped that brute with a snap of your fingers, Senator," she said with awe. "Just the sound of your name."

"Yes. Well, shall we go up?" Hagerman preened and offered an arm. Jessica laughed and walked out of the blinding sun back into the bank.

"You see? Nothing diabolical," Hagerman said.

The office on the second floor was furnished with pieces from his factory. Pictures framed in silver memorialized the various enterprises controlled by the bank, from a photograph of the C. and S. W. Engine #1, a sixteen-wheeler decorated with bunting for a Brotherhood of Locomotive Firemen's outing, to the smokestacks of Consolidated Belshazzar on which the prosperity of the bank rested. A portrait of a large-faced handsome man hung over a marble fireplace—Mr. Clare Gresham, founder of the bank.

"Was this Mr. Gresham's office?" she wondered.

"Yes. Why?"

"It's this strong sense of history, I reckon. I'm in the Historical Society, you know?"

"Can't say I do," Hagerman smiled.

"Oh, history's darn important. You should join," she said with severity. "You've made so much of it yourself. No, I've always had this feeling for Mr. Gresham." She twirled about, grasping the sense of the moment. "What's that?" she asked, pointing to a door.

"Mr. Smith's office." Hagerman opened the door. A spare, handsome man with silvery hair and sunken cheeks, who seemed the epitome of New England's rectitude, rose and entered. "Oh, Mr. Smith," Hagerman said carelessly. "Miss Roux is one of our depositors. Friend of Dora's. Needs a small bit of credit. How much would that be?" he asked.

Jessica thought carefully and began to explain the transaction—a plot of land owned by the Ursuline Order which no one else could acquire because of the Mother Superior's intransigence. However, since she knew the Mother Superior, she could swing the deal. Hagerman held up a hand. "Really, Miss Jessica." He smiled. "I only want the amount."

"Oh. I'd feel safe with two hundred," she said tentatively, "just to hold the deal. I'll have it covered by the fifteenth. I've got these shares in a box at the Nevada Bank."

"No hurry." Hagerman nodded to the secretary. "Make it out, Mr. Smith." Smith called attention to a board meeting and left without a second glance at Jessica. "Now then, Miss Jessica," Hagerman began gallantly and paused. "May I call you Jessica?"

"May I call you Senator?" she drawled.

"Reckon so. Only my intimates call me Senator," he replied. "Strangers and inferiors call me Lew. Seems to prove something. Jessica," he asked ardently, "what's Ophir selling for?"

"Five dollars at the opening," she said promptly.

"Gould & Curry?"

"One ninety."

"Con Belshazzar?"

"One hundred and eight."

"Why, so it is," Hagerman said agreeably, "and now you understand why you're so distinct in my memory. You were talking mining shares a blue streak over that dish of ice. I found it enchanting. Now can you explain the different performances of those shares?"

"Why, sho! It just means that some leads play out faster than others. Or there's advice from the mines. Or someone's booming it up or down. The main thing is to have good information. I think that's the thing—good information," she concluded with conviction.

Hagerman's glance was most respectful. "Let's see now. We like to know something about our customers. You're staying with your brother?"

"At the Purdue. Well, actually we're in Oakland right now at the Hindenberg Hotel."

"Oakland? What in thunder would send you to that backwater town?" Hagerman said, smiling broadly. "Sure you're wasted on the desert air."

"Personal reasons," she said lightly, "and it was so convenient, you see."

"Convenient to what?"

"Why, sho! The State Convention!" she exclaimed. It appeared that the sunny creature was an emphatic and informed advocate of the suffrage for women, free colleges, the rights of organized labor, the Chautauqua Movement, and a score of reforms on which she had decided opinions.

Hagerman was fascinated. "Incredible! Are you really that involved?"

Jessica raised a finger. "If enough of us women march in the streets, there's just nothing we cain't accomplish. I put in a lot of good hard work, but I couldn't get a darn delegate to listen." The sots were bemused, she complained, by an abortive attempt to put over Justice Sickels, the most notorious judge in the country, as a serious candidate for the Presidency of the United States. The attractive, rather cold blue eyes widened. Was it reasonable for Sickels' forces to hope to capture the nomination at the National Convention without the California support?

"Why not? Anything's possible when you've reached that eminence. The whole country knows Judge Sickels. Tammany was for him, we know that. So were Ohio and Pennsylvania. He's really a most famous man, don't you think?" Hagerman drawled, amused by the assertive, positive air of his guest.

"Mrs. Lawes was telling my grandmama . . ." Jessica paused and forced a light laugh. "Oh, politics! You wouldn't want my opinion."

"Oh, but I would," Hagerman said. He lit a cigar and wondered how well his guest knew Mrs. Malvinia Lawes.

"Sho! Why, she made this lovely dress for grandmama.

17

She's got all these tips . . ." Jessica paused in the spate of information and went on intently. "Mrs. Lawes says it was absolutely ridiculous for that man to hope for the nomination the way labor feels about him. Not after all those decisions he wrote in favor of the Chinks. I swear, his record is a crying shame."

Mrs. Lawes was a striking Negro woman of sixty or more whose appearance with her driver, Tom Digges, a former prizefighter, and a spirited team of chestnuts was a daily sight in San Francisco. Her coloring was dark, her accent indeterminable, her voice husky, her influence with the Negro population not admitted but understood. She knew everyone and everything and followed many pursuits. She was one of the city's established personalities.

Hagerman strolled to a sideboard and poured two large glasses of sherry. "Oh, a judge has got to write the law the way he sees it," he observed. "Sickels has had no personal use for the Chinaman, I'm sure of that. I think he shows a liberal spirit. He's really for the workingman."

"Oh, my foot!" Jessica burst out with feeling. "Since when? He's just a despicable old man who'll still do anything to get into the White House—but everyone knows his record. That's why he flopped so miserably. He is the most hated man in this state. I don't care what kind of money's behind him." She clapped a hand over her mouth. "Oh, this big mouth!"

"Try this sherry," Hagerman said dryly. "It's over one hundred and fifty years old."

"That old? Oh, my! I didn't think wine could last that long."

"Well, it's fortified. Just try it and forget politics and see how it goes."

"Oh, lands! It's like honey and gold. I never tasted anything like this. D'ye have another drop?"

"Sure do," Hagerman replied, laughing with the moment's pleasure. "You can talk freely about Justice Sickels. You can't say anything that hasn't been said. "But I'd rather hear about you."

"I'll bet I know something." She pointed a finger. "Where you'd like to land up if Sickels should ever make it?"

"Oh, where's that?"

"The Court of St. James," she said sunnily. "And I hope you get it. I'll bet you'd be an ornament."

Hagerman laughed uncertainly. "Well, there's not much chance," he said and looked thoughtfully at his guest. His preference was Paris.

"Oh, I do run on!" She turned in a rustle of silk and strolled about the office, absorbing its details. A wall map of the Pacific Coast made a fascinating display of bank holdings —red for mining properties, blue for railways, green for vast land tracts granted by the government. Heavy purple crayon marked the Pima Depression. She peered close up and squinted. "I know a secret," she said mischievously. "Promise not to split?"

"Do tell."

"Well, I need spectacles," she laughed. A disorderly reticule produced silver-rimmed spectacles. "I'm blind as a bat," she proclaimed, returning to the map of the extensive railway system of the West. "Lands! Why will they raise the tariffs? Volume makes profits, not prices. Can't understand why they cannot see it."

"You don't think the railways ought to be free to fix tariffs without regulation?" he asked.

"Why, no . . ." she began and halted. "Oh, lands! I just put my foot in it again. You just about own the C. and S. W., don't you?"

"Do I?" he asked stolidly.

"Eighteen percent of authorized and outstanding shares comes to working control," she replied cautiously. "Don't it?"

"It depends," he agreed.

"Ah," she said wisely. "On what?"

"Mainly on who holds the outstanding paper. Or nominates the board of directors."

She laughed liltingly. "And that's you?"

"Oh, let's say this bank has a sacred trust to its depositors. Can't let these Wisconsin communists in Congress ravage private property, can we now?"

"Fascinating! I declare," she breathed with respect, "but I wouldn't exactly call them communists. The communists are entirely different," she said, and went on to explain a nice distinction.

"How'd you come to these notions?" Hagerman asked, much amused. Jessica paused. "I just hate Wall Street," she said vehemently, and then smiled doubtfully and got onto safer ground. "I'll bet you've got a poor view of Mr. George too," she suggested.

"Which Mr. George is that? We had a Lafayette George in Virginia City, but he got the spotted fever."

"No, no! Mr. Henry George! The Single Tax?"

"Oh, him! Say, can I refresh that glass?"

"Well, it is delicious," she agreed, sipping. "What were we discussing? Me? Oh, yes! Well, I did stay in Jackson Street with Grandmama when we first came from the Cape. Cape Badeau, you see? But sho! I shook that dust. You'd think she was the general, not poor Grandpapa."

"Was Grandpapa a general?"

"Right down to Culpeper Courthouse," Jessica said sharply. "Don't get me started on *that*! Grandmama thought she could pick my beaux and run my life. Then my uncle Will agreed I'd be better off with Dudley at the Camden."

"Uncle Will?"

"Will Fitch. He's in real estate," Jessica said, surprised at this hole in the banker's knowledge. "He's making money hand over fist with these new row houses in the Western Addition. He's practically a brother, he's that young and sporty, but he's guardian of my property. Or he was till I got my share of the estate. Or what was left," she added discontentedly. "All those expenses! I tell you."

"Your share?" Hagerman asked.

"Why sho!" Jessica tossed her head. "Me and Dudley. Papa died when we were kids and then poor Mama succumbed and Uncle Cyrus wound up the estate. Now there was a tale!" she said with slit eyes of resentment. "Sold all those poor slaves except those he bought in for himself with not the least effort to work up the bidding. Candy and Tandy went for beans and they were really sweet girls and very willing workers, I was told," she said. "All we finally got was a measly thirty thousand apiece. I'm sure we were entitled to more, but Dudley wouldn't help me get an accounting and just about then . . ." She paused. "Oh, but you can't be interested, Senator."

"Oh, but I am, I am," he protested.

She glanced at him speculatively. "I was more interested in my heart than business. It's always been my weakness. I'm terribly emotional and I was being courted by this handsome boy. He was really godlike with black curls and dark eyes. I got too heartsick to pay attention to business." She paused and picked up a bronze ornament. "What's this?"

"Hindu piece," Hagerman said. "I've got a collection I'd

like to show you some time. I've got 'em in this cabinet in my apartment. Feller who buys for the British Museum gives me the pick. Quite interesting stuff. Mostly religious objects."

"I'd like that," she said politely. But other things were on her mind and a storm gathered in the cold blue eyes. "Lands!" she brooded. "If I hadn't raised Cain with Uncle Cyrus and those lawyers, that fool Dudley wouldn't have seen a red cent. Then how could he have bought into this importing business? I fixed him up there!" she cried indignantly.

Hagerman returned to his desk and folded his arms. "That's Smathers & Company? Notions and dry goods?"

"Why, yes. I reckon you bankers just about know everything," she laughed. "People's weaknesses and things like that."

"Weaknesses?" Hagerman stared penetratingly but saw nothing more than an appealing sunniness of light banter. "Dudley Roux's a respectably fixed young man," he said amiably. "Pays his bills. Let's see how it stands. You've got Uncle Will Fitch and Brother Dudley . . ."

Jessica swirled about and began to laugh. "And Grandmama Bannister and Cousin Delaney."

Twinkling eyes met her own. "Now what's that catalog of relatives for?"

She laughed and shook a finger. "Just to let you know I'm about as darn respectable as a girl can get in San Francisco and still walk out in the sunlight. And that I can manage."

"I reckon you can," Hagerman agreed. "And I promised to recite." He grasped his lapels and a loud and penetrating drone launched forth:

> "There is a pleasure in the pathless woods,
> There is a rapture on the lonely shore. . .

"I can keep that up for hours," he announced to applause. "And I'm letter-perfect. Letter-perfect." He bowed and smiled and expressed only the smallest vexation when Smith finally tapped and entered with a sheaf of currency and the necessary instruments of commerce for Jessica to sign. So ended that first visit at Hagerman's office.

Jessica stopped abruptly in Sansome Street. "Lands! What a ninny!" she exclaimed, slapping her head. "I never once asked him for points on a stock. And the old coot must be full of 'em." She stamped a foot and sauntered off.

No sooner had she left than the door opened and there entered a dark man of middle years, Tony Galindez, Hagerman's son-in-law, legal counsel to the bank, looking, as was said of him, as though he hated the world. Galindez found his father-in-law at the window, staring into Sansome Street in a state of complete befuddlement.

Hagerman looked up. "Oh, it's you," he said foolishly.

Galindez inclined his head. "What's she want? Money?"

"Not much," Hagerman said with an embarrassed grin.

"Lew," Galindez said, "will you keep your mind on business?"

"Yes, yes, yes," Hagerman said testily. "I can't say I like your tone of voice. Damn it, my private life's my own. What d'ye know about her?"

Galindez shot the old man a dark glance. His wife, Dora, had had no use for Jessie Roux and neither had he, he said briefly. The woman had been his law partner's client. That partner, Andrew MacGowan, had found her hard to represent and had never collected fees on scores of impetuous transactions that always fell through. Hagerman's grin was complacent. Quite frankly, he was not interested in fees from women, he retorted, returning to the financial statement. He was in another world of conquest, and the beguiling episode was dismissed.

The encounter remained on Hagerman's mind through the next few days. Soon after, he left for Virginia City. He spent a sleepless night at the International Hotel enduring the effects of a hard session of poker and an oyster-and-champagne supper. Toward morning, he arose and hobbled across the cold board floors and stared over the mining city. He loved the Comstock with all his avaricious soul, for there in the bowels of Mount Davidson lay the pockets and shelves of silver ore with all their dips, angles, and bends, and on the surface all the auxiliary enterprises created in the years of desperate strife and toil which had made him one of the rich, powerful men of America. A full moon drenched Mount Davidson in a silvery and magic glow. Along the shoulder of the mountain lay the series of mines at various levels which had brought up wealth amounting to hundreds of millions of dollars—Belcher, Crown Point, Yellow Jacket, Imperial Alpha, Exchequer, Bullion-Ward, Consolidated Belshazzar, Savage, Gould & Curry. But none of this was on his mind.

He was in the grip of something he could not understand or believe. A sense of dread overwhelmed him. He had no idea whence it came. He felt drawn to the illimitable reaches of the sky. His mouth was dry and his heart was beating. He was miserably aware of every defect of his body. His fingers and hip socket ached with rheumatism. He felt bald and mangy and inferior, like an old dog, and he knew the draining energy of age. And yet alive in his thoughts was the glorious young woman who had stepped out of nowhere into his office, bubbling with laughter, rattling with wit and nonsense, raising a twanging and charming voice in amazed wonder and appreciation at his least utterance.

"Oh, my God!" he groaned.

In the first flush of dawn the miners would be trudging past the site of Maguire's Opera House on D Street toward the pits from which ore and wealth would flow to the milling plants on the ridge. He had come to inspect the most serious problem of the Comstock, the flooding waters in the lower levels. Inspection had shown that it would take thousands of bricks to hold the tremendous weight and thrust of new machinery to control conditions on the 2,500 foot level, but that expense was inevitable. Belshazzar's four pumps were no longer adequate and the decision was to import larger, double-cylinder Cornish pumps from England. He was staring with unseeing eyes at the mining and industrial complex which bore his mark—and none of this was on his mind.

He was thinking of the message which had passed at his office a week earlier and wondering how much it would take to get the woman laid. It was a plain, blunt thought, but then he had spent a lifetime in mining camps. He had to be crazy, he muttered fearfully. There was nothing there but trouble. The trip back to San Francisco found him in agony of impatience to learn the answer.

> "There was a sound of revelry by night,
>   And Belgium's capital had gathered then
> Her beauty and her chivalry and bright
>   The lamps shone o'er fair women and
>   brave men. . . ."

"Oh, I love that, Sen," Jessica sighed, rolling her eyes. "But I cain't be sure I ought to listen."

"Oh, the sentiment is true," Hagerman replied ardently.

23

Having established a mood, he took Jessica's hand and asked that she take off her clothes. He offered one thousand dollars to look at her body. Jessica laughed uncertainly. "You must be joking, Sen. I never heard of such a thing."

Hagerman lit a cigar. "I'm dead serious. Make it two thousand?"

A colder look came and she took a deep breath. "That's money," she agreed, frowning with realistic concern.

"You're beautiful," Hagerman said with fervor. "I just don't throw money around. Of course," he added fairly, observing that her breath was coming faster, "I wouldn't put out that kind of money just for a look. I'll be frank. I'd want to make love to you."

Jessica looked aside thoughtfully. "Sen, you shouldn't say things like that," she said in a low voice. "I'm respectable, and that's sure not proper talk for me to hear."

"You're not worried about my credit?"

"Lands, no!" Charming and infectious laughter rang out in the paneled office. "I refuse to be offended, Sen. You're just teasing, but I do declare you're a sweet boy."

"Not that sweet," Hagerman said grimly, "and I'm not a boy. Hand-holding's not my idea."

"No. Well, thank you," she said, rising. She picked up a parasol and prepared to leave.

He held the door. "Are you angry, Jessie? Because you shouldn't be. I'm lonely," he added, drawing his mouth into plaintive lines.

She softened immediately. "Why, no," she said amiably. "I guess it's flattering in a way. Say! You sure didn't have this place in mind for you-know-what?"

"No," he said hopefuly. "I'd find another place, if that's what you want. Is it?"

A glance turned from an engraving of Beaufort which dominated the wall. "Well, that would be telling!" she said lightly, and with a brilliant smile left, humming the latest tune picked up at the Woodward Gardens.

Hagerman came to a final offer.

"Five thousand dollars, Jess," he said distractedly, "for one night, and that's money. One night, and nobody has got to know. It can't hurt you and it would give me lots of pleasure."

For once she was silent, staring at gloved hands folded in her lap. "Say something," he said hoarsely.

24

"I'm thinking," she replied. She looked up. "I'm just wondering if you're sincere," she said softly.

Hagerman went to a cabinet and took a straight whiskey and turned a burning look at the radiant creature. Jessica Roux was the most beautiful woman he had ever seen, he thought. A superb figure was bountiful with promise. Her skin was milk-white and her nose and mouth delicate and sweet. Her russet hair was abundant. "Then it's not impossible?" To his surprise, his voice was hoarse.

"Well, I've just got to think of my future," she said practically.

"Oh, sure," he said.

The conversation took a curious turn and before she left he was fumbling at whalebone stays.

"Now, Sen," she said firmly, stepping back. Her color was heightened, there was an odd look of animation in the frosty blue eyes. "I'll be able to decide after I hear what you've got to say tomorrow." She paused. "Lands! What would Grandmama Bannister say if she knew about all this?"

Hagerman smiled desperately. "She'd say her little girl's nobody's snap."

Jessica laughed and gathered her things to leave. "Sen, how old are you?" she asked curiously.

"I'll be frank," he said finally. "Fifty-seven."

"Fifty-seven? Lands! Why, that's not one little bit old," she said gaily. She patted his cheek and left, twirling her parasol. Hagerman finished the whiskey and went off to a meeting of the board of directors of the bank. He took his place in a haze of remembered delights, hopes, and fears.

Oh, God! he had thought desperately. What in hell was he in for?

Hagerman awoke, aware that Li had returned from his errand to Kitty Machonichee.

The lilting laughter rang out again. It directed him to the secretary. He unlocked a cabinet and drew a curtain aside from a votive recess. A statuette glowed in the dusk. It was not six inches high, but it suggested enormities of scale. The god Indra stood naked, legs apart, knees bent, arms flung back, hideous with passion. Half in size, the goddess hung pendent from the swollen neck, impaled on his rod, engulfing godhead's fertile principle. A twin of the object in the British

Museum was chaste embodiment of cosmic processes. Here it was an obscenity.

The laughter rang out.

He drew the curtain and locked the cabinet and waited, restless and panting. After a moment he picked up the envelope from the silver tray and studied the jagged scrawl in brilliant green. Against all will, he opened the seal.

18 Wisteria Place

Wednesday

My dear Senator:

Hopefully this letter will reach you on your return from Virginia City. Perhaps I should write there to the International, but I am never sure my letters get delivered. I am prompted to call on you—to see how you are, to know you are well—but what can I do when Galindez and the pack guard you and exclude me like the plague from your rooms where certainly I have some rights? I cannot believe you know these things, for certainly you could never, never wish me this unhappiness.

They are not your friends, believe me. I am your true friend, in spite of what you hear from that sordid and accumulating bunch who have not the slightest love or concern for anything but your great fortune. I am dreadfully unhappy.

In the meantime I must tell you that I have asked Mr. Horatio Pettibone to represent me in a small matter. He was very helpful to Mrs. Leffingwell and he feels the injustice of my position so keenly that he has undertaken the commission as a public service. I have put my entire trust and confidence in his discretion. Do not, I beg you, treat him lightly or let anything dreadful happen, but do obey his request. In the long run you have some obligations to your fortune and your name.

Please believe that I am writing out of love.

Jessica

The letter dropped from Hagerman's hand. He threw aside the comforter and stared at the wall. A snarl twisted a thin, bloodless mouth.

Whatever had happened, he wondered, to that real estate deal with the Ursuline Order?

At six o'clock that evening the MacMillan Theatre was still locked and closed. A side door opened, and there entered the concessionaires with lemonade and siss-water, chocolates and biscuits and cracked ice. The safety curtain with its advertisements for Turkish baths, hotels, jewelry shops, and emporiums was high in the flies.

"*La donna è mòbile . . .*" A strong and resonant tenor came from the darkened boxes. The manager's door opened suddenly, and George Cooley looked out with annoyance. "Who's doing that?" he shouted. A smiling ruddy face thrust over a box upholstered in velvet. "I'm-a testing the house."

"Try another aria. And get that box especially clean. You hear?"

"Ah, *sì!*" the workman called. He touched a taper to a series of mantles while an assistant turned a master cock. The house with its gilt ornamentation came to pleasant light as jets of flame mounted everywhere.

George Cooley returned to his office and stared with distaste at the poster which proclaimed that the San Francisco Light Opera Company was presenting Miss Mollie Hooper in a benefit performance of *Clari or The Maid of Milan*. Who ever heard of that antiquity?

A committee of ladies were in his office intent on the seating arrangements. Two preferred seats on the aisle had been reserved for friends of Mrs. Malvinia Lawes. How had that come about? It appeared that Mrs. Lawes had disposed of two hundred pairs of tickets for the benefit of wayward girls.

"This *Clari*," Mrs. Helen Vassar grumbled. "Who made that selection? Never heard of it."

"It's the first American comic opera ever composed," Cooley said wearily. "Pity Mrs. Bannister ever heard of it." Mrs. Stephen Bannister was chairman of the benefit committee. The effort had bogged down at once. The wrong people staffed the committees. Newspapermen were ignored. Printing jobs were spoiled. Meetings were not called. No one had heard of *Clari* or wanted tickets. Volunteers had melted away and finally in despair the committee had turned elsewhere for help. Mrs. Lawes had worked miracles in selling tickets, but then her resourcefulness was as galling as it was

27

baffling. What were her resources? Those who knew were not telling.

An early group of patrons were descending from hansom cabs and milling about the marble-paved lobby of the theater. A harassed assistant manager advised that the doors would not open until eight o'clock for reasons he could not explain.

Police Captain Billy Pritchard rubbed a blunt scarlet face and grinned good-naturedly. He was in formal dress. White tie and tails went awkwardly with the bulky shoulders.

"One minute, folks," he said in a strong Cockney accent. "I'll 'ave it all organized in 'alf a moment, *if* you please."

"Doubling in brass, Captain?" someone sang out. Pritchard grinned. "Something like!" He motioned to his platoon, also in formal dress, to follow him into the theater.

Celebrities began to arrive. A schoolgirl broke into a delighted squeal and presented an autograph album to a golden-haired stoutish man with baby-blue eyes. Mr. Rudolf Lang, editor of *The Hornet*, had an established reputation as woman hater, poet baiter, errant satyr, drama rater, and other things.

Pritchard meanwhile had conferred with the manager. "Lads," he said to the platoon, "you'll keep a sharp eye. Watch for the wrong ones. We'll have no trouble and after the show it's beer and oysters at the American."

"What trouble, Captain?"

"Who knows?" Pritchard said genially. "Perhaps some bomb-throwing anarchist. See that box?" All eyes went to the box overlooking the stage. "Nobody approaches that box, eh? Not without the nod. I'll be standing right *here!* Understood?"

What was happening meanwhile at the Imperial House was to become a matter much in dispute. Hagerman was in long underwear after a tender half hour. Miss Machonichee—a marvelous girl with the build of a cow—was snoring in the bed. He was considering a choice of cravat when the knock came.

Li said, "Miss Roux down in lobby."

"Tell her to go away."

"She not go way. She say she make trouble."

"Trouble?" Hagerman frowned dangerously.

28

"She here with Missy Nellie, Cousin Delaney, and big-big red-faced man. She not leave lobby."

Minutes later a wrathful ex-Senator emerged from the elevator. He was seen to draw the small party behind a potted palm and there confer excitedly with Miss Roux and a companion, Miss Nellie Driscoll, the tempestuous Pettibone, and a pallid, thin young man in an elegant waistcoat, Mr. Gerald Delaney, who was Miss Roux's cousin.

According to one set of witnesses, Pettibone seemed unusually aroused. Miss Roux was in an evening gown of green watered silk, looking pale and uncertain but most striking with her milk-white skin and abundant russet hair which fell in a fringe over a low brow. Miss Driscoll, a sharp-nosed girl with a short, exaggerated figure, looked plump in an ordinary frock. Both females stood apart while the discussion went on. Delaney, limp and whimpering, begged the other men to lower their voices. Finally, fists being shaken, voices being raised, Miss Roux came between the males and said something in a joking Missouri twang. Hagerman laughed, then grasped Pettibone's lapel and said something distinctly foul.

". . . damned blackmailer," was heard.

Pettibone turned color, wheeled, and left, vowing to return ". . . with an officer."

According to the witnesses, Delaney and the females went with Hagerman to his apartment on the fourth floor. That apartment looked to the court, which with its skylight was a main feature of the hotel. The doors and windows were guarded only by shutters. It was later to be sworn that Miss Roux looked through the shutters and, espying a woman in the bedroom, chided Hagerman spiritedly, at which Hagerman laughed and suggested the empty apartment opposite to talk.

Listening at the transom, Delaney was to swear that he heard his cousin affirm, "Senator, you know I am your legal, lawful, and wedded wife, and you dare not deny it, and you have led some of the smartest and best men in this city to believe I am your mistress."

According to this evidence, Hagerman then said, "I swear before God Almighty I never hinted or said to any human being that you are my mistress." Miss Roux then said, "No more than a week ago, when I consulted Mr. Brawn as a lawyer about my legal problems, he came and told you everything about my case and told you he believed I was your wife and you should make it right with me. And then you promised Mr. Brawn double any fee to take your side of the case and at least one hundred thousand dollars to do so."

Still according to the evidence, Hagerman said, "Brawn would not dare repeat that before me, because it is a damned lie from beginning to end. Honey, darling, don't worry your head about troublemakers, because it will come out all right in the end." Miss Roux wished Hagerman a happy trip east, but told him not to bring back any woman claiming to be his wife. Hagerman then said pleasant and flattering things that got her in a good mood. Miss Roux emerged from the apartment, tucking a check in her bosom. As a sign of high spirits, she patted the doorman at the exit.

Hagerman's version was to differ in particulars. The demand for money had offended his sensibilities, he was to swear, and he had approached the party in the lobby in some excitement and passion; in fact he had called Pettibone a blackmailing son of a bitch and ordered him out. According to this version, Miss Roux had looked imploringly at the shaken Pettibone, begging to know his next move, but Pettibone had left when menaced not with arrest but with a caning. Hagerman was to concede that "somebody" seemed to be in his bedroom—perhaps of the sex opposite to that of the male sex, not to be too precise about it—but that he had gone into the next room only for ink and paper for a receipt for $250 on account of a note for a larger sum which he had refused to pay.

As to the rest, Hagerman was to profess complete bewilderment and deny all.

Miss Roux was to say that her pique was merely that Hagerman had led the most intelligent men of the city to believe that she was not socially on a par with him—in fact that she was *déclassée*.

Mr. Brawn was to call the farrago a scheme for extortion that had gone wrong, and that, while she, Miss Roux, had indeed consulted him on her problems, he'd told her he'd not touch her case with a ten-foot pole.

In any case it was agreed that Miss Roux left with a check for $250.

Police whistles began to blow. A nightstick rapped the pavement. Pritchard ran with the speed of a younger man. " 'ere now! Murphy! Fitz! Wot's this?" he asked.

"Sorry, Cap'n!" A sweating officer was clubbing a youth without much success. "Damn anarchists! Oy got bit!" he said indignantly. "Ow! Ow!" A kicked shin sent him dancing. "Catch 'im, Fitz!"

Bearded and slovenly students from Berkeley had organized a parade of signs. "Remember the Pima Murders!" "Chop Suey Jack Sickels!" "The Comstock Tiger!" "The Chink Lover Must Go!" The crowd surged back and forth, groaning and howling. A two-headed effigy appeared: Hagerman with a tiger's head and a slant-eyed Sickels wearing a pigtail. A chant went up. "Two! Four! Six! Eight! Who do we abominate? Sickels! Hagerman! Yay! Team!" A knot of students surged forward with a manifesto denouncing the Money Power and a corrupt minion federal judiciary.

"Clear off!"

"Make us!"

"Dee-loighted!" Nightsticks rang out. A paddy wagon came clanging and the students were dragged off, singing songs of protest and revolt.

"Shocking!" was the verdict.

"Half hour, ladies! Gentlemen, half hour, if you please!" The call boy went through the dressing rooms, beating a gong.

Two raps sounded. Houselights dimmed and went up. Musicians began to test instruments. The warmth increased. A horn tooted and ended abruptly on an embarrassed burping sound. Amidst the gathering array of claw-hammer suits of the men, the dazzle of bare shoulders and half-exposed breasts flashed seductively. It was the day of tiny waists and opulent bosoms and swelling hips. The audience turned opera glasses about the house, searching out the celebrated personalities of their city.

Mrs. Fanny Woodruff lifted her monocle. It was an instrument she had acquired in England, but in her case it did not seem an affectation. She was a tall, handsome woman, vigorous and direct, whose long nose and air of cool intelligence allowed for this singularity. She was most interested in the scene as a writer whose stories and articles on California had been well received in England. She saw a man with a pendulous face talking earnestly to the house manager below.

"Who's that?" Fanny asked.

31

"Captain Pritchard," Galindez replied. He raised his hand and made a signal.

Captain Pritchard returned the signal, then went on a stroll about the theater. At each exit, he spoke briefly to a waiting man and came back to the entrance. He folded his arms and stood rocking.

Galindez made an expansive gesture. "How does this compare with London?"

"Fair," Fanny said. "You should ask me about the music halls of Paris."

Galindez grinned. "Are they all we read about?"

"Mustn't say in mixed company," Fanny replied. "But Paris has nothing to teach San Francisco. The standards run high enough, I'm told."

The curtains of the box parted. "Mr. Galindez?" A worried George Cooley looked in to say that the curtain was late and the audience restless. "I cannot hold it."

"Let's wait for the Senator," Galindez said.

"Is he really coming?" the manager asked. Galindez turned sharply. "Eh? What? Why wouldn't he come?"

"Sorry," the manager said apologetically, "but there's been a rumor. Some process servers are out." Galindez opened a penknife and began to trim his nails thoughtfully. "Give it five minutes, Mr. Cooley. I'll give the signal."

Fanny said, "Process servers, what's that about?"

"Oh, just another lawsuit," Galindez explained, closing the penknife. "We get them all the time, but we'd rather not get diverted just now."

Leaning forward, Fanny studied the colorful scene. It was all part of a background receding swiftly into the past—more swiftly than the men who had made that world and who lived on as legends in their own self-conscious times. She had returned after a few short years in London and already the city had changed. Strange faces were scattered about the audience.

Down below, Mrs. Stephen Bannister, the General's widow, a determined old woman with a ramrod spine, stumped down the aisle to her seat. Her nephew, William Fitch, trudged behind. The old woman slipped out of a velvet cape and sat erect, studying the scene with distaste. She nodded about with the impartiality of a woman of absolute social status. "Is that fool girl Jessie here?" she boomed.

Fitch glanced at a pair of empty seats. "No, Auntie," he replied.

"She's a minx!" the old woman said darkly. "I wonder that she shows her face in public. Minx!"

Fitch glanced uneasily at the empty seat in the Hagerman box. "For God's sake, Auntie," he begged helplessly. "Will you kindly button up?"

"Running after that despicable Hagerman!"

"Auntie!" he pleaded.

Violins gave a flourish. The conductor mounted the stand to a patter of hopeful applause. A limelight spot flared magically. The theater was transformed.

Suddenly a sigh went through the audience. All heads craned as Jessica Roux appeared and swept forward followed by a slender youth.

Ta-ra-ra-ra-ra . . .

The gallery chant accompanied the full-breasted undulations.

Fanny Woodruff brought her monocle to position. "She is beautiful!" she exclaimed. Jessica was blushing furiously, eyes downcast, wearing the sweetest imaginable expression. "If you like the type," Galindez growled. The dark scimitar face was drawn in a grimace of intense antagonism.

Mrs. Bannister turned to confront her granddaughter, but there was no scene. Instead the old woman put out her cheek to be kissed.

"Sorry, Grandmama," Jessica whispered. She kissed her grandmother and slipped into an aisle seat. Gerald Delaney began to arrange her cloak. "Stop looking like a scared rabbit," she whispered. "And fix your tie, you ninny. It's a show, not a hanging."

"Yes, Jess," Delaney said.

"And don't look at the box!"

"No, Jess."

"And don't fidget!" Jessica began to fan, gazing about with eyes of calculation. She raised her hand gaily to a moon-faced balding man of forty. Andrew MacGowan, member of the bar, smiled painfully and waved back, slumping into his seat. The whole theater was staring with interest at the exchange of Miss Roux with her former beau.

A French horn sounded the motif. The curtain rose on a rustic scene outside Milano. A pair of comic servants came forward and began a nasal duet.

The house sank back in warmth and sentimentality.

Hagerman entered the box and took his seat, unseen from the orchestra. He leaned forward with a smug grin. "Tony? How are the kiddies? Fanny, my dear girl," he went on, "I'm darn glad you could be with us. It's old times."

Fanny forced a smile and wiped a wet and lingering kiss on her cheek. Really! she thought. The stench of cheap perfume was overpowering.

The intermission was without incident. At the finale, Miss Hooper stepped into the spotlight and began:

" 'Mid pleasures and palaces though we may roam,
    Be it ever so humble, there's no place like home . . ."

Backstage, a man in rough corduroys touched a fire ax for luck and quietly mounted the hidden stairs and waited at the portieres of the box while a thousand voices joined in song.

"Home, home! Sweet, sweet home . . ."

Handkerchiefs came out. Noses were blown. The voices outside the box went unheard.

"Where d'ye think ye're going?"

"I'm on the force," an Irish voice said. "Here's the tin."

The portieres parted.

Galindez looked up and scowled. "Matt, what the hell's this about? If it's a summons, bring it to the office. Get out."

City Detective Matthew Canavan shook his head mulishly. "I don't understand this myself," he muttered, "but, signs and wonders! If they can make a fooking crime out o' this, they can make a crime out of anything at all." He turned to Hagerman. "It's a pinch, Senator. Let's go."

Pritchard hastened to the vortex of disturbance. The entranced audience, singing as one man, saw nothing. The slender figure on stage held them enthralled.

". . . there's no pla-*hace* like home!"

The whole world joined in.

As the audience streamed into the fog, the extras were hitting the cobblestones.

Not since the shooting of Marshal Richardson by the gambler Cora had the San Francisco theater had so diverting an incident as the arrest of Senator Lew Hagerman of Nevada on the quaint charge of adultery.

Rudolf Lang, wit and editor, put a finger on the essential question as he drove Fanny Woodruff home. Adultery? How was it possible? As everyone knew since the death of his wife, the man clapped behind bars like a common criminal was an outwardly respectable widower and had been for seven years.

The Crusader had the scoop, under the by-line of Horatio Pettibone. Jessica Roux claimed to be married to the Senator. The laughter was a shout of universal delight.

Chapter Two

A month or so later, Mark Trumbull passed a restless night at his home in the quiet and peaceful city of Stoddard, slightly over a hundred miles east of San Francisco. It was a large and pleasant house on the outskirts of the city. Warm in winter, cool in summer, it faced a small lake and was surrounded by flower beds and well-watered lawns. It was an important house, but it needed repairs and had gone shabby.

Sometime near dawn he heard or thought he heard a sound of bugles, but even in sleep he dismissed this as a dream. He stirred and changed his position and became aware of pain. For a moment, it seemed an old wound of his youth, caught outside Mexico City in that ferocious fray known as the Battle of El Molino del Rey when the First Texas Mounted Volunteers had charged the Mexicans through enfilading artillery fire and the whistle of flying grape. It had a tendency to grow painful in cold weather. On such occasions his hip went lame. A grimace touched his mouth at the madness of that moment. The Texans had charged to the sound of guns, yelling their high-pitched cries, throwing themselves in abandon at mutilation and death. He would not be so improvident now of life, but in those days it had seemed important to be brave. Why? He had no explanation. It seemed a condition of life.

He turned restlessly and listened for the sounds of the

night. A distant train whistled hauntingly as it raced north and west hauling passengers and freight from the fertile watered valleys to the south. He threw back his head and stared into darkness.

He felt anger, for no cause. His hands slid to cover the ache of his loins. He felt deeper into the soft folds of his thighs, probing the humid tangle, feeling something that slid like calcifying pits. Whether he was still a man he did not know.

"Mark? Mark?"

He turned with distress. "Yes, Alex?" The moon now had arisen over the distant hills. A faintest light fell on the pillow where she lay, supine, staring at the ceiling. Her eyes seemed to shine with pain.

"Can I do something for you?" she whispered.

"No."

"But I want to."

"It's all right, dear. Really it is."

"Let me try." She reached out to explore him, slid deeper into the bed and flexed her knees. "It will be all right, darling. Really it will."

"It's not necessary," he said.

"But I want to. Please, let me try!"

Reluctantly, cursing himself, he knelt to position and covered her, and then he flung himself off. "Oh, damn! It's worse than nothing!" He strove to master his anger. Her shaking had been unusually bad. "What was especially wrong tonight?" he asked.

"I was thinking of young Mark," she said. "If we hadn't sent him out to work that summer . . ."

"Oh, damnation!" He checked his temper and touched her face. "Oh, what's this?" He found a handkerchief and blotted the wetness. "Accidents take place," he said gently. "It was years ago. You've got to put it out of your mind."

She flung her head aside. "That note. . . ."

The sense of irritation, unwanted, unbidden, flared again. "It was never in evidence. The Coroner found it an accident."

"Mr. Gillespie told the Coroner—"

"Damn that blithering farmer!" Trumbull cried. More than eight years had passed since their youngest boy had been sent to spend the summer working for a farmer in Tulare County. He had been found in a field of barley with a bullet through the roof of his mouth. The gun used was a rusted old fowling piece, and no one knew he had taken the weapon along. It was that summer that his wife's tremor first began—a small affliction which would grow worse until she had withdrawn to the seclusion of her bedroom. Trumbull forced a reasonable tone, cajoling and logical. Their son might have written something foolish, but, he urged, it had never gone into evidence at the inquest. He had written merely that he loved his parents, that he was sorry for what he meant to do, and he begged forgiveness. But such notes meant nothing. If anything, they showed every intention to live. They had no relevance, no probative value; they were outside the record.

"Yes, Mark!" she said hopelessly.

"Why do you say things you don't mean?" He went to the window in agitation. The moon was bright. Against the horizon a row of black poplars marked the Spanish Mission-style buildings of Stoddard College. It was a college he had helped to establish with a first subscription of a thousand dollars. He thought with a pang that he had hoped to have young Mark enroll in that college after the summer of the fatal accident. For it was an accident, he told himself fiercely. It could not have been otherwise. It had seemed the right thing, he told himself, to give him a summer of hard work. Who could have known how it would come out?

"It's the formal position that counts," he said heavily. "All the newspapers agreed with the inquest. I don't want to go behind the record."

"I want to see the grave, Mark. Could you take me out tomorrow?"

"Are you up to it?"

"It's the anniversary. I can't let him be forgotten by everyone."

Trumbull drew back. "Do you think I've forgotten that boy?" he asked painfully. "Sometimes you don't care what you say, Alex."

"I don't mean to. Only you never mention his name."

"It's not easy to talk." His mood softened. He found cologne water and wet her forehead.

Her slow shallow breath ended in a snore. The iron-gray braids fell over a coverlet.

Let her sleep, he thought. He dressed with care and went down the worn stairs, restless and savage, and left for the stable.

An hour later, he was on a hill overlooking the darkened city.

The roan snorted and pawed the ground. He patted the animal. The tension had passed, but he was thinking of the woman who soon would awake out of drugged sleep.

Many mornings for years he had come to this point of vantage. The dim hills before dawn were California in winter —subdued browns and grays. Far below, the city slept in darkness, with only a scattering of lights, but soon enough it would be vivid with red tile roofs. A channel from the river cut through the Civic Center. Other waterways wound in and around the city. The Pio Pico Channel had been built at his instigation when the city was young. His mark was on that city. His shingle had swung in the breeze for almost two decades at Courthouse Plaza:

Trumbull & Yates
Counselors-at-Law

He missed Yates badly.

Stoddard sat on the estuary of the Santa Ynez River on the upper reaches of the bay. The network of channels formed a shipping point for produce of the valleys to the south—the San Joaquin, the Central, the Pima Depression. In the pre-dawn darkness, flotillas of barges and launches, locally called the Mosquito Fleet, were departing for Oakland and San Francisco. These craft ranged from tiny fishing boats to oceangoing steamers which brought the sea into the heart of the city.

A hoarse train whistle sounded in the distance. The whistle sounded again, faint and receding, wailing through the country-side. A baleful gleam smoldered in his deep-set-eyes. There was the enemy he had fought through the years, winning some victories, more often accepting defeats, engaging that corporate personality with his own strength of purpose. All that now was coming to an end. He felt tired. Tired, and defeated, he thought somberly. It was too much to carry, and this thing at home weighed on him.

"Yo, boy." At his shifting weight the roan turned back and followed the downward path, bearing the ponderous man with ease. Trumbull favored a Texas cavalry saddle—high cantle, high pommel, silver decorations, tooled, ornamental leather. That saddle had a connection with Bragg at Chickamauga but even that thought seemed thin and remote. He swayed along a trail which led him through fruit orchards and meadows past a series of white rail fences. Dark-faced peons in wool serapes bowed as he passed. He rode with reins free, head bowed, sunk in gloom.

Alexandra rattled the door. "Mark?"

"What is it?" he asked.

"Murray's here. He's waiting in the study."

"Jim Murray? What's he doing here?"

"I reckon he wants to talk."

Trumbull thoughtfully whipped the lather in a silver shaving cup. He had a cold feeling that something was wrong. Murray was secretary of the Stoddard Branch of the Workingmen's Party. "Does he say what he wants?"

"My lands, no! I wish you'd get up a head of steam. I find it impossible to make talk with that man."

"Now, Alex," he said reprovingly. "I've got time, and if Murray chooses to call at this hour, I'm not the one to be hurried. Ask him to breakfast?"

Trumbull daubed foam on throat and jowl and massaged slowly. He heard footsteps going downstairs and frowned with disapproval. She was too active for her own good, he thought. Without varying the rhythm, he stropped the fine edge of Sheffield steel and pulled the skin taut at his throat. The triple-image displeased him. He was too heavy and clumsy, almost bearlike under thick underwear, but in fact layers of muscle were well distributed over a large-boned frame. He leaned forward and studied the large pores of a strong fleshy nose. It was a face he did not recognize.

A quick stroke brought the razor along the tough skin. He applied a cake of alum and enjoyed the astringent sting, then reached for a bottle of cologne water, an elegant preparation he had imported from the East. Each move was precise and without hurry, and meticulous in a routine which never varied from the smoothing talcum powder to a last hair snipped from a nostril. He dressed and left the landing. The living room below showed his wife's touch. The furniture was heavy but good Spanish Colonial—straight backs and simple, stern angles, hard benches and flat cushions. Oil portraits of the Hennepins, dark and obscured by time, hung on the walls. The Hennepins had had aristocratic pretensions in Mississippi. The Trumbulls seemed to have had none.

39

Jim Murray, a stocky, muscular man of sixty, looking more merchant than workingman, was waiting in the study with a telegram. "Sorry, Judge," he said apologetically, rising. "I wouldn't bust in, but I got this from our man in Sacramento."

Trumbull studied the telegram with disbelief. *City of Stoddard against C. & S.W. Railroad,* a tax appeal to the Supreme Court of California in Sacramento had been pending for seven years. Years of tax assessments turned upon the decision—a decision being watched throughout the state with painful anxiety. It was a matter bitterly contested, and now, with the result assured, the high court was to adjourn without decision. It was a form of pocket veto from which there was no appeal short of impeachment. "I don't understand this, Jim," Trumbull said slowly. "I know that court. Two of those judges were pledged to us. Damnation, they were elected by us. It's fishy, confounded fishy! Is there any reason for haste in bringing this news here?"

Murray looked uncomfortable. "Well, it's the question of your fees, Judge. The Board meets this afternoon. I've got two votes lined up out of five, but I dunno if it's a good time to press. Artie Garland hates to pay a fee."

Arthur Garland, Mayor of Stoddard, dominating the Board of Supervisors, had postponed voting on appropriation for legal services for several years.

"What d'ye suggest?" Trumbull asked.

"I don't have to offer the resolution for your fee at this time. I could wait till the Court gives the city a good tax decision against the railroad. You'd command a real good fee, Judge. But at this time?" A shrug indicated doubt. "Oh, I could always get expenses."

"No, I want more than expenses. I want a fee."

"It ain't a good time to press it."

"There's never a good time to press it. Tell Mr. Garland I have no relish for this niggardly attitude. Now, sir! Will you join me and Mrs. Trumbull for breakfast?"

"Thank 'ee, no, I et at the Chink's this morning," Murray said hesitantly. "Say, why not talk to Garland yourself? He's kind of hurt by the silent treatment."

Trumbull turned full about. "Mr. Garland knows where to find me," he said curtly. "I'm not running after politicians for the best fee in the world."

Murray looked at the ceiling. "That's an easy program—

not to chase after fees. Well, I'll do my best, Judge, but don't count on anything. Not till that tax decision comes down from Sacramento." He put on his hat and left.

Alexandra was seated at a wicker table filled with breakfast dishes. It was a prospect she loved. From the bay window she could direct Asaki, who daily came to tend her roses and magnolias. An immense oak stood in the center of the lawn before the blue lake on which the property fronted. Trumbull kissed his wife's forehead. The skin was dry with the texture of paper and this hurt. An arm encompassed the frail shoulder and he drew her close. She looked aside. "I'm doing the mail," she said in a low voice.

"Yes, dear," he said hopelessly and took his place. He sniffed a delicious aroma. "Smells good."

She touched his wrist. "Mark, dear?"

"Yes?" he asked abruptly.

Her fine clear eyes were directed at his own. "It was the laudanum last night," she said. "I simply had to sleep."

"It don't matter," he said, forcing a smile. "And I will not let you vex yourself. Where's that confounded Julian? Julian? You, boy?"

"Right there," an old man's voice called out.

Trumbull looked across the breakfast table with some dread. His wife was still a handsome woman, he reflected, feeling a pang. Now, with hurt, he saw processes of change— a mottle of brown spots on her hands, crepe at her fine eyes, thinness of hair—but none of these things mattered. It was the pleasant time of day, and he wanted not to think of the painful dry moments of the night and her flesh which had changed to something he could not recognize. A constant restlessness now and dishonorable thoughts were unpleasant. He looked forward to that first bitter cup, hallowed by years of habit. A sterling pitcher poured the jet of coffee, iridescent in the sun. He opened the newspaper and met her glance. "I could have this with you upstairs," he suggested.

She shook her head. "No, I want to come down just as long as I can. I wouldn't keep in that tower. I'm not Sister Anne."

He forced a smile and looked at the blue-and-white willow pattern. It was a Hong Kong import bought when Alexandra disembarked the *Panama Queen* in San Francisco. She had a feeling for things, he reflected, and she loved the pretty pottery just as she loved the fine pieces of English silver inherited from her mother and all else that marked their lives together. For a moment he stared; then, for want of something better, wiped his eyelids, and ran down the news. "It's so sickening," he exclaimed.

Alexandra looked up. "Yes, dear?"

"Grover Cleveland."

"Oh, not before breakfast," she exclaimed, but he was buried in a political note from New York. A Democratic rally at Cooper Union had ended in cheers for the Governor of New York for President. "You cannot stop a man without a candidate," he said worriedly.

"What brought Murray out here in such a tear?" Alexandra said, opening a letter. "Is something wrong?"

"No-o," he replied, showing the telegram from Sacramento, thinking that his wife knew too much of his business affairs for her own good.

"You're not concerned about money, are you, Mark?" she asked.

"No," he said heartily. "It's just the law's delays, as usual. It'll all work out."

"I hope so," she sighed and went back to the mail. "She's expecting," she murmured.

"Eh? Who's expecting?"

"Cousin Lucy." Cousin Lucy was a mine of information. Marriages, deaths, inheritances, sicknesses of an extensive family of Hennepins scattered through Mississippi, Tennessee, and Texas were all covered by that pregnant young woman in far-off Galveston. She looked up. "Aren't you eating?"

A dish of rhubarb conserve was before him. "Must I?" he grumbled.

"Would you like an orange?"

"Yes! Well, no," he said irritably. "I don't think I want a change from rhubarb at my time of life. Alex, sugar?" he said lazily. "Why'd you ask about money?" She was silent. He repeated the question. "Mr. Jungman came to remove the new gas fixtures," she said finally. "He says you haven't paid his bill."

Trumbull continued to eat. "He did, hey? When was this?"

"Yesterday," she replied. "He was acting queer, I must say. Very sullen. He said you threatened him."

"Did he now?" A grim smile appeared. Pooh! Jungman's

42

stock-in-trade was overpricing bad merchandise, Trumbull said good-humoredly. A bill for $25 had indeed been rejected as contrary to representations made by Jungman's clerk. "Blockhead," Trumbull scoffed. "I offered the agreed price—ten dollars—and he walked off. Truth is, he's a Swedenborgian fanatic, and that's fatal to good business relations," he joked. "Nothing to it."

Alexandra was not amused. "He said you showed a knife."

Trumbull was astonished. He put aside the newspaper and thought profoundly. "Oh, that! 'Twasn't a knife. It was a letter opener. Knife!" he said derisively.

"Was it flourished at him?" she asked.

"Now, Lordy! What makes you ask that?"

"Because he complained to the sheriff that he'd been menaced by a bowie knife. He said you called him a name and said that if he persisted you'd alter him. He was smoldering so, I could barely understand him."

The deep eyes were twinkling. Trumbull was a dignified leader of the bar. He was also out of the Texas blacklands, one of that hard-drinking, hard-fighting breed who grew up to violent horseplay, practical joking, and other crudities. Quick sensitivity to affronts and a coarse sense of fun were traits that lingered still. "It's imagination," he said smiling. "I merely told him that when his clerk sold the fixtures for ten dollars, nothing was said about the automatic regulator. Now he wants to impose an extra charge. I was holding him to the deal just as I'd precisely expect to keep it myself. It is true I had occasion to open some mail in his presence. It is also true I made some observations on animal husbandry. But, Lordy! I thought you'd know better, Alex. I h'ain't had a thing like that in my hands in twenty years. I'm too old for that." A broad smile brought no response. "Oh, come, sugar," he cajoled. "I'm as mild and well behaved these days as any member of the bar. At most I had some fun. What did the sheriff say?"

"Mark! You simply have a dreadful reputation." Alexandra sighed. "You're impulsive and you've been reprimanded too many times. Sheriff Rivers advised him to forget his claim if he valued his future. I'm not proud of that."

"Pooh!" Trumbull scowled irritably. The mood was all wrong. One fist fight in ten years before a Justice of the Peace was hardly brawling. And that other episode in Fresno . . . well. The trouble was that everything got exaggerated.

43

"Fact is," he said dourly, "I swallowed intolerable insults by that storekeeper. He was fortunate I treated the matter as a joke. I am not responsible for the fool."

"Will I return the fixture?"

"Why?"

"We cannot keep it unless it's paid for. It's all so trivial," she said.

"He fixed the price at ten dollars," Trumbull said obstinately. "If he wants more, let him go to law. We'll see whose word is accepted—his or mine." A tide of rage out of all proportion swept him. "Let's not talk about it." And then a dignified black man who had waited behind the kitchen door for a moment of silence appeared with a napkin over his forearm. "Morning, Mister Judge."

"Morning, Julian."

Julian was an old hand at Trumbull's moods. He took a stance of familiarity, cupping his ear. "What else would you like, Mister Judge? I've got this good ham or you could have pig sausages or scrapple or anything you like. Rosita's got some river fish, she says, but I'm not recommending it."

"How's your beef?"

"No different. Same side's been hanging in the cooler."

"Then you know what to bring," Trumbull grumbled.

Julian hobbled back to the kitchen from which came a banging of pots on a wood-burning range, then snatches of a woman's high-pitched laughter. Trumbull listened a moment to the lilting border Spanish of his youth and went back to the newspaper. He scanned the obituaries, then put the newspaper aside.

"Yes, it's trivial," he said grudgingly, "and I shouldn't yell at you. Don't know what comes over me, Alex. What d'ye want me to do?"

"I want the fixture," she said. "I need a better light for my eyes. I'm finding it hard to read at night. Let him have his price."

He looked up anxiously. "Something wrong?"

"No," she said, returning to her mail. "I'm fine in sunlight, but I find it a strain. I just need a good light, and now that we've installed the gas, I don't see why I shouldn't take the benefit."

Trumbull considered a disagreeable and foolish situation. "All right, but the man's not to know I'm in this. Tell him it's from the household money."

A smile touched her mouth. "Oh, Mark! You're such a child. Truly you are."

He was restored to good humor, then anxiously he said, "I'm not too happy about you, Alex, sugar. What about a vacation? We could take the steamer to Redwood City for a spell."

"Redwood'd be fine," she said. "I've had an invitation from Dolly Sinzheimer. She writes that Judge Sinzheimer'd love to have us for a weekend. It'd be a chance to get together."

"Any special reason to hear from the woman?"

"None, except I think she's clinging to old friends. Would you like me to accept? I'm feeling up to it."

Judge Isaac Sinzheimer, who had sat with him on the Supreme Court of California a quarter century past, was his oldest friend in the state. The Chesterfield of the California Bar had been the first Jew elected to that high court by popular vote. Sinzheimer, J., a name attached to earliest law reports of the state and a legend in his own day, was now a dapper old gentleman of great prosperity and geniality.

"I've had a letter from Sinzheimer myself," Trumbull said slowly. "Wants to see me on some business, but I ain't sure I care for all that Bible scholarship. He's a good feller but tiresome when he's on his hobbyhorse."

"What on?"

"Oh, some confounded theory the Gospels need to be revised and that our Lord could've done better before Pilate than to plead *nolo contendere*. Western civilization would've been changed if He'd asked for legal counsel. Sad," he added humorously, shaking his head. "Now wouldn't it be marvelous if somewhere in the archives those trial minutes were to turn up? We've never had the prosecution's side. Another coffee?" he asked.

Alexandra glanced up suspiciously, but the blunt heavy features were enigmatic. "I suppose that's funny," she said tartly, "but I wish you'd not spread it in the wrong place. This is a city of the righteous."

"I do my share," he replied good-humoredly. "But if you exclude hearsay, what's left of the case?" It was a fond joking mood. Alexandra was not done, "Are you going to see Sinzheimer?" she demanded.

Trumbull frowned. It was years since they had spent time with the couple. Nor had he any idea why letters were coming out of the blue. Alexandra seemed to read these thoughts. She said, "He might be able to put something your way, Mark, with all those business connections he's kept up. Or is that why you seem so reluctant to see him? Is that your point?"

"No, it's not my point." He tucked a napkin into his collar. "I don't like the politics Ike Sinzheimer keeps," he said and closed the topic. She would not let it rest. "Mark, there's no point in going on like this," she said. "Antagonizing everyone, taking on public causes and neglecting every valuable friend and association. Really, you must be sensible."

"I'm the most sensible man in the state," he said firmly. "Now let me be." A spoon rattled in her nerveless hands. "Mark? What time did you get to bed?"

"Late enough."

"Working on the book?"

"No, I've gone stale on Calhoun. Can't seem to see much application to conditions. No, I'm preparing a eulogy. Well, not exactly a eulogy—an address." He returned to the newspaper.

She saw the guilty look. "Address?"

He hesitated. "I've been asked to memorialize the McCabes next month."

Luke and Buddy McCabe were the celebrated victims of a vitriolic dispute in the Pima Depression between a group of settlers and the C. and S.W. Railway Company. In that dispute the railway had invoked the powers of the Federal Circuit Court in San Francisco to evict the settlers from several hundred thousand acres of the best-irrigated lands on technical defects in their titles. One thing had led to another, and eleven men one bloody morning had been killed—settlers and lawmen alike. Reprisals had been taken. The McCabe brothers had been convicted and executed at San Quentin for the murder of two railway detectives who had acted to help the United States Marshal. The matter was now eight years old.

"The McCabes? I thought you were done with that business. I didn't think those people would want you to be the speaker."

Trumbull thought back to a hot summer's day in the Pima Depression. He had been asked by the Settler's League to defend the McCabes. It was a most inflammatory situation. His appearance at the railway depot in the Pima had been cheered by the rough armed men who formed his guards and supporters. He recalled a glaring sun, the mutters of anger, threats of direct action, and incredible hatred directed at the Money Power in San Francisco. A leathery ranch-woman came through the crowd to pay his retainer with funds provided by the League. Guns were everywhere.

"Keep the money, ma'am," Trumbull had said courteously. "I h'ain't taken this retainer. I've got to talk first to the boys."

"Talk? Talk about what?" the woman had asked.

Trumbull had removed his hat and wiped the rim slowly, eyeing the watchful armed men. "Why, ma'am," he said, "to see if those boys want me to represent 'em. They're charged with murder. We've got to make sure we're eye to eye on their defense. Now, cheer up, ma'am," he said heartily. "This is the Pima. I can't imagine a Pima jury not giving 'em every benefit of the doubt."

That night Trumbull had conferred in the county lockup with the prisoners. Buddy McCabe, a fat, overgrown boy of nineteen and of poor intelligence, lay whimpering on his cot with an agonizing toothache. The talk had been taken over by a sullen older brother of thirty—Luke McCabe, whose field of hops had burned and whose sickly wife had been killed in the first exchange of gunfire with the nervous lawmen down from San Francisco.

The following morning Trumbull returned to Stoddard and for reasons never made public declined the retainer. His popularity had vanished overnight.

"How did they come to invite you?" Alexandra was saying. "I didn't think those people'd want you to be the speaker."

"There's factionalism," he agreed, "but that's just a small group. The committee understands my position in the matter. Anyway, the request came from San Francisco." He returned to the newspaper. "Besides, I've got some reflections to get off my chest."

"What sort of reflections?"

He stirred restlessly. "Well, the legal implications. I've got some observations about the federal courts. Their interference in that Pima business was simply a prime example. Outrageous. Simply incredible. They do anything at the behest of the railways and the worst of it is the perversion of law. They're driving this notion of judicial supremacy beyond all bounds. . . ."

She closed her eyes. "Would it mean a long trip?"

Trumbull glanced over the newspaper. She lived in pain,

he knew, with a will that came from sources he could not understand. Her hand was quivering, dancing with a dreadful life all its own. "Just overnight," he said uneasily. "I'll turn that engagement down, if you'd rather."

"Will you let me read it first?"

"Read what first?"

"Your address," she said.

Trumbull twisted his beard. "Oh, that," he said evasively. His wife was still the energetic woman with cool eyes and an abrupt manner of intellectual competence. All through their marriage, she had always been his sounding board. In his first days of law practice, she had rehearsed him over her sewing basket nights as he paced, trumpeting jury exhortations in the passionate style of the period made popular by Colonel Henry O'Grady—a style she had brought him long since to moderate. He depended still on her judgment, for except in her mirror he was never sure of his effects. Her comments were cold water damping his fires, corrections he could only welcome. Someone had said that while Mark Trumbull had the talent, Alexandra Hennepin had the character. He had no quarrel with that. Even now she ran the household from her sickroom, paid accounts, supported causes, took positions, and gave his life structure. The best thing he had ever done was to marry the strong-minded woman who had taught him his grammar and rhetoric in the Galveston Free Academy when the world was young. That she was wasting into grayness was a burden to his heart.

"It's not really in shape. I'll have it done by the typewriter." He found himself restive under a dry smile of irony. "Well, it's the latest thing. I swear, Alex, what's got into you?"

The moment grew quiet with the whistling of red-winged blackbirds in the sunny garden.

"Oh, say!" he exclaimed.

Alexandra was slitting envelopes. "Gambetta again?"

"No, the Reserve Fund Cases!" Trumbull beamed with pleasure. A small paragraph advised that his former partner, the Hon. Zacharias Yates, now of Washington, D.C., was scheduled to argue the appeal in those celebrated cases on behalf of the State of California before the Supreme Court of the United States.

"How nice," Alexandra said abstractedly. Zacharias Yates was not among her favorites. He was, she felt, profane, violent, oratorical, diligent, and extravagant—a Mississippi fire-brand whose unreconstructed views were an embarrassment even among diehards of the Confederacy. His departure from Stoddard to Washington had been a "good thing."

"Nice?" Trumbull looked up with a grin. The Reserve Fund Cases, the largest matter ever to arise in the nation, amounted to nothing less than an effort by the Government to force the Western railroads to set aside reserve funds of 25 percent of earnings to ensure repayment of all sums plus interest loaned by the Treasury in the aftermath of the war. All prior attempts to collect interest had been thwarted by rulings of the Federal courts. The matter was now being pressed under a recent Act of Congress passed under an uproar of radical labor and farmer criticism of those decisions. The validity of that Act of Congress was now on appeal.

Four hundred million dollars was at stake.

"I told Zack he'd make it big," Trumbull said, smiling with pleasure. "Of course he's intervening for the public interest, which means he'll be fortunate to clear expenses. The railway's lawyers will make the big fees. He'll be up against the biggest noises in Wall Street. Should be a rousing argument. I'll have to send him some suggestions."

Alexandra looked up with calculation. "The old one's too shabby. I'll get a new one at the Mart."

"What are you talking about?"

"A portmanteau," she said patiently. "You are going to San Francisco?"

"I hadn't actually decided," he said.

"But of course you're going," she said abruptly. "If you've got something to tell the world, Mark Trumbull, get it off your chest. You can pick up my spectacles at Lundy's."

"But you're wearing your spectacles."

She went to another letter, holding it in the direct sunlight. "What? Oh, well, it's a stronger prescription. I can't read in this overcast." Trumbull saw no overcast. The sun, if anything, was brilliant, he thought with some disquiet.

"Outrageous," he growled, turning a page. "Simply beyond belief."

"What is?"

"The effrontery," he exclaimed. He was glowering at a further report of Yates' case. Clearly the case was collusive—a fake attack by a dummy plaintiff in the lower federal courts to declare the Act of Congress unconstitutional. The point was that Sickels was to sit on the appeal in Washington.

"Why shouldn't he?"

"Why? Why, because he manipulated that decision in the Circuit Court. He'll be reviewing himself." It was one of the monstrous abuses of the system that the Supreme Court Justices sat in the circuit courts and then often sat in the higher court in review of their own decisions in the courts below. Ostensibly they were expected to absent themselves from the argument, but it was a cozy club in Washington. Back-scratching was the rule. Sustain me and I'll sustain you.

But at least that was done in the open. In this case, something more subtle had taken place. In over twenty years Sickels had not missed a chance in the Circuit Court to pass on every application by the railways for relief against the ravages of legislatures and taxing authorities—and now, on a test case of vast significance, the decision and opinion had been assigned to that numbskull, Circuit Court Judge Jeremiah Goff. Why Goff? The fool could barely count his toes! The hand was the hand of Goff, but the voice was the voice of Sickels.

"But how d'ye know?" Alexandra cast a worried glance at her husband, thinking that a fanatical streak which so often had served him poorly was getting worse.

"The style!" Trumbull exclaimed. "The blamed sanctimonious style. Who else'd have the coarseness to mingle Virgil, the Sermon on the Mount, and Felicia Hemans in the same quotation? So damnably transparent. Where are the decencies? He's got those spineless federal pimps around his little finger."

He subsided, breathing heavily. A vein was throbbing at his temple.

"You've got Sickels on the brain," she said after a pause. "If you had any sense, you'd make your peace with the man. Will you let me see that eulogy?"

"What eulogy?"

"To the McCabes."

He looked aside. "It's not a eulogy."

"Very well, the address," she said sharply. "Mark, I want your most solemn promise to behave."

Ever since the request had come to eulogize the McCabes, he had awaited this moment with dread. Above all it was her judgment that he feared.

50

"Promise?" she repeated firmly.

He stared solemnly and suddenly felt a wry grin twist his mouth. It was certainly nothing he intended, but it had the usual effect of disarming resolution. "Well, well," he drawled, going Texan, "I might have a word on bias and incompetence of the federal judiciary, but, I promise, not a word against personal integrity—especially Sickels'. I doubt the world's ready for that. Satisfied?"

She said tartly, "Mark, you're a fool."

"Sho! We both know that," he said agreeably, and they laughed. "Only I'd like one more good crack at 'em," he said vengefully, eyes gleaming. "I'd tear down that temple of lies and deceit."

"And your hot sauce, Mister Judge," Julian announced, entering. Trumbull replaced his napkin and ate voraciously.

Alexandra looked up. "Mark, have you heard from Mary Bannister? She writes that she's sent you a letter."

"I've had no letter," he said. "What about?"

"That limb, Jessie."

"Who's Jessie?"

Alexandra frowned impatiently. The scandal in San Francisco had been in the newspapers now for months, she reminded him. Jessie Roux was Mary Bannister's granddaughter—the Cape Badeau side. Surely he knew about the case? The headstrong young woman seemed to be taking advice from disreputable people. The family was prominent and worried about the girl. Would he be available for consultation in San Francisco? Trumbull shook his head.

"I'd rather not. I'd only be forced to refuse."

"Oh, why?"

"Oh, but you know why. I won't take law business outside this county. I've told you so. I wish you would accept that."

Her eyes closed. "But I cannot always be in this position. The practice is your life. If you give things up, I'm afraid what will happen to you. I cannot endure to be such a millstone."

He would not forget that moment, he thought. Alex in quilted robe, the dapple of oak leaves in sunlight, squirrels nickering, the uncanny feeling that a door was about to open on a world he could not envision or understand. "Oh, Alex," he cajoled, chucking her chin affectionately, "you're my life. None of these other things count. I'm perfectly satisfied

51

with a quiet country practice. Nothing wrong with it at all. Now smile?"

"Yes, Mark," she said.

"Check me out?" he asked, turning his imposing bulk and swelling his chest. "What? Oh." She sighed and eyed him critically. "I wish you'd be more careful. You're as slovenly as a hog. Stand by!" she ordered, scraping a spot on a sleeve of heavy blue serge. "Mark?" she murmured. "Don't worry about things?"

"I won't," he replied. He kissed her cheek and left. Alexandra waited for the outer door to close before she called for help and went upstairs, wondering at her own persistence. Her heart was cold with dread. I want my comfortable room, she thought.

The wind from the Sierras had died off, but the chill remained. The shabby offices of Trumbull & Yates were comfortable enough. A blaze of logs in the Franklin stove gave out a pleasant glow.

There was a knock on the door.

"Come in."

A neat white-haired man opened the door and looked in. He pushed up a dark eyeshade. "Mr. Green of Finch and Greeen is here, Judge. I've got him sitting with Miss Coolth."

Trumbull was immersed in the morning's work. He raised a pair of steel-rimmed spectacles. "Which Finch is that?"

"Sidney Finch."

"Oh, yes, I almost thought Sidney was dead."

"No such luck, Judge."

Trumbull sniffed the business card of the firm. Thick cheap white stock. Imitation engraving.

"Should we really see him, Joe?"

Joe Cudahey, who was a scrivener, had worked for the firm from the start. He shifted a wad of tobacco and squinted against a distant sun. "I'd see anybody, Judge, things being as they are," he drawled in the accent of East Texas.

Trumbull followed a glance at the diary. It had not been a good day. "Now, now," he said, uneasily aware that the morning had fled on the memorial address to the McCabes. He spat ringingly at the cuspidor and glanced at a timepiece and agreed to give the visitor an hour. "But, mind'ee, Joe," he said severely, "that's the last interruption."

Trumbull had been working in shirt sleeves. Yawning with

fatigue, he slipped into his coat of heavy serge. He adjusted his cuffs and went forward to shake hands with his visitor. He sat and studied Nathaniel Green with an expression of lurking irony reserved for young lawyers.

"I don't think we've met, mister?"

"I'm new," Green said with an Eastern accent.

"New to the practice?"

"Not exactly. I read law in Rochester. That's upstate New York, and I had some practice in Syracuse. Mostly conveyancing and wills and horse cases. None of these big mining corporations you have out here," Green said with a professional smile.

Trumbull nodded solemnly. "How d'ye like California practice?"

"Well, I was surprised. It's the same Civil Code, so the terminology's the same. People are different, though. They're so—so miscellaneous."

Trumbull considered the matter unsmiling. "Reckon so. Riffraff and kings. Sump hole of the world. Utopia in a sluice. Man's dreams of perfection end here." He noticed haggard eyes rimmed with soot. "You look beat."

"I was up all night organizing my notes, then I couldn't sleep on the train. I can't be sure it was worthwhile," Green said with an odd abruptness. "You'll probably tell me you're not available." His eyes darted about the large shabby office. Trumbull assumed an office pose, palm on cheek, finger extended, slowly tapping. He read the visitor's expression easily enough. It was a young lawyer's wonder and envy for the products of an older man's lifetime. A section of bookcases held bound records and briefs marked CASES AND POINTS in matters argued up and down the state for thirty years. Prominently displayed was a buckram set stamped in gilt *Proceedings of the California Constitutional Convention 1876-1878.* Green turned back with a tart observation. ". . . or give me some other excuse, like the rest. Oh, what's the use," he muttered. "This thing's just too big. Mr. Finch is crazy to take it on."

Trumbull took out a gold case. "Cigar?"

"No, thanks. I'm sorry to take your time."

Trumbull struck a match. His earlier black mood had lifted. The young lawyer had something of the farm boy in his clumsy height and large hands. He was soberly dressed, good but threadbare and without ornaments. He was the proverbial

53

Yankee—sharp features, fair skin, keen penetrating eyes, and a brisk manner. He seemed under an intense strain.

Trumbull brought the cigar to life with quick short puffs. He said mildly, "Unavailable for what sort of things?"

"It's the Hagerman situation," Green said.

Trumbull swiveled about. The sky was clear, he saw, with fleecy white clouds building in the blue. He pursed his mouth and turned back.

"So it landed in your office?"

"It's been there some time on the quiet. An old client recommended Mr. Finch for this case, but he needs help."

Trumbull was polite. "How is Mr. Finch?"

Green hesitated a moment. "He's a remarkable practitioner," he said in neutral tones. "He's laid up with the wind but he sends his best. He thinks you're the only man for the job."

"Me? What job?"

"It's been suggested that we need special counsel."

Trumbull continued to study his fingertips. Well, there it was! he thought, guiltily. He looked up. "Who made that suggestion?"

"An old client of the firm."

"The client in this case?"

"No."

"Was it Mrs. Bannister?"

Green looked puzzled. "Oh, the grandmother? No, it was someone else. An extraordinary woman, Mrs. Lawes. She says she knows you from the early days."

A grim smile appeared. Trumbull recalled a tall, remarkably handsome woman with a dark skin of velvet and the features of an Egyptian queen. "Reckon so," he agreed. "Everybody did. The state was small then and she had plenty to say. Flattered that she picks on me."

Green opened a new cowhide briefcase and produced a memorandum entitled *Matter of Hagerman with Hagerman*. It was a bulky sheaf of light manuscript with blue covers pierced with brass fasteners. Trumbull said, "Well, let's see what we've got." He put on his spectacles and brought the document to the window. He turned the pages and read swiftly.

"Have you had any trouble about this?"

"Only threats. Nothing more."

"You must expect that."

"Well, we're not deterred, Judge. I don't see that a lawyer can consider his own position in these circumstances. Not with self-respect. I should think you know that." Green paused. "The woman's entitled to justice."

Trumbull's face remained in shadow, and this concealed a sour smile. "True. But the case must have merit and carry a fee. There's no special obligation to assume the burden of private litigants."

Green frowned. "Oh? I think there's an obligation on the profession."

"You think that?"

"Oh, yes," Green said confidently. "It takes more'n a hornbook to make a lawyer. Or a smart man. The world's full of smart people but that's no substitute for character."

Trumbull looked up blankly. "Do tell?" he grunted. "Who said that?"

"Why, Judge! You did!" The serious young face broke into a smile. "You made that speech to the first graduating class at the Hastings College of the Law. It's still being quoted."

Trumbull frowned. "Did I actually say that?"

"Oh, yes."

Trumbull kept turning pages, surprised to find his cheeks growing warm. "What we tell students is one thing," he said. "Practice is another. I wouldn't expect it from Sid Finch. What made you join that firm?"

Green shrugged. "He pays me. It's a busy office and I want to learn trial practice." He waited. "What d'ye think, Judge?"

Trumbull failed to answer directly. He studied the memorandum with close attention. "I'd feel better if your client hadn't preferred criminal charges. What way is that for a wife to act against her husband?"

"He's getting what he deserves. After the way he's treated her, he ought to be tarred and feathered. Or lynched. I swear, if I thought it would help, I'd do it myself."

"Have you ever attended a lynching?"

"N-no."

"Then don't be so quick with that wish."

Green sat forward, squeezing his hands for warmth. "Mrs. Hagerman's told me some things she's had to endure. Honestly, Judge, I didn't know men like Hagerman existed outside the Turkish harem. You wouldn't believe what she's had to put up with."

Trumbull suppressed an amused smile. "Everybody knows

Hagerman's a disgusting libertine," he observed with a grimace. "Did your client actually confide these details to you?"

Under a level stare the young lawyer flushed. "It's part of the case," he said uncomfortably, "so of course she told me. Had to. The man has the habits of Caligula."

"Ah? What's the relevance of *that?*"

"It shows the relationship. It shows why she's been so submissive all this time to the man's wishes."

Trumbull felt something queer indeed turn inside. He lit a cigar and turned back to the memorandum. "Well, this is California," he said finally, "and it's seen everything. But my gracious," he exclaimed, "where's my manners? Mrs. Trumbull would never forgive this thoughtlessness. I'd invite you to the house for lunch, but she's not quite up to it. You must be right tired. Let's get up some coffee." He pressed a buzzer. "Miss Coolth?"

Almost instantly a pretty young woman, Myra Coolth, entered. She glanced at the young visitor with some curiosity and returned with coffee.

The room was filled with cigar smoke and the smell of coffee. Trumbull went back now and read the factual background of the scandalous matter in San Francisco. Names, dates, places, and circumstances were automatically noted and classified for use by an orderly, powerful, and retentive mind.

Trumbull raised a hand which though large was delicately formed. It might have been a violinist's. A gold marriage band gleamed dully in the sunlight. When finally he spoke, he drew small circles on a yellow pad and made notes. His manner was now formal.

"Lemme see if I've got all this straight, Mr. Green. Your client came to California about a dozen years ago from the East. She lived off and on with relatives or, not getting on with 'em, in the leading hotels in San Francisco and Oakland. She's done business and bought and sold property in her old name. She's had engagements of marriage broken off. She is an emancipated woman who manages her own affairs. So far as anyone knows, Miss Roux—"

Green interrupted. "Mrs. Hagerman."

Trumbull paused. "But for clarity let me call her Miss Roux. Miss Roux—"

"No, Judge. I'd prefer her true name."

Trumbull stared at the young determined lawyer and accepted the point with grudging respect. "Very well. Mrs. Hagerman has outwardly lived the life of a *femme sole*. Three years ago she moved into the Camden Hotel annexed to the Imperial House in San Francisco. A year later she left in haste—"

"Forced out," Green interrupted.

Trumbull accepted the point. "Very well—forced out. After residing some months in boarding houses, she rented premises in Wisteria Place, where she presently keeps house with this young companion, Miss Driscoll, and a cousin . . . let's see . . ."

"Gerald Delaney."

"Ah, yes! Gerald Delaney, who has no income of his own and whom she keeps as a dependent. Throughout this period, no living soul was aware of her supposed marriage to Senator Hagerman."

"Not outside a limited circle," Green said.

Trumbull stared a long moment. His eyes were hot electric gray. The effect was startling. The clear glance estimated every bit of candor and honesty of the visitor.

"Hagerman denies the marriage?"

"Yes."

"There was no ceremony?"

"No."

"You rest on a written contract of marriage?"

"Exactly."

"Did anyone see the alleged contract being signed?"

"Not quite."

"What does that mean?"

Green clasped and unclasped his hands doubtfully. "Well, it was signed at the bank. The client was ushered into Hagerman's office by Mr. Smith—the bank's secretary."

Trumbull was thoughtful. "Why, sho! I know Ben Smith. Perfectly honorable man. Was he present at the signing?"

"Well . . ." Green replied.

"What makes you hesitate?"

"We wrote to Mr. Smith asking his recollections. He hasn't replied."

"What were you hoping?"

"Oh, that he might confirm the circumstances—presence of legal books, writing paper, ink, pens, things like that. He could fix the date." Green shrugged. "But we don't reckon to get any help out of bank employees."

57

Trumbull swiveled about thoughtfully. "Was anyone else present at all?"

"Not exactly. When Mr. Smith opened the door, Hagerman was in conference with a Spanish man. Or Mexican, she cannot be sure. It was a brief introduction and he left."

"Did she get his name?"

"It was a common name. Ramirez. Pedro Ramirez."

"Ramirez, hey? That's common enough. Could she describe the man?"

"Oh, yes. Dirty white hair. Sunken cheeks. Burning consumptive eyes and reddish cheekbones. Carbuncle on his neck. Old-style Mexican suit with ruffled cuffs and dirty collar. Tall for a Mexican—if he was a Mexican. About as tall as you or me, Judge. Six-foot-something, but he couldn't weigh more than one ten, one fifteen. Oh, and one eyelid droops. Smelled of wine."

"White wine or red?"

"Hey?" Green squinted and frowned, then looked up. "Can you tell that by smell?" he asked naïvely.

Trumbull grunted. "She's got everything else," he said skeptically. "Carbuncles! Consumptive eyes! Ramirez! Too much, mister. Too much. Which eyelid droops?"

"The right."

"Does it indeed?" Trumbull murmured heavily. "The right. Well, well. So we have a Mexican named Ramirez who had consumptive eyes and a carbuncle and who left. My question is whether anyone saw the paper besides the parties after it was signed?"

"Oh, yes."

"How many people?"

"Three or four. Perhaps more."

"Have you met these witnesses?"

"Some, not all."

"Oh? Why not?"

"Some are out of the state," Green said. "Mr. Finch is working on some others."

Trumbull went on without comment. "In any case, this supposed marriage was kept secret. Why?"

"Senator Hagerman imposed that condition."

"You say this marriage was conditional?"

"No, no!" Green said quickly. "The marriage contract speaks for itself. It's unconditional except for a clause by

58

which Mrs. Hagerman agreed not to make it public for two years."

"Why would she do that?"

"There were political reasons."

Trumbull made a note and glanced up without expression. "If you don't mind, Mr. Green, I'll refer to your client in my own way. I don't have to tell you how the law looks upon secrecy in these matters. Certainly it creates a presumption against your claim. You have at best a state of affairs concealed from the world. Outwardly all was cordial and polite and marked by mutual regard but nothing more. Now suddenly Miss Roux announces that she and Senator Hagerman were living together for some time and enjoyed, if that's the word, sexual relations whenever his medical condition allowed. She claims now that they were secretly married by this written contract over three years ago. Ordinarily her family should announce her marriage. But this disclosure was made in a sensational way at a time and place and manner most calculated to degrade and humiliate her husband. Come now, Mr. Green, why ever would a decent woman engage in those tactics?"

Green said thickly, "She had no choice."

Trumbull's brows rose. "Indeed? I can name a dozen courses open under the civil law to establish her position. She deliberately had recourse to the criminal law. Was it her intention to brand her husband a felon?"

"Oh, damnation! This whole thing's a farce!" Green exclaimed. He rose in agitation. "I sure expected more understanding from you, Judge. You must know what she's up against. The woman's holding to the last shreds of reputation under threats and humiliations of the worst kind. Hagerman has deliberately set out to destroy her. She had no reason to expect it. He introduced her to friends. He paraded her through that hotel like a woman held in high regard. He invited her to Beaufort. He endorsed her credit at the White House and other stores. He sent furniture to her suite at the hotel. He called on her grandmother and brought eggs and cheese from Beaufort. He let her tell people they had an understanding of engagement. She was a guest at his daughter's wedding. What else could she expect except honorable treatment? How could she expect him to act like that at the end?"

"Like what, exactly?"

Green strode to the window. "Judge, the time they had

trouble he had detectives throw her out of her hotel suite. He threatened everyone who might come to her help. He promised to ruin her and drag her to the level of a Pacific Street whore if she'd make any claim against him. She was terrified of the man."

Trumbull drew a series of loops. "Nevertheless she took his money?"

"Oh, sure! Money!"

"How long did that go on?"

"About two years."

"And only then she launched this action?"

Green stared helplessly. "Judge, it had nothing to do with money. She has a world of pride. She's a real aristocrat. My goodness, she had as a child an estate from her parents and all in slaves and waterfront property. She's related to the best families of Missouri. Her governess was ex-Congressman Spencer's sister. She's got bankers and lumber deals in her lineage. Can't you see that she'd put her reputation above her life? That's not just our say-so," he said warmly. "You can read this tomorrow in the *Examiner*."

Cape Badeau, Missouri

To the Editor:

Sir: The matter between Senator Hagerman and Miss Jessica Roux is a matter here of speculation and excitement, for this is the city of her nativity. The public opinion is entirely with Miss Roux whose qualities and family are well known.

Contrary to assertions, Miss Roux was never a tomboy. Her father, the late Lucien Roux, a distinguished grain merchant, was often urged to run for the legislature. On her mother's side, she is descended from wealthy lumber dealers of Revolutionary stock. She is a niece to the Honorable Cyrus Fitch, a gentleman of activity in banking circles, who was her guardian but is said to have held a slack rein.

It is generally felt that Senator Hagerman's millions would hardly compensate a handsome young woman of Miss Roux's accomplishments for an alliance with one of his age and notorious reputation.

Mr. Fitch desires me to say (a) that there is on file the report of City Marshal Giles T. Clarke who sold at auction city lots and slaves for a substantial sum pursuant to an order of the Court of Common Pleas to partition the Roux estate among the heirs: (b) that every humane effort was made to sell children and mothers to the same buyer; and (c) that receipts for the final distribution of the estate are on file and that by court order he has been discharged as administrator of the estate, all time to appeal having expired.

Yours, etc. Henly R. Smarr, City Clerk.

Trumbull shot an ironical glance at the young lawyer but saw nothing more than naïve indignation.

"Slaves and waterfront property, eh?"

"Prime lots, Judge. Back at Cape Badeau."

"Very aristocratic," Trumbull agreed. "I've got to respect prime lots."

Green said uncertainly, "What else should she do, Judge? What would you do?"

"I can tell you what I wouldn't do," Trumbull said with a glint of anger. "I sure wouldn't let her lodge a criminal charge of adultery against her husband. Not in California. Adultery!" he repeated, mouthing the word with distaste.

Green stood his ground. "Well, it is a crime," he pointed out. "Hagerman was openly debauching those young girls. I think the prosecution is justified in the public interest."

"Public interest? Mister, don't insult my intelligence," Trumbull said harshly. "A criminal prosecution for adultery could hardly produce a thing for your client that's useful. There's sure another and more likely motive."

"What motive?"

Trumbull returned to his cigar. He sucked slowly. "I'd rather not speculate. Who figured to swear out that warrant? You? Mr. Finch? The lady?"

"Actually, she didn't want to bring the criminal charge. It was Pettibone. Can I explain how that happened?"

Trumbull waved his hand. "Not necessary, Mr. Green." The arrest was a blunder. The main thing seemed clear. A powerful and cruel man had been thrown into the clink and exposed to ridicule by the woman who claimed to be his wife. He was being made a laughingstock. It would not rest there. Strong forces would line up on either side and no simple resolution could be forseeen. Wife or not, the woman and

61

her advisers were riding the tiger. What really was intended? he asked. An action for seduction? Breach of promise?

Green shook his head emphatically. The firm had prepared a complaint in an action for divorce—a proceeding pending disposition of the criminal proceeding in the Police Court. Trumbull twisted his beard, accepting the information for what it was worth. "You'd first need declaratory judgment," he observed precisely. "How d'you hope to prove the marriage?"

"We'll prove it," Green said confidently. "The man won't deny that he used the woman sexually. He's said the vilest things about her before witnesses." He broke off uncomfortably. "Never mind that now. It would be monstrous to let him prevail. Judge, what do you think of the claim? Legally, is the marriage valid?"

Trumbull studied a smoky patch in the whitewashed metal ceiling over the gas mantle. It was not simple, he said slowly. The real question was whether Finch & Green could persuade a California court to give judgment against Hagerman. "She's married if a California court says she's married. Can you get it to say so?"

Green looked up oddly. "With your help, Judge. What do I tell Mr. Finch? Will you take it on as counsel?"

Trumbull swiveled restlessly. He riffled the memorandum and threw it aside. "I'll tell 'ee what I don't like," he said angrily. "It's the secrecy. Something's queer. I don't care for it."

"Well, I'm sorry too, Judge," Green said resentfully, "sorry that I took your valuable time. I reckon I'm in the wrong place." He stood.

Trumbull turned. "Oh, sit down!" he said testily. "No case is pure or simple. This woman must have talent between the sheets," he added coarsely. "What's she like?"

"Well, she's very beautiful. Everyone agrees on that."

"That's something. Look 'ee, mister, I've been in the filthiest matters and I'm not delicate. If the justice of the case warrants it, I admit there's an obligation." The younger man, somewhat sulkily, sat. "Is there something else?" Trumbull said after a pause. "Something you h'ain't disclosed?"

Green drew a breath. "Well, it may call for a special appearance. We may need you to argue some special motions."

Trumbull swung about. "What motions?"

"Oh, sorry," Green said apologetically, looking flustered. "Actually we've got some prior obstacles to overcome before

we start our action. Mrs. Hagerman got served this morning
—before daybreak—by the Marshal with a bill of complaint
in the United States Circuit Court."

"Why didn't you mention this before?"

"I'm mentioning it now," Green said.

"Jesus!" Trumbull said.

He rose and strode about the room, in despair at the ways
of young lawyers. "Mr. Green," he said severely, "you've
taken all this time to describe a divorce case—gamy and li-
centious but as you know solely within the jurisdiction of the
state courts of California. Where in hell does the Federal
Court enter the picture? What's in that bill of complaint?"

The young lawyer looked sick. "It's a suit in equity to
compel Mrs. Hagerman to produce the marriage contract to
be canceled and annulled. Also for injunctive relief against
its use elsewhere."

Trumbull blew his breath. "And you waited to tell me
this?"

"Sorry," Green said.

Trumbull came back to his desk with wonder and incredulity. "Canceled for what?" he said. "Annulled on what
ground?"

"As a forgery, I believe."

"You believe, Mr. Green? You believe?"

"I didn't actually see the papers," Green replied. "Mrs.
Hagerman got hysterical and disappeared with 'em before we
could get to her." He sighed with fatigue and shivered.
"We've got to do something about it, mustn't we?"

"I should think so," Trumbull said. He sat down in his
deep leather chair. "Precisely what sort of motion does Finch
have in mind?"

Green turned to a discussion of procedural remedies. He
was not sure he fully understood the equity procedures of the
federal system, but he was hopeful of various lines of attack
outlined by his chief—from a demurrer for want of equity to
the glittering generalities of the Fourteenth Amendment to
the Constitution. "I'm sure there's some way to knock that
action out of the federal courts. It doesn't belong there at all.
Does it?"

"It wouldn't seem so," Trumbull agreed without expression. "What d'ye want me to say?"

"Is there any basis for the federal courts to take over this
matter?"

Trumbull failed to answer immediately. He stood and went to the window, favoring his lame side, and stared into the plaza. "I've no idea," he found himself saying. "I've never heard of this precise action. Wouldn't've thought of it myself. Evidently it stems from an ingenious mind. Generally courts of equity have wide powers to compel production of fraudulent documents which might threaten property rights, but even that has limits. Offhand I cannot recall an instance of a case in point—on these facts. Trouble is, we're in a complex field." He paused at the bookshelf and glanced at a title— *Story on Conflicts of Laws*. "Mister, you've got a clash of jurisdictions. You're on a sea of storms without a compass. However—"

He broke off abruptly. There was new activity across the busy plaza. A group of men had stepped out from the City Hall, an imposing stone structure of modern design erected by a building committee of which he had been chairman. Mayor Gardner was in earnest conversation with Jim Murray. It was evidently not a happy moment. Murray glanced up with blank eyes, then buttoned his coat and stalked off.

"Well, even precedent don't matter," he said in a wave of gloom. "You're in the worst court since Star Chamber. If they've got no rule of law to hold the case, they'll invent one. That court does whatever it pleases." He halted suddenly, struck by his own rising voice, wondering at his own fervor. "By all means be ready to challenge the federal jurisdiction," he advised, "but I'd also be ready with my appeal to Washington."

"What's the rule of law?" Green asked simply. "What court does this case belong in—state or federal?"

Trumbull turned to the array of calf-bound volumes of California Reports which contained his early notes. All other states of the Confederacy (he had written and noted) had entered the Union with established governments. The people of California had formed their state government out of political and legal chaos. A large amount of labor therefore had been imposed at the beginning on their high tribunal—the toil of searching for authorities in an unfamiliar language in an unfamiliar system of jurisprudence as laid down in the codes of Spain; in royal ordinances and decrees; in laws of the imperial congresses of Mexico; in the acts of the republican congress; in presidential regulations; in decrees of dictators and acts of governors. Many of those laws had not been printed even in Mexico, and all the sources had been assembled only with great difficulty and expense. And all that had gone in the rush of laws and customs of the flood of American citizens who had settled in California with their own notions of laws of status and contract—all superimposed on a society in which the units of law were the missions, presidios, and pueblos of a patriarchal nature.

Well, he had lived through all that. The early volumes were filled with his own decisions laying out the jurisprudence of the state of California and its true and proper relationship to that of the federal power in distant Washington. There was in those early writings symmetry and balance, he thought wistfully, a blazing energy, and its memory filled him with longing for an old and forgotten vision of perfection.

"The case belongs in the State Court," he said with finality.

"But the Federal Court might take it away?"

"It might try."

"Then we'd have to convince the Federal Court it has no jurisdiction?"

"It would be advisable," Trumbull said grimly, "and you might even succeed. They're voracious for power, but there are limits. It's a divorce case, when you come right down to it. And mebbe there are limits to how far this Constitution can be tortured out of shape. It'll depend on how the problem's met. Should be a rouser," he added with a grin. The thought of the sickroom on the outskirts of the city came back. "It's tempting, but . . ." He shook his head regretfully. "No, mister, I'm sticking to local matters. I'm really no damn divorce lawyer. Sniffing sheets, studying chamberpots. No, no. Your chief's a persistent old dog. He don't need me to gnaw his bone. He wants a club to beat Hagerman and his crowd. Sorry. He has all the qualifications himself."

Green made no attempt to move. "Would you argue the motion?" he asked persistently. "Judge, please! If we face a federal injunction, someone of stature must appear in the Federal Court. Frankly, Mr. Finch is not the man. He knows that you're the only man in California who can walk into the Federal Court and make that point stick!"

"I'm gratified," Trumbull said after a moment, "but flattery—"

"It's not flattery!" Green exclaimed. "If you weren't the man, I'd be elsewhere, wouldn't I? It's a small matter—just

65

one woman's right to justice—but if her rights can be destroyed, as you say, by a pack of lawless judges, where are the limits? What's to stop 'em from snatching power from the other branches of government? How'll we ever stop sweatshops? Or raise wages? Or do anything decent if they can cripple the states and hobble just about everything they hate? What's to stop 'em this side of chaos if they won't stop themselves? And I won't even mention Dred Scott," he added recklessly. The young lawyer halted suddenly. "Sorry," he muttered, staring at his hands. "Maybe I shouldn't have mentioned that case."

Trumbull looked up. "Not a bit," he said. "Taney was a dangerous fool. I said so at the time."

Green was surprised. "You did?"

"I did indeed," Trumbull said, almost enjoying the moment. "I was just about your age and doing lots of stumping in places where it wasn't popular. It was the Kansas situation that opened my eyes—Kansas, and a lot of other forgotten issues. There was no justification for that decision in the Constitution. Not even in the case itself. All that the case required was a simple hands-off. The status of that slave was determined by the lower courts entirely, as everyone saw. But something lustful got into Taney. He saw a chance to knock out the Missouri Compromise. Why? Oh, I couldn't say precisely. Maybe because it was there—a feeble thing, but an Act of Congress, keeping the nation in balance with some small chance for a peaceful outcome of all its woes. The Missouri Compromise—product of statesmen and legislators and abhorrent to that stolid blockhead sitting as Chief Justice of the Supreme Court. What more tempting target? No, no, I understand all that. I've been a judge. I know the hellish pleasure of handing down a bad decision, knowing that between you and God there's no further appeal—knowing it must stick. Taney does not stand alone in history.

"Was the Compromise unconstitutional? Certainly not, and we no longer pretend that it was. But Taney and the others declared it so. They thought to tilt the balance in favor of the South, and once they did, the war was on. If you look at the cases, you'll find that the Supreme Court never once before dared to void a law of Congress. Not once. It was an absolute judicial invention that it could be done. But so they did and so they do."

Trumbull was breathing hard. He forced a smile and low-

ered his voice, which had been rising to an oratorical pitc.
The typewriting outside had stopped.

"I fought for the South, sir," he went on, "and I abominated the Missouri Compromise as a surrender to fanaticism. But it was a law passed to preserve the Nation by the Congress in which the political power entrusted by the people for good or ill reposes. I was practicing here in Stoddard when that decision circulated, and I thought, Jesus! It meant war! How in God's name could those fools commit this desecration? Six hundred thousand dead because of those silly old men!" He broke off with a gesture of futility. "Every folly and stupidity that able men can contrive have since been let loose upon this nation.

"I tell 'ee, Mr. Green," he went on darkly, "the destroyers of the Constitution are always with us. They all always have good reasons! Today they are the reactionaries, but tomorrow all our socialists and communists streaming here from Europe will be first among 'em when it'll suit their purposes. These people will always find indulgent ears and willing hearts. They're the parricides among us.

"Now I know people are surprised to hear these views from me," he went on, smiling slightly at the younger man's expression, struggling between respect and dissent. "I fought the Chivalry cause in California. I carried a commission for the Confederacy. I—well, never mind all that." A strong gesture put bitter memories into the past. "But that's just it, d'ye see? I saw where all those careless thinkers and reckless judges had led this country—into a bloody monstrous war this country never wished—and when I came back I had to think it all out very hard indeed.

"I accepted the logic of the situation and looked to another day. But what was the outcome? I won't dwell on the War Amendments. Wise or unwise, they were designed to uplift the slave and protect his freedom. Have they done so? Can you show me one decision to that effect? Not so! The Court has tortured and robbed those Amendments out of any meaning. They now serve monopoly, wealth, and the interests of moneyed corporations solely by the dishonest inventions of the Court. So what was the war about?

"That's why these supposed great constitutional cases revolt me. They're not law. They are betrayals of law—politics disguised as law, stealing the vast freedoms and powers that were once our birthright. I do not think the Trumbull who

Green Mountain had this in mind when he took his
. . to meet the British. And the people? The people are

. . . They are blind," he repeated somberly. "They do not see
what is being done."

He roused himself, smiling ruefully, then came back to the
original thread. "Well, well, we mustn't blame Taney too
much," he went on more comfortably, striking a match. "The
real culprit was John Marshall." Green looked shocked.
"Marshall's notion of the supremacy of judicial power was a
disaster and an insult to the civilized political mind. Jefferson
thought so. I'm secretly convinced that Jefferson's tragedy
was his failure to shoot Marshall while he had the chance.
There's a direct line from *Marbury against Madison* through
Dred Scott to all the shit that today passes for jurisprudence.
Slavery—" He broke off, seeing that he was losing his young
audience. "But you're right. *Sed quis custodiet ipsos cus-
todes?* Quite true, then and now. And with special application
here, hey?"

"Huh?"

" 'Who's to guard the guards themselves?' " Trumbull
smiled. "*Cauta est et ab illis incipit uxor?* 'For your wife's as
cunning as you and begins with them.' Seems especially in
point, hey?" he joked.

Green seemed fascinated by glints of sunlight on the jutting beard. "I'm not sure I get it, Judge," he said doubtfully,
not sure of this banter. "Reckon I've got a literal mind."

Trumbull sighed and let it pass.

"Well, anyway," Green went on doggedly, "We need your
help. I've only been pointing out what you've just said yourself about the federal judiciary. You stand for something,
Judge. Your views circulate. That speech of yours in Galveston last year was exactly in point. I cannot see how you can
denounce corruption of the Constitution in Galveston and
run from a test in your own back yard? Or didn't you mean
what you said in Texas?"

Trumbull stared at the ceiling. "Oh, but I wasn't discussing
the True Constitution," he said sardonically. "That disappeared in Philadelphia the moment the ink dried. When the
first lawyer raised the first point and the first court took over,
it vanished like a dream. No, I was defending something else
—the Nominal Constitution under which labor is kept in
bondage, monopolies are justified, human rights subordinated

to formalisms, railroads nourished, and true rules perverted to serve the rising materialism that's rotting the land. I recall my words in Texas, but I'll tell 'ee something. It's too late to stop the process and I've lost interest in futility. I'm out of it all." He sat back with a grin, reflecting that it was a year since he had addressed the Bar Association of Texas on a hot day in Galveston where all this had come up. That speech had been widely printed. The *San Antonio Law Docket,* one of the nation's best local law journals, had devoted all twelve pages to the occasion.

Green said, "Please, Judge. I cannot take a refusal. We really need you; I cannot tell you how urgently. And it's not just this one case," he added with inspiration, "There's a principle at stake."

"Oh, tshah!" Trumbull said irritably. "I know all about the verities, but really the matter's not that exceptional. There are no principles. The calendars are choked with these claims. I know five prior attempts on the Hagerman fortune. They all failed. I can't help you—certainly not while the criminal proceeding is pending." He strode to the door and grasped the knob. "If you'll excuse me?"

Green failed to move. "I cannot believe this," he said with wonder. "Maybe it's my fault. Maybe I'm not persuasive. Maybe I said the wrong things, but I didn't come for legal excuses or refusals, Judge. I came because this woman is lost without help—and because I've read and believed all you've ever said. I didn't think it was just so much wind."

"Confound it, you're damned persistent! Just because I show the courtesies . . ." Trumbull threw up his hands in despair. "Damnation, no! Let be! I cannot. That's absolutely final."

Green stared. "I'll give you another reason, Judge. The community property is anywhere from five million dollars up. Merit, and a fee, I think you said?" he added pointedly.

Trumbull tapped his cheek and finally the younger man lowered his eyes. "Sorry," he said reluctantly. "I shouldn't've said that."

"Why not?" Trumbull said after a moment. "The ability to command fees is part of the art—the main part, maybe. It's the best argument you've made to date." He paused, thinking, shaking his head. "Too speculative," he said finally.

"I'm authorized to say there might be a good retainer in advance. Would you discuss it with Mr. Finch?"

Trumbull failed to answer for a long moment. "I simply cannot. I'm that regretful."

"All right, Judge," Green sighed. "I took you seriously, but perhaps that's part of my education. Well, I won't take that as a refusal," he said in a strained voice, "not till you've digested the materials. We'd like a written opinion on the law of the case—if you can see your way clear." He closed the briefcase and rose, blinking with fatigue. "You're not thinking of the law, Judge. Just about your prejudices against this woman, but what choice has she got? I know what they say, but she's not run of the mill at all. She's got ideas and feelings and convictions. She's up against all the powers in this state, and her life's at stake. Hagerman threatened to mark her and anyone who takes her part, but she's not deterred. Only the men are scared. Well! They said it'd be like this, but it's sure a surprise in your case, Judge."

An ominous and suspicious glint appeared. "Who told you to say that to me?"

"Say what?"

"You say he threatened to mark the woman?"

"She told me that herself. Why?"

Trumbull returned to his desk and studied his hands. Green waited, not daring to breathe.

"I dunno, I dunno," Trumbull muttered.

He looked up. "Let her take a money settlement and leave California. Really, that's best."

Green shook his head. "That's impossible. She won't take that way out. She feels it's a question of honor. I should think you'd understand that. You above all." He smiled without mirth and turned away.

"Mr. Green! One minute!" Trumbull said. "You'll get a written opinion, but no more. Leave the memorandum. I'll sleep on it and let you know."

Green nodded and left. The outer doorbell jangled. A clatter of steps shook the wooden building.

Cudahey appeared with documents and a hopeful expression. He sat and listened to an outline of the interview.

"Something happened there," Trumbull concluded with a gleam of anger. "Just like Hagerman to promise anything to get a woman into bed. Lustful little maniac."

"Think there's a case?" Cudahey asked.

Trumbull shrugged. "It has the smell of truth. Whether they'll let her prove it is another question. It's more than I

70

want to tackle. And don't start on me," he said testily. "I've had all the stump water I want for one day. No more distractions, hear?"

"I'm only the scrivener," Cudahey said unsatisfactorily, snapping his colorful sleeve garters, "but that pile of bills has been waiting for a week." He left.

"Joe . . ."

Trumbull waited for the vexation to drain. After a moment of thought and a half-tumbler of whiskey, he set out on a long-delayed and disagreeable errand to the German Savings and Loan Society. He returned to his office flushed and disturbed, but his mind was not on work. A letter to Zack Yates in Washington was put aside for a calmer moment. He found himself impatient and ragged, striding the office with a heavy muscular prowl, and the worn carpet was gray with ashes. Finally, with an exclamation of impatience, he brought the Hagerman memorandum to the fading light and began to make notes. The hours passed.

Myra Coolth looked in. "Good night, Judge."

"Hum? Oh, yes. Good night, Myra."

"Will you want me anymore?"

"No, no. Run along. I'll lock up."

When Trumbull looked up with a start, it was near midnight. He locked up and left for home. He had not touched the memorial address to the McCabes.

He entered the darkened house and listened at the stairs to the silence. Let her sleep, he decided, and then like a clumsy bear stole into the kitchen and raided the icebox. In the midst of milk and cold hash a phrase kept echoing. How could a man in his right mind threaten to mark a woman?

It would all go into a file marked *Hagerman*.

Chapter Three

"Junction! Junction Point!" A door banged open and a grizzled man in a blue jacket came through in haste. "What's holding us up, Mr. Wilson?" Trumbull asked.

"Taking on the Chicago Section," the conductor replied

halting. "Judge Sickels' private car from Washington's been standing. Should I let him know you're aboard, Judge?"

"Not this trip," Trumbull said. A month had passed. The promised opinion was done. He felt released and indolent indeed. After a moment he went to the vestibule and looked down the line of cars. In a swirl of cinders the Pullmans slid past, nudged by a clanking donkey engine. In the rear platform of a private car marked CHIEF SEQUOIA, an extremely tall woman with a robust figure was emptying a flower vase of water onto the track. A burly bald-headed man with a long white beard appeared, smoking a cigar, and joined the woman in conversation.

Trumbull stretched and breathed the fresh salt smell of the distant sea before he returned to the desk in the parlor car, afraid to lose a train of thought. He had been steadily drinking whiskey since boarding the train at Stoddard.

"Board. Bo-oard. Franklin, Antioch, points west and Oakland. Step lively, folks. Board."

A door banged and the vestibule roared. "Whaddaya wead?" a hoarse voice shrieked. *"Alta, News, Examiner.* Uproar in Police Court. Sweet Jessie Roo. Senator's Vow. Latest papers! Magazines? *Atlantic? Century? Hornet?"*

"I'll take 'em all, Billy," Trumbull said.

Trucks on stiff springs began to clack across open switches. Shanties and open fields slid past, then all California's opulence lay under the morning sun. The train picked up speed and turned west and the glittering blue waters of the bay swung into view. Trumbull turned to a crude caricature in the *Examiner.* All reports of the woman as a flaming beauty were belied by the unflattering drawing. "Sweet Jessie Roo!" the title read. But she was anything but sweet. The hair was a Medusa tangle of snakes, the mouth a witch's mouth of cruelty, the figure raddled. Hagerman to the contrary was sedate and effulgent with idealism. Well, well, Trumbull thought. Considering the incestuous relationships of California's newspapers to her financial houses, the savagery was not surprising. He turned a page. The few short weeks had seen extraordinary developments. The Affair was now in full halloo in rival courts. The Superior Court of San Francisco and the United States Circuit Court were contending for jurisdiction over the action for divorce—absorbing energies which might have gone to a better cause. And both major courts were awaiting the outcome of proceedings before Judge Lester

Strumpf in the Police Court of San Francisco at the Old City Hall. The pall of that minor criminal court hung over the state. It was embarrassing. Foreigners were derisive. Sarcastic items were appearing back east. The *New York Sun* had said it would be a reproach even to Tsarist Russia.

Tom Wickwire in the *Examiner* had found the crowd gathered by eight. By nine, he reported, Kearney Street was blocked. By ten, fists were flying in Washington and Merchant streets. Flower sellers and pickpockets had done brisk business. At least one miscarriage and several heart failures were charged to the excitement.

The courtroom, Wickwire noted, was not a nice place. It had a stench like a slaughterhouse festering in the sun, like an old soap factory decaying into slime. One could not imagine what that horrible hole was like, the account went on. Its few doors were never opened—and if so, only onto airless courts and closets. A sole window was blocked. Along the aisles prostitutes, chicken thieves, and local ordinance violators stood in foul-breathed ranks, waiting summary disposition of petty offenses. In the perpetual dimness gas burners heated the fetid atmosphere. Trumbull sighed with nostalgia and turned to the activity outside the building. Captain Pritchard's helmeted force had kept a surging crowd behind barriers until the arrival of Hagerman's carriage. From that splendid equipage, inlaid with red morocco leather, chased with silver decorations, there had descended a key trio in the drama yet to come—a plump, excitable lawyer, General Solomon Brawn, a pompous leader of the San Francisco Bar; then Galindez; and finally the dandified and apprehensive chief actor of the harlequinade.

A vast twittering like a rising flock of sparrows had gone up and then, screaming and squealing, an audacious group of schoolgirls had rushed the barriers, bowling aside the constabulary, and had pounced on Hagerman with autograph books and cries of delight. Hagerman had retreated in alarm, brandishing a goldheaded cane. "God God, Tony! Keep 'em off!" he had shouted to Galindez, but then had submitted, blushing and grinning. He had been hauled through the mob, struggling and promising autographs. Three buttons and the cane had disappeared in the melee.

Considering the massive crowd which had gathered in expectation of fireworks, Wickwire found the proceedings inside disappointing. "People against Lewis Hagerman!" Almost before the bailiff had done crying the case, Brawn had bounced forward, brief in hand, cholerically demanding permission to address the Court. "One moment, General," Judge Strumpf had said disagreeably, according to the report. "I'm out of ink."

Ink was brought.

"May it please the Court—" Brawn began.

Strumpf had looked up. "Give your name to the stenographer, General."

"Now then," Strumpf went on, "I haven't got the complainant. Where's the prosecutrix? Bailiff!"

"Yes, Judge?"

"Call the prosecutrix."

The bailiff scratched his head. "How do I call her? Miss Roux? Mrs. Hagerman?"

"Just call the case," Judge Strumpf had said, "and let's see who responds."

Wickwire reported that an excited Pettibone had struggled through the crowd assisted by Messers Finch and Green of the San Francisco Bar. The Court came to order.

The gong interrupted the reading.

"Last call! Last call!"

Trumbull looked up with surprise that he had lost track of the time. He took the *Examiner* and went forward, thoughtfully tugging his beard.

The dining car was full. He took his place on line and waited.

"Morning, Judge," the steward said cheerfully. "If you'll come this way, I've got your table."

"Thank'ee, Mr. Hill," Trumbull said. "I'll wait my turn."

"I don't reckon nobody would mind," the steward replied. "I've been holding a place."

Somewhat embarrassed, Trumbull let himself be guided through a warm sunny car delicious with tantalizing smells to a table near the galley. He had the feeling that all eyes were on him. A waiter presented a menu card. He groaned and turned over the bill of fare. "What's good, Claude?"

"Squab on toast is getting favored, Judge."

"No, no," Trumbull said doubtfully. "I'd favor the steak, but you'd bring all those fried trimmings."

"I could keep 'em back, Judge."

"Wouldn't be the same thing," Trumbull muttered. "Lordy,

I'm weak as water. Tum, tum, tum. Oysters? No, no. Poached salmon steaks? I swear, you railroad people are trying to ruin two constitutions," he added. "Mine, and the United States. If not the one, they'll get t'other."

"Eggs Benedict never hurt no one," the waiter advised judiciously.

Trumbull sighed and wrote out a Spartan order: melon, grits with honey, eggs Benedict, cornbread, marmalade, and coffee, then reconsidered. He struck out honey. "I'm supposed to be against corporations," he said humorously, patting his belly. "Don't hold up the coffee."

Trumbull propped the *Examiner* against a sugar bowl and returned to the proceedings in San Francisco.

Judge: Proceed.

Pettibone: We're not ready. We cannot proceed, Judge. Mrs. Hagerman is not present.

Judge: I see that. I'm ordering this case to proceed. Mr. Finch?

Finch: Yes, Judge?

Judge: Do you represent Miss Roux?

Finch: Do you mean the former Miss Roux?

Judge: I mean the lady in the case.

Finch: I'm glad we agree she's a lady.

Judge: I mean the person whose Christian name is Jessica and who claims she married Senator Hagerman.

Finch: You mean the former Senator Hagerman?

Brawn: You see what we've got to put up with, Judge? Unmitigated insolence—

Judge: Please, Mr. Brawn. I can handle Sidney Finch if I can handle anybody. He just likes to be dramatic.

Pettibone (interrupting): Mrs. Hagerman can't be present this morning. She's been threatened—

Brawn: Objection unless specified.

Judge: Mr. Pettibone, can you specify who threatened the lady?

Pettibone: No, but I can't go on this morning with all this intimidation. Other witnesses have been told not to come by ruffians and police officers.

Judge: Oh, that is serious.

Pettibone: Yes, and they won't serve subpoenas on our witnesses—

Brawn: Objection unless specified.

Judge: Mr. Pettibone, can you specify which police officers refused to serve what subpoenas on which witnesses?

Pettibone: I can tell you who offered a packet of money to stop these proceedings—

Brawn: Your Honor!

Judge: Don't interrupt, General. You have bad habits of interruption. If anybody's offering packets of money, we ought to get it into the open. Was it you?

Brawn: Gracious, Judge! Certainly not.

Hagerman (interrupting): That's denied, denied.

Judge: Well, it's denied. Perhaps the District Attorney's Office has something to say. Mr. Tallboys? You've been silent.

Tallboys: I haven't had anything to say, Judge. This city likes to think it's cosmopolitan. We don't prosecute people for adultery.

Judge: And yet it goes on?

Tallboys: I'll have to look that up.

Voice: Home rule for Ireland.

(Commotion.)

Pettibone: I will not be diverted. Nor will I be intimidated. Stand back, Senator.

Hagerman: You——.

Pettibone: Where's Sadie Keenan? How did you get her to disappear?

Hagerman: Well, that's denied too.

Judge: Will someone please identify Sadie Heenan?

Finch: Keenan.

Pettibone: Keenan, Judge, she's one of the women—

Finch (simultaneously):—the alleged adulteress.

Judge: Oh, that! Is that denied too?

Hagerman: Miss Keenan lives in Philadelphia. How can anyone disappear from Philadelphia? She's a fine young Christian girl.

(Laughter.)

Judge: Order!

Hagerman: I have instructed General Brawn not to let anyone make an issue of my private life. I neither admit nor deny alleged relations with anyone in this state whatever.

(Laughter.)

Judge: Order! Very well, if we can get on.

Brawn: Before we come to that—

Pettibone: Will he deny that he paid Miss Keenan five hundred dollars to get back to Philadelphia?

Hagerman: Quack. Quack.

Pettibone: You see?

Brawn: See what? Good Lord!

Finch: Let Mr. Pettibone talk.

Brawn: That's all he does.

Pettibone: I will not be intimidated. I'm not a lawyer. I'm a journalist and I will not be bought—but Miss Keenan was bought. Others were bought. Driscoll was bought. Explain Patrick Driscoll.

Judge: Driscoll now? Can I be enlightened?

Pettibone: I'll be glad to. How did Pat Driscoll turn up suddenly five thousand dollars to a blocked account in the Hagerman bank? Why is that account blocked?

(Commotion.)

Bailiff: Quiet. Quiet.

Judge: That man! You, there!

Voice: Me?

Judge: Step forward. What's your name?

Man: Well, sir . . .

Judge: I will not have these indecencies in my courtroom. Off the record.

Judge (resuming): Two days. Now, then, who—? Order. Who is Driscoll?

Hagerman: Mr. Driscoll is a fine Christian piano tuner. He voluntarily—

Galindez: Not now, Lew.

Judge: Let's have decorum.

Finch: Your Honor, let me explain. Patrick Driscoll is Miss Nellie Driscoll's father. He's listed as a speculator who lives at 824 Ellis Street, but actually he's an unemployed piano tuner. Deaf, you see?

Judge: So Driscoll's deaf—

Finch: Yes, but his daughter, Miss Nellie, is a witness to these circumstances, and she's not deaf. Nor is she blind.

Judge: I see. Or do I see? Will somebody tell me what I see?

Finch: Let me put it legally. Miss Driscoll an Hagerman are friends. They met after Mrs. H

77

was ousted by Mr. Hagerman. It was a natural propinquity between them—

Judge: What was between them?

Finch: Propinquity.

Judge: Ah!

Finch: Yes. Thereafter Miss Driscoll had talks and conversations with the defendant Hagerman. Talks and conversations. Now the defendant Hagerman made admissions to Miss Driscoll that clearly show the *corpus lutem* of the case—

Brawn: Objection.

Judge: Yes, you mustn't enlarge on that, Mr. Finch. I'll only have to strike it. Is Miss Driscoll here?

Pettibone: She is not.

Finch: Let me explain that.

Pettibone: Oh, why won't you let me talk?

Judge: Order.

Finch: But that's the point, Judge. Miss Driscoll can testify that Mr. Hagerman admitted that he signed the marriage contract between the parties—

Brawn: Well, you slipped that one across.

Judge: Would you like me to strike that from the record?

Brawn: No, we know all about that unfortunate girl. She's really a case for the truant officer.

Judge: I don't need finger wagging. Go on.

Finch (resuming): And now her father, a deaf piano tuner, turns up with five thousand dollars. Tampering, Judge. Tampering.

Judge: I don't see how—

Pettibone (interrupting): Miss Driscoll is afraid to come to court. Father and daughter. He's threatening to assume control of the witness.

Judge: I don't see the relevance, and frankly, Mr. Pettibone, I don't see your standing in this case. Can the District Attorney explain what Mr. Pettibone is doing here.

Tallboys: The District Attorney is not responsible for this man. Mr. Pettibone's a common informer.

(Commotion.)

Judge: Another outburst and I'll clear the court.

Pettibone: Oh, this is monstrous. Every witness is threatened. Every lawyer is intimidated or bought off.

Hagerman: It's all denied, denied.

Judge: I'm ready for a motion. General Brawn?

Brawn: Thank you, Your Honor. Tampering? Nonsense. My client, who is universally known for the sweeping plenitude of his benefactions to this commonwealth—

Voice: What benefactions? Oh.

Judge: Order.

Brawn: His proposed benefactions, then—

Galindez: Not now, General.

Judge: Do I have a motion to dismiss?

Brawn: No. Emphatically. The defense demands that they produce this alleged marriage contract in court.

Voice: Remember Feeney Park.

Judge: Order.

Brawn: I should add that a complaint has been prepared to charge forgery, extortion, blackmail, and false arrest.

Judge: Order! Can the District Attorney produce such a document?

Tallboys: I haven't been able to see it.

Judge: Why not?

Tallboys: They won't produce it.

Judge: Is this true, Mr. Finch?

Finch: Mrs. Hagerman has it in a safe place.

Hagerman: I'm tired of this shyster.

Judge: Gentlemen, gentlemen. Please, Mr. Finch. Less levity and more docorum. Will the lady submit the document to inspection?

Finch: She will, but only in the forum of her choice. Not where they can grab and run. Your Honor, I implore you.

Judge: Yes?

Finch: That officer is glowering. It is intolerable to have the police menace and glower at counsel.

Judge: Captain Pritchard?

Captain Pritchard: If the District Attorney will allow me? The police have procured a warrant of search. We've been trying to glimpse the document in question without success.

Judge: Well, do not glower at counsel. Mr. Finch, what's your application?

Finch: A two weeks' adjournment. At least they admit the fornication.

Judge: What about the document?

Finch: It will be produced at the right time and place, Your Honor. It's not here now.

Judge: Application denied. What does the District Attorney say?

Tallboys: I move to dismiss the complaint on the ground that the statute against adultery has in fact been repealed.

Brawn: We waive that technicality. We want a hearing. We demand to see that damnable forgery.

Judge: I'd like to accommodate you, General, but I'll grant the motion. If that document is not produced, the Grand Jury can take action. The defendant is discharged.

Pettibone: Your Honor, I am being threatened.

Judge: What can the Court do about it? See the police. Court's adjourned.

Voice: Free silver and fornication.

A tall, deep-breasted woman in her late twenties entered and was shown at once to the seat opposite Trumbull. "May I join you, Judge?" she asked in a pleasant, crisp voice.

Trumbull looked up reluctantly. "It's not taken," he said gruffly and returned to the newspaper.

"You don't mind?" she asked.

"No."

"Going to San Francisco for long?"

"Not too long," he said.

The train hit a bad stretch and swayed.

"What a lark," she said.

Trumbull looked up. "Ma'am?"

"Oh, that newspaper account," she said, smiling. He followed her glance to the small print. "Lark? Oh, that? I'd call it something else."

"What? Blackmail?"

Trumbull paused curiously. "Why do you ask that?"

"Because that's what Mr. Hagerman calls it." The woman smiled. "Do you think it's true?"

A southbound express hurtled past with a scream. Dishes rattled and then the hum and clatter of the dining car resumed. Trumbull looked up with a frown of suspicion. "Do I think it's blackmail, ma'am? Have you any special reason to ask?"

"Have you any reason not to answer?"

"I'm not sure yet," he said.

"I see your point," she said lightly. "An idle question deserves that answer, but it's being discussed everywhere. Mr. Hagerman stated that he'd put that bloke Pettibone in jail for threats to his reputation. Why isn't that blackmail?"

"Reputation?" Trumbull stroked his beard sardonically. "Good God, ma'am! Hagerman's got no reputation. Any disclosure of this kind can only benefit the man. In comparison with his general iniquity, any specific instance of wrongdoing will seem so trifling as to soften the public judgment. It could only abate the rancor of those he's not yet wronged. He's a cruel scoundrel, and it's well known. So I don't see how the man can be blackmailed. Now, if you'll kindly excuse me." He went back to the newspaper, thinking he was talking too much and unwisely. But that was not unusual.

"Dear me," the woman said and turned to the menu card.

"Judge Trumbull?" said a voice.

Trumbull looked up. An elderly rancher was swaying in the aisle, beaming. "I just want to shake your hand."

"Thank 'ee," Trumbull said. "Mighty kind of you, Mister . . .?"

"Stickney," the rancher said. "You don't know me, but d'you recollect that lecture on Evolution and God's Law back in 'seventy?"

"Ye-es," Trumbull said.

"The Playhouse at Lakewood? The night the balcony caved in?" Stickney went on in triumph, "Well, by Joe! I was there! Just thought I'd tell you that some of us still remember those days."

"Sure good to meet," Trumbull agreed. "How's it coming?"

"Fine, fine," Stickney chuckled. "Never missed a Trumbull lecture. Never have, never will. I see you're giving this memorial at the Hibernian? You going to let 'er rip?"

"I'll try," Trumbull said.

"Good, good," Stickney said heartily. "Let 'er rip, Judge. Let 'er rip."

"I'll do my best," Trumbull said. He turned back to the page, but his fate was upon him.

"You always do. One thing about Judge Trumbull. Once he's in a cause, he's there to the death. Everybody knows that. Can't do better than you did at Sweetwater." Stickney turned to the woman. "Started the Resistance and that's the plain fact. You can be mighty proud of the judge, ma'am."

"Oh, I am," the woman said gravely. "Mighty proud."

"Thank 'ee," Trumbull said, glancing around with embarrassment. "My very best to Mrs. Stickney and all those fat grandchildren," he said heartily.

"Why, how'd you remember them, Judge?"

"Oh, I just do," Trumbull said. "Here, take these," he added, scribbling on a business card, "they'll be complimentary. Now if you'll excuse me?"

"Sure, sure! Remember Sweetwater!" the old rancher exclaimed and went off chuckling.

Trumbull was conscious of an amused smile. "Well, I usually *can* place a man," he said lamely, "if I know the occasion." He returned to the newspaper.

"Then I wonder if you remember me?" the woman said. "That early bonfire rally for the State Constitution years ago."

"Which one, ma'am? There were so many."

"Mechanics' Pavilion in San Francisco. You made the point that the infirmity of popular government is that liberty is merely power cut into fragments so that popular government becomes immobilized and impossible."

Trumbull stiffened. "Oh, but I don't agree with that at all," he said sharply. "Liberty is an absolute. If invaded or diluted, it ceases to be liberty. The argument against liberty is common to tinpot dictatorships and vindictive Utopians, but both are equally odious. I was citing a viewpoint I reject. Hobbes . . ." He paused and snapped his fingers. "Of course!" Center aisle, third bench, a tall, rawboned girl in braids taking notes in a gray notebook. White middy blouse with sailor collar and red sash. What was the name?

"I introduced myself," she said. "I was Fanny Smith."

Recognition dawned. "Oh, yes, yes! You're Ben Smith's granddaughter?" And of course the pieces fell into place. That bonfire rally had climaxed an early abortive campaign for a new state constitution. After that impassioned address, she had come forward to pin him down to details of a radical proposal to fix liability for debts on the directors of business corporations. She was that rarity: a native of San Francisco, born to a family which had arrived in the first Gold Rush days, and of course she would know everyone. Her grandfather, a handsome tall spare Yankee with silvery-white hair, was one of the city's most distinguished men. So that was why that long nose had seemed familiar. Well, freckles were gone, and so were stooped shoulders. She was now a handsome woman with a quirky smile and a robust, assured manner.

And with a connection to the Hagerman bank.

"How is your grandfather?" Trumbull asked. "Does he still attend every opening night?"

She laughed. "Oh, yes. We were both there at that benefit performance the night Mr. Hagerman got arrested. Grandfather put up the bail and berated the police. He's in splendid form. His handwriting is the same copperplate script it always was and I love to get his letters. It's marvelous how he holds up."

Trumbull said nothing for a long moment. "Well, now, Miss Smith, you must let me help order breakfast."

"Not Miss," she interrupted, smiling. "It's Missus now. Mrs. Woodruff. I'm back from England."

Trumbull looked over the bill of fare. "Are you? I had not heard. Is Mr. Woodruff with you?"

"I'm a widow."

"I'm sorry," he said after a pause.

"Rafe was all right but he had a poor hold on things," she said crisply. "I expect that was the Spanish side. Mamacita Woodruff was an Otero. Lovable people, but when the family lost the land, Rafe didn't know what to do with himself. It all went in that lawsuit that had something to do with a Spanish land grant, or what was left of it." In any case, she resumed, her husband had gone adventuring to Peru, where he had died of the cholera. "No children, so that was no problem," she went on cheerfully. "Fact is, I wasn't cut out for marriage, or perhaps Rafe wasn't cut out for me. I gave him and *la familia* a devil of a time, I'm afraid. At least it left me free to travel and work, and that's something. So perhaps it was all for the best," she concluded heartlessly.

Trumbull cleared his throat, thinking he had received an unusual amount of information in a short space of time. "I think women should work," he said. "And hold political office, of course. What work d'ye do?"

"I write," she said. "I've just been seeing publishers in New York."

Trumbull nodded profoundly. "What name do you write under?"

"My own," she replied.

What the devil did one say to that?

"What d'ye write about?"

"California. Short pieces. Chatter. Articles."

"Articles? What sort of articles?"

"Whatever's wanted," she said. "California is all the rage in England," she went on. "I wonder, Judge Trumbull, if I might call on your recollections of California?"

"You wouldn't want my recollections," he said grimly.

"Oh, please!"

"Sorry. At this moment I've got enough on my plate. Who's now printing this stuff of yours?"

"Oh, it's mostly the English." California painters, singers, actors, writers swarmed in London and the call for items, she advised, was astonishing. "Then you're essentially a reporter?" Trumbull asked. "Well, it's nothing to be ashamed of, I reckon," he said after a pause. "But I'd feel easier if I knew precisely why you decided to have breakfast with me here."

"Eh?"

"It could just as easily have been ordered from Judge Sickels' private car, could it not?"

She looked up to find a gaze of most peculiar intensity fixed on her. She laughed uncertainly. "That's clever," she said after a moment.

"Not a bit. I saw you empty a flower vase back at Junction. Didn't I see Senator Pike with you? That white beard can be recognized a mile—like a mule deer's flag."

He was referring to Senator Josiah Pike of Nevada. Pike was a respected opponent out of the Comstock past.

Fanny stared coolly. "Yes, he's in the party. He joined us in New York."

Trumbull studied the open, arrogant face for a long moment and for the first time saw the woman. She was almost as tall as a man, he judged, but her large frame was poised and balanced. He had an impression of a keen satiric mind and extreme competence. There was a disconcerting twinkle behind the monocle. He considered various implications possible in that gathering in the private car. Aloud he said, "Is there anyone else in that party I might know?"

"Well, of course Justice Sickels and Mrs. Sickels. I'm sure they'd adore to see you, if you'd like to visit."

An ironic smile played. "Me?"

"You don't seem enthusiastic. I thought you were old friends. Can I be mistaken?"

"Does Judge Sickels know I'm on the train?"

Her laugh was a rich contralto. "Oh, I think he knows if a sparrow falls."

"Yes, he's a great collector of droppings."

"Oh, Judge Trumbull," she said reproachfully, half laughing. "He's a dear old sweetheart. What are your feelings against him?"

"What makes you think I have such feelings?"

"Tone. Your voice sharpens. Your eyes narrow. A pulse beats. Your mouth tightens and I feel dread. Come, Judge. What's it about?"

"Nothing much to talk about," Trumbull said abruptly. "I'm disappointed in him, I reckon. He's got ability and application, though he ain't the prodigy they say—but then, who is? He could be a great judge. With his insights, he could make a true contribution to the nation. He knows the central issues of our times. He has talents."

"But they're not realized?"

"No. He has great powers of rationalization. He's supposed to be a strong judge, which means that he's bold in aggrandizing power for his Court, but that virtue's questionable. He's forgot where the Court's power ends and where the nation's begins. Like those Egyptian priests, he makes noises in the echo chamber to simulate the god, then listens to the echo of his own voice with awe and adulation for the god he has become. Then he's beguiled by political ambitions—that last ridiculous campaign in Cincinnati to get the presidential nomination disqualified him forever in my opinion for the bench. I'll tell you one thing I like. He's not dull, but that's about the limit to my praise. Now I'd rather not get started on Sickels, or I'll use up this hour and I'm finding it much too pleasant without him," he said in a burst of gallantry and found his cheeks reddening.

Fanny saw the touch of color. My word, she thought. He's thinking I'm a widow—and what are the prospects? And perhaps exactly that thought was there in Trumbull's mind. "I have a feeling it's more personal than political," she said aloud.

The grunt was enigmatic. "Well, ma'am, what else d'ye want to talk about?"

"The Affair," she said.

"Shall we see about that breakfast?" he said after a pause. "If you'll allow me."

"France is sexual, England is obscene," she said decidedly, licking her fingers. "Loathsome beyond words. It's something murky in the climate, I daresay. The place abounds with twittering men and horsey women. Simply cannot get too much of *that* in their dreadful penny press."

"Ah?" Trumbull followed her glance back to the *Examiner*. They were enjoying each other thoroughly. London and its social and literary scene had come under discussion. Fanny Woodruff had a gift for small talk, he observed. A retentive mind, sharp eye, and dramtic flair had thrust her into the business of writing, and her marriage into the Woodruff y Otero family had given resources she could exploit. Spanish society was formal but small and affectionate, and everyone knew everyone. Family chronicles were for the taking, and her first short pieces, rooted in legend and social observation, had found a market in England. She was passionately Californian, attached to places, people, legends, and, surprisingly, the political institutions of the state. One would not call her beautiful—until she smiled, and then the arrogant features lit up with warmth and friendly intelligence.

Trumbull came back to the story in the *Examiner*. "But why should England care about this nonsense? Haven't they got their own scandals, with all those duchesses getting divorced? This is so remote."

"Well, it's not that remote. Emily's making it a local item, I hear." She swept into a description of the social uproar in Belgravia and Kent. Lady Emily Haskell-Frobisher, Hagerman's pretty younger daughter, lived in London. Since Lord Edward, her amiable husband, was younger brother to a duke whose title went back to the Wars of the Roses, and since her fabulous wedding reception at Beaufort—(second in vulgarity and extravagance only to that of the Duchess of Marlborough)—had been splashed all over England, the family scandal in California was meat and drink to Fleet Street. An English girl might have met the storm with freezing indifference, Fanny smiled, but poor distracted democratic Emily was babbling denials and explanations in a fury of mortification all over London. "I say, is this boring you?" she asked abruptly.

"No, no," he said gravely. "On the contrary, I find the

English exotic and interesting. Inscrutable Asia, I submit, starts at the Bristol Channel."

Fanny laughed.

"Did you see much of Emily Hagerman in England?" Trumbull asked.

"Ra-ther! Californians, unite!" Fanny said, mopping up the last remains on the plate. "The poor girl's beside herself with this thing. She's burning up the Atlantic cable, although I cannot imagine why this peccadillo should be so especially distressing. She's rallying the family. Loathes the idea of a stepmother. *Any* stepmother, but especially Jessie Roux. Claws are out."

"I could suggest another basis for all this."

"Ah?"

"Half the Comstock," Trumbull said dryly, "and perhaps Lady Emily's marriage settlement was not quite that vast. Hagerman's not King Lear. He's got a tight fist."

"He's an affectionate father," Fanny said after a pause. "And grandfather."

"So they say," Trumbull said, "affectionate and doting. It's the one flaw in what otherwise is perfection."

Fanny laughed uncertainly. "My word, this looks heavenly," she exclaimed, sniffing with pleasure at the iced melon. "But it's all interesting. Wot?"

"Is it?" Trumbull said noncommittally.

"Interesting enough for the London *Telegraph*," she said coolly. "It's a dreadful rag, but I've got a good offer to report the Affair. My word, every editor in Fleet Street is cabling for special coverage, but what can I do? I cannot furnish what's expected. Or be fair or ruthlessly honest, which I'd have to be. I know both sides, you see."

The moment was suggestive.

"Does that mean you also know Miss Roux?" Trumbull asked slowly.

Fanny saw no more expression than she might in a courtroom. "Well, of course I know Jessie Roux," she said slowly, "but I cannot say I know her too well. Not . . . my cup of tea," she said briefly.

Trumbull drew a design on the tablecloth.

Fanny's eyes had narrowed. Damn vixen! she thought. She smiled thinly, "I think you must be a good lawyer."

Trumbull looked up. "Ah? Why, ma'am?"

"Because you're listening and I'm talking," she said. "And

yet you need not be so wary, you know. I can't say I want to tackle this story. How can I hope to make clear our fantastic legal system to others when I cannot understand it myself?" A writer's opportunism flickered. "I wonder if I might draw on you for information. I cannot understand why those other courts should grind to a halt to wait on that harlequinade in the Police Court."

"Not important," Trumbull observed. "Both sides are sparring for advantage. People don't understand the minor courts. It's the little things that determine larger issues. Each side tries to get concessions or admissions into the record. In this case it was nonsense to try. The court stenographer is deaf. He garbles the record."

"Oh? Shouldn't he be replaced?"

"Depends. It can be enormously useful for later cross-examination. Nothing like confronting a witness with prior garbled testimony he's bound to deny he ever said. The man's invaluable."

She laughed uncertainly. "But the judge there was not a regular police judge?"

"No, he's a Superior Court judge."

"What's he doing in Police Court?"

Trumbull found the question most perceptive. On a special order, he explained, a Superior Court judge could preempt the lower court judge if he chose. He said, "I imagine some special purpose to protect the record was being served."

"The assignment was manipulated?" she exclaimed. "Oh, ruddy hell!"

He was amused. "But why are you surprised, ma'am? You know the politics of this state. The essential thing is not always the law of the case. It's who decides the issue of fact. That's what will continue to happen here—an intense struggle on the factual issue. If that breaks down, the courts will manufacture law to suit the case. In the real sense there's no such thing as law in this country. Or any other, I reckon."

"I cannot believe you're in earnest, Judge Trumbull. If that's your feeling, why keep at the game?"

Trumbull paused. "Oh, I dunno. We strike wet matches in a high wind," he said, smiling slightly, "and hope one will sputter. The law's not something Platonic. It's not up there in Eternity. The law essentially is nothing more than the ability to predict the Court's behavior in specific cases. No guarantee of the next case, but it has a short-range value and guards against surprise. It's the modern view," he said drily. "Why else ring in a special judge except to ensure the outcome? It accounts for the struggle to establish a favorable forum that's now going on."

"Oh, what's that?"

The latest development, Trumbull explained, was an application by Hagerman's lawyers to transfer Jessica's divorce action from the Superior Court of San Francisco to the United States Circuit Court for trial of all the issues.

"I don't grasp this. Can that actually be done?"

"It can be tried," Trumbull said, "under a recent Act of Congress—in a proper situation."

"Is this a proper situation?"

Trumbull shook his head. "Not one bit—and his lawyers know better."

"Then why have they done it?"

Trumbull smiled at the look of shock. "Their audacity is not limited by conscience or legal knowledge. The federal courts constantly enlarge their jurisdiction at the state courts' expense. I daresay they're relying on a favorable judge to get a ruling."

"What's Jessica doing about it?"

"Something appropriate. Her lawyers have filed a motion in the Federal Court to remand the case back to the State Court where it belongs. It's up for argument in a few days. The decision will be critical."

"Oh? Why so?"

"Oh, because in the State Court she has a chance to proceed on the merits. One or two judges, recently elected, are known to be honest. More than can be said of the Federal Circuit Court."

"My word! That's a bit strong."

Trumbull was enjoying the moment. "Perhaps it won't come to that. In view of the precedents, it'd take a bold set of judges who'd keep jurisdiction. I doubt Judge Goff and Judge Abernathy will summon the courage to deny the motion to remand. It'd stink like a rotten herring from here to Massachusetts. But I'm sure this cannot entirely be news, ma'am."

"Oh? Why not?"

"Because I'm sure it was discussed in that other car," he said with a hard smile. "Judge Sickels must've talked about it. He's real talkative and an old intimate of that crowd—Stanford and Colton and Hagerman—and quite indiscreet. It'd be odd if he didn't voice his opinions on this topic of the day."

Fanny laughed good-humoredly. "I'll not pretend," she confessed amiably. "The whole world's talking about the Affair. We've been following the newspapers since Chicago. I think a lot can be said for Jessie's side of the case—at least Grandpapa Smith thinks so. But I don't suppose that's something I can discuss with learned counsel, while the matter is pending."

Trumbull looked up suddenly. "Counsel?"

"Well, I had the distinct impression . . ." She paused. "Have you been jollying me along? I'd heard that you'd decided to enter this case. Was I misled?"

The deep eyes suddenly flickered with suspicion. "Who told you that, ma'am?"

"No one told me. It was something I heard in passing," she replied. "It's nothing, really. I hope you don't mind my talking about it?"

Trumbull shrugged. "Nothing's yet decided. If it is, I'll make a statement where it belongs. In court."

He mashed a roll of crumbs to dough. All the pleasure had fled. "What else did Justice Sickels say?"

"That it was a pity all this arises at this particular time," she replied, flushing under the penetrating stare. "Really, Judge Trumbull, that's all that was said." She became intensely interested in the linen napkin. "I'd also heard that an offer would be made to get you to drop out of the case. I gave it no belief, of course."

"Offer?" he said.

"That's what I heard," she said. "That's all it was. Just something I heard. I'm sorry if I'm wrong. I feel embarrassed."

"Not a bit. It's a public matter. You're entitled to speculate." He crushed his cigar ash and paid the bill. He spoke with deliberation. "I'm counsel to no one yet, ma'am," he said with emphasis. "I've had no 'offer' from the other side. I'd be surprised if I did. Brawn's talents may be for sale. Mine are not. But if I should finally undertake Miss Roux's cause," he added, leaning forward, and the short broad nose was suddenly slick with moisture, "I'd advise Mr. Hagerman's friends to be most circumspect in any suggestion they might wish to make. Excuse me now." With a curt nod, he took up the *Examiner* and left for the parlor car. Wrong! All wrong! he thought, breathing heavily. What had led him to a denial which at best was only technical? That rodomontade had long since gone out of style.

The waiter appeared, "Will that be all, ma'am?"

"I rather think so," Fanny said, thinking of the man who had left. It was only when he rose that she had seen the enormity of his bulk—the deep broad shoulders, the extraordinary arms. Something in the man was assaultive, she thought, struggling against repressed, tightly held feelings—feelings that could smolder and suddenly, she suspected, burst into flaming violence. But there was something else. The dogged mouth was too thick for strength, the lower lip too sensual, the deep eyes too indolent and lazy and almost—what should she think?—yes, almost feminine. She reminded herself that she had good insights, read French novels, had had passionate love affairs in England's country homes, and had met the Prince of Wales. Men like Trumbull did not often come into the life of a woman five feet ten in stocking feet and almost ten stone in whalebone stays and with a mind of her own. What was it she had found so attractive? The easy drawl? The intelligence that warmed and respected her own? "Ruddy hell," she murmured, turning from these thoughts. She had not learned a thing from the man. But she was stirred and did have an idea for her notebook that could bear fruit in the fullness of time and that was worth the pleasant hour.

"Oakland! Oakland and last stop!"

A brisk wind was ruffling the blue waters of San Francisco Bay. The sun was uncommonly bright in a clear blue sky. The waiting ferry returned the signal as doors opened and the passengers stepped down.

"How lovely!" Fanny exclaimed, breathing deeply the salty wind. "Why would anyone want to live anywhere else in the world?"

"It is kind of nice," Sickels agreed. "I always feel refreshed by that sight." San Francisco on all her hills was gleaming across the bay beyond Yerba Buena Island.

A large yacht, the *Encantada,* blowing plumes of smoke, was lying at a nearby wharf. "My dear," Sickels said to Fanny, "you'll enjoy the *Encantada.* Finest appointments in the world. Gold fixtures, marble tubs, genuine English antiques. You'll love it."

"Excuse me," she said abruptly. She strode off with long

strides to the end of the platform. "Hullo," she said. Trumbull nodded gravely and introduced Green. "How d'ye do," Fanny said, taking in the young lawyer at a glance. "Judge Trumbull, will I see you again in the city?" she asked without ceremony. "Perhaps you'd like to see my grandfather. I'm at home Wednesdays for tea. I promise not to probe."

"Perhaps," Trumbull said. "I'm sure it would be nice, but I doubt there's anything in it for your pieces."

"Maybe not. But a chat with Grandpapa might be useful. He keeps banking hours and generally manages to get there on time. Not later than five o'clock, eh? Mr. Green might like to join us. It's all madness," she added abruptly. She left for the private wharf where the *Encantada* was taking on passengers.

Hagerman was waiting for the party. "Welcome aboard," he said genially, turning to Sickels. "We've got tubs of fried chicken and all the wine you can drink, Jack. Let's forget courts and law business for the afternoon, hey?"

"How are things, Lew?" Sickels asked.

"Bully. Splendid. Couldn't be better." Hagerman grinned. "I've got a lot to tell you. If the ladies will come this way," he added gallantly, "we'll have refreshments and then we'll talk. Fanny, my dear, I've got regrets from your grandfather. Just couldn't face this choppy water."

"Neither can I," Sickels said. "You'd better hold back on that fried chicken."

Blowing her whistle, the *Encantada* plunged into blue waters. The C. and S. W. Ferry blasted an answering signal.

Trumbull met Green's eye with raw embarrassment. "Writer," he said uncomfortably in total explanation of Mrs. Woodruff. Green had other things in mind. "I'm so darned grateful you've come," he said fervently. "Mr. Finch won't admit it, but we sure need help. Let me take those valises."

"Thank 'ee, no. The day I cannot heft these books, I'll tear down my shingle. But you can tell me what in hell Finch thought he was accomplishing yesterday by that Police Court fiasco."

Green had lost weight since his visit to Stoddard. "Not our idea," he replied exhaustedly. "We tried the worst way to withdraw that charge. But he did his best. He was satisfied to show Hagerman up in a disgraceful light."

"Disgraceful light?" Trumbull followed the yacht disappearing toward the west. Hagerman had looked more like the cat that had swallowed the cream.

"You might as well have this," Trumbull said, handing over a thick sheaf.

Green whistled in appreciation. The memorandum, fastened in brass, covered in blue, ran to hundreds of pages. It was thick as a book. "Gosh, I didn't expect this much, Judge. I reckon Mr. Finch'll be more than grateful," he exclaimed, riffling the pages. He was longing to get into the extended text and sick with envy at the glimpses of a bare, terse style that stated the law with strength and economy. "Excuse me," he said and became absorbed in the text. Trumbull was smiling.

As the ferry nosed into the slip, the sound of newsboys could be heard. Even before the hawsers snaked out, they were leaping aboard with the latest developments of the Affair.

"Sagamore House," Trumbull finally said to the driver, when the dust had settled. He sank back and spread the afternoon edition as the hack went jouncing along the cobblestones of Market Street. Well, there it was. A simple announcement in the Federal Circuit Court. All motions in the Hagerman case were set for the next-motion calendar day before a special three-man bench. Mr. Justice Sickels of Washington was scheduled to preside.

Chapter Four

Nevada Block was a large office building with wide tiled floors, ornate gas mantles, high ceilings, and dignified brown-oak and frosted-glass partitions. It ran heavily to note brokers, speculators, and lawyers. It was a respectable address, not quite as prestigious as the new white stone buildings rising elsewhere in the financial district, but good enough.

Sidney Finch was aware of these subtleties. He was not happy with the Nevada Block, but he made do with the galling less-than-first-rate. He had knocked two offices together to make one large chamber overlooking Montgomery Street. From this point of vantage he commanded a view of the Hagerman bank and other institutions of a terrain peculiarly his own. In large gold-leaf letters the plate-glass windows proclaimed: SIDNEY FINCH, ATTORNEY-AT-LAW and in smaller script: Finch & Green.

A massive desk of polished redwood burl, very ornate, stood on a platform. A high backed chair commanded a room of fine appointments with deep-seated leather chairs, a working hearth, lithographs of the Comstock, and a bookcase of leather-bound memoirs of the generals of the Civil War. Something queerly generous in Finch's intemperate nature was pleased to claim that no book agent and expecially not a demobilized veteran of the Union forces had ever been turned away without an order for some compendious work of great length, printed in large type, lavishly illustrated and bound in gold-stamped morocco covers. Finch was staring at this array in temper. Everything was going wrong with the current matter, which had his office in an uproar. Alfie Buchholz, an underslung but dogged investigator, was getting the blast. A knock interrupted a monotonous stream of Irish obscenities.

"Come in," Finch said harshly.

Nathaniel Green entered and announced that he had Trumbull in the anteroom. "How does he feel now?" Finch asked. Green waggled a hand. Finch spat with disgust and hit a brass spittoon. "I'll be with him in a minute."

Green nodded and left. Finch stood morosely cracking his knuckles considering the litter of telegrams, letters, and hastily scrawled notes to himself. "Memo to Self," he wrote. "Keep temper. Apply soft soap. Vain old bird. Avoid politics. Keep your big mouth shut. From: Sidney Finch." He studied the reminder and put it aside. "All right, Alfie," he growled. "Find out what's happened to Pettibone—and where's the lady? Hey? Jump." With an air of suffering, Buchholz left.

Trumbull meanwhile had pursued an old routine at his hotel. The Sagamore House had a pleasingly gloomy lobby decorated with potted palms and rubber plants. Cuspidors and sand boxes accompanied deep and comfortable leather chairs inhabited by drummers, out-of-city lawyers, and the theatrical fraternity.

The wizened bellman staggered under a set of heavily laden valises.

"I'll git a towel, Judge," the bellman gasped, lingering.

"Thank 'ee, Lem." Trumbull searched through keys, penknife and found change. "This should hold you," he said, flipping a silverpiece. "Why, this is too much," the bellman said.

"I'll be the judge," Trumbull said gravely. The door closed. Now why, he wondered, had he parted with a half-dollar? What had that proved? He removed tie and collar and sat heavily on the bed. Lord, Lord, Lord, he murmured. He was suddenly tired. The headlines had provoked a violent swing of mood. He was sunk in gloom.

He began to unpack. Military brushes were placed on the bureau. His razor and toilet articles—soap cup, soap, fine badger hairbrush imported from London—were placed at the sink. Books were organized on the mantel. Shirts, underwear, and socks were stowed neatly away and extra suits hung in a large oak wardrobe. He lay on the bed and thought back to the pleasant hour in the diner.

An hour later, he awoke, feeling refreshed and in a better mood. He brushed his Prince Albert and lifted a thread from his topper. He fastened gold links and studs into a white broadcloth shirt unmarked by travel grime. When his heavy tread brought him into the lobby, he was humming a Mexican hat-dance tune. A message was in the box.

"I'm always at Lucchetti's. I. Sinzheimer."

He crumpled the paper and left. He refused a hansom and strode off toward Montgomery.

"Give 'em hell, Judge!" a swarthy laborer called from a trench where a new gas main was being laid. "Skin 'em!"

"I'll sure try," Trumbull said good-naturedly. A crowd of idlers were gathered at *The Examiner*, reading a display of latest headlines on The Affair. A flatbed press could be seen, clanking out the news. He paused and strode on through the busy street. San Francisco! The most marvelous city in the world, he thought.

He was now in Finch's anteroom, enjoying the atmosphere of the profession. Finch & Green had an active though minor practice that ran the gamut from divorce cases to Chinese laundries. A wild-eyed litigant was thumping a manuscript at a bored clerk.

". . . a clear case of plagiarism," the litigant was saying excitedly. "I need a lawyer who's good at plagiarism."

A toothpick shifted. "We don't take those cases anymore. Not without'n a consultation fee. It would be five dollars in advance."

"Ridiculous! Have you got another lawyer you'd recommend? I want the best."

"Oh, I could recommend Mr. Brawn's firm," the clerk said solemnly. "But I should warn you that he's got high charges."

"Higher'n yours?"

"Reckon so. Even more. Maybe fifteen dollars."

"Well!" The disgusted litigant glared angrily at Trumbull. "Are you a lawyer, sir?"

"Yes, but I charge even more," Trumbull said quickly.

"You *do?*"

"I most certainly do!" Trumbull said firmly. "And moreover, I don't handle that kind of case anymore."

"Ain't there anyone interested in justice anymore?"

"Oh, I reckon so," Trumbull drawled, "but some firms charge more for justice than other firms. I'm that sorry."

"I see I'm wasting time," the litigant exclaimed bitterly and slammed out. Finch was at the door, twirling his spectacles. "Come in, Judge," he said affably. "Dee-lighted you've come. Very good of you."

"Hello, Siddy." They shook hands. Finch turned white and a grunt showed the agony of crunched bones. "This way," he gasped.

A short hall lined with engravings of Presidents of the United States led to the private office. Trumbull put his topper on the hatrack. He sat and studied the room with appreciation. "New carpet?" he asked.

Finch was wringing out his hand. "Actually," he said in a strangled voice, "it represents a fee."

"Ah?"

Finch mopped his neck and put it finely that a client in Pacific Street had been forced to close down at a moment when her cash position was poor. Trumbull's expression was prim. "Oh, that? Glad some of us find the practice rewarding. It's a dying profession," he said, taking a cigar.

"Trumbull," Finch said with a broad smile, "Mark Trumbull!" he marveled, savoring the moment. "Lost hair, put on weight, but it's becoming. I cannot tell 'ee how gratifying I find this. By rights,"—a broad smile appeared—"I should've called on you. Not you on me."

Trumbull said nothing.

Green entered and took a chair near a side table.

Trumbull said, "Siddy? Did you expect this last development in the Circuit Court?"

Finch blinked. "I expected something," he replied slowly. "Not this exactly, but I was never too sanguine there. I've been telling Natty to expect the worst, but he's still under the illusion that the federal courts are here to dispense justice. I must admit, however, that Sickels' appearance in the case is unexpected. Has that affected your decision?"

Trumbull failed to answer. "Mr. Green," he said, turning to the younger lawyer, "I had thought to meet the client this morning."

Green said, "She was supposed to be here."

"Unfortunately she's missing," Finch said with regret. "This morning's news seems to've upset her. She's a night bird. Reads late, sleeps late. This early we cannot expect punctuality. Natty takes the night shift," he added with a wink. "I hope she'll behave better toward you. She's got the most intense admiration for you."

"Very flattering," Trumbull said. "Well, what do we discuss? The law of matrimony in general, or this move by Hagerman to take your divorce case into the Federal Court?"

"First things first: the general laws of matrimony," Finch said, smiling broadly. "I've had no chance to look into your memorandum of law, but I do hope your opinion is favorable." He produced the memorandum with an air of deepest respect. It was obviously a work of scholarship, far more than expected, and undoubtedly the foundation of any line of action to be pursued. However, the morning had been so fraught with that really vile news from the Circuit Court of Sickels' arrival that he'd had no chance to do the work justice. Natty had given him the most favorable report on its contents. It was really marvelous, stupendous. Incredibly persuasive as far as he'd gone.

"Not too bad," Trumbull said, gratified. "Some weak points, but it indicates a universal rule. Marriages are made in Heaven. They're favored by the laws of all civilized nations including Canon Law and Natural Law. I wouldn't doubt the Talmud's favorable, although since it ain't indexed I couldn't get too much out of it. I say, Siddy, d'ye know any good rabbi I might question?" he asked.

"No, I don't," Finch replied.

"Too bad," Trumbull said with regret. "I like to be thorough. You'd be surprised how useful the Jewish authorities can prove—Josephus, and all that." He looked up with a

97

teasing grin. "Well, Siddy? *Semper presumiter pro matrimonio.* Stick to that and hope for the best."

"Does that mean the law's on our side?"

"Yes."

"Well, I'm relieved," Finch said. "I just like it said plain. I kind of reckoned it's come out like this. But it is good to have authority."

"I'm just wondering," Green said hesitantly, "if the Judge found a case that's really in point?"

Trumbull took the question with good nature. "Not quite in point," he said easily. "But no case is ever exactly in point. That's the charm of it all. The uncertainty principle. D'ye know anything about quick clay? It's like quicksand but more deceptive. It's clay saturated in water and any shock—a falling rock, a horse, can turn it to soup. Encountered it once in Louisiana and I tell you—a countryside can disappear while you look! Think on it." He puffed thoughtfully in the respectful silence. "I've been at this game a long time. Used to think it a quest for logical certainty. But, hell! The life of the law ain't logic. It's experience."

"Oh, that's good!" Green said.

Trumbull cocked a brow. "Ain't it, though," he said and looked creative and modest.

An early case in the House of Lords was discussed. New York. Wisconsin. A minority line of decisions in Massachusetts was distinguished—constipated bunch, but one could not brush Massachusetts aside. It was that pleasant communion so rare in a lawyer's life—legal minds united on a point of law. Trumbull finally started a fresh cigar. "So much for the law," he said through the fragrance. "How's the preparation shaping up?"

Finch brightened. "Oh, it's a good case," he said warmly. "Natty's been devoting himself exclusively to this matter. We're getting all sorts of help even from total strangers. It's amazing how kind and generous the common man is. You'd think all these rumors and slanders might be damaging, but quite the contrary. There's a tide running in our favor. Aside from the marriage contract itself, we'll have no dearth of persons offering to prove the marriage. Natty, bring those folders. . . ."

Over a score of large file envelopes were stacked on a long side table, boldly marked and flagged with names of witnesses.

"Please, Siddy," Trumbull protested. "Later, perhaps. What's it all designed to prove?"

Finch halted. "Well, the respectability of the connection," he said warmly. "We've got all sorts of people ready to testify that he always treated the lady with respect and deference, not like those other hired sluts of his. She was no ordinary lay," he added aggressively. He opened a cabinet. "Snifter, Judge?"

"Please."

Trumbull smoked thoughtfully and considered the statement. Whiskey and tobacco were easing the strains of travel, and his nap had done marvels. "I wouldn't paint her too respectable. She ain't applying to be canonized—merely recognized. More to the point. Have you got any witnesses to show admissions by Hagerman that Miss Roux was his wife?"

Finch paused in midflight. "Dear saints!" he exclaimed with a disagreeable scowl. "What d'ye take me for? Of course we've got witnesses. If . . ." He hesitated.

"Yes?"

"*If* they'll stick, of course," Finch said grimly. "It's surprising how much they forget on the second interview."

"What about the family?"

Finch arose and went to the window under a surge of deep feeling. "Oh, those people," he said venomously. "We have our difficulties with the lady, Judge," he said angrily, "but under the circumstances she's a model of behavior. As brave and dignified as she's beautiful. I can forgive Hagerman—he's what God made him, a disgusting debauchee. But that's a natural weakness of the flesh. But that family? Unspeakable, how they've turned on her. No, no, Judge. Don't ask me about those people."

"That bad, eh?"

Finch returned to the desk morosely. "Yes, that bad, Judge," he said in discouraged tones. "Oh, there's no doubt Hagerman called on them with our client. Tea, sociables, things like that. Paid his respects to the grandmother and extended unusual credit to her uncle on some doubtful real estate, but not one will come forward with helpful testimony. Their understanding, they say, was that an engagement was in prospect. What in hell good does that do the poor woman —an engagement? I cannot squeeze out an extra syllable of testimony—not from that uncle, nor that brother. Both, in fact, have found it convenient to leave for the East. And they won't put up a nickel. The expenses are already intolerable, and I'm not sure where it's all coming from. However," he said, forcing a pained smile, "that's my end of the problem. Can we refresh that glass?"

"Please," Trumbull said. Then he looked up with a sniff of appreciation. "Where *is* it coming from?" he asked.

Finch laughed. "Well, Judge, I'm still entitled to one or two office secrets. Let's just say that the lady is not entirely friendless. However," he added hopefully, advancing on opportunity, "I could make a disclosure under some conditions."

Trumbull twisted his beard thoughtfully. "What's the situation in Superior Court? Trouble with the Pee Jay?"

"Why, yes! How'd you know?"

"Oh, there's always trouble with the Presiding Justice. What's he doing to you?"

"That's another thing," Finch said grimly. "He's pressing us to waive a jury."

"I should imagine he would," Trumbull said tolerantly. "On what basis now?"

"Ostensibly to save time. If we don't waive a jury, he threatens to send it out to Strumpf."

"Hm. Yes."

"Strumpf? He's a scut!"

"What about one of the others?"

"What others? None of 'em any good," Finch said with feeling. "Only possibility is this new feller, McArdle. Catholic, so supposedly against divorce and shenanigans, but he's honest and there's a labor background. If we could get him, I'd waive the jury."

"Any chance for that?"

"McArdle? Not a chance! Meanwhile the Pee Jay says he won't tie up a trial department while he's likely to get hit with a federal injunction. I was distinctly told to get rid of that federal action or get short shrift in the Superior Court. We'll never get on that trial calendar."

The deep eyes began to smolder. "He actually said that?"

"Almost in those words," Finch said.

"Outrageous! What's happening to the courts?"

"Exactly." Finch sent a flickering glance to the younger lawyer. "We're between two stools. Now suddenly, just as we are ready to press ahead in the State Court, we're on the federal calendar before Sickels and Goff and Abernathy. I trust you understand why we've been so urgent for your help? It's bad enough in the State Court. It's the damned Federal Court that's got us worried. Your appearance there would be challenge—a sensation they'd be forced to recognize. It'd change the entire atmosphere of this case."

"I ain't that unique," Trumbull protested without conviction. "I merely promised an opinion, and that you've got. There must be someone else."

Finch shook his head emphatically. "No one of your stature," he said strongly. "I've canvassed every list down to the border. You're the only practitioner that's conceivable. Judge, I wonder if you can possibly appreciate what's happened since your name began to circulate—what fear you've struck in the other side? Just last week, I got word from a certain prominent attorney in Los Angeles. I cannot mention his name, but he's held highest posts of honor in this state. He was approached by the other side and offered a large fee to enter the case if necessary to oppose you. The gentleman has a reputation for physical fearlessness, Judge, quite equal to your own. Without question you'd know his name. He's been mentioned for Collector of Customs. He's had a reputation for rashness thrust upon him in the past. Quite unjustified, to be sure. Those few incidents in his record were actually imposed by rowdies and hired bullies. Los Angeles—" A gesture ended this interesting line. "Well, let's not discuss that outpost. This lawyer is most distinguished, a man of ability and integrity, and he turned 'em down cold. It was a big fee, Judge, large and flattering, but when he heard the part he'd have to perform, he withdrew. I think you know what would be expected of him. He'd be asked to affront you."

Trumbull stirred, "Nonsense," he said. "It's just too preposterous."

"I have the gentleman's letter," Finch said. "Would you like to read it?"

"Was it sent in confidence?"

"Yes."

"Then keep it in confidence," Trumbull said. How the violent past lingered into the present, he thought in a wave of gloom, and how incongruous it all seemed. "I'm past all that —and you don't need to lay it on with a trowel. I know it's a good matter."

Finch let a moment pass. "Would you like to review the files?"

101

"Not now. T'ain't necessary." Trumbull looked up curiously. "Siddy? How'd this matter get into this office in the first place?"

Finch smiled broadly. Miss Roux, it appeared, had presented herself several months before Hagerman's arrest for adultery, bringing a copy of the marriage contract. She'd been in frightful agitation because of discouraging advice from other firms. Some had denied the basis for any action, others had called her marriage contract so much excelsior, still others had tried to seduce her. In fact, she had been recommended by the firm which previously had handled her personal affairs—MacGowan & Galindez. It was MacGowan who had said that Sid Finch was exactly the kind of lawyer she required.

Trumbull raised a hand. "She'd left Galindez's firm?" he asked sharply. "Then Galindez knew all about this before this lawsuit?"

"Oh, yes! Indeed, she also consulted Solly Brawn," Finch went on in tones properly ironic among lawyers. "She's quite a digger for help."

"Go on," Trumbull said slowly. The story was coming out in bits and pieces, not too agreeably so, he thought.

Finch went on. "Well, I examined the language of the marriage contract. I was satisfied that it met all requirements of the Civil Code of California. I dictated an opinion. She paid the fee and left. I should add that she was using a *nom de guerre*—Miss Rambeau, I recall. She wore a veil, spoke in whispers, and left a lingering perfume that caused me embarrassment at home. Mrs. Finch, you see, has extraordinary olfactory powers. Hey, Natty?"

Green looked uncomfortable.

Trumbull said, "Did she name the supposed husband?"

Finch looked shocked. "Dear saints, no! Merely that the man was wealthy, owned an important mine in the Comstock, controlled a bank in Sansome Street, and operated two hotels in this city. I had not the least idea whom she had in mind. Wouldn't've affected my legal opinion one bit. No more'n yours." A solemn look went to the white painted metal ceiling. He added sturdily, "I based that opinion solely on my professional experience, my study of the statute, and the prospective fee. Anyway, she must've been impressed because when the storm burst, she came back for help. I must say, I felt gratified."

Trumbull turned a sharp glance to the younger lawyer, then came back to Finch. "You're sure she brought a copy of the marriage contract? She didn't come for instructions and then return another day?"

A laugh was without mirth. "Now, Judge," Finch said with a hard look, "Natty's my witness I did not concoct the instrument. I merely reviewed the language and furnished a written opinion. It's in proper sequence in our letter press volume."

"I'm relieved you've got that proof," Trumbull said after a pause. "I trust you're ready to authenticate the document with expert testimony?"

"Pooh! No problems when the time comes. In that respect the client has done a job of work herself. I haven't seen the original contract yet, but I have solemnly warned that anything fake will not be countenanced by me. So we can assume the instrument to be genuine."

"Quite an assumption," Trumbull said. He stirred, considering a far deeper conflict that the other lawyer with all his persuasive powers could understand. He looked up disagreeably, frowning. "Where's the complaint for divorce?" he asked.

Trumbull had seen the first drafts, but the final document brought a special clean sense of pleasure. A sense of confusion and vagueness lifted. In a contingent world it set boundaries and parameters to that special truth which only the courts could establish. The simple and clear statement did credit to the good lawyer who had drafted it, he said generously. Green flushed with honest pleasure. The signature was jagged and brilliant with green ink. A final paragraph attracted his attention.

"Mr. Green, it was less than half this figure when you called on me at Stoddard."

Finch interrupted. "We've had further intelligence this week, Judge. We then had no idea that the C. and S.W. had effected a merger with Central Western. We've also just learned that those new Cornish pumps in Belshazzar are now emptying the twenty-five-hundred-foot level satisfactorily. All that has affected the size of the holdings," he concluded with a grimace of satisfaction.

Trumbull laughed and stepped to the window. The sun was now high and bright.

Thirty million dollars.

Not fifteen.

Thirty.

One half of the Hagerman fortune.

It seemed ludicrous and unreal to find the audacious claim resting in this second-rate office where now he found himself.

He looked up with a hard glance of suspicion. "I tell you something I still find disturbing. You had all these facts long before Hagerman got arrested. Yet you failed to act on your client's complaint in good time and let him beat you to the Federal Court. How could you let a dandified fart like Solly Brawn catch you in a snap? Were you asleep?"

"Oh, shit!" Finch threw aside his cigar. "Look here, Judge. It's not easy. The lady has other advisers, and she don't listen to her lawyers. She procrastinates. Anything puts her off. A black cat, an unlucky day, a bad horoscope. She's in her monthlies. Or too fatigued to get out of bed. She's changeable. Serene one day, suspicious the next. Bibble-babble, bibble-babble. Not easy to control. Not," he added quickly, "that it matters. The most difficult client is entitled to her day in court."

"Suspicious of what?"

"Well, really, it's so hard to know," Finch said seriously. "That first day she showed up, she was so grateful to find a firm willing to take her cause, I could've laid her on that couch. Might, too," he added with a grin, "if not for Natty. Natty swears by the angel." Green flushed uncomfortably.

"Sounds interesting," Trumbull said. Finch chuckled. He could not understand such scruples. The rules of the matrimonial bar were quite liberal. A lawyer's first duty was to his client's wishes, he winked. And that occasion had been quite special. Gaspy voice, tearful cornflower-blue eyes, dainty nose-blowing, white helpless fluttering hands—and a lawsuit worth millions. Dear saints! He was only human.

"And then, you say, she changed? How? When?" Trumbull asked.

"At the first feeler for settlement. You'd think," Finch marveled, sorely aggrieved, "that I was betraying the woman. At the mere suggestion the storm broke. She attributes hellish powers to the other side. Everything's a trick. No one can be trusted. Everyone can be bought. Even Natty's under suspicion. God knows what's on her addled mind." A crooked smile was painful. "Judge, I thoroughly understand that you only promised your opinion on the law. Quite so. We're delighted, gratified, but frankly I'd hoped to persuade you to

104

take a more positive position where Natty failed. Has anything I've said changed your mind?"

Trumbull shook his head.

Finch rubbed his skull vigorously. "It's a big case," he said angrily. "Too big to be destroyed by qualms and second thoughts." He caught himself and forced a calmer, more equable tone. "Now, Judge," he said cajolingly. "I've shown every courtesy and respect, you'll agree. I don't understand this reluctance. I don't want much. I just want your appearance in the Federal Court. Write your own ticket as to fee, but I feel entitled to a fair answer. Well?" A pause. "Judge, what's disturbing you?"

A cold look passed between the trial lawyers—a glance that belonged to the bear pit. Trumbull made an angry gesture. "Dunno," he said. He strode ponderously, thinking out the shape of the case. It eluded him now. Finch was no bother. He envied trial lawyers like Finch—unthinking men, bulldogs trained to tenacity, advocates as instinctive as animals, goaded by greed and by burning zeal of narrow intensity. The fantastic grimaces, the accessories of low-grade courtroom behavior—rattling coins, portentous leers, masturbatory diction, fancy dress—were marks of function. His own style—if he had one—was a torment of worry and doubt and the crutch of principle. "I'd sure hate to find I'm eating rotten meat," he muttered.

Lord, Trumbull thought dismally. What in hell was he doing in this place? The younger lawyer, so intelligent, so serious, understood nothing of what was passing in that room. The truth was an ache in his heart. "Let me see the list of witnesses," he said slowly. "It's no commitment, but d'ye mind if I sniff around to satisfy myself? But don't count on anything."

When the door had closed, Finch returned to his desk. The reminder to himself of caution was in a middle tray. He tore it to bits. The pieces fell into a Navajo woven wastebasket. Why, the son of a bitch! he thought. A rancorous grin illuminated the vulgar domain.

Chapter Five

Mashers were always a problem to a girl with an hour-glass figure, but Nellie Driscoll had not the time of day for the toughs and dandies at the windy corner. A secret knowledge of important happenings had given the day purpose. She jumped off the Market Street trolley and then hurried ahead, through incredulous whistles, smacking sounds, and low remarks, the short distance to Wisteria Place, sweeping her skirts through the muddy wet crossings. Her eyes were popping with excitement as she opened the door.

"Chew?"

The kitchen range had gone cold and a frying pan was gray with hardened fat and bacon specks. "Chew?" she called. Dolly Varden, the misnamed white rabbit, a buck in his outside hutch, and Stanford, the pet bantam cock, had not had their rations. "Darn that Chink!" she exclaimed.

She went to his lair. It took a climb, but she was young and vigorous and swarmed up the ladder like a navvy. The attic room smelling of cedar shingles was dim and empty but for a torn pallet, a pipe with a sweetly sickish smell, and slips of paper with mystic ideographs. The pipe was for opium, she knew that, and the ideographs, taken from the scriptures of Confucius, served the purposes of a Washington Street lottery called *bok-a-bu*, which she did not know; but in any case Ah Chew, the house boy, was gone.

"Jesus, Mary! I'll rip the dirty hide off him, if I lay my hands. Why can't she ever keep a servant?"

She climbed down and entered a small room overlooking the back yard. The room was strewn with pencil drawings, gorgeous cravats, a nobby velvet jacket, roller skates, and a bowl of hair pomade. Goldfish were swimming in a tank. "Sonny?" she said automatically. There was of course no answer.

"What the devil now?" she wondered.

106

Perfume filled the front bedroom. A dressing table was garnished with oils, essences, and powders. Tortoiseshell boxes were choked with hair—russet puffed from the one; jet spilled from the other. Stockings, shoes, and whalebone devices peeped from a closet. Powder streaked the carpet and a large brass double bed was unmade.

All that could wait, she decided. She filled a portmanteau with blouses and skirts. Shifts, handkerchiefs, bloomers, corselets, gloves, stays, dresses—all went into the bulging luggage. Panting with effort, she took a bench with the carving LOVE to the closet. High up among discarded hats, fans, gloves, and shoes she found a box of japanned metal. She muttered with relief and climbed down slowly, clutching the precious burden. The doorbell jangled.

She put the box on the bureau. The jangle resumed. With a wary expression, she checked the lock. Across the way a freckled schoolboy, confined with the chicken pox, was staring. She strode to the casement, eyes flashing. "Johnny Prior," she said sharply, "you get away from that window this instant!" The jangling resumed. She clattered down the stairs and threw open the front door.

"Oh, you again!" she said resentfully, pausing. "What d'ye want now?"

Green took off his hat. "Hello, Nell. We were hoping Mrs. Hagerman would be here. Is she in?"

The girl's eyes were dark with hostility. "She's not here," she snapped and tried to close the door. Green put out a foot. "Is she coming back?"

"No idea."

"D'you know where she is now?"

"Can't say."

Green found all this tiresome. "Well, suppose we talk inside? It's all right," he said wearily. "This isn't the truant officer. It's Judge Trumbull."

"Oh, yes!" The girl was a sharp-faced little thing, no higher than the watch chain hung across Trumbull's vest. The gloomy face broke into a smile. Trumbull lifted his hat. "I've been looking forward to this," he said pleasantly. "Sho, now, Miss Driscoll, you won't deprive me of the pleasure of a few moments."

"Well . . ." Nellie said uncertainly. She stepped past the lawyers onto the porch and glanced about suspiciously. Wisteria Place was not far from Rincon Hill. The old Spanish building lots, measured in *varas*, were narrow, and the houses constricted, but the amenities were kept up. Most of the residences were brick and stone, with long French windows, opening, Southern style, on decorative iron balconies. Others were wooden frame houses with porches set with wicker furniture, chairs, and hammocks, and front yards with rose trellises and enclosing hedges. Magnolias had been planted by the first Southern families.

A police officer strolled into the street. "That's the second one today," the girl muttered.

"Second one of what?" Green asked.

The girl looked up with anger. "They've changed the one on post. There was a different one this morning. They've got an eye on this house. They're all in on it, working against her. That's why Digges was supposed to be on watch, the black devil."

Trumbull asked, "Digges?"

The girl flicked a cold, estimating glance at the stranger. "Tom Digges. He's Mrs. Lawes's driver and he's supposed to watch out. Not that he's much good at it," she sniffed.

"Watch out for what?" Green asked.

"Why, they might try to get into the house," she replied. "You know they're working against her, Mr. Green. She was warned against the police and what they can do. Them, and the newspapers and the courts. Don't you know that?"

Green turned to the older lawyer. "I said it'd be like this, Judge. We're wasting our time."

"Oh, I think not," Trumbull said good-humoredly. "Sho! It's just to get acquainted, if nothing else. I'd like to know more of this." And a twinkle was at once weakening and irresistible. "Now, we cannot properly talk on the porch, miss, can we?"

"Guess not," the girl said sulkily, "we've got enough of a name in the neighborhood. Come in. But don't think I'm imagining things," she said waspishly. "Some men broke in last week and stole the majolica, but would the police do anything? All they did was muddy the carpets, and steal things, and ask dirty questions, the scum. Come on." She turned and led the lawyers into a dark narrow parlor filled with heavy furniture and smelling of gas. "I can turn up the lamp," she said.

"Not necessary, miss," Trumbull said. "We'll only stay a minute."

"Well, I was just getting dressed to go out. Take any chair you like except the Queen Anne. It's an antique," the girl said with a meaningless giggle. "Or try the Chinese Chippendale. It's got a broad bottom," she added impudently.

"Thank'ee," Trumbull said gravely.

"You know the Chinese began to imitate the Chippendale right after the English landed in Hong Kong?" she said informatively.

"I did not know that," Trumbull said.

She studied the bearded face penetratingly. "It's a fact. They can imitate anything. Oh! I'd offer you something," she added, remembering manners, "but last time I brought out the cooking sherry, you should've seen the faces. Excuse me." With the same meaningless giggle, she ran upstairs.

Green said, "D'ye see what I mean, Judge?"

Trumbull followed the sound of footsteps overhead. Old instincts were stirring and it was vital, he reminded himself, to remember that he was still an onlooker. "She's just a child," he said indulgently. He strode about classifying each article with the retentive powers of a strong and orderly mind trained for the purpose. Tarot cards were strewn on a pedestal table.

He was at the fireplace, examining a bronze peacock, when he heard a clatter in the hall.

"It was a present from *him*," Nellie sniffed. She entered and sat, twining her ankles about the legs of a chair covered in striped satin. The ornament had come from Beaufort, she added with a watchful air, from the East Room, where it had been an important decoration. It was worth scads, but it was not for sale or pawning, not at any price. It was a French import and the feathers were real. Trumbull found himself smiling. "So they are," he noted, touching the feathers and marveling. "I'll have to ask Mrs. Trumbull about this. It looks all right."

"All right?" The girl looked amused. "I should think so!" The peacock had originally been presented to Beaufort at a great reception given to the Japanese Ambassador on his first visit of state to California, she went on animatedly. That was before the Senator had acquired Beaufort from Mr. Clare Gresham. "Course, that was before the bank crashed and Mr. Gresham committed suicide. The Senator snapped up Beaufort. Snapped up everything. That's how he got his real big start. Him and Gresham were partners in the bank and the Comstock and—and, oh, all sorts of deals."

Trumbull adjusted his spectacles and studied the girl more closely. He was not sure he cared for her expression. There was something hostile, something not quite pleasant. The little plump heart-shaped face should have been pretty, but her skin was pasty and something missed. Perhaps the pointed chin. Or the nose. A thin septum dipped uncomfortably below flared nostrils, showing almost translucent cartilage. The stout breasts, thrusting forward like twin guns, were too large to be interesting. But there was undeniably a sparkle in the child. "You seem to know a lot about the Senator's affairs," he said curiously.

"Oh, yes. He was always talking business and giving recitations and presents. And a lot he wouldn't like to get out. We could a tale unfold on that," she said with satisfaction. "Well, never mind. We just do know more than he thinks we do. Jessie could've had anything she liked from Beaufort, before the separation. There was that amber necklace that belonged to his aunt. That pearl brooch he brought back from Washington. Oh, yes, and those two hundred shares of Belcher after that musicale she gave in his honor. Of course she never wanted expensive things," she added quickly. "That peacock was entirely his idea. You should see the things she threw back at him," she concluded with a giggle.

Trumbull waited, but there was no explanation. "Two hundred shares of Belcher?"

The girl tossed her head. "It was going at one dollar a throw at the time. They had a lot of transactions between 'em. And I don't care what lies he's dreaming up!"

"Where are all those presents now?"

"Took 'em back," the girl said resentfully. "Actually he stole 'em back and took her letters and things, but of course that's just her word against his. Will you want to ask questions about that, mister?" she asked cynically. "If it wasn't for the papers he stole, she'd have a lot more proof. He's real smart!"

"Well, that's what we'd like to discuss," Trumbull said. "But if Miss Roux ain't home? Well, it ain't that urgent," he said carelessly. "Too bad she's not in. Perhaps she'll get back later in the day. Mr. Green, can we adjourn for luncheon?"

"Sure," Green said.

"Well, she's got nothing to hide," the girl burst out. "She's

110

just terribly upset by the news this morning and—and afraid. She just didn't want to talk to reporters or—or—"

"Or her lawyers?" Green interrupted.

The girl turned in a flare of anger. "Lawyers! Much good they've done her. All they think about is fees and not about her. Jesus, Mary! She doesn't need lawyers!"

Trumbull studied the girl closely. "Miss Driscoll, I wonder if you appreciate the problem Miss Roux's lawyers are facing in Federal Court?"

"I was here the night they served the papers," the girl said venomously.

"Then you must know what was in those papers?"

She nodded bitterly. "They're trying to take away her marriage contract." She hesitated. "Judge Trumbull, can they really do a thing like that?"

"It's entirely possible." Trumbull opened a timepiece thoughtfully. "Lordy," he sighed forebodingly. "I wish people'd understand how many lawsuits get lost by delay. Coming, Mr. Green?"

"Sure thing," Green said, rising.

"Well, I'm sorry," the girl said uncertainly. She followed the lawyers into the hall. "Aren't you going to ask me questions? I've been with her ever since the Senator had her thrown out of the hotel."

Trumbull looked interested. "But not before?"

"No-o," the girl admitted.

"Then you have no direct knowledge of the marriage? Too bad," Trumbull said with a kindly smile that dismissed hearsay.

"No, but she told me lots," the girl replied. "That was before the lawsuit began. So it was . . ." She threw a questioning glance.

"*Ante litem*," Green supplied.

"Exactly! *Ante litem!* Before the lawsuit! So it should count for something!"

Trumbull was deeply impressed. He threw a sharp glance at the younger lawyer. "Indeed! What was the date of that eviction, Mr. Green?"

"I'm not sure," Green said.

In fact, Trumbull knew every important date of the case.

The girl looked from one lawyer to the other with suspicion. "It was before Christmas," she burst out. "She just came back from her grandmother's into a real shambles—

carpets ripped up, door off the hinges, all her clothes higgedly-piggledy, and smelly detectives ready to throw her out. Her maid was terrified. Then Captain Webster—ooh, there's a black villain!—Captain Webster wouldn't release the trunks until she paid every last trifling charge. She was too proud, too lofty to do anything except call that upstart a name. She wrote the Senator the most heartbreaking letters, pleading how it was practically their first anniversary, reminding him how happy they'd been the last Christmas, appealing to him not to treat a girl so dishonorable and without cause—oh, the most wrenching appeals, but it was useless. What a Christmas present!"

Trumbull threw a side glance to Green. "Then you met and became friends?" he asked sympathetically.

"Not right off," the girl replied. "Not till after New Year's Day. I know because the kids had a New Year's Party and we were up celebrating." She thought carefully, moving her lips in rote. "That's how I fix the date," she added, satisfied.

"What happened after the eviction?"

The girl thought back, frowning. "Well, she was so distraught she stopped over the night with Mrs. Martha Watson, the colored woman who keeps this restaurant she used to eat at. Then, in her misery, she stayed with her grandmother. She got very little help *there!* Dudley—he's her brother you know. He was told to take her to San Jose to recover from the prostration, but it was no use. Then just after New Year's Day, Dudley took rooms for her with Mrs. Olafson next door to us and that's when we met. She had this brain fever. She was laughing and crying and imagining all sorts of things. My bedroom faced hers and it was scary. Mama told Mrs. Olafson to send her off to the Female Hospital. They would've too, except that I came over and nursed her. She almost died. Fat lot anyone cared."

"What was she doing in San Jose?"

"She was in retreat, I guess." The girl sighed. "You can bet she wasn't playing games. She kept sending entreating letters Mr. Hagerman never even answered—let alone got. I could tell you lots. D'you really want to know the truth? How he tricked and swindled her and all the rest?"

"Later perhaps," Trumbull said carelessly. "What happened at Mrs. Petersen's?"

"Mrs. Olafson's!"

"Didn't I say Olafson's?"

"No, Petersen's."

"Lordy," Trumbull said, "I reckon I'm kind of vague. Now you say she had brain fever? How'd you know it was that?"

"Well, she was cowering and talking about imaginary monsters," the girl said with an absorbed look, "and whimpering how everything was phosphorescent—her toothbrush and the toilet paper in the outhouse. That kind of thing. That's how."

The girl went on to explain that when the fever broke and Miss Roux awoke, a clear sun was shining in the room. Miss Roux had turned and wondered where she was. Nellie had replied that the place was next to her mother's boarding house in Ellis Street in San Francisco.

Miss Roux had turned weeping to the wall. Then later the girl had brought a good breakfast of soft-boiled eggs, rose-hip jelly, toast, tea—and, oh, yes, a rose from the garden, which had brought more tears. Miss Roux had wept, moved by the kindness of strangers, and revealed the circumstances. "The villain!" Nellie had exclaimed, appalled at the beastliness of senators and millionaires. Finally Jessica had wiped her eyes and invited confidences in turn and suddenly Nellie was not a schoolgirl with no future but a real person with a brilliant woman of dazzling social distinction for a friend who was treating her like an equal. It all came in a spate.

"Can't we skip all that?" Green interrupted. "How did you get to know about Hagerman?"

He got a sulky glance. "Well, about six weeks later I overheard some dirty gossip," Nellie went on animatedly. "She was the talk of the boarding house, of course. This Sunday morning—Papa and Mama were at church—I went to her room in a pretty angry mood. I told her I'd heard she was Mr. Hagerman's mistress and I didn't want to be associated with her. All that talk about the new woman, I said, was just so much stuff. I told her she was nothing but a charlot."

Trumbull looked up. "A what?"

"A charlot," Nellie replied.

"Oh yes," Trumbull said. "Then what?"

"She laughed," Nellie said simply. "She told me she was sworn to secrecy but she was married to Mr. Hagerman and it was all right. Actually, she said, she had no use for him or any other man, and it was a shame how women were subjugated and, oh, things like that. They'd had a quarrel, she said, and she was through with the man. He was nothing but

113

an old scorfulous without family. Just a nobody from Oberlin —Oberlin is a town in Ohio," she said informatively, turning to Green. "End of the Underground Railway, so you can see! Ohio was one of the worst states of the Union. . . ."

Trumbull sat, spreading the tails of his frock coat. He was apparently struck and impressed. Yes. Yes. But did she have more direct knowledge of the marriage?

A questioning glance went to Green.

"You can tell Judge Trumbull," Green said.

The girl bit her mouth dubiously. Well, it was this way, she went on. The marriage was understood. Their friendship had ripened and Jessica had moved into her mother's boarding house and took meals with the other guests. No one except Nellie knew the awesome secret of her marriage, and all the talk and gossip about the beautiful woman could not shake their friendship. Nellie revealed her dreams and aspirations, her disgust with kissing games at the public school and her longing to escape the tedium of Ellis Street. In return the fascinating woman confided her own determination to strike out for a new life in business but was willing to take advice from Nellie. Nellie was astonishingly mature, Jessica thought.

"Miss Roux wanted nothing from Mr. Hagerman," the girl said firmly, "but I made her see that a husband was obliged to support a wife. Miss Roux revealed that she had a series of promissory notes from the Senator plus the promise of a house. I insisted that she protect her rights and she agreed. We attended Mr. Hagerman's office many times to collect on those notes. Usually I waited downstairs near the cashier's windows while she went up to the private office. I despised the man from the time I met him."

Trumbull nodded sympathetically. "You met him? How? Where?"

"At the bank," Nellie said promptly. "Sometimes she'd come downstairs in ten minutes. Sometimes it took longer, and she'd look excited, usually when she got less money than she wanted. One day she said on impulse—she's very impulsive, that's her big fault—she said, taking me by the hand, 'Miss Driscoll, I want to introduce you to a Senator. He's a very great man.' So that's when I met Mr. Hagerman for the first time. My! It was a shock. I thought he'd be twelve feet high with muttonchops and a corporation. Like all those drawings of him in the magazines—and Mr. Morgan, and Commodore Hofmeyer and all those other despicables. I

114

thought how insignificant he looks! He's no taller than me and I'm the shrimp in the family. I said so later to Miss Roux and she laughed and said that size wasn't always the thing. I was very innocent at the time."

The girl sighed. "So I was there. He talked to me about my father's circumstances, which he seemed to know. He was very sympathetic. He told me Beaufort had ten pianos, and if my father was a good piano tuner he could let him have the contract, and would I like that? He has a good singing voice, which I thought surprising."

"How d'ye know that?" Trumbull asked.

"Well, he often sang for us," Nellie replied. "He tried hard to be affable to me but, knowing how abominable he had treated Miss Roux, it set my teeth on edge. I must've showed my feelings because later Miss Roux reprimanded me. She was married to the man, she said, and had a duty, and would expect a close friend to understand her position, and not show a pickle face when her husband was showing the courtesies. She could understand how I despised him but I had to behave like any lady in the circumstances. I finally agreed, but we didn't speak for days."

"Remarkable," Trumbull murmured, turning about. "Don't you think so, Mr. Green?"

"Most remarkable," Green agreed. "Miss Driscoll hasn't told you about the receipts for the promissory notes."

"Receipts?" Trumbull said with apparent surprise. "What's that about, Miss?"

"Oh, those. Well, on that first occasion she said, 'Senator, your little wife is here to get some money today.' He said, 'How much d'you want this time?' She said, 'I suppose two hundred and fifty will do for now.' Other times it'd be three hundred or five hundred—whatever the necessities, or the bills. She wanted charge accounts, but he was against that. Sometimes he'd pretend he was busted, but that'd be teasing. Usually she signed receipts—which I expect the other side has."

Trumbull stirred. "A wife gave her husband receipts for living expenses? Didn't you think that strange?" he asked doubtfully.

"No, I didn't think it strange," the girl retorted. "She explained that to my satisfaction. She had lent him money to invest for her—so when they parted, they made a settlement. That's why he insisted on notes and receipts—to prove it was

115

business to Galindez, who was dogging him. Mary, Joseph! It wasn't her idea. He had these sayings how records were important for her own protection. But if you ask me, he was just playing with her to—to make a record. She gave receipts because he'd play irritable and mean, and when she charged him with frenzied bookkeeping and petty tactics he'd put on these terrible furies. I got fed up with how he was making a rag of her, how she was letting herself be trod upon. I upbraided her, but she was too much a lady to cope with him. Every time he fussed about money she fell into one of her states. When that happened she couldn't go out, she got so ill."

"Ill? How?"

"Une crise des nerfs," the girl said precisely. Every now and then, Miss Roux would draw the blinds of her bedroom, lie down on the bed, announce that she was not to be disturbed. She would remain so for days, touching nothing, huddled under covers, whimpering. Suddenly she'd call for a hot bath and dress herself, then stroll the fashionable streets, shopping, and she'd write furiously to friends all over the country.

Well, on one such day of moping, bills simply had to be paid. Nellie had plucked up courage and had appeared alone at the bank and asked for Hagerman. Hagerman, she said with narrow slitted eyes of suspicion, was being held incommunicated.

"Incommunicated?" Trumbull asked.

"By Galindez," Nellie said bitterly.

"Then what happened?"

"I threw a fit," Nellie said, grinning suddenly. "I was taken upstairs to the private office by Mr. Ben Smith, who was real nice and considerate. Mr. Hagerman had this jaunty smile—more a smirk, really maddening. He asked why I called on him. I said I knew Miss Roux was his wife, and we had to settle her finances."

Trumbull said, "What did he say to that? Yes, that she was his wife? No, that she wasn't? Or what?"

"Well, he didn't deny it," Nellie said firmly. "He just said, 'Oh?' like it was natural. So far as I was concerned, it meant yes. I know what you'd like me to say, but I can't go that far."

"I don't want you to say anything," Trumbull said, "except the truth. Go on."

116

The girl shrugged. "He said not to talk about it, but he was pleasant and smiling, I must say. I described how Miss Roux and I were thinking of renting a certain house for thirty dollars per month, because the situation in Ellis Street was getting irksome. Mr. Hagerman laughed at the proposition. He said that house shouldn't rent for over fifteen dollars per month, and there was a better house he planned to buy for Miss Roux in Golden Gate Avenue if she was nice to him. He didn't think Miss Roux should live poorly. It reflected on his standing, he said, him being a United States ex-Senator and a millionaire, and he said the house would cost eight hundred to fix up including wallpaper. I thought that would do Miss Roux fine. Then he talked about converting the house to flats and he'd let Miss Roux have a flat for an investment. I thought that was mean. I argued that a flat was not a house. Then he told me the plain truth—that he wanted to do more for Miss Roux but that Galindez had got wind of the matter and so it was just impossible. I then asked point-blank why he didn't acknowledge the marriage and he got agitated. He said he was surrounded by spies and mischiefs. The family was making his life hell. He begged me to tell Miss Roux that he'd do the right thing in time but not to press him just then or send letters which could fall into his children's hands. They were the bane of his life."

"The letters?"

"No, the children!" Nellie said seriously. "Emily was especially a trial, he complained, raising hell all over England! Theo was just a college boy, but still it was vexing to get these reproachful letters from Yale, of all places. Then Galindez . . . well, Galindez is a tale unto himself. So I advised that he had to expect those feelings from grown-up children, but Miss Roux was not mercenary and would be glad to work out a settlement. He seemed to appreciate that assurance and said emphatically that Miss Roux was acting bully —real bully! Those were his words—and he appreciated her concern. He wanted me to understand he was not really a vile seducer but a helpless man living in the public eye, and that he was working hard to get the family to accept Miss Roux. I said that didn't help Miss Roux, who was miserable. He laughed and promised to take her and me on a drive to the Antelope Springs and wondered if we'd like that. Then he rang for lemonade with a whole bowl of powdered sugar. I ate the sugar, every blamed speck."

117

"Was it good?" Trumbull asked.

The girl looked startled, then giggled. "Most delicious," she said demurely and went on. Finally, when Wisteria Place became available, Jessica concluded to move. Cousin Gerald Delaney who had just immigrated to California had no friends, so Miss Roux asked him to move in with her and they made up the family.

"Why should she do that?"

Nellie paused, twitching a pointed nose. "She felt responsible for the boy. He's not strong-minded. Miss Roux felt her circumstances required an establishment. I began to stay over nights, and I moved in too."

The months passed quietly, Nellie went on. They attended lectures and amusements and visited Woodward Gardens and such places and studied real estate investments. Jessica poured out her troubles, fiscal and emotional. They visited the Senator at his office, his apartment, and at Beaufort and planned picnics and excursions. The Senator accepted Nellie into the circle and had no secrets from her. All in all, she knew just about everything that happened in those painful months. But there was never any question of the marital situation within the intimacy of the circle.

The silence was profound.

"Fascinating," Trumbull said finally. The girl was aching to talk—indeed the information was coming like bullets from a Gatling gun. Did it ring true? He no longer felt able to distinguish truth in the young. "It's a good story. Real Good. One of the best. Wouldn't you agree, Mr. Green?"

"Up to a point," Green said. "But I'm not sure where it's getting us. It's fuzzy. Not conclusive, and it's all after the event."

"Well, that's true," Trumbull agreed. "Still it's their word against his. Wish we had more documentation. However!" He yawned and went to the stairwell and looked up. A rail ran along a short hall. Trumbull committed the layout to memory. A ladder led to the attic. A white light filtered from the skylight. "Where does Mr. Delaney live?" he asked.

Cousin Gerald had the second-floor back bedroom. Ah Chew, of course, had the attic. The guestroom was empty. Trumbull stood smoking thoughtfully. "D'ye think Mr. Delaney could make a good witness?"

"Why d'you ask?" she said warily.

118

"Ah, Lordy," Trumbull said ruefully. "Miss Roux had a deficiency of witnesses, Miss Driscoll. So each one's got to count, y'see? What d'ye think of him, confidentaially?"

The girl joined the lawyer in staring up at the skylight. "I've no idea," she said with contempt. "He's supposed to testify he heard the Senator admit that Miss Roux was his legal, lawful, and wedded wife, but he gets such flutters! He's a sissy boy," she explained.

"Is he? Well, they're on the increase these days, poor things," Trumbull said, pursing his mouth. "Cannot say why that should be happening." He turned back thoughtfully. "Which is Miss Roux's room?"

The girl frowned. "The big room up front."

"Which is yours?"

There was a sudden pause. "Why do you ask?"

Trumbull heard the change of tone. "Is there a reason not to answer?" He found himself staring into hot angry eyes. "We have the same room," the girl said. "Is that anybody's business?"

"No, I reckon not," Trumbull agreed, "but I gather that your father and mother object to your living away from home. They might also object to your acting as a witness."

"Let 'em try," the girl said viciously.

An unpleasant vista suddenly opened up. "Let's get back into the parlor," Trumbull said. When they were again seated, he unwrapped a cigar band and bit the tip. "How old are you?" he asked.

"Just turned eighteen, thank *you!*" the girl snapped in triumph. "Let 'em try to get me back. If it comes to that, I know a place where I can go. Then let the priest come crying!" She stood, bristling with anger. "I'm not sure whose side you're on, either! You haven't asked one single word about the marriage contract. Why? The Senator cannot deny his signature. It's genuine. I know it's genuine. It's his very hand—down to the loops. Why must she endure this suffering?" she burst out.

Trumbull struck a match. "You've seen the original marriage contract?"

"Yes! I told the lawyers!" She turned to Green. "Didn't I?"

Green closed his eyes. "Yes, you told us."

"Well, there! And she'll have experts when the time comes, you'll see! Lots of experts! Everybody's talking against her, but it wasn't her idea to get the Senator arrested. As though it matters where that old devil puts his—his dirty thing."

Trumbull glanced quickly at Green. "Are you saying now that Miss Roux had no idea the arrest would be made? I find that curious."

"I am that! She almost had a fit, she was so vexed. It was that villain, Pettibone. Why, just a few hours earlier we were recalling that the Senator had been just that agreeable to us both . . ." She halted and bit her lip.

"Go on," Trumbull said after a pause.

"I'd rather not," she said.

"Why not?"

"Because . . ." the girl began impulsively, then halted and sat back, thinking that that was how lawyers trapped girls: with quick hard questions and staring eyes. She drew back with an alert and wary look. "Because it has nothing to do with anything."

"I give up," Green said wearily. "Let's go."

"One moment," Trumbull said reprovingly. He came back to the girl. "Why was it so wrong to arrest Hagerman?" he asked curiously.

The hostile eyes blazed. "It wasn't just wrong, it was stupid. The Senator was going to return to California in any case, so what was the rush? It could all have been talked over. Pettibone wasn't thinking of her. He was thinking of the dollar, and now they've dug up this criminal record in Melbourne and where is he? Now he's disappeared—the coward. Jesus, Mary, what's she got to do with criminals? She wouldn't listen, and now she's in the soup and it all comes from people who don't care. That wasn't what she wanted at all," she said passionately. "She . . ." She halted and bit her lip.

"Go on," Trumbull said after a pause.

The girl studied her hands. "She don't really want to sue the Senator for divorce. Not like they say."

A moment passed.

"What is it that she does want?" Trumbull asked.

"Her good name," the girl said simply. "Everybody says she's—she's a mercenary. That's not so. All she ever asked was for the Senator to acknowledge her position. She was even ready to go quietly without trouble if only he'd be nice about it.

"Everybody thinks the worst. But, Jesus, Mary! She *is*

120

married to the man. I *know* she's married. Why is it so hard for people to believe? It's not money at all. She hasn't got a mercenary hair in her head. She'd divorce him for nothing if he'd admit the marriage! It's not fair how they're treating her! She's sweet and kind and she's been put in this terrible position by other people. They didn't even wait for her to dress, the villains, when they broke in that night to serve that summons. Just showed badges and came trampling!" The girl stared into the deep eyes, appealing for understanding of horrors beyond description.

"How actually d'ye *know* they're married?" Green interjected impatiently.

On the edge of a precipice the girl paused. "I heard him say it," she said.

"Where? When?"

"All sorts of places! Oh, make this stop!" she shrieked and burst into tears. "No more! No more!" the girl sobbed, wiping her nose on the flats of her palms. Green threw up his hands.

Trumbull sighed. The girl was young, but nothing, not even youth and energy, could make the tears and snortings less unlovely. "Come, now!" he said sharply. "That don't help. Mr. Green, can we go now?"

When the door had shut, the girl ran upstairs and watched the lawyers off toward Market Street. The japanned box went into the portmanteau. She left through the back yard, threw the bag over the fence, climbed after, and took the Mission Street trolley to the end of the line. The few other passengers stared at the girl whose lips moved as though in prayer. What matter? the girl thought, smiling with secret knowledge. Jessica was sure to be pleased.

She had been letter-perfect.

"What d'you think?" Green asked.

Trumbull shrugged, thoughtfully considering the matter in all its aspects. "Seems to exaggerate a bit," he said, "but she's convincing enough in the main. There may be more than she's telling us. She'll need preparation, I'd say."

They were shouldering through the noonday crowds in Montgomery Street. Trumbull's long legs were striding purposefully. "What d'you think of her yourself?" he asked.

"I wish she were more stable," Green said, panting slightly. "I'm not happy. I don't care for those hysterics."

"I thought she was colorful. Terribly important—to paint the scene. You could see it, couldn't you—those conversations with Hagerman? Little vixen, ain't she? What d'ye think's going on between 'em?"

"Between who?" Green asked.

"The woman and the girl," Trumbull said with a grin. "Odd business, wouldn't you say?"

"Odd? In what way?"

"I dunno," Trumbull drawled. "Just odd. Lemme tell you about Lucchetti's," he went on more cheerfully, thinking that at present more was green than a name. "I was there with Mrs. Trumbull the day Lucchetti's opened thirty years ago. Learned to eat calimari in ink sauce, much to Mrs. Trumbull's disgust. I've been devoted ever since."

Chapter Six

Lucchetti's was in full swing. That the sporting crowd favored the house was tribute to many things—potent liquor, good food. Mama Lucchetti presided over the register with moustached dominance. Her lively personality made the hangout accepted—and discreet. A staircase to private rooms upstairs told that story.

"Well, now," Trumbull drawled, taking off his hat. "Any room for an old-timer?"

"Ah, Judge! Judge!" Mama Lucchetti was all smiles.

Trumbull glanced around with pleasure, nodding to acquaintances. An eagle-beaked old lawyer with white hair was waving an elegant hand. Green saw the signal and the hesitation. "Would you like to join him?" he asked.

"No, no," Trumbull said in good spirits. "That's Judge Sinzheimer." Sinzheimer was seated at a round table with a group Trumbull had no wish to meet. "I'll see him later," he said. "Hardly looks good for two ex-judges to be seen together, at loose ends. There's nothing more unemployable. Suppose we sit facing the garden."

Lucchetti's was an old-fashioned restaurant with endless alcoves and many fireplaces. Autographed portraits of prize fighters, jockeys, and opera stars were everywhere on the spotted, shabby walls. The seafood was fresh from Meiggs' Wharf, the smells were beyond dreams of Paradise.

"Over there," Trumbull said, shouldering through the crowded tables. Green followed with a fixed smile. It was a lively scene he was viewing for the first time.

"Well, well," said a hoarse antagonistic voice. "It's Mis'ther Th'rumbool!" A splinter-mouthed, malcontent labor union official, John Quinn, was blocking the way.

"Yes, Quinn?" Trumbull said quietly. "What is it?"

Quinn swayed, belching gin, and spat into the sawdust at the lawyer's feet. A sober-faced companion, Frank Mooney, got up hastily. "It's only Quinn. Inebriated," he said apologetically. "I disassociate! Come on, Quinn," he begged and dragged the troublemaker back to his seat.

Trumbull had spotted a table in an alcove that faced a garden. A group of federal marshals were seated under a steel engraving of the King of the Two Sicilies. One of the hardfaced men, Harry Finerty, was making a signal. "D'ye mind that table?" Trumbull asked.

Green frowned. "Judge, do you think it's such a good idea?" he asked uneasily.

Trumbull smiled. "Ride to the sound of guns," he said jovially. "Maybe there's something to pick up." He joined the group with a feeling of sliding back into something worn and familiar.

He made a gesture of introduction. "Gentlemen, meet Mr. Nathaniel Green of Finch and Green. His strength is as the strength of ten, because his heart is pure." There was laughter. "Mr. Green, meet the knights-errant of the Round Table. That"—indicating a vacancy— "is the Siege Lucrative. Sir Emanuel Jessup, Marshal of this chaste band, is mayhap on a Quest?" Someone snorted. More laughter. Green found the warm leathery grip of Harry Finerty not unfriendly. A rawboned man with killer moustaches, Wilbur Patterson, was one of the deputy marshals who had seen the action in the Pima Depression. Green drew Trumbull aside. "I must say, Judge," he whispered, "I don't get all this camaraderie. You're supposed to take a public position on the Pima at the Hibernian."

"Sit down, Natty! This is Lucchetti's," Trumbull drawled good-humoredly, pulling the younger man into place. "Sacred ground! I'll skin these fellers later on. Gentlemen, you're invited to the lecture. Free tickets," he added expansively. There were responsive grins and promises and a stiff moment had passed. More introductions. More jocularity. They were pleased to meet the newcomer, quite interested in his connection with Sidney Finch, sage with advice to stick to a grand profession. It was a blur of unexpected impressions, but although the mood was relaxed, Green could not forget his role as lawyer. He felt stiff and uncomfortable.

Lucchetti came forward, rubbing his hands. "Everything satisfactory?" He beamed. "First class," Trumbull smiled. "Keep the whiskey coming for my young friend. Mr. Green, what's your pleasure?"

Green looked uncertain. "Oh, not this early, Judge. We've got work ahead."

"Oh, pooh! Bourbon!" Trumbull said firmly. "Dino! Bring it in a dirty glass."

"Ha-ha! One dirty glass. Is-a good."

"Judge, please!" Green protested.

"Pure bourbon never hurt a case. Or a cause," Trumbull said sternly. He loosened a button and a look of pleasure lightened his heavy features. The babble echoed under the low ceiling. He tossed off the whiskey and sat back, mopping his neck, catching up with the latest. It was incredible how quickly this world changed. In a few short years Eddie Shields had retired. George Dunphy had opened a detective agency. Jim Anselmo was running a restaurant in Mexico City and complaining of the altitude's effects upon his potency. Nick Looram was a grandfather. Hughie Potter was in the cattle business. Old-timers were leaving. Greenhorns were coming in. It was all California—changing, yet the same, a world of gigantic forms, crudenesses, and beginnings, a world he knew and understood. These were men of direct action and quick intelligence, confused not by learning nor by conscience, who lived on their senses, who slept easily at night. Not one bit like himself, Trumbull reflected, lighting a cigar, and perhaps this was their attraction for him.

Finerty raised a glass. "Gentlemen . . ."

"Mud!"

A Texas drawl. "Remember the Alamo!"

"And Goliad!" Trumbull completed the cry.

"Goliad!"

The whiskey was beginning to work. Another round.

Solemnly: "Up Charlie Crocker."

"Up Lew Hagerman."

"Up Jessie Roo."

"Judge, is it true what they say?"

"What do they say?"

"Oh yew know!"

"Well, that's not true," Trumbull said, smiling slightly. "It's denied, denied," he drawled, in Hagerman's grinding Ohio accent. He looked up hungrily at the arrival of soup. The whiskey had a pleasant heating effect. It was surprising how many old-timers stopped to congratulate him on getting into a good case.

"Oh, that?" Trumbull said with a show of disingenuous surprise. He wiped his beard of soup. "I'm not in it yet. I've yet to meet the lady. She might not care for me," he said jocularly. "Anything known about her?" he asked casually. Norman Kipp, a mild-mannered deputy marshal, grinned. That Jessie Roo padded was denied, denied.

"Tell 'em, Norm," Will O'Hare said. "Norm has got the feel of the theng. He's f'om Missoura."

Trumbull was interested. "Oh? What part of the state?"

"Jonesboro. Just a holler from Cape Badeau." Kipp gulped a whiskey and winked. The Rouxes were prominent all along the river and subject to gossip. Now theah was a girl spoiled rotten—a willful tomboy with her own fortune and an indulgent uncle with no control. "Two engagements before sixteen," Kipp said with enjoyment, "and I wouldn't guarantee the hayrides. One of the boys went into politics and t'other moved to St. Louis. Missoura moon," he sighed. "Sure was fast."

Trumbull glanced at the deputy. "Was her name attached to scandal?"

"Scandal?" Kipp grinned and shook his head. No, not scandal. Not exactly. He had nothing in mind, not really, just the usual porch talk of a small town—wild hayrides, boys feeling up girls in moonlight, nothing much. A girl generally regarded as tyrannical in love affairs. Iron rules and eccentric whims were the common complaints. A one true love affair with a socially prominent medical student had broken off with mutual jiltings and recriminations, all of which ended in the lady's flight to California with disgust and broken hopes. Her lineage . . .

Lineage again! Trumbull thought.

Yes, yes, he broke in. He was not concerned with lineage

or schoolgirl flirtations. Was there anything in California, he asked carelessly, that might have tarnished the lady's name? Looks passed. No, no. The lady's reputation in California—except for the current matter—was untarnished.

" 'Scuse me," Green said suddenly in a slurred voice. He stood and left in haste. Finerty followed the young lawyer's progress. "Know much about him, Judge?" he asked, buttering crusty French bread.

"Not much. Why?"

"Just asking," Finerty replied. "Some people wonder what you're doing on that team. Kind of disappointing to find you blowing your nose on that bloody rag. Not your kind of case at all, Judge."

"No? Why not?"

Finerty shrugged. "Lie down with dogs, get up with fleas. Whole business is queer—queer and smelly. Hagerman does things to women I'd be ashamed to admit. Woman who'd lay for the man has got to have a name. Can't see you in her corner."

Trumbull stirred restlessly. "You're talking like a child. I wish people wouldn't treat me like a Hindu idol or some inscrutable object of veneration. I'm a lawyer with bills to meet like anyone else. People come for help. I can no more consider their morals than a physician can turn away a pocky whore because he don't like the color of her discharge." He smiled grimly. Then, more seriously, "All my life I've been fighting these people in the areas where they're strong. This woman's case strikes home. I'm not in this yet, but it's a chance. Oh, hell!" he said sourly. "All I need is a nail to hang my hat, a cause of action, a court of competent jurisdiction. Only . . ." He hesitated. "Finerty, what in Christ is going on in the Federal Court?"

"Something going on?" Finerty asked innocently.

"Come now," Trumbull said impatiently. "What was that service of papers on the woman at night? Why an entire posse? Why couldn't she've been served in daylight?"

"I imagine that was possible," Finerty agreed, "but Jessie told the Marshal she'd meet him with a handgun." A pause. "Hadn't you heard?"

Trumbull glanced across the table. Green, who had returned, was flushed, confused, and apparently deep in a metaphysical discussion with O'Hare.

". . . Zeitgeis?" Green said thickly. The rest was swallowed up in noise. "Gun? No, I heard nothing like that," Trumbull said. "What's more, I don't believe it."

"Fact," Finerty said. "Marshall Jessup was called in, oh, just about midnight by the lawyers and handed the papers and sealed orders. The little girl, Nellie, opened the front door and started squalling when we rushed in. Jessie was on the landing with this derringer aimed square at the Marshal. She gave him the count. 'One! Two!' 'Hey, hold it!' the Marshal called. Nellie had bit his thumb and he was bleeding. Jessie really glared. She said, 'You git, Marshal! I'm a dead shot and you better know it. I'm aiming at your guts.' The Marshal looked real respectful. 'Now, ma'am,' he said, 'put that popgun up. We got a legal paper here. You take it like a lady and we'll serve it like gentlemen.' "

Finerty paused. "That stopped her. 'Paper? What kind of paper?' she said. 'Read it and find out,' he told her. He dropped the papers on the stairs, and we scrambled out. The woman was real pretty, I thought, with all that red hair, and that nightgown, but I couldn't say that for the derringer. Popgun? It looked like a cannon."

Trumbull was grimly amused.

Grand fellow, he thought. Old Jessup, one of the old bunch, quite decent as lawmen went. The picture of the white-haired old lawman howling and dancing, with the Driscoll girl hanging like a ferret to his thumb, had its appealing side. He glanced at Finerty, who seemed to read these thoughts. "But what was the purpose?" he persisted. "Some suspicion she intended to evade service? Hardly likely," he said doubtfully.

"Can I be frank?"

"Sure thing."

"She'll never get away with it," Finerty said. "Not in any court in these United States. The word's out on her."

"Th'rumbool?" said a harsh voice.

Quinn was swaying in the aisle. "So ye're going to sh-peak for the McCabes?" he said sardonically. "Is that the truth now?"

Trumbull sat back from the table. He removed and folded his spectacles in their case. "Yes, it is," he said.

The room went quiet.

Quinn spat and threw a pamphlet on the table. Trumbull was familiar with the frontpiece—a line drawing of Luke and Buddy McCabe, the Martyrs of the Pima Depression, hang-

127

ing from the gallows at San Quentin. "Fine company!" Quinn grated mockingly. His eye went around the table. "All the King's Men. Finerty! Patterson! Kipp! O'Hare! George-o White! Minions of the Money Power! What a scene to remember when ye're memorializing the dead! Where in hell were yez when the McCabes needed a lawyer?"

"Those men had trial counsel," Trumbull said slowly. "Able lawyers of their choice."

"But not you! Whoy not? Whoy?"

"It was not a matter I wanted to take on," Trumbull said.

"Not what he wanted to take on. It's enough to make a pig laugh. Oh, damn the Money Power, says the man. Damn the corruption! Damn the blacklegs sh-poiling the dream of America! Adopt this or that and we'll cure everyt'ing from the curse of the Chink to the common clap! We'll clean out the Au'gan sh-tables of—of monopoly—only follow the common cause. And the McCabes followed, God help 'em. We all followed, and what's come of it? Look at the man. Hobnobbing wit' Hagerman's blacklegs! Full of gas and poses," he cried, turning to the room of watching men. "Quick wit' the gun when it suited him. But when it came to the poor McCabes, whoy couldn't the man remember his own bloody, bloody record? The man who killed poor Paddy Gore? He could have sh-tood up in court for 'em. He was asked."

"Not what he wanted!" Quinn turned back to the main object of wrath. "Whoy not? Too dainty for that old durty case?" A finger stabbed out in derision. "But not too dainty to sit wit' Sid Finch's faggot? Not too dainty for Hagerman's whore?"

"The poor bitch!" he jeered, swaying. "You fooked the McCabes. You'll fook the poor woman! A-a-h, what's the use, Mooney?" he snarled, turning about. "He'll sell out. He'll sell out."

"For God's sake, Quinn," Mooney said.

Quinn stood his ground. "What does the fooking poet say? For a handful of bloody silver? For a ribbon to sh-tick in his hat?" he intoned.

"Quinn!" Trumbull said.

The drunken man turned. "You silly man," Trumbull said in a low, tired voice. "Get out before I deal with you."

Quinn stared uncertainly, but as Trumbull made no move, a grin split his face. "Oh, I'll get out," he said. "I find the slave-catchin' atmosphere highly unpleasant, Mr. Fancy Fandango Th'rumbool!" He went to the cashier's and put down a silver dollar.

"I disassociate," Mooney said apologetically and followed.

"Dino," Trumbull said finally, "if you'll be so kind, I'll have that filly of beef now."

He ate without appetite, sunk in gloom and whiskey, wondering at himself. The truth was that he had taken two insults—the duel with Gore, the desertion of the McCabes—and perhaps would swallow others yet to come. Something was happening to him. What? The heavy shoulders sagged deeper.

Quinn was as fake as his brogue, he reflected gloomily, really no account. He was a disaster, a fanatical droning bagpipe, a chronic nuisance. No one took him seriously. The labor movement of the Pacific Coast was the hardiest in the world. It was made up of workingmen and thinkers fresh from the ideological cockpits of Europe—English Chartists, French Communards, Irish and Polish nationalists, German Marxists, socialists, anarchists, men schooled in intellectual strife. It had absorbed native movements—Grangers, Single Taxers. It could and would survive violence. Could it survive the likes of Quinn?

He drew a breath, feeling the trembling of his legs. What else should he have done? He could not be insulted by Quinn. Everyone would understand that. Why then the gloom? He thought he knew. The free expression of anger had been his life. It refreshed and cleansed the soul, but how long was it since the last occasion? He had not acted in rage in a quarter century, he recalled. Not since that quick puff of dust that marked the bullet fired into Gore's chest in early dawn on that meadow in another world.

Gore? He could still hear the barking of seals, the roar of surf hurled upon the California cliff by the endless seas.

He groaned, thankful and regretful for a hellish temper kept in check and noticed that amused eyes were on him.

"Forget Quinn," Finerty said.

Trumbull shook his head. "He was quite specific about an approach to buy me off the Hagerman matter. Don't like it," he said gloomily. "Not the first time today I've caught that rumor. D'ye know where it's coming from?"

Finerty waved a cigar. "Oh, there's always that talk about Hagerman. Have you ever before been approached?"

"No-o," Trumbull said uncertainly. Across the table Green

was hazily describing the unwritten constitution of England and making the point that in a country not without freedom and democratic liberties, the damned judges might interpret acts of the legislature but never their legality.

Sinzheimer was signaling across the room. Trumbull nodded and returned the signal. "Mr. Green," he said, "are you all right?"

Green looked up tipsily. "Huh? Sir?" Trumbull repeated the question. "All right?" Green fumbled for words. "Judge, I'm discussing . . ." He paused with dignity. "Discussing the Case of . . . of . . ." The effort eluded him. "I was just getting to . . . to . . ." He blinked and turned to O'Hare. "What case was that?"

"Sedley's case," O'Hare supplied. "How this English lord was caught peeing on the crowd. Disorderly conduct."

Trumbull smiled somberly. "Most misunderstood decision in history," he observed. "Better leave, Mr. Green, and take your papers. Remember the first rule in the book: Never leave your notes behind. Gentlemen?" he said, rising. "If you'll excuse me?" He drew Lucchetti aside. "Get him into a cab," he said and left for the rear. He was thinking that if young Green could absorb a dozen whiskeys and wind up learnedly expounding the development of Anglo-Saxon jurisprudence to that bunch, he had the makings of a good lawyer and bore watching.

Sinzheimer was examining a silver coin with intensity through thick spectacles. "Why, Mark Trumbull!" he exclaimed. "I've been waving and snapping. What do I do to catch your attention? You know Mr. MacGowan?" he said cheerily, turning about.

Andrew MacGowan, a pudgy, well-dressed lawyer of forty, nodded warily. "I don't believe we've met," he said.

Trumbull ignored the proffered hand. "I don't get into the city these days," he agreed, sitting at a tablecloth spotted with gravy. They were partly hidden from the other guests, and there was a sense of privacy. Evidently something was expected.

"I'm mortified you couldn't join us earlier," Sinzheimer said cheerily, "but then you're not answering letters these days either. Have a brandy," he said expansively. "Dino Din-oh! Two *fines*."

"I really shouldn't stay," Trumbull said.

"Pouf! Nonsense!" the old lawyer said gaily. "You, too, Andy? Hey?" He was unusually cheerful. "Dino? Make that three *fines!*"

"I'll have a whiskey," Trumbull said.

The order was changed. Sinzheimer specified the brands with an air of solicitude and concern and made sure of roasted almonds for nibbling. "Sorry about Quinn," he said cheerily. "Son of a bitch had no right to embarrass you."

"He was drunk," Trumbull said.

"Drunk or not, I'd've caned him myself. Dunno why you didn't. It was disgraceful." Sinzheimer sipped thoughtfully. "The Pima's a dead horse, Mark. You see how labor rewards its friends? Most bitter taste in the world."

"Please, Ike," Trumbull said uncomfortably.

"Very well," Sinzheimer replied. "But as I was saying thirty years ago, you hate advice and never take it. What brings you here?"

"You left me a note at the Sagamore."

Sinzheimer laughed and turned to the younger lawyer. "Go on, Andy," he said.

"Judge Trumbull," MacGowan began and stopped.

"Yes?" Trumbull said.

"I've been hearing the talk," MacGowan said in a thin tone, "that you're being asked to get into Jessie's lawsuit?"

"Reckon everybody has," Trumbull grunted.

MacGowan turned to Sinzheimer but saw no help there. "Well, I know it's being said that she originally brought that case to my office," he said reluctantly. He was distressed, he went on, because of rumors that made his behavior in that matter—in view of his partnership with Galindez—improper. "Well, I want to square myself. I never discussed her case with Tony. Never."

Trumbull rolled the whiskey glass. "So?"

"That's all," MacGowan said unhappily. He wiped his palms and came to a point of decision. "Judge Trumbull, I'll say this as a responsible lawyer. I want to urge a quick settlement of Jessie's case. It wouldn't help to drag me into something messy—or Jessie either. I'm thinking about her too, although she won't believe that."

"Messy? How are you affected?"

MacGowan drew a shuddering breath. "She's likely to say I took advantage—that there was some breach of confidence," he said defensively. "It wasn't so at all. She was my client only in one serious matter and that one never really got started. She wanted me to bring an accounting action against her uncle in Missouri but I never did. Never saw any basis for it. I had some unpleasant scenes before I could convince her."

"Did you take a retainer?"

"No-o," MacGowan said.

"Then where was the confidential relationship?"

"Oh, well . . . naturally, I saw her a lot and we'd had dinner together off and on. I don't know how it started but . . . you know how it can get with a woman client. A lot of intimate talk and before you know it you're her confessor and godfather and—"

"And engaged?"

MacGowan looked pained. "That was her idea, not mine. I'll swear, Judge Trumbull, I never misled her. Trouble is, she misleads herself. Great capacity for that. Not an easy client, you know." MacGowan was wearing pince-nez rimless glasses. He put these aside carefully and suddenly he was no fool but a keen lawyer with insight and ability. "She's got the memory of a fiend and more invention than Eli Whitney. If you're not careful, she'll be running you, the case, and everything else, down to buying your neckties."

Trumbull looked at Sinzheimer. The old gentleman was looking detached. He came back to MacGowan. "Indeed? Why tell me all this?"

"Because I cannot get through to Finch," MacGowan said. "Mother has a bad heart and I don't want her agitated. She's had enough of Jessie Roux."

Trumbull lit a cigar. "Mr. MacGowan. You look old enough to run your own life. Why should your mother be agitated by Miss Roux?"

"Never mind," MacGowan said blackly and with passion. "It's easy to get involved with Jessie and not too easy getting loose. I thought I was finished with her, but it seems to go on and on. I want to say one word of warning—it's in her own interest to keep my name out, or I'll have some disclosures myself. I hope that's clear."

"Quite clear," Trumbull said, unimpressed. "What's the worst you can reveal? Scandalous relations with the lady? Pooh! She's got no legal claim, and that's about all that counts."

"Really? I hope you're right," MacGowan said. "Judge, it's

in everybody's interest to halt before it really gets started. Let's hope I'm not brought into it. Good day." He nodded angrily to Sinzheimer, put down a tip, and left.

"Too bad," Sinzheimer sighed. "Good lawyer, too. First in his class at Harvard."

Trumbull watched MacGowan leave. "Ike, how far d'ye s'pose he got with the woman?"

Sinzheimer grinned. "Deponent saith not," he said. Jessie Roux was a looker, slender ankles and marvelous breasts, but with that ass MacGowan, vestryman in Trinity Church, under Mama's thumb, it was anybody's guess.

Trumbull found himself smiling. What had Mama got against the woman? he asked.

"Mothers are mysterious," Sinzheimer said cheerfully. "But I must say that white skin always gave me shivers of delight. What a waste of womanflesh." A reminiscent gleam came and went. He made a gesture of dismissal. "We don't see enough of you in San Francisco anymore. Getting fat, Mark. Hear you're writing a book. Well, the sedentary life don't become you. Or anybody else. Blisters the arse and bad for the bowel." He sat back and beamed. "You don't answer letters, Mark. Avoiding me?"

"Not a bit," Trumbull said. "I'm engrossed in things, Ike. Pulling in my horns. Or trying to. I'm past all that. I'm too old for travel and turbulence."

"Oh, pooh!" Sinzheimer scoffed. "All you want is the call to arms."

They picked up where they had left off. Sinzheimer knew everyone, from Archbishop Tosefa to Alfred Sutro. He was an old friend and a mine of gossip and political information. He found life good, he remarked, except that, tragically, an only grandson had decided to shun the law for the academic life. "Political science," he added in explanation. "Princeton."

"Anything I can do?" Trumbull asked.

"Nothing," Sinzheimer said bravely.

More whiskey materialized. Necessity versus Free Will and other burning topics of the day were touched on. "I vow you look glum," Sinzheimer said. "Mark, boy, are you committed to help Finch in the Federal Court?" The shrewd eyes had a disconcerting twinkle.

"Not yet," Trumbull said warily. "But I'm close. These tactics of the other side are outrageous. I dunno how you stay friendly with those abysmal villains."

"It's a friendly trough." Sinzheimer chuckled. "I find the villains more interesting. Othello's a howling bore, but when Iago comes on moralizing, the stage sparkles. Think on it."

A sharp gaze turned. "Is that a message?"

"Now why must I be charged with that?" Sinzheimer complained. "Be smart for once, hey?"

"What's that mean?"

"Mark," Sinzheimer said, "you've wasted every chance you ever had. You were on the ground floor—pioneer, good lawyer, and all that—but you took on every losing cause in history. Take that McCabe business. Oh, I know, I know!" He waved a hand. "So you are making a speech on the McCabes. Just shows that Mike Larkin's bunch of radicals as usual are short on talent, so they're giving you a chance to come back gracefully. Meaningless."

"D'ye think I shouldn't make that speech?"

"No, no. Depends on what you want more—that privacy you profess, or the turbulence of action? You've still got a following, Mark. Small, but devoted, and every group counts —that's the glory of the system." An odd expression, estimating, judging, flickered. "Mark, how old are you?"

"Old enough," Trumbull said.

"Don't get huffy. From my perspective, you're a boy. Question's not idle. I've got something in mind."

"You generally do," Trumbull said. "Why are we chasing the devil around a stump?"

Sinzheimer gestured at the empty table across the room. "What was all that drinking with the enemy about? Scouting the Roux matter?" Trumbull shrugged. "Why look so unhappy about it? Nobody's got a ring through your nose."

Trumbull looked up. "Ike? I believe the woman's probably got a good claim."

"Do you now?" Sinzheimer grimaced. "Well, I agree." A delightful laugh relished the effect. "I thought so when I read those headlines. I cannot breach confidences, but just about that time the lady met the Senator—when was that? Three years ago? Well!—Hagerman came to the Archbishopric and broke into a meeting of the building committee for a private talk with the Archbishop. I'm on that committee, y'know. I've represented the Archdiocese since I brought that replevin action against that Mexican curate to recover a stolen chalice. Well! Hagerman left, looking remarkably ruttish. Almost immediately the old man was rubbing his hands, talking about stained-glass windows and what not. I don't say that's proof, but Mrs. Sinzheimer immediately heard all the rumors about the connection. Now, Mark, I distrust testimony but I most firmly believe in malicious gossip. So I'm sure she's got a claim. A good, good claim. Delighted when I heard you might get into the matter. Couldn't happen to a more deserving practitioner. Hope you make a pile," he said, cheerfully blowing smoke at a mezzotint of Vesuvius.

"But actually," he went on, staring into space, "actually there's no assurance that you will. Don't have to tell you about the courts. It's dice with the devil and it all turns on the accidents of life and litigation. I wish sometimes we could return to the water cure or trial by combat. Just as reliable and much tidier. It'd be just like Hagerman to promise the moon and the stars to get a woman between sheets. He's a sexual maniac, lustful and impetuous. So to the extent she swears he promised marriage, I'm inclined to believe her. But did he keep that promise? Ah, there's the rub."

Trumbull was the picture of gloom.

"Mark," Sinzheimer said gently, "what's on your mind?"

"I dunno," Trumbull muttered. "That feller Quinn depressed me. Shouldn't be affected by those trifles, but I am. I've got a theory you'll laugh at."

"Yes?"

"Well, I've noticed that I get these fits when I ought to feel angry, but don't. Does it mean anything? Can we possibly have thoughts and feelings we ain't aware of? That affect us below the conscious level? I've often wondered."

Sinzheimer looked up anxiously, disturbed by the bizarre notion. "I wouldn't think so. If we ain't aware, how can they be thoughts or feelings? Forget Quinn. What about this new case of yours?"

Trumbull shook his head in wonder. "I don't know what to do about it. Ain't it odd, Ike? At my time of life? Not to be able to decide my own mind? I've gotten to rely on Mrs. Trumbull so much over the years, you see. I had no realization how much I've depended on her judgment. Took her for granted and that's wrong. Now I cannot bring her these vexations of the practice. We cannot talk anymore. We're living in separate worlds and we don't know what the other's thinking. She's going through something of her own. Something she can't confide and I dare not intrude." Sinzheimer was silent, fearful of naked revelation. The deep eyes were without expression, turned inward. "They don't know what it is. Don't even have a name for it. Just something wasting, and every day it's worse, inexorable. She knows what's happening, but she never complains or gives me a moment of anxiety. The thing of it is . . ." Trumbull halted the flow, conscious of a strained look. "She's dying, Ike," he said simply. A fixed smile was a grimace. "Oh, not today. Not even tomorrow. It could be a year, two years, but it's going on and she knows it. Meanwhile she wants me to keep up the practice. I don't know now what to do about this matter. I'm full of doubts. Oh, I can argue that motion in the Federal Court easily enough, but then what? A trial could take months. Or even years, with appeals. Mrs. Trumbull may not have those years."

"Sorry," Sinzheimer murmured ineffectually, wishing desperately the burden would shift.

Trumbull read these thoughts. "Well, enough of that," he said abruptly. "What d'ye think I should do?"

"Oh, don't ask me that," Sinzheimer replied, accepting the change of mood. "You've not changed your obstinate mind once in all your foolish life. I think you've made it up right now."

"No," Trumbull said slowly.

"Oh, bosh!" Sinzheimer said with feeling. He broke off as the waiter approached. Places were being set for the dinner hour. "Well, I'd like to help," he said finally. "I'm just wondering how seriously you do take the lady's business."

"Hard to say, Ike. It may be my deficiency of character, but I do tend to take these things to heart. She's facing very large forces indeed. I'm torn, for a fact. Torn."

A small hand covered with brown spots touched Trumbull's wrist. "Look 'ee, Mark," Sinzheimer said. "Is it that earth-shattering? So the lady lost her cherry. I regret it, but is it important? Look at the stars. Read Blake. On the cosmic scale, has it more than minor surgical interest? *De minimis non curat lex.*" The law, he admonished, smiling, did not concern itself with trifles.

"Trifles?" Trumbull said stiffly. "I had an impression your message to meet here meant something."

Sinzheimer paused. Raillery was getting no response. "Very well, Mark," he sighed, "I did have something in mind that might—just might—help you resolve that question. Let me explore it. That is, if you don't mind self-benefit for once."

"Self-benefit? Is it something political?"

"I'll let you know," Sinzheimer replied, smiling evasively. "Sit tight until we talk more. Time you stopped fishing in muddy waters, hey?"

Trumbull snapped open his timepiece. "Well, I've got some errands," he said, rising stiffly. "Ike, I was born on the Mississippi. I've fished in muddy waters all my life. Not the best fishing, but it does have its rewards." He nodded and left.

Sinzheimer remained seated, smiling oddly as he followed the bowed hulking figure into the street. Queer man, displaced in time, he thought. What could one do for *that*?

When Trumbull returned to the hotel, a cold wind was blowing and the lobby was full of guests. The comforts of the Sagamore were never more welcome. A message was waiting in his box.

"Tomorrow at eleven. Driver will call. Malvinia Lawes."

He folded the message with a frown, listening to the rumble of voices and laughter from the saloon bar. He was longing to rest and went up to his room, where he stretched out on the bed—torn, full of conflict, and, to his intense surprise, thinking of women he had not seen in years. He opened and, with an exclamation, slammed the city directory shut. There was no point, not the slightest to that damned nonsense. He felt at loose ends and full of something he did not understand. A nap was impossible, but later, after a dinner in the cheerful dining room, he felt refreshed, with purpose. He smoked a cigar in the lounge, exchanged yarns with a drummer, and went up to his room with a bottle. He spread out his notes but lost the sense of the matter. Whiskey, he thought.

In the midst of a letter to Alexandra, he fell asleep.

Chapter Seven

Trumbull awoke and stared at the faint light of dawn at the window. Some mysterious process was going on. He was thinking of an old affair, almost forgotten, with a lively married woman. It was a business in which he had no pride, briefly conducted under risk to both on a solitary occasion. That affair had happened after an invitation for lemonade and he had found himself in something not expected. Delicious woman, he recalled with a qualm of guilt, with a sweet mouth and small breasts. He'd not thought of the woman in—how many years? Fifteen? As many as that? And yet he had awakened smiling with that pleasant recollection. There was another such occasion in Bakersfield—well, that was a hotel situation that never truly got started. Then some recollections of being on the brink in San Jose. It did not add up to much to show for a lifetime. What in hell was bringing it all up now?

His eyes went wider and he saw the morning fog. He got up and went out. He tramped the damp pavements as far as Sacramento Street, head bent, shoulders bowed, sunk in thought till the restlessness had worn off. The hour was still early when he returned. He bought the newspapers and entered the dining room, now noisy with commercial gentlemen. He sat at his usual table overlooking Market Street, smiling, self-conscious, feeling at last back at his profession. The whole world was reading about the Affair.

Breakfast was a matter of ham and eggs and fried potatoes. He shoveled down the food to the last sticky morsel, and read the remarkable news that his appearance in the Circuit Court was expected. He returned to his room and put his notes in order. The sun was high when he stepped into the street. A carriage was waiting. The liveried driver raised a silk hat.

"Judge Trumbull?"

Trumbull squinted suspiciously. "Oh, you, Digges! How long've you been out?"

"Eight years, Judge," the driver replied. Tom Digges was an ex-prizefighter, a black insolent man with scarred, brutal features. "Mrs. Lawes has asked me to give you this note."

"Mrs. Lawes, hey. I'm honored." Trumbull held the scrawl of misspellings at arm's length. The shrewdest business woman in San Francisco had the handwriting of an illiterate child. He brought it close and sniffed. His brows rose. Expensive paper with the smell of chicken fat. The note advised that Miss Roux was waiting at Las Flores. "I'd rather see her at Mr. Finch's office."

"No, sir, Judge," Digges said emphatically. "Not there. She wants this talk confidential—Miss Jessica insists. She don't want to see Mr. Finch."

"Mr. Finch will be informed," Trumbull said.

"I wasn't told about that. Mrs. Lawes instructs me and that's what I do." The near chestnut nervously backed a step. "Ho," Digges said, drawing a check rein. "Well, sir?"

"Very well," Trumbull agreed, "but first I've got an errand. Take me to Lundy's." He sank into red morocco, enjoying the luxury.

"Yah!" Digges threw the reins. The superb team started at a fast pace, smooth as silk.

Lundy's shop dealt in optical supplies, curios, scissors, cutlery, and photographic supplies. Displays of spectacle frames covered the walls and a reading chart faced Benjamin Franklin in bifocals. Trumbull turned to the counter display of cutlery. "Fine steel," he said, absorbed.

"Finest in the world—Sheffield," Lundy said energetically. "Anything there you'd like?"

"No, no. Can you fill this by tomorrow?" Trumbull asked, handing over a paper. Lundy examined the paper and looked up with a start. "Who made out this prescription?"

"Young doctor we've got," Trumbull replied. "Why? Is something wrong with it?"

"No, no, Judge," Lundy said. "It's just stronger than anything I'd expect. Of course," he added, frowning, "we expect change. You could stand a new prescription yourself?"

"Me? Pooh! I've got an eye like an eagle."

"I'll have it ready," Lundy agreed and returned to his work.

Trumbull hesitated, then left for the carriage. He did not like Mr. Lundy's manner one bit.

It was now a jolting but swift drive. Digges was a good driver. He sat forward, feet spread, spine rigid, cigar jutting, intent on the chestnut rumps before him. A light touch guided the spirited team. Trumbull sat asprawl the carriage, smoking, noting the changes. Real estate developers were extending the city boundaries beyond conscience. Houses became fewer. Cobblestones turned to rutted dirt and the countryside appeared. Every so often Digges turned about, chuckling.

"Digges?"

"Sir?"

"What d'ye hear about the woman around town?"

"Well, she's got good manners."

"What made her run off like this? Why can't she make up her mind?"

"Well, she must've had some reason."

"I'm not after anything confidential. Just the general talk?"

"Judge, sir, I keeps a shut mouth."

"Quite so." A pause. "Have you any idea why Mr. MacGowan would fear to get mixed up in this?"

Digges addressed the overhanging trees. "Mr. MacGowan is real respectable. He handles law matters for the Third Baptists on Powell Street. Real aristocrats, the Third Baptists. They're poor but active. Mr. MacGowan has been kind to them and they has been kind to him."

"Kind? Kind how?"

"The firm don't charge for legal advice. In return they bring him information." Digges grinned broadly. "So maybe he knows something we don't know."

"Could you find out?"

Digges brandished a fist of broken knuckles and chuckled complacently. He'd try. He was not in good standing with the Third Baptists, but he could keep his ears open. "Judge, sir, you going to help the woman?"

"I'll tell 'ee something, Digges. A shut mouth is a good idea."

A rambling white farmhouse stood behind a stone wall, shrouded by enormous oaks which were old when Fra Junipero Serra had walked the land. The white gravel road was taken with a rush.

A black strong-featured woman appeared at the door,

squinting in the hot sun. "You, Digges," Malvinia said in a deep voice, "you're running those animals too hard. You git 'em cool first, you hear?"

"I hear," Digges agreed, bored.

"You're late!"

"You ast me to stop off for parcels."

"Hump. Well, git 'em into the sewing room. Now, git!" she ordered. "Well, come on in, Judge," she said. "You're expected."

He entered the hall, bowing under a low lintel. Narrow stairs led to a warren of bedrooms and attics from which came highpitched laughter and sniggering. A child with black ringlets and yellow skin was at the landing, solemnly sucking a thumb. At the sight of the stranger, she burst into tears and ran off, wailing. A slurred voice scolded, a door slammed.

"Go right in," Malvinia said, indicating a parlor room.

A fire was blazing, but the room was cold. Low ceilings and pine plank flooring, stained yellow and highly polished. He had a glimpse of peach trees and a white picket fence enclosing a lawn. The furnishings were luxurious.

"Real nice," Trumbull said with grudging appreciation.

Malvinia had followed him into the parlor, smoothing her dress. A dark face followed his glance of appraisal. "One thing I know," she remarked, "is how to buy and sell."

"Mrs. Lawes, I'd just like to know why I was so confidently expected?"

Malvinia smiled.

"I reckon, like the whole world, you're just that curious to see the sideshow freak. Well, you're in for a surprise." Noisy scuffling upstairs attracted her attention. "Damnation!" she muttered, then her face cleared. "This is sort of a second home," she explained. "Jessie just loves to come out here, go riding, maybe give a hand around the house. I'll git something for the chill, if you'll excuse me?" she said abruptly and left. Trumbull was alone.

As always he classified the room and smelled its purpose. He knew something about Las Flores. Las Flores was a large and comfortable house set on a hill. It was plain, but country houses were expected to be plain. It had come down from an earlier period when the style in fashion was no style. It had been acquired years earlier by Clare Gresham from the widow of the last Mexican Governor of California. Originally it was part of a larger spread Gresham had assembled. On his death the title deed had not been found among his effects. How it had come to Malvinia Lawes was something never explained—not even upon demands by Gresham's executor, Hagerman, who had aggressively marshaled all other assets of that bankrupt estate.

It was an interesting line of speculation, he thought, when the woman returned with a decanter and glasses. "Try this, Judge," she said.

"No, thank 'ee, I'm on business." He hesitated. "Well, one. Now that I'm here," he said abruptly, "what in thunder's this about?"

"I'll tell 'ee, Judge Trumbull. Since your name got noised about, the woman's in a state of expectations. She had these high hopes and now we heard you're still skeptical—still blowing hot and cold. I concluded a little talk might help decide your mind."

Trumbull struck a match. "Mrs. Lawes," he said, "what's your interest in this matter?"

"Let's say it's a business interest," she said with a grin. "If he wins, she's a good account and she wears my dresses like an angel."

It was strange and odd that the woman could shift at will through accents from Creole to Tidewater Virginia.

"Business? The issue's marriage. All the rest is wind."

The woman's eyes were mismatched, blue and brown, and the effect was remarkable. "Maybe so. I just ask you to listen to her side." She rose stiffly, rubbing her hands. "There's no real question about the marriage," she said. "Everybody knew it at the bank, the hotel, at Beaufort, other places—even if not everybody's got the sand to come forward. You just git 'em under oath and you'll get surprising testimony." She went out to the hall. "Jess?" she shouted. "The Judge is waiting. You hear?"

The answer was distant and faint.

Malvinia came back. "Sick headache," she explained. "Takes camomile tea." She threw a log on the fire and resumed. "If they say she's got no witnesses, 'tain't true. I'm one even if I'm colored. Of course she's married."

Trumbull considered this. Malvinia Lawes had resided in the city since the Gold Rush. She had arrived from New Orleans with a dozen trunks and a sack of gold coins and a Creole name quickly discarded—Mme. Nicole Malacquait. She was known for shrewd business dealings in many lines.

Her first ventures were in laundries, boarding houses, and the import of merchandise. She knew everybody. She became acquainted with Hagerman at her boarding house in Powell Street. Later she kept funds with him in the Anglo-Pacific Bank. She was reputedly in money lending and many other things. And so, when the rumors first began to circulate, it was only natural enough for her to be summoned for a discussion by Jessica's vexed grandmother. If a woman could not consult her dressmaker, whom could she consult? She described that scene.

Mrs. Bannister had closed the door and turned in wrath. What truth was there, she had demanded, to the disgraceful rumors? Mrs. Lawes was commanded not to evade, not to lie, but to investigate the circumstances of her stubborn granddaughter's residence at the Camden House. "Mrs. Lawes," the old lady had said imperiously, "I want you to make sure it's respectful. Miss Roux is no longer a girl—she's past foolery. If she makes a name for herself, she'll get shipped back to Missouri sure. Your mission is to scout and report back."

Trumbull smiled faintly. Then what?

Malvinia smiled. "Mrs. Bannister," she had said earnestly, "Miss Jessica is too moral to do anything disrespectful!" But she had promised to sniff around.

"Let me see," she said, closing her eyes. "Jessie moved into the Camden late in September. Early October she'd given a musicale in the Senator's honor. So it was just before Christmas that I called on business. I told her that this chambermaid, Edna Crooms, had reported that she, Miss Roux, was seen coming from the Senator's apartment at the Imperial and flitting across the bridge to the Camden in the small hours of the morning—and that her grandmama'd be sick if it got out. 'My lands,' I told her, 'your grandmama's no prude—after all, she's army and she knows something too—but you can't just go flitting through halls and across bridges.' I warned that the colored help were telling that story all over the city—which was true. Well, she laughed and said to tell her grandmama not to worry because she'd be around to explain. She was really engaged to the Senator, she said, and it'd be all right.

" 'Engaged?' I said. Miss Jessica had professed engagements before with half the eligibles in town—including Mr. MacGowan. . . ." She paused. "But I reckon you know about Mr. MacGowan?"

"Go on," Trumbull said.

"Exactly. There'd been a flutter there too about a wedding dress, but in Mr. MacGowan's case I had wanted to see the ring. Well!" Malvinia made a gesture of dismissal. "So this time I said, 'Miss Jessica, let's have no more scenes of heartbreak. This time are you sho?' 'Why, sho I'm sho!' she replied gaily. She was more winsome than ever. Then she told how she was publicly served meals on the family silver service—the chafing dish with the Hagerman crest which the first Mrs. Hagerman had got for a wedding present from the late Mr. Gresham. She was going with the Senator in public, attending theaters and restaurants, and using his carriage. I said she was simple to imagine that that carriage was a sign of anything respectful. Half the actresses in town had commanded that service. Then she showed me the guest list for the musicale she had tendered the Senator—the finest capitalists had attended with their wives: Mr. and Mrs. Joe Leffingwell, Mr. and Mrs. Cyrus Jaeckel, Mrs. Helen Bjornson, her bosom friend—whose husband travels but who has the children, so it's the same thing; and people like that. Now the importance is this . . ."

Malvinia paused to dip a pinch of snuff. She waited for the sneeze. ". . . that the list survives. The musicale was catered by the hotel. Captain Webster even charged extra for flowers and champagne—so you've got records to subpoena—and it was in the social notices. It would be inconceivable if she was not on a respectful footing. Whether the help will testify is another thing, but I can assure you," she said with vague menace, "that you'll have that chambermaid, Edna Crooms, and Henry Venerable. He's the Imperial's senior waiter, so he's bound to make a good impression."

She paused with satisfaction, rubbing her hands. Trumbull drew down his mouth, not sure how much of this was useful. The husky voice with its slurred accents, the dark splayed hands like a man's, the shrewd eyes had an emphatic quality. Malvinia read these thoughts with a chuckle.

"Now I'd heard she'd gone with her friend, Mrs. Bjornson, on this gay moonlight drive to the Fourteen Mile House for oysters and beer with Lieutenant Haddock and Lieutenant Garson. I brought this up and told her the sooner the marriage the better, because an old horse like the Senator might not last the course. So she laughed and told me there was more to it than met the eye and one day soon she'd reveal

144

all." Malvinia paused meaningfully. "Meanwhile she wanted me to make her a dress for Emily Hagerman's wedding reception to Lord Haskell-Frobisher. She had a printed invitation to attend, so how could there be scandal?"

Trumbull looked up. "Has she got that invitation?"

"Why, sho!" Malvinia said emphatically. "Now would a Senator invite a mistress to attend his daughter's wedding? He'd have to be low. Of course," she added critically, "it wasn't the ceremony, just the reception, but that can be explained."

Trumbull looked thoughtful. "So she was living at the Camden, and she was engaged—?"

"Not engaged. Married."

Trumbull made a precise point. "You were not present when she contracted this marriage?"

"Reckon not. You'll have to get that episode direct from Miss Roux. Miss Emily's wedding was right after Christmas, so Miss Roux was then four months married, as I was soon to learn. This invitation got Miss Emily furious because Lord Frobisher was beginning to ask questions about Miss Roux. She objected to the invitation but the Senator took iron control and made it clear that Miss Roux had every right to attend a family affair. Now for that reason she needed a real gorgeous dress and I was not to make mountains, she said, unless I wanted to lose a good account. She's got a real old temper, I tell you. So I got her undressed and took measurements. She's got a perfect white body without blemish. It was not an account I'd care to lose.

"Now there the point there," she went on, fixing her mismatched eyes on the lawyer, "is that I called next day on the Senator to confirm the order. Would he guarantee it, I asked. Which he said he would—not in writing, of course, but I'll say this —his word's good in small things. He paid by check—so you can demand its production. Then we had a real old intimate talk on how to handle this problem—and I counseled that he pay a call on Mrs. Bannister to reassure the family, which he did. Not that it helped. Mrs. Bannister treated him like a bad smell but that's neither here nor there. He paid that family call and will not deny it."

Malvinia watched a log fall in the hearth, sending up a shower of sparks. "That dress took extra fittings and four good women around the clock, but it was beautiful—blue velvet. I provided a dozen dresses for that occasion, worn by

145

the best ladies. She was treated at that reception like family. Miss Sprye, the Yankee housekeeper, gave her a room to change and stay over. She inspected the wedding gifts while hanging on Senator Hagerman's arm and laughing out loud at his jokes. Mr. Hagerman had a medical reason for not dancing, but he arranged her dances with all his friends. She's a wonderful dancer, light on her feet, and witty. Judge Sickels knows her from that time because she was joking him about his latest flip-flop decisions in Washington. I don't reckon he was pleased. But it was the greatest social event of this century and she looked outstanding in blue velvet with her white skin and red hair. Everybody was commenting on her. I catered the ice cream and I heard the compliments from my ladies on that dress—it was that striking. She danced till sunup. Thousands including waiters saw how respectful she was treated. Now *that's* when she told me of the marriage. It got blurted . . ."

She paused to listen to sounds of quarreling above. "It got blurted," she resumed, "when she came to bed about sunrise. I had fallen asleep in her room. She woke me up and told me —kind of laughing and weepy because she was full of champagne—that Theo Hagerman got excited by the smilax and tried to feel her up behind the circular stairs and the Senator caught 'em at it. 'No, he didn't!' I says. 'Yes, he did!' she says, laughing in this ringing laugh. 'What did the Senator say?' I says. 'Well, he was more amused than angry,' she says. She had got angry because the Senator then said, 'Who'd the boy have a better right to feel up than his own mother?' She didn't know whether to laugh or what. It was a terrible remark, but just like Mr. Hagerman, and those were his words. She had wanted him to thrash the boy, but he wouldn't. So she had stopped giggling and began to weep, because after all it was a dreadful thing to say.

" 'Mother?' I said. 'How's that, Miss Jessica? You mean you're expecting to become his mother?' 'No,' she says, laughing and crying. 'No, it's the living truth. I am that boy's mother, right now!' Then she hit her head and exclaimed, 'My God! That means I'm Tony's mama-in-law.' It struck her into hysterics—and with the champagne and excitement she started to laugh and cry together. I got her into bed with a sleeping draught and then she said earnestly, clutching me, that it was a secret and implored that I was not to tell a soul because it was all in writing and so forth. So I can give the time and place when I was told about the marriage—and I am willing to take my oath!" Malvinia said firmly, flexing hard strong hands. "Now you're surprised?" she said.

Trumbull smoked quietly. "It's new to me," he acknowledge. "You didn't tell this to Mr. Finch?"

"Quite a few things we haven't told Siddy Finch," Malvina agreed. "Not till we see how it's going." A pause. "What d'you think?"

"I gather you had a further talk with Hagerman? When was that?"

Malvinia thought back, counting. "I'll have to skip a year. I called on her at Ellis Street where she was supposedly recovering from the brain fever. That sprat, Nellie, brought me to her bedroom. She was exhausted by the ordeal, crying all over the place, but clear-minded. I sure didn't care for those cheap lodgings. Too many cats, and this smell of spoiled milk. I was shocked to find Miss Roux living among immigrants. She said it was temporary and she wanted to buy and furnish a house. She was sick of hotel life, she said, with its sordid hypocrisies and unbearable expenses, and wanted to start a new life. I estimated all that would cost several thousand dollars. Then to prove she had means she showed me the marriage contract." Malvinia paused for dramatic emphasis. "It looked all right and I advised her to ensure its safety."

Trumbull said precisely, "So you say you actually saw that paper at least two years ago in Ellis Street?"

"I did."

"Pray go on," he said enigmatically.

The crooked smile was discerning. "I know she told that girl, Nellie, that she was through with the man—like she was still sixteen with boys languishing for favors back in Cape Badeau—but, sho! That was just acting up. I was another thing. I had dressed and undressed her and talked intimate and she had no airs with me. We talked sober. She wished me to carry her abject apologies to the Senator if she caused him any unease of mind and to say she promised to be good and not make trouble if he would reconciliate to erase the public humiliation. I was most emphatic against that. I know men like Senator Hagerman, I told her, and that was the wrong way. I advised more show of pride and left when she got weepy.

"I called on Mr. Hagerman at his apartment—well, frankly, to look around. Mr. Hagerman received me in his dressing gown, looking sallow. I told him Miss Roux desired to live apart and wanted me to furnish a house. I said I knew he had had relations with her and owed her money. He just sighed and said it was complicated. It wasn't something he could deny—not to me, you see? The Senator and I had always been frank about these things and for good reasons, and would talk plain to each other. I asked if it'd be all right to deliver furniture and things. He replied Yes, if I brought an order he'd pay it. He pressed me to tell Miss Roux that he was regretful about his bad temper and what had happened, but that even kings had to courtesy to great customs. He said it was a quotation and I guess it was. We had some wine and talked about things—mostly how these broken-down old-timers and old actresses were costing him a fortune—but then Lew Hagerman always was a complainer, as we all know."

Trumbull stirred. "Can't we come to something more precise?" he said mildly. "More than respectful treatment and bill paying? Have we got a specific admission to you of the marriage from the husband?"

"Yes," she said emphatically, "but that comes after the trouble broke out. I—" She went out to the hall. "Miss Roux?" she called. "You git off that commode and come down. Hear?"

"Coming!" a distant lemony voice floated down.

Malvinia returned. "I'll take my oath on that whenever I'm asked. I h'ain't scratched the surface yet and I've restrained the language, out of respect for you. I've got a feeling for this case, Judge Trumbull," she said strongly. "It's something I've got in me for all these years. Look here," she said suddenly, thrusting out a hand the color of mahogany. "There's African. Cherokee. Something French or English. Jesus knows what makes the rest. Whatever 'tis, something inside there don't rest when these things happen. What's happening to the woman tortures and sickens me. I've laid for men, Judge Trumbull, from when I was a child of ten. I had no say in that. I just did what they said. All kinds of men came and went and I remember how they acted. When I was sixteen, I got to wonder why they kept on their filthy boots and never took off hats. I asked a simple question—Why did they act so?—and I still got the marks to show. It took two men twice the size of Digges to hold me in ropes while they laid on the whips, I was that big and strong. I cursed 'em out and they laid it on thicker, till they whipped me senseless. I woke in a kennel with dogs and just as naked—just for asking that question. I will carry this to the grave," she added bitterly, slipping open the front of her dress.

The dug was a split purple stub. The queer eyes held Trumbull's—and with the same quick motion the dress was closed. "I did something to the man who had it done," she said in low tones of anger. "I won't say now what. It was a long time and a war ago. I came out here to change my life, you'll recollect. I had good times and bad. I made my pile and lost it. I sued and got sued. I helped a lot of poor slaves in dire circumstances. I've dealt with men and helped girls—and I'll tell 'ee this, Judge, I never treated any girl unfair. I never stood for any gross abuse. As to unnatural appetites, I always satisfied myself that the girl was willing. I never stood for cruelties. I'm out of it all now, but I have never forgotten how it feels to stand helpless when they finger you and there's no recourse in God's earth.

"Now, Judge Trumbull," she said strongly, coming back to the center of the room, "if that's how I feel about the most common kind of girl, how d'ye imagine I feel about Jessie Roux? That woman's got a fine mind. I can tell you she's rare and delicate, without a mark or blemish. And Hagerman? That low sucker had a good thing there. He got her with promises and tactics. When she begged for fair treatment and regard for her good name, he pissed on her feelings and threw her into the gutter. Now he's saying because he's got power and runs the courts she'll never get justice. She was pitiable when she begged my help—weeping, distracted, crazy, and talking odd. I told her I'd been in her position. I knew what it is. I promised to get her due. I assured her of help.

"And it's not the first time Hagerman's acted like everyone was insignificant," she said with deep anger. "Somebody's got to take him in hand. Now the question, Judge Trumbull, is simply if you're that man. But I don't know," she said abruptly, "how much you accept. You look so disbelieving."

A clack of French heels at the door interrupted them.

A pale, slender woman entered with an air of grief and determination. "Oh, Judge Trumbull," Jessica said wanly, extending her hands. "I suppose I should be grateful you've come!" She took Trumbull's hands with a nervous grip, peering with intensity, searching for something. "Yes, yes, of course," she said, studying the large head, the somber, deep, unwavering eyes that met her own. "You're amazingly like your pictures, Judge Trumbull. I feel reassured. I feel hope—and it's no snap judgment. Well, can we sit?"

"Thank 'ee," Trumbull spread his coattails and sat stiffly in a chair with a straight back.

"Lands! I don't know where to begin," she said. "It's all such a jumble. I'm exhausted," she proclaimed, "just exhausted."

Trumbull did not think she looked exhausted at all. If anything, she looked remarkably self-possessed.

"Mrs. Lawes tells me you're old friends," Jessica went on conversationally. "She has spoken so highly of you."

"The Judge don't have too much time," Malvinia said. "Suppose you git down to cases?"

"Isn't she marvelous!" Jessica exclaimed. She touched her mouth in thought, then sat forward with an air of decision. Her tone was a trifle loud. "I hear you're to speak at the Hibernian Temple. I'm that pleased, I cannot tell you, Judge. It's exactly what my case needs—someone who thinks, who cares. It must not become just another sordid divorce case. It should be understood for what it is—a fight for principle."

"Of course," Trumbull said.

"Because if not," she said emphatically, "I shall lose all friends, all support. You'd be surprised how quickly that happens. Now where would you like to begin?"

"Wherever you like," Trumbull said. "I'm told you delayed signing the complaint? Why was that?"

"Well, I've not been satisfied with the proof," she said with sudden impatience. "I've been working hard to get the evidence—without much help either."

"Ah? How's it been going?" Trumbull asked.

"That's another thing," Jessica exclaimed. "When the story became public, I wondered who could help me. I thought, well, that first year at the Camden, lots of people knew we had an understanding. Also, Senator Hagerman wasn't always discreet. He wanted secrecy but sometimes he'd let the cat out of the bag. In wracking my brains, I thought, who could've been aware of the marriage? I wrote to all our old friends—people we'd entertained at Beaufort and places—begging for help. At first the replies were marvelous. Everyone was so helpful and sympathetic—because they knew the truth, of course."

150

Jessica fell back in the same thoughtful pose, biting her mouth. She turned to the old woman. "Where was I?"

"Letters," Malvinia said drily.

"Oh, yes! My mind keeps racing," Jessica said apologetically. "If not for sleeping draughts, I'd be a wreck. I am sustained only by my will and full determination not to lose this fight. I began with Congressman Reichbart. I wrote reminding him of that time the Senator had told the whole crowd that I was secretly Mrs. Hagerman. It was that day we all went to the racetrack together—Commodore Vanderbilt, Mr. and Mrs. Starke, and others. I asked if he was willing to recollect that Mr. Hagerman told him I was his wife. Well, I don't have to tell you what happened. The Congressman was full of manly help at first. Then he merely sympathized. Next he felt he could help more by staying out. Then he refused to promise to testify in court for me. Finally he stopped answering my letters. My God, Judge Trumbull! The nation's filled with cowards! Not one will antagonize the railroads—and do you know what's happened to those letters I wrote? The Congressman has turned 'em all over to Mr. Hagerman. I learned that yesterday. It was far more upsetting than anything else that's happened—to learn how alone you get. And I don't have to tell you the downright filthy things that happen to a woman in my position."

Trumbull listened to the rapid fire summary of an important area of the matter. "Then none of those people are available as witnesses to the marriage." It was a statement, not a question.

She halted in mid-flow. "Well, that's blunt," she said with an uncertain laugh. "But, yes, I'm afraid Mr. Hagerman has seen to that. I've been working hard, very hard to establish my case, Judge Trumbull, but everywhere I see the power of the man. He has isolated me. Even my best friend, Mrs. Bjornson, has given her diary with particulars of our mutual affairs to the other side." A strong gesture struck out against betrayal. "If not for Mrs. Lawes and Miss Driscoll . . . well, I'm alone," she said with stark realism. "Even Mr. Finch— and that's another thing," she burst out angrily. "Finch!" She walked to the window, hugging herself. "I could be sold out tomorrow," she muttered. She turned about. "He's a limited little man, don't you think?" she said with contempt. "Really not much of a lawyer."

Trumbull removed his spectacles. "Ma'am?"

151

She paused at the rebuke. "I suppose I shouldn't have said that?" she asked with scorn.

"Not to me," Trumbull said.

Jessica retreated a step. "Oh, sho! There I go," she said with a forced laugh. "I knew it was wrong when I said it, but it popped out. Can you excuse me?"

Trumbull said, "Is that why you asked to see me out here without Mr. Finch? To suggest that I represent you separately?"

Jessica flushed. "I've had bad experiences with lawyers. I'm not too sure of Mr. Finch."

"But you are of me?" he asked.

"I begin to think so," she said slowly, "but you haven't given me your views of the case."

Trumbull glanced at Malvinia and shrugged. "I'm not sure this whole thing is such a good idea," he said, rising.

"Judge! Sure you're not going?" Jessica said strongly. "You cannot go. I forbid it!"

Trumbull looked up. "Cannot, ma'am? Forbid?"

Jessica hesitated. "Well, I'm sorry," she said reluctantly. "I shouldn't have said that, only I get impatient with fools and cowards. I was told to expect more from you." She sat suddenly and averted her face, touching her eyes with a damp handkerchief. "You must excuse me," she said in a choked voice. "I'm not always like this. It's just that I got so upset yesterday by that announcement in the Federal Court. Judge Goff was bad enough. Even Judge Abernathy. But now that horrible Judge Sickels! Mr. Hagerman's friends are all rallying, while I have none. If you hadn't responded to my cry for help, I think I'd end my life."

"Pshaw!" Malvinia said impatiently.

"Well, I would!" Jessica said defiantly. "Life isn't worth that much, let me tell you! Judge Trumbull," she said, "what's happening to me is incredible. It's unbelievable. When I married Mr. Hagerman, I thought finally the sun was shining in my life. He raised me from a situation of despair you cannot imagine. I was financially embarrassed, heartsick from personal cankers, facing dreary prospects of life with strangers and hotel transients for companionship. Then Mr. Hagerman came into my heart. He was the kindest, sweetest, dearest man you can imagine before his mind was poisoned —poisoned by people who care for neither God, nor the decencies of life. Powerful, cruel, and vindictive people with lust for lucre. They turned him from me and now I am in the world's eyes an outcast. God! If I'd shot the man, I'd get more sympathy."

She suddenly leaped up and strode the room, gesticulating strongly. "It is terrible. It is outrageous. Nobody comforts me or supports me with one kind word. Not one of my family. I cannot persuade my own brother how outrageous the position is. They want me to run like a cur. God, oh, God!" she stormed. "That Hagerman should have one night of rest while he carries on against me like this! I should never have nursed him through that last disgusting, vile sickness. I should have let him rot and die of disease. I should have let him welter in vomit like a mangy, sick old dog!"

She stood, hand on hip, brandishing a fist, glaring at the unseen enemy. Then the mood broke. "No, I don't mean that," she said bitterly, "but I feel so alone. No one cares. No one feels."

Malvinia spat without expression into the fire.

"Oh, you! You're no better!" Jessica said angrily. Then, instantly contrite: "No, no, Vinnie! I don't mean that either. What do I mean? Oh, God! Have I come to this? Dependent on lawyers and hirelings?" A gesture took this back. "Oh, forgive that, Judge Trumbull! I don't mean anything I say. It's just that so many people have let me down and now you too look so disbelieving. How I came to let Senator Hagerman put me in this position galls beyond words. I am fretting away my life on this case. I have no money. I have lost my character. Miss Driscoll . . ."

She hesitated and went to the door and peered down the hall. She came back with renewed bitterness. "I am distracted to death, Judge, for fear they'll take Miss Driscoll from me. I have been like an older sister to that girl. I took her from a sty. I have taught her accomplishments. She can go out in company. She has stopped biting her nails and—and all other unpleasant mannerisms. They say I'm an influence. If that's being an influence, let 'em. I know those people—they're scum. Dirt. Unspeakable filth. And that immigrant trash who were so delighted to have me take the girl in hand and get my patronage—those disgraceful people are trying to take the child back to that shabby middle-class dreary life. Why? I'll tell you why! The bribery is beyond belief!" A finger stabbed out. "Did you know they have offered the police ten thousand dollars to catch me in something?"

"Oh, come," Trumbull said.

A skipping step was in the hall.

"Don't say anything to *her*," Jessica said quickly, gesturing to the door. Nellie entered with a quick look of inquiry. She stared sulkily at Trumbull and announced that lunch was ready.

"Oh, good! We'll be right there," Jessica said. "Or would you like to nap first, Judge?" she asked solicitously and was surprised at the irritable refusal.

He had one thing in mind, Trumbull said shortly, and that was the marriage contract—the how, the when, the where, the who! Would she kindly get to that? "Very well, but first lunch," Jessica said with managerial positiveness. "Country style. Mrs. Lawes has these marvelous Creole receipts you cannot refuse!" She paused. "Unless you mind eating in the kitchen, because it's sure no simple story to tell."

He could see why the kitchen was preferred to the dining room. A tall yellow-skinned man ruled an immense cast-iron range on which kettles simmered slowly through the day. Malvinia was up and down—tasting, adding, skimming, sampling, criticizing with authority. Pensioners of both sexes and all ages and colors came casually through what evidently was a communal kitchen. The young women with swollen bellies explained the function of the establishment. It was not only a residence and place of business, he gathered, but a not-so-secret house of refuge, less than an orphanage, better than a common baby farm. Malvinia through her network did a good traffic in getting babies for adoption—performing a needed service that the best families knew about but of which little was said.

Jessica seemed perfectly at home. Her own troubles cast aside for the moment, she was able to carry on animatedly and familiarly with the chattering young women who came for trays. The talk was obstetrical. The big problem in married life, one gathered, was that once respectable women married and had their babies—cinching their positions—they shunned relations with their husbands out of fear of more babies and disease. And could one blame the poor men if they acted as they did?

Good God, Trumbull thought, shaking his head. Bastardly? Yes! But the extent and ramifications were staggering. If one were to believe the talk, Mrs. Lawes was not only an angel of mercy but had something on every prominent family

154

in the city. He suppressed a smile. He felt like an accomplice in crime—and for a moment the interlude was enjoyable.

The afternoon was going, he observed finally, and suggested they get back to the case. Jessica led the way, sucking her fingers. A tumbler of whiskey was at his side.

The shadows in the garden had grown long. Trumbull had been listening without expression, tapping his cheek. He was considering the long, circumstantial, not entirely satisfactory narrative that had ended in heartbreak and despair. He finished a last cigar and turned to the weeping woman.

"Who signed first?"

"I did. Mr. Hagerman showed me law books and described the law and I relied on his word. Then he signed and I became Mrs. Hagerman. *Ex post facto,* I think he said," she added significantly, wiping her eyes.

"And next you say he read the secrecy clause?"

"Yes, he did!" she said. "I asked why I had to agree to keep the secret for two years. He said that was needed for the dust to settle. I didn't question it."

Trumbull tugged his beard. "Was that clause written before or after the signatures were put to the body of the contract?"

"Is that important?"

"Most important."

She sank back, breathing hard. "It was after the signatures. It had to be."

"Why so?"

"Once we signed, we were married. Anything subsequent couldn't affect the marriage, could it?"

Trumbull crossed the room, chewing his cigar savagely. "I've been in business for myself, Judge," she flared. "I've signed contracts and had 'em explained. I was dealing with a brilliant financier and I didn't see why I had to check my brains with the office boy."

"Is that what you'll tell the court on oath?"

"Yes. It's the truth."

"Then you didn't rely on Hagerman's word after all?" Trumbull said with contempt. "You rested on your own knowledge of business practice? Is that what you call reliance?"

She was silent.

"I only know what happened," she said after a long moment of realization. "I need not tell the operation of my mind, need I?"

"No!" Trumbull said. "But you do see, ma'am, that it's one thing to tell this story to your own lawyers. It'll be another to face cross-examination in the courtroom—your naked word against his as to the total circumstances, without supporting letters and documents?"

"How many times must I say this? They were mostly burned when my hotel in Oakland caught fire. The rest he stole."

"I see," Trumbull said dubiously.

"Well, I did not burn his letters myself," she exclaimed. "If I had all his letters, I wouldn't be in this situation. But they sure were written. He cannot deny that we exchanged notes and letters. Too many people carried 'em between us—Li, oh, I don't know who! If he'll criticize me for not having more letters, I'll criticize him! We'll see who's believed."

"Ma'am, you're the plaintiff," Trumbull said heavily, pursing his mouth. "You've got the weight and burden of this case. Not Hagerman." He shook his head. "Are there any points you'd care to clear up now, before I leave?"

"You're going to leave? We've not begun."

Trumbull glanced at his timepiece. "I see no reason to prolong this. I've got all I need to form an opinion. Trouble is, the vital act rests so heavily on your own word. That's what's so deplorable about the secrecy. It would be helpful to recall if those law books were seen by Ben Smith or that Mexican, Pedro Ramirez, before he left the office?" It was a suggestive question, testing, probing.

She thought carefully and shook her head. "I cannot say that. I have no idea what they saw." She turned aside. "I am the greatest fool in the world. Fool. Fool. I should've held out for a marriage in church, but I trusted the man. God!" She turned to the wall for composure. "What will satisfy you? What is missing?" she asked in a strained voice.

"Ma'am, it's a good circumstantial story—except for one thing I find impossible to grasp: Why still you've not shown anyone, not even your lawyers, the original marriage paper?"

She was looking at the high molding from which paintings darkened by time were hanging. "Mr. Finch has the text," she said. "I'll produce the original at the right time and place."

"You've shown this to experts?"

"Only photographs. It seemed sufficient."

Trumbull studied the slender back, baffled. It was a tone he found strange. "I've got a feeling it's in this house. Ain't there an iron vault in Las Flores?"

"I see," she said bitterly, and turned. An expression of intense suspicion narrowed her eyes. "You've been after that all along," she charged, "haven't you?"

Trumbull said, "I won't play blind, ma'am. I must insist."

"And after you've seen it, what assurance have I got of your help?"

"None, I'm afraid."

She ground her teeth and went to the hall. "Mrs. Lawes?" she called. "Mrs. Lawes? I need you." She returned to the room and stood before him, arms limp, staring with hot challenge. "Is there anything else?" she said, stepping closer. "Anything else you'd like to have?"

"Here 'tis," Malvinia said, and entered with a japanned box of gold-leaf dragon design.

A smell of dust wafted from the box. A dirty brown envelope was spotted with grease.

He brought the paper to his nostrils. What was it? Soil? Mold? A doggy stink mixed with old dust? A musky perfume so faint as to be merely imagination?

"Satisfied?" Jessica said in a frozen voice.

Trumbull studied the creases in the paper. "This paper looks worn. Where was it kept?"

"I kept it here," she exclaimed, defiantly indicating the fold between her breasts. "It was then put in that box, buried in the cellar. Judge Trumbull," she drew herself up with anger, "if you continue to look so doubtful, take your lawyer's scruples and go to hell."

"Doubtful?" Trumbull faced the doorway, buttoning his coat. He considered the pose of indignation, outthrust breasts, flashing eyes, clenched fists—yes, it might work. Finch's case could have possibilities—life, something was stirring. "Don't worry about my doubts. Worry about the Court's. If this signature's genuine—as you say it is—and if the testimony will hang together, you'll get judgment. If not? Well—" He finished the last button. "Look, ma'am, you best know the truth. You know what Hagerman's lawyers can bring against you. The story ain't too edifying even now, but you're not yet under judgment of any court. You can still decline to face the pillory, still live it down. The world's really not as censorious as it's made out. The relationship, whatever it was, is tolerable so long as it ain't flaunted. It ain't the world in which I choose to live, but many do.

"But once you go ahead with your lawsuit, you'll have surrendered yourself to the public judgment. You'll become what the courts with all their fictions say you are. You're up against cruel men. They'll search out California for materials to degrade you in the public eye. What they don't find, they'll contrive. You'll be paraded and stripped and flayed, and indecencies heaped upon you. So it's still entirely up to you—but before you finally go ahead—think! Is there anything else your lawyers ought to know?"

The solemn, foreboding words had their effect. A nervous glance went to Malvinia. Jessica retreated to the casement, hugging her breasts. She stared out at the profusion of wildflowers—lupines, yellow and purple—growing riotous in the poor soil. All the torment of the moment was before her. "I want to know your judgment," she said, troubled.

"I'm a lawyer," Trumbull said, "not a judge. I have no judgment."

"Why then do I feel judgment? I still want your opinion. For God's sake, do you believe in my case?"

Malvinia stirred. "Let up, Jess, or Judge Trumbull'll decline entirely. Think it over, Judge," she said quietly. "There's no hurry."

"Dear God," Jessica said. "Judge Trumbull, what shall I do?"

"Do?" He picked up his hat and went to the door. "I think you know what you've got to do—you can press that complaint for divorce without delay—or run and be degraded forever. I wish I could be more definite," he said, and left.

Nellie entered with a rush. "Well?" she said anxiously. "What did he say?"

"Sagamore," Digges said.

Trumbull climbed on, groaning with the stiffness of his wound. "I don't need help. I ain't ninety. Thank 'ee, Digges." Suddenly the air was cold and dank—San Francisco after dark. He entered a lobby blazing with lights and stopped at the desk, longing for his room.

"Anything wrong, Judge?" the clerk asked.

"No, no," Trumbull murmured, frowning at the message. Intense preparations, he was advised, were going forward at the Nevada Block. Offices would be open past midnight. Signed "Nat'l Green."

Sinzheimer was waiting in the friendly hubbub of the saloon bar.

"Did you commit yourself to those females?" he demanded. "You have, haven't you?" he said, drawing back in vexation. "Mark, you're a confounded fool. You came for help. Couldn't you sit tight till after our talk?"

"Now, Ike—"

"Ah! Look at you!" Sinzheimer said in disgust. He threw a coin on the bar and picked up his hat. "I wash my hands," he said angrily.

"Ike—"

"Ike me no Ikes," Sinzheimer snarled. A gold-headed cane tapped Trumbull's chest. "I said I'd make certain inquiries. But would you wait? It's characteristic, Mark. You're hot-headed, impetuous. It's got you in trouble all your life. Head in the stars, feet in the mud. You could've had anything this state has to offer. I weep, Mark. I weep. Go back to Stoddard—"

"Ike!" Trumbull said angrily, breaking through. "I have not promised to enter the case."

"Bourbon, Judge?" the bartender broke in.

The wretched expression gave Sinzheimer a pang. He suggested a booth in a paneled room hung with pink-and-white callipygous beauty. Two rounds of whiskey went down. Trumbull sat back, letting the warmth spread, and described the interview at Las Flores.

Sinzheimer said, "You saw the marriage contract?"

Trumbull nodded slowly. "Yes."

Sinzheimer reminded himself that Trumbull with all his repressions, passions, and weaknesses was an experienced lawyer and a man of great parts. "You must have pressed them very hard," he said respectfully.

"Hard enough," Trumbull said gloomily. He was thinking of the paper now returned to its vault at Las Flores. "I was hoping to find some gross fraud, a blatant forgery, a scheming adventuress. It'd let me out, y'see? But it's none of those things at all." He looked up with a grimace. "It's Hagerman's hand, Ike. And I wish it weren't."

"Have you decided what to do?"

"Not yet." Trumbull stared into his glass.

Sinzheimer studied the obstinate, unhappy man. "Mark,"

he said carefully, "I want you to come with me and listen to a proposal. It's an entirely respectable matter, of course. It could work out to your advantage and maybe to the client's. Would you listen to an old friend?"

The dead stare was fixed. "Listen how?"

"Just listen," Sinzheimer said.

"Why can't you tell me now?"

"Because you've got a damned impulsive temper," Sinzheimer replied. "Will you trust me that far?"

Trumbull waited uncertainly. "I trust you implicitly, Ike," he said, "but I promised myself a quiet dinner. I need to prepare my address for tonight."

"This will not take time." Sinzheimer was not to be put off. "Forget your own plans. Do what I say. Don't be weak, Mark. Be strong."

"Well, I sure don't want to seem weak," Trumbull sighed. "Tell me, Ike," he said crossly. "I'm beginning to sense what people've got against the Jews. What d'ye suppose it is?"

Sinzheimer laughed. "It's not hard to understand. After all," he said, complacently studying his fingernails, "not everybody can be one. Shall we go?"

"Come in, Ike. Mark, I'm delighted," Pike boomed. Pike came forward with a smile of intense cordiality and a strong grip. "Gentlemen, find seats."

"Joe," Trumbull replied warily. He felt cold and stony with a clarity of vision that held a warning. The Presidential Suite at the Purdue Hotel was splendid with ornate furnishings. A haze of tobacco smoke and a litter of notes were evidence of a recent conference. Voices could be heard in the next room.

"Is it still bourbon?" Pike asked.

"I'd be grateful," Trumbull replied, accepting a tumbler of whiskey. Something was in the wind. Pike was grinning and stroking a flowing white Walt Whitman beard. That beard, and an immense bald dome of intellect, gave Pike a grandfatherly appearance—an appearance belied by the hard eyes of shrewd good humor. Josiah Pike was a legend—friend of Lincoln, first Senator from Nevada, advocate of bimetallism, Wall Street lawyer, and biggest fee earner in the nation. Short on scholarship, Trumbull thought, but that was an overrated asset. "Now, Joe," he grunted, "I ain't here for a talk-fest. What's this about?"

160

Pike turned to Sinzheimer. "Any trouble with this feller, Ike?"

"Came like a lamb," Sinzheimer said.

The courtesies were exchanged. Old lawsuits in the Comstock were recalled, the split in New York politics between Tammany Hall and the Governor was touched upon, and Pike came to the purpose. It was of course the Hagerman matter. Messy, of course, unfortunate scandal. Good people getting hurt. The effort to get Trumbull into the notorious case was the talk of the profession; rumors had even reached Wall Street. It was naturally of concern to old friends. "They'll never let you win, Mark. I think you know that," Pike said with pitiless realism. "It could ruin you. Might even be dangerous, though I know that won't impress you. However, there might be a way out."

"Go on," Trumbull said.

Pike stroked his beard. "I've had a talk with Lew Hagerman—he's incensed but not wholly obdurate—and in my opinion he can be made to listen to reason. That is, if he's reached by the right party. Could even be good for you, Mark," he added smoothly. "I put that with respect. Will you listen?"

Voices murmured behind the sliding doors. So there it was! Trumbull thought, facing the discerning eyes. The whiskey left him cold, unmoved. Why was he still seated there? The noise was distracting.

"Oh, I'll listen," he said grimly. "How's all this to be done?"

Pike and Sinzheimer exchanged a glance. Pike said, "Hagerman wouldn't refuse Sickels."

"Sickels? What in hell would I have to do to induce him to do anything for me?"

"This is entirely in confidence, I trust—not to go beyond these walls?"

"Go on," Trumbull said.

Pike smiled. "As it happens, Sickels sends you his particular regards. Refresh that glass, Ike," he boomed and outlined a proposed line of action in a voice that rattled the windows. In a few months the major political parties would convene to nominate their candidates for President of the United States. Not Sickels necessarily—for having failed once, he was loathe to try again—but his name was being persistently advanced and his reluctance, he had indicated, might be overcome if his own state's support were assured. No one who joined the effort early enough could fail to benefit. . . .

As the import sank in, Trumbull's face darkened.

"Well?" Pike said finally.

Trumbull put aside an empty tumbler. At the door he turned to Sinzheimer, "I'm astonished, Ike, amazed that a man of your sense would bring me to this room. Most preposterous thing I ever heard. Good night." He left, shaking with anger.

Chapter Eight

The annual memorial meeting for the McCabes had in a few short years dwindled to old friends and family. Now the hall was packed. Fanny Woodruff arrived early with Rudolf Lang, who introduced her to Tom Wickwire of the *Examiner*, a strongly opinionated Southerner. The three found chairs together at the press table. A small man tiptoed to the lectern, organized pencils and notes, and tiptoed out.

A stocky man with radiant white hair came forward and took a prizefighter's stance, hands aloft, palms outward, waiting for silence. "Brothers! If you please!" he bellowed.

"So that's Mike Larkin," Fanny said. It was her first glimpse of the turbulent demagogue who had in a burst of ranting created the Workingmen's Party of California and whose faction now was raising havoc within the Democracy of the state.

"Larkin for President," an excited voice screamed. Groans responded. A drunken voice whooping, "Sickels for—" was stopped abruptly. "Ow! Who did that?" the voice complained. Larkin raised his fists, smiling desperately. "Brothers! Brothers!" he bellowed. "Respect! Silence! D'ye hear?"

There was laughter and derision. Larkin announced that the principal speaker, the Honorable Mark Trumbull, was delayed. Boos, catcalls, and laughter came from the balcony.

"Dolf?" Fanny said, focusing her monocle, "D'ye think this could make the milieu of a novel?" Lang turned, puzzled. "What would?" he asked. "This!" A gesture encompassed the scene. "The class struggle—monopoly of wealth and power—cruelty, greed, industrial warfare—well, all this!"

"You mean write about strikes?" Lang said thoughtfully.

"Yes!"

"And long hours? And the crushing power of monopolistic capital and its corrupt influence upon the political structure of the state?" Lang shook his head. "Absurd," he said with finality. "California's the Land of Heart's Desire. Romance or nothing," he added firmly, making a mental note to steal the idea.

"Th'rumbool!" Johnny Quinn arose and made a vulgar sound. There were boos, catcalls, applause, more laughter, and offers to settle differences outside.

"Who's that fellow?" Fanny asked.

Lang outlined Quinn's theory of treachery and betrayal of the McCabes. "Oh, impossible! Trumbull would be incapable of anything like that!" Fanny exclaimed. "If he refused to defend those men on a murder charge, I'm sure he had a good reason."

"Incapable?" Lang murmured, amused. "Have you got the Trumbull bug too?"

"Well . . ." Fanny replied, thinking. "But I know something too. Men don't change, and his life's too well known. He's always acted out of conviction."

"Has he really?" Lang said skeptically.

"Yes, he has," Wickwire said, joining in. "Trumbull was hired by the League simply to defend their lives. He withdrew when the defense—because of their guilt—became impossible to maintain. He wanted to make a deal and save their lives. Didn't work out."

"Deal?" Fanny said.

Wickwire nodded. "Why, sure. A deal to get Buddy released and a prison sentence for Luke. It meant they'd have to plead guilty. The League wanted martyrs, a sensational fight, charges of frame-up, and refused to string along. Trumbull was caught between politics and his duty as a lawyer. Couldn't prove innocence and wouldn't risk hanging, you see? People like Quinn still haven't forgiven him. They won't accept that he withdrew on a simple point of principle. And perhaps they're right," he said with a neat smile. A mantle was unspotted, but two men had died. Perhaps the excess of purity was a form of higher corruption, he concluded, enjoying the game of words.

Fanny found it convenient to search for a handkerchief. There was an answer, she was sure, but it eluded her. Wickwire was not much to her liking. She looked up, fascinated by the tumult. Most of the audience were rough-clad workmen. Welsbach gas mantles on the stage cast brilliant light on the proceedings. Mingled with the workmen were the pale faces of city dwellers, smug with high-mindedness. Leathery tanned men represented the Pima. "I don't understand the catcalls," she said. "I thought Judge Trumbull was so popular, at least with the rest of this crowd."

"It's the Hagerman matter," Lang said, smoothing his blond moustaches with enjoyment. A tide of suspicion of attempts by the Senator's forces to keep Trumbull from entering the scandalous lawsuit accounted for the big turnout for what otherwise was a routine affair.

"What damned nonsense!" Fanny exclaimed. "Dolf, how can people believe anything like that?"

Lang shrugged. "Not everyone's Trumbull's friend," he observed. "No one's reputation's a perfect shield, especially a man who's fought a duel and killed a man. He hasn't lived that down either. Come, Fanny. Is an approach to Trumbull so unthinkable?"

Fanny paused. "What could anyone offer him?"

"What indeed?"

"Well, perhaps not," she said reluctantly, recalling Trumbull's stiff behavior on the train at the same suggestion. She had always had a strong feeling about Trumbull, she went on, fanning herself. The hall was intolerably hot. "Ever since I was a child," she said reminiscently, "Grandpapa used to love to talk at the breakfast table about Old California. I remember as a girl, his pacing the parlor, describing the magnificent conduct of a man called Judge Trumbull. I had no idea what he meant, but the sound of that name rang in my ears. A man with a Minotaur name—Trumbull. What a funny childhood memory."

"They're the best," Lang said.

"Then when I was older, I found a pamphlet in the library. It showed Judge Trumbull being sentenced to death by the Vigilantes Court for resisting their usurpation of the law and that letter of resignation to fate that he wrote to his wife. I read it endlessly, over and over, I committed it to heart. I kept it next to a life of Joan of Arc. I was in love with 'em both at fourteen," she smiled. "I was carried away by the concept of heroism pure unto death."

"Yes. Sad about Joan," Lang murmured, smoothing his moustaches with a covert grin. "Just because the poor girl wore male dress, slept in ditches, refused, ah, sexual relations, claimed divine inspiration, and heard voices—that's no reason to think she was mad. The main thing is to remember that Joan's voices—as we now know—were real. Why not Trumbull's?"

He cocked an ear. Doors slammed. "People think the worst—and there's no reason to grant good motives. No one with common sense would undertake a fight he couldn't win. Here he is now," he said, rising with the rest and joining in the applause.

Gas jets flared, casting a soft yellow light upon the chair and podium. Heavy, uncouth men were lolling in chairs of honor. Trumbull was staring at a distant point in space, unmoved by praise, unhearing of discontent and hostility. He knew every third face in the hall. Once he had known every one of them. A swift glance went to the press table—the reporters were friendly enough but unconvinced, skeptical. Good enough, their job was skepticism. Larkin was bawling an endless introduction—every political honor and achievement in his life was labored in garbled form. And then: " a great Californian, friend of labor, Judge Trumbull of Stoddard!" The applause rose as Trumbull stood. "Don't take long," Larkin said, grinning, and sat.

Trumbull waited for silence. He grasped his lapels, robust and easy, and, suddenly, seemingly good-humored. It was Trumbull at his best—drunk with the moment.

"Mr. Chairman . . ."

Larkin nodded.

"Honored Brothers . . ."

A panel of labor union men, horny-handed, scarlet-faced, glanced up impassively.

"Member of the Clergy . . ."

The Reverend Norman Townsend gave a toothy liberal smile.

"My young friends . . ."

A group of students came to order.

He glanced at the press table. Fanny Woodruff, looking much amused, raised her brows. A blink acknowledged her presence. "Ladies, gentlemen . . . and reporters," he drawled provocatively and halted. "So far so good," he said and waited for an uncertain patter of laughter. He placed a set of notes on the lectern.

"The blindness of the privileged classes of France to the Revolution which was about to overwhelm them . . ." he began on a low note.

"Louder! Can't hear that!"

He looked up to the gallery. "Oh, you'll hear me soon enough," he promised. A few chuckles were friendly and encouraging.

A bellow: "Don't fall asleep, Mark!"

Trumbull turned to the balcony. "That you, Senator?" he drawled. A moment of silence, then a wave of laughter. Then another, and another as it caught on. Men gasped and howled, slapping their thighs, bursting with mirth. Old Trumbull had put it across again. Trumbull, somewhat surprised, let the storm subside. "Sorry, Lew," he added, cupping an ear, "cain't see you against the dazzle. Speak up." More chuckles. "No? Oh, now, folks," he said with mock disappointment, "seems we've got a blushing shy capitalist up thar. I'll tell 'ee what, Lew. I wasn't asleep. But if . . . if . . ." The heavy features darkened and an expectant hush gathered. "If perchance I should slumber, beware, sir! Beware lest I awaken!"

A gasp, and the storm of applause burst. He let it die. A leisurely manner now commanded attention. He put aside the notes and faced a sea of expectant faces. "Now I *did* have an intellectual beginning," he said solemnly, peering over his spectacles amiably. "I had expected to draw an analogy to the conditions of France and those which prevail now in this state and nation. The celebrated Mr. Maine points out that the aristocracy of France was blind to growing irreligion, to gross inequality of taxation, to class privileges, to financial disorders, and to all other immediate causes of revolution. But they at least had not the benefit of hindsight, for the French monarchy had survived a thousand years, and seemed destined to last forever. It was impossible for them to see that the entire structure of a stately and scandalous court was undermined on all sides. Beautiful Armida Palace—where the inmates lived enchanted lives, lapped in soft music of adulation, waited on by the splendors of the world—nevertheless hung wondrously by a single hair. When that hair was snipped, France fell."

Now the silence was uneasy as the ornate prose reached every corner of the hall. The roaring of gas jets was a continuous murmur. He had also hoped, Trumbull went on, glancing at the press section, to point out how strange it was that worse conditions should exist in California, spurred paradoxically by the very liberty and popular suffrage of her free institutions. State government, like that of the nation, he had intended to show, resting in theory on universal assent, in fact had come to rest on no assent at all but that of the strong. Government without restraint, government coercive, government of the rich, the powerful had sprung up in the midst of democracy. Never had history in fact seen a community in which the weak had been pushed so quickly, so pitilessly to the wall—a state in which so quickly the rich had become so strong—in which so quickly there had risen great inequalities of private fortune and domestic luxury.

But these things, he added ironically, peering over his spectacles, were not the things he had finally come to say. "I wrote all that for the young folks—just to show I kin. But I find I cannot make the analogy between this state and France, because unlike the aristocracy of France, we had the benefit of hindsight and the lessons of their experience. We can see where we are going. They could not. The point is too clear to labor and so I won't. So much for Mr. Maine." He put aside his notes and waited for a titter to die off.

He had come instead to memorialize two brave young men who had resisted force and injustice. Without theory, without ideology, without education, without organization, moved by nothing but manhood and blind instinct, they had struck at a Power stealing the land and destroying their lives. It was a hopeless gesture doomed before it started. And wrong. . . .

A murmur of uneasiness went around the hall. Wrong? What in hell did he mean—wrong?

Trumbull read the mood and went on to the events of the Pima Tragedy when Luke McCabe and his young brother had taken direct action against the railway—action which led to their own tragic deaths at San Quentin. The matter-of-fact drawl rehearsed the history of the state since the earliest clashes of the people—ranchers, farmers, workingmen—against the pitiless instruments of a rising industrial power:

167

events they all knew, head-on clashes which led finally to the Constitutional Convention and reforms imposed on the state of California by those listening to his words. Those reforms were known and their fate too, the corruption which had stolen from the people the fruits of victory. . . .

The argument went on in silence, carrying his listeners with a vivid reconstruction of horrors felt most keenly. Staring eyes were dry and fixed. There was a mutter of assent.

But it was all wrong, Trumbull went on, drawing down the deep lines of his mouth, returning to his theme. Wrong because they were charging the wrong target—like bulls charging the cape and not noticing the muleta poised for death. Was there sense in killing railway people—brakemen, conductors, station agents, or even yard police and hired detectives? Or even the federal officers? Were they the enemy? Who was the enemy? Courts? Judges? Court officers? Or the apocalyptic beast whose tentacles of steel stretched across the nation? The hand they knew—but whose the voice? The question lingered in the ominous silence. Whose?

Trumbull stood rocking, fixing his glance at a point in space. "Well, now, Senator? We know, sure enough, don't we? Hey? Don't we, Senator?" he asked, cupping his hands as before. Laughter started and died nervously.

An expression of mock regret gathered. "No answer? Cat got your tongue? Lordy, where does that leave us?" He stood peering into space. A note of rancor crept in. "The tree of liberty must be refreshed with the blood of tyrants, it's been said. It is its natural manure.

"There's another name for manure," he added somberly. "If we must have it, we must. But where shall we seek it? Hey, Senator?" The cupped hand, the attitude of concern, the humorous pose expressed earnest attention—followed by disappointment. "Ah, silence. Too bad, too bad."

Trumbull turned to the audience. "Reckon the Senator cannot be roused," he said with regret. "But he knows where we've got to follow him. Upstairs, downstairs! Into"—a humorous penetrating look went to the press table—"my lady's chamber. . . .

"Strange place to follow, but if follow we must, follow we will. Small consolation for murder and pillage and corruption of the courts, but the smallest consolation is better than none. So be it, so be it." The great head remained lowered ominously. "Now let's see," he said, "I was to memorialize the dead, wasn't I? But wouldn't that be the memorial to the departed?"

There was no peroration, no exhortation, no final appeal to the deeper feelings. A question lingered in the void. Trumbull picked his timepiece from the lectern, and returned to his seat.

The applause was feeble, uncertain. What in hell was it all about?

"He's taking the woman's case," Lang exclaimed. "The confounded fool." The applause, at first feeble, uncertain, broke into a sustained roar.

Chapter Nine

Sickels had awakened at dawn in savage temper. He had lost over six hundred dollars at poker in his annual game with the boys, had eaten too much liver paste, had swallowed too much beer, and had listened to unsatisfactory political reports. He had a thick tongue and heavy head. "Oh, God," he groaned, wending his way to the convenience where he poised dully, waiting for ease to come, too dispirited to force the issue. Those burning ambitions were farther away than ever before. He had a childish and immense vanity, and why he should be denied a term of residence in the White House by intrigues and small-mindedness was beyond his grasp. However, he was obstinate and had not yet given up.

Only gradually as he dressed did a knot of wrath dissolve. Mrs. Minerva Sickels, most patient and gentle of women, wondered whether or not things had gone well the night before. "Well enough," he grunted sourly, slipping a set of dentures into place. The splashy speech immediately improved. "Minnie, we're walking a tightrope," he said finally, kissing his wife. "But we'll make it yet. I'm convinced on it."

"Yes, Jack," the woman sighed.

Each year Sickels looked forward to visiting the Ninth Circuit, where he held undisputed sway—not diluted by the rule of nine. In that Circuit he ruled with an absolute hand— the subordinate judges were his nominees and not likely to

169

forget the source from whence their tenure flowed. The commodious suite at the Imperial House was fitted out for housekeeping and ordinarily he dined there with his wife with the greatest pleasure, but when business called, he would breakfast in the grill room screened from the public by potted palms. This morning the breakfast room was still deserted but the smells were delicious.

Galindez and Fanny Woodruff were waiting. Galindez stood. "I had a bit of trouble getting her up this early," he joked, "but she has an infinite capacity for forgiveness."

"Judge Sickels," Fanny smiled, extending her hand, "this man is not to be denied."

Sickels shook hands, studying his guests with ominous intensity as though to commit the moment to the extraordinary filing system of his memory. He put great weight and comfort in that memory—and recently a few lapses had caused him concern. He longed for coffee to clear the sensorium. Fanny was looking hollow-eyed and fretful. Galindez, freshly shaved and pomaded, was plucking the red lips and pointed chin of Mephistopheles with an air of vindictive amusement. This was no clue to his mood. So far as Sickels knew, Galindez never looked otherwise.

Sickels began by dropping a few words in Turkish to Galindez. Sickels had picked up the tongue in his boyhood when he had accompanied an older brother on a mission in Smyrna. He had also learned Demotic Greek and French. How Galindez had picked up Turkish, Sickels never learned, but the pastime was innocent. It was a kind of bond.

"Well, Fanny?" Sickels said finally with friendly indulgence. He was intensely—for the moment, at any rate—interested in her activities. He asked polite questions and pressed her to convey compliments to her grandfather. Fanny brought her monocle to place, listening with interest to the flow. In its horrid way, she saw, it was a form of flirtation.

One of the senior waiters, Henry Venerable, a thin black man with affected manners, brought the bill of fare and newspapers. Venerable departed hurriedly. A knowing look passed: Venerable, witness for the enemy, it said.

Galindez shrugged significantly.

Sickels nodded.

Fanny glanced from one to the other—a cryptic message had answered an equally obscure question. So men of affairs communicated by primitive means, she thought, almost on the animal level—by shrugs, sounds, who knew? Perhaps by scent and other such means. Something was going on. Sickels excused himself and turned to the headlines.

"Fried caviar?" Fanny wondered out loud, staring at the bill of fare with awe.

When it became certain that she was joking, Sickels laughed. "My dear," he said with forced geniality, "I gather you were at the Hibernian Hall? How was Trumbull received?"

Fanny made a precise business of arranging the silverware. "They cheered like mad," she said compactly. Sickels looked thoughtful indeed.

He wiped his mouth and reached for a cigar. "I'll tell you what we have in mind," he said finally. "It's that biography on me by Professor Nock. What d'ye think on it?"

Oh, dear! she thought. "I think it's good," she said with a straight face. "A bit too adulatory, of course."

"Too adulatory?" Sickels said.

"Perhaps that's not the word," Fanny said without dropping a stitch, "but too legal . . ." She turned to Galindez for confirmation.

"Too legal? What's that supposed to mean?" Sickels demanded.

"Confused," Fanny said. "Ambiguous. Overemotional. Lacks precision. Inflation of ideas . . . but I suppose it's all right. Professor Nock was trying to show the legal side . . . your preeminence as one of the ten greatest jurists the country has ever seen. You are, aren't you?"

"Well, yes," Sickels said judiciously. "I reckon I am. I've given it thought, Fanny. I've weighed the others and I think, I *think* I'd put myself among the top four, if not the top three. I wouldn't question Marshall's contribution. He comes first, of course, then . . . well, the fact is, I'm not sure who does come after Marshall.

"However, I reckon it does come down to campaign literature," he said abruptly, with a practical air. "It's always too black and white. Never gets the human touch, Tony," he said angrily. Galindez managed to look patient. Nock's *Life of Judge Sickels*—to give its short title—has been distributed at the Democratic National Convention four years earlier like confetti. The railway lobby had strewn copies throughout the country. It had been serialized in all their newspapers. As

171

campaign manager, Galindez knew the cost to the penny. Lost money.

Sickels came back with a broad smile. A man's life was too serious to be left to pedants, he agreed. It was really a writer's job, his advisers saw that now. As to that book, was there comment? he wondered. Were there mistakes? Suggestions were welcome.

It was evident that hurt vanity, more relentless than the grave, was seething. "I'm no lawyer, of course, but I think Nock might've explained some decisions better," Fanny said carefully, pausing at the quick frown, reluctant to push on. Certain cases, especially the line of Chinese decisions, still excited public feeling. In *Ah Luk Fow,* for example, he had ruled for free Chinese immigration; but more recently, the case of *Chang Ping* reversed that ruling. The lack of consistency was puzzling. It was not clear how one might reconcile those cases—and the diametrically opposed opinions gave no clue.

Sickels looked vexed indeed. His long tenure on the Supreme Court bench had touched thousands of situations. Why the curse of China was upon him he could not fathom. "I don't know what to do. If I admit the Chinese, I'm damned by labor. If I exclude 'em, I'm suspect. I ought to wash my hands—" He broke off, coughing with vexation. "Too much," he muttered. "Too much." Ah Luk Fow had been an immigrant prostitute from Canton detained by California's Commissioner of Immigration for failure of the steamship line—an affiliate of the C. and S. W. Railway—to post bond for good behavior as required by state law. Mobs had assembled that hot summer's day at the United States Assayers Building on rumor that the steamship's lawyers has applied on her behalf to the United States Circuit Court for the great writ of habeas corpus. In defiance of the mobs, Sickels had limped to the bench and there despite shouts and imprecations from the street had gone to judgment. There was no proof, he had ruled in that orotund and sanctimonious manner famous throughout the nation, that Ah Luk Fow was a prostitute. True, her sleeves were long and her feet were large. Ordinarily these were signs of that unfortunate class, he had conceded, but, he noted, the steamship's lawyers had proved that she was wife to one Ah Kim, an employee of Mr. Clare Gresham, who had vouched for these facts. She was thus *prima facie* a woman of worth.

It was certainly desirable, he had added with fine sarcasm, that lewdness be suppressed. But he had little respect for that discriminating virtue which, shocked by the frail daughters of Cathay, yet allowed painted harlots of other races to parade the streets of San Francisco without let or hindrance from a corrupt constabulary. In a harsh and sonorous voice, he then turned to the legal side. He had rebuked the state's attempt to override the Treaty of 1868 between the United States of America and His Celestial Majesty, the Emperor of China, which entitled the citizens and subjects of each freely to enter the other's domains for all lawful purposes.

Federal law, he announced with brutal directness, would prevail over state law. It was basic to the Constitution for which men had recently fought a bloody civil war. Then, reproving hypocrisy, citing Acts 17:5, recalling the Federalist Papers, the Constitutional Convention of 1787, and the Admiralty case of *The Thistle*, he noted that discriminatory laws of any state against any class, sect, creed, or nation were prohibited by the Brooding Spirit and Undeniable Intent of the Constitution. In short, more than prostitution was involved in the person of Mrs. Ah.

"Let the prisoner be discharged!"

The decision brought a volley of gunfire and a charge of federal marshals into the street. The decision pleased no one. Every pulpit denounced the judge. He was burned in effigy by Mike Larkin's laborites. The suspicion was voiced that the ruling was prompted by railroad need for cheap and sexually contented Chinese labor—suspicions which still dogged his political career. It was *Ah Luk Fow* which more than any other single legal act had brought him labor's enmity.

"Ah Luk Fow! Ugly hag, you know? Wasn't worth the fuss!"

Sickels muttered savagely. "Besides, she died of the cholera, so what was it about?" He forced a broad smile. "Look here, Fanny," he said weightily. "The thing to bear in mind is that the law is a science whose principles are settled. Settled, mark you! Men rest upon the stability of the law—hold property, make contracts, assert rights, claim protection. The law rests on reason. It stems from the general intelligence, learning, and traditions of mankind—not on the individual reasoning of any one judge. So it cannot change.

"However, it is possible to become a slave to this notion. It is also possible for man's intellect to rise above the errors of

173

man—including its own. I reversed myself in *Chang Ping* because I changed my mind. That is how I reconcile those cases," he concluded belligerently.

The waiter removed dishes and poured coffee. The grill room was beginning to fill up. The old judge pressed his mouth, regaining control. "But you're right, Fanny," he said. "Nock's book is wrong and clumsy. A political campaign ain't an argument on appeal. It calls for verve. Snap. Romance. Something colorful to get to the voter.

"Well, it's preposterous," he went on with vigor. "This notion I'm a disembodied brain, a logic machine, is ruinous," he said, spitting a flake of tabacco. "It should've been another kind of book with guts and thunder. Truth. Actuality. Ought to read like a thriller, like—well, like something you might dash off, Fanny," he said with inspiration. "Has Tony told you what we've got in mind?"

The silence was uncomfortable.

Fanny turned in reproach. "My word, Tony, you never said you wanted a book. An article, at most. I'm not sure I'm qualified," she said uneasily.

"But you are," Sickels exclaimed. "I've read your articles in the *Overland*—Mission Fathers, Bear Republic, Pioneer Days, Gold Rush—and you show real knowledge of that colorful setting. True, I'm no rail splitter. No Indian fighter. But I've had a real colorful career," he went on argumentatively. "Just missed forty-nine, but I was on the ground floor. I could easily be pictured as a pioneer. I hung out my shingle when Marysville was still overrun with thieves and bad men. I was elected to the first legislature from the county. I practiced law with a six-shooter in my belt. I defied lynch mobs. Tony, didn't I defy lynch mobs?" he appealed.

"It's documented," Galindez said with his Mephisto smile. "Give it thought, Fanny. Justice Sickels is a gold mine of colorful recollections. Actually most of it is already in shape. It's already dictated to a stenographer. You'd only need to touch it up here and there."

Except for the soft voices of waiters showing guests to tables, the silence was painful and profound.

"Lynch mobs, you say?" Fanny murmured.

"Oh, yes, but that wasn't too unusual," Sickels chuckled. A smile softened the threatening features. "There were a bunch of us in Gold Hill and Virginia City. Claggett, Pike, me, Hagerman, others. We all went through lynch mobs and river floods and mine fires. Claggett and Pike have got out their reminiscences—stretching truth. Pike has all this stuff about facing down those miners' delegations. Stuff! He had the compromise from the mine owners in his pocket—four dollars a day plus hot showers. Those books sell. Why shouldn't mine?"

"Now as to manliness," he went on, ticking off on his fingers. "I had my own affair with Senator Patrick Gore, years before Trumbull's encounter. Gore and I had words at Sacramento where I served in the Legislature. Gore was so impressed by my indifference to threats that he asked to become fast friends. Later when I had trouble, Gore, who was then the Speaker, warned that the first wrong move would result in gunfire from posted marksmen. You didn't know about the posted marksmen, did you, Tony?" he demanded, ticking off three other such episodes from those early days—a fist fight with a police justice in Wilmot, the thrashing of a cowardly blacksmith in Gonzales, an encounter with a fiery Virginian, John Lee . . . He paused and laughed self-consciously. "Oh, I reckon you'd not want to hear about that one," he chuckled, embarrassed.

"What one?" Galindel asked.

"Oh, just a silly thing." Sickels smiled broadly. "It's just my old nickname I got in Sacramento—Fearless Jack. Fearless Jack," he repeated with relish. A startling whinny was squeezed out under forced draft—in reality laughter. It was simply, he explained, that his opponent in Sacramento, John Lee, had had a failure of nerve. "Lee displayed a pistol," he went on. "But I walked up coolly to Lee and said, 'Give me that instrument, sir!' Lee just handed over the pistol and said with awe, 'You're fearless, Jack. Absolutely fearless. Let's not quarrel.' That's how I got that nickname. Did you ever hear of that?" he demanded.

Fanny said respectfully, "No."

The old judge looked disappointed. "Well, that's understandable," he said grudgingly. "Sacramento was a small village in those days. Not many do remember. They're all dead, or scattered. Come to think, all those people are gone. Still, it's as vivid now as the moment it happened—that gun, John Lee. Well, he died of consumption," he concluded, shaking his head. "Fanny, could you use such anecdotes? I mean, revive those stirring days so people see 'em?"

"Um. I see. My word," Fanny said, staring at dregs of coffee, visualizing a most extraordinary career that stretched from Haddam, Connecticut, where the old judge was born— one of eleven quarrelsome, brilliant offspring of a Congregational minister—through law practice on Wall Street and in California, then finally participation in the great political and legal battles of the nation's history. "I'm so terribly flattered," she murmured. "Would I have a free hand?"

There was a perceptible pause. "Well, of course," Sickels said. "One or two touchy matters could be held out. Otherwise, you'd have perfect freedom. I certainly don't want anything artificial. I want a literary product, your own views, based on questions, records, letters, files, my manuscript. It's all at your disposal. I rather think you'll enjoy it."

Fanny sat thinking. "Well, of course I'm flattered, Judge Sickels."

"Then it's done?"

"I'm not sure I can manage a whole book," Fanny said slowly. "I'm being asked to do some pieces for the *Herald* here, but perhaps a series of articles could be strung together. If we can make terms."

The ingratiating smile narrowed. "You'd want to be paid?" Sickels said with a touch of wonder. "Just for writing?"

"Oh, yes," she said.

There was a prolonged moment of silence. "Well, I'm sure Tony can make arrangements," Sickels said finally. "I just ask truth—warts and all."

"Of course," Fanny said. "My word! Time's flying! You must excuse me. I've got an article to get off by the mail train. I was up half the night getting that Hibernian Hall affair on paper. Quite exhausting. However, I'll be glad to think about it. I'll see you later at court. No, don't get up, Tony. Judge Sickels, it's been charming," she said with a cool smile, and left.

"Glad to think about it! Damned bluestocking," Sickels muttered. "You'd think she'd jump at the chance." What had she meant—lack of consistency? He was famous for his consistency, he glowered. "Next case!" he said, rousing himself. "Tell me what's supposed to happen this afternoon." He listened carefully, then shrugged. "I'll do what I can," he scowled, "you know that. But I'm going to handle this matter in my own way. I want no suggestions. No interference. Just go along with me and I'll go along with you. Is that understood? I swear, you and Lew are putting me in a hell of a position. I don't relish this—especially not at this time. Not with Trumbull making the argument. No, I'll take that check," he said quickly, snapping for the waiter.

On the drive to his chambers Sickels sat back in the carriage, nursing his grievances.

Ah Luk Fow! Such an absurd trifling matter then, but fraught with such consequences for himself. Chop Suey Sickels was the least offensive sobriquet he had earned and his reversal of field in *Chang Ping* had come too late to help. And now this latest damned approach to his judicial ear, he thought resentfully: It was the wrong case at the wrong time.

Finch said haggardly, slipping into his overcoat, "That's that. Briefs?"

"Ready," Green replied, checking.

"Last minute corrections?"

"None."

"Any thoughts, Judge?"

Trumbull was seated with closed eyes, shivering with fatigue after a night of hard work. "I cannot think of anything more. If I could, I wouldn't change the line with last minute improvisation. I would, however, like the twenty-first of Howard's Reports in the courtroom."

Green left for the library. He returned with a dusty volume, and forced it onto a canvas bag packed with other books. Deep rings encircled his eyes.

The drive up Sansome Street was uneventful. Trumbull sat asprawl in the back seat, legs out, hands braced, eyes closed. He was exhilarated but tired. The cheering had scarcely died away in Hibernian Hall before he had joined the others in the Nevada Block to plan the argument ahead. The work had gone on late into the night.

The carriage jounced. Trumbull fluttered open his eyelids and leaned forward. "Mr. Green," he said, "change your face."

Green looked startled. "Beg pardon?"

"You're scowling," Trumbull said. Suddenly his heavy features contorted in mimicry—nostrils wrinkled, anger frowned, misery was displayed—it was a comical parody that got a snort of laughter from Finch. "How d'ye think the judge feels to stare at such a mournful phiz?" he demanded. "Can only feel dislike."

"Do I look like that?" Green said in consternation.

"You most certainly do. Try on a smile. And bear in mind not to indicate joy or disappointment, pleasure or misery—nothing but courtesy to your fellow practitioners. Never show your feelings. I learned this from a judge in a lower court," he added reminiscently. "Just a police justice, but the best we ever had in Galveston. In those days I was so concerned about a client, I walked around like a thundercloud. Every time I got a wrong ruling, I ground my teeth and threw murderous glances of protest and anguish at the judge. Lordy! Dunno what I thought I was doing—maybe hoping to reverse him by mental force—mesmerism at a distance. I remember I had the defense of this fellow on a charge of selling whiskey to slaves. I was putting up a hell of a clamor of objections, ranting all over the courtroom. This judge finally took me aside and gave me the dressing down of my life. I was just twenty, and I'd never heard anything like that. Called me down for upsetting his digestion. Said I was poisoning his life with my discontent. Threatened to cut off my privates if I failed to stop. Strong words for that time, and I'd fought fights for less—but I reflected he was right and I thanked him. He was a judge and talking for my good. Thereafter, I put on a watermelon smile like a happy field hand, bowed low, thanked His Honor for every ruling, groveled abjectly, and I have conducted myself like a lawyer before every pipsqueak on every bench ever since. I lost the case but I had learned courtroom behavior. You see?"

Green nodded. "Yes, Judge. You found it intolerable to lose a point but you learned control."

Trumbull squinted sharply. The younger lawyer was serious, innocent of guile. "Hm," he said. "The secret is always to be a gentleman. Never burden the Court or impose your feelings. You must affect ease. Act as though you couldn't care how it goes. Your private opinion of the corrupt son of a bitch is another thing. That's morals. Not manners." He was smiling, but as the carriage stopped before the great building, the pleasant mood vanished. "I'll tell you what preys on the political judge's mind—not the lawyer's scowl but the force of public opinion. Now Sickels knows that the woman has the general sympathy. He can hardly relish to hand down an unpopular decision between a hated capitalist and a pretty woman. That's the problem; he'll be looking for a way out—maybe to try to give over writing the decision to Goff and Abernathy. We'll have to watch that."

"Yes, Judge," Green said.

Trumbull smiled grimly. "We've got one advantage, Mr. Green—that fanatical self-righteousness and that blind obstinacy that maddens him like a stuck bull. We'll have to play a precise game." He closed his eyes. He was considering a letter brought in the night by Digges:

My dear Judge Trumbull:

I am eternally grateful for your decision to support my cause. That you chose a public forum for the occasion—placing my case in its larger aspects—was a stroke of statesmanship. I feel not alone. I am a symbol. I repose my life in your hands.

Yours gratefully,

Mrs. Jessica Hagerman née Roux.

P.S. I hope you like the package. Mustn't lose the battle for want of a nail. Again, eternal thanks. J.

The nail was a pair of gold cuff links, artfully wrought in the design of a miner's pick and shovel.

"All out," Finch said cheerfully, leaping down. Green followed. "Judge?" Finch said. "We're here."

Trumbull was staring at the monstrous building with a strained expression. "Judge?" Finch repeated. A gleam of hatred in the deep eyes faded. "Well, gentlemen," Trumbull said, "let's do a lawyer's job."

A loud voice commanded the spectators to rise. The door opened and a procession advanced: Goff, Abernathy, then, after a pause, Sickels, who limped to the center with a hard look of absolute impartiality. The United States Circuit Court, District of California, was commended to God and called to order. Two raps and all sat.

Sickels formed a tent of fingers and leaned forward, eyes closed, lips moving in prayer. He could smell ink, feel the blotter, enjoy a Cupid and Psyche inkwell, sense a calendar and desk lamp and all the artifacts of decades past. Refreshed, he looked up.

Clerk Nolan rose. "Number one on the Motion Calendar. *Hagerman against Hagerman*. Ready for argument."

There was a stir at the press table. The rival groups went forward to the counsel tables. Trumbull, Finch, and Green sat stiffly, placing memoranda and authorities in place. Brawn sprawled out in ease and indifference. He was accompanied by Colonel Harley Evanston, a tall spare lawyer of renowned scholarship.

Sickels noted that neither Hagerman nor Jessica Roux were in the room. "Will counsel step forward?"

The lawyers trooped forward and formed a group before the bench. "Mr. Finch," Sickels said severely, "I'd rather counsel not put hands on my bench." Finch hastily withdrew.

Sickels was an experienced judge, sensitive to the subtleties. There were pleasantries and a forced smile. He nibbled his pen and wondered aloud whether there was any chance to resolve the issue amicably. If so, the Court would be pleased to mediate. Mr. Brawn? Mr. Finch? He stared about hopefully, but all faces were blank. "Well, my brothers and I find it disappointing," he remarked. "Most painful. Let's see what's here."

Motion papers and briefs were placed before the judges. Sickels riffled through the papers. "Don't see too much of you in this court, Judge Trumbull," he remarked conversationally. "Real pity."

"I have generally found the courts of California sufficient for most purposes," Trumbull said humorlessly, "when their jurisdiction is not invaded or diminished. I am here when I must."

Finch turned color. Sickels closed his mouth like a knife. "Judge Trumbull," he said after a pause, "I am aware of your dislike for the rulings of this Court. I will remind you that our decisions when sustained are the law of the land. However disagreeable, they are to be accepted. I am ready to listen with an open mind and rule with my brothers on the merits of your argument."

"I should expect you would," Trumbull said stolidly. "I merely find it amazing to find a special bench of three where two are sufficient under the rules."

The courtroom strained forward, trying to determine the burden of the rumble forward. Sickels sank in the deep chair. "Judge Trumbull, do you suggest any kind of impropriety?"

he asked dangerously. "If so, and if you can support it with proof, I will consider to remove myself."

"I suggest nothing," Trumbull replied. "I am raising a question. What brings about this extraordinary bench today to pass on a simple motion to send back to the Superior Court of San Francisco a divorce case which should not be here in the first place?"

"Do you ask that I disqualify myself?" Sickels said after a pause.

"On the contrary," Trumbull retorted. "I prefer that you decide on the issue—and sign the decision."

Sickels was drumming the bench, "I find myself vexed, Mr. Trumbull. The Court does not relish this language."

Trumbull shook his head. "I am not disrespectful of the Court. The Court is commenting on my state of mind. I am free to remove any error or illusion it may entertain."

The silence was breathless. Green, for one, thought he would choke. It was Sickels who lowered his eyes and deliberately made an inscription in his book of minutes. "Proceed to your argument," he said. "We will listen with interest."

The lawyers trooped back to place in a ceremony to be repeated a thousand times to come.

Finch begged piteously for an explanation. "What are you trying to do? You have antagonized the bench beyond remedy. He's a most vengeful man. Why? Why?" he whispered in a trembling voice.

Trumbull turned to the shaken lawyer. "I know this man," he said in a low voice. "He is caught in a dilemma. He does not at this time want to give an unpopular decision. I could not let him give the decision to those flunkies who would do his dirty work. He now faces a challenge—as I thought I explained."

"Proceed!" Sickels ordered.

Trumbull stood and thoughtfully touched a handkerchief to his mouth. The silence deepened. Goff was staring blankly, nursing a straw. Abernathy's nostrils were wrinkled by a bad smell. Sickels was gazing at a point in space. Trumbull began first with Hagerman's action to compel the production of the marriage paper—

A rap cut him off.

"Stick to the point," Sickels said sharply. "I confess to irritation when lawyers don't stick to the point."

"I am trying to make my point," Trumbull replied.

"Please do!"

"If given time!"

"Beware, Judge Trumbull," Sickels growled. "Beware. The Court is losing patience."

"I will wait for the court to regain patience," Trumbull replied. The courtroom was buzzing.

"Come to the meat," Sickels said finally. "Do not confuse the two actions."

"One is prelude and background to the other."

"Proceed," Sickels said testily. "Good God," he muttered aside to Goff, "the man's impossible."

Trumbull leaned against the rail, scratching a cheek thoughtfully. "May the Court please," he said finally, staring at the angered judge, "the best point is not the technical question of this motion but the personality of Senator Hagerman. It is Senator Hagerman who is responsible for the two actions which disgrace these courts—his wife's action for divorce in the Superior Court of San Francisco and his action to stop her by recourse to this Circuit Court. Let us see how this came about—"

"Do not be prolix," Sickels interrupted.

Trumbull folded his arms. "Unless I am allowed to talk, the Court will never know what is in my mind."

Sickels threw down his pen, and sank back. "Go on," he said. "but I must warn you not to go too far."

Trumbull let a moment pass. "It is Senator Hagerman's personality that links these two matters. The best thing that can be said for Senator Hagerman is that he's a man of remarkable will and energy seeking to embroil this honorable Court in his disgraceful affairs because he fears the swift and deadly justice of another court to which his wife has entrusted her life and honor.

"It is of course not sure that Senator Hagerman controls these manipulations—or whether is not himself being manipulated and controlled by the superior will of others." Trumbull glanced at Galindez. "But no matter, no matter," he said. Galindez began to trim his nails with a penknife.

"What is the issue here?" Trumbull went on. "Isn't it essentially the question of underlying equity and fairness? When Mrs. Hagerman first discovered her husband was denying the marriage agreement, she proceeded in a straightforward and honorable way to demand her rights as his wife. The secrecy clause had expired, and she was free to take ad-

182

vice. She found it impossible to see or talk to Mr. Hagerman at his bank. Captain Philip Webster guarded the approaches at Imperial House. She sought to consult lawyers, and these efforts were immediately made known to Mr. Hagerman. How do we know? Well, first she called on General Brawn . . ."

Brawn smiled cherubically, but as his associate, Colonel Evanston, flashed a startled look, he blushed. Trumbull went on.

". . . and then upon her former lawyers, Messers Galindez and MacGowan, begging intercession. Mr. MacGowan gave her inglorious advice to forget her cause. Mr. Galindez stated that her marriage paper—a paper he'd never seen—was a forgery. Coarse expressions by Mr. Hagerman were conveyed to her. She was put to a campaign of terror and intimidation and was told that her husband had every judge in this state in his pocket—that she could never get a legal decision in her favor. She was kept penniless and helpless and cut off from legal advice. She was put in doubt—not indeed as to her moral position—but as to her ability to assert her legal position against the weight of wealth and ruthless influence. It was not until she took independent legal advice that she learned she was a victim of lies and propaganda and that indeed her marriage document complied with the Civil Code of California."

Trumbull wiped his mouth with a handkerchief and called for the Civil Code and read with precision and clarity. The impact of the dry formal language was remarkable. He threw down the book and resumed.

"Now, reassured, she did all a woman could do to persuade the man to behave with honor. Of course that was a mistake since the man has no honor, but how was she to know that? She told him in plain fashion that if he would not respect his written word, she would sue for divorce in the only court where such an action would belong—the Superior Court of San Francisco. The exclusive jurisdiction of that court is undoubted. That too is so provided by the Civil Code of California and a line of decisions as old as this state.

"I need not, I am sure, further read the Civil Code," Trumbull went on ironically, "for the relevant parts are copied from the first Civil Code of California, which was introduced to the Legislature a lifetime ago by the Presiding Justice of this Circuit himself. I am sure he remembers."

There was a murmur of amusement. Sickels flushed and

made a notation. Trumbull went on. "To go back to the eve of the battle, Senator Hagerman was at all times aware that these claims would be presented in open court. I understand his regrets and unhappiness. The ardor had passed. The marriage was now tempestuous. His daughter and son were incensed. His son-in-law"—a bleak glance flicked at Galindez—"was concerned for the inheritance. Quarrels and recriminations took place, and somehow, somewhere a canker began to gnaw."

Trumbull drove on, "I can understand the temptation to repudiate a contract signed in the heat of quick courtship. I can understand the temptation to buy peace with turbulent children clamoring against a second wife taken in old age—it is a story as old as David and Abishag—but I cannot understand the dishonorable way in which the honest claim to marriage and divorce was met.

"How was it met? Was it met head-on? Was she told that he would accept a summons and appear in court? Did he prepare to meet her complaint with denial and proof in a court where it belongs?

"He did none of these things.

"What instead did he do? Before she could prepare her complaint for divorce, he fled, evading the jurisdiction of the State of California. He showed up at the chambers of Wall Street counsel. The Honorable Mr. Pike was consulted . . ."

Galindez looked up.

". . . and then he went to take advice from someone else—in Washington." A dead stare locked with that of the Presiding Justice. After an ineffable moment, Trumbull resumed. "Having made preparations, the Senator returned to California in the dead of night. All was ready, all prepared at counsel's chambers, where a petition for injunction was waiting. Swift and willing lawyers applied to a judge of this Court"—a glance went toward Goff, who seemed stupefied at these ringing thrusts—"who signed the writ of subpoena himself."

Trumbull studied and threw aside a copy of that writ with disdain. "The United States Marshal, Mr. Emanuel Jessup, was commanded to assemble a band of armed men to effect service of the Court's process. All these astonishing acts were done between dark and dawn in the most menacing and savage manner. Why? Was it merely preemptive? Merely to block the wife's action for divorce in another court? Or was it not rather a warning of violence to come?"

The chamber was utterly silent.

"What is the basis of that petition? It is really simple," Trumbull said, picking up the petition. "What does Mr. Hagerman tell the Court? He comes to say that he is a rich man. A very rich man," he added with contempt. "He says he is a widower who had three children, the issue of a previous marriage, one of whom—his daughter Dora—has died, leaving grandchildren and their father, Mr. Galindez, who sits here now as a spectator." All eyes turned to Galindez. "He says that he conducts a large business and had important social connections. He says that Miss Jessica Roux—as he calls her, and as she now understandably prefers to be called —is an unmarried woman who lives in the City of San Francisco and that she publicly claims to be his wife. He says the claims are false and untrue and are made to get credit from merchants and money from himself or—in case of his death —from his heirs. He claims that he never heard of the marriage declaration, that it is surely forged and false, null and void, and prays it be so declared. He says all sorts of things but omits to say that his wife—far from waiting for death to attack his heirs—was about to sue him for divorce in the state courts of California.

"Why did he omit that allegation? Why, clearly because he knew that otherwise to ask this Court to prevent her appeal to another Court would appear too raw to swallow. For then it would be seen for what it is—an attempt to shop for a favorable forum—"

Sickels looked up angrily, flushed. "The Court will not tolerate insinuations against its process, Judge Trumbull. This is unforgivable."

Trumbull's jaw set. "I insinuate nothing against the Court. I am making charges against the party. He comes here for equity? Let equity be done. Equity looks through sham to substance. The substance is a background of conspiracy to use this Court's equitable powers to defeat the straightforward, honest legal claims of the wife in the only court which truly has the right and power to determine her status. I do not say this Court will succumb to this conspiratorial intent. I merely say that the attempt should be firmly rejected in the interests of justice. Of course," Trumbull added, "the Court is impartial and will pass on these issues, I am sure, with its customary detachment and objectivity."

185

Sickels sank back ominously. He glanced at Goff, then at Abernathy, whose frowsy brows were raised in astonishment. "Beware, Judge Trumbull," Sickels said. "I recognize your strong compulsions, but do not press the Court too far. I must say all this sits poorly."

An involuntary groan escaped poor Finch, who turned aside. His eyes piteously disavowed any connection with the strident argument.

"I must follow truth," Trumbull said simply, "wherever it takes me. Let me come back, then, to Mr. Hagerman's petition for injunction. What does he ask? He asks that this Court compel his wife to deliver up physically to this place the very evidence she needs in the other court to establish her claims to marriage and a decent regard in the world's eyes. He asks that this evidence be mutilated, destroyed, obliterated from sight and memory. He asks this Court to decide the very issue which belongs in another court—to destroy the justice of another court. Could anything be more openly disgraceful?

"It is outrageous. It is monstrous." Trumbull paused wrathfully. He was now striding the room, oblivious to the careful notes on the counsel table, sunk in the thread of argument. He placed a hand on the rail, facing the reporters.

Fanny glanced up from her notes. Whether or not she was impressed by the flow of argument he could not tell. He seemed not to see her nor anyone or anything but the construct of logic in his mind.

"It means—not only that this man is seeking to use this Court for personal ends—but that he feels no compunction, no shame, no fear that he may fail. It staggers me to find this in California. One would expect a man who stands besmirched as a liar, welsher, fraud, fornicator, and seducer to welcome an open contest and full disclosure of evidence before an impartial court if only to vindicate himself before the world. Instead he flops like a fish on a line, struggling frantically not to be dragged before the forum where the stink and corruption will be exposed, begging this Court to shield him from proof that will establish him as unprincipled and without honor. That is what Senator Hagerman's action against his wife means—an action to intimidate a helpless woman whose male relatives have proved a feckless lot indeed. It is an attempt to win by threats what cannot be gained by submission of the justice of the case.

"But did he succeed?" The clear penetrating voice rang like a trumpet. "Another woman might have quailed before the writ of this Court. But to her honor, this woman was not intimidated by armed men nor the menace of the federal injunction. She was instead fired with determination to vindicate her name. In a plain and straightforward way, she instructed her lawyers to bring her action where it belongs—in the Superior Court of San Francisco—an action for divorce on grounds of desertion and of more adulteries than one might imagine possible for a man of Mr. Hagerman's age and infirmities." An uncertain titter was instantly quelled by hard looks from court officers and deputy marshals. "Miss Roux might have alleged the marriage in a general way, but to her credit she frankly set forth the circumstances of the marriage —the marriage document's text and so forth—thus inviting her husband to meet her on even ground and openly contest that issue.

"But what happened? Mr. Hagerman says that the document is a forgery. Mrs. Hagerman says it is genuine. But who, *who* is seeking to hide it from the public gaze—the husband or the wife?" The strong trumpet voice now commanded entire attention. There was some nodding of assent. The dark glittering eyes of Galindez were staring with intensity. Trumbull went on. "Instead of answering his wife's complaint for divorce in the proper court where brought, he has caused her case to be removed to this Court on the spurious ground that he is a citizen of Nevada. Imagine what this means! He has removed the case from the only court where it belongs and which alone can give judgment, to a court where it does not belong and where it cannot by any stretch of imagination be tried. To put it mildly, this was most irregular and in a moment I will submit the authorities.

"Now this finally brings us to the motion before us," Trumbull went on. "What is that motion? It is Mrs. Hagerman's motion to remand her action for divorce back to the court from which it was wrongfully taken. I can see no denial of that motion. The case must be sent back. For one thing is certain: It is impossible for this court to try this divorce case in any event."

Trumbull picked up a book, pursing his mouth with hard humor. "May the Court please?" he said with lurking fun. "I refer in my brief to *Mannheim versus Hills,* Volume 125 of the official United States Reports, where the Supreme Court

187

in Washington passed on similar issues. For all the reasons set out in that opinion it is clear that this Circuit Court has no jurisdiction whatsoever over this or indeed any other divorce action. The motion to remand must therefore be granted. I wonder," he said, halting provocatively, "whether I need read that decision, considering the strong retentive mind of this Court. Especially since that opinion was in fact written by Your Honor, the Presiding Justice of this Court." He ran his tongue over his lips. "Well, perhaps I can read from the opinion."

There were covert smiles of amusement.

Trumbull turned to a marked page and read slowly and emphatically. He then shut the book and with folded arms faced the mural of the Figure of Justice. "Senator Hagerman seeks dark clouds of obscurity. His wife seeks the light of day and submits that the motion to remand her action for divorce back to the Superior Court of San Francisco be granted with costs." He sat.

Sickels sat back, scowling unpleasantly. "Judge Trumbull, I have never heard a more indecent farrago in all my years on this bench. I will later decide how to deal with it. General Brawn? Colonel Evanston? A moment with you both first." He rose and strode off, white with rage, black robe billowing. Goff and Abernathy followed in bewilderment.

An hour later Brawn and Evanston emerged from chambers. Brawn sat smoldering while the courtroom came to order.

Brawn stood. "May the Court please. We stipulate that the action for divorce in the Superior Court of San Francisco, entitled *Hagerman against Hagerman*, No. 9984, be remanded back to that Court. Under the circumstances, we will not reply to the really disgraceful tirade to which we have been subjected."

Sickels tapped. "Is that agreeable to counsel?"

"Yes!" "Certainly not!"

Finch and Trumbull spoke at once, confusing the stenographer. They stopped, began again, then stopped. "It's agreeable, it's agreeable," Finch sputtered excitedly.

"Well, which is it?" Sickels demanded.

Trumbull asked to approach the bench. "Judge Sickels, I have challenged the Court to make its ruling. I am not satisfied with a stipulation. It decides nothing and leaves us hanging. Is there any reason not to have the Court decide on the motion from which an appeal can be taken and thus establish the law of the case?"

"Challenge?" Sickels said unpleasantly. "I find that language strange."

Trumbull gripped the bench. "You dare not write a decision against this woman," he retorted, "and you will not write one for her. I find that singular. If that's a challenge, make the most of it." Finch bleated with pain. Sickels mastered his anger with effort. "Judge Trumbull, you're unwise to press me. I never prophesy, but I warn you not to rely on *Mannheim versus Hills*. You raised a laugh at my expense just now, but I have distinguished harder cases in my lifetime. Now, sir," he said harshly, leaning forward with a disagreeable scowl, "If you can stipulate with Mr. Brawn, the matter need not proceed here in what you're pleased to call the corrupt court over which I preside. Well, isn't that what you wish?"

Trumbull said, "Judge Sickels, if you have some good reason not revealed not to sign the decision, I am sure Judge Goff or Judge Abernathy will be glad to accommodate."

The silence was deathly.

"Go back to your place," Sickels choked, "and put your answer on the record." He sank back, shaking with rage.

Finch dragged Trumbull aside. "What in hell game is this?" he hissed. "Take the damn stipulation or I'll take it myself before the son of a bitch changes his mind. I'm the lawyer of record. Not you."

"Confound it, I want to nail him down," Trumbull growled. "Can't you see that this is not the end? It's only the opening round."

"No, I don't see," Finch replied.

"Oh, go ahead," Trumbull flared. "She's your client. Do as you please."

Finch rose. "So stipulated," he croaked.

A gavel banged. "Draw your stipulations. Submit order."

Sickels stared with intensity. "Judge Trumbull, I'll assume that certain things were said only in the heat of argument. I'll expect appropriate expressions of regret without delay. Fortunately they were not said on the record." He nodded and left, followed by Goff and Abernathy, whose manner was somehow furtive and ashamed.

189

Ya-hee! A cheer went up. A cluster of well-wishers gathered. Fanny came forward with a quizzical smile.

"My word," she said. "This will not be believed at the Inns of Court. You just walked into and out of the jaws of hell."

Trumbull laughed. "The descent into Avernus is easy, but the return? Ah! There is the toil, there the difficulty." He paused somberly, peering into the future, then shook himself. "We didn't settle a thing. Now I wonder, ma'am," he added good-humoredly, "whether you'd permit me to offer you a glass of sherry one day?"

"Sherry? Oh, my eye! You'll have to do better than that," Fanny said lightly, taken by surprise but pleased by the invitation. "But I am delighted to accept. I'd really like to know what made you change your mind about taking on this fight."

Chapter Ten

The dark mole thrusting into blue waters of the bay was empty. As the launch approached, Trumbull leaped to the wharf. A steam whistle howled and slowly, then with gathering speed, the Overland Express, thrusting bursts of black smoke into a darkening sky, receded to the East.

"Oh, damnation!" he exclaimed in dismay. Stuck in Oakland and the Express gone. It all came from missing the ferry and frantic efforts to catch the last train to Stoddard. A short, energetic man came over with a knowing smile. "Judge Trumbull, remember me? George Gorham."

"Why, George Gorham!" Trumbull exclaimed. "What in hell are you doing with that tin?"

The man grinned and fingered a badge. "I'm in the law business, Judge. Sheriff of Alameda County. Between fees and findings, I do right good. Can I help out?"

"Can't say," Trumbull observed, shading his eyes. "Confound it, I don't want to stay the night in Oakland."

Gorham squinted. "Judge, you could lay over with us, if you like. Mrs. Gorham would be right pleased. Potluck, of course."

"No, no. Wouldn't dream of imposing." The launch was steaming back across the darkening bay. There went all chance to return to San Francisco for the night. Blast! "Ain't there anything running east? I'd rather be in motion than in Oakland."

Gorham scratched his head. The station master would be along soon and maybe find something running. "Been reading about the fireworks, Judge. Good to see you back in action."

"Why, thank'ee, George," Trumbull said, pleased. "Good to get back. It calls for a mess of details, but the trial should be kind of pleasurable. Damnation, I shouldn't miss ferries at my age. If a lawyer can't catch a ferry, what can he catch? Where's that station master?"

"Oh, he'll be along." Gorham paused. "You could stay over at the American. Or the Union. The Sutter burned down, you know. Nothing left there but a fire-insurance claim."

"The Sutter?" Trumbull asked sharply.

"Yes. Why?"

Trumbull hesitated. "Oh, nothing," he said stiffly. "Let's stroll, hey? I'm that creaky with all this office work."

"Sure thing," Gorham said agreeably. "Hey, these are heavy!" he gasped, hefting a portmanteau and canvas bag. "What's inside?"

"Oh, books. Couldn't endure travel except for the chance to read. Just leave them there." Trumbull took the other man's arm and walked the platform, smiling and pleased with himself. It had been a busy several weeks, longer than he had planned: conferences around the clock with Finch and Green, tactics laid out, points of research indicated. He had not felt so young in years.

A group of Mexican cholos were coming along the right of way wrapped in wool serapes against the chill. "Sheriff," Trumbull said, "know anything about the Hotel Hindenberg?"

"Hotel? It's no hotel. She's a boardinghouse. What would you like to know? Have they got fleas?"

"No, no! We have information that Senator Hagerman called there on Miss Roux that summer when she was living here in Oakland. What kind of joint is that?"

"No joint at all. Old Hindenberg's a retired Latin teacher. Mrs. Hindenberg's a dear sweet thing. Lutherans, but respectable."

A semaphore bobbed. The station master, an abrupt and

191

efficient official, arrived and listened to the problem. A freight train was going south, he suggested. It was not a Pullman sleeper, he warned, but it had benches and would serve. "Come on," he ordered. They picked their way in darkness to a siding where a freight and mail train was being loaded in the flickering lights of the yard.

Trumbull put a foot on the step. "Sheriff, you're sure it was the Sutter that burned down? Not the Hindenberg?"

"Definitely the Sutter," Gorham replied.

"Well, I may have something wrong," Trumbull said slowly. A lantern swung, green in the black. The great driving wheels turned and the train rolled into the night. Trumbull found a bench in a converted baggage car. A few farmhands were trying to sleep in the midst of cinders and smoke pouring through roof ventilators. A pair of kerosene lamps in brackets barely dissipated the gloom. And then he struck his forehead. Damnation! In the excitement and turmoil he had put off and then forgotten to pick up Alexandra's spectacles at Lundy's. He said, "Skipper?"

The conductor approached, a white-haired man in shabby blue. A sleeve was empty. "Yes, Judge?"

"Can I drop off a telegram at Hog?"

"Reckon so. I'll get a form," the conductor said. He left and came back with a green telegraph blank. Western Union, he advised, was closed, but the railway lines were working. "Judge," he said hesitantly, "mighty honored to have you with us."

"Honored to be on board," Trumbull said pleasantly. Yankee accent, he noted. "What time do we hit Stoddard?"

"Oh, bar delays, accidents, and the like—maybe four A.M."

Trumbull sat bolt upright. "Tomorrow morning? I was told about midnight. Don't you keep a schedule?"

"Now that's a laugh," the conductor said.

"Lordy," Trumbull said with dismay, seeing all the horrors of travel upon him. Evil water, stinking windy privy, straightbacked benches. Frowning against the dim light, he wrote out a message to Finch & Green in San Francisco to forward the package waiting for him at Lundy's. His thoughts drifted and then the train jolted to a halt and stood throbbing at Hog Junction.

"I'll take that now," the conductor said.

"Thank 'ee," Trumbull said, rousing himself. Through

dirty opaque windows silent hulks were outlined again[...] night sky. Green and red lamps made small arcs in the dar[k]ness. The conductor left with the message. When he returned, Trumbull looked up. "Will that go off? It's important."

"Oh, sure," the conductor said with a broad grin, and advised that the wire tickler had sent an Irish valentine home and someone with age would get the message delivered first thing. By which he meant that the telegraph operator had sent a railway telegram to the home office to someone with seniority who would attend to the errand. "Why, I'm most grateful," Trumbull said with surprise. "I didn't know I rated all that attention from the company. I'd like you to thank that feller for me."

"Oh, he's the dispatcher's delight," the conductor chuckled, suddenly quite friendly. "No matter what the head office thinks, Judge, you've got lots of friends along this right-of-way. Oh! He had this for you. That is, if you can find the appetite?"

"For me?" A paper bag, translucent with butter stains, held thick slabs of bread and juicy slices of pot roasted beef, pickles, and a jar of sauerkraut. "Say, he's not giving me his supper?"

The conductor shook his head, grinning. "Nope. He had his wife make it up for you. He knew you were coming along on this crate. He's one of your devoted followers, Judge. Collects your lectures, so it was entirely his pleasure. Don't you know the strings've been singing since you left Oakland?"

Of course! Up and down the line the telegraph operators were chattering, exchanging news, passing along the word. It was a network of intelligence that never failed to astonish him. "Skipper, who's following me?" Trumbull asked slowly.

"Oh, now! Just some dicks passing the word," the conductor said. "Just want to know your moves. Where you go. When. Nothing special."

"I do feel flattered. Who's getting this intelligence?"

"Can't be sure," the conductor replied. "Law department, I reckon. Just don't let it spoil your appetite. I could get up some hot java?"

"Sounds good."

With a friendly blink, the conductor stood, then had a moment of doubt. "Oh, say, Judge. You wouldn't mention about getting those sandwiches? Because it wouldn't help the feller."

"Wouldn't dream of it. Thank him, hey?"

hing. Now let me get this rattler rolling," the con-
d. He went forward and made signals, and came
coffee. "Judge," he said reproachfully, "you
actly fair to the railway, y'know."

Trumbull ate methodically, strong cheek muscles bulging.
"That so?"

"Well, I read your speech at the Hibernian."

"Oh, that." Trumbull looked up quizzically. "I thought you
had that courtroom argument in mind."

"They're connected," the conductor said thoughtfully. "But
the Hibernian one was violent."

"Do tell? I thought I kept it down."

"Down? Well, maybe. Actually, Judge, why blame just the
one side? The railway has never wanted nothing but peace."

"Everybody wants peace," Trumbull said somberly. "Peace
ain't the absence of war. It's the presence of justice."

The conductor was silent, groping with this thought. He
was not sure where the strife between the people and the railway had begun, but surely, he urged, the railway was the
main victim. "I know these people," he said earnestly. "These
farmers has been getting away with murder. Ever since we
came through the Pima, they've been making fortunes—vast
fortunes, sir, at our expense from all the produce in this area
—wheat, hops, wool, minerals, what-not. Out there"—a gesture encompassed the night—"it'd still be desolation if not
for us." He paused cracking his knuckles and staring doubtfully at his passenger. "Can I be frank, Judge?"

"Why, sure."

"I've been traveling up and down this line more years, and
I know 'em. It's the deep Pima that's giving the trouble. That
element comes with a tradition of violence—people who supported the Rebellion and they're still unreconstructed. Once
people think they can go against the government with guns,
they're hopeless. That's why the radicals get support out
there—it's the appeal to violence. All of us in the railway see
it. We can't hardly walk these towns without black looks and
threats against our families. It may not be so clear in the big
cities, but we feel it out here in the wilderness. The police are
political and the children get marked by the other children.
You talk about the railway! Well, sir! I admit we've did some
wrongs, but on the other side? Nobody's safe . . ."

"Oh, come!"

"Oh, come, what? You made a big speech for the poor Mc-

Cabes, but did you say anything about the men they killed? These men got their heads shot off without a blessed chance. Joe Bassett! Henty Willicutt! Two of our best men. They started with this road when all we owned was the right-of-way, five hundred Chink laborers, and two thousand tons of iron rails from around the Horn. They deserved better'n they got. You say it was a reprisal for the Pima? They had nothing to do with that. The marshals kill some ranchers. The McCabes kill some railway men. The railway hikes the tariffs. More men get killed and the dynamiting begins. Next you're chewing on Mr. Hagerman's arse from a public place and attacking him in the courts. The muttering starts and the lines get drawn. And it can't be right."

"Oh? Why not?"

The conductor stared cautiously about the darkened, rocking car. The few passengers, curled up in sheepskin coats, snored and mumbled in fitful sleep. "Well, I know Lew Hagerman, Judge," he said defensively. "I worked the old narrow gauge we ran to Gold Hill when he had the Agency in Virginia City. It made a woman a promise, he'd keep it." The conductor fell silent, going back to a painful thought. "I'm against lawlessness."

Trumbull said seriously, "It's not the gun, sir. It's the intent. Injustice can blow up the world. Almost did not long ago. You saw action, I'd expect?" he asked, glancing at the empty sleeve.

The conductor nodded. "The Massachusetts Seventh. Mustered with General Butler."

"Vermont originally?"

"How'd you know?"

"I've got an ear for sounds." Trumbull steadied himself as the train took a curve. "Six hundred thousand men died," he said somberly. "D'ye regret marching with Butler?"

The conductor thought. "No, honestly, I can't say I do. It was a necessary thing."

"Because of your sense of injustice?" Trumbull suggested drily. "Come now, sir. What was the Pima? Such a little violence compared with the constant, unremitting brutality and injustice of this insane world."

"Sometimes there's no choice. Those people had other recourse."

"Recourse? To what?"

"Why, the courts! Judge, I don't have to tell you! Without

195

the courts where are we? People would claw themselves to shreds. I actually saw that, Judge, and so did you. When you go against the courts, who's safe?"

"The courts? Ah, yes! I'd forgotten, hadn't I? Trouble is, Mister——?"

"McDade. Tom McDade."

"Yes, McDade. Trouble is, Mr. McDade, that it calls for faith. Tell me: You truly have faith in the courts of America?"

"Why, sure."

"Well, well," Trumbull said. "I've spent a lifetime in those courts. I've read widely, thought much, and wasted my years in that arena. I know every judge in this state. I know his weakness. I know his follies. I know the trough where he shoulders and grunts. I know who feeds him. If I don't know, I can guess. What if there are no courts, Mr. McDade? What if they are only counterfeits of courts?"

The conductor stared at a horrid possibility. "Judge, I'm puzzled by the one thing," he said finally. "Was that the time or place?"

"Time? Place? For what?"

"For that announcement about the divorce case?" the conductor said. "People who don't know might think you took the case for a personal vendetta. You don't mind if I'm frank?"

"No," Trumbull said.

"Because it gives the other side a chance to rake you. That's what made me wonder. You'll excuse it?"

"Oh, yes," Trumbull said. "Point's well taken. I get impulsive, Mr. McDade. I'm judicial, but not, I fear, always judicious. I drink my own words and that can be fatal as hemlock. But I hope it is not a vendetta. Excuse me now."

"Nice talking, Judge," Conductor McDade said. He stretched and yawned and went back to the potbellied stove radiating heat in the cheerless car and shoveled coal.

Trumbull sat back. After a moment he reached for a telegram now ten days old.

CALENDAR CLEAR STOP READY FOR FIGHT OR FROLIC STOP
WHAT APPEAL QUESTION MARK

ZACHARIAS YATES

He picked up a pen and became absorbed in writing.

196

My dear Zack:

Forgive this wretched handwriting. I am writing by kerosene lamp in a vile freight car and my eyes are tired beyond words. It is the penalty for missing the Overland. I feel like a tired horse too old for stud and not worth the boneyard. Ah, the years!

I miss your empty office. How many times, confused and aimless, have I not unconsciously opened the door, half hoping, half expecting to interrupt you in something inflammatory, hopeful for wise counsels. God knows I need them. This firm I'm helping isn't much—Finch is basically a minor court practitioner, shoddy, tricky! and Green is dominated by his senior. How I got into this situation I do not quite know.

Let me explain my telegram and why I asked whether you could entertain taking an appeal on our behalf. It is of course the Hagerman matter and I cannot imagine that any of the other Supreme Court practitioners in Washington would take that matter with your devotion to our interests. It would of course take courage to tackle—(not Hagerman, pooh! we've dealt with the creature before)—but Sickels himself in his own den.

I cannot explain all that passed in that courtroom, but perhaps one day you will know the real forces at play. It was evident that Sickels meant to repeat his usual villainies of your Reserve Fund Cases by assigning the decision to Goff, keeping his own skirts clear.

This time I was determined to force the man himself to write the decision—one way or the other—from which to take our appeal. We never learn. I have known Sickels over thirty years, yet I was naïve enough to hope that he was still a lawyer, still guided by personal honor, still mindful of the few pitiful rules which still are thought to govern the conduct of judges—that he'd affirm his own prior opinion in *Mannheim v. Hills* which stated the sole jurisdiction of the state courts over marriage and divorce. If so, we'd be home and dry with the decorous removal of the threat of federal intervention. But, if not, I meant to ask you to represent us on that appeal.

Credit the devil with guile. He wriggled out by coercing Finch to make that foolish stipulation which settles nothing—which puts off the issue to a future day. For the moment the divorce case is back in the Superior Court of California where it belongs.

I cannot complain too much. The case will be tried before Peter McArdle without a jury. I know you will question waiving a jury, but it was a compromise. McArdle is thought to be honest. I am told that the other side finds him acceptable because he is a Roman Catholic and hence supposedly against divorce. But this very Romanism may be helpful. We shall see.

I do not want you to think I took this case on blind faith. I overstayed my visit precisely to satisfy myself and questioned the lady more minutely than one might think decent. I pressed her hard and, I tell you, Zack, she'll do beautifully. She is quick-witted. She has a remarkable memory for details that might be tedious in a wife but helpful for litigation. Some details are not edifying, but she has been frank in a way that carries conviction. And although the newspapers are seeking to convert a conjugal situation into a bordello mood, what of it? She makes a profound impression of sweetness and purity which is hard to convey.

Credo quis absurditatus. She is too clever to have invented this farfetched story—which surely derives from the greater implausibilies of life—unless it rests on truth. The difficulties indeed dissolve when examined—for example that Hagerman had discussed the possibility of a secret marriage ceremony with the Archbishop. I called on the Archbishop. . . .

Trumbull coughed and looked up at the kerosene lamp jouncing at his head. The cold night air, mixed with soot and cinders, smelled of the estuary ahead. He was thinking of his interview with Archbishop Juan Tosefa. The old churchman had been all expostulations of pleasure when his good friend Judge Trumbull appeared.

They had lunched in a warm sheltered garden at a table of oak under a pepper tree. There was stone flagging underfoot and roses on two sides. A meal of cold lamb and hot saffroned rice, washed down with good wine, was delicious. The talk covered many topics of worldly and philosophical interest with some observations on Herbert Spencer's recent concepts of social evolution—a doctrine the old churchman found more entertaining than alarming. Archbishop Tosefa looked like a Raphaelite cherub, but the disarming lisp and delightful chuckle were belied by a shrewd twinkle in the flat blue eyes.

He wondered if his old friend was there with a purpose. Trumbull nodded. Between them was something called the Pious Fund, a charitable foundation established by the Jesuits and later—when the Jesuits were expelled from Mexico by the Spanish Crown—transferred to the Franciscans. Much had happened to the Fund after its spoliation by Santa Ana and its disappearance into the maelstrom of the Mexican Treasury. On Trumbull's advice, all Church claims to compensation from Mexico guaranteed by the Treaty of Guadalupe Hidalgo had been preserved—advice for which the Church was grateful. Trumbull made deprecating sounds. The scholarship was its own reward, he observed, but perhaps one good turn deserved another.

The Archbishop said demurely, "I was rather expecting you, Judge Trumbull."

There was a pause while a boy brought a tray of pastry. "I read the newspapers, you see. I get up early not only for devotions but to study this busy scene. I love the land, the city, the people. What interests the world interests me—the business, the turbulence, the follies, the excesses of this beautiful city. What drives them? What do they seek? I am concerned to understand, and where Saint Augustine leaves off, the newspapers instruct. The world comes to me. It is what we call *un gran galeoto*—a great go-between, a gossip factory—that brings the news. *Ai, delicioso!*" he exclaimed, licking a morsel of custard. "You are not eating," he said reproachfully.

"Watching my weight," Trumbull murmured, patting himself doubtfully. He took a spoonful of custard laced with vanilla.

"There is the business of the Church," the Archbishop went on. "Administration and finance teach me so much about the people who follow those pursuits. I am talking not of money itself but of feelings for money. Nothing is more revealing. I wish the love of God were as powerful as the love of lucre. Your unhappy client interests me. And you—I

199

have an impression this struggle has nothing to do with money?"

"Why so?"

"It is merely an impression, Judge Trumbull. Or is that indeed your purpose in the matter?"

Trumbull was silent. "No," he said reluctantly. "It's not the money, although the big fee marks a lawyer's distinction."

"Ambition then?"

"Not that either." Trumbull cursed the discerning glance that mocked his own insights. "It's just . . ." He went silent.

"A sense of perfection? An ideal?"

"I really don't know," Trumbull said, putting aside the plate.

"Is it justice?"

"Perhaps. No, not even that," Trumbull exclaimed restlessly. "I cannot abide the arbitrary tyranny of these judges. Great power calls for great restraint. For compassion and . . . and a sense of limitations. I had all those powers. I sat on the bench. I have looked from its heights at litigants and my hands have trembled when I signed orders or made judgments, sometimes in matters of life and death. The power was too much, and when I see it treated like a bauble, crudely, for personal satisfaction, I cannot endure it. I must act. D'ye understand that?"

"The sense of injustice?" the Archbishop murmured. "Oh, it is rare. Rare, and when we encounter it, the world trembles. No, I do not understand it—but I believe you do. And I am afraid for you. There is no limit, no end to where it will bring you, and your enemies are many and strong.

"But I see why there is only one Judge Trumbull," he went on jestingly. "For the same reason there is only one Leviathan. If there were two such primordial monsters, the world, according to legend, could not contain them and would end." He smiled and changed the subject. "Can you tell me something of your investigations?" he asked curiously.

Trumbull found the wine good. It was not easy to determine what had happened, he observed slowly. The courtship —if such it was—had proceeded on two levels. It was at first *sub rosa,* a secret affair which fed on excitement and intrigue. There was then the story given to the world—the engaged couple whose honorable intentions looked to matrimony. And there was the sharp issue of fact—the marriage contract executed when the Church had refused consent to secrecy: Was it genuine or forged?

One could see how narrow that made the question. Every word and act of the parties was double-edged, proving or disproving the marriage, depending on the slant of the Court. He was himself in doubt how to separate fact from fantasy, rumor from legal obligation. Hagerman too was a puzzle. Often he treated the woman with respect and deference. At other times he had acted with unbelievable coarseness. Was she wife or mistress? Nothing in their outward behavior was conclusive.

"And yet you will proceed?" the Archbishop said ironically. "Another coffee?"

"Thank'ee. You said you were expecting me? Why?"

"First, by instinct. Then your name has been raised by someone."

"Oh? Who?"

"Our dear friend and adviser, Judge Sinzheimer," the Archbishop said pleasantly. "A week ago—or was it ten days?—he requested to confirm if Mr. Hagerman had indeed discussed with me the possibility of a secret marriage with Miss Roux." Trumbull looked up sharply. "I told him I could not discuss the matter. It was a simple matter of gentlemanly discretion."

Something significant was being imparted.

"Before I was a priest, I was a gentleman," the Archbishop said with amusement. "I conceivably might—I barely might violate the sanctity of the Confessional," he added teasingly, "in some remote case—under torture, or illness, or other extremity. But I could never violate the canons of gentlemanly conduct. You understand?"

"Of course," Trumbull said, smiling. "Then why tell me this?"

The cherub eyes sought the ceiling. "Well, because there is always the court's power of subpoena. Someone might summon me to testify. I would be on oath to tell the truth. *Verdad?*"

"Quite so."

"It would be highly inconvenient to become a witness. And the alternative would be arduous. I love Rome, but a trip at this time would leave certain matters in a mess. It'd be a pity to depart San Francisco to escape."

"Why try to escape? Who would have an interest in concealing your testimony?"

There was a most unpriestly mutter of impatience. "If I tell you I am loath to give testimony in a public scandal, I'd expect you to exhaust every other possible remedy. I have practically imparted what you need to know. If Mr. Hagerman is called to the witness stand, you will know what questions to put. But I have not actually told you! *Dios mio!* Must I stick a finger in your eye?"

Trumbull apologized. "Plain enough," he agreed. So Hagerman had indeed consulted the Archbishop about a secret marriage! The discovery brought a grimace of satisfaction. The Archbishop searched his face. "You expected this, no?"

Trumbull made no direct answer. He was more concerned with the third party in Hagerman's office when the marriage contract was to be signed. He put aside his cup. "May I talk in confidence, Archbishop?"

"As one gentleman to another?"

Trumbull smiled faintly. He described the man called Pedro Ramirez. "I want to find that man," he said.

"Ah? Why?"

"To affirm or deny those circumstances," Trumbull said simply. "He is a possible independent witness to that vital episode. Possibly the only one we can produce."

"Why do you come to me?"

"Because I think you might know how to find him."

"Ah, who? Find who? Ramirez? It is a name as common as dirt. Why not get detectives—?"

Trumbull cut this short. "We've tried that. I've got little to go by, Excellency. Just the extreme height, the drooping eyelid." He paused, troubled. Did the Archbishop recall the Maldonado Fraud Case—a vast claim that involved church lands and other lands—a dim matter three decades old? It was an audacious fraud based on forgery which involved a simpleminded padre of the Santa Ynez Mission, Fra Santander, and a man named Pedro Maldonado, who had just such a drooping eyelid.

"I do not see the relevance," the Archbishop said.

Trumbull said, "Hagerman bought up that claim, more than thirty years ago, but those men knew each other—Hagerman and Maldonado. Miss Roux is said to have strong powers of invention. But it is hardly possible that she could invent a man with that precise physical defect—a description of a man last seen in this city almost before she was born?"

"Maldonado—Ramirez?" the Archbishop murmured doubtfully. "Before my time. A tall man with a drooping eyelid? Where would I find him?"

"I have no idea. He was Castilian. Born in Madrid. Perhaps by now he's back in Spain. Or Mexico, or somewhere in South America. Would you help find him?"

The Archbishop rose in dismissal. "Judge Trumbull," he said, "I cannot become a party to scandal, you'll agree. You are entitled to information. But I cannot become your investigator. Why should I assume such a burden?"

"In the interests of justice," Trumbull said.

"Now that is unfair," the Archbishop said resentfully, "and you know it." A servant appeared with Trumbull's hat and coat. "Good-bye, Judge Trumbull."

The door closed.

"Maldonado," the Archbishop muttered. "What a mess."

The newel post felt smooth and cold. Except for a small flame winking in a wall bracket, the house was dark and mysterious with shadows.

A face, dim against a pillow, looked at the ceiling in a shaft of cold moonlight. A pair of iron-gray braids fell over a coverlet. A slow shallow breath ended on a light snore.

Let her sleep, he thought.

He undressed and emptied his pockets. Studs and cuff links went into a box. Finally he slipped under covers and lay supine, waiting for body heat to warm the sheets.

A dry frail hand slipped into his own. "Was it a good trip?" Alexandra whispered.

"Pretty good." He kissed her head. "Glad to be home," he yawned.

"What's she like?"

"Who? Oh! Miss Roux?"

"Yes. I feel sad for her, Mark."

"Sad? Why?"

"She must be so alone."

"That? Oh, yes. Reckon so. Not my problem," he yawned again. "Let's sleep now. We'll talk at breakfast."

"Good night, darling."

"Night, sugar."

He lay stretched out, thinking back. The woman had totally surprised him, he thought. Sharp mind, acute perceptions, grasp of details. But somehow sad and withdrawn. It wasn't easy to know these things about women. Faces of angels, dispositions of fiends. He'd neither predict nor evaluate anything about the woman. Still, something bothersome gnawed, something elusive. For the first time in his life, he was unable to foresee how a line of testimony would strike the court.

And something else about the woman. Brilliant, snapping eyes, but cold. Most remarkably cold eyes he had ever seen. Pure or not, he thought with conviction, the woman was entitled to her day in court. He drifted into sleep.

Chapter Eleven

Superior Court Judge Peter McArdle was astonished at the activity as the trolley stopped at McAllister Street. It was a bright morning with a clear view of the hills which lay beyond Van Ness Avenue. An unusual number of people were gathering at the rotunda which stood before the Hall of Records. His heart lifted. The splendid new Civic Center had been established in a park hacked out of shabby stores and disreputable factories on the outskirts of the city. The triangle, seeded with grass and planted with conifers, was the center of his world. He crossed the wide street and made his way to the new City Hall.

Four flights of Romanesque columns soared to a gilt dome. Flagpoles were hung with the American flag, limp in a windless sky. Peter McArdle was a young judge, newly elected, and everything ardent in his soul swelled to the symbolism of the moment.

The Superior Court of San Francisco consisted of ten departments. Five still functioned in the old City Hall in Kearny Street, a malodorous building long outmoded. Five were now located in the new City Hall at Larkin and McAllister streets. McArdle paused at the directory which listed his name and title and chambers: Room 5 on the second floor—large chambers coveted by judges with greater seniority. A wide grin split the boyish Irish features. Fate having given him the juicy plum, it would not be withdrawn. He mounted the stairs, unnoticed by the crowds. Still smiling, he slipped into chambers through a private entrance. "Shut that door, Jack," he said.

"You're late," his law secretary, Jack Dinesmore, said sourly, closing the door. "I cannot deal with this list, Judge. Everybody wants a seat up front. You'll have to take the responsibility yourself."

"In a minute." McArdle opened a package and displayed its contents. "How d'you like it? Not too ostentatious, is it?"

"Looks all right," Dinesmore said glumly.

The black silk robe, specially tailored, was elaborately embroidered about the wide drooping sleeves and short stiff collar. It floated in the room, light as gossamer. "Justice should not only be done," McArdle said seriously. "It should *visibly* be done!"

"Yes, Judge," Dinesmore said. "Now here's everything you'll need—marked pleadings, file, memorandum of law, citations . . ."

"I see," McArdle said.

"Good. Now let's go over the sections of the Code—"

"I know the sections," McArdle said.

"Yes, but it's easy to get mixed up," Dinesmore said with forced patience. "Just remember that the issue is a simple one, Judge. Don't let 'em get you confused."

"Why d'you think I'll be confused? I can read English."

"I know you can." Dinesmore closed his eyes. "I just want to go over it again. We've got about an hour—"

"Oh, they'll wait, they'll wait," McArdle said with a grin; then, more solemnly, "You think it's important? The Code, I mean."

"Very important," Dinesmore said. "I've got it all written out with topic headings. Don't comment on the law at all. In a pinch look thoughtful and reserve decision and rule later—after we decide the point. You begin with the common law . . ." McArdle nodded soberly. Yes, the common law of England—adopted by every state in the Union after the Declaration of Independence—would govern. Quite simple, quite clear. Except where modified by the Code. Good. Under the laws of England, down to the Marriage Act, 26 George II, like those of every civilized country in the world, a simple promise to take each other for husband and wife constituted marriage—except in California, which required something more. Ah, yes! But what? he wondered anxiously. His prior judicial experience in the minor criminal courts of the city had not prepared him for these issues.

Dinesmore paused with a sense of despair. "Look 'ee, Judge, it's all right," he said gently. "Just remember that the whole thing will depend on the marriage contract. If you find that the contract's a fake, that's the end of the case. If you find that Hagerman signed that contract, we'll have to get into the other problems."

"Other problems?"

Dinesmore let a moment pass. "I'll be there," he promised. "Just don't make any snap judgments. Now, Judge, there are four Codes, but they form one complete statute. They're construed as one law. Title 1, Section 55, defines Marriage as a personal relationship arising out of a civil contract, to which the consent of the parties is necessary. But consent alone will not constitute marriage. It must be followed by a solemnization or mutual assumption of marital rights, duties, or obligations—"

"I know all that," McArdle protested.

"Sure you do, Judge," Dinesmore said, "but it never hurts to get it clear in mind. Now, what in the first place are the rights of marriage?" he intoned. "Cohabitation and sexual relations, naturally . . ."

"Naturally," McArdle nodded.

"Now duties," Dinesmore went on, pacing the floor. "What duties devolve on the husband? He's got to support his wife. He's got to give her a home. If he don't—"

"She gets alimony and support," McArdle said quickly.

Dinesmore paused above a crack in the polished wood planking. "Yes, but only if—if, Judge—if she's his wife. If she's not his wife, she's not entitled to anything."

"And counsel fees for the lawyers?"

"Same ruling," Dinesmore said. "Judge, you do understand that you've first got to decide whether the parties were ever married?"

"Yes, yes," McArdle said intelligently. "That means that I've got to find whether Hagerman signed that bloody piece of paper, Jack-o? If he didn't, then it's over?"

"Not quite," Dinesmore said precisely, "but, yes. Roughly, yes. Now, what point were we on?"

"Cohabitation and relations?" McArdle said with a gleam of interest.

"We covered that under 'rights,' not 'duties,' " Dinesmore

said, and resumed, ". . . but he cannot insist on unnatural acts," he concluded. "Let's hope it don't come up."

"Let's hope so," McArdle said.

"It's clear from Section 57 that the marriage can be proved under the general rules of evidence—and from Section 68 that the written contract should be recorded with the county register, but, Judge . . ."

"Yes, Jack-o?"

"You will remember that failure to record does *not* invalidate the marriage—if otherwise lawful. You won't be misled?"

"Misled? Why should I be misled?" McArdle complained. "It's a simple case, really. Now help me with this robe. I don't care what they say, it's worth every penny."

McArdle gazed at a mirror. Life was good, he decided, and who would have thought that the poor boy from Tyrone could have reached this point so early in his career. "Now, Jack-o," he said gravely. "The entrance is important. I don't want 'em to think they can put anything over on us, just because it's a civil case. Oh, Jack-o," he asked, halting at the door. "What d'ye really think? Privately? Did Hagerman sign that bloody contract?"

Dinesmore frowned. He was, he thought, reaching the limits of human adaptability. "I have no thoughts at all, Judge. I expect you'll listen to the evidence, weigh it carefully, and make your findings. When I know what you think, I'll know what I think. But if you ask my opinion . . ."

"Yes?"

"It was crazy to accept the assignment."

"All rise!"

The resonant voice, speaking the authority of all court criers since the beginning of time, rang out.

The door at the rear opened. McArdle entered and mounted the bench with a bounce, the silk black robe floating behind. A good-humored smile lit up the handsome young face.

A bang. "Be seated, please. This court is now in session."

McArdle straightened his sleeves and beckoned. "What's the date?" he asked profoundly. "March tenth," came a whisper. "Ah! Why are we whispering?" "I've got a cold," the stenographer whispered. "That explains it," McArdle said in a natural voice. "Hope you make a fortune, Manny," he added with a friendly nod. "I hear you've got a real windbag there." The reference was to Brawn, asprawl at the defendant's counsel table.

Messers Finch & Green were Ready for the Plaintiff.

Were there any other appearances?

Judge Trumbull was unexpectedly delayed in Stoddard but would appear to act Of Counsel, Finch advised.

The Defense was Ready.

McArdle glanced covertly with satisfaction at the crowded courtroom. He had been sitting in Superior Court only two short months. Those months had been a learning process, sitting with older, more experienced judges in the various departments of the court—motion, trial, probate, and so forth. Their swiftness of decision, apparent certitude of knowledge, expert handling of turbulent and difficult lawyers had filled him at first with despair. He could never, he felt, equal those men, but he was young and optimistic and sure that he could master at least the outward mannerisms of a good judge. For the rest, he depended upon the court clerks and Dinesmore.

The important thing was the press. Four benches were set aside for reporters. They were a raffish crowd—a disrespectful and contemptuous bunch much to be feared. A new face was among them. A tall woman with a monocle turned from a disconcerting stare to speak to the fearsome Rudolf Lang. Her remark drew a grin. Talking about me! McArdle thought, flushing.

A scraping sound drew his glance to his right. Hagerman was seated somewhere apart from his advisers, scribbling in a notebook. As he watched, the man tore off a page and handed it to Brawn. Brawn studied the notation, frowned, shook his head severely. Hagerman sniffed like a hurt child. Good God, McArdle thought. What a runt! Pathetic, more than anything else—a squat bantam cock sucking at lozenges, looking oddly forlorn.

Lastly, McArdle turned to the center of interest. Miss Roux, seated at the counsel table, hands folded in her lap, had the sweetest expression imaginable. Her gray skirt was severely cut; a full waist with starched collar and cuffs showed refreshing curves; the sunny pose reminded him of his own dear mother in a pensive mood. By Jesus! She don't look like a bloody whore, he thought with astonishment.

"Will Counsel step forward?" The lawyers trooped up for a low-voiced conference. The judge looked at the circle of grave faces and wondered how the matter stood in the other court. He had an intense and irrational respect for the Federal Circuit Court; until the last moment he had feared the intervention of its mighty writ of injunction—a writ that even now might pluck the trial from his hands and wipe out his day in the sun. He was assured that the issues of law and fact were entirely before him.

"Well, I'm pleased," he said, accepting a sheaf of documents marked in crayon. "How long d'ye think this will go on?"

The lawyers glanced at each other warily. Really, there was no telling. Weeks, perhaps months.

"Hope it don't go into June with the National Conventions taking place. I imagine you'll be attending?" The question was directed to Galindez.

"May have some hand in that business," Galindez said. The deep voice carried a barest hint of family influence. McArdle looked respectful and turned to the marked pleadings in the action before him. He began with the complaint.

"Oh, Jesus!" he exclaimed under his breath. Twenty-seven separate counts. Adultery with Sadie Keenan, diverse occasions. Adultery with May Cuff, aged seventeen. Amy O'Toole, a girl under eighteen, enticed from her guardian. He ran down paragraph after paragraph, turned over a page, and looked up with outrage. "Mr. Finch!" he exclaimed with honest anger, "d'you mean actually to bring out all this filth?"

Finch stared at the ceiling. "We did not commit those adulteries. They were," he said suavely, "the lamentable product of the defendant's own lust."

McArdle thought this over. "General Brawn? Is there any concession? Or is it your wish to see all this on parade?"

Brawn looked worldly. "Pooh! Mr. Hagerman's a widower. There's no obloquy."

McArdle scowled. "Maybe not obloquy, but the man's got grandchildren. Mr. Galindez might like to give that thought."

Brawn begged time to confer. Heads bent at the defense table. Hagerman shook his head, making rapid angry observations. Galindez' deep voice rose. Brawn looked up. The defense had no concessions. None whatsoever.

McArdle drew down his mouth unfavorably. "I'd like a solution."

Finch announced that his client, more solicitous of decency than her husband, would proceed on charges of desertion

209

alone. Adultery was withdrawn. A mutter of disappointment arose. Brawn stood. "She was not deserted, Your Honor. She was dismissed." McArdle caught a signal from Dinesmore. "Decision reserved," he announced with aplomb. "Let's have your opening, Mr. Finch."

Finch took an hour to outline the case.

McArdle finally stirred. He stared with disgust at the squat fornicator before him. What a prick, he thought. He was completely convinced.

Brawn took two hours to reply. He was a surprise—fat and fluty, intemperate and wordy, mincing like a dancing master across the courtroom well. Finally, indignant, mopping his neck, he sat. McArdle was bewildered. What a bitch! What a cheap dirty lay! He was completely convinced the other way.

"Proceed!" he said sternly.

Finch took a legal pose, tapping his spectacles. He took in every face in the room—the throng who gave his sleazy world structure and meaning. It was that best moment when fantasy is still perfection, tactics infallible, traps unsprung, and no surprise lurks. No one sneezed, no one coughed. There was total expectancy.

"Call Miss Driscoll," Finch said impressively.

Joe Cudahey came through a pouring rain before dawn to drive Trumbull to the depot. He put the carriage in the stable and stamped to the warm kitchen.

Trumbull in flannel underwear and dressing gown was at breakfast in the kitchen. Julian was hovering at the iron range. Rosita was rattling a skillet. Trumbull wiped his mouth. "Julian, bring Mr. Cudahey some coffee. Now, Joe, what've we got?"

"I've put away the shotgun," Cudahey said, pulling up to the oilcloth. "That situation washed out."

Trumbull nodded. "I told you so." For some weeks, Cudahey had taken to sleeping in the office nights to protect the files. All sorts of types were drifting through town—two strangers named Hogan and Scotti had been seen by Myra Coolth talking with the C. and S.W. agent at the depot; then the office had been entered, or thought entered; no one was sure. Sheriff Rivers had questioned the men, who had claimed credentials of a dubious law investigation outfit back

210

East; they had then faded out of town. "I said there was no real harm in those fellers," Trumbull said, pouring coffee.

"Seemed menacing to me," Cudahey replied.

"If they want information," Trumbull said precisely, "they'd better learn how to get it by legal methods than by rummaging. What'd they expect to find?"

"No idea. Myra thinks mebbe they were trying to locate the famous marriage contract. Why they'd expect to find it in our tin box I cain't imagine."

"It's a fine safe," Trumbull said stiffly. "Latest thing."

"Sho, sho!" Cudahey said reassuringly. Je-sus, we're sure in a mood! he was thinking. Three hundred dollars for an office safe was sure extravagant for a country law firm.

Trumbull was following another train of thought. "How's the trial going?"

Cudahey studied the ceiling, gaily festooned by Rosita with strings of red and green peppers and ears of drying corn. "I'm just the scrivener," he drawled. "I've got no opinion."

"Indeed? What does Myra think?" Trumbull asked acidly.

"Oh, Myra!" Cudahey repeated, brightening. "Well, I reckon she thinks that Little Nell showed she was quite a go-between. She's testified to all these visits where Hagerman confided his guts—loves, hates, finances—in precise detail. Pree-cise detail," he stressed. "The *Herald*'s got more'n eight columns of her story—exactly how Hagerman repeatedly failed to deny the marriage. Thank'ee kindly, Julian," he said, sitting up at the appearance of coffee. He filled a saucer with extreme care. "If this Judge McArdle, even if he believes our Little Nell . . ." A pause for slurping.

Trumbull adjusted his spectacles. "You sound doubtful."

Cudahey continued to suck. "Well, I don't like these emphatic truthtellers. Between Little Nell and Cousin Delaney they almost made out a *prima facie* case. Almost, not quite. The thing of it is they go just so far with Hagerman and no further. It didn't come out quite like we expected."

"Never does."

"Yup, yup. Still . . ." Cudahey sipped. "Well, they testify how they both told the Senator how Miss Roux was known to them as his wife but strangely he failed to answer. Just smiled and joked and parried. So really, Myra says, what does it prove?"

"Let's see that," Trumbull said gruffly. He scanned Mrs.

Woodruff's account in the *Herald*. The attempt of Miss Roux to proscribe Mr. Hagerman as a married man might be deemed a blessing *en manque* to him rather than a curse, she wrote. The longer the parties were in court, the more justice and expense they could expect to get—much as lobsters grow redder the longer they boil. It was her opinion that the world could contemplate with pleasure the beauties of lawyers' law. The question, she thought, was simple: Was Miss Roux the wife of Mr. Hagerman? Miss Roux sought affirmative answer by proof that Mr. Hagerman had signed a contract of marriage with her. Obviously the sane and honest question would be: Did he?

If one could imagine so alarming an innovation as a Chief Justice of California with dictatorial powers, she imagined the suppression of any lawyer except to answer that single question first. Yet since Hagerman's arrest for adultery weeks and months had elapsed and no progress made toward its determination. By now all sorts of actions were pending or threatened—criminal and civil—and the question lay in a clueless maze with no court able to decide a single point of the case. It was hard to believe the state of affairs. Its preposterous absurdities were never equaled in Satire's most incredible dream.

Trumbull smiled. He was now becoming most respectful of Mrs. Woodruff. Satire's dream? He tucked the line safely in memory and read on. Miss Nellie Driscoll had entered in a rush. She was described as a sharp-nosed girl with a short exaggerated figure whose adoration of Miss Roux was evident from smiles and nods that passed between them. She had told the familiar story down to the final outrageous scene at the Imperial House with surprising maturity and poise. The encounters with the Senator, while amusing, showed merely that she had been treated with indulgence and ambiguous banter. Certainly, Mrs. Woodruff concluded, while a liaison of some sort was established, thus far at most Mr. Hagerman was shown as a man who kept his own counsel.

Trumbull considered all this with pressed lips. "Didn't we get anything more positive in?"

Cudahey looked up with a squint. "Yes, they . . . I mean, we . . . that is, our Little Nell got in some of those self-serving letters where Miss Roo was characterizing in her own favor, managing conveniently to keep copies—"

"What's wrong with that?"

"Nothing, nothing. Except it would seem she was making a record."

"Yes? So?"

"Well, then, they weren't quite the spontaneous letters she'd have the Court believe, were they? Read for yourself, Judge."

Trumbull studied four columns of Nellie's story. The testimony ended with a letter delivered by her to Hagerman.

18 Wisteria Place

May 20th

Dearest Sen:

I am sending this note by Nell to make sure you get it tonight. It's impossible for us to go to Beaufort this Saturday for reasons that Nell will explain. I am afraid I am "being a woman" and that cannot be too bad, can it? I think you know what I mean.

It is all so bewildering. I sit in this little house looking at the garden with the sweet smell of wisteria at the window. It attracts humming bees and that always makes me melancholy like the remembrance of sweet things past and all you have meant to me. This is a strange sort of life. One is thought to be single and yet one has all the responsibilities of marriage, because I must keep house and look after children—Nell and Sonny are children, in their way—and all the chores of laundry, setting out mouse traps, shopping, managing the servant, and thinking of the household head who should be here but is not. I have had some strange experiences since I have been seemingly alone. The few men I have met all seem to think—well, I don't have to tell you, Sen, what they think, but nothing wrong can happen, I am glad to say. My pride and moral code would just not allow it.

Hush! Nell is rushing upstairs now either to burst in with news of some outdoorsy excursion or to go past to curl up with a book for the afternoon.

No, the sewing machine just started.

Now we must talk serious, Sen. I know you still want to keep this business quiet and of course I will abide by our agreement but this terrible suspense is killing me. I am not sure I can keep the secret much longer.—Grandmama has made plain that we either announce a date or

I'll get sent East to live this down. She will not much longer accept assurances that we are talking reconciliation.

I am torn by your strange refusal to deal with me openly. First it was politics. Then it was Emily's wedding. Now you accuse me of divulging our secret to strangers. But how can you be so unfair when you know how I suffer by keeping silence? Have I not been snubbed by the world? Would my family treat me so badly if I came right out and told 'em the truth? Your reproaches confuse me. What have I done to deserve this silence? I have ministered in sickness, rubbed your feet like a tender nurse that Christmas you almost died, read poetry aloud of the most upsetting kind, and waited like Griselda to be lifted as promised from the mire back to a state of honor. I surely have no wish to interfere with the smooth running of your declining years but I am selfish and I want my proper place in your heart and life. Oh, please, please, don't feel offended. If I write boldly, it is because I love you and look to you to act according to your honorable nature. I have a world of pride which rebels at this strange position you have put me in—especially when only the other night you said in such a loving and tender way that I was your own little wife and only us two knew the secret.

Those words still run in my ears and in truth no one else in the world does know the secret. So, while I hate to trouble you, bills have got to be met and could you let Nell have the balance of what you owe me?

So, good night, darling Sen, and flights of angels, as you once said, see that you get lots of rest.

Your loving Jess.

P.S. By the bye, Nell and I have again looked at that house in Golden Gate Street. It's behind in taxes and repairs, so I'm not sure 'tis such a bargain after all, although better than living in your little flat in Polk Street. But we can always talk about adjustments lest the cloud on the title prove a cloud on the horizon. At this stage of the game I am tired of stocks and would relish the tranquillity of real estate.

J.

Trumbull looked up with a frown. "What's wrong with it?"

"What's it prove?" Cudahey asked. "Self-serving stuff. It's denied, so what good is it?"

"The whole case is denied," Trumbull said shortly, "but it's an artifact." He scanned the page with concern. What was Finch sparring for? Why not go for the throat? "Anything useful get established?" he asked with an edge.

Cudahey touched his nose. "Read on," he said. Trumbull turned back to the account. As Brawn rose to cross-examine for the defense, Miss Driscoll, overcome by the heat, had fainted. A commotion followed. General Brawn with Christian charity had waived his right to immediate cross-examination, observing that the testimony and letters were lies and vulgar concoctions of that crafty old woman, Mrs. Lawes, the Black Eminence of the conspiracy, and he looked with relish to expose her in the fires of his cross-examination. Trumbull smiled unwillingly.

Black Eminence? Not bad.

Cudahey grinned crookedly. "Mrs. Lawes was quite a help too. Quite a help indeedy."

Trumbull continued to eat, now silent. He was respectful of Cudahey's insights and vexed at the raillery. "What's so funny now?" he asked.

Cudahey grinned. "Myra was showing me this article in the *Hornet* where this wit, Rudolf Lang, discusses McArdle's capacities. He writes that there's no judge on the bench but forgets more law every night asleep than young Judge McArdle is capable of to learn awake. He says what's needed are men o' the world—sly old boys well grounded in knowledge of evil and not unacquainted with the Devil's daughters."

"Devil's daughters?" Trumbull frowned.

"Harlots," Cudahey explained. "Myra was real amused. She was marveling where men get these flowery conceits. She was saying when it comes to contracting to sell oneself to a sporty old millionaire, she might be tempted to succumb herself. Joking, of course," he added, seeing no response.

Trumbull put the newspaper aside. "I'll read it on the train," he said impassively. "Now have done with Myra's talk."

Cudahey knew every mood and all their shades. An obstinacy was settling into the case, he saw with apprehension. "Judge, do you really feel bound to go in this hard weather?" he asked unhappily, finding courage.

It had been pouring rain for weeks, and washouts were everywhere. Trumbull had the best excuse in the world not to leave the warm and pleasant kitchen or the woman in the sickroom upstairs. "I'm already days late as it is. Weather's no reason to put it off further," he said. "Why d'ye raise this now?"

Cudahey started to speak, then stopped. "Oh, dunno. Me and Myra can't hold down the office without'n your presence. Myra was wondering if you shouldn't turn that retainer back."

Trumbull stared. "Turn it back? Joe! I've taken a public position. You tell Myra I appreciate her solicitude for Mrs. Trumbull, but she's paid to typewrite. Not to wonder."

Cudahey hunched over the oilcloth, elbows forward, sucking at the saucer. "It could drag out," he said.

"So it could, but I've made arrangements. If anything unexpected happens to Mrs. Trumbull, telegraph. I'll get back in a hurry. I'm not taking the main burden of the trial—fortunately. Come now, Joe," he said impatiently, "have done with spaniel looks. And you can tell your crony, Myra, I have never abandoned a client during a trial. I won't now. And look, it's the total, final effect that counts. These first witnesses are only laying the foundation. It's the client who's got to cinch—or lose—the case. Give Mr. Cudahey what he wants, Rosita," he ordered and left, bending under the doorway.

The huddle of bedclothes was indistinct in the dim rain-filtered light from the streaming windowpanes.

"I'm getting dressed now," Trumbull said, letting his hand cover her breast. It had once been a full breast, he recalled with a pang, springing to touch, and now its tissues were shrinking from life.

"What suits are you taking?" Alexandra asked.

"The black broadcloth. I've also got the worsted."

"The worsted?"

"In case it gets warm," he said. "We could have a warm spell."

"I forget it's spring," she replied.

"Let me dress now," he said, rising.

"No, wait," she said. "Let me feel you." And her hand slid over the enormous biceps, pectorals, hair bristling under flannel. "Hard, Mark. Hard as a lion. You're my strength,

216

my support," she said, sliding her hands, feeling warmth and a man's bulk. "You'll be sure to write?"

"Oh, it's not for that long," he protested.

"I want you to write," she said.

"Sure thing," he agreed with suppressed irritation. "But I'll be back Friday for the weekend, sure."

"I would like you to write," she repeated. "I want letters. You tell me things in letters you never say otherwise."

"I'll write," he promised. "And you'll be reading about me," he said, forcing a light tone. "Don't be too critical when I get back."

"Reading?" she murmured with despair.

"You know how I mean that. Myra likes to read to you. Feed her lemon cake, and she'll jump through hoops."

She smiled faintly. "How is the trial going?"

He hesitated. "Too soon to tell."

"Oh, Mark, Mark! I'm that sorry I've tied you down. You should be there."

"It doesn't matter," he replied.

"No, but it does. It matters a lot if you're not leading. You've already missed the opening. I feel I've robbed you of something."

"Hush, now," he said gruffly. "I'll miss the train."

She felt a light kiss and the familiar beard on her cheek, smelling of tobacco and bay rum and coffee and whiskey. He started off, then: "Mark?" Her voice called him back. She sank back breathless and the sweat of weakness stood on her forehead. "I'm concerned," she said after a panting moment. "You cannot have the woman exposed to this besmirching campaign. Can you bring her here for a weekend? I could make a reception for her."

Trumbull paused. "Why should you do that?"

"It'd help to get a social note in the papers. I've got respectability enough for a regiment. And besides," she said with wan humor, "you've been talking a blue streak about the creature. I'm like the rest of the world. I'm curious about her."

There was an excitement he did not like, a febrile quality that was new, a deepening exhaustion.

The rapper sounded at the front door below.

"I'll think on it," he promised gently, "but I don't think it's such a good idea. But perhaps . . . if the occasion comes up. Good-bye, dear," he said, kissing the hot forehead. The heavy tread crossed the room and went down the stairs, shaking the building. Voices rumbled below at the front door. She faced the window, feeling the draft of air, rain-wet and cold. Quick steps ran upstairs. The door opened.

"Well, well, well! How are we today?" the young doctor sang cheerfully, rubbing his hands, entering with a breath of the wet outdoors. "Ma'am, you look blooming."

The worn face turned about. "You have a very nice face, Doctor," she said. "Let me feel it."

Trumbull watched Cudahey drive off and sank back in the parlor car. The rush of blindness should not have come entirely as a surprise, he thought. Off and on, for a year, she had been complaining of mistiness and reading difficulties. The optometrist Lundy's surprised reaction in San Francisco should have alerted him. Nevertheless something in Julian's voice that day had brought him racing up the stairs two steps at a time. He had burst into the room to find her staring in fright. The new spectacles lay on the floor. "What's wrong with the lamp?" she cried.

A fist had gripped his heart. "Why?"

"I cannot see," she cried.

He had never seen fear in her before. He had kept his voice in strong control. He took her hand. "I'll turn up the lamp," he said.

"No, no. I can't see anything. I cannot see the lamp at all. I want the doctor! Mark, I'm blind."

He prayed a moment. "No, you're wrong," he said with forced calm. "It's just a spell. You've had this before. I'll get a compress and you'll be all right."

"Mark, I cannot see a damned thing," she had cried, her voice rising. "It's gray, almost black. There's just a faint heat when I turn toward the lamp. It's lit, isn't it? Isn't it? Oh, dear God! I'm blind."

Julian was in the hallway. "Oh, Mister Judge," he quavered. "Mister Judge. Mister Judge." Rosita was weeping.

"Christ!" he had prayed, gripped with terror, feeling the dark closing in on himself. For months vision had flickered—darkness, light, grayness followed, more terrifying than the complete night. The young doctor, newly graduated from a medical school in St. Louis, had come, full of theories. It was not the eyes at all, he thought, but some blood disorder,

218

something systemic or focal not yet understood by medicine. An aging process, he speculated buoyantly. Functions were ending, he said cheerfully.

"Would rest help?" Trumbull stared in helpless desolation. "If I took her east for a vacation? The baths?"

Nothing would help, the young doctor advised crisply. He promised to write to specialists in Vienna and Paris, but offered no hope. There was nothing to be done, nothing at all, but to endure and wait.

It had torn him asunder. In preparation for the trial, he had made a dozen hasty trips back and fourth to San Francisco. Each trip was aborted by fears and concern for Alexandra, and only half his mind was on the case. On the surface the case was going well; the city was enjoying an old rake's discomfiture; Hagerman, it was felt, was getting what he deserved; but underneath it was not so satisfactory. Finch, he discovered, was less than methodical, surprisingly reckless, a slovenly practitioner neglectful of minutiae. In their frequent clashes Finch often had exploded with exasperation, inviting Trumbull to take over. Only too often Trumbull had cut short the visits to return to Stoddard, smoldering at the straitjacket into which he had put himself.

The client was part of the difficulty, Trumbull reflected. Nine in the morning meant three in the afternoon. She would arrive late, breathless, apologetic, complaining of pains and sleeplessness, then plunge into furious railings at the villainies of the other side. The business of preparation went late into the night; she depended on him, she exclaimed only too often, assuring him that life and honor were in his hands. It was a theme constantly repeated. She was self-engrossed, obsessed by her case, taking no account of his difficulties; when he reminded her of his limited role, she flared into recriminations. On the last visit, he had brought her up short. One more outburst, he had said coldly, and he would drop the case. She'd told him to go to hell, slamming the door, then returned, contrite and begging forgiveness, blaming Finch. As on each such occasion he had patiently explained that nothing mattered but to win. The trial called for an intense discipline—an unswerving zeal to reach a single goal—and that tantrums had no place in the struggle. And finally, she had seemed to accept the rule firmly laid down. Oh, lands! she had sighed with a nervous smile, it was just that she felt so fearful of the ordeal ahead. He would not leave the case? she had beseeched. The brilliant cold blue eyes, here called, had searched into his own with an intense message. He shook his head, unable to promise. At home he had made a final offer to abandon the trial in San Francisco. Alexandra had refused. "You know you want that trial," she had said. "You'd never forgive yourself if you stopped now—nor would I. Dear God, Mark, don't pretend to me. I will not tie you to this room." Her exhaustion was dismissal and end of the argument.

Trumbull ordered a whiskey and opened a newspaper. The heavy rain drummed on the metal roof, streamed in runnels down the misty windows, formed a froth on the dim fields as he read the San Francisco papers.

The last witness for the day was Mrs. Malvinia Lawes, described as an old Negro woman well known in San Francisco for her shrewd business dealings. He could almost hear the husky voice with its slurred accents, see the dark splayed large hands folded in her lap, see the shrewd twinkling eyes, hear the thrust and riposte of a native wit. She had given testimony in a clear loud voice. Called the "mystery witness," she had been greeted sarcastically by General Brawn, who begged leave to examine the witness preliminarily for capacity to take the oath.

Brawn began with a deep bow. He felt, he said, like the Hindu before his idol. He saw that she was ugly but felt that she was great—great at least in certain arts. Waiting for a titter to die, he wondered with deference if he might put some questions. The idol stiffly inclined her head and was asked whether she had sprinkled fresh chicken blood on her morning grits, and what were her views on voodoo.

Mr. Finch was instantly up. Really! he complained. What was the purpose?

It appeared that Mr. Brawn was having a bit of fun, but the witness took this insolence with composure. She had no faith in greenbacks, she explained, so how could she have faith in voodoo? Voodoo was not something to talk about. Only the credulity of some gave currency to that foolishness. She believed neither in voodoo nor fortune telling nor palmistry—all of which she left to those who made it their profession.

Finch was again up and down with objections, but the witness was allowed to observe that voodoo in fact was widely misunderstood. She had heard that it was all right in some places, but not in San Francisco. She had better places than dolls to stick pins, and if some people thought she, Mrs. Lawes, was a voodoo queen, why, let 'em! It was a religious belief. Yes, you could summon spirits from the vasty deep, she agreed, but would they come? She was glad to learn that maxim, and what else would anyone like to know?

All this, Fanny Woodruff noted, was said with a hard ironical smile directed at the defendant, who complained that the witness was trying to demoralize him with a cross-eyed stare.

Brawn had one last question. Was it true that the witness was financing Miss Roux's lawsuit? Now reluctant, the witness admitted that she had at times lent sums at ordinary interest to Miss Roux but had no other stake than friendship in the case.

However, she had added, Miss Roux had repaid all loans and she had notes to prove it. Did he, General Brawn, want those notes produced in court?

Brawn was seen to stare at the wall, the press, his client, the ceiling, and the witness. Then, with irony, he bowed and withdrew and the witness was sworn.

Trumbull put down the newspaper and turned to the soaking landscape. Voodoo? What in hell was it about? he wondered. It had a smell of danger and Finch had been too quiescent during the exchange. Too much leeway, he thought uneasily, and returned to the account.

The witness went through a personal narrative without surprises. To begin with, she had not thought it curious to be consulted by Miss Jessica's grandmother. She called on the finest families and they called on her. It might seem strange to some but not in Old San Francisco, where everybody had come in the same one Rush. If it came to that, she, Mrs. Lawes, was received by more people than Mr. Hagerman, because there were houses where he couldn't get past the dog.

She wanted to explain that she often gave advice without charge. Young women could be foolish and needed older heads in their dealings with men. She reckoned she had a wise old head, maybe not older than some but old enough to know the world. She might be called a mammy, but not a manager—there was a difference. In any case she had heard independently about the Secret. San Francisco had no secrets. If you wanted to know things, you called the nearest child. So actually, the so-called secret was all over town.

Yes, Miss Roux was a frequent visitor at Las Flores, but it was entirely social.

Miss Roux had been brought up in the Old South, so that was the bond. She felt natural and easy with people who understood her. Color had nothing to do with it.

Now the newspapers had printed letters from Cape Badeau that Miss Roux had had the reputation back home of a heartless flirt. That was not the witness' opinion; but if it came to that, some of the finest married women in San Francisco had started out heartless flirts, so it proved nothing. In the Old South girls were taught to be willful and tyrannical in heart matters, it was supposed to lend charm, and maybe it did. She claimed no authority.

The witness was most emphatic about bills and could show that Mr. Hagerman had paid for draperies and furniture. She most assuredly had seen the marriage contract when Miss Roux was recovering from brain fever. She had also seen that Miss Roux sure needed help.

The long detailed narrative went on. It was late before she got to a final crucial episode. Trumbull adjusted his spectacles and sat closer to the text.

Shortly before the arrest for adultery, she went on, she had received a visit from Captain Pritchard of the Police Department, who ominously had refused a glass of her finest whiskey.

". . . he said that he had this bad complaint that Miss Roux was putting this forgery—he meant the marriage contract—on Mr. Hagerman and he was tipping me off. Forgery being a crime, he said, Miss Roux had better come in to see himself than wait for the District Attorney to take action where everybody would be sorry. I thanked him but asked what else was on his mind. He laughed and asked exactly how the marriage contract read. I declined to speak of it and pointedly told him that Mr. Hagerman had a precise banking memory and ought to know what he signed and not to send somebody else to worm it out. He apologized about a certain other matter we both understood about and left. But I was surprised because I was expecting a commissioner and not a captain. Captains are less important than they think."

Trumbull looked up with a grimace of satisfaction. An atmosphere was beginning to gather.

". . . so I summoned Miss Roux for a frank talk about the matter. She was irresolute and begged me to intercede. I then called on Mr. Hagerman at his apartment. It wasn't easy to get in because I had to talk sharp to the hotel detective who was posted. I found a changed man. He was drinking hard, in a bad temper, and wasted with this suppuration and complaining about a wind he had caught that was supposedly brought by this ship from Yokohama. Things like that were on his mind, and he was not standing the usual treat. I must say that room was real fetid. I am just trying to show what us advisers sometimes have to put up with in situations.

"I told Mr. Hagerman that Miss Roux begged me to tell him her life had become impossible. She could not visit respectful people and respectful people would not have her. He had placed her so bad in society, she was an outcast even with her family and would have to take action. I admonished him he'd better put her right with a divorce because now she had less wise advisers than myself—but she'd give no trouble and quit-claim all claims against the estate if he'd do right, and she'd even return those mining shares he gave her for a wedding gift.

"He was not his usual joking self. He said not to mention Miss Roux's name, that she was a filthy, you-know-what. He'd have nothing to say about her; he knew nothing of her claims; he'd see her dead; he'd heard she was talking to divorce lawyers and this other blackmailing—well, I won't use the words Mr. Hagerman used—he meant Mr. Pettibone—but she could not prove her claim, he said, he'd never pay another cent in this life. He said he didn't give a something what she did, he'd see her in jail first. He got choking and had to swallow pills to catch his breath.

"So I told him a few things too. I was not impressed with bad language, I reminded him. I could call names too—and I did then, but I won't now. I told him exactly what he was in plain English and some French. Then I warned he might end up in jail himself, and the matter should be settled. But he got excited and stamped about and swore and blurted something most pointed about Miss Roux. Then he stopped and turned green when he realized what he had said."

A storm of objections brought a hail of rulings from the bench.

"We looked at each other like two cats on a fence, and then he advised me not to test the word of one of my race against a millionaire's. Then he put on this sick smile—that same sick smile he's wearing now—and said that maybe he was wrong and he was troubled. He wanted my opinion on Miss Roux—was she pure when he met her?—because at his age he couldn't afford to make a fool of himself. I most emphatically vouched for Miss Roux and said he must have had the living proof. He said, well, he wasn't unreasonable, and he'd pay five thousand dollars if I could get Miss Roux to give up that paper. Money didn't grow on trees, he reminded me, saying he didn't care how I cut up the pie. He'd settle for nuisance value. 'Nuisance?' I said. I told him five hundred thousand would be more like it but Miss Roux wanted nothing but her good name. She'd sign away anything if he'd put her right social. He screamed something real filthy at my race. So I told him exactly what he was and left. He ran after me down the hall, begging me to come back, but I said, while I could understand his behavior to Miss Roux—a craving for relations being a powerful compulsion—I would not forgive that final slur against me and my kind."

The witness wanted the Court to know that she would not pass judgment but she had known human beings of high honor and the defendant was not among the highest. He was an old catfish with a hook in his mouth and that was why he was so enraged. The main thing was his remarkable statement—it was not in writing, but her two good ears were not stuffed with wax, and it was conclusive of the matter.

"Now, Your Honor, maybe Miss Roux was foolish, but Mr. Hagerman's conduct is so unspeakably bad that no force on earth can make me think different—because what he blurted was that he'd be damned to give Miss Roux a divorce; that Miss Roux, he said, was still seeing Mr. MacGowan in French restaurants; that he had a dozen men to swear they had relations with her and—if it came to it—he could divorce her himself without a dime because she had never been true to him since he signed that damnable marriage contract."

Trumbull dropped the newspaper with a grunt of relief. So there it was! The vital admission in Hagerman's mouth. There were slight elisions, small changes, a shift in emphasis —but it had a ring. The case had been made. If anything, it was going in too easy, he thought; the resistance too perfunctory. Malvinia Lawes had been a strong witness, but Brawn was not yet done with Nellie. Ahead lay the girl's cross-examination with all its dangers. The outcome would turn on the plaintiff herself.

He was thinking constantly of the woman, he found. He could not make her out. There was the physical delicacy that was so engaging, a winsomeness that fascinated him. He thought constantly of that, but he was uneasy. She had special attitudes for everyone—intimacy with Malvinia, tenderness for Nellie, contempt for Finch, fondness for Green, respect for himself. She seemed to fear his opinion and he was content to keep it so. What he could not escape was something within himself—something which he had thought was dead.

He had rented rooms from a widow in Farley Street and an office on Kearny Street near the Nevada Block for his private use. It was small but sunny, with casements rising to the ceiling, and utterly bare of decoration. At their last meeting he was behind the desk with the woman opposite reviewing a list of personal expenses. Her lips moved, conning the accounts; the spectacles had slid down her nose; her breasts were pressed against the desk, making a flat ridge in a crisp taffeta street dress. He was suddenly aware that he was staring with intensity at delicate pierced ears which held small pendant pearl earrings set in gold. She looked up and caught his stare.

The thought between them was unspoken.

"Mrs. Lawes will know how much I spent for those shoes," she said thoughtfully. She adjusted the spectacles and returned to her calculations, looking down. After a moment, she shifted her position, dabbed a beading of sweat on her mouth, smiled, and left.

He was deeply troubled by the episode.

Even now, leaving Stoddard, the moment was a shock—unexpected and absolute. In years no such thing had happened—nor struck so hard. It was not merely the effect of a woman, he thought, but the thought that something was about to happen for which he had waited a lifetime. As the door had closed the last thing he had noticed—the thing that still recurrently came to mind—was the deep curve of a woman's spine. He had protested his reluctance every inch of the way, but the truth was that now the whistle howling ahead, the forward motion of the train, the jerk and clash of iron couplings and gushing steam brought only an overwhelming sense of wonder—at his own feelings of relief to escape into the lawsuit, to feel nothing but impatience and zest for the conflict ahead. The sickness at Stoddard, he thought resentfully, had gone on too long.

It was past midnight when the railway ferry finally crawled into the slip. The city was asleep, shrouded in fog. Nevertheless he ordered the hack to detour past Wisteria Place. He paused outside the house. It was dark, asleep, and he had no idea what he was doing in that spot. "Go on," he ordered finally. His rooms in Farley Street—a small *pied-à-terre* with a kitchen—were waiting.

Chapter Twelve

He threw back the covers with an exclamation and reached for the clock. The bright sunlight slanting through lace curtains told him that he was late for court. It would be the first time in a lifetime of practice that he would fail in the courtesies. He had begun to shave when he heard the knock.

"It's late, Judge," said a tart New England voice. "Would you like coffee?"

He paused in the midst of a stroke. "I'm not sure I have time," he said doubtfully.

226

"Do I leave it or take it?"

"Put it on the table," he said finally, "and I'm much obliged." He continued to shave methodically while light footsteps entered and left and a door was firmly closed. It did not amuse him much to live in bachelor quarters, but he had a separate street entrance and Mrs. Coles—a war widow of the Northern persuasion—held to a low rent and was incomparably clean. Somewhere back East a daughter was expecting to give birth, which might require that she vacate the house in his care for several months.

The notion of an empty house was not without its attractions.

The full New England breakfast of eggs and pancakes, slabs of bread and butter and coffee, was more than he could decently leave in haste—and all set out on good bone china. He ate quickly, rereading a letter to Alexandra written in the small hours. It would be satisfying, he thought, just the right touch of optimism regarding the trial. He licked the envelope and fixed a stamp, then walked down a narrow flight of stairs and paused at a kitchen door. "Mrs. Coles? I'm off."

He was astonished at the crowds near the Civic Center. City police and deputy sheriffs were aiding court officers to keep the crowd calm. He was recognized. Good-humoredly, Captain Pritchard made a path through the crowd. "Nah then, good people. Nah then. Let 'em pass." He turned panting. "Judge Trumbull," he said with a hard grin, "would you convey a message to Mrs. Lawes? Tell 'er commissioners come, commissioners go, but captains are forever. See?"

"Glad to," Trumbull said heartily. Pritchard was his own height, a tall man with a large bulbous nose on which every vein stood blue and glorious. "Proves Mr. Darwin was right —the lowest forms of life have the strongest powers of survival." Pritchard laughed under forced draft and turned to the guards. "Open up, you bleeders. Move it!" And the portals swung open.

At the stir, his name ran through the chamber. Finch turned with vexation and relief. Trumbull strode past the rail and with a courtly bow to the bench sat at the table.

Jessica turned her face, white with fury. "Where in hell've you been?" she whispered murderously.

"It's been raining here too." Young Judge McArdle smiled, aware of a friendly warmth that radiated from the large man

227

across the bench. He was honored, he said respectfully, and he'd read all Trumbull's opinions in the early California Supreme Court Reports, or his law secretary had, so it was the same thing. The lawyers smiled painfully and returned to their places like boxers waiting for the bell.

"Recall Miss Driscoll."

A woman screamed and struggled. "Oh, no! Holy Mother, no! Don't let 'em do it to my baby. God in Heaven, not to my baby girl! My baby! My baby child!" the woman clamored. "A-a-h take ye'r hands off, you bummers," she snarled. "I'm the mother. . . ."

A distracted woman was brought before the bench. A thin ineffectual man cupping his ear apologetically explained that they were the parents of the girl.

"What a laugh! Parents!" Nellie said scornfully. "A fat lot they know!"

"What about my baby?" the woman wept. "Can they do this to her? They're corrupting her morality. Ooh, that woman! There she sits, the unnatural creature!" she shouted. "How can they let this happen?"

McArdle got order and swiveled about sternly. "Miss Driscoll, just exactly how old are you?"

"Eighteen," the girl said with venom.

"Only eighteen?" McArdle said with rising temper. "You hear what your mother's saying? Are you putting your judgment against your mother's? You? A mere eighteen?"

A cold look flicked across the bench. "I may be only eighteen, Judge," the girl said, "but you'd be surprised."

A titter went around the courtroom.

McArdle leaned across the bench. "Well there you have it, madam," he ruled. "Wait outside!" The door closed on a spitting, snarling woman and timid man. "Be seated!" the court officers said, ordering the spectators to resume decorum. The judge eyed the white-faced girl a long speculative moment. "Decision reserved," he said firmly.

He motioned his secretary and left the court in recess.

Five minutes later he returned. "Proceed," he ruled weightily. Dinesmore's sigh was a passing mark.

"You don't mind if I call you Miss Nellie?" Brawn said pleasantly, "considering the difference in our ages?"

"Call me what you like," the girl replied haughtily.

Trumbull opened his eyes. He was now seated, hunched

forward, eyes closed almost in sleep. It was a characteristic pose caught by all the quick-sketch newspaper artists in the room. The girl was white-faced and nervous, but determined.

Brawn put a foot on the step before the witness chair. "Now after Miss Roux recovered from her, ah, brain fever, you met again. How did you meet?"

The girl shrugged. "She was walking in Mrs. Olafson's yard. She heard me yelling at my brothers and she walked through a loose board in the fence and asked me about taking meals with my mother. That's how it all began, when she was boarding with us about two weeks and began to tell Mama how to improve the recipes for goulashes and stews. Mama was incensed to have her meals run down, but I told Mama to listen to Miss Roux. Miss Roux had lived in the world and knew Southern cooking and all sorts of things. It was just the first of the arguments. But I have testified to all that."

Brawn let the rush of information go on. Then: "Your mother did not care for Miss Roux?"

"No."

"You say because she criticized the cooking?"

"Yes. And the decorations."

"And not for other reasons?"

"I don't know what you mean."

"Well, that your mother thought you were spending too much time with Miss Roux?"

"I don't know that I did."

"Did you visit her at Mrs. Olafson's?"

"Yes."

"How many hours a day?"

"I don't know."

"Would you say that you would daily visit Miss Roux from between seven in the morning and ten at night? Almost every day in the week?"

"Well, not solidly, because I helped in the house. Mama was trying to make a servant out of me. I didn't care for that. If my brothers could have careers, why not me?"

Brawn looked informed. "What sort of career was contemplated?"

"We had not yet decided," the girl said. "What's your next question?"

"Ah, yes! My next question?" Brawn murmured. "Well,

there came a time when you stayed the night with Miss Roux without letting your mother know in advance?"

"Yes."

"How old were you then?"

"Sixteen."

"Wasn't that extraordinary behavior?"

"I don't know that."

"You were still going to school?"

"Yes."

"And you neglected your homework?"

"Just geography. It was only state capitals."

"State capitals are not very important, I agree. But why did you call on Miss Roux?"

"Because Mama was saying insufferable things."

"Because of this association with Miss Roux?"

The girl paused. "Because of what she had heard from the boarders, especially Mr. O'Mara. Mr. O'Mara keeps the Gun Hill Cemetery and he picks up all kinds of gossip. He was talking about Miss Roux and Mama commanded me not to see her. I asked why and I was told. That's when I called on her because I was so incensed that she would demean and debase herself for a mere man. She said she had no interest in men. But I have testified to that."

"So you have," Brawn agreed, standing on tiptoes. "Did Mr. O'Mara tell you anything else not pleasant about Miss Roux?"

The girl frowned. "Such as what?" she asked, puzzled.

Brawn stared at the girl. "You don't know?"

"No."

"Then never mind. In any case," he went on, "Miss Roux told you, I think you said, that she was married to Mr. Hagerman. Were you satisfied with her explanation?"

"I was not," Nellie retorted. "I told her very decidedly that I would not want to be married like that. So then she told me how she and Mr. Hagerman had come to make the marriage contract and—"

"I didn't ask for all that," Brawn said.

"Well, you just got it," Nellie replied pertly. There was laughter, but the lawyer seemed not perturbed. A significant look of skepticism went to the reporters. He turned back to the witness, rocking on his toes. "But actually Miss Roux did not show you the marriage contract at that time?"

"No, but I saw it," the girl said.

"Saw it? How? Where was it?"

"In her bosom."

Brawn stood back. "Her bosom? How could you see it there?"

"She showed it to me."

"Showed it? How?"

The girl looked irritated. "How d'you suppose? The usual way."

"Did she take it out?"

"No."

"You just peered into that mystic region and saw a piece of paper?"

"Yes."

"Then how could you know what it was?"

"She told me," the girl retorted, exasperated. "And when Mrs. Lawes came to discuss the furnishings, she verified Mr. Hagerman's handwriting in my presence. I think that should establish it."

Brawn glanced at the clock. "You say it was verified by Mrs. Lawes? This charming lady now whispering to Miss Roux in a shell-like ear—?"

Throughout the proceedings, Malvinia, seated behind Jessica, had leaned forward with a running commentary on the progress of the case. At the question she sat back with a hard stare. The girl nodded. "But I later verified the signature myself," she added.

Brawn affected astonishment. "You? How? Did you compare it with a genuine signature?"

"How else is it done?"

"How indeed?" Brawn meditated. "But then you'd need a genuine signature. Where'd you get the sample?"

"Where'd you think? When Miss Roux got a check from Mr. Hagerman for two hundred dollars, I looked under a glass, and it was just too plain for words. I knew the check was the real thing because I had it certified by Mr. Smith, who's listening right here." All eyes turned to a handsome silver-haired man. The frosty eyes stared at the girl with indifference. "You call Mr. Smith and ask him under oath and he'll not deny that he certified that check," the girl said in triumph.

"Strike that," McArdle said. "Sorry, Mr. Smith. Mr. Brawn? Will you be on this much longer?"

"Not too much." Brawn strolled forward, now more wari-

231

ly. "But to get back to that first delectable glimpse in Ellis Street," he said carefully, "it could have been any piece of paper?"

"Why would she keep any piece of paper in her bosom? It was the marriage contract."

"How can you be sure?"

"Miss Roux has only got one bosom."

"Can we get away from Miss Roux's bosom?" the judge asked and looked surprised and gratified at the laughter.

Brawn bowed and smiled pleasantly and returned to the attack. "Very well. You stayed the night? And did what?"

"We talked."

"Talked about what?"

"Different subjects. Things girls talk about."

"Did you talk about men?"

The girl made a sour face. "There are more pleasant topics than men, I'm sure."

"Surely you could not always omit men?"

"Well, no, but only when unavoidable. She needed someone to confide in."

"Why you? When you were so young?"

"Miss Roux was bursting to talk, and I was glad to listen. I had no idea such things went on and she was telling me about Beaufort and all the people at the Purdue—she made many friends at that establishment—and at the other hotels. Some people live only glittering hotel lives, you know. But I s'pose that's not relevant and if I go on you'll object, won't you?"

"I had thought of that," Brawn agreed.

"Well, then, let's go back. Oh, yes. So I advised Miss Roux to stick to her rights and make Mr. Hagerman put her right with society, and before I knew it was too late to go home. So she showed me how to make a cheese rabbit and we went to bed. She's a very good cook."

"I'm sure she's good at many things," Brawn agreed. "Tell us, Miss Nellie," he went on casually, "what sort of bed was that at Mrs. Olafson's?"

"A double bed," Nellie said.

"Was it comfortable?"

"Comfortable enough."

"More than your own at home?"

"Yes," Nellie said. "Mrs. Olafson has goose down and my

own mattress was cotton batting. Any other particulars, mister?"

A titter went about. "No, no," Brawn said pleasantly, "though I'm delighted with domestic details. Are you still using a double bed at Wisteria Place?"

"Of course," the girl said. "Why not?"

"No reason I know of," Brawn said, caressing his neck. "But is there any reason not to have two beds?"

"It's a small house," Nellie replied slowly, "and it came with the furnishings. I don't see what difference it makes."

"Perhaps none," Brawn agreed. "But tell the Court: What happens when you go to bed?"

"What happens how?"

"I have no idea. You tell me."

Nellie frowned. "Well, we talk a lot, and tell jokes and giggle or confide secrets. Sometimes we read. What d'ye suppose happens?"

Brawn folded his arms and stared in a now silent courtroom. "Do you kiss each other good-night?" he asked.

"Not usually," the girl replied. "But sometimes, naturally. What else d'ye want to know? Do I brush my teeth? Mary, Joseph! Where's this getting us? Oh, yes!" she said suddenly. "There's something I forgot."

"What?"

"Sometimes we tell ghost stories. Is anything else on your mind?"

The judge leaned over. "Mr. Brawn, I cannot see where this is going."

"I'm not too sure myself," Brawn replied. "Let's go to other things," he said, noting Trumbull's sardonic smile of derision. He shuffled through notes and reviewed the girl's earlier direct testimony. Green leaned over and cupped his hand. "What d'ye think, Judge?" Trumbull frowned and shook his head. "Can't say," he murmured slowly. "Silly feller's just reinforcing her story. What's he really after?"

"What's that? What's that?" Finch demanded in an undertone. Green conveyed the thought. "Brawn's a fool!" Finch said emphatically. "A mincing, dancing fool! That's the entire explanation."

In wearisome detail Brawn retraced the turmoil in Ellis Street, the move to Wisteria Place, the various excursions to the bank in the two years that followed. As to Hagerman,

233

Nellie had despised the man from the moment of her first visit with Miss Roux to get money.

Brawn folded his arms. "Tell us about that."

"Again?" the girl said exhaustedly.

"If you don't mind," Brawn said. "We have all the time in the world."

It was the story heard in Wisteria Place, Trumbull thought, almost verbatim.

Counsel clustered at the bench. "How much longer with this girl?" McArdle asked. Brawn carelessly thought cross-examination would soon conclude. "Oh, good." The judge sighed. "Wouldn't like to go too long with this girl. Dirty situation. Mr. Brawn?" He lowered his voice. "Can you get me two tickets for Madame Patti's concert? I'll pay, of course." "No trouble," Brawn said heartily. "Madame Patti has asked for tickets to attend this trial." "Fair exchange," McArdle chuckled. "Gentlemen, can we hope to finish before the summer recess?" Counsel could not estimate time. So vast a trial could easily take months—summations alone would need weeks to prepare. The lawyers returned to their places, smiling. The room buzzed. What was that all about?

Fanny struggled through the barriers in the recess and pressed down the aisle. She spotted a thatch of silver. "Am I late?" she asked breathlessly, plumping beside her grandfather.

"Oh, not too much, my dear," Smith said, smiling at his handsome granddaughter. "That child has been attributing the most dashing things to Mr. Hagerman but I cannot say he's pleased. Now I've been included," he added ruefully.

"You, Gramps?"

Smith summarized his role in the testimony, remarking that he was somehow in the spiderweb of scandal. Fanny was amused. "My word! Did that actually happen to you?"

"Certainly I caused a check to be certified," Smith replied, "and those women were a nuisance at the office; but I never saw that alleged marriage contract, if that's your question."

Fanny smiled fondly, catching a subtle reproof. "Well, Gramps, I won't pump," she said. "Excuse me now?" She went forward, nodding to a dozen acquaintances. The mood was almost festive. She found a seat among the press. "Dolf, darling," she whispered. "Was there anything significant?"

"Just rehashing," Lang yawned.

"Dolf, this is funny," Wickwire said.

A snigger was attracting attention. Copies of a magazine were passing from hand to hand. "Here, let's see that," Fanny said. Wickwire handed over the *Hornet*. She studied the colorful lithographed cover and laughed softly. On it was a savage caricature entitled: "A Delectable Family Resort." The central court of Imperial House with its tiers of balconies was shown in bright colors as something between a Turkish seraglio and a French bordeloo. Pimps, toughs, prizefighters, houris looked down at the center of attention— turbaned Sultan Hagerman, narghile in mouth, reclining at lecherous ease on a mound of pillows, fondling an amorous odalisque—Jessie in breastplates, stroking the monarch's cheek. From an upper tier a Satanic Galindez dangled a naked trull. Lady Emily in hunting garb centered in the background. A pug-nosed McArdle presided. Finch and Brawn simpered in a minuet. A tall, coal-black Malvinia brandished a cat-o'-nine-tails, holding in triumph a sack with a dollar sign. In the wings, wrapped in villainous black cloat and slouch hat, an epicene Trumbull clutched a law book, beard bristling, eyes aflame with fanaticism.

Fanny smiled. "Senator Hagerman'll have your head, Dolf."

"I doubt it. He's taking bows," Lang said.

The chamber went silent. Trumbull filled the doorway as he entered. He sat at the counsel table, planted foursquare over a transcript.

"My word," Fanny breathed. "And what was Trumbull's comment?"

"Just laughed," Lang said. "He said fortunately it was meant in fun and no one'd take him for a capon—but I'm not sure he liked it."

"One day you'll get shot. Or kicked," Fanny said.

The court officers were walking the aisles and urging people to find seats. The court was coming back to order. Hagerman and his lawyers sat with stony faces. It was a corvine scene, she thought. Got to catch up, she decided. She borrowed Lang's notes and scanned rapidly. "Nellie seems to've done well," she remarked, turning pages.

"Just the first slap and tickle," Lang replied. "She's too pert. Don't underestimate Brawn. He's just begun."

A small disturbance marked the return of Finch. Scowling, he skirted the Hagerman camp, smirked at the press, and slumped into his post of command. "Judge Trumbull," he said discontentedly, "the bitch is impossible."

"Oh? What now?"

"She's giving me a dreadful time," Finch said, rubbing his eyes. "I knew it was a mistake to lend the creature my Blackstone, and she's only half through Prerogatives of the Sovereign. Tried to forbid me to recall that slut Nellie for cross-examination. Will you please talk firmly to her? She's still stuck on you, and I'd like it kept so."

"Stuck on me? What the hell does that mean?"

"Oh, please, Judge Trumbull, save that for the court! We've all gone through this. I was Christ Returned to Earth. Now I'm Judas hawking fake pieces of silver. She's done with me. Done with Natty. But not with Saint Mark. I'd be obliged if you'd service her and the case together because"—he studied a timepiece—"I give this mood of trust and faith in you exactly one month. Pray do not be absent again. She has been in an incredible rage of disappointment."

"Has she now?" Trumbull said angrily. "What's keeping Mr. Green?"

"Talking still to the other draggle-tail," Finch said glumly. "God knows what's coming out of those creatures. I don't!" He lapsed into scowling contemplation of the wall.

Jessica entered and sat apart. Fanny felt a pang. Jessica was alone, looking tranquil enough but sad; somewhat pensive, she thought—and, well, isolated. Fanny went to the rail. "Hello, Jess," she said in a friendly voice.

Jessica turned. "Fanny Smith!" she said, forcing a bright smile. "I'm so glad you decided to speak to the pariah. I was afraid you wouldn't."

"Pariah? Don't be a fool." Fanny smiled. "I didn't want to break in. We don't all think like that."

"Oh, truly?" Jessica said pleasantly. "I wouldn't think so from your articles."

"Oh?"

"Well, they're not too unfair," Jessica conceded, dabbing her mouth, "but you shouldn't make fun of my witnesses. Still, I suppose you write what you're told to write. I'd rather have satire than the hateful libels the rest are printing." A hard glance encompassed the press, fixed Lang, then Wickwire with resentment. "Just remember, Fanny, that this disgrace was forced upon me. If you make that point, it's all I ask. But I think *you're* being brave," she said quickly. "My husband's staring daggers."

And indeed Hagerman's black scowl was unpleasant. Fanny wondered whether old friends could not have tea one day. She went back to her place. All this was followed without pleasure by her colleagues.

Jessica sat with folded hands in a studied pose. She was still in an angry mood. Trumbull had his back to the woman, but he felt her presence: her rage, bitterness; and a glacial misery seeped through his shoulders. He was infected with that mood.

"Judge Trumbull?" Jessica whispered. It was an overture. "Yes?" he said ungraciously. "You ought to've been out with us last night to Romeo's," she whispered. "The clam sauce was out of this world."

Trumbull turned full about. "Glad to hear it," he grunted with some astonishment. He felt a light pat on the wrist. "Oh, *you!* You need a haircut," Jessica said with a quick light laugh and popped a lozenge into her mouth. Trumbull stared at Finch and turned back to the transcript.

"Now on the next visit Mr. Hagerman made a very important admission," Nellie went on. "That was six weeks later. I can give that date. It was Tuesday, June fourteenth. I stayed over that night because Miss Roux was in a state of nerves and talking how life was not worth living. I told her that no man was worth that misery, but then she revealed that she was in a condition . . ." The girl paused and went on resolutely to describe a moment of anguish.

"She didn't know what to do," the girl resumed. "She appealed to know if she should go east or talk to someone like Mrs. Lawes who knows about these things. She seemed absolutely incapable to decide. So I marched to the bank. I told Mr. Hagerman that his wife thought she was in a delicate state of health. That's how I put it. Flat out. His wife, I said. He gave me a funny twinkling look of disbelief." She paused. "He's got that look right now."

The whole courtroom looked at Hagerman. Whatever look was described, it vanished.

"Mr. Hagerman said he was an old hand at the game, and who did she suspect? I couldn't believe my ears. He had this vulgar laugh. I said, 'She don't suspect anybody, Senator. She knows it's you, and so do I.' Imagine! I gave him a piece of my mind, and then he tried to placate me. He said he would believe the miracle when it became actual, for if I was right it had happened only once before in history. You'd think she was I-don't-know-what!" The girl sat forward, quivering with indignation.

"And was she in a delicate condition?" Brawn asked sympathetically.

"No."

"She forgot the calendar?" Brawn said with the understanding. "Well, we all do at times," he agreed, "especially the motion calendar." Lawyers laughed and every man and woman counted off the weeks. "Then how could you be so sure of the fatherhood?" he asked gently.

The girl started to answer, then stopped. "I mean, it could only be the Senator's fault, if true."

"Ah! Why so?"

The girl went round-eyed. "Why? Because Miss Roux was his wife," she said naïvely. "So who else's could it be?" An innocent look of triumph went to the judge who swiveled a full turn. In any case, the girl went on, she could swear on oath that Miss Roux had had lawful relations since their acquaintance with Senator Hagerman alone.

"You know that?" Brawn said.

"Yes."

"How can you know?"

"I just do."

"You seem to know a lot for a mere girl."

"Mere girls know more than you think."

"Perhaps so," Brawn agreed, "but in what school are these lessons learned?" He folded his arms. "Miss Nellie, have you any feeling for your mother?"

"Of course I have, but she's limited."

Brawn agreed that this was a common fault of parents. "Limited or not," he said, "she objected to your intimacy with Miss Roux?"

"I guess so."

"Why, miss! Isn't it a fact that after your last disturbance you let her follow you and Miss Roux from this courthouse to Wisteria Place? Begging and pleading with you to return home and abandon this scandalous lawsuit?"

"And made herself a disgrace!" the girl retorted angrily.

"Berating every inch of the way! Screaming in the streets! Sure, that happened."

"How did Miss Roux reply?"

"What d'ye expect? Not too nice. But Mama wasn't too nice either. Just stuff and lies for the newspapers to carry. No wonder she's losing boarders. She's going off her chump," the girl said vengefully.

"What did she say that wasn't nice?"

"She said we had an untarnished name and I ought not drag it down like a little you-know! That's what she called me, my own mother. Mary!" The girl choked. All Wisteria Place had witnessed the scene. Reporters had caught the episode and the world knew the turmoil in the family. "She promised me money and a trip to Europe to stay out of the case. But I told her no, not for all the tea in China! And where was it coming from? Mr. Hagerman? I couldn't see why she was down on me because I told the truth. And that's all I'm doing, mister!" She raised her hand in oath. "It's not fair!" she burst out, glaring at Hagerman. "Just because he can bribe them don't mean he can bribe me."

"Can't someone stop this?" Hagerman said aloud.

Finch arose wearily and wondered at the line of questioning.

"Yes, Mr. Brawn?" the judge agreed.

"I'm questioning as to bias," Brawn replied. "I am trying to show that the witness has kept up this relationship against her parents' wishes, that she has broken away from her home and every barrier of protection that surrounded her as a child, that this woman's influence is unnatural—so much so that the witness is under her control. She has been kept prisoner and not allowed to see her father or mother except in the presence of counsel. I am trying to show—"

A storm of objections broke into the flow. Finch was up and howling. Trumbull turned to Jessica in surprise. Imprisonment? What had gone on in his absence? "Ma'am?" he said dangerously. "Were the parents kept from their daughter?"

"It was my idea," she whispered, taken aback. "I feared those people'd tamper with her. She's vital to my case. Please understand."

Her eyes were inches from his—urgent and intense.

"We'll talk later," Trumbull said shortly.

"Will counsel come forward?"

239

McArdle faced the angered circle of faces. "Just what kind of 'unnatural' are you driving at, Mr. Brawn?"

Brawn looked gelid. "Oh, I'd rather not run ahead of the proof," he said with a grin. "I'm suggesting only that it's unnatural for a young girl not to obey her parents."

"Well, all right," the judge said sternly, "but she's a nice Irish girl from what I see, and I don't want her abused, d'ye hear? Go on."

Brawn contemplated the girl and returned to Ellis Street. The roster of guests was established. "Now, Miss Nellie, can it be that you refused your mother's so-called bribe because you were tempted by a better offer from another source?"

"Tempted?"

"Didn't you recently tell Mrs. Spencer that you expected ten thousand dollars from Miss Roux if she won this case?"

The girl's face was pure astonishment. "Me? I never! You're making it up. I wouldn't expect a penny. Mrs. Spencer's off her chump."

Brawn walked about the courtroom, scuffing thoughtfully. "Is everybody off his chump but you and Miss Roux and Mrs. Lawes?"

The girl stared at the lawyer. "Oh, no," she replied with a grin. "People are like lawyers—some are, some ain't. I wouldn't specify."

Every lawyer in the chamber felt a pang of sympathy. Brawn smirked painfully. "Well, didn't you tell Mr. O'Mara that nothing, not even damage to your reputation, would stop you from testifying for Miss Roux, even though you found the notoriety unpleasant for a girl your age?"

A burning look of scorn stabbed out. "I never said that. I know you're trying to show I'm partial to Miss Roux. Well, I am, but that's because she's in the right. I'm under oath and you're not—so of course you can insinuate anything you please."

"But you agree that the notoriety is unpleasant?"

"Yes," the girl said, "but I cannot help that. Or what they're writing about me in the papers. It just shows that writers have dirty minds."

The writers in the chamber looked gratified.

"So they have, poor souls," Brawn said philosophically, "fortunately for literature. So much for that." Then, abruptly: "Have you ever visited a house at 290 Pacific Street?"

The girl's mouth dropped. "Wha-at?" The question was re-

240

peated by the stenographer. The girl bounced about. "I've never been to that kind of place!" she cried, aghast and furious. "I never have, and you know it. What a dirty thing to say."

Clamor from Finch. More from Jessica. Order! Silence! The gavel banged a warning against demonstrations. Brawn rode through the storm. "And you've never visited that or any house on Pacific Street?"

"No!"

"Objection!"

"Sustained!" the judge said severely. "Mr. Brawn, you will drop that line of questioning. Now go on and keep within the bounds of decency."

Brawn took a confidential stand. "Your Honor misunderstands," he said suavely. "I am not now trying to degrade the witness through these questions. I am trying to show the opposite—that the witness is too young, too inexperienced to have been employed—as she now claims—by a married woman as go-between on nasty errands of vice and lucre. That's all I mean by this line of questions."

"Get on," the judge said angrily.

"What's he talking about?" the girl asked.

"Let's get back to Pacific Street," Brawn said, holding up a hand. "Does the name of Lightfoot ring a bell? Mrs. Mary Lightfoot? Or the term Dragon's Blood?"

Comprehension dawned. "Oh, that!" The girl sighed with relief. "What about it? Why didn't you say that in the first place?"

"What is Dragon's Blood?"

"It uncrosses you in love."

"What does that mean?"

"If you've been crossed in love," the girl said simply, "it uncrosses you. Mary! That's not hard. It's made from dragon's blood. That's why it's called Dragon's Blood. It comes from mysterious Cathay. Mrs. Lightfoot sells all kinds of things."

"Now, in fact you've been to Mrs. Lightfoot's shop in Pacific Street with Miss Roux?"

A long pause. "Well, yes," the girl said reluctantly.

Brawn relaxed imperceptibly. "Because Miss Roux was crossed in love?"

"What else would you call it?" the girl cried. "She's had the biggest cross to carry since Jesus." The witness was ad-

241

monished against irreverence. Brawn was imperturbable and sunny. "Now, miss," he went on easily, "did you not hear Miss Roux tell Mrs. Lightfoot that she needed Dragon's Blood to get an old man to the marriage altar?"

"That's a lie," Nellie cried. "She said nothing of the sort." Only after most persistent questioning would she admit that Miss Roux indeed had some, not much, faith in the occult. "Lots of ladies in San Francisco have," she snapped. "So what does it prove?"

"Yes, Mr. Brawn," the judge said. "I don't see the relevance."

"Nor do I," Brawn said drily, "but I sense it. Miss Nellie," he went on, turning over his notes, "did you visit other tellers and sellers of fortunes and charms with Miss Roux?" A nod. "How many?"

"I don't know."

Finch was up. "Really, Your Honor," he complained wearily. "What is this all about?"

"Yes, Mr. Brawn?" the judge said.

Brawn said innocently, "We intend to show that after Miss Roux was barred from the Camden Hotel, she began to seek out the occult to get help. It will show that she did not then believe she was married—nor had in her possession a marriage contract, forged or otherwise, on which to make this claim—"

"That's not so," Jessica called out, clenching her fists.

"Hush!" Finch said harshly.

"Yes, madam," the judge said severely. "You'll have your turn. Mr. Brawn, will you produce those fortune tellers?"

"Most assuredly." Brawn bowed.

Jessica cupped a gloved hand and leaned over. "Judge Trumbull?" A fresh strong scent filled his nostrils and he felt her warmth. Suddenly in all the tedium his heart stopped a beat. Her face was close and the clear skin, covered with scented powder, was marred only by a black spot on the delicate mouth. "He's getting that girl to exaggerate," she whispered urgently. "Best thing is to let all this alone," he said. "But Mr. Finch is letting too many things alone," she said vehemently. "Later," he repeated, conscious of others following the byplay.

A dozen questions established that Mrs. Lightfoot had sold Miss Roux and Miss Driscoll three ounces of Dragon's Blood with a manual of instructions. When were those instructions followed?"

"The next Christmas," Nellie said reluctantly. "It was sprinkled around in Mr. Hagerman's apartment."

"Sprinkled on what? Just how did the conjure work?"

"It was sprinkled in the four corners, that's what. But it was just a charm. You're making too much out of it."

"But if she was then married to the defendant, as you claim, what was the purpose?"

Nellie stared with pity. "If you were crossed in love, mister, wouldn't you make an effort?"

"I've never been crossed in love," Brawn said sunnily, "but I'll study that." The laughter brought a gavel.

"Charms are nothing," the girl said.

The judge intervened. "In that case, why use 'em?"

The girl turned about, thinking deeply. "Well, it seemed to give Miss Roux comfort," she said honestly, "because when she felt helpless it was something to do. And how could it hurt? Li was there. He let us in."

"Ah?" Brawn said. "Bribed?"

"Of course not," the witness said, wrinkling her nose and starting to laugh like any other young girl as she described a ridiculous scene. The fact was that she had got Li into a game of cards, she said, to divert his attention while Miss Roux sprinkled powder. "What-you-doing? What-you-doing?" Li had complained, Chinese style. "Play, Li! Play, Li!" Miss Roux had commanded, sprinkling. It was a comical imitation and the court, including counsel, were smiling. And all the time, Nellie giggled, poor Li had protested querulously: "What-you doing? What-you-doing?"

Brawn waited for the laughter to die. He ticked off the special occasions when the pair had visited Hagerman's apartment surreptitiously.

"Surreptitiously? What's that mean?"

"Like a sneak," Brawn supplied.

The girl hesitated. "We visited Mr. Hagerman constantly," she said slowly. "I'm not sure how you're counting."

Brawn stared peculiarly. He mopped his neck, then wheeled. "You claim to *know* that Miss Roux was a married woman?"

"Yes, and I have so testified on oath."

"May I again have Exhibit 23?" Brawn said.

He held up Jessica's letter of May 20. "Doesn't Miss Roux

state here that only she and Mr. Hagerman knew she was his wife? Isn't that what it says?"

"Ye-es."

Brawn turned about with satisfaction. "So Miss Roux admits in writing that no third party—you, for example—could possibly know that she was Mr. Hagerman's wife? Aren't those her written words?"

Trumbull's pose was somnolence, but every intonation was followed with exquisite care. He looked up and met Finch's jocular wink. The girl nodded slowly.

"Good."

Brawn took up the beat. "Now, Miss Nellie," he resumed amiably, "apart from this lawsuit, what are your feelings for Mr. Hagerman?"

"Feelings?" The girl made a sour face. A titter arose and died.

"Do you not hate him?"

"Hate?" The girl hesitated. "No I wouldn't say I hate him. It's Miss Roux's business, not mine. I have sworn an oath and that's all."

"Good answer," a female voice said.

Brawn evidently thought so. He nodded with gratification. "Then if anyone were to suggest that you ever expressed strong partisan—almost fanatical feelings against Mr. Hagerman—feelings so strong that you'd stop at nothing to cause his downfall—would he be wrong?"

"Yes, wrong!" she said firmly. "I have nothing against Senator Hagerman as an individual. I just feel sorry for him."

Pure scorn was registered. "Were those your feelings when you brought him the May twentieth letter? Or were you not there even then to contrive evidence against him?"

"My feelings have always been kindly," she retorted, "until he forced this disgrace upon Miss Roux. That's what made me change. It's because I know he's doing a job on her, and if you ask me how I come to know I'll tell you more than you like."

Brawn seemed struck with the retort. "Ah?" he said, recoiling. "Hm." He handed up a letter. "Is that your handwriting?" he asked softly.

"May we see that first?" Finch demanded.

"She may answer," McArdle ruled.

A burning glance went to Jessica. "Well, I see he kept that

244

letter, the villain," the girl said with vindictive triumph. "I said he would. Yes, it's mine!"

"Show it to counsel."

The letter passed from lawyer to lawyer. "One moment, Your Honor," Finch begged. Trumbull turned to Finch and Green and put questions which drew low, inaudible replies. Jessica entered the conference. Malvinia leaned over and there were hurried whispers.

Lang nudged Fanny. The moments were drawing out. Finch ambled forward with an air of contempt. "No objection," he said scornfully, handing the letter to the clerk, and returned to his seat, looking wrathful indeed.

"You still say your feelings were kindly?" Brawn said with menace.

"Answer the question," the judge said.

Nellie was staring at Jessica. "Well, now I shall tell all," she said vengefully. "That was written last July, when everything blew up. Everything was going bad for her—money, people whispering and ostracizing, and she was so lonely and brave. The Senator kept making and breaking all sorts of promises, teasing and joking and never a straight word out of him. Then it was her birthday. So she sent me with a note to ask him just for once not to mind the family and have a pleasant dinner with her. She had the blues, she wrote, she was so discouraged, and would he be the same kind and sweet Senator he always was? I thought she was too abject, but she said No, she knew Mr. Hagerman. He could be awful nice if approached right, and maybe I could effect a reconciliation. I took the note against my better judgment.

"So Mr. Hagerman asked my advice. I said, 'Well, Senator, she's your wife, but she's only human, and I'd advise respect and courtesy.' So he said, 'Fine, Miss Driscoll, let her come, and tell her I'll have a good bottle of wine and it'll be like old times.' I was pleased on her account because I thought at last the old man would set things right. I helped her bathe and dress in this pale-green dress with shamrocks and a simple blue bonnet with an egret feather we'd made. I wore—"

"Miss Nellie," the judge said.

"Sorry, Judge. Mr. Delaney came along," the girl went on, "to make sure that Miss Roux'd not be stood up, for that'd been known to happen. If so, the plan was to dine out and not waste the evening."

"Then what happened?" Brawn asked.

"Well, we came to the fourth floor," the girl went on. "Me and Mr. Delaney stood out of sight while she knocked. There was no answer, and while she was asking one of the help for pencil and paper, a hotel detective named Norris came and asked Miss Roux what the deuce she was doing there. Only he said something stronger than that. Miss Roux said she'd come to see Mr. Hagerman, and we'd wait below.

"The man said No, she'd not, and orders were to put her out.

"Miss Roux said if Mr. Hagerman wished her that treatment, let him tell her that himself. She was in tears, she was that upset. Mr. Delaney was cowering and she was disgusted, but that comes later in the story, shall we say.

"Then this Norris said he didn't claim Mr. Hagerman gave those orders himself, but it was somebody else; only if she said he told her that, he'd deny it. He said she had got to go, because it meant his job. And he gave her a shove. It's lucky Mr. Delaney was clinging to me or I'd have gone for the man's eyes.

"Then there was talk about getting us arrested. Miss Roux defied the man and asked what he'd do if we just sat on the floor and screamed bloody murder. But then she relented and said in a kindly way that the poor detective was only there to execute orders and had a wife and kids, and to go home. The man nevertheless pushed and cursed to show his powers. I got hysterical, I guess, and got dragged through the lobby. The next day I wrote that letter," she concluded indignantly. "I didn't mention it before only to protect Mr. Hagerman from the effects of his own vulgar, cruel behavior. Your Honor," she said, turning about, "I offer this letter in evidence."

There was amusement.

"No, no, Miss Nellie," Brawn said gently, "not you. I have that honor."

"As you like," Nellie said haughtily. "I was trying to save time."

"Mark it," the judge said.

Brawn took the letter, gazed at the press, who had been provided with copies, and read with dramatic emphasis.

Wisteria Place

Old Hagerman:

When I first met you I felt honored to think I had on

246

my list of acquaintances a United States Senator, but today I feel it a double disgrace to know you. If you are a specimen of our rulers, then I pity America, for a bigger coward or upstart never existed in my opinion. I was present with the lady who called on you, and to think your conscience would not let you see her in person to excuse yourself, but you must blame others and send hirelings to do your dirty work.

I hope God will punish you with the deepest kind of sorrow and make your old heart ache and your old head bend. You did her a mean dirty trick. You tried to disgrace a motherless, fatherless girl, because you knew she leaned on you and was alone in the world. Instead of holding her up in the world, you've tried every way you can to disgrace her. It is well I am not her or I'd advertise you from one end of the world to the other. But she's so much a lady that she tamely submits to your insults. You're not good enough for me to wipe my shoes on, much less her.

If you knew how insignificant you looked today at the bank, although I, a poor girl, and you could ride in your carriage, I feel so much above you that I asked Mr. Smith to take in my message rather than come in contact with yourself.

The insult you sent back by Mr. Smith was so farcical that I had to laugh in Mr. Smith's face and ask, "Don't you think that man's crazy?" I am a poor girl, but I feel so much better than you. I'll do anything in my power to bring you to justice—you horrible, horrible man.

                                              Miss Driscoll

The reading came to an end in shocked silence. Finch, who had been up and down a dozen times with vain objections, settled for an expression of contempt and disdain.

" '. . . I'll do anything in my power to bring Mr. Hagerman to justice?' " Brawn repeated heavily, quoting. "Would that include telling lies at Miss Roux's request?"

"It don't take lies," the girl said thickly. "Just truth."

Brawn strolled forward frowning at the document. "You call Miss Roux 'a fatherless, motherless girl'? Is that how one describes a married woman?"

"Yes," the girl said strongly, stung. "Because at that time

247

every lawyer was telling Miss Roux her marriage contract was not worth excelsior! They were telling her it was not legal in California. Mr. Galindez was saying it. Mr. Mac-Gowan repeated it. Others advised her to pack up and leave the state. Nobody gave her a Chinaman's chance to make it stick. So if I too was under that impression—"

"Even so—" Brawn interposed.

"Let her talk!" Finch shouted.

"Mr. Hagerman has got the money," the girl went on excitedly. "He buys everybody and everything. She felt it was hopeless until Mr. Finch told her that if Mr. Hagerman thought to trick her into submitting to him when she really loathed that disgusting old man, the law too had a few tricks and he would learn something about solemn legal instruments under seal, and that's Judge Trumbull's opinion too." All eyes turned to Trumbull. "A fatherless, motherless girl? If she is cast out? Yes! If she is menaced and disgraced? Yes! If she cannot get justice? Yes! If she finds cowards and poltroons everywhere? Yes!"

The girl paused for breath. "But let me tell you, Mr. Brawn! That's why we're here! Everything Mrs. Lightfoot prophesied is coming to pass. His Honor has the last word. Not you with all your fancy handkerchiefs, and not, thank God, that cowardly old wretch! I'm not a lawyer," she shouted. "I'm only a girl, but I know what I heard and saw!

"Mrs. Lightfoot told Mrs. Hagerman that a secret document would reveal all, like the Star of Bethlehem. That one day she, who was down, would be lifted up! The Venus Line was so strong, like signs and wonders. You're so smart, but I heard the prophecy. If Mrs. Hagerman wasn't married, how would that woman know about the secret document? You can ask that woman yourself."

"Perhaps we shall," Brawn said dryly.

The girl turned to Hagerman, "Not too long ago, Senator, God took away your wife and older daughter. I don't generally wish people evil, but with all my heart I wish it now for every cruel trick you've played on her. Take care, Senator, that God does not bring you more grief, more misfortune. I hope He will."

Jessica was on her feet. "No, don't!" she cried with an appealing gesture. "Nellie, sweet, you mustn't!" "Order!" The gavel was banging. "Be seated." Lawyers crowded forward, snarling objections and arguments. "I can't get all this," the stenographer complained. "Order! Quiet!" The yammer went on. "Where's the justice? What about all her letters he stole? Why isn't he struck dead where he sits? Oh, my God!" the girl screamed hysterically. "How can this be happening to her? What kind of a country is this anyhow?"

Bang! "Silence!"

Suddenly there was quiet. The girl was shaking. "Coward! Scut! I hope you die!" she shouted and fell into convulsions of hysteria—laughter mixing with frantic weeping. She was taken off by a police matron.

"Gentlemen? Ten o'clock tomorrow morning," the judge said and fled, looking churned.

Finch glared at his client.

"Tonight, madam," he said venomously. "Be prompt and come without that piano tuner's mistake. Judge Trumbull, I'll expect you too. I'm most upset. I hold you accountable for being so soft with that slut. Natty, gather the papers," he commanded and left abruptly. "Darn those smelling salts," Jessica exclaimed, agitatedly, searching her reticule. "Oh, the poor child. How could he let this happen?"

"Oh, Jesus!" Trumbull muttered disconsolately. He looked forward to the council of war without pleasure.

Chapter Thirteen

Jessica was facing a black window of night. A few offices were lit, but the street was dark and vacant. "But I have tried to explain," she said. "I was trying to keep Nell out of the court. I did not want her to return. It was you who insisted."

"But once we started," Finch said, exasperated, "I explained that we could not keep her out."

"I know that!" she exclaimed in a temper. "I know that very well. You have explained it." She turned, clenching her fists. "Judge Trumbull, I regret her outburst in court. She promised faithfully to watch her temper, but she was baited. If Mr. Finch had protected her, this would not have happened."

Finch struggled for self-control. "Very well, it turned out

poorly with that girl," he agreed angrily, "but that's the chance you take." He turned to Trumbull. "Miss Roux was urgent to prove certain things—that letter, for example. How else could it be proved? I yielded to the needs of the case."

"We're making too much of this," Trumbull said. "Did you know about that berating letter the girl wrote?"

"Ask the client," Finch said bitterly.

Jessica interrupted. "Mr. Finch was not told."

"Why not?" Trumbull asked.

"Why? Because it was not necessary. I knew about Nell's letter," Jessica said, "and had aplogized for it myself to Mr. Hagerman. He was quite airy about it. He assured me it was a childish thing. He was charmed to see her loyalty to me and said falsely that it had been destroyed. That's why Mr. Finch was not told. It seemed not too important at the time."

"Not important? Who are you to say?" Finch retorted. "We begged for every scrap that ever passed. We spent endless hours prodding and reviewing. You know best the agonies we've suffered on your behalf."

"Oh, tshah!" she retorted. "Mr. Finch, you have not sought truth here at all," she said firmly, facing the bloodshot eyes. "So don't impute dishonesties when you yourself have spun webs of trickery and deceit about me. You don't want real truth. You want lawyer's truth—"

"Go on, go on," Finch said, baring his teeth. "Let's have the rest. Here it comes. Pay heed, Judge."

". . . and I'm not too sure how much you are in communication with the other side," she concluded.

Finch smashed his palm on the desk. "Madam," he said, "one more damned insinuation, and I'll break your neck." He strode aside, scarlet.

"Siddy," Trumbull said strongly, "come back. You're acting like a boy."

Jessica said, "Never mind, Judge Trumbull, I will not be provoked. Mr. Finch, I instructed you not to call Miss Driscoll to the stand."

Finch wheeled, incredulous. "What?"

Jessica retorted, "You'll not deny our conversation in this office Wednesday last? When I expressed my wish not to put the girl on the stand?"

Finch stood back a step. "Jesus!" he said simply, staring. "Natty? Did that happen?"

"I'm not sure," Green said.

Finch turned to Trumbull. "I'm on the moon. I marvel," he exclaimed, clasping his cheeks. "Natty? Is this woman so mesmeric you cannot recall 'twas I who urged not to call either the sissy boy or the little bitch? And this woman who insisted?"

Jessica said angrily, "This morning—in court I was against recalling Nell to the stand."

"This morning was too late!" Finch screamed.

"But I was against recalling her," Jessica repeated obstinately, "and I now again urge that she not go back tomorrow. She is resting now. I do not want her troubled any further—"

"Christ!" Finch yelled. "Bloody, bloody Christ! Can you not grasp that having started she must inexorably go back to finish or we face a damned mistrial? Is that what you want? I think you're feared—not for the slut but for yourself. You daren't face it. That's turned to water," he said with unbelievable coarseness, pointing to the woman's belly. "You're afeared, you damned bitch." He gasped and rushed off. It was a moment of embarrassment. Trumbull apologized for Finch, thinking the whole business most bizarre. "Oh, never mind that," Jessica said impatiently. "Words mean nothing."

"As you like," Trumbull said sorely. "Well, Natty, you see what this foul profession is about," he said ruefully. Green shrugged, wordless. Finch returned, pale and wiping his mouth, grudgingly apologetic but not retracting one word.

"I think we should listen to the client," Trumbull said, "and think more about the case. Let's discuss this tomorrow."

"No!" Jessica exclaimed, coming to a decision. "Judge Trumbull," she said with determination, "I want you to take over direction of this case."

"No objections," Finch said strongly, flinging himself aside. "Take over, Judge Trumbull. Pray do. I have been begging it for weeks. Saints! It's more than flesh and blood can endure."

"Confound this," Trumbull said. "Be quiet, both of you. Very well, Siddy, the girl flew into hysterics, but what did it prove? That she's partial to your client? It should be laughed out of court on summation. Natty, must we have these scenes?"

"Not my doing," Green said calmly.

Trumbull pointed the cigar. "Siddy, you're simply ridiculous. There's work to do. Natty, be seated. Ma'am, we'll get a medical excuse for the girl for a few days, so compose yourself. Now then, what's this all about?"

"I shall be calm," Finch told the portraits on the wall. He assumed a cajoling manner. "Look, Judge, I had a broad hint from Brawn during the recess, that they'd welcome an end to this. He thought his client might go to high figures plus, well, our counsel fees."

"Counsel fees!" Jessica exclaimed bitterly.

Finch ignored the interruption. ". . . but that was before the little slut made that display of herself. Now there's no assurance the door is still open. Why should it be?"

"Why wasn't I told about this offer?" Trumbull demanded.

Finch accepted a rebuke. "I was waiting for the right moment," he said sourly. "You've been taking a most obstinate line, Judge, quite absolute. I feared you'd shut things up out of hand."

"Did you think that indeed?"

"Natty will bear me out. Frankly, I've been puzzled, Judge. Your attitude. Don't get it at all. You seemed so blamed unperturbed today by that girl's lack of candor."

"I'm not concerned with minor points," Trumbull said, "but with the affirmative proof of our own case. What does one upset matter? What d'ye actually fear?"

"Thank God for this," Jessica exclaimed.

Finch grimaced. "I fear surprises yet to come."

Trumbull turned to the younger lawyer. "Natty?"

Green knocked an ash from his pipe. " 'Fraid I agree."

"Hm. Well, I'll recall all that eloquence when you first came to my office in Stoddard," Trumbull said. He turned to the angry woman. "Ma'am, I've tried to explain the position," he said in a hard voice. "This lawsuit is unlikely to turn on any one thing alone but on the total picture presented to the judge—the relationships, the probabilities. Nasty unclean hints have been coming out that color the picture. We're prepared for that. Hagerman's life lends itself to that, but it engulfs you. You were part of that life. You cannot escape it. That has no bearing on your legal rights, but we must not have surprises."

"I've no criminal record," she exclaimed, "if that's what you mean."

"Is there anything more we should know?" Trumbull was unmoved. "We must talk plain."

"No, no, and no!" She leaped up and paced. "It's a trick,"

she exclaimed in agitation. "Galindez put up this business. He's got no intention to let Mr. Hagerman concede one red cent. God! If I had my hands on him! Can't you see what they're doing?" She strode the room, seething, kicking at the carpet. "Settlement? Don't you believe it. It's merely to corrupt my advisers."

Green looked up. "Ma'am? Why d'you say things like that?"

"Because it's true," she shouted. "Mr. Finch can't see his finger before his face. It is not money or even the marriage. Mr. Hagerman is acting with dishonor. He wants to injure me. That is why he has this venom. And another thing," she added emphatically. "On Monday I will tell the world my story. That is what they fear—the voice of truth. Mr. Hagerman fears me. He knows I will be believed. He trembles at that. Since he cannot swerve me, he is seeking to reach my lawyers. Christ! Mr. Finch is calculating fees and to hell with Jessie Roux. Judge Trumbull, I am shocked that you countenance this man. I have a world of pride! Pride! Or have you forgotten?" She walked off, choking. After a moment, she turned. "Can't you see? This is just the wrong way to reach me and Mr. Hagerman knows it. He knows all my feelings. He knows that if he spoke right and gentle I'd melt. He could have anything he wants if only I'd get a kind word."

The men exchanged bored glances. Really there was no end to these surprises. "Galindez!" she said darkly. "Galindez! That's the one! If I could talk to Mr. Hagerman without Galindez it'd sure be another story. No, he'd never let it happen. Judge Trumbull, what d'you think? Should I try to settle with Mr. Hagerman? Mr. Finch shakes me so."

"Mr. Finch will stop shaking you," Trumbull said. "Sit down, ma'am."

She sank down. Trumbull drew up a chair and sat forward. "Nothing has changed the issues," he said firmly. "It is not merely your own case that's involved. It is the machinery of the entire fabric of the law. Now, Siddy," he said, "I'll speak for myself. I do not believe Hagerman will settle. There is only one path ahead—the path we started on. Unless they withdraw the defense and consent to judgment of the court, we must finish out the trial. I see no other way."

Finch groaned.

A cold wind from the Golden Gate brought a dank smell

of fishy things, hinting the endless fetch of the vast black seas of the Pacific.

"Let's walk," Jessica said. "I feel so darned stifled. It's such an infuriating business trying to recall, let alone explain, your life. D'ye mind walking?"

They strolled past dark office buildings and business houses. A light was shining in the Bank of California. A policeman's stick was hitting the pavement. Otherwise the financial district was as empty of life as a dead planet.

"I love to walk," she sighed, leaning toward him. "It's what I loved best back home—walking under the Missouri moon under a cold sky back at Cape Badeau." Evidently Cape Badeau was on her mind. The war had swirled about Cape Badeau—she remembered Fremont and fighting about the city's outskirts and outrages of the cowardly Northern forces. Really, he thought impatiently, all that was barely a memory; she was trying to establish a common basis and it was not necessary.

"Poor Judge Trumbull," she said smiling. "I shouldn't say these things. He's too dignified and I put him out. Well I'll try to be good," she went on lightly, taking his arm and clinging. The dark wet streets were a refreshment after the noisome office.

"I'm very troubled," she said.

"Oh? Why so?"

"I cannot truly say, but it sure seems that more than a trial is involved. What kind of a woman must I be to get into this scrape, and how does it look to people? You, for instance: What are you thinking?"

"Not thinking a thing."

"Sure enough that's something," she said disconsolately. "Judge Trumbull?"

"Ma'am?"

"I feel I can talk to you. Can I?"

"If you like," he agreed.

She sighed, leaning toward him. She recalled a studious boy who used to walk her home from socials, real tall with impossible notions about girls that made her want to shake him. She had scratched that boy's hand invitingly, she confided, and had leaned against him and sent him lines from Tennyson, and nothing had worked until one special night after a hayride.

"Were you fond of him?" seemed to be the question.

"No, not truly," she said. "I just wanted his scalp, I reckon." Trumbull smiled. "Why?"

"To know I could get it," she said. "Well, I did get it and a lot more besides. Maybe it was this other girl who'd put me up to it. Maybe not."

"Don't sound so dreadful," Trumbull remarked, amused. "Why d'ye want to tell me this?"

She glanced up. In the dark, the eyes deep in shadows within shadows seemed to be twinkling. "I feel I must," she said in a low voice. "I want you to understand. That's the trouble with this case. Finch doesn't understand anything. Nathaniel listens, but he's just a sweet boy. I need to feel reliance in great strength. Judge Trumbull, I think you have that strength. D'ye mind if I talk? Lands! I haven't talked to anyone like this in all my life." She went on recalling the uncertain times after her mother had died. She was beautiful as a girl, she had known that from the mirror, from the attention of boys and the comments of men, some kinds of comments she was not supposed to hear. But all that had had no satisfaction. She'd felt uneasy in a frantic search for an answer to something of disturbance, a feeling for which she had no name—just a kind of impatience and dissatisfaction with things.

Now that boy was one of many, she came back, who'd been her partner at church socials and picnics, a nice boy who had hand-holding privileges. His agitation at her touchings was amusing, she recalled; he'd been roused and allowed so far and no farther. There were other hardier, rougher fellows whom she'd rallied and sometimes fended off, and sometimes not, and teased at hayrides and theatricals, but it was that nice boy who kept coming back to mind. She recalled precisely that moment. It had been a cold night, she remembered. They had come to a parting moment under a drooping larch. The quiet was unbearable. "Oh, Jess, Jess," the boy had groaned, pushing his mouth toward her in desperation. She had kissed him with a girl's kiss only, more sister than anything, firm and quick; his nose had been warm and dry, she remembered thinking, and then her mouth had opened. That kiss had remained for all her life. "You aren't listening," she said, drawing away.

"Oh, yes, yes," Trumbull said, rousing himself. They had turned at Fremont Street. He was expected to say something. "Go on," he said abstractedly. After a suspicious glance, she went on. She wanted him to understand a point of realization in her life. The thing of it was that the boy had said that she had looked frightened.

"Frightened?"

She nodded. "And I was, but not of him, poor thing, but of myself. I was nestled inside his coat because of the cold." Her glance was troubled, hesitant, but the story was coming. "I pressed closer and then, well, he went off, you know? He had suddenly to excuse himself and he was so ashamed. I could've cursed myself for that shame. I read his thoughts: that it had to be an accident; that it was his fault; that maybe I didn't understand, but of course I did. I said, 'Who's frightened now?' It sounded like joking, but it wasn't joking. I have always said the first stupid thing that always pops out. I asked if I could help him, which sure made it worse." She forced a painful smile. "Well, what d'ye think of me now? Now that you know some things?"

He turned about and he could not to save his life understand the moment. Something was missing, he thought; there was a magpie intelligence, darting at her life's incidents, but at the center a shallowness of feeling. She was showing a surprising naïveté, an insensitivity or grossness, he could not say which, that made him uncomfortable. She drew away with an exclamation of distress. "I thought you said we could talk plain, and now you're offended. We're both living in the world, aren't we?"

"I'm not offended," he said. "Lordy, what's your concern? A boy that age is on hair trigger. Happens all over the nation, and you cannot except Missouri."

"It's not amusing," she said resentfully.

"Reckon not," he agreed.

They continued to stroll. The short flirting motions of her knees were kicking her skirts rhythmically. She went on. "The thing is, I didn't know why I did it. The boy meant nothing. I had coldly got him in that position on purpose and for no good reason. I had driven that boy to distraction. He was wild for me and I had shamed him, but he was no more to me than the kitchen pump. I felt so queer and guilt-stricken because I didn't have feelings of . . . of compassion, if that's the word. The fact is I have always had my mind on older men. It was a terrible feeling because suddenly as clear as anything I realized that I was heartless.

"It was terrifying to know that nothing in life could ever

change that in me. And to this day I have never loved any man. My heart has never been touched. No matter what I say, that remains the very truth." She went silent. In the passing lamplight her face was white, troubled. "The truth was that I did not care. I have never cared. Now why I did it all I will never know."

They had crossed to the Embarcadero and were facing the bay. Lights of shipping were riding the waters.

"You look so stern," she complained.

"I am really thinking of the case," he said.

She dropped his arm. "You haven't heard a word I said."

"I've many things on my mind. Now, look 'ee, ma'am," he said thoughtfully, "Finch is right. You've been making it damned hard."

"I get upset," she interrupted.

"Never mind that," he said. "You cannot afford to get upset. The court's judgment is your answer to the world. Can we not keep that in mind and leave out the atmospherics?"

She was breathing hard. "Well, I reckon you mean my good," she said in a strangled voice.

"I do not care about your good," he retorted precisely. "I mean to help you to get judgment. I am thinking of the evidence and you keep telling a life story. How does it relate to the lawsuit?"

"God! You too? I am concerned to be believed and understood. Finch is my lawyer and he will not understand me or how I came to this marriage. Now you seem to doubt me too." They walked in angry silence. The absurdity struck him. "Ma'am," he said. "After all my years at the law, what sort of notions of you d'ye think I've got?"

"What does that mean?"

"For one thing, that you're not seventeen."

"Nor are you," she retorted. "You don't care about me. I'm just a case, and that's all. You don't even believe I'm married. You think I'm a common woman. Isn't that so?"

Too stupid, he thought.

"Now, look 'ee," he said, grasping her arm, "you've been in the man's bed and he's had you, and there's no point in not facing it. The world's watching with a pretty clear idea of what that means. It's the piece of paper that gives it honor. I have nothing else in mind but that legal fact."

The wind had died and the air was comfortable. The rank harbor stench was refreshing.

"Forgive me?" she said timidly.

"Nothing to forgive," he said shortly. "You're in sore straits and striking out. I am being hard to bring you about. Nothing more."

They walked on. "Oh, my lands," she sighed. "I'm always like this. I get such a riding impatience and dissatisfaction. I don't always know why. I reckon my greatest fear now is you. I'm desperate afraid you may leave the case. Can I say something?"

He was silent.

"I cannot tell you how my heart leaped up when you entered the court today, I'd been so nervous about your absence—oh, I know, I know," she said hastily. "I'm not reproachful but explaining. Finch kept losing points, backing down, losing the ascendancy. This morning when you came late I was in a temper. But when I saw your face in that crowd, you looked so distinguished—all head and shoulders above those small people, with that look of authority and determination. . . . Oh, lands! It was like that first sight of you at Las Flores, standing in Malvinia's parlor, almost reaching the ceiling. I felt safe, reassured. If I did not feel that now, I'd stop here and lose myself in those waters."

"Ma'am," he said impatiently.

"I don't mean it," she said quickly, "but that's how I feel. You saw how Finch treats me. How he curses and reviles. It's you alone who gives me the strength of purpose. The feeling that you really do believe in me."

Trumbull halted. "Ma'am," he said, "I've tried to tell you that I believe you totally on the only thing that concerns me now—the legal issue of marriage. If not, I'd not lend myself to this business. So far as you're concerned, it don't matter what I think—only how I help your lawyers to advance your case."

"But there is some question? There is—isn't there?"

He felt most uncomfortable. "Well, there've been the broadest hints in court about you and that girl. D'ye know what Brawn's driving at?" To save his life he could not put the direct question.

"D'ye think I'm a dunce?" she said angrily. "Of course that's the dirty charge against me. D'ye wonder I'm fighting back?" She walked off, tight and frozen. He followed at a slower pace, angry and sore at himself for the damnable street quarrel. She was waiting under a street lamp.

"Judge Trumbull," she said with determination, "all sorts of stories are coming out. I get 'em all from Mrs. Lawes, and I'm not simple. Suppose they're true? Suppose Mr. Brawn's famous double bed were a couch of unnatural behavior? What then, Judge Trumbull? What would you do as a lawyer?" The nasal voice trembled with anger. "Would you abandon my case?"

He looked deeply and saw dreadful fear. "It's no concern of mine," he replied, disconcerted. "What d'you imagine a lawyer deals with?" They were standing in a cone of light cast by a street light, and the world was beyond in the darkness. "If it affects the case, I'd have to think, wouldn't I?"

"Judge Trumbull, I have never touched that girl. I had only one experience of that sort in my entire lifetime—back home, with an older girl. I was a child myself and once was enough, I assure you. I'll swear that on my poor mama's grave."

"Oh, don't swear," he said. "It's just something more to consider. I regret I asked."

"I wouldn't want us to be less than honest with each other," she said and took his arm.

"Let's not stand here," Trumbull said.

They had made a long circle and a dark street had brought them back toward the Embarcadero. "If need be, Judge Trumbull, could you take on the entire case?" she asked.

That's what it was still all about, he thought wearily—Missouri, the boy, the unclean confidences—and now the clear eyes were cold, the pure rounded cheeks drawn, the soft mouth thin and tight.

"Ma'am, I take on all I can," he said in brusque reproof. "You know the position. Nothing has changed."

"Are you afraid not to get paid?"

"You have been told the reason," he said obstinately. He relented and took her arm and again sought to explain the sickness hanging over his life. There was no consistency in her, none at all.

"I swear I'm a chinch," she cried in consternation. "I had no idea what you were going through for me. Why are you here at all?"

Trumbull shrugged. "Mrs. Trumbull insists I continue the practice. I couldn't be here except for her."

"Tell me about her," Jessica said.

He was a man of great restraint, but as they walked the

dark, quiet streets, he found himself talking freely and easily about matters he had not in his life discussed with anyone else.

He opened the gate and took her to the steps. She turned about, studying the large somber face and touched his cheek. "Mrs. Trumbull must be a wonderful woman," she said mournfully. "I wouldn't come between you for the world."

Standing on the step, her eyes in the dark were level with his. Lordy! he thought with total surprise, the woman's thinking of me as a man.

"Would you like to come in?" she asked.

Her face was soft. He felt a stir to clasp the slender waist, he ached to cover the thrusting breasts.

"It wouldn't be wise," he said. "You have an ordeal ahead to prepare for."

The light hand slid slowly down his neck and rested on his chest. A gentle look was quizzical, tender. "Oh, dear," she said tremulously. She brought his hand to her cheek. "Oh, I wish all sorts of things," she said. She turned and ran into the house.

Trumbull waited a long moment and walked off. A strong perfume clung to his hand. For no reason he could assign he laughed. He was panting like a hard-run colt and he was not quite sure that he liked the woman at all.

Chapter Fourteen

"Can't you lie still?" Nellie complained. "Oh, damn!"

Jessica sat bolt upright in bed, feeling the sweat clinging to her body. "Listen."

"Listen to what?" Nellie asked in exasperation. "Mary, Joseph! What? Oh, let's sleep, Jess. You'll need a clear head."

A tight clutch gripped her shoulder. "Did you hear that?"

"Hear what?"

"I heard my name called."

"You're imagining. It's just a dream."

Jessica pulled away her nightgown and blew between her

breasts. She muttered, "It keeps going around and around. Nell, I'm that scared, I don't know what I'll say. How do I begin?"

The girl raised herself on an elbow. The profile, silhouetted against the faint sky glow of the window, was troubled. "Don't worry about that," Nellie said. "You're a brilliant woman, Jess, and there's nothing you ever forget. Just let old Finch ask questions and make your answers."

"Finch!" Jessica said bitterly. She leaned back against the brass fluting. The cold metal was comforting. "Dates, talks, names, amounts. Oh, shit!"

"Language," Nellie said.

"Well, that's how I feel," Jessica said savagely.

The girl came only up to the round shoulder silhouetted against the window. "I don't think I did that bad," she said, offended.

"No, sweetie, you were upset," the woman said. "I couldn't have asked for more." She sat brooding, clasping her knees. "Finch!" she said vengefully. "I'm just a cow to the slaughterhouse—so much a pound. I have an intuition, Nell. Why did that vase fall this morning?"

"Mary, Joseph!" the girl groaned. "Again?"

"Don't say 'Mary, Joseph'!" the woman ordered.

The girl tossed about. "Now, what's wrong?"

"I think I've got a lump," Jessica said.

"You're imagining."

"I'm scared, Nell. Feel."

The girl sat up, yawning and sighing for sleep and reached out. "Underneath," Jessica said, troubled. She sat forward, clasping her knees, letting ripe breasts fall pendant. "Don't you feel anything?" she asked anxiously. "Like a little hard worm inside?" The girl prodded the soft moist flesh. "You're such a worry bug," she scolded. "There's absolutely nothing at all. What makes you dream these things up?"

Jessica was staring off into darkness. "I don't know," she muttered. "My mama had a lump and she died of it. But I don't know. I just don't."

"Well, there's not a blamed thing," the girl said. "Now go back to sleep."

"All right. I feel better," Jessica said, "but I get so scared of every mark and blemish. I have a lovely bosom. Don't you think so?"

"Sure I do."

261

"It's the one thing Senator really liked," Jessica went on, hugging her knees. "Most lovely he ever saw. I just don't know what went wrong." Nellie threw herself about. "Darn sheets," she exclaimed. Sleep was hopeless. She felt the woman's body, its fragrance and its sharper smells and something was happening. She got to her knees. "Oh, Jess," she said and put her mouth to the woman's.

"Nell, please," Jessica said irritably. "I'm going to go over my notes." She threw back the covers. "Try to sleep," she commanded and left. Footsteps went down to the kitchen below. The girl tossed and clapped a pillow over her head, but it was no use. She got up swearing, then trailed to the bathroom. The pipes were roaring when she entered the kitchen.

"Castor oil?" Nellie exclaimed in horror. "Jess, are you crazy? You'll be running all day!"

Jessica was intent on a saucepan. "I'm not taking it, you goose. It's a remedy. Take that rag and get it ready."

"Pooh! It stinks," the girl said, wrinkling her nose.

"Now, put it on," Jessica said, taking a chair. She slipped the nightgown off rounded shoulders, letting it fall to her hips. "Ow! It's hot," the girl complained, passing a soaked strip from hand to hand. "Hurry, before it cools," Jessica said. She closed her eyes and arched back. The breasts were innocent things, pink-tipped and pure. "Go on," she said. "What are you waiting for?"

Nellie was smiling. "Lovely," she said with an intent look.

Jessica looked up. Their eyes were swimming into each other and their breaths mingled. "Hold still," Nellie said, moving close. "Jess?" she whispered. "Why are you so mean to me? You know I love you. I'd do anything for you. Is there anything I'm doing wrong?"

"You're not doing anything wrong," Jessica said softly.

"Then let me love you. Let me. How can it be wrong when I feel so? Please. Please." A spider's touch traced the breasts and slid down to the slender waist. "Oh, Jess, what's wrong? What's wrong? Is it something about me? I'm sorry about my complexion, but I can't help it." The girl knelt forward, clasping the woman's waist, burying her face against the delicate fragrant neck. "Jess," she begged, kissing the woman frantically, searching, reaching. "Let me love you." The woman threw her head back, eyes closed. The moment was unendurable. "Nell, dear," Jessica said, troubled, turning her

262

head away. "You mustn't, really. This is silly." "But you want to?" the girl cried. "You must want to when I want to so much!" "No!" the woman replied. "Why not? How can it be wrong? What's wrong with me?" Nellie wailed.

Jessica reached down for the searching hand. "Nell, listen," she said earnestly, taking the hand to her breast. "I'm scared. I'm scared of the lawsuit. I wish I'd never started it. I don't want to go to court. Maybe if you went to the Senator for me . . . ?"

The girl sat back. "The damned lawsuit," she said bitterly. "You only want me for that. You don't love me at all. You've changed!" She came back and held the woman's face in both hands. "Jess, you're up to your ears. You cannot withdraw. You've got to go through with this or leave California. I couldn't stand that. I just couldn't. And if you leave, I'll kill myself."

"Please, Nell," the woman said.

The girl went on in a commanding manner. "Here's what you'll do," she declared. "You'll take a sleeping draught, and in the morning you'll be fresh and ready. Jess, you've got to get control. You must."

There was a cough.

"Excuse me," Delaney said. He was at the door, rubbing his eyes sleepily. Jessica placed an arm across her breasts. "For pity's sake, Sonny. Can't you see we're busy? What now?"

"I heard noises," Delaney complained. "I thought if you weren't sleeping, you might want me to talk to you or something. I want to help, y'now. Oh, don't mind me," he said with a sniff. "I'm not interested."

"Very well," Jessica said. "I reckon we're all up. What time is it?"

It was almost five.

Jessica decided. "I reckon I'd like to review the tactics one more time. Sonny, make the coffee—and look the other way," she commanded while the poultice was applied. Finally, she felt better and went to the dining room, where a sheaf of notes was spread on the table. Nellie said, "If you don't know it now, you never will. Must we?"

"Yes, we must!" Jessica said firmly. "If I make any mistakes, I'll die. Where are my spectacles? After all," she added, "it's a kind of debut, isn't it?" She spread the notes with purpose, then, clenching her fists, gave up. She reached for the tarot cards. A dark man had come into her life, she said mischievously. King of Clubs? Diamonds? Spades? Or Hearts? Slap, slap, slap. Lands! The fool cards meant nothing —nothing at all. Just rubbish!

When the carriage arrived, Nellie and Delaney were drooping and hollow-eyed with fatigue. Jessica was sparkling fresh, ready for her day in the sun.

Long before court had assembled, the lobbies were crowded. Standing room was occupied.

"What's up?" Fanny whispered, arriving late.

"Nothing definite," Lang said. "Just that Finch and Brawn have been conferring. Something funny's going on. Settlement talk's rumored."

She turned to Wickwire.

"Oh, why?"

"Pressure. It's costing a fortune. Read this," Wickwire said. Fanny began at the top.

There are rumors on every street corner of a probable compromise of the Roux-Hagerman divorce suit and the end of threats of criminal proceedings. The public has a right to hope that no such end of the entertainment shall occur. The Affair is a pleasant relief to taxpayers and a change of bill from the supervisorial rascality and school trustees flip-flappery. . . .

"Oh, bosh!" Fanny said.

"Shush!" A court officer frowned for silence.

Trumbull looked about and met Fanny's eye and nodded gravely. She handed back the writing. "Tom, if you're thinking of compromise, I don't think you know your man."

"Call the plaintiff," Finch said.

Jessica arose in a neat gray suit with pearl buttons and swept forward. She took the oath with downcast eyes, then faced the court. Trumbull folded his arms and stared. She felt a chill as she gazed into the emotionless eyes. He was a tree in the great mountains—a giant formed at the beginning of time. He would judge and weigh with a terror worse than any of the court's terror, and she had no idea what his thoughts were of her. How would she start? What tone would she strike? Dates, times, places had fled. She felt blank, unreal. Cold hands, colder feet, suffocation and a choking for air set her skin crawling.

She was sworn. She gave her name to the stenographer, and suddenly the senses of her mind were clear. She saw the case in all its clarity. She knew what to say and do.

She leaned forward with a sweet smile. A shaft of sunlight fell on russet bangs over the low forehead. Something new was noted by the press. The plaintiff was wearing spitcurls. She seemed unusually pale, but her answer, though low, was firm.

"I have read the complaint and sworn to it before Almighty God. Every word of it is true. I am the wife of Senator Hagerman and I am entitled to judgment. So help me God!"

There was immediate disorder.

Soon after her arrival in San Francisco, it became clear that she could not live with relatives. She had moved into the Camden for the first time. The Camden Hotel, she said precisely, was then the most fashionable hotel in town, its builder and owner, Mr. Clare Gresham, being still alive.

There was a stir of interest. Some spectators saw the lines deepen in Trumbull's face. The financial history of California with its bitter memories had been recalled.

Fanny lowered her head. "Dolf, what's this about?"

Lang grinned. "It's the master's touch," he whispered back. "Trumbull cannot be happy without the larger implications. Purely prejudicial. Watch Brawn."

Brawn was trumpeting objections, but to no avail. "I'll take it," the judge said, "and see where it gets us."

Jessica was gracious and friendly to the colored staff, she resumed, coming as she did from the same background. Oh, and bellboys too. She had good relationships with all except for a quarrel once with Captain Philip Webster about a matter of no consequence at all.

Well, it had been about mice. The hotel had mice, scampering and whispering in the old walls, and it was impossible to convince the man of the mice and the smells of gas and drains. She was not afraid of mice. She was not afraid of anything. She was physically fearless, for a fact—a good horsewoman and a dead shot. But the blamed things had ruined a good merino dress, and the management would take no responsibility. It was all to come back later to plague her,

265

but how could she know how that silly episode would rankle the man through the years to come?

"Mice," the judge noted. He looked up. "Well, go on."

She now had the attention of the entire court.

It was there she had first noticed an energetic little man bustling about the lobby, darting on mysterious errands, talking animatedly to the ladies and to financial friends. It was Dora and Emily's father, Mr. Lew Hagerman, already celebrated as a financial wizard for astonishing feats in the Comstock—the narrow-gauge railroad, the consolidations and speculations, the milling, irrigation, and water companies.

Jessica smiled silghtly, with a hint of roguish fun. He looked like nothing, she recalled, compared with Mr. Clare Gresham. Everybody knew that Mr. Gresham gave the real orders in the bank. Mr. Gresham was the most important officer and chief stockholder. Mr. Hagerman, for all his bustle and boom, was only in charge of its Agency in Virginia City. He was, she thought, completely insignificant. But then . . .

Well, to be fair, it was all so dramatic. One day in August —precisely a year before the great Centennial Ball at Mechanics' Pavilion—the Bank of the Anglo-Pacific Company had crashed. It was the greatest financial disaster in the history of the state. Strong men wept like children. Some tried suicide by jumping from fourth-story windows. Men and women filled hotel lobbies in all stages of undress. The bottom had dropped out of the world of finance. Mr. Gresham had been such a wonderful big bear of a man with a hearty laugh and such big splendid ideas to beautify the city and advance the welfare of the laboring classes. He had been more than great, he'd been famous and beloved. No one of importance who visited California had ever come without letters of introduction beseeching to be entertained at his great palace at Beaufort down the peninsula.

It was therefore a great shock when Mr. Benjamin Smith had locked the bank's doors and posted the closing. The next day Clare Gresham was dead of an apoplexy, according to Dr. Sawtelle's certificate, of suicide according to rumor. It was a triple shock when the examiners announced embezzlements and defalcations and removal of bullion to cover a short position in Belshazzar. She folded her hands and waited for the storm of objections to pass.

Lang was grinning with delight. "Look at the mood," he whispered. Half the spectators had been caught in that bitter disaster. Hagerman was rigid. Jessica waited patiently while the admissibility of her evidence was disputed.

"Yes, madam." Judge McArdle scratched his crest in perplexity. "There's a point. It's kind of remote, isn't it?"

"Isn't it obvious, Your Honor?" Jessica said earnestly. "I am derided by Mr. Brawn for saying I trusted this man—for who in her sane mind would rely on the promises of a banker and Senator?" A hoarse laugh whooped in the balcony. "So I am trying to explain the background—why when we met again I was taken in. Mr. Hagerman is now behaving badly, but I was young then and I thought him splendid. He spoke calmly to merchants. He telegraphed to Lord Rothschild. I felt that there was a new financial savior. I and my friends and family faced ruin and when he took over and saved the bank, it left an indelible impression."

Objections were continuous and troublesome.

McArdle beckoned his secretary. The court was filled with a buzz of uneasy interest.

Fanny covered her mouth. "I remember that, Dolf," she whispered. "Men howled like beasts for Gresham's blood and Hagerman's too. Grandpapa was crushed by that dreadful news. I shiver still."

Hagerman sat bolt upright, every string in his squat short neck taut. The judge came out of conference. "Well, I see all that now indeed," he said. "I hadn't known that Mr. Hagerman was that thick with Nate Rothschild. I'll take this testimony, subject to connection. There being no jury," he added with defiance. "Madam, can't you get quicker to when you lost whatever it was you lost?"

"I shall try," she said humbly, but with a twinkle. Decidedly, the mood had swung in her favor. She glanced at Trumbull and went on, gathering strength. "Lands, let's see . . ." she said. "Oh, yes. Mr. Hagerman was superb. He issued statements and managed the biggest funeral the city ever saw. He caused Judge Sickels to deliver that famous eulogy which guaranteed deposits and brought comfort to thousands of mourners. Later Judge Sickels granted a federal court order to let him handle Mr. Gresham's estate. Everyone said it was the most brilliant estate settlement ever had in California. Even the creditors sang his praises but, lands! What really happened?

"While he bought up the claims and got voting control of the bank and the whole job—what did the creditors actually get?" She removed a speck from her eye critically. "Peanuts," she said, rubbing her fingers.

A snarl ran through the gallery.

Fortunately, Miss Roux had a sixth sense, for a fact. She had smelled something and she had moved gold notes into a safety box at the Nevada Bank—about $7,500.

And life went on. The bank reopened, with new officers and new directors.

"I gave credit to externals. It was a mistake, and like Hamlet, grievously am I paying for it. That is why I am fighting back. This is not just a case," she exclaimed. "It is a Cause!"

"Cause? What Cause?" the judge asked.

"The Cause of Justice," Jessica said with simple fervor. "I am not in this fight for myself. I have no relish for scandal. I would rather live on crusts than expose my private life. I am in this fight to vindicate the law and for all who might stand in my position in the future." Her eyes were flashing, her breast heaved with emotion. A patter of applause broke out and died. "Perhaps if Mr. Gresham's widow had fought back, she'd not have died a pauper in a foreign grave," she exclaimed poisonously. "I am not that woman." A burning glance rested on Trumbull, who was seen to nod. "I stand for justice, and, thank God, I do not stand alone. That, your Honor, is my Cause!"

McArdle swiveled in the silence, tapping his cheek. All eyes had turned to Hagerman, who was rigid, immovable, but except for a pulsating temple showed nothing at all.

"Go on, madam," Finch said suavely. "Where next did you reside, and may we not stick to the issues as His Honor rules?" With a broad wink to the press, he took a comfortable stance. Trumbull put aside his doodling and stretched his long legs, letting his eyes close. The heavy lines cutting into the beard formed a theatrical mask of sardonic satisfaction.

It was late afternoon. Jessica returned to the stand, having described the first visits to Hagerman's office. Finch came forward.

"Now, madam, did there finally come a time when you got a distinct proposal?" Jessica smiled timidly. "Tell the Court what happened. Omit nothing," Finch said firmly and went back to the rail.

Jessica glanced at Trumbull, who nodded. "Well, I don't remember the date exactly," she said. "I know I went to the bank. We could fix the date because Mr. Hagerman was talking about this issue of Belcher stock his bunch was fixing to boom—rig, you know?" Hagerman wriggled restlessly. "Three days later it jumped ninety points. Mr. Hagerman and associates unloaded and then it dropped. That should give the date."

"Go on," Finch said, noting the effect.

"He was talking silly, how he liked the girls and how the girls liked him. D'ye want those details?" she asked.

"It's your story, madam." Finch shot a glance of suffering to Trumbull.

Jessica touched the corner of her mouth. "Well, he sat me on the sofa and took my hands gently. He told me softly he admired how I was conducting myself—with nobility and sagacity, he said. Those were his words—I had real brains and I could be another John Law of finance. He had investigated and found I was a nice girl, not like the rest, and then he repeated those earlier things I have described about . . . about being nice to him. I said, teasing, it was not a question of money. I would want to be sure of sincerity in a man. Would he, for example, throw Emily's white horse into the bargain? It'd be a test, you see? Well, Emily might not like that, he said, but it might be arranged. Two could play the wheedling game. It was a lovely afternoon, he pointed out, with a nice sun coming through the blinds, and the air so fresh, and would I relent? Now is all this important?" She broke off.

"His Honor might think so," Finch replied.

Blame it, she muttered, it was all so darned simple once. "Yes, well," she said wearily, smoothing her hair, "he said he knew why I was putting him off. He'd heard I had had this personal disappointment—alluding to Mr. MacGowan—and he was surprised I could still seem interested in a cheap lawyer when I could get a rich client like himself. He said it joking. Then he said he knew I was a serious woman and he'd be serious. I said airily, 'Go ahead.'

"Well, he said he'd like to love me. I said I had no objections to any gentleman loving me. He offered sherry and said he wanted me to love him back. I said there were very few people I loved in the world. Very few indeed." A glance of understanding went to Trumbull. "I was absolutely frank on that score. Finally his words got so pointed that . . ."

She paused, and a mantle of crimson mounted. She looked to the high windows, silent.

Finch folded his arms. "You must come to the pointedness of that question," he said severely, thinking that life had its compensations. To put a beautiful woman in a predicament like this did not come to every man.

Jessica drew a breath. "Well, he said he'd give me Emily's white horse and a thousand dollars a month if I would—" She stopped dead, still flushed. "I find it hard to use that word," she said in a low voice. "Must I?"

Derisive amused glances went about among the press, the bar, the clergy, and everyone else.

The judge leaned over. "Can you write it out, madam?" Jessica scribbled and dropped a chit on the bench. McArdle looked up. "I take it you know what it means?"

"I'm a woman, Judge," she said with a hint of temper, "not a child. It's just a word you hear around stables."

Brawn stormed forward, requested to inspect the word, and asked if it would go into the record. Judge McArdle scowled. The record would show that the court had seen a word describing the act of carnality according to ancient usage. Did counsel insist it be read aloud? he asked dangerously.

Brawn sniffed. "I will not insist," he said, "but I should like to know what we are to make of a self-styled young, virtuous woman who will go to a private office and from a man old enough to be her father get propositions such as these which should strike the soul of any honest girl with horror?"

A groan went up. "Oh, balls," someone said distinctly. Brawn flushed and rode on. A girl who could receive that proposition in a man's office and not leave in indignation might just as well go upon the town. He enlarged on this theme at tortuous length. That was all he wished to say, he concluded, breathing hard. He turned to meet stony faces and universal derision. He hesitated and sat with a feeling that his own client held him in disgust.

"Can we go on?" the judge said.

Jessica resumed with an effort. "I wasn't sure I'd heard it right. I got up and said, 'I think, sir, you've made a mistake in the woman. If you wish to make love to women in that style, you can get plenty for less.'" She had not felt indignant, she mused, but rather, well, surprised; then Hagerman said something to make it right. He had put his back to the door and said he was a man and she was a woman and he had wanted to make it plain. He wanted to marry her.

A messenger made a dash for the rear. She glanced at Trumbull and saw the faintest nod. And then Finch was under her nose. "Did you believe that statement?" the man was demanding.

"Not at first," Jessica said. "Well, he worked up to it," she went on. "He said he liked me better than any girl he'd met since his wife died. He got emotional about how wonderful she'd been although they hadn't had, well, relations after Theo was born. He said how Mrs. Hagerman had always liked me, how Dora and Emily never really liked him, and how they were always on their mother's side, and that I was more like a real daughter than them. How it was a burden to be so undersized and how it was always humiliating to have the other pupils make fun of his real name, which wasn't Lew but Augustus. He talked about his struggles and then he cried real tears. Oh, lands! Here I go myself!" she exclaimed, diving for a handkerchief. The mounting scarlet in Hagerman's cheeks was balm in Gilead.

"Lands!" Jessica gasped. "I'm such a baby. Such a fool. I could never stand to see men cry. I told him I'd been burned and I was suspicious. I just didn't see why he'd want to marry anyone. He had all the girls he wanted and it wouldn't make sense. Then he promised to be entirely frank.

"He said it was hard to trust the people around him. They were vultures waiting for him to die, like . . . like some Oriental potentate. He complained that Galindez was using methods to get him out as head of the bank."

There was a frozen silence, and then a dark hand with a massy gold wedding ring pushed back an inky lock.

Jessica went on. "He said that Galindez wanted him kicked upstairs as chairman of the board, away from any decisions. Galindez, he said, wanted to take over the entire estate, supposedly for the grandchildren, and was pressing him to sign a trust indenture. But he was not giving up a blamed thing while he could still sign his name. Then he said he needed somebody he could absolutely trust, with financial brains, and that would fix 'em. Then we talked about the children. I knew Emily disliked me but Theo, I felt, would be understanding, not being tied to his mama's memory. I was thinking of my own mama . . ."

She sighed. "So I said Yes, it'd be an honor and I'd be a

271

good wife and hostess, and that I wanted to consult Grandmama about arrangements.

"Then he said No, that was impossible because he'd have to marry me secretly. I found that offensive. What was wrong? Why secretly? Then he said he had a girl in Philadelphia who had this baby. She could come to Nevada and make trouble at his reelection. She had nothing to lose and lots to gain, and he had to be careful. Well, I doubted that yarn. I had never heard of a Senator or Governor who had ever been affected by such a tale—not even that case in Massachusetts, where the relationship with that stableboy was unnatural. The American nation as a class just don't care about such things. So I said I was from Missouri.

"He laughed and offered to prove it. He took out a letter for me to read. It was from a Miss Sadie Keenan."

"Just a moment." Finch excused himself and brought his head to the counsel table and in an undertone asked for advice. "Offer it," Trumbull said, "since it's been mentioned." "Are you taking the responsibility?" Finch demanded. "I'm taking nothing," Trumbull retorted. "I am giving advice." "Very well," Finch said with resignation and offered to place the letter in evidence.

The letter was passed around. Brawn looked up. "Your Honor, I object to this document. It is disgusting. Its filth cannot be mentioned aloud in this court. It is inherently improbable. My client might be the most corrupt man who ever lived. He might have had the worst designs against this confiding innocent girl. But it is contrary to human nature to suppose that a man of his age and shrewdness would ever try to assault the fortressed heart of a virtuous young woman—as she pictures herself—and urge a secret marriage based on a filthy letter that he had a child by another woman. Did ever mortal woman conceive so degraded a tale?"

"Let me see it," the judge said. He placed his elbows forward, clutched his cheeks, and studied a childish scrawl. He looked up finally. "Madam, this is a private letter from another woman. D'ye actually want to use it in this court?"

Jessica turned about. "If I must," she retorted, flushing. Was that lovely jaw just a trifle large? "They're doing the dirty on me," she said resentfully. "I don't see why I've got to be nice. Mr. Hagerman gave me the letter. He shouldn't complain now."

A glance went to that gentleman. "How does Miss Keenan come into the picture otherwise?"

"She was to be the tragic cause," Jessica said bitterly. "But that day I fully accepted Mr. Hagerman's disclaimers. He was crazy about babies, he explained, and could never abandon a helpless child, especially one of his own contrivance. He had this photograph. It was the cunningest thing, a cute little morsel that wrenched my heart with envy. I have refrained from producing that photograph," she said apologetically, "there being limits." She paused, struggling with softer emotions. "About baby photographs, I'm just mush. Bruno . . ."

"Bruno?"

"The child," Jessica said with some impatience. Hagerman had sworn he was through with Miss Keenan, she went on, but that he could never let Bruno down. Yet it was Bruno who was to break up the marriage. A year later she, Jessica, had come in to find Hagerman playing on the floor with Bruno, smeared with oatmeal, grinning like a fool. Miss Keenan was on the bed naked as a fish, eating vanilla ice cream topped with whipped cream and a red cherry. "Choose!" Jessica had exclaimed. She had stalked out, laughing and weeping, and had sought advice and refuge with her friends in Oakland, the Hindenbergs. It was heartbreaking, and the only solution seemed separation and a Paris divorce. She had sought to patch things up, but the bloom was off the rose, and there was no turning back. "So that's why I offer this letter," she said, wiping her eyes, "on legal advice."

"I'll take the letter," McArdle ruled.

The letter written from a watering place near Washington was most explicit about the aftereffects of childbirth. Miss Keenan was in sorry condition, she had written, not able to exert herself without pain. She was dreadfully torn and flowing freely but hoped to recover in time to enjoy the Senator's sweet society on his next trip east. She was writing in bare shoulders and bare feet. Baby was lovely. Photograph enclosed. Yours, forever, Sadie. P.S. Wasn't she naughty?

The judge said, "Have you got the photograph?"

Miss Sadie Keenan—a small-boned blonde with roguish dimples and, clutched to her cheek, an adorable baby who had the unmistakable receding Hagerman chin—seemed about seventeen. All that and Bruno too? Most unwise of Miss Roux to throw that gauntlet, McArdle thought. "Mark it in evidence," he said, handing the exhibit to the clerk.

Jessica brooded on that moment, so vivid in memory. "So I was satisfied," she resumed. "I wanted to go to the Catholic Church to get married by a priest secretly, but he said No, it'd have to be called out in church. Finally, he said he'd talk with the Archbishop, but meanwhile there was such a thing as getting married by a written agreement which would be secret. He promised one or the other. I promised to give my answer and left in a trance. That's all I have in my notes for that particular day. Lands! I don't know why I'm shaking. It seemed so natural at the time."

A day later, Jessica went on, she returned to find Hagerman nervous and alone. It was after hours. "The bank was deserted of people," she recalled precisely, "except for Mr. Smith. Mr. Smith showed me to Mr. Hagerman's office. He took Mr. Hagerman's signature for a notice of a meeting of the board of directors, so I have the date. August twenty-fifth. Mr. Smith opened the large safe in the private office, took out papers, and left. He was thus a witness to the circumstantiality. Of course he's a creature of the bank, but there was this dilapidated old Spanish man in the office. Señor Ramirez. But he left just as I came in."

Hagerman then had closed the door, she went on. He had books on the table, a small book and a larger which showed that marriages by written agreement were legal in California. The larger was bound in three quarters calf, she recalled, and had red panels on the spine. Her impression was that the larger book was the Civil Code of California.

"Such as sold at Bancroft's?" Brawn interrupted with sarcasm.

Jessica ignored the interruption. Hagerman had apologized for the smell of brandy. He said that the Archbishop had refused to sanction a secret marriage. She had wondered that he had so little influence there. Hagerman had laughed and said gaily it'd cost a fortune, and he wasn't ready to put up a cathedral, and after all it was Mrs. Hagerman who'd been the Roman Catholic. "Now, if Mr. Hagerman talked to the Archbishop, wouldn't that prove something?"

"Go on," Finch said.

"Well, we had wine and we talked endlessly about this matter. He showed me this book where people'd got married and some case in New York where Mr. Choate, the famous lawyer, had got this woman all this property on a marriage contract—" A warning light in Trumbull's eyes brought this

274

garrulity to a halt. The fact was she had trustingly accepted that such things were done.

Well, as stated, she was in a trance. She had obeyed, overcome by the powerful will of a domineering man. "I know for sure I got married because while he dictated, I wrote. I supposed it was a sketching or draft which would afterwards be properly written out, so I wasn't careful. It was so unreal. I blotted and scratched a bit, Your Honor, as you'll see. I was wearing gloves and excited. I hardly knew what I was doing. It was hot and I felt mesmerized. I just did what Mr. Hagerman bade. When it was done, Mr. Hagerman put his arm about me and asked would that suit me. I said, 'Lands, Senator, that's not our sure-enough marriage certificate, is it? It looks so scraggly. It ought to be on parchment.' He laughed and said I was charming; he was busy and had to go away for a few weeks, but to get the fanciest parchment in town, and he'd sign it fresh. Meanwhile I could keep the rough. So we both signed and it was done. He said gaily—toasting it in brandy—Mrs. Hagerman, you've got the binder, now how about the consideration? A kiss to start off?" She choked and paused.

"Here come the waterworks," Lang whispered.

Jessica was indeed weeping. "It was such a queer sunny day. So lovely and strange. I kept thinking of my poor mama! Mama! Why wasn't she there? Why wasn't somebody with me? I was married, all right, but I'd always wanted a real church wedding with the trimmings—bridesmaids and distinguished guests and a satin gown. I deserved better, and there I was alone with this man. I had this cold premonition and my heart was a stone." She looked to the high windows and the brilliant blue sky beyond. "I could've married anyone," she said in a tremulous voice, "and there I was in that strange position. Maybe Mr. Hagerman was right. Maybe if Mr. MacGowan was more the man, I wouldn't . . ." She wept again, blotting the tears with a ridiculous patch of lace. She had the tribute of silence. "Sorry, Your Honor," she gasped contritely, "but when I think back . . . Oh, lands, lands," she said mournfully.

The judge swiveled full about.

At this point the press noted the plaintiff covered her face with a handkerchief, remaining silent and weeping.

"Oh, I forgot to say," she continued, wiping her eyes, "that we signed in each other's presence and pronounced our vows before Almighty God. Are there any questions?"

Brawn interrupted. "You pronounced those vows before God?" he demanded with disgust. "Under these circumstances? Before Almighty God? God Himself?"

"Yes," she said.

"Before or after the brandy?"

"Before," she replied, smoothing her hair. "I take a serious view of God, Mr. Brawn. He is everywhere. He is within me, I believe. And if so, there is none I fear, for He is with me. As a Grace Church vestryman, how do you feel about that?"

"I feel regretful that I asked," Brawn said philosophically and sat.

Jessica was between tears and laughter. "Can you understand my anguish, Judge?" she asked.

"Go on, madam," McArdle said.

Jessica struggled for composure. "Well, he was tender and considerate. He saw it wasn't easy for me and asked if I wanted to back out. I said No, he had my oath and I'd be a good wife. I just wanted time, but he'd never regret it."

"What else happened?"

Jessica threw a questioning glance at Trumbull. She seemed to read his expression and sat forward with an opulent effect. "Well, he wanted a keepsake."

"Did you give him one?"

"Well, we *were* married," she said defiantly, "and I reckoned he had rights. He bade me sit in the big chair while he turned up my dress. I was still in this mesmerized strange mood while he touched me. I had no objection if it gave him pleasure. I just threw my head back with shut eyes while it happened. He was breathing so hard I was concerned he might keel over. I could feel him, but he was very gentle and nice about it—tentative, kind of—and then I fluttered my eyes and saw he was as white as paper and sweating buckets. I said, 'Senator, are you all right?' He kind of groaned and said not to bend my knee because it was my garter he wanted. I said, 'Oh, is that all? Why, Sen, sweetie, I'll help.' He said No, he preferred to do it himself.

"Anyway he got off the garter and straightened up with a cry of real pain. It was a muscle cramp, he said, and not to mind. He went limping around the room, rubbing his chest, cursing, he was that vexed. Then he apologized and took some more brandy and sealed the garter in an envelope. He was quite recovered except for this pale look. He put it with his wallet—next to his heart, he joked, and we both laughed. In a funny way, I was touched by the poor man because he looked so humiliated and ashamed and yet he was trying to show he loved me."

He had chaffered and joked her into a better mood and they had toasted the occasion. They had wished each other health and good fortune, and then he had caught his train for Virginia City to examine a new shaft in the Belshazzar Mine. She had left in a mood of exhilaration and wonder at her brilliant future. Would anyone believe that her main thought was the good she would do as the chief influence in the life of a United States Senator?

Hagerman was slumped low, glaring murderously, held in iron restraint by Galindez.

She resumed. "I went back to the Purdue," she said, biting her lips. "But actually the Purdue lasted only a few days. Mr. Hagerman paid me one visit there but he got uneasy and broke an engagement. Instead, one day he sent me these frantic notes by Li—three within two hours—to meet at the Camden. He proposed to pretend to meet accidentally so he could explain something important because he was afraid the city was getting wise to our marriage.

"When I got there, I found him agitated. He said someone had learned of his interest in me. He was sure people were out to do a job on us. He suggested I now move into the Camden Hotel while he remained at the Imperial. With the bridge, it'd be like being under the same roof. I didn't like that one bit. I was displeased by the suggestion. I told him I had lived at the Camden and it held unhappy memories for me. Besides, the Camden had become second-rate. I wanted to move into the Imperial, where I belonged. But he said No, it wouldn't be wise. I said I had no other objections to the Camden and of course I'd do his bidding. I had good relations with the staff except for Captain Webster. Unpleasant villain," she muttered spitefully.

In any case, she had moved into that hotel one month after the marriage to the day. It was like an omen. The air was charged with importance and excitement. She had in her bosom a secret of awesome dimensions. Ahead lay a year of happiness, to be followed by the years of exile and heart-break, but at that moment she had felt exalted beyond other women.

277

Finch said carelessly, "May we take it that the marriage then was consummated?"

Jessica hesitated. "Would you repeat the question, please?"

Judge McArdle looked up. "D'ye understand the question?"

She nodded.

"Then answer it," he said.

The courtroom was silent. She glanced at Hagerman and drew a breath. "I reckon you could call it that," she said with a droll twinkle, "so the answer's got to be Yes."

There was a burst of relieved laughter. Guffaws rang through the courtroom. Thighs were slapped. Oh, glory! In all the immoderate laughter Hagerman's excited protests were lost. "What's the point to all this?" he cried, struggling with his lawyers. "Where's the marriage? What if I poked her up? What does it prove? What kind of a court is this? Damnation, let go!"

"Be seated, sir! Bailiff, if that man's not seated by the count of three . . . One! two! three—"

"I'm seated," Hagerman snarled. "But I'll have something to say." He bounced with anger, turning upon Galindez with rage. A murderous whisper was distinct that it was crazy not to have paid up in time ". . . make me look like a laughing-stock!"

Brawn stood. "Your Honor, I have begged for the document. We've had Acts. May we go to Revelations?"

The judge leaned over. "Mr. Finch, is that document in court?"

"I cannot be precisely sure," Finch said, rocking on his feet, "but it's eye-ther in that purse"—eyes went to Jessica's lap—"or secreted on her person."

"Which is it, madam?" the judge asked.

Jessica let a moment pass. "I have it," she replied, "but I am afraid to show it to those men, Your Honor."

"Oh, Your Honor," Brawn bleated in suffering tones. "I will swear on my honor as cotillion leader to concede judgment if harm comes to that forgery—"

A new voice, deep and low-pitched, broke into the discussion. "Counsel should not testify," Trumbull said quietly. "He should argue from the evidence and nothing more."

Finch and Green turned in surprise. Brawn paused in mid-flight.

"It may not be called a forgery," Trumbull said precisely, "before it is in evidence."

"I was not testifying. I was characterizing, as Judge Trumbull knows," Brawn retorted. "Oh, Lord!" He threw up his hands and sat. Trumbull returned to doodling impassively.

"Well, unless it's produced at once," the judge said, "I'll have to dismiss the complaint and give judgment for the defendant. Make up your mind, madam."

"Well, it's not here," Jessica said, placing a slender hand below the cleft of her breasts, smiling suddenly with infectious fun. There were answering smiles. "But I do have it in court." Then grave, she opened the purse and took out a small package of oilcloth. The entire courtroom craned as the lawyers approached in a body. "Stay back!" she cried in alarm. "Stand back. Order!" the bailiff said sternly. "Order!" "I'll be the one to call for order," the judge said, vexed.

"Oh, be careful," Jessica cried in alarm as the stenographer marked the item. "No! Give it back," she exclaimed, snatching back the exhibit.

"What does she mean, No?" Brawn exclaimed, bewildered.

"Madam, counsel has a right to see the exhibit," the judge said, frowning, "you must really show the paper."

"I cannot get myself to do it," Jessica said, whimpering. "Emotionally," she added.

Exclamations all around. "Well, you'd better overcome that emotion," McArdle said sternly.

"I just don't desire that those men handle it," she cried with an edge of hysteria. "I have held it as my honor for three long years. No one knows what this dreadful secret has cost me," she exclaimed. "Mr. Hagerman knows all about it."

Brawn broke into the clamor. "I object to this woman making statements. Mr. Hagerman knows nothing about it. It is a fraud and forgery from end to end."

Jessica cried, "So help me God, Mr. Hagerman dictated it to me on his Axminster carpet, and knows all about it."

"Can't she be stopped?" Brawn begged. "She goes on, and on, and *on!*"

"Millions! He's got his millions!" Jessica said bitterly. "He's cheated me out of my money, and I've got no money to defend myself with." She went rigid, fists clenched, trembling violently.

The judge quelled the disorder, puzzled. The woman's behavior, he thought, was decidedly odd. "Now listen, madam!"

he said firmly. "I'll have to ask the sheriff to remove you unless you behave. You don't want that?"

"But why must I leave my paper?" she asked childishly. "Why aren't photographs enough?"

Finch closed his eyes in prayer. "Mr. Brawn don't want photographs," he said, exhaustedly. "Oh, but I do," Brawn said quickly. "Well, I've got an apparatus at home and he can come there and photograph it," Jessica said. "If only this tongue could be stopped," Brawn exclaimed, mopping his neck, "I could get a ruling."

"I'll tell you something," the judge said finally. "If you fail to deliver that paper, I'll have to dismiss your complaint. Is that what you want?"

"Mr. Trumbull?" Jessica said imploringly. "What shall I do?"

Trumbull looked up from doodling. "You must always do what the Court requires," he said quietly.

"Very well," Jessica said. "As Your Honor orders, I, Jessica Hagerman, before witnesses, deliver this paper to the Court. And I hold you, Judge McArdle, responsible for my life and honor."

The judge looked into blue eyes of desperation. What the hell does the woman expect? he thought. What's the bloody business about? "You can save the speech," he said sorely. "There's no responsibility in the matter. Mr. Clerk, take that document and show it to counsel."

Brawn curled a lip in derision. "Not your signature, sir!" he said to his client with contempt. "Rank forgery."

"Forgery," Evanston agreed. The exhibit was passed among counsel. "Clumsy beyond words," was said distinctly.

Finch was outraged. "Your Honor, we object to language like that at this time. It will be observed that the paper was produced at their demand. It is monstrous that this man should stand in a court of justice after they've compelled the production of the paper and make such a remark. The remark is entirely out of order and may not be tolerated."

The judge looked uncertain. "Mr. Brawn?"

Brawn took a studious pose. "Ordinarily I would agree with learned counsel," he said urbanely, "and reserve my remarks for later. But this is not an ordinary paper the lady offers. May the Court please? This looks suspicious. There are dangerous and venomous animals which God has endowed with such physical repulsiveness that man on sight recoils.

Nature warns him to avoid them. If man and creature meet, it is because man is pursued and caught, not because he voluntarily touches the rattlesnake or the tarantula.

"So with this paper," he said with distaste. "Something taints it with suspicion of fraud. It is soiled. It is scraped. It is scratched and creased. It looks ironed out and pressed—but the gloss is gone. It looks scorched. It has a ragged, disreputable, and disintegrated appearance. It has seen careless times. It shows stains as though exhumed from dirt and carried intimately where sweat or other fluids may have drenched it. It looks anything but a valuable paper treasured by a woman of honor. Why, sir, there is not to be found anywhere among Christian people anyone who would not turn up something better than this diseased exudation of a perfervid and scheming mind. A Piute squaw who had her marriage contract on pine bark would guard the muniment of title to her Indian chief, squatting on his hill, and the badge of legitimacy of her papooses with better care than this thing which now Miss Roux brings to this court.

"And on the basis of this scrawl with its dirt and abrasions does she now saunter into this honorable Court to lay claim to fifteen million dollars?" he trumpeted in passionate disgust. He held the paper like tissue from a diseased corpse. "For this? It stinks of the jakes! Marriage contract? Never! It was always a scrap of paper, creased and folded in the noisome depths of a feminine pocketbook, resurrected for criminal purposes and used in this present dirty form out of foul need. Faugh! I object—"

Hagerman applauded, rising excitedly. "She stole that signature and got that black she-vulture to fix it up—ow!" A hand of steel dragged him down.

Finch leaped in triumph. "Mr. Stenographer? Did you get what just was said?"

"Don't answer!" Brawn exclaimed.

"I got it," the stenographer told the judge. "Do I keep it?"

"Got what?" the judge asked with asperity. Everyone was talking at once. What precisely had been said? The stenographer read back the colloquy. Reporters were scribbling notes ". . . stole that signature . . ." was read back. A motion to strike was denied. Silence was got. "I've warned against this," the judge said grimly. "Mr. Brawn, your client cuts no special ice with me. One more interruption, and he'll be jailed. Did you get *that*, Mr. Stenographer?"

Galindez was seen in most strenuous conversation with Hagerman. "I stand to it," Hagerman said loudly, struggling, "and say it's a fraud."

"Don't you dare repeat that before the Court!" Finch cried.

"Mr. Hagerman. Be quiet, sir."

"A-r-r-h!"

"Mr. Sheriff, remove that man!"

The Comstock millionaire was ushered out, uttering words that never reached the record. "How can I consult or show the paper to my client," Brawn demanded, "if he's cooling his heels outside this room?"

"That is your affair," the judge retorted warmly. Order was restored. An objection was made.

"Judge Trumbull? Have you some comment?"

Trumbull looked up without expression. Throughout the tumult, he was sunk in thought, recalling the moment at Las Flores when he first had seen that document. He could recall his dismay at its appearance—and more at the substance. It had an unusual order of vows—first the woman's, then the man's, contrary to custom. It was replete with queer, pompous phrases. There was triple repetition of the senatorial title, and other redundancies. It had all the defects pointed out by Brawn and more—but it was without doubt a mutual acknowledgment of marriage in writing between the parties.

"The signature has just been admitted," Trumbull said. "The issue is up to the Court."

Bloody bitch, the judge thought. The whole business was too bewildering. "Overruled!" he said defiantly.

Brawn turned to Trumbull. "Well, well! That was well prepared," he said with a grimace.

Trumbull did not stir. "I'm sure counsel did not mean that," he said in a cold voice.

"Eh? What?" The judge looked up.

The chamber went quiet.

"I assume counsel meant no reflection." Trumbull's voice was without tone.

"Watch La Roo," Lang whispered, the light of mischief dancing. Jessica was leaning forward with concern. The lawyers faced each other in the sudden hush.

"Order!" McArdle said strongly, dealing with a situation he understood. "This case will be conducted proper and gentlemanly. I am determined it will be so conducted."

Trumbull said nothing.

Brawn said weakly, "I mean nothing," then rallied, "but if I ever make a direct charge, it will not be misunderstood."

"Let it be so," Trumbull said.

"I know Judge Trumbull's reputation and why he is in the case," Brawn retorted, recovering his voice. "I would not dream to excite him without purpose."

"Order. Order," McArdle insisted.

"I am content," Trumbull said, and went back to doodling. Bang. The court stood adjourned.

After a stir, it was reported that Miss Roux stood down and strode to the defense table. She was seen to engage General Brawn in gracious and bantering conversation, after which, patting his wrist, she laughed and with Mrs. Lawes departed the courtroom on Judge Trumbull's arm. Counsel followed to winks and smiles of encouragement on the sunniest day of the year.

"Please don't rush me," Smith said sharply. The waiter bowed and left and he returned to his cocktail with annoyance. A most precise sense of the occasion put highest value on leisurely drinking, good food, and civilized talk with his striking granddaughter, but he was not too sure of her mood.

It was astonishing how the Affair had taken over the city. There seemed no other topic of conversation at Schoenberg's, a comfortable family restaurant. Fanny had been talking steadily about nothing else. She thought that Jessica had had a good day; Nellie's hysteria had been neutralized; the marriage contract had gone into evidence; Jessica's version of the marriage proposal with its farcical elements had seemed convincing, and yet . . .

Smith lowered the cocktail. "What's wrong, my dear?" he asked.

"It's this trial." Fanny sighed. "I'm not sure what Trumbull's at or why he's in it. At first I thought he wouldn't take it. Then today . . . well!" She looked up. "He won't like my piece tomorrow at all."

"Ah?"

Fanny said with wonder, "I found his behavior disgraceful. Threats in open court like a ruffian! My word!" She took refuge in her drink.

"Oh, I dunno," Smith said unexpectedly, "Trumbull made some gains with that show of force."

283

"Gramps! I'm shocked! How can you condone that display of violence?"

"I condone nothing," Smith said. "A challenge has nothing to do with violence. Its real purpose is to gain ascendancy by a show of character—same reason mating baboons show their blushing behinds."

She laughed. As a child she had loved her grandfather as one loved God—fearfully. Now that he was somewhat tipsy, he was delightful. "Of course if it's a beauty contest, I've nothing to say, but I had hoped lawsuits were more than lawyers displaying their vulgar parts. Shouldn't the judge be incensed by that behavior?"

"Yes, and no," Smith said genially. "It has its logic."

"D'you suppose Trumbull could really have meant to challenge Brawn?"

"Brawn might have thought so," Smith said.

Fanny was appalled. "In this day and age? It hardly seems possible."

"What age is this?" Smith asked. "I don't think you understand men like Trumbull. Trumbull has always acted as he feels obliged to act. He's never backed off from a point of principle and he's never reckoned the cost. I think he'd walk into a cannon's mouth if he'd said he would. His whole history shows that. Take that business of Gore. Gore, who picked the fight, was a skilled shot and a fierce man, totally combative. He expected without doubt to kill Trumbull, and Trumbull knew it. Gore had fought three duels successfully. Trumbull in fact had never fought a duel in his life. Trumbull knew the risks, the hatreds he was cultivating. He also knew he could not back off and still live in this part of the world. Today these notions are considered romantic nonsense, but then a challenge simply enough meant homicide or death. The notion of honor was not sentimental at all, but vital. A decent man would no more lightly insult another man than enter his home at night. The outcome could be the same.

"But it was ironic, really. Trumbull never wanted to fight and would not yield. He succumbed like everyone to fear of ostracism and disgrace. He was a moral man in an immoral situation. You can only say that he was brave. The effect lingers though. He's still under a cloud."

"Still? Oh, come."

Smith said drily, "When Gore died, the uproar of disapproval forced Trumbull to close up his law practice and get up to the Comstock, where his reputation preceded him. Your friend, Senator Pike, could tell you all about your hero."

Fanny looked down. "Who says he's my hero?"

"Have I said something?" Smith went on good-humoredly to tales of legal brawls of the Comstock where both lawyers —Mark Trumbull of Texas, Josiah Pike of Indiana—with their armed followers had battled across that crazy lunar landscape until the outbreak of the war. It had all ended when Pike had secured title almost at gunpoint of the largest single producer of ore in the Comstock for the San Francisco syndicate headed by Gresham and Hagerman—the great Belshazzar Mine, the foundation of the bank and the basis of the Hagerman fortune. "Pike got a three-foot interest in Belshazzar and made a fortune from that single verdict," Smith concluded. "Trumbull got nothing. We tried hard to hire Trumbull, but the opposition were a raggedy lot of single miners and naturally he took their cause against ours."

"Naturally," she said.

Smith smiled. "Fool, too. He's a blind advocate. He sees everything the client's way. No other truth exists, and that makes him a great force in the courtroom—the display of fervor and conviction to the point of death. That's how he survived—the universal respect in which he was held. Now, you want to understand what really happened today? Brawn's no match for a man like that. He doesn't understand the courtroom. Trumbull does. Trumbull overawed the man, got him to back down, put him in fear. From now on, he's got the moral ascendancy. I'd say that Trumbull calculated that effect pretty well. I just wish it were a better cause."

Fanny said, troubled, "I don't think the effect was calculated at all. I think he lost control."

"Eh? What?"

"I think something's going on between them," she said.

Smith stared. "Trumbull? With her?" he exclaimed, incredulous. Fanny nodded. "But . . . but he's a perfectly honorable man. How's it possible in his position?" he said.

"Oh, Gramps," she said, smiling faintly. She drew lines on the cloth, thinking back to the courtroom scene, wondering how she could have been so blind. It was all so clear in a flash. She came to something which had gnawed her mind for weeks. "If I arranged it, would you see Trumbull? You might make him see where he's headed. You'd know about that marriage paper and you've got the confidence of both sides. You might be able to suggest a way out."

Smith blew his breath. "Be a go-between?" he said, disturbed. Confound it all! he thought resentfully; the genial mood had fled. "My dear girl, I could only say that Mr. Hagerman has repeatedly and solemnly told me that he never signed that marriage contract. I wouldn't have anything useful to say."

"You can't be sure," she said.

The broad thin mouth was pressed tight. "It'd be futile. Your precious Trumbull has evidently made up his mind. He's Lazarus and it's too late. If Moses and the Prophets have failed, an archangel couldn't hope to change him. Just too absurd. Oh, dear!" He broke off and turned.

Fanny followed his glance to the entrance. Frau Schoenberg, a tremendously endowed blond woman, was welcoming a high-spirited party. "Fritz," she called in Wagnerian strength that carried through the half-dozen dining rooms. "Fritz!" she sang gloriously. "Judge Trumbull's table? *Schnell, schnell!*"

The entire restaurant turned about. Trumbull in a rumpled clawhammer was escorting a smiling Jessica and the Driscoll child through crowded tables, followed by a serious Nathaniel Green, who was looking self-conscious indeed. And, bringing up the rear, splendid in purple and gold, Mrs. Lawes, bedecked like a maharani. They were recognized at once and got some smiles and some hostile stares as they passed on to a table in the rear. Trumbull removed Jessica's wrap with utmost good humor. His deep voice lauding the roast goose went to every corner of the establishment.

The banking business had made Smith an observant man. He leaned across the table. "My dear," he said gently, "the man's a fool, not worth your while. If he had sense, would he bring that woman here? It's not as though he's got some little brown hen at home."

Fanny dropped her eyes. "But hasn't his wife been an invalid for years?" she asked in a low voice.

Smith paused on the brink of something quite ungrandfatherly. His granddaughter had developed beautifully, he thought, since he had started her off on Plutarch. She had grown to a companionable woman whose assurance matched his own. He had some notion of her life abroad and a shrewd idea that she had enjoyed at least one affair, if not more. And somehow this put them on a worldly footing. She spoke and wrote like a man, he thought; she was self-engrossed, completely ambitious, determined on career. These were qualities he appreciated. He liked her looks very much indeed. If he had any regrets for her, it was that although splendid in his own eyes, she was quite tall and thus, when fashion called for the petite and plump, with tiny waists and full busts, handicapped. A troubled expression sent a pang through him. "Yes, Mrs. Trumbull's been sick," he said slowly, "but she's an extraordinary woman, and Trumbull's been devoted to her. That sort of thing is all very well for creatures like that"—a nod indicated the animated woman at the far table—"but not you, Fanny. You should have better sense."

Fanny made a pleasing discovery—she loved her grandfather with a simple and old-fashioned affection. It was indeed nice to know that such feelings still existed in a rotten world. "Let's talk of something else," she said forcing a smile.

"Just ahead," Trumbull said several hours later, striking the roof of the cab.

The clopping sounds went on. "Are you all right?" he asked anxiously. "All right for sure," Jessica said. Her sides were aching; she had been laughing too hard, too long. The sense of triumph was passing. Her temples were throbbing.

"All right," he said, sinking back in the hansom. He felt heavy now with goose and wine, conscious of his girth and stiff muscles and the strain of carrying off that public appearance. Schoenberg's was out of the way, but still anyone might have walked in. The table had been a nice question; it had had to be somewhere open—not furtive, not hidden, so ordinary and respectable and chaperoned that it would convey an innocent intent. Now they were alone and still he was not at ease, not even in darkness.

How had he got to this point? he wondered. It had been a good dinner, animated by triumph and flowing champagne. Malvinia had been surprisingly full of smutty stores matched unexpectedly by Green. Where had Green got those limericks? Trumbull could not tell; an expression of round-eyed innocence was more than droll. It had all been jolly enough. Nelly, avid to discuss the case, unexpectedly had turned pale and sick. Green and Malvinia had trundled the girl out of the restaurant to a cab. Trumbull and Jessica had a moment alone. They smiled uncertainly.

"Jess?" he said, lowering his voice.

"Yes, Mark?"

"I cannot always meet you in offices, you know."

She leaned forward, smiling, the small lines crinkled about her eyes. "D'ye mean you want my fair body?" she teased. It was that kind of moment. Their eyes met.

"Yes," he had said simply and had felt a clutch at his throat. Lord God, he had thought, surely this was not his voice speaking.

"Oh!" Her voice went small and she shrank back. "Lands, I wasn't expecting that!"

"You don't mind?"

She looked away, silent. "It's just that I wasn't really expecting it."

"Think on it," he said hoarsely—and then Green and Malvinia returned.

Jessica was silent through the rest of the meal. When done, Trumbull summoned a hansom to see her home. He was sunk in humiliation. Unexpectedly she had said she wanted to see his place. "Farley Street!" he ordered. And now they were driving in silence and she had not given an answer. "I ought to take you home," he said.

"No, no," she replied, taking his hand. She slid her hands deeper, up his sleeve, seizing his wrist, and felt the beat of a strong heart. What was he thinking? she asked softly.

"Oh, that Schoenberg's was a poor choice of a place to put the question," he said with dour humor. "I'm a clumsy fool."

"Well, you're not a fool," she said with dubious comfort. They had not ever before touched each other. She leaned over and put her head to his chest, feeling hard muscles through heavy cloth. A gold watch chain was at her nose, the rise and fall of his chest was a tidal effect.

The sound of hooves stopped.

"I'll see if it's clear," Trumbull said in a strained voice. He got out and looked about, then came back. "All quiet," he said and reached up to span her waist. "More to you than meets the eye," he joked.

"Color in the pan," she said gaily and swung down. The house was dark. "It looks deserted," she said.

"I told you it was," Trumbull said. "Just come this way." A flagstone walk brought them to a backporch. A latch fell.

She stepped into deeper blackness. Behind her the door closed. She had a sense of a kitchen somewhere and the emptinesses of a vacant house. "It has a smell," she said, wrinkling her nose.

"Just that it's closed down," Trumbull said. "Actually the woman is very clean. Real Yankee housekeeper."

"Oh, they're not so much."

"In that respect they're fine."

"I won't argue that," she said. "You're sure she's gone east? How long?"

"Oh, till this grandchild is born."

"Oh, good. I just wish . . ." She paused.

"Yes?"

"Oh, that we'd done this earlier." The house was strange, it was dark, both were whispering. "Take my hand," he said. "Here's the stairs." She went ahead, her thighs and hips moving rhythmically. The steps creaked under his weight. "Lands," she said breathlessly, halting, "I just got dizzy." They stood motionless, his arm went about her hips, holding her close. "Silly," she said and went on.

"This way," he said, guiding her along a short hall. "Here it is."

A door creaked on its hinges, the room lay there, dark and remote, heavy with male smells of tobacco and sweaty wool. "Oh!" she exclaimed, retreating.

"What?"

"Oh, nothing, I expect," she said nervously, entering the dark room. "I'll get the matches," he said, following. "You stand still." He moved off and she followed. "Darn," she exclaimed. "I hurt myself."

"Then don't move," he said, groping. "Oh, Lordy! I'm out. I'll have to get to the kitchen. D'ye mind?"

"Help me find the watcha-ma-call-it?"

"Can't you wait? I'll be right back."

"Must I be indelicate? I've had a quart of beer," she giggled.

He chuckled, amused. "Well, all right. Take my hand." He led her past vague forms. "What about you?" she said mischievously.

"Never you mind me. Now here," he said, throwing open a door. "You've got everything—towel, soap, what-not."

"No perfume?"

"Eh? What would I want with perfume? But there's bay rum—real stuff from the Virgin Islands. Special recipe I import. Very rare."

"Sounds real racy," she drawled. "Don't be long now. Hear?"

"You'll be all right?"

"Sure will," she said. "Here, catch." It was her cape, scented with her body, warm, velvet-soft black in blacker darkness. He waited, crushing it against his face. "Now go!" she commanded. The heavy footsteps went downstairs and she was alone.

Cold water was running on her wrists when he returned. The match spurted blue and the Welsbach mantle glared in the outer room. Trumbull came to the door. She was at the basin, frowning with concentrated thought, unhearing. "Jess? Something wrong?"

"Oh?" She looked up, confused. "Sorry, I'm still squiffy, I reckon." She came to the door, drying her hands, glassy-eyed. "Oh, say! It's real nice," she exclaimed. "The way you've been talking, I expected some pig wallow. Ever watch pigs make love?"

Trumbull chuckled. "Who ain't? Can't say it's instructive, though it has its entertainments. Glad you like it." He threw the matches on a bureau and turned about. In the soft glow, standing with clasped hands in a low-cut gown of blue satin, she was graceful and slender. "It's all yours," she said, indicating the bathroom.

When he returned, she was staring into the dark street. "You're all right?" Trumbull said, coming behind her.

"Sure thing," she said dizzily. "Ooh, I'd better sit." She fell into a worn morris chair with a sagging bottom. The far wall held a divan covered with a shawl; a curtain of beads divided the parlor from an alcove with a bed. "So this is how a lawyer lives?" she joked. "I'd say it's three dollars a week with board?"

"Without board," Trumbull replied.

"The woman can't make money at that."

"She's finding it out," he said humorously. "Here, let me straighten things. Sure's no way to receive you." Slippers were flung into a closet; socks went to a bureau; he moved restlessly, fixing pictures, talking about things. What a hell of a place for this! he was thinking, cursing the shabby corners, the furtive sense of defiling the house; that he had not chosen another time, another place; the woman was expectant, charming, melting toward him, and still he could not step

290

across the void. "Jess," he said, halting. "I may be too old for this."

There was a fearful moment.

"Oh, no, no," she said quickly, and his heart took a bound. "Have you got a comb?" she said.

"Only mine," he said.

"I don't mind," she replied. She rose and went to the bureau. "Is there a drink?" she asked, smiling over her shoulder.

"H'ain't you had enough?" he asked.

"One more and I'll do anything," she said impishly. "Mark? Let's forget the blamed lawsuit."

"Last thing I want to think about."

She pulled the comb through her hair. "Sit where I can see you."

"Not if you want that drink." He brought the tumblers and sank in the morris chair, breathing heavily. She sat facing him. "Mark?" she said in a troubled voice. "I don't want to hurt anyone. Have you ever done this before?"

"I don't seem to be doing this right now," he said humorously. They laughed together. "It ain't a question you ought to ask," he said.

"Oh, no!" she exclaimed, contrite. "It's not my business. I sure say the wrong things."

"No, 'tain't that. Only, what can I say? If I say No, I'm a ninny. If I say Yes, I'm a braggart. Either way, I'm a villain."

"Villain? Why?"

"Getting you here," he said. "Ain't fair to let this happen. You're in no condition to know what you're doing."

"That's when I'm at my finest. Ooh, lands!"

"Something wrong."

"No, just that I'm stuffed. D'ye mind if I loosen something?" She put her hands behind her back and felt for the stay laces. "Oh, gosh!" she gasped. "Would you give a hand?"

"Reckon I can." He came behind her and began with surprising skill. Well, why not? she thought. He's had a lifetime of experience. He's a real man, a married man, he's had women and he knows these things. The loud whistling was his breath, she heard with satisfaction. He was excited, she thought. His heat suffused hers. She looked back and his head, inverted, was looking into her own. "Oh, Mark," she said with a gush of feeling. "I don't know what I'd do if not for you. Mark?" She reached back, touching his cheek. "Mark?" she said more urgently.

He was above her. He reached out, a hand was at her breast, but made no move to touch her. Their breaths were one cloud of desire. She drew him closer; a small reluctance refused the gesture, then the strong mouth, bitter-tasting of tobacco, met hers: his taste, his smell, she thought. A vise crushed her breast and brought a scream. A hoarse voice said her name. She twisted about and held his face and plunged her tongue into his mouth.

"No!"

He threw her off and walked aside. "Jesus!" he gasped, leaning for support on the wall.

"Is something wrong?"

"No. Give me a minute."

She went beside him. He was facing a chromo of a New England farm, staring with unseeing eyes at a winter scene. "I sure didn't expect anything like this," he said. "You're sweaty!" she cried, taking the bison head in both hands. "Let me get something."

"No, let be," he said. She pushed him without resistance into the chair. He sat back, arms hanging, leaning against the headrest. She left and returned with a towel. "Stay off, Jess," he said. "I'm too indelicate. I stink."

"I've tended horses, I can tend you. Sit still." She unbuttoned his shirt and dried him, feeling the deep swell of his chest. "So strong," she murmured, slipping her hands into a denser matting. Something hard and large leaped up. Their eyes met.

"Jess," he said. He seized her nape and pressed her face down. He was thinking with cruelty that the bones were delicate, they could snap, a squeeze would end her life, but there was the fragrance, the years of drought. "Can't breathe," she choked.

With a quick twist he turned her face about. Her eyes were swimming, her mouth was his mouth. She struggled free, gasping for air, and threw herself at him. She chewed his beard, her claws raked his cheeks. "I want to make you happy," she said desperately. She struggled against the cruelty that constrained her. He reached into her dress. "Let me do that," she gasped.

"No!" He had her pinioned, out of her dress, she was a toy in his arms.

"Don't hurt me," she said. "I don't want to be hurt. Please?"

"All right." He stood and a deeper darkness blinded him. Lordy! What was this? He was almost fainting. Nothing like this had ever happened in his life. He groped for support and waited for the spell to pass. A light step crossed the room; the bead curtain clicked and the bed springs squeaked.

"One minute," he said.

Both faucets gushed cold water. He dipped his hands, throwing the water over his head, slapping his neck, tasting the special moment. He stared down at himself. He had not been so hard in years. What was it? he wondered desperately. What was it she had done? Tiles were cold underfoot, then wooden flooring, then carpeting. He found himself at the bed and beneath him something lovely and delicate beyond words. God is good! he thought, sinking to one knee. She reached up and with a strong hand took him to herself.

Chapter Fifteen

Jessica arose and went forward, skirting the defense table. She sat and faced the world with amused good humor, wearing a demure dress with neat white collar and cuffs. Every hair was in place.

Brawn took a stance facing the witness, leaning on the rail of the jury box, outwardly grave, inwardly smiling, considering the woman. And since he disliked her, he had a great impulse to step close, to see her stiffen, to see her recoil from the reek. But that would wait. For the moment he was content to keep the distance.

Jessica waited with a smile. She knew every filthy thought in the man's mind. A glance of amused understanding went to Trumbull and away. She had made a faithful promise to testify with care and guard her impulsive tongue. Well! That would not be hard, she decided, and forced a smile.

"Let us review," Brawn said in coaxing tones. During that

first year she had received a series of letters addressed to her by Hagerman as his "Dear wife"?

"Quite so," Jessica said pleasantly. "They are in his handwriting. Admittedly."

Brawn smiled agreeably. "Admittedly? That remains to be seen. You say that the word 'wife' is neither traced nor forged?"

"Certainly not." Jessica smiled.

Brawn beamed. "Well, let's see if these are the kind of letters a man writes his wife." The letters were read aloud.

Dear Wife.

In reply to yours of the ult., I have instructed Captain Webster to give you room as cheap as possible. Trust this satisfies. Kindest wishes,

L. Hagerman.

Dear Wife.

That's too much for a chair. $50. busts me.

Yours,

L.H.

Occasionally Hagerman was less formal.

Dear Jess.

Cannot make the trip to Beaufort. Take your friends.

L.

Jess:

Come over the bridge and join me in a nice bottle of champagne. Let's be gay and misbehave for our first Christmas.

L.H.

A kindly note ended the year at the Camden.

Wife:

Inclosed find $550 till I'm better. Will then discuss

294

your eastern trip. Am worried about your chest cold.
Fear I'm getting it.

Truly,

L.

The courtroom was tittering. Brawn looked up with a
pursed mouth. Were those the sort of letters written by an ardent bridegroom to a bride? "Tender, aren't they?" he asked.

"For a banker, yes," Jessica retorted. "I understood it was
a financial note, written in a countinghouse mood. But he *did*
write 'Wife.' And if you examine his letters to the children,
you'll find he always signed off, 'Yours truly, Your father,
L.H.' Get Emily here to deny it! Or Theo! Let Mr. Galindez
produce one family letter not written like a banker's circular.
Mr. Hagerman wrote 'Wife' because I was his wife. It sure
wasn't how a man writes to a sweetheart."

There were nods among the ladies.

"He was offhand because we were married," Jessica added.
"He was madly in love and expected to acknowledge me, as
my letters emphatically show. If my hotel in Oakland had not
burned, I'd have plenty of wifely letters."

Brawn examined a note. "I believe you stayed at the Hindenberg? Wasn't it the Sutter that burned?"

"I stayed at both," Jessica said sweetly and lowered her
eyes. "But yes, the Sutter burned. I'm not sure that he didn't
arrange that too," she added darkly.

Brawn looked up quickly. "Arson now?"

Jessica's lawyers had looked up in concern at the sally. She
bit her lip. "Well, of course not. All I meant was that I
wouldn't put such things past him. A man does not become
King of the Comstock by throwing cream puffs," she said
with a sudden appealing smile. "He also sure did burn all my
early love letters—and that's arson, isn't it, Colonel Evanston?" she asked, appealing to the scholar of the Brawn team.

"No," Evanston said distinctly.

"It should be," she said with conviction. There was laughter. "And if I were his mistress," she drawled, "I'd sure have
got more than five hundred a week."

Still smiling, Brawn said, "By the bye, did you ever examine letters from Mr. Hagerman to his children?"

"If you mean without permission, no! But it was natural to
discuss the children's problems. He often asked my advice,

as, for example, when Emily's wedding plans came up. I felt our daughter should be married in the Church, not at Beaufort, but Mr. Hagerman deferred to Emily's wishes." She smiled sunnily and arched her spine with satisfaction.

Brawn picked up the exhibits thoughtfully, recalling his opening offer to prove that the letters were tracings and the word "wife" forgery. Now, if Hagerman should so swear, would he be lying?

Jessica considered the matter gravely. "It'd be perjury," she said firmly, "but what's that to Mr. Hagerman?"

"Would you make the same answer as to your marriage papers?" Brawn asked with a hint of menace.

Jessica smiled. "No, but only because that's not your question. Mr. Hagerman will claim, as I get it, that he signed his autograph all right, but that I wrote the contract above it later."

"I haven't asked for this," Brawn interrupted petulantly.

"You're getting it," Jessica retorted. "But that's ridiculous, and I'll nail that point right now. The signature is genuine. So where's the forgery? If he was only giving an autograph, why did he add the date and residence? Most ridiculous!"

Brawn took time to ask for water. "You did not steal that paper with his autograph?"

"Never did!"

"And if the creases in the paper show that the so-called contract was written after the paper was creased?"

"What does that indicate?" Jessica scoffed. "That I wrote on a folded piece of paper. Too silly!"

Ten minutes later Brawn was directed to go to something else. He went on, less polished now, more overtly insulting. Now, of course, he continued, in preparation for her trial, had she not consulted experts to support her claims? And indeed combed the city for supporting opinions? A nod. And she was aware of the science of questioned documents? "Yes, yes," she replied less patiently.

Brawn turned about. "May we have Mr. Dabney rise?"

A scholarly man with tired eyes came to the rail and gave his name. Ethan B. Dabney was Archivist of the Spanish Archives at the United States Surveyor General's Office. Brawn turned back to the witness. Had she not called on Mr. Dabney July last to request that he testify as an expert witness on her behalf?

"I called on Mr. Dabney," Jessica said.

She glanced at Trumbull, whose face showed nothing.

"Did you not show a photograph of your document and a canceled check and ask Mr. Dabney's opinion of the disputed signature?"

"Yes."

"What opinion did he give you?"

An objection was sustained.

"Very well," Brawn said, rubbing his hands, "but you know that Mr. Dabney has kept the Spanish Archives for the past thirty years? And that he has during that time studied writings to determine their integrity and to trace titles to Spanish grants and documents?"

"Yes, I have heard that," Jessica said.

Brawn went on smoothly. "And you know that Mr. Dabney organized those archives and testified in many trials to settle fraudulent Spanish and Mexican land title disputes when Mr. Edwin Stanton came to this state at President Buchanan's direction?"

"Well, that's history," Jessica said.

"I asked your knowledge," Brawn replied.

Jessica shifted about. "Mr. Stanton was later Secretary of War to President Lincoln and the most notorious member of that man's cabinet, so I cannot admit anything about him. Yes, I have heard that about Mr. Dabney."

"If Mr. Dabney will swear that the signature to your supposed marriage document is a forgery, would that too be perjury?"

"No," Jessica said precisely, "It would not be perjury exactly because that would only be his opinion, but it'd sure be a switch from your other theory, and my own experts will swear the opposite. We'll see what Mr. Grimble has to say. Mr. Grimble was paid a thousand-dollar fee to act as Mr. Hagerman's expert, but after seeing my marriage contract he threw back your fee and said he'd knock the case higher than a kite if you dared call him because he could not in conscience lend himself to a despicable fraud. And you know that, Mr. Brawn, because Mr. Grimble refused twice that fee from you and told you how contemptible the business was. So I'll appeal from Mr. Dabney to Mr. Grimble," she concluded with spirit.

Brawn let a moment pass. "Are you finished with this?"

"Yes," she retorted. "And I can promise more testimony

from Mr. John Throckmorton, who is a famous expert in these matters."

"Do you have any more experts in mind?" Brawn asked.

"Yes," she replied, "but I won't name names. You might try to buy 'em off."

"Then we're done with this?"

"You started it," Jessica said. "But it's pure nonsense, because I saw Mr. Hagerman sign in my presence and have never let the document out of my hand. So it can't be a forgery."

"That is for the court to say."

"That is the fact."

"And Mr. Dabney's expert opinion . . . ?"

"Pooh! You can buy experts," Jessica said insultingly. "I sure can't put out Mr. Hagerman's kind of money to buy opinions. But if Mr. Dabney dares claim forgery, I will swear that he personally told me he couldn't say positively, yes or no, whether the signature is Mr. Hagerman's. I challenge him to deny that conversation. Lands! Look at the man. He's blushing."

Brawn looked at Dabney, who slowly turned red. Brawn shrugged. "We shall return to this," he promised ominously. "Let's see now. Aside from letters and documents, you ask the Court to infer the marriage, do you not, from all the defendant's behavior—letters, finances, circumstances, and so forth?"

Jessica removed her spectacles; they flashed iridescent in the sunlight. Brawn was a blur; she restored the lenses and he leaped back to horrid clarity. "I understand the law permits that type of proof," she said pleasantly, "in the ordinary case where people just live together under common law. But this is no common-law marriage. It's a contract marriage. I rest on the contract. Behavior's not always the criterion and I'll tell you why: Mr. Hagerman's no model," she drawled. "He's a law unto himself."

Even Hagerman joined in the laughter.

"On the other hand," she went on judiciously, "aside from gifts, Mr. Hagerman arranged my support while I lived at the Camden Hotel. He sent me furniture from the Sierra works and paid my bills. Mrs. Lawes' testimony too showed further significant marital behavior."

Brawn let the moment pass. "What about your own behavior?" he asked significantly.

298

"What about it?"

"Wouldn't you agree that your behavior shows that you did not for a single hour believe you were Mr. Hagerman's wife? Did it not show the mental, moral, and physical impossibility of the lie on which your case rests?"

The gavel quieted an uproar of objections.

"Now, now." Judge McArdle tapped in reproof. "If I get this," he said with a gleam of interest, glancing at his notes, "you're talking about whether the contract was followed by an outward assumption of marital rights and duties by the parties?"

"Exactly," Brawn said, bowing.

"As called for under the Code?"

"Pree-cisely."

"I thought so," the judge said, flushing with pleasure. A glance of satisfaction went to Dinesmore. "Go on," he said, "and let's see where it gets you."

"You did quite well," Trumbull said at the luncheon recess. They were at Gallagher's, a restaurant near the Civic Center that ran to corned beef and cabbage and good draft beer. The moment was their own. "Experts are important, Jess," he went on, wiping his mouth, "but there ain't an expert who cannot be torn apart by a good lawyer. Don't worry about that."

"But I do," Jessica sighed. She was toying with oysters. "When Mr. Dabney appeared, I got this awful cold feeling they'll try any trick to besmirch my marriage paper. I'm nervous. Here, feel." Her tight grip was wet, cold.

"Don't be," Trumbull said reassuringly. "We'll deal with Dabney when the time comes. It'll focus on the marriage paper—it's got to, of course, because that's the gravamen of the complaint. But no one thing will decide this case. It'll turn on the total impression—the Court's confidence in your testimony. That's why the attack on your character. But, sho! The signature's the thing. Don't let 'em get you into diversions. Hear?"

"Yes, Mark."

Trumbull put down his fork and began to chuckle. "Oh, that blush! Poor Dabney! I told you he'd blush if a dog raises a hind leg. Most foolish sight I ever saw. He can't get away from it now."

"But he did make that statement to me."

"I'm sure he did," Trumbull replied, still amused. "Typical of that cautious man. When he went to work for Stanton in 'fifty-eight, he found the land titles of this state in hopeless confusion. Governor Castro and General Pico were still alive, lurking in Mexico City, selling their signatures to any predated document of title stuck under their noses. Those fraudulent claims exceeded the land mass of the nation—over twelve billion acres of California soil.

"Now the only way to attack those documents was against the records, and they were in hopeless disorder. Four hundred volumes were removed by the Mexican Army to Benicia and San Jose. Some were down in Mexico City. Dabney and Stanton pulled the records together, reconciled 'em, canceled forgeries, and put titles together with indexes. Many of those forgeries were later validated by Acts of Congress or approved by the Supreme Court in Washington, where your friend Sickels had his usual venal say—"

"My friend!" she exclaimed, wrinkling her nose.

Trumbull was in good humor. "Oh, Sickels had a finger festering in every pie. Some forgeries were incredibly skillful. At that time an old widow, Señora Quintana, sought my help after one of these fraudulent claims had wiped out her inheritance—a ranch in McClelland County. My partner Yates and I had long conferences with Dabney and got his ruling in her favor. Dabney's honest but predictably hesitant before he gets to an opinion."

"What are you driving at?"

"Oh, just this," Trumbull drawled, teasing, yet suddenly not teasing. "The same thieves were in the Maldonado Fraud. Ever hear of that?"

Jessica frowned. "No. Should I?"

"Hagerman did," Trumbull said after a moment. "In that case, they had genuine signatures but false documents. So I expect the same line of attack here. They have partially conceded Hagerman's signature—what else is possible?—but now claim you wrote in the contract later. Cardinal mistake. They shouldn've claimed outright that you forged the signature too."

"But I didn't," she said sharply.

"Didn't say you had. I'm just pointing out their best tactic."

"D'ye think I could do such a thing?"

"Could? Lord! You're clever enough," he chuckled. "You

had every cause. Not a man in California would blame you if you had."

"You're joking!" she exclaimed.

He paused and saw pale fury. "Oh, now," he said uncertainly. "Course I'm joking. What d'ye think?"

"Mighty stupid joking."

"Well, I declare. I meant nothing by it. I'm sorry."

"Let's get out," she said dismally.

"Come now, I was not serious. I wish you'd change your mood."

"Very well, but Dabney sure told me the signature looked genuine," she reiterated obstinately. "If he now says No, he's a liar."

"Dabney's no liar," he said, "but he'll make a poor witness. We'll tie him up in knots. Brawn made a mistake." Jessica looked up. "Having produced Dabney to discomfit you," he said with renewed relish, "they must now put him on the stand. They're stuck with his honesty."

She was nervous, abstracted, unable to eat. Finally she pushed aside her plate and put a gnawing question. "Must the judge take the expert's opinion?" she asked. "If it challenges mine?"

"That's what makes the lawsuit." Trumbull patted her hand. "Now if we hurry, we'll just be in time."

She looked over her shoulder. "Everybody's watching us," she said.

"So they are," he drawled with forced humor, "but it's broad daylight. We're in full view and I'm a well-behaved man. Let 'em watch."

"That awful courtroom," she sighed. She took his arm and walked with him into the sun. They crossed the street, smiling at each other, and stopped before the City Hall entrance. "Jess?" Trumbull said soberly. "A pleasant mood influences the judge. You must keep it so."

"Yes, Mark," she said.

"You look charming," he said, glancing at her breasts. "Just stick to the marriage paper and you'll be all right."

The same leisurely pace marked the resumed cross-examination. The first year of residence at the Camden was probed with an easy but increasingly searching touch. She was questioned in detail about a moonlight drive with her former friend, Mrs. Helen Bjornson, and two army lieutenants to the

301

Fourteen Mile House for beer and oysters. Her answers were quick and spirited. She was expected to behave like a single woman, she retorted.

On the whole she did well. With light deprecatory laughter, she was forced to admit errors as to time, place, dates, and such details—but then, lands!—she had no head for such things. The smile became more fixed, the laughter less spontaneous. Trumbull was in his characteristic pose, eyes closed, doodling, memorizing the record as it went along.

Brawn kept his coaxing pose. He turned to the complaint. Miss Roux understood, did she not, that Mr. Hagerman's wife would have a large claim to community property running to millions? Jessica nodded agreeably. However, after that episode with Miss Keenan, Brawn went on, she had taken as payment in full for, ah, services rendered, a paltry lump sum of money?

"That had nothing to do with my marital claims," she said pleasantly. "I'd given him seven thousand five hundred dollars to invest for me before we were married. He returned precisely that sum. It was a distasteful argument to get it back because he claimed this stock had collapsed and I was wiped out. I said that he had no business to hold the investment when with ordinary prudence and foresight he'd know that the speculation was a bust. How was it my fault? He gave me"—she went on, consulting her notes—" three thousand in gold currency, a demand note for one thousand, and notes for the balance at two hundred and fifty a month. He also added mad money, but I have no records on that."

"Very complete answer," Brawn said.

"Quite so," she replied.

The bland tone went on. "Those notes were made to you as Miss Jessica Roux, were they not? And in the following two years when you got cash, you signed receipts in that name. Why should Mrs. Hagerman have taken notes and given receipts to her husband in her maiden name?"

"Well, I sure was no maiden," Jessica observed good-humoredly. "So I don't know if that's correct in any case."

"Would you call it a *nom de guerre?*" Brawn bantered, smiling.

She stared long and critically at space. "I used my maiden name not to antagonize him. He was testy and irritable at that time because of these boils."

"Boils now?" Brawn said wearily, feeling his client wince. "Can we not leave the medical side to medical men?"

"The medical side finally had a very important effect on our lives," Jessica retorted with warmth. "After the Miss Keenan episode, he was never again the same. He fell sick and was woried about his age. He was no longer his masterful self, but guarded by nurses and detectives, having his life run by the family. I often came to nurse him and rub his feet. Dr. Sawtelle knows all about it. In those last months when he was so unhappy and fearing death, he called for me and I always came. One night I found him crying like a baby because of what they were doing to him.

"He told me what truly was upsetting him. He was worried about this terrible wrong he felt he'd be doing the children, especially Emily, who was plaguing him about the estate. He was daily getting letters and even cables from England, and he was too cowardly to come out with the truth—that the marriage had taken place. All of 'em, you see, had swallowed that story about the engagement—except Mr. Galindez. I always felt that Mr. Galindez knew the truth," she added with a spiteful stare. Galindez shrugged. "Then he asked me to give up my marriage contract. Well, there I stopped. I said I'd lost it. . . ." She paused.

"But you hadn't?"

"Well, what would you have done?" Jessica said with feeling. "I wanted time to think. I was afraid he'd contrive to steal it. You must remember that every time we quarreled— and we sure raised the dust, I can tell you—he'd threaten the most brutal things, screamed he'd throw me out on the street, reduce me to shameful things. To be fair, I said some strong things myself, but I reckon all married couples have their ups and downs, so I took it in an ordinary way. But I was determined not to surrender my honor."

"Oh, honor!" Brawn made a flirting motion.

"Yes, honor!" Jessica retorted with spirit. "And that smirk's uncalled for. Mr. Hagerman may be small but he's wiry and can be dangerous in a temper. He's got quite a bite," she added ruefully, rubbing a shoulder with a suggestive hint.

Another laugh. La Roo was holding her own.

"But I did agree to settle our fiscal accounts," she added nicely.

"And you want the Court to believe that you—a business

303

woman—took that seven thousand five hundred dollars to settle your account without interest?" Brawn wheeled and stabbed a finger with incredulity. "Without *interest?*" He might have charged violation of an eleventh commandment.

Jessica drew a breath. "Mr. Brawn, you'll not anger me by aspersions. I was not his mistress but his wife—and by his invitation, not mine. No one put a shotgun to his head. So have done with innocence. You are twisting things. I will not be angered."

"So much for receipts," Brawn finally said, apparently baffled.

"The fact is that I was aghast," Jessica went on. "I hadn't been thinking about myself at all, I saw. I had been entirely too confiding, I concluded. I'd had this skylarking attitude expecting Mr. Hagerman to confront the children in due time and present me to the world. Why not? The alliance could only honor him. Now, suddenly, I saw the forces I was up against. I consulted my lawyer—"

Brawn said casually, "That was Mr. MacGowan?"

"You know it was."

"Why Mr. MacGowan?"

"Oh! Well, he'd been my lawyer," Jessica replied. "I thought perhaps he'd help me, but that was being credulous. I should have realized that in business nothing's more important than the partner who won't let you do the right thing."

Galindez smiled grimly.

"Mr. Hagerman got wind of that," she went on, "and accused me of meeting Mr. MacGowan in French restaurants and began to make scenes of jealousy, objecting to his wife dining with other men. Mr. Hagerman, I am afraid, has two standards in these matters. Now I am sure you know that I had hired a maid companion, Miss Blake, to be my chaperone going east. I understand she has been bribed to testify against me, so let me say that I met Mr. MacGowan solely for legal purposes."

"In French restaurants?" Brawn asked.

Jessica considered this gravely. "There is nothing wrong with French restaurants unless people make it wrong. This is San Francisco, and us married women have a freedom elsewhere unknown."

The married women nodded.

Brawn faced the woman with blank contemplation.

"Madam, didn't you at that time tell Miss Blake you were engaged to Mr. MacGowan?"

Jessica waited a long moment. "I think you know it never came to that. Mr. MacGowan was a dear friend, nothing more, and Mr. Galindez knows all about it. I think men and women may be dear friends, don't you?"

"I have no opinion," Brawn said. "But wasn't Mr. Mac-Gowan more than a dear friend? Did you not confide to Miss Blake that you regarded Mr. MacGowan as your sweetheart?"

Jessica knitted her brows. "I did not say Mr. MacGowan was *my* sweetheart—I said he was *a* sweetheart. Quite a difference."

Brawn let the moment pass. "Did you tell Miss Blake that you planned to marry Mr. MacGowan when the old dragon, meaning his mother, tired of breast-feeding a forty-year-old son? Would a married woman say that?"

Jessica stared. "Well, *that* I cannot recall, but if I said such a thing—and I might, I'm impulsive and I rattle on—bear in mind I'm thirty years younger than Mr. Hagerman. I sure had no wish to end up a rich lonely widow with a fancy man for company in some foreign land."

The coarse expression brought a sucking in of breaths.

"I'm afraid," she added with realism, "that women look to the future. We must." The smile was now more set. "All charges about Mr. MacGowan and myself are without truth."

"I have made no charges," Brawn said with quiet menace.

"Good!" Jessica said with force. "My circumstances were painful and perhaps I confided my secret thoughts to Miss Blake in a vagrant, wishful way. I have done that all my life. When I said I could marry this man or that, it was just fanciful. Maybe I take comfort in thoughts but that's not too unusual. I felt trapped. I was kept impoverished. My life was in danger, I felt. So was my sanity. Mr. Hagerman would not release me nor sustain me. I found no way to appease him. One moment he was his old loving self, calling me to spend the night. Next he was yelling, picking pretexts, getting Captain Webster to vex me by unconscionable petty charges, or putting vermin in the bathroom, and a thousand maddening tricks.

"Yes, I poured out my heart to Miss Blake. Why not? I was not the scheming adventuress you are making me out. I was a distracted heartbroken woman whose marriage was piling on the rocks. Mr. Brawn," she said ringingly, "you are degrading that poor old woman, but you cannot turn my daydreams into evidence." There was a burst of applause. "Miss Blake is over seventy and not reliable. She steals things."

Brawn wheeled. "Steals things?"

"Silver mustard pots," Jessica said with regret. "That's why I dismissed her. Poor thing."

Brawn turned on his heel. "Call Miss Blake!"

Miss Charlotte Blake, a thin, white-haired gentlewoman, entered and identified herself with an angry sniff. There was marked constraint between the women as she turned to leave. "What can you expect for ten dollars a month?" Jessica said nastily. "I heard that; I'm not deaf," Miss Blake snapped as the door closed.

Finch passed a note. "Can't she keep her mouth shut?" Trumbull wrote a reply. "Was Miss Blake planted to spy?" Finch looked up, startled. Trumbull was perfectly serious.

Jessica pressed her temples and mentioned a headache.

"Mr. Brawn," she said exhaustedly, "you're making a fool of yourself. If I was just a mistress. . . . Why would Mr. Hagerman go to such lengths except to find cause to divorce me? That's the sense of linking me to Mr. MacGowan. But it's false."

"But if you discussed a marriage with Mr. MacGowan," Brawn retorted, "wouldn't that show you were not then conscious of legal ties to Mr. Hagerman?"

"How was that possible? I was married to Mr. Hagerman. Do you think you get divorced from a written contract by tearing it up—piff-paff? It can only end like any other marriage—by a court judgment or in death. I'm now divorcing Mr. Hagerman because I tragically must, but I was then still living at the Camden Hotel and very much aware of my position as Mr. Hagerman's wife.

"Very much," she repeated in a strangled voice, suddenly overcome. She covered her face. "Sorry," she said apologetically after a moment, wiping away the tears. "Do you think I'd be such a fool? Married to Mr. Hagerman, worth millions, to give him grou.ids? If I'm the money-mad adventuress you're trying to make me out, why would I be so foolish? Pray credit me with sense, if nothing else. I'll tell you another thing: Mr. MacGowan's the safest man in San Francisco. That was always the trouble there. It put a crimp on everything."

There was no laughter. The strain was beginning to tell.

A darkening picture began to appear. Jessica's smiles were more fixed. Brawn was pressing hard. Miss Roux denied giving Miss Blake an exaggerated idea of her financial position to conceal an illicit source of income. She denied sending frantic notes to MacGowan by Jimmy Riley, a bellboy; denied visiting MacGowan's offices after hours; denied eluding her grandmother one Sunday to spend an hour with Mac-Gowan while Miss Blake waited in a cheap oyster bar; denied returning from MacGowan's offices on that occasion with flushed cheeks, denied pirouetting and crowing to Miss Blake that she'd marry her dearest Andy; denied dining with Mac-Gowan at the Verein Club on the fourteenth; at the Bay City Oyster House on the sixteenth; the Antelope on the seventeenth; let alone the Poodle Dog and other such places; denied telling Miss Blake that she had decided not to go east but would stay in San Francisco, and keep the sweet, sweet company of her dearest Andy. No, no, Miss Blake was a clear case and needed to be sent to Melrose for her own protection.

"And how would you describe a woman who'd behave like that?" Brawn asked.

"She'd have to be crazy," Jessica exclaimed. "But I'm not. It never happened."

"Well, let's see now," Brawn said, calling for a memorandum. "Let's get back to your fortune-tellers."

"That again?" Jessica said exhaustedly. "Ye gods!"

Brawn was sweating now. Did Miss Roux recall a visit with Miss Blake to Mrs. Lightfoot's establishment?

"Yes," Jessica said, recovering. "That old fraud? Go on."

"You recall that parlor? It has the zodiac signs about? Long drapes? A table?"

"There's always a table."

"King Solomon's Seal is on the door?"

"Smells of onions, too. What of it?"

Brawn came back with some effort. "Mrs. Lightfoot told you she knew the old man you were worried about? It was Mr. Hagerman?"

"Yes."

"Did you not tell Mrs. Lightfoot you had given Mr. Hagerman things to drink to make him love you? Things like comparity leaves?"

"What are comparity leaves?" Finch wondered.

"The plaintiff knows," Brawn replied. "And so does Mrs. Lawes. Madam, did that happen?"

"Of course I gave Mr. Hagerman things to drink," Jessica replied, "but for a chest cold. Mr. Brawn, you're very credulous if you don't recognize home remedies. It was mainly honey and lemon."

Brawn came back to the rail. "Miss Roux?"

Jessica assumed a straightforward, slightly mocking, expression. "Yes, please?"

"Did you ever tell Mrs. Lightfoot that you wanted to buy a graveyard charm?"

"Graveyard charm?" she asked, puzzled.

"A charm which required one to wear the gentleman's clothes for nine days, then bury 'em in a newly made grave at midnight?"

Jessica frowned, bewildered. "I sure don't know where you get this from, Mr. Brawn. I wouldn't go to a stinking graveyard to save my life."

Brawn turned to his associates. She saw Galindez' shrug and Evanston's sniff. Brawn studied his notes. On that visit had she not complained to Mrs. Lightfoot that she had bought such charms from other fortune-tellers—Mrs. Laura Scott, Mrs. Ida Massey—which had failed to compel the gentleman to marry her? That she had taken a bull frog, cut it open, taken out its heart, and stuck nine needles in it? That the needles had been buried in the sea?

The harsh questions were compelling attention; the mood was unpleasant indeed, but the mocking smile was untouched. "Never happened!" Jessica scoffed.

Had she not then opened her famous bosom to Mrs. Lightfoot? Had she not displayed a red silk bag with a little dried thing—a frog's heart—to prove her statements? Had she not told Mrs. Lightfoot that she had been wearing the gentleman's shirt at night and his stocking around her left knee as part of the charm?

Left knee? An ironic laugh was empty. Why the left knee?

Was that knee not supposedly nearest the heart?

Jessica studied her knees, and the dipping cleft between her thighs. Lands! She couldn't see the difference. But she sure had never opened her bosom to Mrs. Lightfoot, and if anyone said so, she'd lay a complaint for perjury.

No one now was smiling.

Brawn advanced in the deepening silence. "Did you not take out a paper with a written charm? And tell Mrs. Lightfoot that it was a graveyard charm that, if used, would make a man marry? That while the body was rotting in the grave, the party must marry or die?"

Jessica looked about with wonder. "I must be dreaming," she said, bewildered. "I never heard of such a charm."

"Did you make that statement?"

"Certainly not."

Brawn was staring unpleasantly. "Then why go to Mrs. Lightfoot's at all if not for charms?"

Jessica smoothed the materials of her dress, thinking deeply. "Well, honestly," she said finally, "sometimes when you're going crazy out of your mind, it helps to talk about your fortunes. I confided in Mrs. Lightfoot because she was a comfort and seemed wise. But only once or twice, and only on trivial things. Sho! None of those disgusting things you're bribing her to say."

"You now say she's been bribed to commit perjury?"

"Yes, and for a clear reason. Mrs. Lightfoot is a member of the Colored Baptist Church. I have reason to believe when this case appeared in the newspapers, she took up the matter with the lawyers for the church, Messers. Galindez and Mac-Gowan, and perhaps got her instructions there. She's sure no disinterested witness. Otherwise I have no idea why she should say such nonsense. What in the world for?"

"Is there anything in this area you do believe?"

Jessica hesitated. "Well, my tarot cards have proved remarkable."

"And what do they tell you?"

"That there is a rich man in my life," she said and raised a wan laugh. "Your Honor," she said suddenly, "I'm exhausted and I cannot think. Could we not recess?"

"I'd rather go on," Brawn said.

"'I can't think!' Jessica said with rising temper. "It's all tied up here." She pressed her temples.

"Ten minutes will finish this," Brawn persisted.

"Damn you!" she burst out, and caught herself. "Your Honor?" she appealed. "I haven't slept in a month and it's just a jumble. Can't we recess?"

"Well, of course," the judge said, frowning. "Half hour!" He tapped and left for chambers. Jessica waited dully, then stirred and painfully left the witness chair. Deathly pale, she joined Malvinia, who produced salts.

The lawyers used the recess to stroll the crowded hall. Green said, "Judge, I'm worried about this business. Suppose they bring in these fortune-tellers?"

"What of it?" Trumbull replied. "Who'd believe 'em? They might as well bring in a passel of streetwalkers. Best thing in the world that could happen. Siddy, d'ye remember that pimp who walked out of the courtroom and hung himself after you had done with him?"

"Frenchy Sam," Finch said. "Quite so."

"Well, if you cannot pulverize that scum, turn back your shingle," Trumbull said. "Which gives me to think we've neglected that area of investigation. Mrs. Lawes could get a line on all of 'em, wouldn't you say?"

"Guess so," Finch said without enthusiasm, "but we seem never to run out of surprises."

Trumbull threw a stub into a sandbox. "Let's get back and try this case," he said abruptly, thinking that Finch was getting difficult indeed.

She found it hard to focus. The first question, thin, shrill, from the distance, was repeated. "Come again?" she said, leaning forward.

It was Brawn's voice she realized despite the confusion. Something to do with what conduct? she wondered. What episode was the creature talking about?

A typescript appeared. It had danger, she saw. "Madam, I want to be fair," the voice said.

"Yes?" she said wearily.

Brawn said, "Madam, this statement by Li describes an occasion just before you left the Camden Hotel?"

"Of course," she said mechanically.

"Li recalls that he lit the parlor fire and rubbed Mr. Hagerman's feet, then thought he heard a noise in the bedroom. He says:

"I go round the dark closet and I find Missy Roux sitting in that dark. She put her finger, so, and say, 'Shush.' Scare me half to death. I holler like everything. I say, 'Hoo-hoo,' and I fall right down this way, you know?"

Brawn looked up. "Did that happen?"

"I have given my views on Li," she retorted. She dabbed her mouth. "No. It did not."

Brawn read on.

"Scare me so, by God! Then Mr. Hagerman come and try to push her by the shoulders and she refuse to go. She pretend she faint. Mr. Hagerman pour water on her and she go off, swearing bad words. She say, by God, she come back again and fix him. Mr. Hagerman say maybe she pay me five dollar for key. I say No, maybe she steal key long time by-and-by ago. Mr. Hagerman take pills and lay down and I say, 'Oh, my, why you nice people cannot get along better?' Mr. Hagerman laugh and tell me next time I let Missy into rooms, he skin me alive. Then I go crying to Missy how she make me trouble. I tell her next time Mr. Hagerman swear if she do crazy things he send her away forever. She say a bad word and tell me she kill Mr. Hagerman he try such a thing and I go away."

"Now, madam," Brawn said, "would a woman hide like that in a closet if she were legally married?"

An intolerable moment passed. "Lands! Why would I want to hide in a closet?"

Brawn turned full about. "To spy, wasn't it?"

"Spy on what?" Jessica asked helplessly. "Why should I want to spy?"

"Why, after the Bruno episode, did you not become suspicious of Mr. Hagerman and have him followed about—as you testified?"

"He was staying out late and I was concerned. I was his wife."

"Quite so. And you upbraided him for being faithless?"

"A bit. But he deserved it."

"Did you not rant and rave?"

"We had our tiffs."

"Ah, tiffs! After one tiff, did you not hide in his closet and spy on him with another woman?" Brawn demanded, raising his voice and stepping close. She sat back, blinking at the force of the question. Was there a distant twittering sound? What was it? Bats? Things flying? She cleared her mind of those annoyances and threw an imploring glance to

Trumbull and Malvinia. Then Brawn was advancing upon her. "Why, madam, did you not return to your rooms and tell Miss Blake in a fit of uproarious laughter that you had watched Mr. Hagerman in the sexual act with a woman named Kathie Dunnock and had overheard Mr. Hagerman call you a tigress in bed with reference to your special accomplishments?" It was a bellow of disgust.

"And did you not roll on your bed, kicking your heels, screaming with laughter on the joke of hiding in that closet? And did you not tell Miss Blake that you were indeed a tigress and knew more ways to give a man pleasure and satiety than all the pipe dreams of the Orient?"

"Never!" Jessica said thickly. "That is too abominable," she choked. "Spy on people in bed? What d'ye think I am? I don't remember anything like that."

Brawn stepped closer. "But you were in that closet?" he said, holding her transfixed.

She stared at the nostril pits, seeing each hair. She was drowning in the nares of that man. "What Li and Miss Blake have got to say are lies. But I will tell the truth now. I had hoped to keep this in the family, but I see it is not possible."

She was now forward in her chair, fists clenched, vehement, strained. "I was not spying at all. I was called to that room after Miss Blake brought these tales about Mr. Mac-Gowan. Mr. Hagerman was drinking and in a jealous insane rage. I had never seen him so. First he began to torment and wrench my heart by telling me indecencies committed with Miss Dunnock. He said horrible things that he had done with that girl—things I'd rather die than repeat before this Court. Then he told me how he had indeed compared me with Miss Dunnock, calling me a tigress in comparison. So much is the truth, but I have never, never done those things with any mortal soul. I was sick and horrified, begging that he release my wrists and cease the torture. I begged him not to torment me with abominable thoughts. I was not brought up so. Then he commanded me to do things I had always resolutely refused to do and finally I was called names and commanded to sign a scurrilous paper giving up my rights as wife. I refused. I had given him no trouble and he had no right to abuse me. He said I had three days to sign that paper or he'd throw me out in disgrace. I told him I'd never commit moral and legal suicide by signing any such paper. Then he went insane. His eyes were rolling like epilepsy. He was frothing and

312

then he tried force. I still have a mark where he struck me. He jumped at me and choked me until I fell on the floor in a real paralyzed fit.

"He was real scared, believing he had killed me. He locked me in that bedroom closet, and left me for dead. I awoke finally and found myself in the dark and began to cry and that's how I was found by Li. I did not go laughing uproariously to Miss Blake. I was weeping and laughing hysterically, which is another thing. Oh, dear God," she burst out. "How could anyone say such abominations? What can be worth it?" She threw back her head, sobbing convulsively.

Jessica blew her nose and resumed. "Mr. Hagerman knows the truth. After that episode, I went to my grandmama's, where I stayed overnight, discussing plans for my trip east. My Uncle Will was all for thrashing Mr. Hagerman to an inch of his life, but I said No! I valued Mr. Hagerman's friendship, and perhaps it would blow over. I wanted no scandals. But when I returned to the hotel, I found poor Miss Blake in terror. Captain Webster's men were ripping up my carpets. They took the door off the hinges. I almost died. I wrote and begged Mr. Hagerman not to make a scandal. I groveled and pleaded with him to have more regard for his wife and to let me go quietly. I sure did not deserve that treatment." Her breast was heaving.

"You say you wrote, begging him to treat his wife with more regard? His wife, you say?"

She nodded and pressed her temples.

Brawn called for a folder. "Madam, think carefully: Is this a letter from a wife or from a discarded mistress?" he asked brutally, displaying a paper.

She glanced at the paper and away. "From a wife, surely."

"Let's see," Brawn said with a hard smile and read the text aloud.

"My dear Mr. Hagerman:

You are wronging me, so help me God, you are wronging me. I am no more guilty of what you have accused me than a stranger. Would you who asked me to come to this place, whom I have been up with nights and waited on, and cared for, and would have done anything on earth to help in his distress, be the one to wrong and injure me? Would a man whom the people

313

have sent to the United States Senate stoop to injure a girl and one he has professed to love?"

Brawn looked up. "What had he accused you of?"
"That I stole the receipt for my seven thousand five hundred dollars, and two hundred shares of Belcher stock," she replied bitterly. "It was all a pretext."
Brawn read on:

"I've written twice without reply except to hear that you have read my letters to others. I heard you were told I said I'd give you trouble. Be too much the man to listen to such talk. I never said such a thing or thought it. If no other woman gives you trouble till I do, you will take your gray hairs to your grave without the slightest care. You have been kind to me. I hope my God may forsake me when I cease to show my gratitude. I'd not give you one restless night upon your pillow through any act of mine. If you are not trying just to quarrel, you will find how you have wronged me.

"You once said no woman alive could look you in the face and say, 'Lew Hagerman, you have wronged me.' Let me not be first to utter the cry. I have hoped to have your friendship throughout life and this outburst is undeserved. How absurd and ridiculous. Why would I do such a thing? What was I to gain in doing so? Pray credit me with sense. I valued your friendship more than all the world. Have I not given up everything and everybody for it? One million dollars would not tempt me to risk its loss. I am humiliated to death that Captain Webster can say I was ordered out of this house. I hope at least in your unjust anger you will let us apparently part friends, and don't make gossip. Think how you'd feel to have your daughters treated so. Don't fight me. Don't send orders through Captain Webster or this, that, or the other relative. You have put me in a strange position, Senator, and all the pride in me rebels. I've been looking at some nice places, but cannot get them until the coming month, so if you want me to go, let me know and I will obey when I know that this is what you really want.

As ever,
J."

The reading was completed in a dead silence. Jessica was staring at the floor.

Brawn said, "Well, madam? D'you anywhere here refer to yourself as this man's wife?"

"No," she said reluctantly.

"Thank you," Brawn said with satisfaction.

"But what about the other letters?" she asked. "Where I pleaded to preserve our marriage?"

Brawn halted, facing Trumbull's wintry smile. "Dear God, is there no end to these inventions?" he said distinctly. "Is that it? Now Mr. Hagerman is keeping back your letters?"

"He sure is," she said wearily, "and it's no invention because I told you about those other letters at your office when I tried to hire you."

Brawn was dead still. "This is intolerable, Mr. Finch—or Judge Trumbull—or whoever controls this creature," he said in a strangled voice. "She said nothing to me about this, now or never."

"That's not true," Jessica said distinctly.

"Oh, be quiet, madam," Brawn said insultingly. "I'm not talking to you."

Finch was up raging. "Counsel has no right to impute perjuries," he cried heatedly.

Bang. "Gentlemen!"

"Why can't she just answer questions?" Brawn complained. "Why must she put me into her lies?"

Trumbull strolled forward. A peculiar light was in his eyes. "Mr. Brawn is not under oath," he said slowly. The voice was dead and without tone coming from a distance. "The witness is under oath. I believe the witness and I do not believe Mr. Brawn."

Brawn stood back. "I do not care what Judge Trumbull believes or thinks. I decline to be provoked or to take notice. I ask that he sit and that we continue."

Trumbull glanced at the mute judge, the silent chamber, the court officers, the press. Jessica was leaning forward with a look of excitement and fear. "I say I believe the witness," Trumbull said in the same remote voice. "General Brawn may believe what he likes."

"Gentlemen! In chambers at once," McArdle said angrily.

"Damnation," McArdle stormed, "how in hell d'ye think I feel when I see the lawyers screwed up like a pack of bully boys? Threats? Menaces? In my courtroom? I won't have it. The next hint of violence, the other party gets the verdict. This ain't France."

Trumbull looked up. "Counsel may argue from the evidence. He may not except under oath make statements of fact."

"I will seek a peace bond," Brawn said.

Trumbull said, "I will resist that."

"I ask that Judge Trumbull be searched," Brawn said. "I am afraid he has a weapon."

McArdle stared. "Is that true, Judge Trumbull?"

Trumbull had remained calm, almost impersonal, saying only what was required. A flush appeared. "I have not carried a weapon in twenty years and need none now. I have the point of my boot."

"I think he should be searched," Brawn said.

The situation was painful with tension. "Well," McArdle said, backing down, "if Judge Trumbull says so, I'll take his word. He has always meant exactly as he says."

"Thank you," Trumbull said.

The young judge drew a breath of relief. "All right," he said manfully. "Shake hands and make up now."

"I'll apologize only to the court," Trumbull said. McArdle insisted—or the trial would be adjourned until they did. Fingertips touched and the moment had passed. The men rose to leave.

Brawn found his voice first. "Judge Trumbull," he said reasonably, "really I'm surprised at a man of your parts. I hope we've got mutual respect. D'ye honestly think I'd state a fact like that to the Court unless true?"

Trumbull stared with absolute contempt. "You've taken Hagerman's money, h'ain't you? After milking the woman of her confidence? What opinion d'ye think I've got?"

Brawn flushed a deep red. "Well, Trumbull," he retorted, "you may advocate that bundle of ignorance and superstition, if you like. My answer to you will be a lawyer's answer—the verdict of the Court."

"Keep it so," Trumbull said.

McArdle ended the exchange. "Gentlemen, if this happens again, it's thirty days in the calaboose all around and I don't care who you are. Get back to court and behave like lawyers." A blink of approval from his secretary was a passing mark.

Finch hung back. "Judge Trumbull," he groaned, shaking his head in despair. "I don't know what got into you. Alienating every judge, state and federal? Are you trying to cut off our heads? What's this about?"

Trumbull halted. "Damn that long face!" he growled. "If we show less than absolute determination, the woman's lost and she knows it. She looks to us and is entitled to strong support. From now on she'll be treated with respect and circumspection. If you'd shown more courage yourself, this intervention'd not have been needed. Let's keep that in mind from now on."

The courtroom was more crowded than ever as Brawn retraced the movements from Ellis Street to Wisteria Place.

"Now, about Li," he said finally. What was Li's role? Was it not that he acted for Mr. Hagerman to get women for his bed? Did she know that?

"Bed?" Jessica dabbed her mouth, showing the strain. "That was never specified to me. I was just told by Li to come because Mr. Hagerman was lonely or wanted my light-hearted fun. When I showed up, Li'd be sent home. He could never wait to get to his family. He's got a flat in Washington Street."

"Did you ever visit Li at that flat?"

Jessica sat forward, blinking. "Yes, I'd heard that Mr. Hagerman had recovered his health. I thought Li could help persuade him to ask me back. I was fighting to save my marriage. I think that I had that right."

"Did you give him money?"

"Five dollars, yes."

"Why couldn't you write yourself?"

Jessica drew a breath. "I wanted to be asked. I would not impose myself. I do have my pride."

"Pride?" Brawn took a step back. "And you—Mrs. Senator Hagerman, the aristocrat of far-off Cape Badeau—saw no wrong seeking help in the stinking lair of a Chinese pander?"

She was undaunted. "Save that speech," she said coldly. "I have never heard anything more undemocratic. Li will tell any lie for Mr. Hagerman, but he was a sweet and good friend. I abominate prejudice, but let me remind everybody that Mr. Hagerman's been very good to the Chinks—California's full of 'em because of him. No wonder there's unrest." The reminder was dropped into the poisoned well.

Brawn came back to Dragon's Blood and the whole business with Nellie of sprinkling that odious powder was reviewed. Now, on that occasion, he wondered, was not a shirt taken from the bureau in the bedroom?

"Shirt?" she asked wearily.

"Or stockings?" Brawn asked carelessly, studying his notes. He consulted his associates, nodded, and came back. "Yes, that's still the question," he said, entwining his hands.

"Well, honestly," Jessica said. "What d'ye think I am? Rummaging through smelly laundry bags?"

"If Li should swear that a shirt and stockings were missing that afternoon, would that be false?"

"Shirts? Stockings? What for?"

"You must tell me," Brawn replied.

Jessica said, "I just have no idea why Li'd say such silly things."

In the witness room, Trumbull was staring at the window. He was thinking that he did not like the trend one bit.

"Oh, don't ask why I sprinkled that damned powder," Jessica said sullenly. "It seemed a thing to do, that's all. Nellie was excited to see the apartment, I expect."

They were alone. The door was locked. "Mark, dear," she said, troubled, "don't be angry with me. I vow, I couldn't endure this if I didn't feel your support. Don't you know that?" She stepped close and searched his face.

"This is a public building," he said uncomfortably. She withdrew, hurt. "What's Brawn after? He's spending too much time on these superstitions. Ain't worth it. What's coming? What's he driving at?" He took her chin, searching her eyes, scowling. "D'ye have any notion?"

His grasp was cruel, hurting. "Blame it! I thought it'd be a straightforward lawsuit and now I'm on a sea of doubts." She took his hand, stepping close, meeting his gaze. "Mark, honey?" she said with a note of desperation. "You won't leave me to Finch?"

His hand stroking her hair was gentle. "No, sugar," he said, summoning reassurance. "I'll sure be here. Just take it cool."

Green knocked and, when he entered, Jessica was fixing a loose button on Trumbull's sleeve.

The day was ending on an ominous mood. Jessica sat forward, her knees together, flashing a wan look of apology to the court. The smell was bad, she thought dully; something like garlic clung. The questions were hard to hear and she strained to listen.

"When was this period?" she asked stupidly.

Brawn was more than patient. Wasn't it true, he asked, that when she first met Hagerman at the bank, she was under no temptation to listen to an indecent proposal? She nodded. That was because she had independent means and social position? Quite so.

"Life was good? The sun was shining, you say?"

"I had a toothache, but nothing worse. I couldn't complain."

Brawn smiled broadly. "Let's see now how sunshiny the day really was. You were there to borrow money, were you not?"

"Yes. For investment purposes," she retorted. "You make money on borrowed funds. No different than a margin account. It's the only way to show a profit."

"When the market rises?"

"Sho."

"And when it falls?"

"It comes back."

"Did it come back for you?"

"It was going to."

"You had just been wiped out?"

"I had losses, yes. I wouldn't say wiped out."

The earlier mincing, lisping manner was gone. The questions struck like hammers. Was it not the fact, Brawn went on, that Miss Roux had no more than eleven dollars at the Hagerman Bank that day?

Miss Roux could not be expected to remember.

Miss Roux was confronted with a copy of her account.

Miss Roux nodded slowly, but that, she added, was merely her checking account. Sho! She had gold notes in her safety deposit box at the Nevada.

Ah! Did anyone else know of that currency?

Yes. Mr. Joseph Morgan, her stock broker.

Mr. Morgan was dead?

Unfortunately, yes.

Did anyone else know of these assets?

Yes, a dear friend, Mr. Melville O'Bannion.

319

Also dead?

No, in Europe.

Was there anyone available who knew of that fund?

No.

Not her brother?

Sho! Especially not her brother. But she sure had gold currency.

Hm. Then how was it that she had left the Purdue Hotel owing three hundred dollars for back rent and moved to a cheap boardinghouse in suburban Oakland? And had she not begged Mr. Purdue to carry her stocks? And had Mr. Purdue not pronounced her stocks worthless? And had she not been wiped out just one month before meeting Mr. Hagerman?

Simply not true! Miss Roux said strongly. She had sold her stocks at a profit and kept the cash in her safety box. She was weary now, arching forward, holding the small of her back with one hand.

Was it not the fact, Brawn shouted, scarlet with rage as the exchange got hotter, that she had been sinking financially for a year? That her inheritance had been entirely lost in speculations? That she had fallen into such sore straits that she had most desperately followed Mr. MacGowan about the city, beseeching marriage?

"No!"

Brawn thrust an ugly jaw forward. His breath was whistling. Had she not spent days and nights besieging Mr. MacGowan's friends and clients with stories, pouring her woes to strangers on the street and threatening something desperate unless he married her?

There was dead silence.

Jessica went white. "Your Honor?" she appealed, aghast. "Mr. Finch? Will you allow this?"

"Not proper cross-examination," Finch cried in rage, "and Mr. Brawn knows it. Purely speculative!" he shouted with other things. The judge wearily asked enlightenment. Brawn besought a glass of water and came forward. The Court was confronted, he urged, sipping, with the clash of human probabilities. His client did not deny indecency. He claimed indecency.

Miss Roux of course saw the implication. Her version was a fairy tale—a chimera of secret documents, mysterious assignations, bizarre behavior, disappearing witnesses, all the claptrap of cheap melodrama. It was ridiculous and insulting

320

to the intelligence. And so she pretended to circumstances of wealth, background, and lineage to suggest the impossibility that she would hire herself out at salary for gross immoral purposes. There was something to that, of course, for indeed her family were substantial people who enjoyed respect and store credit—

"Thank you," Jessica interrupted.

—but not too much, Brawn went on, for in the best families—who did not know this?—were offspring so turbulent and headstrong, so reckless and despairing, so driven by immoderate and vengeful passions, that medical science had no explanation and no name for 'em. Those people were torments to themselves, and afflictions to all. The West was full of such remittance creatures—and he did not need, he said angrily, the savage grimaces of derision which Judge Trumbull was pleased to display!

Trumbull shrugged. What was the question?

The judge nodded. Yes, what was the purpose?

Brawn wiped his hands and went on, breathing heavily. "I am questioning her, Your Honor, now to show that when she met Mr. Hagerman she was in fact neither honest nor respectable nor solvent—that in fact her life was in such hopeless insolvency and personal misery that she turned with alacrity to the indecent but blunt proposal of this coarse and sensual man as a desperate way out of a suicidal frame of mind. That is the heart of the case—and what I now seek to bring out," he concluded. He sat, scarlet, conscious of the racing pens of reporters.

Hagerman cupped his hand. "If that prick calls me coarse and sensual once more, I'll kill him," he whispered.

Galindez bit a thumb and slid a glance of contempt at the woman on the stand. Jessica was staring daggers. "Judge Trumbull, must I answer?" she said.

Trumbull rose and came forward, conscious of amused, derisive faces. "Counsel may question your credibility here, ma'am, and you must submit," he said gently. "In this courtroom, counsel are privileged," he went on, fixing a level glance at Brawn. "It would be another thing elsewhere." With a curt nod he returned and sat in gloomy silence.

"Rephrase your question," the judge said.

"Now, then, madam," Brawn said, "one month before you called on Mr. Hagerman, did you not intrude in Mr. MacGowan's office, so hysterical, so desperate, so burdened with

321

fiscal woes, so burdened with sin and sorrow that you took laudanum . . ."

There was a shock of silence.

". . . from which you could have died and been carted to the morgue, to be stripped naked and exposed to public gaze, had Mr. MacGowan not carried you to Dr. Sawtelle's office . . ."

She was shaking her head.

". . . where you lay the night alone, your family not notified, giving your stomach contents to a bucket brought by a nurse?" Brawn stuck his face directly into hers. "Did that not happen?" he shouted. "Did you not take laudanum?"

"Well, that's not the way it happened," she said, shrinking back. "I was agitated because Mr. MacGowan chose to believe slanders by Mr. Galindez, and I took the wrong pills which I keep for my nerves, but it was an accident. Sho! Kill myself for love? That's silly. No man alive is worth that."

Evanston handed over a folder. Brawn stepped forward. "Must I produce the nurse?" he shouted, thrusting a medical form under her nose. "The bucket? The vomit and the retchings?" An imploring glance went to Trumbull. No comfort was there. Reporters stopped writing. "Did you not have your stomach pumped in Dr. Sawtelle's office?"

She made a weary gesture. She was tired, tired. "Yes," she said, sunk in humiliation. "But lots of ladies have got their stomachs pumped. What's that got to do with anything?"

A sigh went through the chamber.

Brawn nodded. "Just this: Were you not still in such a mood of personal and financial despair when you met Mr. Hagerman that you were glad to take—and did take—any immoral offer you could get?"

She sat thinking, feeling the horrid stare of the Argus-eyed monster—the ranks and ranks of faces. A scream died in her throat, and then words saved her. She sat forward and managed an amused ironic smile. "Well, if it took death's door to get me to that point," she drawled, "I couldn't be all that immoral to begin with, could I now?"

"Ten minutes," the judge rapped and fled.

"Not immoral?" Brawn repeated grimly, when the court had resumed. "Well, let us see." He glanced at Trumbull. "Miss Driscoll was only sixteen when you introduced her at the bank?"

Jessica frowned. "Actually, seventeen. Why?"

322

"Is this your handwriting?"

Even at a distance the bright green ink, the jagged scrawl were familiar.

"Yes, I wrote that," she said. "What of it? It was just a social note after a pleasant afternoon of banter."

"Is this a wife's banter?" Brawn asked.

"My Dear Senator:

Won't you please try to remember about those Springs you were talking about today, which you say were so lovely, and let me know tomorrow when I see you? I wish you'd decide and go down to them with Nellie and me on Saturday."

Brawn glanced significantly at the bench.

"I wish you were here. I am out at Nellie's mother's for a few days in Ellis Street. The old lady is a trial to me but she has the loveliest garden where I sit with birds singing, and I feel so sentimental for you, dearest. How I wish you'd come along in your carriage to surprise us two lone birds and take us for a moonlight drive. But gracious! It's too nice to think of, and I always disappoint myself by wishing too hard, so I really wish you would. 'Twould do you good to get out of that stupid old hotel and we'd both make you forget business cares and go home feeling happy.

"I am crazy for you to see Nell try and swallow an egg in champagne. I haven't told her of my own feat and I am looking forward to her going through that performance. Anyways a jaunt would do you worlds of good and us girls would take best care of you and mind you in *everything* you might wish!!"

Brawn rephrased the letter with intense loathing. "Us girls." "Us two lone birds." "Moonlight drives." "Eggs in champagne." "Go home feeling happy." He said each phrase in turn with disgust. "What did you mean when you said, '. . . us girls would mind you in everything you might wish'?"

"Just to laugh and joke and things like that," Jessica said, flushing. "It was to get him out of the dumps. What did you think that letter means?"

323

Brawn bowed profoundly. "No man can fail to understand what it means," he said suavely. "Except perhaps the lawyer saints on the other side of the case." Trumbull looked up blankly. Jessica was scarlet.

"I know what you're driving at," she burst out, "but it's a lie. If Mr. Hagerman had touched that girl, I'd have shot him —and I challenge him now to say he did!"

Hagerman half rose. "A-a-ah!" he said angrily. "Who says I touched her?"

"Aha!" Jessica said, triumphant.

"One minute!" The judge leaned over the bench. "Madam, were you, the man's wife, proposing moonlight drives for the Senator with that young girl? Well, I want that girl brought back on the stand promptly tomorrow morning. Hear that? Understood, Mr. Finch?"

Finch bowed and understood.

Brawn glanced at the clock. "Did you ever tell Senator Hagerman he could have Nellie stay the night?"

"Never," Jessica said angrily. "And you have no right to suggest that."

"Well, then, I'm sorry I asked," Brawn said, and the ordeal was over. Jessica received a nod of dismissal, stared at Mrs. Lawes, then swept to her place at the counsel table. "I just hope I pleased you," she whispered, convulsively seizing Trumbull's hand. "How'd I do?"

"Very well," he said with a heavy heart.

"There was nothing wrong with that letter," Nellie said stubbornly, running a tongue over white lips. She was pale, laboring under strong feelings after a session at Finch's chambers in the Nevada Block. Judge Trumbull had been uncommonly severe. There had been another, even stronger session, late into the night at Wisteria Place. News of her return to the stand had brought out the crowd. Every seat was filled, spectators lined the walls, the balcony was jammed.

"Quiet, quiet!" McArdle said. A bang and threat to clear the chamber brought order. What in particular, he demanded sternly, was meant by "us girls would take best care" of the Senator? Exactly how?

Nellie pressed her mouth tightly. Well, in questions of diet, she replied, and exertions. Senator Hagerman was under doctor's orders, so that's what it probably meant.

"Quiet!" the judge repeated automatically, although the

chamber was silent. But what was meant by minding the Senator in "everything" he might wish? Mind how?

"Just mind him," Nellie said.

"Did Miss Roux instruct you on that?"

"Yes."

"What were her instructions?"

Nellie glanced at Jessica, then shrugged. "Oh, not to get the sulks," she said resentfully. "Miss Roux said I'd been acting like a mean little something. So I was to act more gracious."

McArdle scribbled a notation and came back to the girl. "You see that the Senator's charged with strong proclivities toward young women? The younger the better? Were you—or were you not—to go along on moonlight rides?"

Jessica was leaning forward with concern and interest. If a signal passed, it was not evident. "Not really," Nellie said. "I was to give an excuse at the last minute."

Hagerman made a strangled sound.

"Oh, I see," McArdle said. "Why?"

"Miss Roux was hoping the Senator would take her alone to the Springs on her birthday. So she wrote a pleasant letter, chatty, you know? We'd had a sociable call at the office—so that's how it came to be written. But she sure didn't want me along, and I sure had no use for him."

McArdle stared at the resentful girl and suppressed a smile. "I see," he said finally. "Well, that seems satisfactory." Really, he thought, that was how to get the truth—firm questioning. "If there's nothing else, the witness is excused."

Trumbull cupped his hand. "Get her off," he whispered.

Finch said, "Step down, miss!"

"You may step down," the judge said.

Nellie hesitated. "But I'd like to say something, Your Honor," she blurted. "If I had gone along to those Springs, what would've been wrong? I knew Miss Roux was the Senator's wife."

"Just a moment." The judge raised a hand. "Miss Nellie, how did you know that?"

Nellie said, "I heard him say so."

"Why, miss?" Brawn bounced up angrily. "Why would a man of his age, sense, and acumen tell you a thing like that?"

"I didn't say he told me!" the girl retorted. "I said I heard him, and I did."

Brawn halted. "When? Where? You said nothing of this in your direct testimony."

The retort was classic. "I wasn't asked," she said promptly. "That's what everybody's trying to keep out of the case, but I don't care. What I heard will blow this case sky-high, and nobody wants to let me talk."

Bang! "Order! Order!"

Order was finally restored. The girl was leaning forward, triumphant. Reporters were scribbling. "Go on, Miss Nellie," McArdle said, staring at the plaintiff. Jessica was on her feet, curiously intent. "When and where did you hear that admission?"

"In his apartment the night that—"

"One minute. I've had enough hysterics." McArdle quieted a renewed babble. "You now say you were in Mr. Hagerman's apartment *at night*?" he asked with incredulity.

An angry glance flicked. "Yes, Judge. That night as she wrote in that letter, when the Senator said she was his own little wife."

"You say you were present?"

"Yes. They were making love."

McArdle swiveled full about, shaking out his sleeves. An ominous glance swept the chamber. Finch was bewildered. Green had broken a pencil. A newspaper messenger raced to the rear. Trumbull rose, "I doubt we need this . . ." he began.

McArdle held up a restraining hand. "Miss, did you ever confide this to your lawyers?" he said dangerously.

The girl shook her head. "No, Your Honor."

"Why not?"

"Because they don't really want the truth. When I try to tell the truth, they want me to trim the story. But I know the truth and I know she's married—"

"One minute!" The judge beckoned to his secretary. "Jack-o," he muttered. "What kind of dump was the old son of a bitch running?" A glare fixed the dirty little millionaire at the defense table. "Disgraceful! Absolutely reprehensible!"

"Wait for the cross-examination," Jack Dinesmore whispered. "This could be a fabrication."

"It could?" McArdle said, startled. Hell of a thing to fabricate, he thought. He pointed a finger. "Miss! I want to know what you heard and how, but if you're lying, this Court will know how to take care of you. Go on," he said ominously. "Counsel will not interrupt. I want all the circumstances."

Mrs. Lawes was seen to whisper to Miss Roux, who nodded. The silence became deathly. It had all come about when Miss Roux had become fearful of the man's intentions. He'd been blowing hot and cold, laughing mockingly and without reason, and so forth. Then, when Li came with an invitation to spend an hour, Miss Roux determined to test the matter and sallied forth with Nellie to the Imperial House.

And then what happened?

Nellie had full attention. She threw Hagerman a glance of malice and went on. The room opposite Hagerman's was used by one of the Senator's friends—Senator Claggett, she recalled. Miss Roux, finding that suite empty, had asked her to wait there and listen to some conversation. "I asked, 'What kind of conversation?' Miss Roux said, 'Never you mind, Miss Driscoll. You wait till I return.' So she left me looking through the crack while she went into Mr. Hagerman's apartment. Imperial House has these thick carpets and paintings and grandfather clocks everywhere. It was awful quiet, and about an hour later, I heard the clocks striking six along the halls. I could hear the rush traffic in the street and I got hungry and nervous, waiting in this strange room. I thought, Mary, I could be arrested! Then I heard Mr. Hagerman's voice in the hall. He was joking with the chambermaid, something that he was not that young anymore, and I heard her laughing. He went right past me into his apartment. The transoms were open, and I could hear their voices. Then I heard him laugh. He was singing some kind of aria, I believe, and then Li left. I could see that big moon grin go past and I thought, Oh, Mary! What now? I wanted to cut out, but the detective was now at the elevator. I had to use the bathroom, I was that nervous, but that was down the hall. I was never alone in a hotel before."

The girl had the world's attention, and she was going on swiftly but with maturity and composure.

"And then Miss Roux came and pulled me into Mr. Hagerman's bedroom through the side door and hid me behind the bureau. There's a big walnut bureau catty-corner, with room for a person. I said, 'For God's sake, Jess! What if I'm caught?' 'Oh, you won't be caught,' she said. 'I just want you to hear some conversation. I thought you were my devoted friend,' she said. I said, 'Yes, I'm your devoted friend, but I could be sent to San Quentin.' 'Oh, pooh! Senator Hagerman's a sport, and he'd just laugh,' she said. Well, that wasn't my idea of Senator Hagerman. Miss Roux pressed her lips for silence and left.

"So I stood there choking," the girl rushed on. "Senator Hagerman came in and, well, washed his hands and things and laid down on the bed. She came in and he asked her to brush his hair. Then he asked her to rub his feet."

The judge looked up. "Rub his feet?"

"They were cold," the girl said.

The judge scowled at his minutes. "You saw this?"

"Not that part. I was behind the bureau."

"Behind bureau. Not really eye witness," the judge wrote. "Did anything significant happen?"

The girl drew a breath. "Well, when he came into the room, he said, 'How d'ye do, Mrs. Hagerman?' And I said to myself: So it's really true! Not that I had doubts, but now it was clear to me beyond peradventure."

Objections were furiously made, sustained, and the witness admonished not to volunteer thoughts. She was merely to tell what she had seen and heard. "Anyways," she said finally, "Mr. and Mrs. Hagerman went out for dinner. When they came back, they were talking about these pearls for her birthday and if they could be ordered from Paris. She said, 'All right, Sen, if you love me so much, why did you turn me out of the hotel?' So he started to fondle her—"

"Did you see that?" the judge asked with wonder and growing distaste.

"No, but I judged it because she said, laughing, 'No, Sen, not until you explain.' What else could it mean?"

The silence was profound.

"Go on," the judge said, writing, choking on the damnedest situation in his career. Seventeen, he was thinking. Seventeen! "And did he explain?"

The girl sniffed. "Well, he said, 'Baby, I couldn't help myself. I was sick and confused and I guess I was hitting the bottle. Then I was getting all these letters about you. The family were making life hell for me, Baby. It wasn't my idea to put you out. I'm still crazy about you.' So Miss Roux asked who'd had the nerve to put her out of her rooms. He said it was Mr. Galindez who'd done that job of eviction— like all the rest. 'Baby,' he pleaded—he called her Baby— 'what can I do?' She said softly, 'Nothing, I reckon, but you're fortunate I'm an understanding woman because I'm swallowing lots of things. Let's see those letters.' He laughed and went to the bureau for the letters—I could hear the drawer next to my ear—and he read 'em. They were poison letters, warning that Miss Roux was carrying on with men, cowardly things like that. Then he burned the letters to prove his feelings and asked would she stay the night? My heart sank. I didn't think I could hold out." She stopped for breath.

Trumbull glanced at Jessica. She was arched forward, following the narrative with intent eyes. Behind her Malvinia formed a dark shadow of watchful judgment.

The girl resumed. "She said she did not come to stay the night.

"He wondered if she really loved him.

"She said she'd like to but she wasn't prepared.

"He said he'd fix it up, and he went out. Your Honor," the girl said suddenly, "I don't like to give these details. Must I?"

The judge looked up with a frown. "Yes," he said grimly.

The girl made a face and went on. "So I whispered, 'Fix up what?' She said, 'Never you mind, you've just got to stay now until he's gone to sleep, or we're cooked.' I started to whimper. I said, 'Jess what am I going to do?' She said, 'Stay there, you silly. I'll think of something!' I said, 'I can't wait!' She said, 'You've just got to!' I began to cry because I didn't know how I'd ever get out, and then I heard Mr. Hagerman whistling in the hall. I froze. Then he came back and took out this Hindu bronze statue—"

Could she see that?

Not at the time, she granted, but later she had. The object was small, about six inches high, like those Buddhas sold in tourist stores in Chinatown—but it wasn't something she liked to talk about. It was set out on the table and that was all she'd say about that bronze. The judge raised a hand. "What about this thing?" he demanded. "Why bring it into the picture?"

The girl blinked. "Why, to show I was there. I can describe every stick in that apartment including that Meissonier painting he bought that spring. Mr. Meissonier's French. Very fashionable."

"Never mind," the judge said. "I'll have to view the scene, I expect. Then what happened? Incense?"

"Why, yes," Nellie said with surprise. How did judges know such things? she wondered. "Then he said, 'Well, Mrs. Hagerman'—those were his words—'Lochinvar has come out of his vest.' They were laughing in a real fond way. Then they undressed each other." She stopped dead.

"Oh, no!" a woman's voice said.

"Silence!" the judge looked about angrily. "This is a court-room." Order was restored. "So they undressed each other," he said dangerously. "Then what?"

The girl dropped her eyes. "You know."

"Yes, I know," the judge said grimly, "but the stenographer can't put it down. Then what?"

"Then they put out the light."

"And then?"

"I heard sounds."

"What sort of sounds?"

"Love sounds," the girl said in a low voice. A clamor of objections rose that the young girl was not qualified to characterize such sounds. "Love sounds," McArdle muttered, making a note. Nellie was staring at the floor, pale and red in turns. Jessica was twisting a handkerchief.

She had remained behind the bureau, the girl went on, listening to conversation and endearments. Only after the sound of heavy breathing did she escape, shaking like a leaf. Fortunately the detective was gone.

Dead silence.

"Mr. Brawn?" the judge said.

Brawn returned to his post. A glance lingered on Miss Roux, then Mrs. Lawes, then to the girl.

"So you claim that you left the married couple?" he said, "and, I take it, went home?"

The white-pointed face began to color. "No."

Brawn looked up inquiringly. "You stayed in the hotel? Where?" The girl shifted. "In the hall toilet," she said reluctantly.

Brawn contemplated the red-faced girl. Finch stood with an objection, then slowly sat. "And how long," Brawn said, "did you commune in the Temple of the Goddess Cloacina?" then explained in simpler language.

"All night," the girl said.

Brawn leaned back against the rail with folded arms and considered the matter. "Were you comfortable?" he asked with concern, and in the burst of heartless laughter, instantly quenched, waited. "No, I was not comfortable," the girl said, glaring angrily. "I was crying, I was that mortified in that stinking place with the help banging on the door. It wasn't funny, without supper, and I was nervous I might get caught by the detective. I know I fell asleep, because I awoke with this knocking. I heard this rough voice say to call the locksmith, so I got out. I walked around for hours, trying to look like I belonged, waiting. Miss Roux didn't come out till noon. She looked real radiant and happy, but surprised to find me still there. I gave her a good piece of my mind for letting me get stuck all night like that."

"Why so? You could have gone home."

"I couldn't leave her in the lurch."

"What lurch? With her husband?" Brawn asked ironically. "Oh, come!"

The girl paused. "He might have choked her, or something; I didn't know, he sometimes got so violent. Oh, I saw black and blue marks, I can tell you. You don't know the kind of man—And I don't see any call for that smirk," she added swiftly.

Brawn came forward. "Your Honor, this cannot be true. It is physically and morally impossible to be true. It is a rotten falsehood imposed on this girl by a mind sunk in the miry depths of moral idiocy—a mind corrupted by slavish faith in the hellish practices of witchcraft intolerable even to the nakedest savages in the jungles of Africa—"

"I'd like to hear the rest of her answer," the judge said.

"Your Honor! Mr. Hagerman desires to say that not a particle of this is true. I ask that this indecency not be allowed to go on and be stricken from the record for the honor of this Court and all womankind." Brawn stood breathing heavily, and when the ruling was adverse, sat though bewildered.

"Miss Nellie," the judge said. "Just cut back to the moment of darkness. What was it you heard Mr. Hagerman say?"

"Mr. Hagerman said it was all a big joke on the family, that Miss Roux was his own little wife and nobody but them knew about it . . ."

Brawn advanced to object.

". . . that her mistake was that she had torn up the marriage contract, because she'd lost the whip hand over the old man, and if she wanted him to write out a new paper, he would because he was losing his head all over again. Then he asked her to pass the peppermint water for his teeth, and the talk stopped." A glance of triumph flicked at the defendant.

The laughter now died in the atmosphere of horror, disgust, and derision. "After I heard his breathing, I left. That, so help me God, is the living truth!"

"Mr. Brawn?" the judge said.

Brawn waited for silence. Was it then that Miss Roux wrote the letter which recalled that she had a world of pride?

The girl stared with hate. "Yes."

Brawn glanced at Trumbull. "I wouldn't dream of adding to this line of testimony," he said blandly and sat, wiping his eyelids with satisfaction.

"Blackguard," the girl muttered.

The judge squinted at the wall clock, adjourned the Court for luncheon, and fled the bench. It had to be true, he thought with agitation. It was too gross to be false. It was the damnedest story ever heard. How could a girl invent such a tale? He was pacing his chambers when Dinesmore entered. "Jack-o," he exclaimed. "How in hell d'ye know when they're lying and when they're not? How d'ye *know?*"

Before the footsteps were on the porch, Delaney, wearing a silk dressing robe, had the door open. Nellie entered with a scowl and ran directly upstairs to the bedroom. She was weeping and red-nosed. Jessica entered and handed over her cloak. "Make coffee," she said. "Come in, Mark."

Trumbull was still on the porch. "It's late and I've had enough of this," he said, in a tired voice.

"No, now! I want to talk to you!" Jessica said imperiously.

"Very well," Trumbull said. The parlor with its gewgaws, smelling of coal gas, was now familiar. He threw his coat at the youth and turned to the window.

"No, not coffee," Jessica said. "Get the judge whiskey."

Delaney hesitated. "Should I start the fire?"

"Just takes a match," Jessica said.

"I'm just trying to help," Delaney whined. He knelt at the gas logs, then went to the back.

With a groan Trumbull stretched out on the sofa and put his feet to the warmth, letting every bone relax. A door slammed upstairs. Nellie came to the landing.

"Jess? You hear me?" she called plaintively.

"Yes, dear?"

"Coming to bed?"

"Not right away."

"We've got another day tomorrow."

"I know. You go to sleep."

"Oh, fudge!" The bedroom door slammed. Delaney returned with sandwiches and a decanter of whiskey. "How did it go?" he asked.

"Get to sleep, Sonny," Jessica said. "Oh, come back first and give me a kiss." Delaney made a face. It was a wet cousinly kiss full on the mouth, and it caused him to shudder. "Oh, Jess," he complained and went up to his room. Jessica laughed. "How are you feeling, dear?" she asked, coming back to Trumbull.

"Dead in every bone," Trumbull said wearily. "Can't stand these scenes." The whiskey went down. Jessica lay on the sofa and put her tongue in his mouth. After a moment she drew back with a hard laugh. "Well, say it!" she exclaimed.

"You've got to do something about that girl."

"Still on that? Ye gods!"

"I said all I had to say at the office," he replied. "It was a terrible, imprudent thing she did."

"I didn't know she'd burst out like that," Jessica replied impatiently. "We talked it over careful last night, right in this very room, and she promised faithfully not to mention it in court. She wasn't to volunteer."

"Then why did she do it? Why?"

"I explained all that," Jessica said wearily. "To help. What's more, I had told her to leave the bedroom while the Senator and I were out to dinner."

"Which she failed to tell the Court," Trumbull said.

"Brawn got her upset, or she'd have made it clear. She still can, if you wish. I don't see the big tragedy. It was her own wish to stay."

Trumbull stood and grasped the mantel, staring at the fluttering blue flames of the gas log. Strange seductive color, he thought, feeling the warmth on his ankles. "The whole thing's too distasteful. What d'ye think people are saying?"

"Anything they like. What do I care?" she said.

Trumbull shook his head. "It's so absolutely vile, all this stuff the girl's volunteered. Who'd believe you didn't put her up to that display in court?"

"Well, I didn't!" Jessica sat, hugging her knees, staring sullenly at the fire, and the graceful pose caught at his heart. He softened, became irresolute. He knelt and took her chin. "Look'ee, sugar, I'm not trying to make you unhappy. I only

333

point to appearances. If you say you didn't expect that outburst, I'll believe it. Now smile a little, hey?"

There was nothing to smile about.

"What's the appearance of things?" Jessica asked. "Sort of thing that goes on in French houses? Is that the idea?"

"Don't talk like that," Turnbull said, pained. "Sounds vulgar."

"Then I'm vulgar," she retorted. "I'm not a saint, even if you are. I'm reckless, but I'm not afraid. D'ye think I'm made of sugar icing? I'm not, and I can't pretend. Suppose Nellie was watching? D'ye think it was the first time for the Senator? How could it hurt him?"

Lordy! he thought; she means it! The blazing eyes were cold, frank, untroubled. "She'd also be staring at you," he replied pointedly.

She turned, honestly surprised. "Sho! We're two women. How can it matter?" she said, then recovered. "Mark, honey, I'm trying to explain how the whole darned thing was unexpected. I never dreamed I'd be asked to stay the night. It'd been months since he'd had the pep."

"How'd you know that?"

"How'd d'ye think I knew? Darn it, don't look so pained," she expostulated. "I always said we had relations down to the wire."

"How do I know you're not still meeting him?" Trumbull muttered.

"You don't mean that?" she said uncertainly.

"Sorry," he said after a moment. "But it's maddening, you'll admit. When I think of you, standing for the man like a damned sow, it's past endurance. I want to tear the man's head off his shoulders," he said savagely. He had turned about. One hand still clutched the mantel. The flames cast odd shadows upward, lit the hollows under the thick brows. She stepped into the ambience of warmth and touched his face.

"What about my head?" she asked, smiling faintly. "Want to tear that off too?"

"Sometimes," he grated. He softened and kissed her hand. "Jess?"

"Yes, honey?"

"Why didn't you tell me about this business of the bureau before?" he asked hesitantly, almost knowing the answer. The delicate nostrils flared. "Because you don't like to hear about those things," she said simply, raising her face to his; and it was, he realized, quite true; his mind stopped at Hagerman's door. "And because nothing really came off that night. I wouldn't let it with Nell in the room. Sho! I have got some sense."

"Why'd you let the girl think it had?"

"It seemed amusing. The look on her face, I mean. She gets so raging jealous." Jessica laughed, then turned sober. "It was more brandy than love, I can assure you, sweet talk and no action—but he did call me his wife and she heard it. Was she to hide the truth from the judge because it's not nice?"

Trumbull turned back to the fire. It was all said with such innocence and indignation, he thought. "I don't know," he sighed.

"You look so doubtful," she said sharply. "Why?"

"Something took place. She testified you looked radiant," Trumbull said.

"I'd been promised those pearls," Jessica replied. Her laughter was free, but he thought a clever mind had dealt swiftly with the thrust. She was now smiling at the man's downcast expression. "Silly," she exclaimed, kissing his cheek, "let me get into something else."

The bedroom upstairs was dark. The girl turned and flopped on her belly, face crushed into the pillow. She was in a fury of silence, pressing the mattress hard, clutching the brass columns of the bedstead. She felt the woman's presence at the bed, a warmth, a new scent. No, no, no, no, no, she was saying to herself. There was rustling of silk, and again she was alone in the bedroom. Ages passed. She got up and left for the landing. The hall lamp was small, almost nothing, a tiny flame in a frosted glass mantel. She crept downstairs with infinite caution, avoiding the creaks, clinging to the balustrade. It took a lifetime to reach the ground floor landing.

She crouched at the keyhole of the sliding doors. Her heart was beating unpleasantly at the moving shapes dimly seen, dimly understood in the darkness. She could see massive shoulders, thick arms extended, the back of a large head against the sofa. Blue flames flickered in the hearth beyond. Then the woman stood, facing the man. With a slow movement, she picked up a robe and covered her naked body.

"Oh, Jesus, Mary!" the girl whimpered. She ran blindly up the stairs. Delaney was at his door, openmouthed.

"If you say a word, I'll murder you, you miserable excuse," the girl choked. She rushed back to her bed, weeping and convulsed.

It was Delaney who found the note that morning charging lies and deceptions, warning that it would be useless to follow, for her mind was made up, and she was returning home to Ellis Street.

Chapter Sixteen

The bedroom disclosures had sent a frisson through the city, but after the first shock had subsided came a fair measure of acceptance. True, stones instantly flew from Christian pulpits, and the newspapers were uncommon preachy with professed outrage, but that sort of bleating was not decisive. Here and there other voices were raised. A dozen bluestockings spoke critically of men. The Bohemian Club devoted a literary meeting to a debate on both sides of the case for the false values of a sick materialistic society.

All in all, the revelations, though disquieting, would not be too damaging, Trumbull thought, not so long as they showed nothing too French, nothing too abominable, nor otherwise offensive. San Francisco was too lighthearted not to favor a pretty woman over the disliked, hard-fisted little capitalist who had cheated and fornicated for a lifetime over the whole Pacific Coast. It was, after all, a tough town. Even the children were skipping rope to surprising rhymes.

The bitter trial continued. Mrs. Lightfoot, a wrinkled crone, trembled under Mrs. Lawes' remorseless stare. A horde of Hagerman's pensioners—old actresses and arthritic miners—came in support of poor shrill Miss Charlotte Blake. Shopkeepers showed books. Waiters became celebrities. Love letters were produced. Captain Webster was hissed. Mrs. Helen Bjornson asserted that Miss Roux had avidly followed every breach of promise, seduction, and divorce case in the newspapers and testified that she, bosom friend of the Purdue and Camden period, had never heard of the secret marriage.

Mrs. Bjornson was a stunning blonde, and the spiteful

courtroom exchange between the beauties was thoroughly enjoyed. Mrs. Bjornson denied any attempt on her part to gain the Senator's affections but under slashing cross-examination admitted to a peppercorn of truth in that charge.

Early in May, Trumbull returned from Stoddard, worried and distressed by his wife's growing weakness. The trial was still in progress; Finch, unable not to dot the last *i*, had presented a surprise witness—an elderly feed and grain dealer from Oregon. "Eighty years old," the old man muttered, hobbling across the courtroom. "Useless old man," he panted, mounting the witness stand. "Eighty years old," he repeated. "Look'ee, Grandpa, most of us don't make it," the judge had said gently. "What have you got to tell us?" And then, in a clear and vigorous voice, the witness had testified that Hagerman, in a rollicking mood, smelling of brandy, had introduced him to the lady outside a Powell Street jewelry shop as the "Prettiest wife in the world; didn't he think?"

Sensation!

Greater sensation a week later, when the old man made a deathbed recantation, gasping of bribes by agents in a put-up job—but by whose agents and whether to testify or recant was knowledge which followed him to the grave.

Trumbull's language that night surprised even himself. How could Finch have been so reckless? he demanded. In the delicate state of balance, one gross error could lose the trial, he stormed. "I am not at fault," Finch said. "I tested that old man thoroughly. I challenged him to pick out the lady from all the people strolling down Montgomery Street, like a police lineup. He passed with flying colors, didn't he, Natty?"

"Yes, he did," Green said.

"Was she walking alone?" Trumbull demanded.

Green hesitated. "She was accompanied by Mrs. Lawes."

Trumbull groaned like a wounded animal.

"If you don't like it," Finch said sorely, "you can handle it yourself!"

"Perhaps I shall!" Trumbull retorted.

The case would turn finally on the marriage document itself, he wearily told Green that night at his own office on Kearny Street. A photographic enlargement of the disputed signature was nailed to the wall. The new science of handwriting study was not universally recognized. In many states, one saw older forms of proof still invoked—rheumy-eyed ancients swearing from old recollections of writings that signatures were or were not genuine, with results often pure farce. In such jurisdiction, the instruments of science, photographs, and microscopes, were viewed with suspicion and reserve. Fortunately, in California the new science was making progress; and there, Trumbull concluded, when all was said and done, was where the case would be won.

The other side, too, had its experts, Green observed dubiously; how could one be sure which would prevail? Trumbull closed his eyes, considering the question. "If they come to curse, they'll stay to bless," he said grimly. "I'll get it from the other side."

The drone of technical evidence went on and the attendance fell off. Jessica's temper got shorter, her interruptions more frequent, her tendency to lose control more evident. She had most positive views of the science, having read treatises and attended lectures. She sat with Trumbull at the counsel table, scribbling suggestions of surprising insight. Ten exhausting days of clashing expert testimony and a parade of useless knowledge ended indecisively. Brawn fell back on an older mode of proof.

"Call Mr. Smith."

Benjamin Smith established his background of more than thirty years in the banking business and called for a magnifying glass. "It's not Mr. Hagerman's hand," he said crisply.

"Your witness," Brawn said with a bounce.

Trumbull rose. "Not Mr. Hagerman's hand, you say?" he said pleasantly.

"Precisely," Smith said.

"Yet you have seen statements by Mr. Hagerman that the plaintiff stole this paper with his signature? Isn't he the best judge of his own hand?" Trumbull went on courteously.

Smith considered the matter seriously. "Mr. Hagerman had not yet seen this disputed signature," he replied. "He ventured a guess."

"On impulse?"

"That is my understanding."

"Is he often impulsive?"

A twinkle appeared. "Isn't that the issue in this case, Judge Trumbull?"

Trumbull smiled. "Very well, but can you say precisely why—without benefit of microscope or photographic enlargements—you believe this signature not genuine?"

Smith hesitated. He could point to nothing specific, he said slowly, but there was something wrong about it. Something which made him uneasy. He had seen thousands of genuine signatures by Hagerman and something, call it instinct, molded his opinion. "I feel suspicious of it," he said finally.

"But you cannot say why?"

"Not precisely, no."

Trumbull came to a grave question. "Sir, if a check bearing that signature were routinely presented to your bank by a holder in due course, would the cashier pay or not?"

A full three minutes passed before the judge quietly reminded the distinguished witness that he should know his business.

"I cannot be sure," Smith finally said, reluctantly. "Although I think he too would be suspicious."

Trumbull waited for a murmur to die, then pressed his advantage. "And with such suspicions, what in practice would you expect the cashier to do with the check?"

"Hold up payment and require the maker to confirm or deny the signature."

"And you'd take his word?"

"Of course," Smith said simply.

"And do you ask this Court to take Mr. Hagerman's word in a matter where the truth might cost fifteen million dollars?" Trumbull asked with broad sarcasm.

Smith flushed. "Mr. Hagerman's word is trusted in business."

"Is his word to women trusted?"

"I have no opinion," Smith said austerely.

"That is all!" Trumbull bowed from the waist. Smith hesitated, left the witness stand, and strode from the courtroom with a cold nod to to defendant.

"Marvelous," Fanny Woodruff said in the recess, chaffing Trumbull on his success with her grandfather. Over the months of easy give-and-take of the courthouse, they had slipped into a comfortable friendship. They could talk easily, and as a member of the press she had information, often useful. She confided that her grandfather had agreed to testify only with reluctance and only upon Hagerman's insistence.

"Brawn must've been desperate," Trumbull observed, "to put an honest man in that position!"

"I wouldn't be that smug," Fanny said. "He merely said

339

the bank could not be sure of forgery. You *might* have got another answer."

"Hardly," he drawled. "Your grandfather's a Transcendentalist. Corresponded with Emerson and that bunch. There's a terrible strong compulsion for truth on those who've got no god to remit their sins, ain't there? I was counting on that."

"You really don't feel sure though of that signature," Fanny said slowly, studying the heavy features. The amusement was a bit forced, she thought. Trumbull shrugged. "It's the client's case, not mine."

"But what's the truth, d'you feel?" Fanny said, slightly vexed. Complicated man, she thought. "You show such fervor in there, I can't believe you're not sincere."

"I'm always sincere," he said solemnly, joking. "Good lawyer is like a good stage actor. He believes the role, not the lines. Mebbe that's what makes us a breed apart."

It was a pleasant moment of satisfaction, especially as the courtroom mood had swung to the plaintiff at the quasi-admission, or whatever it was, wrung from the secretary of Hagerman's bank.

"I'll predict what they've got to do," he said, smiling.

"What?"

"Put Hagerman on. He's got to deny or confirm the signature."

"He'll deny it, of course," Fanny said.

"Will he?"

"My word, won't he?"

"Don't count on that," Trumbull replied with a grimace.

"Don't count on anything yourself," Fanny replied, vexed. "You may know less about all this than you seem to think." Jessica came from the ladies' room, and joined Trumbull and Fanny with a questioning look. "Lands!" she said gaily, taking Trumbull's arm. "Thick as thieves! What have you two jolly giants got to talk about?"

After some inconsequential matters, Brawn informed the court that Senator Hagerman had decided to take the stand. As the expectant silence deepened, the shovel-nosed little man walked forward. He was sedately dressed in a banker's morning suit with a prim carnation in his lapel. A pearl stickpin was thrust in a black four-in-hand. His reddish cheekbones jutted; he seemed unusually testy. His motions were

340

painful and his irritability marked. He refused to face the plaintiff, and in a toothless mumble apologized to the court, explaining that he was too upset to wear his teeth. After frankly admitting the gross indecencies of his life, and prayerfully hoping forgiveness of his dear ones, the living and those gone to the other place, he described a painful climb from an obscure Ohio boyhood to the pinnacle of capitalistic success and marriage. The hardships of early years—blizzards, grizzlies, Indians, the loneliness of mining camps, and Christmases away from home and family—brought tears. Jessica wept in sympathy. Hagerman stopped and the pair wept noisily and in unison. Twenty minutes later, Hagerman was struggling with bailiffs and screaming for a missile with which to brain the bitch.

The upshot was a two-hundred-dollar fine and stern warnings to both sides. Resuming, still under Brawn's questioning, Hagerman denied every element of the case. Damnable lies. Never heard of any damned Mexican named Ramirez. Never knew of the document. Never had those talks in his office except of stocks and points. Decided to take action only after the blackmail started. Not a moral man but never abused a woman in his life. Relations began in quite another way than claimed, he said to Brawn, warming to his version of those events:

Brawn: You first had sexual relations when?
Hagerman: Actually when she came to my private rooms, had champagne, expressed desire to see my curios.
Brawn: And did she see your curios?
Hagerman: She saw more than my curios.
(Laughter.)
Brawn: I am referring to your Hindu curios.
Hagerman: Exactly so, and she was amused by that item. I said, "It is too late to go back and you might as well stay. It's safe here." There had been no other amatory talk. I said to her, "Miss Roux, I will give you two hundred a month to sleep with you." She said, "I will not take that." I said, quite rapidly, "Miss Roux, I will give you five hundred a month." She said, "I sure want the money, but I don't want to sleep with you." I said, "You take that bed there and I will take my own." I undressed and got into bed while she waited in the parlor. After an hour she crawled into my bed and that's how it was done. Had to thank the brandy, but we pay for

341

our mistakes. Treated her honorably until place turned into bedlam. I admit she could rub feet.

Brawn: Did you ever have the Civil Code in your office?

Hagerman: Never did. Didn't even know existence of any such law. Learned about it after the arrest. I was in Wall Street and called on Senator Pike, and we first discussed the statute. I was thunderstruck. Saw the plot in a flash. Could only conclude such document was forgery. Absolute damned forgery. Could never have signed such paper. I got fond of Miss Roux's chatter, that's true, and I had the good out of her, but I would not cheat her. I am a widower with grandchildren. My wife, rest her soul, was a pure woman who suffered my follies and weaknesses without complaint. Could I ask a woman like Miss Roux to take her place?

Miss Roux (interrupting): Did you not say you would crush me?

Court: Madam, you will be seated.

Miss Roux: I will not be seated.

Court: Then stand.

Miss Roux: I will not stand.

Court: Then sit. Judge Trumbull, control your client. Proceed.

Brawn: Now I show you Plaintiff's Exhibit 23 and ask if you signed this so-called marriage contract.

Hagerman: Never did.

Brawn: Now finally: Are you sure it bears your true signature?

Hagerman: No. On reflection I say No. Denied emphatically.

Brawn: Your witness.

Trumbull earmarked a set of minutes and came forward with ominous purpose.

Trumbull: You've signed your name on checks, papers, and hotel registers innumerably?

Hagerman: Guess so. Why?

Trumbull: Then how do you know you didn't make that signature?

Hagerman: I know my own signature, sir.

Trumbull: Let's see if you do. I show twenty photographs and ask to have them marked.

(Plaintiff's Exhibits 105A to 105T are marked for Identification)

Trumbull: I show you Exhibits 105A to 105T. I will advise that nineteen of these exhibits are photographs of your signature taken from checks, letters, papers, and hotel registers. One is the claimed forgery. Can you pick out the forgery?

Hagerman: I'll need my glasses.

Trumbull: Take your time.

Hagerman: The light's bad.

Court: Raise the shade.

Hagerman: That's too bright.

Court: Lower the shade.

Hagerman: Don't rush me.

Trumbull: Don't look at Mr. Galindez. Look at the exhibits.

Hagerman: I'm no expert, damnation. I'll say 105G is the forgery.

Trumbull: Why did you close your eyes?

Hagerman: (Word deleted.)

Court: Once more and I'll double the last fine.

Hagerman: (Word deleted.)

Court: Five hundred dollars. The next outbreak will be one thousand.

Hagerman: I'll stay with 105G.

Trumbull: You know one Senator John P. Claggett, don't you?

Hagerman: Yes. Why?

Trumbull: I will advise that 105G is actually a photograph of your signature to a letter, Exhibit 2,678, introduced at the last Hearing of the United States Senate's Commission to Investigate Frauds and Fiscal Irregularities of the Pacific Railways in which—

Hagerman: Hey! What's this?

Trumbull (continuing):—in which you advise Senator Claggett that all records of the Aurora Railway Construction Company pertaining to collusive construction contracts had been safely incinerated and that the United States Treasury could whistle for its money.

(Commotion.)

Court: Judge Trumbull, go to something else. Court won't be influenced. And, Senator?

Hagerman: Yes?

Court: Watch it.

Trumbull: Let's turn back to the marriage document. Exhibit 23. Take a hard look.

Hagerman: I'm looking.

Trumbull: Is it your signature?

Hagerman: It looks like it. . . .

Court: Order. Order. Senator, then you're not denying it's your signature?

Hagerman: Not denying, no, but . . .

Trumbull: Then what are you saying?

Hagerman: Damnation, I have signed my name a million times. How can I remember every time I used a pen? I must have signed in blank.

Trumbull: Signed what in blank?

Hagerman: How do I know? An autograph, some letter. How do I know? You've got me excited.

Trumbull: Why did you add the date?

Hagerman: Habit.

Trumbull: Ah. And why did you add the word "Nevada"?

Hagerman: It must have been the place where I signed.

Trumbull: But on that date, August twenty-fifth, you were in San Francisco.

Hagerman: I see.

Trumbull: Do you generally sign papers in blank?

Hagerman: Well, no.

Trumbull: Why this one?

Hagerman: Can't recall.

Trumbull: Do you ask this Court to believe that a man of your wealth would blindly write his name, date, and state of citizenship for a purpose you can no longer recall?

Hagerman: Not when you put it like that.

Trumbull: Then what do you ask the Court to believe?

Hagerman: I cannot account for that signature, but it was not put to any damned marriage contract. It must've been stolen from my effects with those two hundred shares of Belcher and the rest of that gibberish written in later. Don't press me too far. Judge, I'm a sick man.

Trumbull: That is all.

The courtroom was silent, stunned, as the gavel banged, and then came the congratulations. Smiles followed Jessica and Malvinia to Malvinia's carriage, and the defense was correspondingly angered and dejected.

"Splendid, Mark," Sinzheimer beamed. "Bully! Dirty business, Mark, quite beneath you, but so good to see that skillful work. Siegfried's sword and the giant, hey? Zip! Snick! Beautiful," the old man crowed. "After that little baggage Nellie left the stand, I was sure your case was down the drain. Absolutely wrote you off until those last few questions. I don't say you've won, but you made remarkable gains with that last bit. How did you ever manage to wring that admission out of the man?"

"I'll tell 'ee, Ike," Trumbull said slowly, amused, "I had that last series of questions—and the probable answers—in mind the day the case came into the office. D'ye think I'd have taken on this monster otherwise?" It was not quite true, but it came close.

Sinzheimer burst into laughter. "Well, don't press your luck." He chuckled. "It can't end on a better note. That Driscoll girl . . ." He paused.

Trumbull waited. "Yes, what about her?"

"Never mind," Sinzheimer said, "but I'd stop now."

So there it stood. Seven thousand pages of testimony and monumental labors had gone into that final expert thrust. And yet, was it final? Trumbull returned to the remaining odds and ends of the trial with an uneasy sense of something ominous yet to come.

A few nights later Trumbull awoke from a disturbed and restless sleep. Every bone and tendon was aching with the strain. He shook himself and sat bolt upright. It was the street-door rapper below.

A hoarse voice at the window whispered his name.

Ten minutes later, wearing a muffler, he left and was being driven through swirling fog on a wide, deserted street. Digges drove with reckless skill, refusing to describe their destination, and Trumbull put no questions. Digges had proved invaluable over the arduous months, bringing most useful gleanings of gossip and information from the sporting world. He commanded every tendril of the Negro grapevine that ended up at Las Flores.

"Here we are, Judge," Digges said with a dramatic flourish. Their destination was the City and County Morgue on Sacramento Street.

Trumbull was undecided. It was too absurd, he thought, reluctant to go on. Dumas-style cloak-and-dagger nonsense.

345

Digges pulled a cord. A dog barked and the portals swung open. A stink wafted into the night.

"Come in," said a deep voice.

The attendant, a muscular, thickset hunchback, came forward with a nervous, lurking smile. A flip of a hairy paw ushered them into a large gloomy chamber filled with marble slabs. Trumbull entered slowly, followed by Digges, and stared at the unpleasant environment. A single gas flame in a protective wire mesh lit the ugly chamber. A series of Romanesque arches held the low ceiling. Cabinets filled with glass containers of human giblets floating in alcohol covered the walls. A saucepan was bubbling over a gas ring, and the sharp stink was tainted by the smell of cooking cabbage.

"Lunch," the attendant said apologetically, putting a lid on the saucepan. His name was John Kelly and he seemed matter-of-fact enough. A terrier was yapping.

"She's death on rats," Kelly explained fondly, scrutinizing the visitors closely. "Let's see the money," he said, coughing. Digges showed a sheaf of gold certificates. "All right," Kelly grumbled, "but it's worth more. Would you like the grand tour, Judge?" he asked hospitably. "We've got a feller here who just ran three city blocks with a knife stuck two inches in his skull. If you'd like to see it . . ."

"Did he make it?" Digges asked.

"No, sir," Kelly replied, "but he set some kind of a record. It's a real phenomenon, they say."

The stink was suddenly too much.

"Let's get out of here," Trumbull growled.

The yard was dark and cold, but the fog had a rank smell and he felt refreshed. A light from the building showed the outlines of a stable and a pile of cheap pine boxes meant for the potter's field. "What's this about?" Trumbull said.

"I'll get to it," Kelly protested, spitting, looking cautiously about. "I'm a working man," he said defensively, "and proud of it. I'm only in this job for the living."

"Quite so," Trumbull agreed.

"But some things are too much," Kelly went on. "I dunno, I dunno," he muttered, then struck a palm with his fist. "Well, it's between us and the lamppost." A few days ago, he began, the police—it was Captain Pritchard and a few men —had called to ask a lot of funny questions, and especially to discover the attendant on duty on a certain night a year earlier.

"What date was that?" Trumbull asked.

Kelly rubbed a pointed skull uneasily. Well, now, it was the night before May first, one year ago.

Trumbull started a cigar. "Go on."

Pritchard had then put a lot of idle, silly questions, Kelly said, but mainly wanted particulars of an old gentleman killed by a runaway horse. The old gentleman was first thought to be an unknown pauper, and had been marked for dissection, when a medical student had recognized him for a Mason. The Occidental Lodge of that order had arranged for burial in their Gun Hill Cemetery. Pritchard had wanted the particulars, how long the old gentleman—whose name was Mergenthaler—had waited burial, his condition, and so on. Kelly had told Pritchard that the old gentleman when taken in was well preserved. It was a standing mortuary joke; Kelly laughed but without response.

Trumbull turned to Digges. "Mergenthaler?"

"Just another old man. Eighty years old," Digges said.

The case was full of harmless eighty-year-old men, Trumbull thought sourly. Was that all?

Well, no, Kelly went on, looking disappointed. Pritchard then seemed unduly interested in the attendance record that week. "We don't keep such records," Kelly said, "but I recollected that poor Rattigan had had the night shift that whole week. When I told Pritchard that Rattigan died six months ago, he stopped dead. Then he argued that maybe, since I was so smart, perhaps I could recollect harder, that maybe I was the one on duty. I said, No, I was positive 'twas Rattigan. Captain Pritchard got annoyed and cursed me roundly. He was annoyed because Rattigan, rest his soul, having passed on, could give him no information, and I was no more use to him than a stiff meself, he said."

"Information?" Trumbull demanded.

"Bloody nasty information," Kelly said, "that the man tried his goddamnedest to impute to me. He said, very well, if I wasn't on duty, then sure Rattigan had passed it on to me. 'Passed on what?' I asked. 'About Mergenthaler,' he said. Sure, there had got to have been some talk about what happened to the body that night. I said I didn't know what in hell he was talking about. He said I was lying and I got mad. I said, 'God strike me; John Kelly has never lied in his life.' I may not be much, nor my category, but I don't lie. I grabbed a broom and ordered him out and he laughed nastily—and called me a bloody hump and said he'd smash me. It curdled me blood.

"When it got cooler," Kelly went on, "he said I could make a packet of money if I'd remember what Rattigan knew. I asked, 'What was that supposed to be?' He said with a curse that sure I was too thick to trust; he couldn't put words in me mouth, and that's how it was left."

Trumbull said, "D'ye know what he was after?"

"Not at the time," Kelly replied. "It was Mr. O'Mara who made me realize. I know O'Mara from the Gun Hill Cemetery. A few days later, O'Mara came around on some cemetery business for the Masons, and somehow Pritchard's name came up. Pritchard, O'Mara said, was more than just a police captain. He was in with the Powers-That-Be and was doing a special job. He knew because Pritchard had been coming around the Driscoll's boardinghouse in Ellis Street for confidential talks. He then said that the Driscoll girl, God help her, could be in trouble and was to give evidence for the Senator in the divorce case. Some parts of her story needed corroboration."

Trumbull walked in darkness to the end of the yard. He stood breathing deeply, and when the shaking was over, he came back to Digges.

"How long have you been sitting on this?" he asked.

"Not long, not long," Digges said.

Trumbull turned back to Kelly. "What sort of evidence?" he asked ominously.

"Evidence against Miss Roux," Kelly said simply. "They're still out to smash her, you know. That's why Pritchard had been to this morgue—they're trying to nail down details of the Driscoll girl's story, and O'Mara was trying to help out. He's Driscoll's great friend, you see, been star boarder all these years with the girl's mother. The Driscolls are fine people, he said. Fine people. But here's the thing!" Kelly lowered the deep voice conspiratorially. "O'Mara confided that Driscoll was expecting to get something out of it—a big new house, one with twenty rooms and large enough to make a real establishment—one of the finest in the city. Now that's important, I'd think."

"So?" Trumbull said.

"Don't you see?" Kelly said impatiently. "Pat Driscoll's been drawing weekly sums from the Senator for months now. In cash, but it's a fact. Now he's got enough to buy a bloody big hotel. I'll tell you something else." The little man stepped closer in the darkness. "There's a box at the German Savings and Loan with twenty-five thousand dollars. That's not for nothing, and when the girl gives evidence against Miss Roux, you can ask about that. You did know she means to give fresh evidence?" Kelly said sharply, glancing at Digges.

Trumbull made a business of lighting a cigar. "Bribery? We've charged enough of that already to sink a battleship. What did Pritchard want you to corroborate?"

Kelly drew a breath. Throughout the narrative, he had paced nervously. "Well, whether Rattigan had allowed Mergenthaler to have visitors just before he was taken for the burial," he said.

Something painful went tight in Trumbull's belly. "What sort of visitors? Who?"

"Miss Roux and Miss Driscoll," Kelly said after a pause. "O'Mara was saying, 'Who cares where or how a pretty woman spreads her legs in this city?' O'Mara was very amusing about that, I'm bound to say. He's a great reader, you see. He said that all the insinuations against Miss Roux about secret lovers and making believe to kill herself for love and such was poppycock to what was going to come out. This thing, he said, had to do with graveyard charms."

Something colder than the fog chilled Trumbull's heart.

"I'm only saying what O'Mara told me," Kelly went on hastily. "I told him I wouldn't believe it. Not of Rattigan. Not with his pride in this establishment. Let females loose among them corpses? Christ, no! If anything like that took place, I said, Rattigan'd sure have told me. I told O'Mara the imputation was too bloody disgraceful. Let people do what they like on the outside, I said, they disgust me with their bloody wars and oppressions, their cheating and conniving. It's hopeless out there anyways. But don't bring it in here. Let the dead be dead, I said, and if Pritchard didn't keep his nose out of this place, I'd come after him. Terrible imprudent, I know," Kelly said ruefully, "but I just saw red. They can bribe some, not me."

The courtyard was silent. A distant cable car was rattling up the steep slope of California Street.

"What did O'Mara say?"

"That he always had the highest regard for me and Rattigan and was relieved to hear my denial."

Trumbull had no idea what to say, and then inside a

349

furious barking broke out. "Rats!" Kelly exclaimed and hurried back to his post. Trumbull and Digges followed. A rat was cornered between two boxes, chittering in terror. Trumbull stared at the indecencies about him. Mouths open. Mouths closed. The nakedness was beyond the nakedness of death. The nearest face was a man's face, sharp, sprinkled with freckles, and seemingly placid. The chest was caved in and the thin arms extended with the palms upturned. Under gaslight the colors were strange, but the skin was dead white. He had a vision of the slender woman and the short, full-breasted girl, walking among the horrors.

"Jesus," Trumbull said wearily. "Jesus!" Kelly came back from his task. "Sorry," he said apologetically, showing them to the door. "I wanted to stay out entirely, but I follow the newspapers, and when I saw what those dirty people were after trying, I couldn't rest. I'm a working man, Judge Trumbull," he said with pride, "and I thought you'd know what to do."

The first light was showing in the east as they drove off. Trumbull was silent, chewing an unlit cigar.

They turned down Market Street, passing the first dim traffic. Hooves passed, slow, plodding, in the ambiguity of mist.

"Monstrous," Trumbull said bitterly. He sank back, thinking of his cross-examination of Hagerman. "With the hook in his belly, you'd think he'd give up. Digges?"

The bloodshot eyes rolled. "Sir?"

"Must be some colored workmen out at the Masons Cemetery, hey?" A nod. "I do believe your work is cut out there. Get me all you can on Mergenthaler's burial." A pause. "Is something wrong?"

"No, Judge," Digges replied unsatisfactorily.

Trumbull had an impression that Digges was laughing at him.

It was sunup when they reached Farley Street. Trumbull bathed and shaved and had breakfast. He ate mechanically. He took the Market Street trolley to the Civic Center and arrived in court clammy with dread.

Jessica vehemently denied everything and swore to fight the slanders tooth and nail. She was beside herself with fury.

Pritchard was waiting on Ellis Street with two of his men. They had a closed hansom cab standing at the curb. At about nine o'clock, Nellie came out of the boardinghouse, button-ing a pair of gloves. Father, mother, and four hulking broth-ers were watching from the parlor.

They drove straight to Market Street and turned toward the Civic Center. The men, McNamee and Fitzpatrick, were facing the girl. They sat with folded arms, stolid, imperturbable.

"I feel nervous," Nellie said.

"Nothing will happen," Pritchard said. "Will it, Tom?"

"Not a thing," McNamee replied.

The girl said, "Will I have to get right on the stand?"

"No," Pritchard said, peering out the window. The whole city seemed to be converging at the courthouse. "You'll have a chance to refresh yourself."

"I hope so," the girl muttered. She lapsed into silence, moving her lips at a memorized speech. "Where's Mr. O'Mara? And the others?"

"They're being brought another way," Pritchard said. "All you have to do is tell the truth. It wouldn't be advisable to play tricks, miss."

It was an unmistakable warning and she shuddered. She was afraid of the police. They were dangerous and could make white slaves of girls. She had heard of such things. If a girl was stripped and broken and kept in chains and starved while Chinks forced her and such things, it wouldn't help to run away. The police would put her right back in a house and she would die of the consumption and end up in a pauper's grave. Pritchard smiled reassuringly.

They entered McAllister Street. "Well, it's her own fault," she burst out, "for making me tell lies and doing things. She's a liar. A darned liar."

"Sure she is," Pritchard agreed. "And we'll stop her from telling lies, won't we?"

Nellie stared with hatred. "She's worth ten of you," she said nastily. "If only she weren't such a liar."

Her hand was caught in a mighty grip. "No tricks, miss?"

"You're hurting me," she whined.

"Will there be tricks?" Pritchard repeated.

"No," she said, wincing. Her hand was released. She turned to the window, suppressing tears of rage. "Black-guards," she muttered.

They entered the Hall of Records, descended to a connect-ing tunnel, and came out in the City Hall. They climbed a hidden staircase to an airless room filled with wooden cabinets.

"I'd like to know what's going on," she said.

"You'll know," Pritchard said. "Mr. Brawn don't want you seen, me gel. The other side's not to expect a thing. Get it?"

"Yes," she said sullenly.

"You haven't communicated with Jessie Roo?"

"No."

"Because if you 'ave . . ." Pritchard said warningly.

"I haven't," the girl said bitterly. "I hate her. She's dirty and mean and full of lies."

Pritchard brought a threatening face to the girl's. "All right," he said. "All right. Just remember that lies can send you to prison, so tell the truth and you'll be fine. It's time to purge the perjuries, hey?" He tapped the girl's shoulder for emphasis, laughed, and left for the courtroom.

"Peppermints?" McNamee said.

The girl shook her head. A ventilator shaft had a murmur of voices. They were directly above the courtroom, she judged. That was the bailiff's voice; then the lawyer's. She hated them all. Fitzpatrick wandered into the hallway and came back, yawning with boredom.

"What's Jessie like in bed?" he asked knowingly. "Is she a tigress?"

Nellie's epithet was unprintable.

"Lay off," McNamee said. "She's a nice Irish girl. We have that from the judge himself."

"I revere Judge McArdle," Fitzpatrick said solemnly, "but by any standard that's a new kind of nice."

"Get used to it," McNamee said.

Nellie turned to the ventilator. Some delay was taking place. The door opened and Galindez entered. "Is she all right?" he asked the men.

"We haven't looked," Fitzpatrick said.

Galindez turned to McNamee. "Is he always like that?"

McNamee said, "When he's excited."

"Oh, so funny," Nellie said.

Galindez came to the girl and sat, studying her speculatively. "Miss Driscoll, we're going to begin with the other witnesses, then we'll call you. Remember that Mr. Brawn has your written statement."

"Yes, sir," she said sullenly.

"That means if you depart from the truth, you can be indicted for perjury and blackmail."

"I'm not afraid," the girl said defiantly.

"But if you stick to the truth," Galindez went on in his deep rolling voice, "nothing can happen to you. If you lie now, you'll regret it."

"I won't lie."

"See that you don't," Galindez said. "Now if you're asked about money, you can say that your father got five thousand dollars for expenses from Mr. Brawn."

"I thought it was three thousand."

"Well, it was five thousand," Galindez said after a pause, "but only for expenses and because of his illness. If you're asked about other money—"

"I don't know anything about it," she said quickly. "I haven't had any promises of money or—or anything. I'm just telling the truth because it's the best thing. I now see how horrible and corrupt it was to make up lies and forgeries. I was misled by an older woman, but I have talked with Father Foyle and come to realize."

"I hope you have," Galindez said.

"Sir?" Nellie said timidly. "Will you send those men outside a minute?"

McNamee and Fitzpatrick left and waited in the hallway.

Nellie glanced at the dark threatening face and looked off. "Suppose I'm asked about things I told Mr. Finch? About the time Pa was told by Mr. Brawn he could get twenty-five thousand dollars if I were to help?"

Galindez' face did not change. "Did you actually hear Mr. Brawn say that?"

"No, it's just what Pa told me."

"Then you don't really know?"

"Well, no," Nellie said reluctantly, "but suppose they ask Pa?"

"Don't worry about Pa," Galindez replied grimly. "Your testimony is your own. Have you personally been promised money?"

"Only witness fees," Nellie said, sniffing resentfully.

"Would you lie for witness fees?"

"Not under oath," Nellie said.

"Then tell the truth." Galindez studied his fingertips. "Now it *is* the truth?" he demanded with special emphasis. The girl nodded. "Good," he said and left. The men returned. Fitzpatrick winked at McNamee and turned to Nellie. "What kind of stockings are you wearing, darling?"

"Ooh!" Nellie stamped. *"Ooh!"* she said bitterly.

The room was close except for the small draft from the ventilator. That black shaft had a curious muffled sound—distant shuffling, interrupted by coughing, from all parts of the building. It cleared at intervals, making audible the sounds in the chamber below.

After raps for order, there was silence. A strong, unctuous voice—it was Brawn's—recalled Miss Roux for further cross-examination. Nellie followed raptly, moving her lips in a rehearsal of testimony to come.

At recess, Fitzpatrick brought sandwiches and a growler of beer. There were cautious excursions to the convenience, where she bathed her temples and smoothed rice powder on her nose. Her name was called.

"Let's go," Fitzpatrick said, jerking a thumb.

Earlier that morning, when the court had convened, Jessica had been recalled by Brawn for further questions. Brawn had abruptly asked whether she had visited the Masonic Cemetery on May 1, the year before, with Miss Driscoll.

"What was the date?" she asked frigidly.

"May first," Brawn said.

"I don't remember," Jessica replied, "but I have been to the Roman Catholic Cemetery at the end of Geary Street when a friend died, if that's a help. I have been to the cemeteries, all the cemeteries, frequently with Miss Driscoll, but only horseback riding. The Masons Cemetery? That's at Gun Hill, is it not? Lands! It means nothing to me, sir."

Brawn turned with menace and called a witness. Dr. Gilliam, County Health Officer, entered with a military stride, holding a court order and a box wrapped in paper. Brawn opened the box and lifted out a pair of stockings and a man's shirt and wondered if Miss Roux had ever seen those things before.

Miss Roux exclaimed, startled, that she had never seen those things in her life.

Brawn waited for attention, then said savagely, "Did you not go to a newly made grave with Miss Driscoll and get down into that grave with a package containing Mr. Hagerman's stockings and shirt and ask the man in charge to help you put it under a box where a gentleman named Mergenthaler was shortly to repose?"

According to some reporters, Jessica sat stupefied under the shout of hate, but then, as realization dawned, she burst

354

out: "I never did anything like that in my life, sir! You may bring all the world here, and that's a falsehood. I defy anybody to prove it. If you think you'll dirty me over the world, you're making a great mistake, sir. I never heard of anything so ghoulish in my life. What day was it?"

"May first. Last May."

"Never did, and I will swear to it."

"Are you not swearing to everything?"

"Yes, and I will double swear. Who says I did? This doctor? I never saw the man in my life. I presume he has had a well-paid fee for doing it."

Brawn said, "Did you tell the man at the grave that the package would work a charm and bring a rich gentleman to you, and get him to marry you?"

Jessica spat murderously, "I did not! No doubt you can hire lots of people to swear to all such dirty stuff to get me into the newspapers—Mr. Hagerman has plenty of money! I utterly deny time, place, and circumstances!"

The testimony ended in an uproar and strong motions to remove the filthy exhibits and strike the line of testimony. Everyone was at the rail, craning. Oh, oh, oh! the judge groaned inwardly, rubbing his skull in perplexity. Confound it, what was the defense intending to show, he demanded.

Brawn made an offer of proof to show that on that certain fair and warm day in May, under the bluest of skies, Miss Roux and Miss Driscoll had gone to the Masonic Cemetery at Gun Hill and had climbed into an open grave waiting for the said Mergenthaler. He would show that a rough box was open to take the casket; that the middle board was lifted and that when Miss Roux went down into the grave, she was seen to mutter charms and make weaving motions like playing a harp—motions from her breast to a loose board where the gravedigger, a certain Goletti, would testify he had seen her put a package; that Miss Driscoll too had gone into the grave and then gave Goletti a silver dollar to make the charm work.

"What of it?" Finch clamored.

Brawn went on with his offer of proof. The defense would show that the grave had remained intact for a year—unmourned, unvisited, but intact. Then, just ten days ago, there had assembled the cemetery superintendent, Mr. O'Mara, Dr. Gilliam, Brawn, the same Goletti, and Captain Pritchard. The grave was opened, the casket removed, water bailed. The loose board of the rough box was lifted and a shovel used to take out a package—the very package now produced in court.

The contents of the package were marked for identification. The court stenographer shuddered. The stockings were gaudy, white and red; the shirt was fine lawn with stripes; the items, Brawn promised, would be identified by Li as those filched during the Dragon's Blood episode. Mrs. Lawes was seen to whisper to Trumbull. Trumbull nodded and begged leave to examine the repulsive objects, then observed sarcastically that, despite a show of tearing and ripping, the rags were too intact to have soaked a year in a wet grave. Mrs. Lawes, having fingered and sniffed, thought the stains to be coffee infusions.

Brawn begged not to be interrupted.

Trumbull said strongly, "I shall interrupt. Something is being omitted from your offer of proof. Who d'you say in fact got into the grave for that package? Hey? Was it not Captain Pritchard?"

Brawn blinked. The judge turned inquiringly. "Judge Trumbull? D'you dispute that the package comes from that grave?"

"Oh, not a bit," Trumbull retorted. "*Something* came from the grave. But how did it get there?"

"Captain Pritchard—" Brawn began.

"Pritchard? Or Panjandrum, the Magician?" Trumbull said with contempt. "Was he searched before he went into the pit?"

"Captain Pritchard will swear—" Brawn said desperately.

"Anyone who'll believe a detective will believe a whore," Trumbull retorted and sat, scarlet.

The judge drummed and then in a marked brogue said that when he had first come to America as a common greenhorn, he had taken employment as a police officer and could not agree with a remark so patently unfair.

Trumbull felt the blood drain. His remark had been stupid and thoughtless, a sign of impulsive recklessness he thought he had overcome. He stood and apologized to the Court, but would not retract the charge. The offer of proof stank worse than the rags, and he was happy that Captain Pritchard was present to hear that comment.

The judge looked over the bench. "That is a strong charge, sir," he said coldly.

"It's meant to be strong," Trumbull said wrathfully. "The whole episode is meant only to besmirch. It's an afterthought as contemptible as it's corrupt, and they cannot prove it. And it is irrelevant. We've done with all the legitimate issues of the case, and they know it."

The judge turned. "Mr. Brawn. After all, we are here to pass on a marriage contract, not on superstitions. How can you justify all this?"

Brawn launched into an ornate address. While not directly relevant, he agreed, the episode, like the fortune-teller business, would show the abysmal mental and moral degradation to which the pinchbeck scion of backwoods nobility had descended. The association with necromancers and voodoo practitioners, the foolish and unwomanly acts of superstition certainly refuted any notion that she was married.

For were she married, could a woman worthy of belief have reached such a state of debasement as to invade a newly made grave and there bury clothing with blasphemous incantation that, while it rotted, the man once appurtenant to that clothing would either marry her or die? Even as fantasy, it was repulsive beyond words—foul, diseased, smelling of corruption and immorality. And more, it suggested a curious psychological problem—whether one claiming to be born to the aristocracy of Missouri—educated, refined, God-fearing—could perform acts so degrading, repulsive, barbarous and unchristian and still be thought worthy of belief. Or even sane. Since Miss Roux's denials were so peremptory, and Judge Trumbull's insinuations of sleight of hand by agents of the defense so violent, the only way to resolve the issue was to call the gravediggers to tell the truth in a matter in which they could not have the slightest personal interest—unless, of course, according to the suggestively contemptuous shrug and bitter smile of Judge Trumbull, he added, they too were bribed to injure his female client.

"Judge Trumbull?" the judge said.

Trumbull rose. There was nothing new in the argument, he said with contempt. The false issue of superstition had been exhausted earlier. The present job was a concocted smoke screen to hide the effect of the defendant's confession of his signature to the marriage document. He objected to prolonging a trial which should have closed long since.

The judge considered the matter grimly. He knew the Gun Hill Cemetery well enough and could visualize the scene—

the wet grass, the open grave, the marble slabs on the sward, the horrid errand. His eye caught the woman's. Christ! What could one think?

"I'll take it," he decided with a stare of doubt at both sides.

"Call the gravedigger!" Brawn said.

It was in this atmosphere that Nellie returned to give further evidence.

Pritchard was waiting at the door. "All right," he said with savage joviality. "All right, me gel. In there, and mind!" Nellie entered the courtroom with beating heart and mounted the witness chair. It was a familiar scene with some changes: Malvinia's queer ironical eyes were smiling (and somehow that was scary); the judge was now wearing a pearl stickpin and new muttonchops. Trumbull seemed haggard and older than she recalled, a streak of gray marked the jutting beard. She shivered—the deep eyes were baleful, the heavy mouth twisted with contempt. She clenched her hands, wishing she had made a last visit to the bathroom.

A cardboard box was filled with the objects of the day's testimony.

"Bribed by Hagerman's millions!" Jessica said distinctly. "Infamous!"

"Infamous yourself!" Nellie retorted, and turned to Brawn, who was rising with ominous intent.

Nellie testified in a breathless voice, crossing and uncrossing her legs, dabbing her mouth, showing every sign of bitterness and nervous tension. She identified the Senator's stockings and shirt, described the graveyard charm, told about planting the package, and denounced Jessica as a liar and a cheat, with not a particle of truth in her.

A sigh went through the courtroom as she denounced the marriage document as a forgery contrived after the move to Wisteria Place, and there aged with a flatiron on a certain night which was clear in her mind.

"Your witness!" Brawn said with contempt.

Throughout the shocking testimony, Trumbull had remained slouched at the counsel table, studying the witness with an intent, baleful stare.

"Your witness!" Brawn repeated with a sneer.

Trumbull came forward. He had never felt so haggard and

old in his life. "You say you are now telling the truth?" he asked heavily.

The girl wet her lips. "Yes, I am," she said defiantly.

"Well, let us see," Trumbull said with dislike. He turned to a transcript of her earlier testimony. On a prior occasion, had not the following questions been put? And had she not made the following answers? And she now swore to the opposite? Which was the truth? The present answers? If so, were the former false? Knowingly false? False on oath? Having lied in most shameful and sordid details, did she now expect belief?

The girl dabbed her mouth. "Yes!"

"When you testified before Mr. Finch, you now say you committed gross perjuries?"

Finch exchanged a worried glance with Green. Too strong, too much! Finch thought.

"Yes, I have committed many perjuries for Miss Roux," the girl said defiantly and braced for a cross-examination less punishing than expected. Trumbull explored the Driscoll family finances and took disclaimers of bribery with a running fire of derisive comments for Brawn's role. It was an obstinate inventive young mind that matched his own. The receipt of money from Hagerman was denied with lofty contempt. The question was flogged to death. Trumbull finally said, "Well, Miss Roux gave you no money for your prior testimony, did she?"

"No," the girl admitted with a flicker of scorn. "I testified out of undying friendship. There's such a thing as that, Judge Trumbull, where one person will give her very life for another. Or don't you think that's possible?"

"That's not so," Jessica exclaimed angrily from the counsel table. "I was your friend, but evidently you were not mine."

"I'll leave that to Judge Trumbull," the girl retorted, wrinkling her nose. "I was promised dresses and a set of amber beads, and you know it! And what about my career?"

"Miss Driscoll!" the judge admonished sternly. "Judge Trumbull, you will stick to the issues and not wander."

"I shall try," Trumbull replied, conscious of amused glances from every corner of the chamber. He closed the transcript and recalled a series of office conferences with the girl. Did she now swear that she had lied to him as counsel?

Nellie sniffed. "Well, if so, it wasn't too hard. I don't think you wanted to know the truth."

Trumbull remained immobile a frozen moment. He walked

359

back to the table and fumbled with a set of notes. What in hell had made him put such a question? He began afresh, "Let us get back. You now deny that you ever heard Mr. Hagerman call the plaintiff his wife—as you swore?"

"That was contrived," the girl retorted.

"You deny you heard such a statement from behind Mr. Hagerman's bureau?"

"Contrived," the girl snapped.

Trumbull stopped dead. "You say you were *never* behind the bureau?"

"Never," she repeated, rolling her eyes, invoking a patience from some unseen power. "It was an invention."

Trumbull frowned. "Invention?" he echoed, seeming bewildered. "But, gracious, why invent a story so unedifying?"

The girl bit her thumb. "Well, maybe Miss Roux didn't think it so," she said with malice, flashing a bitter glance at the plaintiff. "Or care. If she cared, she'd have settled, but she don't want settlement, she wants revenge, and she's got a blind spot. She didn't have to disgrace herself like this."

"Somebody invented something," Trumbull said heavily, "and the Court must say who—the person who perseveres in truth or the admitted liar. Did you not swear to the furnishings, even to that indecent Hindu object?"

"It was all described to me by her in precise detail. She's great for precise detail, which shows what a liar she is. Mama had an engineer boarding with us once who would always tell the melting point of everything. It was just to cover the lies and not pay rent."

Finch coughed and passed over a slip of paper. Trumbull shook his head. Finch ambled back, swinging his spectacles, and sat with inward anger. What was the man trying to do?

"Any more questions?" the judge asked.

Trumbull looked up with a start. A shaft of sunlight touched the clock. The girl was showing strain, but his own seemed deeper, as though he were not sure of his legs. "Tell us what happened in the graveyard."

"But I have done so," the girl protested.

"Do so again, pray!"

The girl's white lips moved, then covered the ground haltingly. The deep eyes seemed to bore through the girl, remote, hostile, dead. "You have heard Mr. Brawn urge that only a diseased mind could engage in such—what did he call it?—hellish practices? D'ye agree that anyone who'd molest a grave must be depraved and unworthy of belief?"

"I—I cannot say," the girl said.

Brawn leaped into the breach with objections. Trumbull waited for a ruling and went on. "You still swear on oath that you molested a grave?"

"Yes!" the girl said. "For her!"

"Then is your mind not diseased?"

The girl stared, wordless. "I don't know what you mean," she said finally. "I have never thought of it, but if mine is, so is hers."

"Miss Roux denies it. You admit it."

"She denies many things, but we were there together. Why would I do such a thing except for her?"

"I suggest you're lying about it."

"In that case I'm not a grave violator," the girl said swiftly, "and you cannot say so."

"Are you not then a perjurer?"

"You didn't think so when you wanted my testimony! And if I am a perjurer, what happens to her case, which depends on me?"

Trumbull stood back. "Which is it you want the Court to believe? That you're a perjurer, or a grave violator?"

The girl paused. "The truth is that I lied for her, and went to the grave with her, and in your heart, Judge Trumbull, you know that! And so does she!"

Trumbull's shoulders sagged. He seemed utterly discouraged and confounded. He pressed his mouth with distress. "And all this," he said with an effort, "was on what date?"

"May first," the girl snapped.

"Lordy," Trumbull muttered with distress. The chamber was quiet. He returned to counsel table and studied a memorandum handed over by Green. "You're sure of that date—May first?"

"Yes, I'm sure."

"How d'you fix that date?"

"It could be no other date," the girl replied. "Mr. Mergenthaler got buried that day, and so the records show."

Trumbull slowly walked forward. "Who supplied you with that date?"

"Mr. Brawn," the girl said simply, "after Captain Pritchard made the investigation."

"And it was not Captain Pritchard who told you in whose

grave those disgusting rags would be found?" Trumbull's voice rose in pitch.

The girl stared. "Why, that's plain crazy," she said, and laughed uncertainly. "How's that possible?"

"Ah, how?" Trumbull said heavily. The air of uncertainty dropped. He turned to a list of names. Did she know Rachel Brown? Sarah Jane Carey? Edward Caines? Eliza Jane Seth? Mrs. Emma B. Sterret? Molly Hudson? He now had complete attention.

The girl nodded, puzzled. They were people from Las Flores.

Trumbull folded his arms. "If I suggest that Miss Roux spent the entire day of May first at Las Flores with Mrs. Lawes and a dozen other persons, and so could not possibly have been at the cemetery, would you still deny you are swearing to perjuries and inventions?"

The girl faced Malvinia. The queer eyes were amused and ironical. "No, I would not!" she retorted, "because Mrs. Lawes can get alibis for people, just as she gets babies for rich ladies, and hides babies for others. I'd not believe her on a stack of Bibles! And I don't care how many people she brings in."

Trumbull said, "Mrs. Lawes is three times your age and has lived in San Francisco since the Gold Rush. Is she not more credible than a creature who admits perjuries and blasphemies against the dead?"

Malvinia chuckled.

The girl stared with bursting feeling. "I helped Miss Roux," she said bitterly, stung, "because of friendship."

"*Undying* friendship?"

"Yes."

"But now it's dead. You are no longer friends?"

"No. I hate her."

"Is that why you are swearing her away? Because you quarreled and now hate her? Is that it?"

"Yes!" the girl shouted. "Yes. I hate her! But I am not lying."

Trumbull glanced at the judge. A brow rose with ironic meaning. "Thank you," he said and returned to his seat. "No more questions," he said in dismissal.

Brawn stood, opened his mouth. "No questions," he croaked.

362

The judge made a note. "You may step down, miss," he said with distaste.

Jessica sighed audibly with satisfaction. Green put aside a check list of questions, relieved. Trumbull glanced about the quiet chamber, noting the effect, then an impulsive question was on his tongue, uttered by another, divided part of his mind. "By the way, what was the quarrel about, miss?" he heard himself say.

Every lawyer in the chamber looked up.

"Quarrel?" the girl said stupidly. A burning glance went to the plaintiff. "It was private. I'd rather not say."

"Step down, miss," the judge repeated.

The girl remained seated, angry and resentful. "But it was her fault," she burst out, "because she lied to me. She said she didn't care for men. She said she only wanted to marry Mr. Hagerman because she was tired of life and didn't care. She said it was all really a farce, that lots of ladies marry to get homes and have babies, and why not the Senator, who at least was fun even if he was old and not much capable of relations. Lots of ladies manage without relations. She always said that she didn't like relations at all—that it's just something to grit your teeth."

The girl paused, eyes glittering with rage, intent only on the object of wrath. "She said over and over that she didn't love the Senator, or any man, and just wanted to be a gracious *chatelaine* at Beaufort. She was always using that word. Her heart really was cold, she said, and there was something finer than that kind of thing—real, true friendship, like sisters, and I was like a sister! She loved me like a sister," the girl said, beginning to sob. "I was the only one, she said, but she lied. She is always lying. Mary, Joseph! She don't know where truth ends and lies begin. She was just using me for this lawsuit. She's just after the money and using me, like she uses everyone and everything."

The yammer went on in the embarrassed courtroom and ended in hysteria and sobs. Trumbull started to rise.

"Dear saints! Let it alone," Finch said hoarsely.

"Can't," Trumbull said and opened his mouth. Nothing came to mind.

"No questions," he said dully, and sat. A dozen witnesses from Las Flores would answer the girl's inventions, he had no doubt, and that dreary prospect lay ahead. Why in hell had he put that one last question too many? He had no idea. He dared not look at Jessica.

"Anything else, gentlemen?"

Both sides rested. A recess was announced, good wishes expressed for a pleasant Fourth of July, and a date set in September for final summations. The trial was over. Slowly, almost reluctantly, the lawyers packed up their books.

That last night at Wisteria Place would always remain with him. Jessica was never more fetching. He came famished and she made an omelette in the kitchen, dressed only in corset, stockings, and black shoes with red bows, and her laughter was as roguish as the costume inciting. She went lightly about the task, beating the eggs with a wire whisk with chatter about a rare recipe of spices and mushrooms that came by way of Provence. Not a word was said about the courtroom outburst until the first exhaustion of bed was over. "Oh, Mark," she whispered in the dark. "What's wrong? You didn't believe that dirty stuff?"

"Lordy, no," he said, closing his eyes.

"I just hope we have no more surprises. The news from home's not good. Not good at all."

She lay against his breast, feeling the great movements of his breathing. "Are you sure Mrs. Trumbull don't know about us? I'd hate that. I don't want to hurt anyone. I just want my own happiness. How'd you feel if she learned about us?"

It had become an accustomed exchange between them, not the first, not the last. "It's not your business, Jess," he said dismally. "Just mine, and I'll deal with it. I'd feel destroyed to bring her pain, I reckon. How else d'ye think I'd feel?"

And then, as always, she pressed against him with demands that added to the unbearable drain of his strength. "Love me," she said insistently. "Love me." He was engulfed in voracity and he did not care. A sweet smell suffused his nostrils, stuck to his fingers, clung to his beard. He had every part of her body clear in mind, every ridge, every hollow. He could think of nothing else. There was a dimple at her spine, a soft curl at her neck, a delicacy poignant beyond words. He berated himself constantly for sinking like a schoolboy into a mire of moral and legal confusions. The courtroom disclosures should have repelled him, he would have thought, but they had not. The woman was full of laughter and a kind of

364

innocence and abandon that stopped his breath; and perhaps it was that sense of abandon which had him ensnared. He had no idea how all that had come about.

He had always thought himself a man of sense and honor, a lawyer of clear vision and sound morals and honest good advice to others. And what now could he say of himself? He did not know. The fact was that he was not thinking at all. A flood of emotion was sweeping him to some unknown destination that he could sense but not foresee. It was all mixed up with the grinding bitter trial. He was committed to a cause and for the first time in his life, had no sense of the trial. What had the judge thought of the degrading revelations? Of the technical evidence? Of the ugly admissions dragged from unwilling witnesses? Of that last minute graveyard business and the alibi? His instincts told him nothing.

Was there anything to that graveyard business? Impossible, impossible, he groaned, and put the nagging thought aside.

Lordy! What in hell was going on with him? That business at Stoddard was getting worse, and he was giving it only the barest thought. The dirty little paragraphs circulating in the newspapers surely had come to Alexandra's attention, and how he would face her he had no idea.

Jesus, God, he thought dismally. For the moment he knew nothing else but irresolution and a torment of hunger for the devouring woman in his arms.

The summer passed and it was September.

Green met Trumbull at Oakland and took the luggage. He felt a pang. Trumbull looked worn, he thought. Lines of suffering cut deep at the heavy features.

They crossed a placid bay in silence. Trumbull sat at the window, staring at the sun. He was allowing himself one week in San Francisco, he said finally. His summation would take five days to deliver, he thought, and then he would return home to Stoddard to help his wife through her last days.

Beyond that he had no thoughts at all.

Chapter Seventeen

Alexandra had made a little world for herself at the window overlooking the garden, and there while the shadows grew long, she sat. She was thinking of the house and their lives together.

The door opened. The breath, panting with garlic, was Rosita's. The woman came with a tray of simple food—soft-boiled eggs with a fragrance of salt, bread toasted on the range and crackling with smoky edges, custard, and tea. Rosita sat beside the sofa and began the feeding. She was full of church doings and family complaints. Alexandra turned away.

"Señora," Rosita said reproachfully.

"Well, just the custard," Alexandra agreed weakly. When it was over, Rosita left with the tray.

She turned back to the garden and listened with growing detachment. Every limb felt weak, and she was now feeling less, caring less, living only for small habits. She counted the hours and lived on small routines between meals and the bathroom. She had become helpless and the humiliation of that place distressed her. It was for that reason perhaps that she had asked that her husband sleep in a room across the hall. Or there was another reason; she could not be sure. That hall was a separation between them. She listened to the house but it was silent—the heavy tread in the library was absent and perhaps he had gone. It was just as well, she thought. Something was going on with the man, she knew from small clues—a new suit of broadcloth, strange cuff-links, lame excuses, and evasive talk after his last trip, his extreme attentiveness. He left briefly each morning for his office, and as quickly returned. He was constantly at her side, reading and making talk—European politics, villainies of monopolies, then end of the obsessive trial in San Francisco. He was nervously impatient at the delay and fearful of the

366

verdict. She let him talk and said nothing. It was easier than to deal with her pain. She was overcome by a deeper fatigue, a lifelessness and withdrawing into herself.

There were thoughts of young Mark and his short life and even that seemed dim and far away. There was something she meant to tell her husband, but it eluded her. Was it that woman in San Francisco? Even that had lost its point. She lay under the quilt, listening to the garden. A medley of whistling and singing could be heard. She could remember the early days when the poor birds of the wasteland, less melodious, grayer than the eastern kind, were few; but the land had changed, the hawks were fewer, singing birds had multiplied and that accounted for the clamor.

The door opened and he entered. He took her hand and said gruff things. He was kindness itself.

A full moon was visible over the poplars in the garden, swollen and yellow, lighting the winter landscape. Trumbull was awake, pressing the lumpy pillow, listening to the sounds. He threw back the blanket with growing alarm— there was a dreadful wait, then the sough of expelled breath across the hall that signaled the flicker of life. He could not sleep, he decided, and dressed.

He waited on the dark landing, listening at her door. The low regular sound was some assurance. Jesus! he though desperately. Let it come easy! Let it happen while she's asleep! Protect and help her through these days! The low moaning sound was too painful to bear. He went down with care to be silent. The library was cold, there was nothing to read. He put on his coat and went out with no idea where he was going.

The waters of the channel were black. He turned on Railroad Avenue and walked past warehouses and commercial buildings. A cantina was still going in a side street and a piano could be heard. He crossed the plaza and stood before his shingle, shivering in the cold. He had every impulse to return home, then changed his mind and went up to the office.

He lit the gas and looked on desolation. Two wooden files bulged with the lawsuit; the long table was stacked. There were exhibits and correspondence, photographs and bursting press books. The coverage was astonishing—articles, linecut drawings, editorials, satirical pieces, gossip. A malicious newspaper item noted Brawn's savage castigation of a woman

367

as devoid of moral sense as a child with a mind blank to right and wrong, to virtue and vice, to holiness and sin— lonely, desperate, and proved guilty. The item twitted "Judge Tremble" on the gallantry that had made the client's cause his own.

He winced. He had felt more than uncomfortable when Cudahey had silently put that item on his desk.

After a time, he opened the drawer. Among the accumulation, a recent letter from Jessica begged his return to San Francisco for the verdict. The weeks had passed, she had written, with no word of his return. The judge was taking forever and the suspense was killing her. She had put her case in his hands and now at the crisis he was not at her side to meet the judgment of the Court. She understood his other obligations—had she not released him when he was most needed?—but she too had her claims: Without his assurances of support, she would long since have abandoned the agony and fled. She had persisted in the fight against all her misgivings only because of promised victory, and where now was he? The writing was stilted, jagged, frantic, reproachful. She could not eat, think, or sleep for fear of that verdict. Except for Malvinia, everyone seemed to have abandoned her, even her lawyers. She lived in dread that the verdict would go against her, damning her forever of unnatural practices with the girl. Oh, God, oh, God! she wrote, she was better off dead! Now finally, the judge had promised a decision before the end of the year, but the outcome was anyone's guess. Please come! Please, please! she implored. Perhaps the enclosure would cheer him for Christmas.

He put aside the letter and studied the photograph taken in a fancy store in Montgomery Street. Jessica faced the camera demurely, holding a bunch of violets. A gown of rich brocade was decorated with large white flowers. A sweet glance, imploring and sentimental, under a low brow fringed with soft curls, stopped his breath. He traced her figure from crown to toe and felt thick blood collect at his throat. Something began to move with hard unwanted life. He replaced the items in the locked box, turned off the gas, and left.

How long he walked he could not say, but when he returned there was a light in the window. He broke into a run. Julian was on the porch looking into the darkness.

Trumbull froze. "Is it over?" he asked. Julian shook his head. Missus Judge was acting strange and calling for him.

Trumbull made a small sound of distress and hastened up-stairs.

The ravaged face turned to the door. "Marcus?" she called. "Marcus?"

She had not used that name in forty years.

He sat and took the cold hand. "Alex, it's me," he said reassuringly. He motioned Julian to get rid of the weeping Rosita. "You're all right, dear," he said over and over.

The sightless eyes burned with intensity. "How did you get here?" she demanded wildly. "How? How?"

He was not sure he understood. "I was just out for a walk," he said, puzzled. "What would stop me from coming?"

She looked uncertain. "Gracious, I was so worried. I can sleep now. Marcus?"

"Yes, dear?"

"I'm so relieved you're here," she said, throwing back her head. "Where is this place?" she asked wonderingly, clutching his hand. She was restless, plucking at the sheets. "Mark?" Her voice was suddenly clear.

"I'm here."

"I'm your friend, you know? I don't want your life to end because of me."

Oh, Lord, he thought wretchedly, she knows! What was going to happen now? "Just try to rest," he said.

"Be careful of yourself," she said. "You've got a very sick wife and I won't always be here to help you." The words trailed off and it was over.

The doctor did all a doctor could do. He applied a mirror, felt the pulse, and tied the dropped jaw. "Gallant woman, Judge," he said, wiping his hands. "She had courage. Courage, and a strong hold on life. I'm that sorry."

He could have said nothing more pleasing.

"They always said I had the talent," Trumbull said, handing over the doctor's coat and hat, "but that she had the character. I cannot disagree. Thank you kindly for all you've done."

"Not a bit." The young doctor bowed, and left. A first light was showing in the east. He drove off thinking the bereaved man had been entirely too courteous, too contained for his liking. He was not sure he cared for the strange fixed smile.

Rosita was struck by the same courtesy. What was it? she

369

wondered uneasily. A husband to one like that blessed one should be tearing his beard, howling with grief; but this one was without feeling that she could see. "*Gracias por todos, Rosa,*" he said. "*De nada,*" she replied, and took a silver brooch as a keepsake with some wonder at the haste. It was too much to expect, she muttered. Could she not make coffee to sustain him?

"Go to bed," Trumbull said. "Mrs. Trumbull loved you, and that's something to remember."

"*Gracias,*" Rosita said and left, wiping her eyes.

Trumbull motioned Julian to the library. "Snifter?" They drank in silence. Did Julian know his last thoughts? he asked. He'd been thinking how important it was that as life had fled, his wife had been warm and safe—and at the end not frightened.

"She was never afraid of anything," Julian said.

"Sure enough," Trumbull said. He started a checklist. People would soon call and the house had to be ready— chairs, refreshments would be needed. Could that be handled? Julian nodded.

Question of undertaker and the minister, Trumbull noted methodically. Nieces and cousins were to get remembrances —rings, brooches, trinkets, and such. Telegrams had to go to relatives. He was not sure he could remember all the Hennepins.

"I remember," Julian said. "Mister Judge?" he went on uncomfortably. "Do you want me to sit with her?"

The old man seemed diminished, frightened somehow, Trumbull thought. "No, I'll sit. You get to sleep," he decided, rising. "You're worn out and I'll want to think." His smile was odd, fixed as he started to climb the stairs. "Oh, Julian," he said, grasping the rail. "Is there any keepsake you'd like?"

Julian paused. "I don't need a keepsake," he said. Trumbull went up to the vacant room. When Cudahey showed up, he was still awake, staring at the sky, the same smile of despair twisted his mouth.

The minister spoke simply. It was a sensible eulogy which began with Proverbs 12:4: that a virtuous woman was a crown to her husband, that her price was far above rubies. In his review of a long and hard life, he said much to shake the emotions. When he came to that historic episode when the woman had written her husband, who sat at Fort Vigilance in the shadow of the Vigilantes' noose, that she would rather see him hanged than accept dishonor, the hush was notable.

Trumbull listened critically, almost with detachment. He remembered the letter and his answer—an answer printed by her in pamphlet form. He had written of two things: his love for his wife and a clear willingness to die to defend simple things. He knew war and death as the reality of a harsh life, he had written, but he was on oath to save the constitutions of the state and nation and was ready to give his life for that cause. That conviction had been expressed with clarity and simplicity, and the two letters, sent throughout the state, had turned public opinion in his favor. It was the thinking of the times. Lord! he thought wanly. What had happened to that younger self? He felt every eye upon him and stared at the floor.

The mourners gathered at the grave, stamping on the hard ground. A psalm was recited, earth was strewn, and it was over.

The visitors were few, embarrassed, and subdued, talking in set tragic tones, but occasionally recalling the dead woman's good humor, her old joking self, her wit, her good works, her kindnesses. He thought they would never go.

Julian looked into the parlor. "Turn up the light?"

"Thank 'ee, no," Trumbull said, looking up. "Oh, you might get rid of all this food," he said. Julian removed platters of cold food and came back to the bleak parlor. "Mister Judge, do you want me to stay on?"

"Stay on? How's that?"

"Can't be sure you want to keep this big house. In that case I'd want to make some plans. Go back home, maybe."

Trumbull nodded. "I won't hold you, Julian. I've not decided on this house. It'd be a wrench to give up, but perhaps you're right. It is big. Good night." Julian left.

Trumbull stared without pleasure at the basket of letters and telegrams of condolence and opened an envelope.

My dearest,

I am heartbroken for you and feel all your sorrow as my own. I have prayed that God will heal your grief as you deserve. I have been reading about Mrs. Trumbull in the newspapers and she was from all accounts surely as wonderful as you have told me. I wish I had known her. I feel so ordinary and insignificant a creature compared with the wonderful person she was. I envy the life she had with you. I'd like you here for the verdict, but if you decide not to come, I'll understand.

I hate to bring up the mundane but I thought you should know.

All love,

Jess

Trumbull read the letter again with resentment. Not right, quite jarring, he thought with a wave of dislike. The house felt strange. He finished a whiskey and wandered to the empty bedroom and waited for something that would not come.

The next day a curt letter went to Green to notify the client that he would not attend the court nor leave Stoddard until after a decent time of mourning. The next few weeks passed in routine waiting for the court's verdict. Just before Christmas a telegram brought the news.

ETERNAL LOVE AND GRATITUDE FOR VICTORY STOP JESSICA

He walked home through the dusk. He sat in the library and felt nothing at all.

A few days later he had an almost empty parlor car to himself on the run to Oakland. The dun-colored landscape sped fast under leaden clouds. He had been drinking steadily since boarding the train and was conscious of a valise filled with letters and telegrams still not answered.

A friendly voice said, "Dining car's open, Judge."

"Thank'ee, Mr. Wilson. I think not."

"Well, it was quite a victory. Quite a few of us were talking about it."

"Oh, that case? Yes, it was."

"Well, I'll be off. Sorry about your loss, Judge. A real lady. You're sure now—about lunch, I mean? You look peaked."

"I'm real sure, Mr. Wilson."

The hours passed. He stirred and opened the valise. A warm affectionate letter from Fanny Woodruff, signed with love, offered sympathy and invited him again to call. Well, that could wait. He opened the newspaper, now several days old.

The *Bulletin* ran to fifteen columns of small type with a sarcastic description of the scene. After months of mystifying delay, Judge Peter McArdle had bolted into a crowded and expectant courtroom like a nervous bridegroom and had plunged at once into reading a lengthy opinion, abusive and unsatisfactory to both sides. An extended disquisition had begun with an impressive Latin tag—*vox emissa volat, litera scriptament,* that it was easier to change words than writings, and for that reason the Court would rely mainly on the written proof and disregard the rest. He was troubled, the judge announced, at the seething mass of perjuries and barefaced indecencies which had distressed the Court. The infamies and the amount of perjury on both sides was not only shameless, but, if he might be permitted to say so, tedious and disgusting. But disgusting or not, the issue was whether the disgraceful conduct was matrimonial or meretricious. Justice might be blindfolded but not blind.

The plaintiff was hard to understand, the Court thought. She was certainly respectable prior to the lawsuit. She had a sharp incisive mind and rattling powers of conversation and a keen eye. She was quick in repartee and seemed endowed with a fine intellect. In some respects, however, she seemed absolutely devoid of moral sense and even when confronted with evidence of grossly indecent behavior had laughed and treated the matter with indifference that was confounding. She had sworn to false matter with such sincerity that the Court could find either no sense of guilt or a hardihood beyond belief. As to her superstitions, her relationships with one of another race and with that unfortunate young girl— ordinarily those elements would compel the court to reject her testimony in toto.

On the other hand, not much more could be said for the other side. The defendant, for his part, had a brilliant mind, ruthless and avaricious and without scruples in business except those set by the needs of business credit. The Court could not dissent from opposing counsel's portrait of a man of boundless wealth, possessed of strong animal passions that from excessive indulgence had become unaccustomed to restraint—a man who knew the weakness of human nature faced with temptation. He had always got what he was after and—with passion stronger than judgment—may have regarded as an airy trifle the miserable bit of paper behind which such a woman might well surrender her virginity and rest her claim to standing in the community. He might have meant to regain that paper after slaking the intensity of his passion—but if so, he had gone too far and the law would make permanent what he might have meant as a temporary ruse.

The testimony was recalled in detail and summarized at length. The temptation to put a plague on both houses was reluctantly put aside. A decision was required.

The fact was that the indisputable evidence and the admissions of the defendant in open court showed that the signature, date, and place were all in his handwriting—and the suggestion that the contract was written above that signature was an insult to the Court's intelligence. Such being the case, after lengthy disquisition of texts and cases, the Court felt compelled to explain that nothing in his religion kept him from administering the secular laws of his state and nation; and to rule that under the Civil Code of California nothing was essential to a valid marriage beyond mutual consent followed by the *copula*—the act of carnality being tantamount to a legal "assumption of marital rights, duties and obligations" under the Code. He found the marriage contract genuine, copulation conceded, and the marriage valid. Counsel were directed to submit proposed findings and orders without further show of personal spleen. The judge looked up at a stunned audience, smiled complacently at the defense, and bolted back to chambers. The reading had taken three full hours.

The ferry nosed into the slip at the foot of Market Street under a glowering sky. Trumbull took a cab to Wisteria Place, then changed his mind. "Sagamore House!" He went directly to his room and found an upbraiding letter from Jessica. He started a dozen replies. Not one was satisfactory. He spread out the messages of condolence. "No good, no good!" he groaned, striking his head with a clenched fist. Finally he went down and found a cab.

"Jackson Street!" he said with relief.

Smith was working on the galley proofs of the annual statement, making corrections in the margin. It had been a mixed year. Through acquisitions and mergers the C. and

S.W. system now covered the Pacific Coast from British Columbia to Juárez: Deposits were down but not too badly; with Hagerman's retirement the scandal was over and a good year lay ahead.

"Four o'clock, sir."

Smith turned to a last-minute urgent invitation from Fanny that he come to tea. Tuesday. Hm. He was puzzled, but despite the weather, pleased to leave early. His life had few pleasures outside the bank—good books, the theater, his handsome granddaughter, who was the nearest thing to a woman in his life. What was up? He brushed the mane of silvered hair with some complacency. The second floor was unusually quiet. Galindez had come late, signed papers, and left early for a conference at Brawn's offices in California Street. Hagerman was at Beaufort hiding from reporters and nursing a cold.

The rain was beating down when he reached the house on Jackson Street. A maid showed him to a warm parlor. It was San Francisco, he thought, rubbing his hands with satisfaction—cold rain and sea winds outside: a wood fire and tea and friendliness within. Hello? It took a moment to see that Fanny's other guest was Trumbull. He stood still, disappointed.

Fanny came forward and kissed his cheek. "Gramps, don't scold about the short notice," she said lightly. "Judge Trumbull just arrived in the city and dropped in unexpectedly. We've been talking about the Affair."

"Shouldn't wonder. Hullo, Trumbull," Smith said laconically. "Sorry about Mrs. Trumbull," he added, shocked by Trumbull's gauntness and bloodshot eyes, and surprised somehow to see a mourning band. "Brr! Dirty weather," he said, taking a hardbacked chair. "Have you got something better than that, dear?"

"Whiskey?"

"Good!"

Smith sipped the golden liquid, considering the awkward situation. Trumbull seemed older somehow, thinner, and wretched. Where was his granddaughter's good sense?

"I'm not sure of this," Trumbull said in a tired hoarse voice.

"Now, please!" Fanny turned to her grandfather with a determined look. "This meeting is my notion," she said firmly. "Jessie's won her divorce, but she and Hagerman cannot seem to end the bickering. If they keep it up, they'll hurt and degrade each other for years." She glowered at the endless columns of text in the newspaper. "My word! Did that ass of a judge have to go out of his way to blacken the people himself? Why couldn't he stick to his job?"

Smith smiled faintly. "It's a conspiracy of brigands. Bench, bar and hangers-on—all together to drag things out and plunder the outsiders. Got to expect it."

Trumbull shrugged. The law was no worse than other institutions, he observed cynically. "There's one sure rule—the more inferior the judge, the more abusive his tongue. Lucky I wasn't there when he read that language."

Fanny said uncomfortably. "We—that is, I—have persuaded Judge Trumbull that it's got to stop here, now Jessie's got her divorce, Gramps. It should be up to the lawyers, but . . ." She paused. "But it seems to need someone who can talk to both sides."

Smith sniffed the whiskey thoughtfully. "Me?"

"I hope so," Fanny replied.

"Have you discussed this with your client, Judge?"

"Not yet," Trumbull said. "I just got back to San Francisco and we've had no chance to talk. But I'd expect her to be generous. Her views to the press seemed to show that. It should be simple."

Smith smiled with irony. Jessica's victory had been celebrated at a reception on Christmas Day at Wisteria Place. She had received the crowd, all smiles and gracious triumph, wearing an elegant wrapper of shrimp-pink satin. Champagne and oysters had been served all around. She had sat on a pillow-strew floor in Bohemian freedom, and announced that she was happy as a kitten, for her cause had won—she was sorry for the poor Sen, who could have settled with her at any time, except for his spiteful family. She was glad he had not, for now, having won and being vindicated, she was looking forward to seeing the Louvre and all those places. She still loved the old sport and wished him Happy New Year. When the reporters left, she was quaffing champagne, an arm around her bronze peacock, earnestly discussing the new woman in broken French with the man from the New Orleans *Picayune*.

Smith said, "Generous? Her claim was for millions. Is that the range?"

"She's not thinking of the money," Trumbull replied.

"Neither is Hagerman," Smith said dryly. "He's thinking

of public opinion. How d'you think a man like that feels to have his nose pulled in public by a woman? I doubt he'd listen."

Trumbull stared. "She's got the judgment. Has he thought where that puts him?"

Smith glanced at Fanny. She sat forward uneasily. "Ah? But has she got the judgment?" he said. "As I understand it, no judgment is final until the appeal is decided by the higher Court. Hagerman will certainly appeal."

Trumbull laughed unpleasantly. "Let him try. We'll have an overwhelming brief to sustain the divorce. Meanwhile she's got a final valid judgment that wipes out the imputed indecencies and puts the perjuries on the other side. As to that gratuitious blathering by McArdle about her morals? Pooh! She'll get half the common property, worth millions. That alone clears the social slate." He shrugged, staring at the purring flames as though to convince himself. "I could throw a stone and hit a hundred homes of worse behavior. You're in banking, Smith. You tell me where half your customers began. Hey?"

"Different times," Smith murmured.

"Pompous hypocritical nonsense! It ain't what the Court says that matters—but what goes into the judgment roll. She's been treated outrageously," Trumbull said argumentatively. "There's no reason to settle or relent."

Fanny found it convenient to tend the fire.

Trumbull stirred. "Still, if Hagerman will recognize the marriage, that is, abandon the appeal and withdraw those infamies, I'll urge a moderate sum to settle the money claims."

"How moderate?"

"Moderate enough," Trumbull said. "But don't put it to the test, sir!"

Fanny had watched the exchange with growing concern. "Please, Gramps," she urged. "It wouldn't be meddling. You've got the bank's interests to consider."

Smith put his bony hands to the fire. "Judge Trumbull, I'd like to help for many reasons, but it's Mr. Hagerman you've got to deal with, not me, and he's resentful. Some of the difficulty is your fault, you know."

"Mine?"

"Quite so," Smith said coldly. "He was initially excited, but not intractable. He's always had a soft indulgent spot for a pretty woman. So it might have been compromised. That is, before you made the case your own."

Trumbull was taken aback. "I don't quite see that," he said stiffly.

But of course he understood. In reply to Brawn's taunts of bad faith in the closing argument, he had stated that no honorable lawyer could knowingly take on a false cause, that he had practiced law a lifetime in the state and was well known, and while he had made enemies, no one had ever before questioned his honesty: that he had gone into the client's account in detail, which had not varied since their first meeting at Las Flores, and gave his personal assurance to the Court that he had not for one moment doubted his client's cause and would make that statement anywhere.

"Sorry, Trumbull," Smith said coolly. "Did you expect to taunt Hagerman so briskly in public on his morals and disregard appearances yourself? And not, I might add, lose a measure of respect yourself?"

Trumbull went pale. "Eh? What's that?"

"Oh, come!" Smith said acidly. "Were you in any position to make yourself the woman's protector? It was an indiscretion, you'll admit. Not my business, but on the other hand, you initiated these talks with my granddaughter. She's sympathetic and clever, but the strong female mind, I'm afraid, is no substitute for knowledge of how these things work." He glanced at the window. "Confounded rain. Fanny, dear, I'll have a last whiskey."

"Of course." Fanny poured a glass in the uneasy silence. Trumbull stirred. "What's all this got to do with the case?" he said.

"Everything considering the gross recriminations. You made Hagerman look like a fool, and that's intolerable. Your closing argument gave him less morals than a Mexican pimp."

Fanny interrupted. "Worse things appeared about him in the press, Gramps."

"That's the press, but this was face to face." He turned to the lawyer. "I'd be careful, Judge. How d'ye think he felt while being roasted to get all those tales about your conduct with his wife?"

"His wife? But . . ." Trumbull halted, confounded. "He had separated from the woman," he said hoarsely. "It was technical, at best. The marriage had gone empty."

Smith glanced up with a smile of ice. "Had yours?"

The sound of breathing was heavy.

"Maybe I'd better go," Trumbull said with an effort, suddenly appalled. "I had no idea to embarrass anyone. Mrs. Woodruff, if I could have my coat?"

"No, wait!" Fanny said, restraining him, "I won't have this nonsense, Gramps. Hagerman's got no claims to Jessie after the brutal things he's done. I'm disappointed in you. I never thought you'd be narrow." She tried a conciliatory note. "Gramps, too many real people are being hurt by this. Someone's got to help. I could talk to Tony myself. The trial's over—"

"Over? What makes you think that? It's just begun," Smith said sharply. "Judge Trumbull, I should tell you that new counsel's being brought in to replace Brawn. It's Senator Pike."

Trumbull was jolted. "Pike? You say Pike's entering the matter?"

"It was decided today," Smith said. "Didn't you expect something of this sort?"

"Dunno what I was expecting." Trumbull put down the glass and walked to the window. He drew a breath and turned about. "Any fee he'd charge would exceed any possible settlement! So what's the point?"

"Haven't you answered your own question?" Smith slapped his knees and stood. "Time to go, Fanny, if I'm to get the rare side of the roast." He turned back to the downcast lawyer. "Sorry, Judge. I've no wish to question your affairs, but I thought you should know what your indiscretions have cost."

"Nothing I've not told myself," Trumbull sighed. "But I've got to see this to some finality. To be frank, I'd welcome a settlement to have done with this."

"Well, I'm no lawyer," Smith replied. "Sorry, Trumbull, about everything. Fanny, my dear girl, if I may have my coat?" Fanny followed him to the foyer.

"Are you all right?" Smith said.

"Oh, yes. I'm just concerned for him."

"Nothing more than that?" he asked gently.

"Oh, Gramps," she said.

He touched her cheek. "Don't make his mistakes yours. I'm fond of you, dear, and for your sake I'll do what I can. You might urge Trumbull to get her to yield before Pike

379

wrings her neck. Pike's not Brawn, by a long shot. Where's his common sense gone?"

He kissed her and stepped into the night.

Fanny returned to the warm parlor. Trumbull was at the fireplace. "So they've got Pike," he said. She stood beside him. "It'll be all right, Mark. Really, it will." The troubled eyes were level with her own.

"What d'you want to do now?" she asked.

"I don't know," Trumbull said. "I don't want to see her at her place."

"Would you like to meet her here? You could use this house, if you need a place to meet."

"No. Couldn't," Trumbull said, shaking his head. "I couldn't involve you. I just know I've got to get her what I promised and then have done with her."

She waited, feeling the nearness.

"Oh, Fanny," he said dismally. There was a strong force in the room. She drew a breath. "You know, Mark, I'm soon going back to England. In England a lady can have all the lovers she likes if they're her own class and if she keeps out of the divorce courts," she said ruefully. There was no response.

She stood beside him, passive, waiting for something impossible to happen. She loosened her hair.

"What about the maid?" a hoarse voice said.

She looked up, and then there was a mouth on her mouth, a grip of iron crushing her breasts, a thing of agony and despair in her arms.

He returned to his room at the Sagamore. The heaps of letters and telegrams of condolence were accusing things. "Christ!" he said wearily. He sat and began. He wrote on and on in a precise handwriting, letter on letter, recalling the past. The range was surprising—Hennepins, a few Trumbulls, Texans, Californians, workingmen. How many lawyers, he thought, wondering at his mark upon the profession. The Comstock. The Governor. Judges. A kindly note from Minerva Sickels of condolences in which her husband shared. The memories were thick upon him. Old soldiers. Galveston? Galveston? That was yesterday! A graveyard with its markers for his mother and brothers was vivid. Suddenly tears were coursing in runnels down his cheeks, soaking his beard. He wrote on and on, blinded with grief. The room in Stoddard was before him. Something ominous should have happened, but he could not escape the truth that had haunted him since that moment of death—the recollection that, except for a mild sense of loss, of strangeness, perhaps of panic, he had felt nothing for the woman with whom he had spent his life.

Nothing at all.

Except perhaps a debased sense of relief and a vision—unbidden, unwanted, startled—of a naked woman in another place.

At daylight the helpless silent weeping was still in flood. For whom or what he could not tell.

Chapter Eighteen

White Rose Lodge

Friday

My dear Mark:

Such a thoughtful note, and so gentle, so little deserved. I had no right to bolt San Francisco without a word of explanation, but on the whole, was it not best?

I've had this month to reflect and come to some conclusions. It was misery that propelled you to me, but what greater misery to continue! I was so moved, but I feel sure that it was not me you wanted, but a reassurance and comfort of a kind I could not, and never will be able to give. I cannot understand it all, but I accept it. No need for apologetics.

Let us stay friends.

Having got here in the winter season, I am dining out everywhere, being a celebrity from the Land of Heart's Desire. Your divorce case is still the talk where I go—with surprising tolerance and amusement. I am asked to explain Jessica and our complex legal system. How can I? I understand neither.

To be germane, I have had a note from Emily inviting me for a weekend in Kent. I am not sure I'll go. I've heard that daily letters go off to San Francisco, vehement against settlement on any grounds at all. Theo (who might help) is in New York, and she has an ally in Galindez—and so if peace can be made, do not, I urge, delay.

Wish Jessica well. Life has dealt badly with her. It will bless you to work things out for her. I long for news of agony's end before my return to San Francisco —but that is some years off. I now haunt the British Museum, accumulating materials for a novel of ancient Greece. I think of Aristides the Just. Such a good man, pure and noble—and so hated for it.

I write in haste. Tonight I dine in Kensington and will meet Mr. James. I am stupefied. In prospect, it is like shaking hands with Mont Blanc, but then so was meeting you.

It was not without rewards.

With devotion,

Fanny

"Villain, villain, villain!" Jessica exclaimed indignantly. A cold wind was blowing, but the slow, jingling trolley car with its potbellied stove was warm and comfortable. The passengers, who had filled the car since the terminus near the Mission Dolores—housewives, mostly, going to town for special shopping—had noticed the slender woman talking to herself, but she wore a veil and was not recognized. She was oblivious to the world, glaring at a copy of the *Hornet*.

Her most private affairs were before the public—a quarrel over fees with Finch, his departure from the case, the infatuation of her chief counsel. As to Finch, the article observed, his departure had been expected. It was amazing, it went on, that anyone could expect for long to do business with the ignorant, vicious, opinionated, tyrannical woman who had been his client. With the inconstancy of a weather vane, the creature had abandoned and been abandoned by everyone fool enough to deal with her—except Judge Trumbull, whose goose too was trussed for the spit, though he was too doting to know it. Jessica ground her teeth. The *Hornet* had not let up on her once since the case began.

"Van Ness Avenue!"

She stiffened with suspicion and hid behind the *Hornet* as

382

a rough man got on, but the man paid no attention. She resumed reading, thinking that perhaps she should have taken the railroad, but that might have been watched.

She did not doubt that she had cause for fear. Directly after the verdict, Hagerman had announced that he would defend in the State Court with energy and prosecute in the Federal Court with zeal. He promised in the first to resist alimony and counsel fees to the death, move for a new trial, and take every appeal known to man. In the second, he vowed to proceed afresh before an Examiner in Chancery just as soon as subpoenas could be served. Deputy United States marshals began their search for Jessica. They appeared at Wisteria Place, at a flat in Van Ness, where she was rumored hiding out, and at Las Flores. It was Digges, blankfaced and ignorant of marriage contracts, who met them at the kitchen door.

Patterson spat on the sill. "Digges?"

"Sir?"

"We don't want trouble."

"I don't want trouble neither."

"You know where she might be at?"

"Might be anyplace."

"Might she be here?"

"Might. Might not. Cain't say."

"Mind if we look around?"

"Oh, I don't mind," Digges replied. "I don't mind what you does, but you ain't looking around."

"There's three of us," Patterson said.

"I cain't count past one, Mr. Marshal," Digges said.

O'Hare wiped his moustaches. "Let's take this prick," he said.

"Washburn?" Digges called. A muscular young man stepped forward with a shotgun. "Sorry, Mr. Marshal," Digges said, pulling his lip. "Washburn cain't count either."

"Never could," Washburn said.

"You see?" Digges said. "Now, I respects that badge, but it won't get you in, Mr. Marshal. Not unless you got something more legal than that."

Patterson studied a pig sticker held in an enormous hand. A triangular iron blade was encrusted with dried blood.

"Don't make us come back," Patterson said, smiling unpleasantly, and left. When all was clear, Malvinia entered the darkened bedroom where Jessica, languishing in one of her

383

more serious spells, had fled for refuge. She was still not able to grasp that her victory was no victory after all.

A week later Malvinia brought a note from Trumbull advising that a meeting with Hagerman at his offices in Kearny Street had been set. Jessica was urged to attend. He promised to give away no points, to listen and to let the parties talk face to face; it was at least imperative to explore every way out. A safe conduct was assured. Jessica threw herself on the pillow in despair. "No!" she exclaimed. "It's a trick! I won't go!"

"What sort of trick?" Malvinia asked wearily.

Jessica said, "The purpose is to disaffect Judge Trumbull."

"That is childish."

"Is it? I'm worried about Judge Trumbull," Jessica said. "He's changed, Vinnie, quite changed. He treats me so indulgent, so kindly and gentle it breaks my heart, but something's happened. He's become so absentminded, so deep in his thoughts that—well, I don't know where we stand. He's not been with me outside the office but only once at Wisteria Place, and then it was a fizzle. He said he was tired."

"Maybe he was."

"Him? He's a bull when he wants to be!" Jessica complained, then clouded over. "Vin? D'ye think it's another woman?" she asked fearfully.

"Any reason to think so?"

"No, except that men are like that," Jessica brooded. "Not that I'd blame him. I can be a real pest when I'm upset and I'm sure in a state of nerves. He was a million miles away. I remarked on it, and he got real testy and left without coffee. And we always had coffee and sandwiches afterwards. Vinnie?"

"Yes, honey?"

"Am I likely to lose him?"

"He'll come around," Malvinia said firmly. "You're a good thing, Jess, and at his age the man knows it. Just keep it less agitated and give it time. He's got more'n you on his mind— the trial, his position in the profession, keeping his promises to you. The main thing is he wants to win your case."

"I don't know," Jessica sighed, clutching the pillow to her breast. "I daren't go back to the city now they're after me. It looks so gray and depressing. Oh, Vinnie!" she burst out suddenly. "Oh, Vinnie, Vin-Vinnie, don't despise me!" she cried passionately, taking the splayed hand to her cheek and kissing it. "Without you, I wouldn't know what I'd do. It's only here I feel peace. I need your strength. Don't make me go!" The dark face was remote. "Oh, tell Judge Trumbull I'll think about it," Jessica cried. She flopped over and buried her head in the pillow.

Suddenly the stove was suffocating and the trolley had passed her stop.

"No wonder you're in receivership!" she said indignantly, addressing the driver. She stepped off and strode back to Kearny Street with rising fury and talking to herself. "Trash!" she cried, addressing the *Hornet*. "Trash! I'll cowhide the mudsill, I swear I will!" She was recognized and followed by knowing winks. Her cloak was open and she strode with the heads-up stride of a grenadier.

She stopped at the corner to catch her breath. A thousand things were running through her mind, but she was resolved to keep calm. No one suspicious was about. She entered the office building and ran up to the second floor and then down the hall in a clatter of French heels on the tiled flooring.

"Mark?"

There was no answer. Cautiously she opened the inner door. A strong sun poured through closed windows and a gas flame was burning. Trumbull, who had been working all night in shirt sleeves, had fallen asleep in a characteristic bulky pose—elbow on desk, cheek in palm, eyes closed. A snore brought an affectionate smile. How sweet, she thought, and touched him. He stirred and then she saw the letter from England on the desk. She read the affectionate opening with a sinking heart. So that's what had happened, she thought with a pang. Trumbull groaned. She replaced the letter and left. Ten minutes later she returned and knocked.

"Come in!" Trumbull said sleepily.

Jessica entered with a strained smile. The letter had disappeared. "Breakfast!" she announced, and paused in surprise. "That's no way to sleep, you fool! If you must work late, at least let me buy you a sofa." She got busy with a bag of doughnuts and coffee. "Say, how late did you work?" she demanded severely.

"Late enough," he said, yawning mightily. "Ow! I'm stiff!" he complained, then paused. She looked flushed and charming. "Say, for a delivery boy you look mighty nice," he joked with an indulgent grin. The thick fingers went through his

385

locks, rubbing briskly. "Ooh! Uh! A-a-h!" He stretched and yawned. "They won't get here till eleven. Ain't you early?"

Jessica turned off the gas. "Maybe I'd better be early," she said tartly. She sat and began to undo her gloves, glancing with disapproval at the room. A half dozen chairs were in a circle, borrowed evidently from the photographer down the hall. Down to the brass cuspidor, nothing could be less elegant. She was ashamed of it. "Haven't seen much of you at all, Mark. I miss you," she said acidly.

Trumbull was rummaging in the desk. "I'm working hard," he replied.

"I hope on my case," she said with an edge. "You've neglected me, you know. You're real unfeeling sometimes, Mark, real stupid, especially now."

Trumbull paused. "Something special gone wrong?" he asked, cracking his knuckles. He was taking a monstrous time to come out of it, she thought. "Wrong? I declare! Have you seen this?" she exclaimed, throwing down the *Hornet*.

"You'd best not read this stuff," he said wearily, turning the pages. "Just has no point."

"Will you do something about it?"

"What? Start a fist fight?"

"Well! You're mighty calm. On the day—the very day I'm here to talk soft to Hagerman, they manage to get these insults into the papers. Don't think it's accidental. It's to upset me. Oh, I'm sorry your name is involved," she said with irony. "Still, don't recriminate me about that. I'm not the one responsible. I did not pursue you. You pursued me, so if we're being discussed, it's not on my conscience. I have been very protective of you, and cautious."

"I know that," he said.

"More than you have been of me!"

"I think very much of you."

"You don't act it!" she said. "You let these things happen! You do nothing—"

"Jess!" he broke in. "Just stop this now," he said. "I do all I can! I'm working unmercifully on your matter and I dare not get diverted. Don't be unjust."

"I'm sorry," she said, halting, "but I get so darned upset for you. I'm made notorious and I don't care a fig, but they've got no right to slur you. Not you, Mark! You're too good, too fine."

"It's best ignored," Trumbull said after a moment. "Now

let me get refreshed." He shaved and washed and brushed out his hair and beard, taking as long as possible, then sighed and examined the mirror. Her eyes, he saw, were tired, pouchier than he remembered. He braced his shoulders and returned smelling of bay rum. Jessica was peering at his notes. "What's all this about?" she asked suspiciously.

"I'm developing the authorities," he said. *Dalrymple vs. Dalrymple* in 4 Eng. Ecclesiastical, 485, a precedent in the House of Lords, was much in point, he observed. The case dealt with a secret misalliance of a noble Scot in the Dragoon Guards with a plebeian woman living in passionate Edinburgh. The practice of secrecy of marriage was more widespread than one might imagine. The research was taking him far afield indeed.

"It seems so endless. What's taking so long?" she asked with some desperation.

Trumbull almost laughed. The table held thirty volumes of stenographic record of a million words. The Court's opinion alone ran to twenty thousand words. A score of lawyers were toiling for the enemy. His own force consisted of himself and Green and outside help of poor quality. Finch had left him with a mess, and the enemy was throwing every harassment known to the book. Pike was fresh and the pressures relentless. How could this be explained? "It's a good case," he said.

"Is it? I thought we're supposed to talk about settlement. Now I find you preparing to answer the appeal. Hardly shows much faith in this meeting!"

"Hardly does," Trumbull agreed. "But they must have something to propose, or they'd not be here. The main thing is staying power. A lawyer has got to take punishment, nail down the law, and come back with hard blows, however long it takes. I want 'em to see readiness." He sipped the coffee, meditating on the endless toil. "It ain't simple to analyze cases. Each has a world of meaning against a vanished background. You've got to feel the life behind the case—the times, the customs, the judges, their dispositions—and try to predict what the next set will do. Take this English case. It states the general rule—but, *quaere,* will it be applied to our case? And if it ain't, what happens to the laws of California? Of this nation?"

Her brow knitted. "Mark, you scare me. I am dependent on the law. If it's so changeable, so subject to whimsical judges, where's my case? Your doubts and skepticisms offer nothing but uncertainties." She glanced resentfully at the Dalrymple case. The man always managed to divert her, she thought. "What's it about? No, don't tell me. Can I read it?"

"If you find that fun," he agreed, smiling indulgently. The session, he saw, would be difficult.

"Never mind the smiles! I have a good legal mind," she said severely. She put aside the cup and placed a reticule on the desk and began to search. "Oh, darn! I left my spectacles! Well, write out the citation and I'll find it in the Law Library. And this time I'll want to see the brief before it goes to the printer. I might have some ideas." She looked up with a trace of challenge. "I trust you don't mind showing it to me?"

"Not a bit," Trumbull said after a pause and began to write out the citation.

"I think my ideas are very good," she said. "I want to help, Mark. I'm taking up the typewriter. I could type it up or edit it. D'you object?"

"I'm not sure it's a good idea," Trumbull said.

"But why not?" she asked persuasively. "We're always working late, and I could be useful, I know I could. Come on, Mark," she wheedled.

"No," he said, shaking his head.

She drew back, offended. "Why not? Mark! You're not keeping me from having some voice about my own case?"

"Of course not," he said.

"I don't believe that!" She paced the office, twisting her hands. "I have to tell you this, Mark. I am not satisfied. Mistakes have been made, serious ones, mostly by Finch, but you've had your share too. I mean to keep a closer watch from now on. I've been too trusting, but no more. I no longer believe anyone. It's becoming such a ludicrous farce. You promised victory! Where is it?"

"I promised you a judgment," Trumbull said, "and you now have it."

"Then why am I still in this fix? Judge McArdle gave me ten thousand dollars back alimony and monthly support. I need that money to clear my debts. I'll never see it!" she smoldered, staring at the street. "And don't tell me about the appeal! I'm tired of excuses. I know only that time is passing and Hagerman still has his women and spends millions while his wife—and I *am* his wife, the Court has said so—lives like a pauper. Other women get alimony. Why not Mrs. Hagerman?"

"Hagerman has filed a bond," Trumbull said, "for four hundred thousand dollars, and has got a stay."

"Oh, a stay!" she exclaimed scornfully.

"Yes, stay," Trumbull said. "I cannot stop the appeal. I can only fight it. I'll win. There is no basis on which to set aside the judgment of divorce."

"I wish I were convinced," she muttered. "Meanwhile you're letting them drag me back to the Federal Court. What chance have I got there? Why do you allow it? Good God, Mark! What kind of a lawyer are you? You said there is no federal jurisdiction. What happened to my demurrer there? To my plea in abatement?"

"The Federal Court has not yet passed on those motions," Trumbull said restively. "Let's wait and see what happens. Judge Goff has personally admitted that he'd regard Judge McArdle's judgment in the Superior Court as a bar to his court."

"And you believe that? Oh, lands! You're real simple if you think the matter's not already determined. All that talk about stopping the federal jurisdiction is so much swill. The federal marshals are chasing me all over the city, trying to serve those papers on me. If that court ever gets hands on my marriage paper, it'll go off to Washington and I'll never see it again! It's enough to make an Egyptian mummy laugh." She fell into a deep chair, indignant beyond words. "Mark! If I can't get justice we must take action."

"What? Write pamphlets?" he asked ironically.

"If anything happens to my paper, I'll shoot Hagerman and then kill myself," she flared. "Well, I will and I can! I'm no fool city girl. I was brought up to ride and hunt. I can hit a four-bit piece at ten paces nine times out of ten."

Trumbull reached for a cigar. "That's better'n I can do," he observed dryly, biting the tip and spitting, "but I'd not be heard to say that aloud. But why the despair? The State Court's judgment will eventually prevail."

"Eventually? When's that? A year? Two years? Ten? I can't live this way! How am I to meet my bills while my lawyers get fat?"

"The lawyers ain't had a cent yet," Trumbull replied, "and I cannot tell when they will. The stay covers all."

"My lawyers!" she jeered. "My precious lawyers! Lawyers? Oh, my arse!" she burst out vulgarly. "Who did I have? Finch the Chinch? Dirty mudsill!" she cried nervously with growing wrath, stalking the chamber. "Shysters! Oh, not you, Mark," she said, pausing. "But you're so darned tolerant, I'm never sure how they're taking you in. You all stick together. And that's another thing," she exclaimed, striking her forehead, "I swore on oath that my lawyers had no interest in the case, and yet you let Finch file that retainer agreement for a half interest in the recovery. Makes me look like a darned liar!"

Trumbull sank back and stared at the cigar. "I was never told about that paper," he said dangerously. "Was I?"

"I forgot about it," she said after a moment, taken aback, "but anyways, I reckoned Finch had told you. Sho! I'm not supposed to know these fine points. But *fifty percent?*" she said blackly. "It was an immoral and unconscionable agreement. It ought to be set aside."

"You're free to try," Trumbull said. "I'll tell 'ee—if you keep this up, it'll be half of nothing."

"Oh!" She flounced about.

Most unreasonable, he thought sorely, turning back to the cigar. "Lordy, Jess," he sighed, glancing at the clock. "What's this about? You've been leading up to something since you came."

She half laughed and got up. "Well . . . D'ye know what day this is?"

"Yes. Friday."

A smile was peculiarly amused. "It's more. Hagerman didn't pick just any day for this meeting. It's his birthday. D'ye know he sent Li to beg me to be sure to come today?"

Trumbull frowned. "Why would he do that?"

"Because he's so darned sure he can get around me," she exclaimed indignantly. "Now, listen! There's some things I cannot resist, and Hagerman knows it. I can tell you exactly what he's aiming to do." She was mysterious, portentous, speaking with peculiar intensity of feeling.

"Do? Do what?"

"He's going to show me a picture."

"Picture?" Trumbull was bewildered.

Jessica leaned closer on the desk. "It's not just any picture," she said intensely. "It's one his mama commissioned when he was six years old. Just the cunningest thing, with that funny nose and ringlets. It always turns me to jelly and he knows it, the darned scoundrel! You may not believe this, Mark," she said, reaching for her handkerchief, "but I'm still

ond of the old man. Oh, what's the use? He doesn't really
want a settlement. He wants total surrender. He knows just
how weak he can get me. Mark," she said fearfully, and then
tears welled and she began to weep. Trumbull waited patiently. "I'm such a softy," she said tremulously, when she had re-
gained control. "Honestly, I'm not sure you should let me go
through with this."

Trumbull glanced longingly at the pad of yellow foolscap.

"Lands!" she said finally. "If I see it, I'm a goner. Mark!
Promise you'll not let him show me that picture! Promise!"

Trumbull began to smile. Really, he thought, sorely, she
was just too comical. "Jess . . ."

She stamped a foot. "No, promise!"

"I'll do what I can," Trumbull said and got a kiss. "I'm
such a baby," Jessica said, sitting on his knee, "but I can be
grateful. You'll see. Once this is over, I'll make you real
happy. Oh, Mark! I do love you so!" she exclaimed, throwing
herself at him.

Hagerman climbed the stairs, pausing occasionally to catch
his breath. A coat lined with Russian sable hung baggily, but
a silk topper was immaculate. He rapped and entered.

"Sen! How sweet!" Jessica swept forward with a glad
smile. "It's like wine to see you again! Are you alone?" she
cooed.

"Hello, Jess," Hagerman said noncommittally. He strolled
into the large shabby room and shook hands limply with
Trumbull. He seemed nettled to have come ahead of time. "I
thought the others'd be here," he said, coughing.

They compared watches. No accounting for it. Precisely
seven o'clock. Jessica smiled knowingly at Trumbull, told
Hagerman that she was reading a real brilliant brief on appeal full of English citations and erudition that went back to
the Ecclesiastical Courts under Henry II. "Kindly take the
Senator's coat, Judge Trumbull," she said with deep concern.

"Thanks, no," Hagerman said. "I've got this chill."

"Here's a good chair. Or would you like one more comfortable?" she asked.

"It'll do," Hagerman said briefly. He sat and bit a cigar.
Jessica sat opposite and stared earnestly. "Oh, Sen! You don't
look well!" she said with commiseration.

Hagerman looked at Jessica, then at the window, the wall,
the ceiling, the floor, and Trumbull. He spat a flake of tobac-

co. "Can't complain," he said with a ghastly smile. "Market's up. That's something." A penetrating glance lingered on the woman—a bit plump under the chin, marked cleft between the brows, spidery lines drifting from fine nostrils to pale mouth! Jesus, he thought, she claimed twenty-seven when they first met. How in hell could he have believed her age? Trumbull was gray, and that was some satisfaction. Good Christ! They were sitting like a married pair in a drawing room—and what in hell did they expect of him? He struck a match. "Any business here besides my case, Trumbull?" he asked crudely. "Or am I supporting the whole show?"

"Are you eating enough, Sen?" Jessica broke in. "Getting enough greens?"

"Greens are bad for me," Hagerman replied. "Give me this black stool. Tarry," he said informatively.

"Sen!" Jessica said, outraged.

Hagerman was surprised. "Did I say something?"

"No, Sen, nothing," she said and stared at the floor.

Hagerman glanced at his watch. "They want me to donate a fifteen-foot public monument of myself," he said. "They say it'd make a good impression."

"Sounds wonderful! D'ye mean to do it?"

"I'm thinking of it," Hagerman replied, frowning. "I find the price a confounded wrench. And who knows if the sculptor is any good? He claims he is, but who knows for sure? I find it worrisome. Lots of things are worrisome. But what in hell do I care for the public? Yep," he meditated. "Tarry. They don't seem to know much about it." A grimace went to Trumbull.

The pause was awkward.

"D'ye hear from Emily?" Jessica asked.

"Oh, she's on her third," Hagerman said with a fond gleam of interest. "Setting fashions, I hear, despite the scandal. Great people, the English. They understand scandal. Had the practice, y'see? God help the world when they go!"

"Give her my love?"

"Yes, sure."

"I hear Theo's marrying a widow."

"Rich widow. Can't say it matters. He's rich enough himself."

"Bruno must be having a birthday," Jessica said reminiscently. "Lands! He's five, isn't he?"

"Shut up," Hagerman said.

"Sen!"

"Oh, hell!" Hagerman said. He stood impatiently and went to the window. After a moment he turned about and saw that the woman was smiling. "Oh, dear, oh, dear!" He sighed, shaking his head. "Seems strange, don't it! I never change, only the world gets less interesting and a lot of things lose importance. I dunno, Jess, I dunno. We had some good times."

"Yes, we did," she agreed warily.

"You behaved bad to me, Jess," Hagerman said reproachfully, "real bad, you know. And I never did you anything but good."

"I'm sorry, Sen," Jessica said meekly. "I say things and I never know why. I've had some awful remorseful nights since. But you did say you'd break my neck that time, and that's what started it, you'll recollect."

Hagerman held his tongue. "I wish it never happened," he said handsomely. "It's this testiness. I just said I *hoped* you'd break your neck; there's a difference. Frankly, I made a lot of mistakes, Jess."

"You sure did!"

"Well, I just said I did!" he retorted. "Look 'ee," he said impulsively, "let's forget this shit, Jess, and try to work this out. I'm not vindictive, and we're still old friends, hey?"

Jessica stiffened and threw a meaningful glance at Trumbull. "I reckon," she said cautiously.

"I say, Judge," Hagerman said doubtfully, "d'ye mind this?"

"Not a bit," Trumbull said.

"No? Well! Now, then, as I see it, Jess, us two could always talk if the lawyers let us. Gaiety and a bottle of champagne always went a long way . . ." He stopped suddenly and snapped his chalky fingers. "Say, I almost forgot!" He fumbled in a pocket. "Now, where in hell is it?"

Jessica rose in alarm. "Judge Trumbull!" she exclaimed, backing off.

"Oh, here!" Hagerman said. "Here's that picture you always liked so much." He looked up expectantly.

Jessica was backing to the wall. "Judge Trumbull, Judge! Please."

"Remember this?" Hagerman said. He had a small silver-mounted portrait cupped in his hand. "No," she whimpered, retreating. "No, no, no!" He thrust the portrait at her face. She stood flat against the wall, frantically moving her head.

393

"Oh, Judge!" She paused, transfixed. "Oh, Sen! Oh! Oh! Oh!" she wailed and burst into tears.

Hagerman seemed surprised. "Well, Jesus Christ!" He scratched his head, perplexed indeed, and put the portrait on the desk.

"Such a scoundrel!" she wept. "You planned this! You know what it does to me!"

Trumbull picked up the portrait and suppressed a grin. Hagerman at six was a wizened parody of his future self—a mannikin shrunk as though by Amazonian headhunters. A tiny duckbill nose and golden ringlets masked a leer of avarice.

"Oh, Sen!" Jessica gasped, blowing her nose. "I don't care what happens now. I'll do anything you say, but let's be loving to each other. No, Judge," she said, raising a finger, "no conditions at all. I'll depend entirely on Mr. Hagerman's generosity. I'm sure he'll be fair."

"D'ye mean that?" Hagerman said suspiciously.

Jessica nodded. "It's Euripides who wrote, 'Once a lover, always a lover.' You told me that yourself, Sen, and it's so true."

"I said that?"

"Sure did! I wrote it in my book."

"Well, all right then," Hagerman said, relieved. "All right! I always said I'd be fair, confound it. Tony will hate this, but I'll work out something real generous. You'd like that, hey?"

"That's sweet, Sen!" Jessica said. "Of course you'll have to discontinue your appeal against my judgment?"

"Discontinue?" Hagerman frowned.

"I can't get married unless I'm sure I've got my divorce. Sho! It's too elemental!" she said sunnily.

By an immense effort, Hagerman held himself in control. "Jess, there is no marriage."

"There is to me!" she said with conviction.

The jangling bell interrupted them.

Green entered with Pike and Galindez.

"Well, Mark?" Pike said jovially.

"Josiah," Trumbull said with forced equanimity. The greetings were antagonistic, but courteous. Galindez sat apart. He ignored Jessica totally.

Jessica's smile was gracious. "Senator Pike, I've looked to meet you for a long while. I vow, I once thought I understood your theory on monetary policy and free silver, but, lands! It's just beyond me!" She laughed appealingly.

"Not if you've got silver shares, ma'am," Pike said resoundingly. Oh, Joe! he thought appreciatively, going back in time to the lonely gold fields when a woman's appearance sent that cry from claim to claim. So this was the little lady who was raising all the dust! A real beauty—graceful, proud, and buxom—he thought with relish. "Life's short. Time's short," he said when the pleasantries were done. "Let's cut the cackle, Mark, and wind this up."

The antagonists eyed each other warily.

"I'll tell you, Josiah," Trumbull said. "We're dealing with people, not cows. If you're here to make some fair deal, good. If you're here for blood, I'll refuse to listen."

The frosty eyes twinkled. "Pshaw, Mark," Pike boomed, "nobody wants blood. Certainly not Mr. Hagerman. Hey, Senator?"

"Quite so," Hagerman said with a start.

An hour later Jessica for the third time left, slamming the door.

Galindez looked up. "If she does that once more, Mr. Pike," he said calmly, "I vote to leave. You've got to control her, Trumbull."

Trumbull's smile was wintry.

A minute later, Jessica returned. "Sixty thousand and acknowledge the marriage!"

Pike was unmoved. "Fifty thousand plus lawyers' fees. It's our best and last offer."

Jessica was aghast. "Fifty thousand? What's that? How can I live on it? Lost! Lost! I knew it would come to nothing. Oh, what's to become of me?" she said in agony, wringing her hands. She crumpled in a chair, broken and moaning, but graceful nevertheless. "Judge Trumbull," she begged in anguish. "Tell me what to do. No, wait!" she cried, leaping up. She strode the room, darting murderous glances at the lawyers, and halted. "Forty thousand, but I must have my honor! Mr. Pike, I appeal to you—"

"No!" Pike said.

"I do not recognize the Federal Court! I will defy 'em. I will trust my lawyer." A finger went out. "All right, thirty, and my divorce. Now that's real cheap."

"No!" Pike repeated implacably.

She turned to Galindez. "You're doing this, you chinch!" she stormed. "Give me my honor! You shall not take my honor! Sen? You cannot mean this after all we've meant to each other! After your solemn and written word!"

Hagerman said with equal passion, "Can't you get it through that skull? I never signed that paper! It never happened! If it had, I'd pay. Why can't you see that?"

"You can stand there and deny it to my face?" she said in horror.

"I can stand anywhere!"

"You swore otherwise in the State Court!"

"I will unswear in the Federal Court!" Hagerman shouted. "Jesus! I am trying to help you. Can you not see that? Go on like this and you'll never live to see a cent!" With a massive effort, he changed to cajolery. "Now, look, Jess! Take the cash and let the credit go," he wheedled. "I don't let go of money easy. They'll say I coughed up because you had the goods on me. It's a real good deal. Tell you what!" he said on final inspiration, affable, friendly, beaming with kindness. "One hundred thousand and done! Now that's capital!"

"No!" "Lew!" Pike and Galindez spoke together.

"No, I mean it!" Hagerman snarled, turning on his advisers. "It's still my money, damnation—and there's an ethic, confound it! Here." One hundred crisp Treasury notes redeemable in gold riffled in the sunlight. Jessica licked a pale mouth with an intake of breath. Hagerman beamed. "I believe in paying my women—and Jessie's not all wrong in this. I can be a real prick sometimes," he said handsomely, "and mebbe I gave false hopes. Anyways, what's money?" He dropped to friendly tones. "Jess? Listen to me. I'm the oldest friend you've got in this room. It's money. Take it."

Jessica stared a long burning moment. "I said it was all a trick, Judge Trumbull," she said with bitter contempt. "Maybe now you'll believe me."

Hagerman took a step backward, and seemed to wilt. He looked frail and small in a suit suddenly too large for his old man's bones. "I'm done," he said. "I don't know why I got talked into this. Tony, Pike . . . Sorry this happened. Let's go. God knows I tried to help this crazy woman."

No one moved. There was expectancy, then Trumbull stirred. "Joe, let me appeal to you. If money claims are fixed in some fair amount, can you not persuade your client to let the divorce stand? How does it hurt him or the estate? It puts Mrs. Hagerman in an impossible position—neither married nor divorced."

"She put herself there," Pike replied. "Come, Mark. Yes or no?"

Trumbull glanced at Hagerman and Galindez. "Mr. Green," he said bitterly, "show the gentlemen out. They didn't come to bargain—just to make impossible conditions."

Pike measured his old opponent with regret. "Mark, just make sure you know what camp your judge is in," he said grimly. "Ma'am." With a curt nod to Jessica, he left. The others followed.

"Oh!" Jessica exclaimed, advancing to the closed door, clenching her fists. "Now, d'ye see?" she cried in triumph. "I said it was all bad faith! It was just to make me look unreasonable. That's why he brought that portrait—to weaken me. He never meant to give a thing!"

Trumbull picked up the picture. The wizened face leered back. "Jess," he said, "what made you induce Hagerman to bring this here? Was it to prove his trickery to me? Hardly needful, y'know."

"What?" she asked. "Why would I ever do that? Sounds foolish." She laughed uncertainly. "He brought it here himself. You cannot think I lied?"

He studied the woman with pain. He was beginning to sense something dreadful—something he put out of mind. "Jess, it ain't his birthday at all. I know that from the file. Why, Jess? Lord, why?"

"Oh! Well, that is clever." She made a small sound and looked unhappy indeed. "I know what I'm doing to you, Mark," she said, "what it's costing. I was afraid you'd make me take the money or drop me and the case for being unreasonable. If that'd happen, I'd want to die."

"But why would I do that?"

"You said you might—more than once; and I was afraid. How can I be sure you'll see this through?"

"Because I have said so," he said simply.

She stared at the threadbare carpeting.

"Lord, Jess," he said gently, "I made this fight mine a long time ago. We'll win no matter what or how long it takes. Jess, I love you." It was the first time those words had ever passed his lips, and what it had to do with the driving force of the fight he was not sure. She gave a cry of joy. "Oh, Mark! Let's be gay!" she exclaimed. "I've missed you so. Let's go out and have a rare time! I'm dying for some fun."

Chapter Nineteen

The Affair had disappeared from the London newspapers, but Fanny, although sunk in her novel, kept a sense of the distant scene. She had the home newspapers, letters from friends, an occasional note from her grandfather which told her that Hagerman's health was failing—spurring his lawyers to end the trial in a race against time. The going was slow. Jessica—after an interlude of gracious behavior—had grown troublesome indeed.

A letter from her grandfather gave the news of the intense struggle at the United States Appraisers Building where the Honorable Roscoe Ives, Examiner in Chancery, was taking testimony from the same roster of witnesses as before. Pike had gotten an order from the Circuit Court to compel Jessica to produce her marriage paper to let the celebrated Dr. Emil Pfeiffer removed four particles of ink for microscopic examination.

Jessica had flatly defied the Circuit Court's order; finally, rather than see his client face jail, or violate her conscience, Trumbull had stipulated to let the Court draw what inference it might from her refusal, complaining that Pike's tactics were relentless and brutal in the extreme. In the end, Smith wrote, Dr. Pfeiffer, who was a wonder of German scientific learning, had pronounced the paper a forgery—but since German science could prove anything, it was no surprise.

With a sinking heart, Fanny read the enclosure—a letter by Trumbull to the Pima *Democrat,* with an unbridled attack on the federal judges, especially Goff, for having resumed the trial in disregard of the written stipulation which had originally sent the case for trial before Judge McArdle in the Superior Court of San Francisco.

The letter charged that Goff had admitted his initial belief that the Superior Court judgment would bar the federal trial, but then had openly stated that he had consulted Sickels, who had changed his mind for him. This was not surprising, Trumbull wrote, for Goff was Sickels' pliable and corrupt tool—and it was notorious that rich men and corporations were always right and always won in the Circuit Court. Everyone knew that Goff shared bribes and fees with his nephew, Orlando Nolan, Clerk of the Court, and got more salary from railroad companies than from the United States.

And that was why the brave woman had obstinately refused to let Dr. Pfeiffer remove even one particle of ink from her marriage paper. For if the Court could remove some ink, it could remove all, and even destroy the document itself. She had supplied photographs, but not the original. If once the original got into that court, it would go off to Washington and there be forever lost.

But that would never happen. The brave woman, Trumbull wrote, was right to resist. She too believed Goff a corrupt tool of Sickels. She was without money, almost without friends, for few would be her friend and thus risk the malignancy of a desperate financial clique. But poor and alone, her cause was just. Time would tell whether the federal judges would compel her to deliver her paper to be mutilated and destroyed.

Miss Roux had resolved to abandon the struggle for judgment on merits and would rely solely on her ability to show that the court lacked jurisdiction. The case had no business in the Circuit Court. She trusted that its judgment would eventually be held void by the Supreme Court in Washington— and if justice there should fail, all the world would know. Much was at stake in those four particles of ink—Y'rs respectfully, M. A. Trumbull.

As for the months passed news trickled out, then stopped. Fanny took off for Athens for further work on her novel about Aristides. Five toilsome months later, a most extraordinary report by the Examiner in Chancery to the Circuit Court sent by her grandfather showed an alarming development.

Respondent: When I see this stuff, I feel like taking that man Pike and horsewhipping him. I could shoot him sure—that man sitting there. Where does he get this stuff?

Examiner: Mr. Green, can you stop this?

Mr. Green: I'm sorry, sir.

Respondent: Who is Pike? He is living with a woman and brought his wife to cover it up. I will expose the whole thing.

Examiner: Will you remain quiet?

Respondent: I don't know. I get so worked up when I see what lies he's getting up on me.

Examiner: Madam—

Respondent: And you're no better.

Examiner: Your lawyers—

Respondent: I am my own lawyer. And stop smiling. You take orders from Pike and are corrupt. Judge Trumbull knows all about it, be sure of that.

Examiner: If you interrupt once more, I'll adjourn and report this to the Court. The Court suggested that I be lenient with you, and I have indeed treated you with forbearance throughout. Shall I report your charges?

Respondent: That's enough. Say no more.

Examiner: No, but I mean to talk. For months now your offensive conduct has disturbed me daily and I have tried in every way to check you—by kind treatment, by ignoring misbehavior, by rebuke, by appealing to your counsel, by threatening to report you to the Court. But the evil grows worse and worse with the passing weeks. This must stop.

Respondent: Don't cry. I'll stop. I reckon it's not your fault, but I have just heard news that those state judges in Sacramento were reached too. They stopped my alimony money, and yet will not pass on the appeal. I am in limbo. It is pure torture. I don't know but what it takes extreme measures.

(At this point, the Examiner's report recited that Jessica drew a derringer from her satchel and placed it in her lap beneath the table, pointing it at Pike.)

Mr. Pike: What's that? Do you want to shoot anybody?

Respondent: Not unless you'd like to be shot, and think you deserve it.

Mr. Pike: On the whole, I'd rather not.

Examiner: Unless you give me that pistol, I shall adjourn and report this to the Court.

Respondent: I'm not going to shoot anybody.

Examiner: I will summon the Marshal and deal with you. This building, I will remind you, is territory of the United States.

Respondent: That cuts no ice with me.

(Mr. Trumbull entered the room.)

Mr. Pike: I say, Mark, did you know the lady has a gun?

Mr. Trumbull: No, I did not. This is dreadful. Ma'am, what's the explanation?

Respondent: I've been threatened, Judge Trumbull. Mr. Hagerman has said I should never live to see the judgment.

Mr. Trumbull: Let me have the gun.

Respondent: All right.

(The gun is handed over.)

Mr. Trumbull: It's not loaded.

Respondent: Well, don't look so foolish. I never said it was.

Examiner: Madam, you must not make such demonstrations. This is a contempt of court and a violation of the federal law for which I can ask that you be sent to jail.

Mr. Trumbull: Well, that's not so clear either. Miss Roux has had provocations and threats against her life. She is justified.

Examiner: Not here. I will take the gun.

Mr. Trumbull: Not without a written order.

Examiner: I am empowered by the Court to cause an arrest.

Mr. Trumbull: No, sir. I say you are not. There can be no arrest but after refusal to comply with the Court's direction and then not without a written order.

Examiner: I do not understand it so.

Mr. Trumbull: I do. I will be responsible.

Examiner: Well, well. Will you take custody?

Mr. Trumbull: Yes. Miss Roux is upset and does not feel well. That is the explanation. (To Respondent): Now madam, you must be quiet and let Mr. Pike go on.

Respondent: May I not defend myself?

Mr. Trumbull: Not like this. It only plays into their hands and is unnecessary while I am here. The judges do whatever Mr. Pike asks.

Examiner: Be sure I will report this to Justice Sickels.

Mr. Pike: Can we get on?

Respondent: Very well. I will obey my lawyer. What's the question?

From the Examiner's written report, it appeared that Jessica's agitation was sparked by probing questions about her attempted suicide in MacGowan's office. The report was considered in chambers and an oral ruling made in a tense and crowded courtroom by Sickels himself that Jessica thereafter be disarmed by a deputy marshal. She was harshly warned that the next outburst would see enforced the severe criminal laws of the United States.

On this extravagant note of tension, the trial came to end. The next day the press reported that Miss Roux was residing in seclusion at the Union Hotel in Stoddard awaiting the verdict of the Court.

The year was waning. Hagerman awoke with the realization that his mouth was drawn in a foxy grin that exposed his gums. He had a sense of happiness, of buoyancy for which he could not account. Something had amused him in sleep. Now what was it?

He turned in his comfortable four-poster. His hand fell to the empty place beside him and he sat upright. The bed was the first piece brought to Beaufort from the old house on Sutter Street.

At this thought, he made an attempt to struggle upright. His wife's full-length portrait—a comfortable flaxen-haired woman with blue eyes—gazed placidly at a clutter of Victorian pieces. "Good Christ, Daisy," he muttered. "What in hell do they want of the old man? Why couldn't you be here to set 'em straight on how it was?"

Later in the morning Emily came to spend an hour, dismissing the nurse with a cold look. She was dressed in a trim riding habit with full skirt, boots, and a jaunty hat. She smelt horsey. England had given her a fluty accent which he found unendurable, but she was still pretty, for which he was thankful indeed.

She was full of social chatter which he could not follow. Something watchful and anxious made him uneasy. He had no illusion why she had made the long journey, nor why she was so heartily reassuring.

Emily stared at her hands. "Pa? I want to talk about this situation," she said with determination.

"Can't it be later?"

"Pa, now," Emily said clearly. "Tony says you've got to sign some papers. Is there any reason why you won't?"

Hagerman turned on the pillow. Five years in England had produced a change in his little girl, he thought. He now saw a sharpness of jaw, a Hagerman look of avarice he found most endearing. A small grin tugged at his mouth. "Fact is, Baby, I'm asking for some kind of memorial to your ma."

Emily's control was admirable. "Why, that's dandy, Pa. What kind of memorial?"

"Oh, I don't know. Maybe a university, or museum, or something like that. I was thinking to go to ten million. Your ma was a wonderful woman."

Emily was staring in disbelief and fright. "Are you really that rich, Pa?" she asked with awe. "It's your money. You can do what you like with it, but that's a little high, isn't it? But . . . but Pa," she said uncertainly, "you're joking, sure, aren't you?" Her accent had gone American.

Hagerman closed his eyes. "Yes, Baby," he whispered, "I'm joking. It's all yours. Why in hell would I give it away? I'm weak but not out of my mind." Emily sighed with relief, then frowned. "Sit down," Hagerman said. She sat with folded hands.

"Why won't you sign the papers?" she persisted.

Hagerman was not clear about many things, but those papers were drilled into his mind. Galindez was urgent that he execute a will and deed of trust to divide the estate among the children and grandchildren in equal shares and appoint Galindez and Theo executors of the will and trustees under the deed. Galindez was a good cold-blooded draftsman of the law, so the papers were probably all right; they would protect the estate against lawsuits and bankruptcies. It was not therefore the general terms to which he objected but the paragraph which charged Galindez and Theo to contest Jessica's false claims and pretensions with all vigor in every possible court in the land and which denounced her as an impostor and perjurer and conspirator. He could not see the good to say that once he was dead.

"Baby . . ." he said weakly. "Is it needful?"

Emily said, "Tony thinks so."

"But why?" Hagerman persisted, focusing on the problem. "Why must I drive the last nail in the coffin?"

Emily plumped the pillow carefully, remembering her

403

briefing. "We're a long way off from finishing this matter, Pa. If the divorce is upheld on appeal, Tony says that Jessie'll get half the estate sure. Unless something's done about it." She forced a sweetly persuasive tone. "Pa, you've been a lawyer. Tony wants you to think like a lawyer. He says somebody's got to be empowered to carry on the fight."

"Why can't we wait for the Circuit Court? Has anything gone wrong there?"

Emily touched the warm forehead. It was dry and rough like a lizard's skin. "No, Pa," she said, finding this business uncomfortable. It had to be done, she reminded herself. "But you've been over this with Tony."

"Tell me again," he whispered.

"I'm not sure I understand," she replied. "He says the federal judgment cannot execute itself. It must be put into effect."

The eyes were unblinking. "What happens if . . . if I cash in first?"

"Oh, Pa! Don't say that!"

"Tell me what happens then?"

"Tony says . . ." Emily hesitated, suddenly wretched in her role. "He says that the judgment abates—loses effect unless revived by your executors or trustees. It's a legal thing. If Jessie's divorce stands up on the appeal in Sacramento, she'll get millions from us—unless he's empowered to do something about it. Why won't you sign? Tony says he'll use it only if he must. He'd rather win the appeal. Pa," she said softly, "this is a responsibility to the children."

The blue eyes were now in focus, unwinking, intelligent, skeptical, penetrating the pretty intent hovering face. "I've got a brown envelope in the bureau. Could you see Jessie gets it? Just to show no hard feelings?"

"Gee, Pa! She'd make capital of it."

"Suppose she does? How would it hurt me?"

"How much?" she said in clipped tones.

"Not too much," he said. "Considering."

She drew a breath. "Pa, I never thought you'd do a thing like this to us. If you give her anything now, even a cent, it'll be taken to mean she has a real hold on you—no matter how you put it. I swear, I don't understand why you want to do it!"

He felt incredibly unhappy. He was no longer clear, he realized, things were eluding him, but he had no doubts what was happening to him, and he was in pain and weak beyond imagination. No one seemed to understand. It was important, he felt, to be understood. "Hold my hand," he begged. Emily took the frail hand. It was shockingly hot. "Listen, Baby, I'm no model," he said feebly, "but no criminal neither. I didn't lead so bad a life. I kept a good home and raised you kids. I'm proud of that. I made a good record in business and politics. I don't apologize for anything. I'm not really ruthless. I liked fun and I never hurt a woman. I respected your ma and she understood me. I never did anything against her health. That was always the one rule. Never go against a decent woman's health. You can see how it was?" he said anxiously.

"You don't have to explain," she said.

"No, I want to. Jessie . . ." He rested a moment, listening to all the sounds of Beaufort—the gas works, the barnyard, a railroad whistle going into the distance. He lost the thread, then resumed. "The thing is, I liked the woman. She was gay and accomplished—real smart in business. I could enjoy the talk. She was a nice companion and I got real lonely. I was a lost soul when your ma died. I wasn't cut out for a widower, that's for sure. Not rattling around in hotels full of women with eyes on my checkbook. That's what was so refreshing. Jessie never cared for money. She thought she did, but she didn't. Actually, she was thoughtless and impulsive, with her eyes bigger than her mouth. Then she comes from real good stock, you've got to admit it. I wouldn't have to be ashamed of her, I thought, and once I got you all married off . . ."

He paused wretchedly. "Fact is, I wanted to discuss it, but I didn't know how to tell you children. What was all the objection to her, Baby?"

"It was just so unsuitable."

"D'ye mean my age?"

"Part of it."

"Oh, Baby, I didn't want to marry a bag of bones. I wanted someone young and beautiful who'd love me for myself. She might have, you know," he said wistfully.

"Might she?" Emily said frigidly. "There's no limit to what she might love. I just don't want her in the family. Not that kind of woman. Pa, nothing that came out in the trial—not even that disgusting business with that Nellie Driscoll—was a surprise. And never mind how I know."

A blinking showed the shock. Well! His little girl was not

such a little girl after all! "It wasn't simple," he muttered guiltily, plucking at his mouth. He was embarrassed.

"Are you saying that you really signed that marriage paper, Pa? That you're trying to square some account?"

"If I say Yes, would that change it?"

"No! I don't want her to get a ruddy farthing. Not one blasted thing!" Her voice was rising with pent-up feelings. "We're a family, Pa! I don't care what you signed, or didn't sign. I won't have that woman acknowledged. Ma would turn in her grave." She stalked closer to the bed. "Well, Pa?" she demanded. "Did you?"

The unwinking eyes looked up from the pillow. "I don't remember, Baby," he said feebly. "I can't be sure now what I know." A weak smile appeared, rueful, self-mocking, and derisive.

Emily stared, aghast. "Pa! Is that the truth now? Or another joke?"

A grin was ghastly. "Joke?" he whispered painfully. "I just want to leave a good taste—in case I did." He turned on the pillow, too tired to go on. Really, it was too much! he thought. His memories were turning back to the sunny moments, the fun, the lighthearted laughter, and a sigh shook him. He was weak and sick and suffering pain, but there were some things he could wish he had done better. What had gone wrong? It was all dissolving. All slipping away. But at least he knew now why that morning he had awakened with laughter.

Ten days later Hagerman died and was buried at Beaufort in the family plot beside his wife and his daughter Dora. The attendance was small and the eulogy restrained. Still the press carried full accounts of a colorful life and pioneer days and the man's rise to fortune—and noted that the imminent decision in the federal court was on everyone's mind. At Beaufort Emily tore a dignified letter of grief and condolence from Jessica to shreds.

Mr. Jim Purdue's hotel, sedate, comfortable, and respectable, had a good location and wide bay windows looking north and east on Market Street. From that vantage point, Jessica a month later had been watching all morning, hoping against dread hope for some miracle of deliverance. She had demanded to be present in the Circuit Court for the decision, but Trumbull, yielding in most things, for once was firm. Goff was to deliver the judgment. Trumbull wanted no demonstrations and all promises of good behavior left him unmoved. He was to bring the news from court without delay.

The Purdue was a logical place to stay. Jessica had spent her happiest years there and a few old friends were still there to call and wish her luck. Jim Purdue sent fruit and flowers and came to wish confusion to a common foe. From time to time she issued bulletins to the press gathered at the bar. She was not concerned with any posthumous judgment of the Circuit Court, she announced, for what would it mean? Death, the King of Terrors, had dissolved the marriage, and her Superior Court judgment still upheld her honor.

She had nice things to say about the poor Senator but thought a family announcement of a cash gift of $100,000 to the city's three orphan asylums—Catholic, Protestant, Hebrew—a spurious device, concocted to impose an aura of philanthropy on a man no longer there to defend himself.

She kept returning to the bay window overlooking Market Street.

The carriage was unmistakable. Trumbull glanced neither right nor left, but sat rigid and unyielding. "Oh, God!" she exclaimed with a sinking heart. "Let it be good news!" but, as the carriage reached the curb below, she knew that it was not.

As Trumbull entered, his face was drained of color.

"Sorry, dear," he said guiltily. He explained the final order of the Court, that she surrender the paper to be canceled and annulled as a proved forgery.

She twisted her hands. "Surrender my marriage paper?" She drew a breath and turned with a forced smile. "Well, it's all right, my dear. We expected this, did we not? Let me get you comfortable while you explain, and then we'll decide what to do." She brought whiskey and slippers and a robe and listened, pale but composed and attentive. She stirred only at the final touch—the pronouncement of forgery which was tantamount to finding the marriage invalid.

"Confounded pimps!" Trumbull said savagely.

Goff had gone on gratuitously to add insult to injury: to conclude that a community which allowed the family—the cornerstone of society—to rest on no other foundation than a secret writing, accompanied by no better behavior than furtive intercourse more befitting a brothel than otherwise,

407

ought to remove the cross from among its symbols and re-place it with the crescent.

There was more, but she was not listening. He kissed a limp hand. "Be patient, dear," he said. "This ain't the end by a long chalk."

"I'm branded, Mark," she said in a strange voice, bitter and remote.

"Lordy! It ain't that bad," he said.

"Oh yes, oh yes," she replied, thinking deeply. "I've got a notoriety put on me now. You say I've still got the State Court's judgment? I cannot trust the State Court now to stand firm. I cannot trust anything. I'm made no better than a prostitute."

"No—"

"Well, isn't that the effect? That I laid with the man for money? Tshah! Get out, Mark, while you've still got some shreds of reputation left yourself! Leave me!"

"Don't talk like that," he said.

"No, I mean it. I cannot live with that brand. I'll do some-thing desperate and drag you with me. I'm destroying you. There's not a federal judge who don't hate you—and the state judges too." She strode the room. "Well, go!" she ex-claimed.

Trumbull drew a shuddering breath. Words were no help; silence was worse.

"Mark!" she cried in sudden anguish, "Mark, d'you love me?"

"You know I do," he said.

"Then why haven't you touched me? Why haven't you kissed me?" she exclaimed, overcome with grief and rage. "Why haven't you asked to marry me! You've got to! Oh, God, you've got to marry me!" she said with rising hysteria. "It's got to be your answer to those men."

A week later every newspaper in the country carried the story that a marriage had been performed between the most conspicuous pair in California by the Reverend Father Dillon in the parish house of the Roman Catholic Church at Stod-dard, California, where they would reside. The marriage li-cense described the bride as the legally divorced wife of Lew Hagerman, deceased.

Part Two

Chapter Twenty

Cudahey spat carefully. "But, Judge, McAllen's so blamed far away!"

Trumbull considered the shambles of his life. The practice in Stoddard was in tatters. Outwardly he still commanded respect, but Jessica's notoriety had had its effect. He worried about Jessica. She was more sedate, and had lost her girlishness, an intent look and perpetually thin-pressed lips showed intense strain. She was talking a lot, bursting under pressure. No one would let her forget that she had replaced an older woman months before death and divorce had made it decent. "So far away from *what?*" Trumbull asked.

"Might as well be McAllen," the scrivener agreed with a heavyhearted sigh. The move from Stoddard would be a wrench, but the choice of McAllen was logical. It seemed desirable to practice law among friends and partisans who would be watchful of his safety—and his wife's.

The move was made on the hottest day of the year. A sweltering committee was waiting at the depot. They had greetings for Trumbull, roses for Jessica. Jessica accepted the flowers with sunny pleasure and a statement to the Pima *Democrat.* With the Senator's death, she said, his federal judgment had abated and the battle shifted from the Superior Court of San Francisco to the State Supreme Court in Sacramento, where the desperate enemy had taken their appeal. But—she raised an admonitory finger—her state judgment when upheld would be invoked to assert all her rights against the Hagerman estate.

All the rights, she repeated emphatically. Meanwhile she was delighted to start her life fresh among her husband's oldest friends—the good, decent people of Pima. She was married now for sure, and by a priest with full solemnization, and this time, she laughed, with no slipups. The crowd laughed uncertainly and dispersed. It was an uncomfortable

411

moment. Trumbull's air of solicitude and anxious pride for the handsomely dressed, painfully talkative woman was gentleness itself.

A wind was blowing, a burning wind hotter than anything in memory that killed young stock, and left rabbits dying in the fields. Jessica was oblivious. She was delighted with her new home—a pleasant house of white clapboard and wide verandas on which to make love at night, the sweatier the better.

She could not wait to start.

"Oh, Jess," he sighed. "Jess, honey. What in hell d'ye want with a tired old dog like me?"

"Tired? Pooh!" she whispered, kissing his ear. "I can't imagine more of a man." Her voracity and tenderness went on to dawn. Lordy! he thought, staring at a full moon in a luminous sky. The barren years were past and under her hand and mouth and tongue he was again alive. It was amazing, astounding, happiness he had never hoped to have in life, but there it was. A murmur of pleasure brought him back. He placed a heavy massive thigh over her hip. She looked up from drowsy sleep and with a loving sigh sank under the covers, seeking him out.

His law business resumed, and calls for lectures again came in. The views of Mr. and Mrs. Trumbull on all sorts of topics began to appear in the newspapers. Their life was marred only by the nightmare struggle which they could not and would not give up. And on that arduous business they made many trips together all over the state. Even Cudahey grudgingly conceded that Jessica was invaluable in a town where office help simply could not be had.

And then in a whirl of dust came the telegram that Jessica's judgment of divorce granted by McArdle in San Francisco—and all her claims—were upheld on appeal in Sacramento, and there it stood at last, except for a demand by Trumbull for books and records and an accounting to enforce his wife's judgment to half the Hagerman estate.

It was April. The days were warm, the nights clear.

"Mark," she whispered.

He had not yet had time to fall asleep. A cool wind was blowing. A dog had been barking now for some time in the garden. "Someone's out there," she said.

He swung out of bed and into a dressing robe and went

forward on dry creaking boards to the front door. Deputy United States Marshal Finerty was sprawled in a wicker porch chair, smoking quietly.

Trumbull scowled. "What in hell are you doing here?"

"Just found out where you lived," Finerty replied easily. "Had to ask a Chink. Nobody else in town would give me the time. Want to invite me in?"

"Certainly not," Trumbull said shortly.

"Wouldn't expect it," Finerty agreed, staring in darkness. "Yup. He's a sorry Chink, but he did point you out. Hate to do this, but you and Mrs. Trumbull have been evasive these past weeks about accepting the federal process. Sooner or later you have got to respond to the Federal Court. You know that?"

"I know nothing of the sort!" Trumbull said abruptly. "When Hagerman died, the federal action abated."

"If you believe that, you'll believe anything," Finerty said calmly. "You're an intelligent man. Were you serious?"

"Serious about what?"

"Demanding books and records and an accounting? Mr. Galindez might've been willing to let it lay—just plain let it lay, if you and Mrs. Trumbull would stop these games. What does he really care about the so-called marriage? Means about as much now as a teat on a brass monkey. But here you go, demanding him to turn over and account for all those millions of dollars. Do you really expect to see that day?"

"Is that a message?" Trumbull asked ominously.

Finerty shook his head. "I'm just asking," he said curiously. "Have you got something up your sleeve? Because unless you do, this don't make sense."

"Indeed?"

"Sure thing," Finerty said placidly. "You ain't out of the woods. This is no country for an unreasonable man."

"Go on," Trumbull glowered.

"D'ye know what they're saying? That your case didn't really add up. That you got your verdict out of McArdle out of respect for you and not on the evidence. It couldn't happen again."

"What else do they say?"

Finerty chuckled. "Oh, that you made your point when you married Mrs. Trumbull. Mr. Galindez respects that.

413

Can't expect you to back down. Said so in public. Practically said, if you'd lay off him, he'd lay off you."

"Anything else?"

"Only that Marshal Jessup retires next month. Patterson takes his place. Quite a different man."

There was a sound within.

"Mark? Is everything all right?"

Trumbull went to the door. "Yes, dear," he said gently. "Go back to bed."

Trumbull listened a moment, then said, "Very well, Marshal, I hoped we were done with you. Have you got some sort of process there? What is it?"

"Oh, just papers for you and Mrs. Trumbull," Finerty drawled. "Will you take service for her?"

"I'll take the service," Trumbull said.

A sheaf of papers was handed over.

"I'd like to say something, Judge." Finerty looked about the moonlit garden. "This is the end of the road. When this new action gets done, the State Court won't mean a thing. Me, or somebody else, will come back and take that marriage contract from Mrs. Trumbull. There's no help for it and you know it. Now I could tear this service up if you want to reconsider." Finerty waited a moment and shrugged. "Well, my best to Mrs. Trumbull." He nodded and left. A whistle brought two hidden men into the moonlight to join him and the three strode off.

At dawn Jessica was still raging at the latest villainies. Her vocabulary was a surprise even to Trumbull—and what incensed her most was her betrayal by a Chink.

Late that afternoon the group of deputy marshals reached San Francisco and went directly to the Marshal's Office to report—tired, scrubby, but grinning broadly. Finerty certified that he had served upon the parties the writ of subpoena commanding on penalty of $5,000 that they appear in the United States Circuit Court to answer a bill of complaint to revive and execute the judgment given to Lew Hagerman, deceased, to cancel the forgeries therein described, and also to enjoin any use of the California judgment of divorce based thereon.

Six months later it came to a head.

Chapter Twenty-One

Trumbull entered the courtroom an hour early and escorted Jessica to the bar. Jessica was in a state of excitement. She waited graciously for the old bailiff to open the gate. "Mornin', Mr. Voight," she sang. "Mornin', ma'am," Voight replied, smiling slightly. Jessica patted his hand and strolled to the defense table. She removed her cloak with a flourish, stared at the assemblage with challenge, and sat, placing her satchel at her feet. Meanwhile, Trumbull went behind the jury box to hang his coat—it was a moment of solitude to gather strength—and came out with the assumed smile of professional discipline. The sweltering chamber—ordinarily hushed and decorous—was a pit boiling with lawyers, and not one would meet his eye.

Jessica was intent on a note written on the train. He sat and covered her hand reassuringly. "I'm all right," she said, looking up with a glad smile. "Truly." And returned to her note.

Trumbull swung about and scowled. The chair to his right was empty. He felt haggard and missed the old friendliness, the rowdy courtroom banter, hard blows up front, brotherhood in the aisle. The fun was gone. Well! It's almost over, he thought.

Jessica put the satchel in her lap. The bailiffs stiffened, then relaxed as a cambric handkerchief came into sight. To some she was showing a peculiar pallor never before seen.

Evidently something was up. Trumbull knew every law officer in the state, and it was obvious that the two regular court bailiffs, Sam Voight and Carroll Asbury, had been augmented by marshals—O'Hare and Kipp were on hand and also a new man, John Blish. The city had contributed some men—Sam Monckton, a detective, and Fred Glennon, a patrolman. Tim Van Buren, a railroad detective, was conspicuous. Some of the rough-looking men were strangers.

"Who's that man?" Jessica whispered, fanning herself. "He's looking daggers."

The man with intent eyes was thin but wiry. Patches of scarlet splashed on protruding cheekbones.

"Dunno," Trumbull grunted. He rose and stretched his muscles, then strolled to the far corner. Finerty, freshly shaved and barbered, was wearing a gaudy silk shirt as though for an occasion. "Finerty?" Trumbull dropped to a confidential tone. "That feller's trying to mesmerize me. I seem to know him."

The thin man was leaning against the wall. "Something wrong?" Finerty asked.

"No, but he's making Mrs. Trumbull nervous," Trumbull replied. "Who is he?"

"Jim Kiser," Finerty said indifferently, "collects licenses from these fruit and flower peddlers in Washington Street. Why?"

Trumbull stared a full moment. "Just don't like his looks. Is he working for the marshal?"

Finerty shook his head. "Nope. Can't say he is. He put in for the work, but the marshal didn't cotton to his record. He did law work in Arizona and other places. I could find out, if you like."

"No, no, 'tain't necessary. Kiser? Kiser? Well! Here we are, hey?" Trumbull muttered. "Quite a welcoming committee," he drawled.

Finerty shrugged. "Judge, it's what I've told you all along. The marshal's had orders on you and Mrs. Trumbull ever since she got troublesome during the hearings. And especially since this last encounter with Judge Goff. Justice Sickels has made it very clear what he expects. They're ready for you, Judge. I think you ought to know. And that other bunch know your reputation." A nod indicated a rough element. "They're out to see the fun."

"Reputation?" A snort was wearily contemptuous. "Lordy! Can't people ever forget? Well, tell Marshal Patterson to rest easy. We've got no notion to play into Pike's hands with misbehavior. But thank'ee for the word." Breathing heavily, Trumbull returned to his seat.

Jessica looked up from her notes. "Well? Who is he?"

Trumbull glanced anxiously at his wife. She was pallid after a sleepless night, and showing signs of strain. The clear oval face was now puffy but tranquil. "Just a feller," he said gently. He was thinking worriedly of the encounter between Jessica and Goff which had called out the show of force.

The day before Judge Goff had tottered into his office, shaking flabbily, and had sent for his nephew. "Lando," he said in agitation, "send for the marshal. Monstrous! Outrageous!" he trumpeted. "Jesus Christ, what are things coming to?"

Clerk Nolan, startled, withdrew and returned with Patterson. Patterson found Goff sucking whiskey through a straw.

"Marshal Patterson!" Goff squealed. "I will not have it! That woman is going too far. I want steps taken. Steps and measures."

Patterson took a straightbacked chair and sat teetering. "Suppose you tell me all about it, Judge."

It had come about while Goff was enduring the hardship of returning by Pullman sleeper from Los Angeles, where he had been holding court. He had not slept a wink through the clanking rattling night, and so was all too fretful.

In the morning, as the train left McAllen, he had returned from the diner to find the sleeper made up and the Trumbulls in the car. Jessica, who was brushing Trumbull's hair, had stiffened as he, Goff, entered and had given him an ugly glare. She'd hissed, "What? Are you here too? Are you following us?" They knew each other well by now—the woman had attended every argument on Galindez' suit to revive the Hagerman judgment—inciting her husband to bitter remarks, deriding Pike, scorning the bench, eating chocolates in court with studied insolence. She was evidently en route to hear the final decision in San Francisco. Goff had felt a surge of hate for the slanderous pair. But, summoning restraint, he had replied coldly, "No, madam," and bowed in acknowledgment of her essential femininity. Jessica bridled and turned back to her husband, sniggering and throwing contemptuous glances.

Every section of the car was empty. Nevertheless, Trumbull chose to move to a section directly facing Goff, remarking that the sun was ungodly hot, to which insolence Goff paid no attention. Trumbull was nonexistent, so far as he was concerned. He felt dozy and closed his eyes and tried to sleep.

Jessica kept changing her seat and then had passed by and seized his hair with a spiteful twitch and went on before he

417

realized what had happened. Trumbull had laughed in his face.

Goff found himself shaking. In all his years as a judge he had never been twitched.

Patterson took out a notebook. "Twitched?"

"Twitched," Goff snarled.

For the rest of the trip, Jessica had moved about, clenching a parasol as though determined to use it, and opening and closing a satchel. Trumbull seemed to be dissuading her from something rash and the trip was without other incident to Oakland—except that the woman never stopped talking.

"Nothing else happened?"

"Not on the train," Goff said, breathing hard. But at San Francisco, he had taken the Sutter Street car and found Jessica and Trumbull in the seat opposite. Jessica had said with a frown, "Are you still here too? What are you doing in this car?" Goff had replied, "I am going to the courthouse." Jessica then said irately, "Well, so are we. You should take another car and not offend people," and made other remarks, less complimentary, to which no attention was paid.

And finally, at Montgomery Street, she spoke in a low voice to her husband, and said something indecent.

"Could you make out what she said?" Patterson asked.

"No."

"Then what proof is there that it was indecent?"

"Good Christ! What proof is there that it was not? Really, Marshal! Are you teaching me evidence?" Goff said, offended, and went on. The woman had said nastily, "Are you handing down the decision in my case?" Goff replied, "No, madam. That will be Judge Sickels' vast pleasure. He is putting off his return to Washington to do so." Then she said with a menacing smile, "Good! Good! I do not blame you for being a coward in this dirty business," and went off with her husband, laughing and swinging her satchel.

"And that's the whole story?" Patterson asked.

"The whole story?" Goff was incensed. "Isn't it enough? The man was waiting for me to resent his wife and then take action. I'm not armed, Marshal, and if I were, what good's that with such parties? If it's come to pass that a federal judge cannot travel in this state without fear of insults and assaults—perhaps deadly assaults—from violent parties to litigation, why, something will have to   done about it. That woman is dangerous! Justice Sickels has made an order

418

against her that she be kept disarmed. And what do you propose to do about it?"

Patterson stood to his full height. "I'll take this up with Justice Sickels. She won't trouble you again," he said. That afternoon Patterson arranged for city police to help his own small force of deputy marshals to back up the old court bailiffs on the decision day. And now there was an assemblage of armed men with cold faces intent on the Trumbulls.

"Good morning, Judge. Mrs. Trumbull," Green said, sitting at the defense table. Jessica looked up with a smile. Green turned to Trumbull and suggested a smoke. "Go on, Mark," Jessica said pleasantly. "I'm trying to concentrate on this checklist."

"Sure now?" Trumbull said doubtfully. "You'll be all right?"

Trumbull strolled with Green down the crowded hall. Green had a report, he confided, that the judges were outraged by Jessica's misbehavior with Goff on the train and would not stand for another episode.

"Indeed? Well, let 'em look to their behavior. I'll look to ours!"

"Sorry," Green said.

"Oh, don't be sorry!" Trumbull said. "Too absurd. It's just the persecution she's faced all along. I'd pay it no mind. It was just an impulse."

They walked in silence. The tousling episode on the train was in fact more disturbing than he cared to admit. Why did she do such things? he wondered. It was so unbecoming, and really with no explanation except an odd sense of fun.

"Goff said you laughed," Green ventured.

"Did I now?" Trumbull said ironically. "You can hardly blame me. Goff was so pompous, snoozing there, Mrs. Trumbull couldn't resist to tousle the old man. Just teasing. I tried to make some pleasantries, but the fool wouldn't have it." He chuckled. "Course, it shouldn't have happened, but then he shouldn't have taken on so. Too comical."

Green studied the older lawyer with surprise. "Well, I wish it hadn't happened," he said slowly. "Marshal Jessup asked me to pass the word to take it easy. He asks you as an old friend to submit to the court."

"Couldn't Jessup talk up for himself?"

"He thought—as an ex-marshal—it wouldn't look right."

"The whole world wants me to submit to this court! Well, at least we've got their earnest attention," Trumbull said darkly. He squeezed the younger lawyer's shoulder. "Oh, forget it, Natty; Mrs. Trumbull will be a model of behavior, I promise."

"Well, I'm relieved," Green said. "Mind if I talk, Judge?"

"Not a bit."

"Have you thought of letting someone else take over?" Green said hesitantly.

"You?"

"Only if you say so."

They were at an open window overlooking the street. Trumbull paused, feeling the weariness in every bone. Oh, the air was good, he thought, breathing deeply. "Think I'm impulsive?" he said sardonically. "Likely to lash out? Say extreme things?"

Green smiled.

Trumbull shook his head ruefully. "Oh, Natty," he said reproachfully. "Why would I want to do it? It's all but over in this court, but there is an appeal and Washington. This won't end here."

Green was perplexed. The suit to revive the prior Hagerman judgment had been fiercely contested in the Circuit Court. He had merely sat in at counsel table, watching the flow of passion and energy, not sure he liked what he saw. Monumental briefs had been submitted, oral arguments had assailed the bench, and every argument against the jurisdiction had been urged not only in court but in pamphlets and letters circulated throughout the state. Trumbull had sustained that burden alone—it was a remarkable show of skill and pertinacity and scholarship—but the points were no longer razor-sharp, the thrust was blurred, the logic labored, random. Green felt uneasy indeed. Trumbull had aged markedly, and there was an emotionalism he found surprising. Green said, "It's been so hard, Judge—all these years devoted to this lawsuit. And the nature of the case . . . Aren't you tempted to let it go? Or let someone else take over?"

Trumbull stared at the sky. "Hard? Let it go?" He took Green's arm and walked on, feeling the impulse to confide bursting feelings. Years of effort had gone into that matter and with the end in sight he felt a loss. "I've thought of it." He sighed. "It's been difficult, I grant, hard beyond anything in my professional life. Sometimes, when I reflect on that

420

hardship, I almost pray the cup could pass from my lips. But I'm grateful too that you brought this case to me, Natty, especially for Mrs. Trumbull's sake. If she'd landed up elsewhere, I dunno what would've happened to her. She'd still be fighting, of course, because she's brave, but she'd be alone and without help. I'm thankful to be here, able to show where I stand in the matter. Her cause is just, Natty," he said earnestly, peering at the younger man with urgency, "undoubtedly just, and she's been villainously persecuted. At this stage, how can I let anyone else take over? My presence stamps the case. I know the evidence. I cannot hand it over without raising doubts about Mrs. Trumbull—and, for that matter, about myself. Can't be done. Can't be done."

"But—"

A strong gesture interrupted. "Yes, I know what people are saying, how ungenerous and intolerant the world is to her because of the scandal. About me too. You'd not believe the vile letters we get—letters that tell me I'm a besotted old fool enslaved by gross weaknesses. But what's that got to do with the cause? What am I to do?" His grip tightened. "Lordy! I'm no Bible shouter, but times I've almost prayed for guidance, for inspiration, and in all my wrestlings with my soul, I've had no doubts on the matter nor on her—no more than you had when you first came to Stoddard. She's an uncommon woman, Natty, as smart as a man, with real brains. As to all that—that stuff about the relations with Hagerman? Fah!" He paused, breathing hard. "Confounded nonsense about women, not related to their true natures, nor ours either! What's it all turn on? Why, the marriage! Granted marriage, all's excused! What else stands between Catherine the Great and Victoria? Damn all prudery! The world's so censorious, so hypocritical, it's abominable. I'd live with Mrs. Trumbull on a desert island and starve on husks because of what she is and has meant. Mrs. Trumbull is the Sabbath of my life, Natty." He paused abruptly and turned aside. "Sorry," he muttered. "Dunno what's overcome me!"

They walked on in silence. Green was never more embarrassed in his life. Trumbull seemed to have lost all his reserve. These were thoughts men simply did not talk about. Real strange, he thought uneasily.

Trumbull blew his nose and went on shakily. "Yes, I'd like to give up if I could. Hagerman's dead and it's only his ghost we're fighting; so where's the satisfaction? But how can I?

421

She's my wife," he said simply. "Pull out? What would the world think? Mark Trumbull, who in all his life never pulled out on a client, abandons his own wife's case? If I give one ounce less than my utmost now, those who have confidence in me—who put my judgment above a wilderness of Sickelses—would damn her forever. No, no! Let Sickels do what he likes! I can no more falter than fly."

Green said curiously, "Can we hope for anything favorable today?"

Trumbull hesitated. "Sickels is a judge of great parts and vast learning. He's also vastly conceited and faces review of this record on appeal by the other judges in Washington, and ultimately by the law reviews and text writers. He's always writing for posterity, so—although he has promised Pike to deliver a result—there's a remote chance he'll be judicial and do right. If not? Well," he said with determination, "we cannot stop the judgment, but neither will Mrs. Trumbull ever acquiesce. Lord! You surely don't think we're still fighting for Hagerman's money?"

"No. Of course not," Green said doubtfully.

"Then don't worry!" Trumbull said. "I'm here to make our point with dignity and keep the record clear. But thanks for sitting in, Natty. It's helpful. Most helpful. I know few who would. Most creditable. If a lawyer needs anything, it's to be brave."

"Well, I did talk you into this, Judge," Green said after an awkward pause.

"All rise!"

The familiar black-robed procession of three entered with a liturgical air. Sickels stumped to the bench, snuffed loudly, and after his customary prayer, turned a baleful glare at the scene he had dominated for almost thirty years. It was still his court, his circuit, he thought with grim satisfaction and, with the full power of the nation flowing in his veins, felt keen as mustard. He studied the clock—it was precisely eleven—and flicked a hard glance at the defense. Trumbull, elbows on table, facing him directly, was seated between the woman and the Marshal. Sickels sat forward with an immense sheaf of foolscap and read the findings of the Court.

"May the Court please!" Trumbull stood.

Sickels looked up. "I want no interruptions when giving an

422

opinion, Judge Trumbull," he said in a hard voice. "Arguments were done months ago."

"I have a question," Trumbull said obstinately.

Sickels sank back and stared. "What is your question?" he asked poisonously.

"Has not a step been omitted from the statement? The court will recall that I obtained an order to allow an appeal from the prior judgment. With all respect, I fear it has been omitted from the record."

Sickels drew a breath. It'd take careful handling; there'd be no rising to the bait; so much was agreed, a warning glance told his colleagues. "If counsel got such an order, it was improvidently made. The attempt was not effective. Counsel knows that where a suit abates by plaintiff's death, no appeal can be taken until after it's revived by a fresh judgment of the Court."

"Is that a ruling?"

"I will include it in the opinion."

"I am relieved."

There was an astonished hush at the impertinence, but Trumbull was not done. "And if the prior judgment is revived, will the appeal now be allowed?"

"The Court will not give advice," Goff exclaimed. "Wait for the decision, sir."

"I simply want to preserve the point," Trumbull retorted, "and respectfully ask to be guided accordingly."

Pike rose, stroking his white beard. "Counsel knows his appeal should have been taken within the statutory period. That expired a year ago. Too bad," he added, regret personified.

"The judgment revives, but not the appeal?" Trumbull said derisively. "Curiouser and curiouser."

Pike turned about and gave Trumbull a broad and disconcerting wink.

Sickels sank deeper in his chair. "You go far," he grated. "Far indeed! If your right of appeal expired, you may seek your remedy with the Congress. This Court will enforce the rules as it finds them."

"I respectfully say that this too can be appealed," Trumbull retorted.

"Do so!" Sickels replied. "You will do well to come to Washington. We know your views, Judge Trumbull, but I assure you that the Supreme Court is a tribunal lifted far above all prejudices, passions, and attachments. It will adjudge any appeal, even yours, sir, without any human frailties so far as attainable under our nation's system of government. And you will surely obey the Court," he added with menace.

Trumbull nodded slowly. "I must always obey the Court," he observed with deeper meaning, "and its judgments, or the world is lost. It is the basis of liberty and civilized life. My assent even to injustice is an agreed thing. I am part of it, so it has no shame. But really, sirs," he went on with barely concealed disdain, "unless you go by the law and evidence, I care nothing for your judgments. You cannot touch Mrs. Trumbull. I know precisely the just merit of her cause. That is enough for us.

"It may be the last time I shall ever again address this or any court, so it might as well be said. As for that other court in Washington, sir, we shall see in time. The best thing I can do for them is resist their lawless drift."

The faces on the bench went granite. Goff was stung. "More respect, sir," he said. "When the Supreme Court speaks, that is the law and you know it!"

"Ah, yes!" Trumbull said, bowing, "unfortunately that is the case because the people acquiesce. But where do they derive their powers? From the governed? Or elsewhere? No, sir! The federal judiciary, I submit, appointed for life and responsive to none, spin the gossamer web of law like political spiders—not from the Constitution—but from the orifices of their bowels. The thought does not command assent."

An astounded silence settled.

Trumbull went on. "Now, sirs, the California courts have upheld the marriage. I say with respect that your own prior judgment here, even if now revived, is too late to undo what was done by the State Court." He sat and folded his arms, staring at space. Green looked aside. He was surprised that Trumbull was trembling.

Sickels reminded himself that in a long lifetime he had dealt with insolences, plots, and malignancies beyond imagination, and had outlived them all.

"Were you talking for the press?" he said with menace.

"Oh, yes!" Trumbull responded with apparent surprise, tugging his beard. "I will remind Your Honor that under our theory of government the ultimate sovereignty still lies with the people. It is sometimes forgotten. I trust the record has all the remarks."

There was a gasp. Judge-baiting was an honorable tradition of the Western bar, but nothing like this had ever been seen. An eruption was expected, but Sickels was an old hand at the game. After a strangled moment, he went on, remarkably flushed.

Now what was the issue? he demanded. The prior case—brought by the late Hagerman—had determined that the marriage paper—which had not yet been surrendered—was a forgery. The issue was whether Hagerman's representatives were empowered to revive and enforce the prior judgment of the Court.

And that, he repeated with emphasis, was the sole question before the Court. Counsel seemed to think that the federal judgment, if now revived, was too late to affect the action of the State Court. Not so! The vast federal power—omnipotent and supreme within its given orbit—having once attached could not be ousted by trickeries or any devices whatsoever, and its scope would be determined by the federal courts and by none other. Did the female defendant seriously hope on such monstrous frivolities in exchange for her chastity to lay hands on so many million dollars? Strictly speaking, the marriage itself was not before the Court nor properly subject as such to review. But since counsel had alluded to the State Court's judgment as the moral basis of that marriage, the Court could not humanly let the matter pass without comment. The supposed marriage had not a single eyewitness but rested solely on the disputed testimony of the female defendant. But if the evidence was any guide, a case was presented which from its enormities would make pirates shudder. . . .

Every lawyer was grinning widely. Sickels was going past the technicality of the case—he was out to kill an old enemy. "Olé!" said a Spanish voice with fat humor. A cold voice interrupted.

"Justice Sickels!"

Sickels paused in surprise, frowning. Jessica was standing. "We may stop right here," she said sharply. "Justice Sickels, there is no need to continue the farce. We want to know if you are going to take it upon yourself to order me to give up that contract."

Goff and Abernathy shoved back their chairs; Patterson took a forward step.

"Dearest," Trumbull whispered, tugging Jessica's elbow. "You must be respectful. Wait till he finishes."

Jessica looked down, pale. "He is ruling against us, but I am not afraid." She turned to the bench with defiance.

"Dear," Trumbull said urgently. "Please, sit."

"No, dearest! I must get this off."

"Madam, sit down," Sickels said ominously, "or you will be forcibly seated."

"Justice Sickels, we hear you are bought," she said in a shocked silence. "We want to know if it is true, and how much you were paid by the Hagerman people, and how on your salary you can afford to ride around in a private railroad car."

"Lordy, dearest!" Trumbull groaned, and half rose. "I should like to explain . . ." he began.

"There is nothing to explain," Jessica said and raised her chin. "It appears no one can get justice in this court without he has a sack."

Sickels contemplated the full pale face, the swelling breasts, the blazing clear eyes. "Marshal, you will remove that woman!" he said with intense dislike.

"No, wait," Trumbull exclaimed in alarm.

"Come on, ma'am," Patterson said, taking Jessica's arm. Jessica resisted, spilling a handkerchief and her satchel. "You cannot take me from this place!" she cried, twisting away. "You dirty scrub, you dare not remove me. Let me go!"

The chamber was in uproar. Everyone was standing, craning to see the action.

"Marshal!" Trumbull leaped up, outraged. "That's my wife. Get a written order, or let be. I'll see her out."

Patterson thrust Trumbull back into the chair. "No writing is needed, Judge, and you know it. Come on, madam," he said, shoving Jessica forward.

"What in hell are you trying?" Trumbull cried passionately, struggling to rise. "I'll see that she goes."

Patterson shoved the lawyer back again.

Trumbull surged forward with a wild glare and a swing.

"All right," Patterson said with satisfaction, examining blood, and signaled. "Hey! What—" Trumbull cried, stumbling under the weight of a dozen men—deputy marshals, city detectives, and bystanders. He would never forget the taste of dust. Boots and shoes were at his nostrils. The flooring bruised him. He heard a scream. "My satchel!" Jessica cried. "It's got my money, my bracelets. Oh, you cowards!" Resisting, scratching, and striking every inch, using appalling language, calling frantically for her satchel, she was dragged screeching out into the hall. "Oh God, oh God!" he gasped, straining desperately. His legs were terrifyingly weak. The struggle moved down the aisle, shouts and growls were everywhere. A horrified face—Green's—floated out of sight. He flailed clumsily, panting with the effort, formed a bridge and rose against the weight of numbers. Snarls and growls rose from the melee. He struggled after, dragging a dozen clinging men, step by step, shaking them off like dogs by a baited bull. He stumbled and was pinned in the aisle. "Let be!" he panted desperately, striving for breath. "Let be, damn you! I'll go quiet. I only want to see my wife."

"Let him up." The calm voice was Finerty's. Trumbull stood, panting, and rushed out to the hall. A terrible constriction squeezed his breast. Oh, God, just so it ain't a heart attack, he thought. A shriek from the marshal's office brought him up cold. "You sons of bitches! Let me through," he shouted. "I know what I'm doing. Let me pass, damn you, or I'll cut you to pieces!" he sobbed, thrusting his weight at the crowd.

"Look out! He's got a knife!" A dozen hands reached out. Someone had his wrist in a vise. People were scattering, retreating from the disheveled panting giant and the swearing, struggling men at the entrance to the marshal's office. The door opened and Patterson looked out.

"It's a Texas knife!" someone called.

A fire went through his hand. A finger was being twisted. It will break, Trumbull thought, agonized. The thin man—it was Kiser—was staring directly into his eyes. "Keep cool, Judge," Kiser said. "Keep cool."

Patterson put a gun to Trumbull's head. "Judge, drop that knife or I'll drop you. Will you let go?"

"I'm going in," Trumbull said. "I have a right." The crowd was watchful during the exchange that followed. "Well, I don't want trouble," Patterson said finally. "Will you give up the knife?"

Trumbull released the knife and was taken into the office. Finerty picked up a fallen satchel.

"What's that?" Patterson panted. Finerty opened the satchel and showed the contents. "I'm damned," Patterson said. "I never saw the like. What's the matter with the woman? Well, let's go," he said grimly. Jessica could be heard in the inner room, denouncing the marshal as a brute, a dog, a hireling, reviling that he had her bracelets and money, that he was a thief sure and she was without a penny. A deep voice said, "Mrs. Trumbull, you're too fast. That's nonsense. The marshal wouldn't take your money or your bracelets. They'll be found and your money too."

"Then where are they?" she cried. "Where are my bracelets and my satchel?" As Patterson entered, she leaped up and struck his face. "Where is my gun? What have you done with my property? You thief! You villain." She continued striking and desisted only when her gun—a Colt .41 self-cocking revolver with one chamber gone—was taken from her satchel and handed for safekeeping to a deputy marshal.

Two hours later the reading came to an end and the Court recessed. After a light luncheon which Sickels scarcely touched, he announced that he was ready to see the marshal. After listening to a full report—during which the other judges and the United States Attorney put precise cutting questions—he came to the specific matter of interest.

"Now, then, Marshal, you say she was complaining that you had taken her satchel?"

"Yes, Judge," Patterson replied.

"What was the manner of complaint?"

"She accused me that I had got her money. That she had a large sum of money and it was gone, and that I was a thief. She was speaking of me in the vilest terms."

"Sounds crazy. Then what?"

"Mr. Finerty returned with her satchel," Patterson replied, "and she asked for her pistol."

"Pistol?" Sickels said grimly. "What happened to the pistol?"

"I gave it to Mr. Finerty to keep."

Sickels turned to Finerty. "What did Mr. Trumbull say to this?"

Finerty said, "He seemed surprised."

"What did he say?" Sickels repeated coldly.

Finerty shrugged. "He said that if Marshal Jessup had been present, there'd have been no trouble. That Marshal Jessup would simply have told him to remove Mrs. Trumbull, which he'd have done. He said he'd not allow any man to put his hand on his wife. Also, that he recently bought the knife only after hearing of ruffianly threats against himself and Mrs. Trumbull. It'd have stayed sheathed, he said, but for the Marshal's action."

"Didn't he know I made a special order against weapons in the courtroom?"

"Well, that's assumed," Finerty said.

Sickels swung slowly, perplexed and cold. "Trumbull's impossible. Simply incomprehensible that he'd be so reckless. Is there any explanation?"

Patterson said, "He says Mrs. Trumbull's gravid. That she's in a condition."

Sickels halted. "Gravid, hey? Well, well! This is one Trumbull cannot blame on the federal judiciary," he said with hard humor. "Mr. Finerty, what else was said?"

Finerty hesitated. "He claims the marshal did it on some prior understanding with you, Your Honor. That you deliberately and unnecessarily created the situation."

Patterson flushed a deep crimson.

Sickels turned to the clerk. "Mr. Nolan, kindly call the stenographer here to take a commitment order for these birds. This has gone far enough."

It was late afternoon when Patterson returned to his office with a certified copy of the Court's order: Jessica was given thirty days for insulting the Court and Trumbull six months for abetting the conduct. Trumbull read the text for the first time, grasping an essential import. "But . . . but it wasn't so, Marshal!" he said slowly. "I drew no weapon till I was in the hall. This is a misstatement of the fact!"

"Lemme see." Patterson read the commitment order. "No, Judge. Justice Sickels states right here you drew in the court."

"But . . ." Trumbull was confounded. He turned to Jessica. "My dear, you see this, don't you? It's a plain lie. I did nothing like this in the courtroom, but only in the hall when I heard your voice—"

"I believe you," Jessica said.

"—and only to make 'em let me through to you. I struck no one. I never menaced anyone, but only to come to you, my dear. Then some ruffian twisted my hand." He turned in alarm. "Mr. Finerty? You were watching. Sure you'll confirm this to Justice Sickels?"

Finerty glanced uncomfortably at Patterson. "Does it make a difference where it took place, Judge?"

"Difference? It's vital!" Trumbull said, striking the desk.

429

"This order is illegal. The Court cannot punish like this—summarily, unless for an act done in its presence. I am entitled to a hearing. It's the grossest tyranny—" He paused suddenly, aghast at the uncomprehending faces. He was going too fast, he reminded himself, choked by the rushing sense of outrage. He strode to the window in renewed agitation. "Marshal," he said formally, "I don't think you appreciate this either. It's one thing for the Court to act on evidence—I have never quarreled with such, as I think the record shows—but this is something else. This order rests not on affidavits or sworn testimony, but on the say-so of the Court itself. The Court is not on oath. The Court cannot be charged with perjury. The record is final—but it rests on nothing. Sickels cannot say I committed this act, since it never happened."

"How do we know that?" Patterson drawled.

"Because I tell you so," Trumbull said in a dead voice. "Marshal, I ask you to convey my request that Justice Sickels correct this mistake."

Patterson shook his head. "I wouldn't dream to tell him how to run his court."

Jessica interrupted. "Marshal, you'll not call Judge Trumbull a liar?"

Patterson turned to the woman with dislike. "Judge Trumbull's excited. He ain't thinking like a lawyer. It's not only a contempt, but you can both be criminally prosecuted for assault by the grand jury—which could mean the penitentiary. And don't think it ain't being considered. I'd button up."

Trumbull halted, seeing an unpleasant vista of danger ahead. "Lordy! As far as that goes, Marshal, I lost my temper," he said uncertainly. "Come! It's a bad temper, I admit, but there was provocation. You cannot take it that serious. It's not worth six months. It's worth a fine at most." He sat thinking, then humiliation came flooding. "Damnation, no! Sickels cannot give me such a barbaric sentence and hold his head up in the profession. It's too mean, too vindictive. It's this damned lie about the knife he rests on to justify. For the last time, will you tell him I demand a hearing?"

"Will you listen to Judge Trumbull?" Jessica demanded.

Patterson said calmly, "The order says to deliver you and Judge Trumbull to the sheriff, and that precisely is what I am doing—nothing more, nothing less. Now!" he said with a grimace of satisfaction, touching a loose tooth. "You've been reviling me steady, ma'am, and I've taken abuse from Judge

Trumbull I'd never take from another living soul. So if you have got a complaint, take it up with Justice Sickels."

Jessica cried, "You whelp!"

Trumbull put out a restraining hand. "Never mind, my dear," he said bitterly. "You were right. This was put up the moment we exposed the vileness of the Court—and there's no help for it now. . . ." He turned to Finerty. "Will you go to Justice Sickels?"

Finerty avoided his eyes.

"I see!" Trumbull said, glaring at the federal men. "Mr. Finerty, I have thought you honorable, but no more. We will submit to this order—but when the time comes, be sure you will be sued for illegal arrest."

It was hardly a wise remark, but Patterson, after stiffening, took it well enough. "In what court?" he drawled.

The Oakland Ferry steam whistle blared. Newsboys were whooping the latest headlines which by now were being carried by every newspaper in the state.

"Ruffianly attack."

"Gun! Bowie knife!"

"Terrible scene in court!"

"Raging lawyer threatens Justice Sickels!"

"Cowardly attempt!"

"Get ye'r paper!"

"Gore's death recalled——"

The hack drove onto the ferry in a rush, crowding back the passengers on the lower deck. The door of the hack opened.

"Hello!" Jessica called out ringingly. "Is any member of the Laborers' Union here?"

"Jess Roo. Hey, Christ! What's she doing here?"

"Anybody? You! Are you a member?" Jessica demanded, pointing imperiously.

A mechanic nodded self-consciously.

"Oh, thank God!" Jessica cried dramatically. "Sir! Everybody! Please!" The crowd pressed about the hack. "Now, listen! Judge Trumbull and I have been sentenced to the Alameda County Jail by that despicable old villain, Justice Sickels. Our friends must be told what's being done to us by that horrible man. . . ."

A friendlier crowd now gathered.

"Listen, please!" Jessica begged. "Tell everybody it's being

431

done because we have defied these people. That's why they hate Judge Trumbull! Because he will not eat their dirt. It's not just our fight. It's yours. Oh, don't you see. . . ."

She fell back into the hack, then looked out again. "We appeal to the working people. Our only real support has come from the laboring classes. The people—workmen, railroad hands, clerks—are our inspiration." She disappeared again.

The crowd was pressing curiously about the hack, peering into the dim recesses. Jessica was expostulating excitedly.

". . . could have killed those old villains!" the twanging voice rang out. "I could shoot down either of 'em. No jury in this state would convict me for killing that old villain. . . ."

"Why don't you shut up?" Patterson said.

"I despise you, Marshal!" Jessica retorted. "You're a dirty dog to treat poor Judge Trumbull so. And at his age too! He's a great man!"

"Sure he is," Patterson said.

"Well, he is and you're a hireling. You're no better than that coward Sickels. When they meet up, Judge Trumbull will make him sorry, be sure of that!"

Trumbull, who had been silent and downcast, stirred. "Please, dearest, it does no good to make such threats. It gives 'em ammunition to report back to the Court."

"I'm not afraid of jail," Jessica said.

Trumbull took her hand gently. "I know that, dearest, but I am afraid for you. You must take care."

Jessica nodded slowly. "Yes, my dear," she agreed. A look of pain crossed her face.

A blustery wind from the north, kicking whitecaps over the darkening bay, was blowing through the vehicle. Suddenly she pulled forward on the strap and leaned out. "Workingmen!" she cried. "Workingmen of the world . . . !" The whistle blared.

"Huh? What'd she say?"

"Cranes? Or chains?"

"What's it mean?"

"Unite with who?"

"Hang Sickels! Hang Goff!"

"Thank you," Jessica said passionately. "Thank you all for your support. This fight is not over. It's just begun," she shouted as Trumbull! tugged at her arm. "Justice Sickels was laying for us and has abused his powers. What about judicial restraint?"

She was pulled back and the blind drawn. The crowd milled about, dispersed, speculated as the ferry approached Oakland. Within the darkness of the hack, Trumbull shrank down, unable to face the federal officers. Finerty was subdued and silent. Patterson stroked his moustaches. Trumbull was lame and hurt, only beginning to feel the beating he had taken. Jessica's outburst could not have come at a more unfortunate moment.

The Alameda County Courthouse was a familiar sight—a large brick building with a clock tower and battlements. The sheriff's office was at the rear of the ground floor. Attached was the county jail, a forbidding mass of stone with a dozen cells, a tank for vagrants, and a wing for female prisoners.

Trumbull got down, painful and stiff after the brutal handling earlier in the day. His palm was cut, a finger was in a splint, a scratch ran down the fleshy cheek into his beard. Jessica stood beside him and faced the crowd with dignity and calm. An old friend, George Gorham, sheriff of Alameda County, came forward in a frock coat, lifted a silk topper hastily found for the occasion, and bowed. It was overwhelming and without precedent to receive a former Chief Justice of the Supreme Court of California and his wife in his humble suburban jail. "Judge Trumbull? Ma'am?" he said nervously. "Welcome to Alameda County."

The crowd surged forward, friendly enough. The newspapermen were clamoring for comment.

"No speeches," Patterson said roughly. "Let him talk!" a voice sang out.

"My dear friends!" Trumbull said, glancing anxiously at Jessica. "The newspapers have published Justice Sickels' version of today's events. But I have this to say. Justice Sickels is mistaken in his findings and deliberately so. I say they are false. I also say that only a wretch would treat Mrs. Trumbull so after giving her such provocation, and I will tell him so when next we meet."

The crowd jostled, went silent. He lingered on the irrevocable moment. "Come, my dear," he said despondently. "Justice Sickels can make what he wants of this. He'll know where to find me," he added with bleak humor.

433

Gorham's office was well lit but it had the look, Trumbull thought, of all such places at night—a dreariness beyond despair. The appointments were the usual—a board announcing sales to satisfy tax liens and judgment creditors, a gun rack, small barred windows, a rolltop desk with stuffed pigeonholes. Gorham had got rid of the federal men and now was beaming at his prisoners. "Judge, if you'd like to take Mrs. Trumbull to some hotel, I'll arrange it. I want you comfortable. I know what you've meant to the people of this state. Sickels and that bunch can . . ." He caught himself and blushed. "Excuse me, ma'am," he said earnestly to Jessica, "but that's how we of Alameda feel about Judge Trumbull. It's just that the county gives me no accommodations for married couples. I'm real sorry."

"Quite all right," Jessica said graciously, "but I wouldn't dream of giving Sickels the satisfaction. No, we'll stay here. It's a nice jail, I'm sure. I just don't want to leave Judge Trumbull alone tonight. The brutes treated him abominably."

"Well . . ." Gorham scratched thoughtfully and excused himself. He returned with his wife, a talkative, compassionate, birdlike creature. Mrs. Gorham—formerly a Lipscomb of Texas—had worked hard all her life and had an immediate grasp of the cause of Trumbull's concern: Jessica was showing fatigue, and blue rings under her eyes told the story. "You'll stay with us," Mrs. Gorham decided. "Let's see. Every blessed room is crowded—it's these orphan children I'm raising! What about our bedroom, Father?"

"I wouldn't hear of it!" Jessica exclaimed.

"It's that or nothing," Mrs. Gorham said. "Father? Get those bags over to the house."

An hour later a supper of Southern pan-fried chicken with trimmings was polished off and a history of running boardinghouses and raising orphan children under hardships thoroughly covered. It was the darnedest prison sentence ever, Jessica said with a tired grin.

"Follow me," Mrs. Gorham said. At the head of the stairs she said proudly, "Now we do have an inside bathroom. Some of the boys has taken to reading there, but they'll get out if you bang. Anything else?" she asked solicitously.

"Just liniment," Jessica said wanly, kissing the woman. "You're a godsend, my dear, and we're enternally grateful for the kindness."

434

Mrs. Gorham smiled and dropped her voice. "When are you expecting it, my dear?" she beamed.

"What? Oh! Well, not too soon," Jessica said and closed the door.

Trumbull lay supine with every bone aching. Jessica was rubbing liniment with exclamations of concern. He was breathing heavily, staring at the gaudy wallpaper, and wondering how the matter had come to such a pass. His lids felt feverish, his finger throbbed.

"You're all black and blue," she said wrathfully. "The brutes must've kicked you."

"Never mind me. How are you? I saw you holding yourself. D'ye want a doctor?"

"Lands, no. I'm not the first woman to have a baby. I'm still young and strong as a horse."

"Well, I'm not. I want you to take care," he said somberly. "I cannot say too much what this child means at my age, and especially after all the misfortunes we—Alexandra and me—had. It was like some curse, you know. . . . Misfortune after misfortune, with the first two children dying of the croup and the mountain fever, and then young Mark . . ." He had to pause. He was overwhelmed with feeling. He was raw and close to weeping. It was his weakness, he thought; for the first time in his life his strength had failed. He touched her breast. "Oh, my dear! I thought I was so old, so old! Old and destroyed like a ruin of myself. This came as a blessing. Nothing'll happen to this baby? Promise?"

"I promise. Now you need rest," she said firmly, "and a fresh mind in the morning to deal with these people. Let me worry about me."

The gentle hands slipped lower, rubbing and massaging the protruding belly. He felt easier, closer to sleep, his eyes were heavy. "You're not angry with me?" she said timidly.

Of course they both understood. If there had been any chance to accept defeat and return to McAllen to live out their lives quietly, that chance was gone. The humiliation was a knife to his heart. "Oh, dearest," he said reproachfully. "You now see what power these men wield? You see the trouble that sort of thing can bring? I thought we'd agreed . . ."

"Don't scold," she begged. "I could not help it, my dear. I could not stop myself. I have got this case now where we always wanted it. The public must not be allowed to forget our case. I knew the villain might send me to jail, and that was exactly what I wanted—to expose what happens in the courts of our land. I saw suddenly there was no other way. That if I had to go down, I would at least strike a blow! But I did not expect what that scut did to you, dear. I never meant for that to happen. Not to you, Mark. You must believe that."

He gazed at the pleading eyes so close to his own. "Well, it ain't fatal," he said with false reassurance. "Mebbe in the morning I'll think of something. Now can we sleep, dearest? I can't remember when I've been more drained."

"Yes, dearest," she said softly. She lay beside him in the deep bed and waited for the labored breath that would tell that he was asleep.

At dawn she woke with excruciating pains and within the hour saw the blood and the tiny form in the basin. The homunculus with its bulging forehead and stubby suggestions of limbs was a parody. "Oh, my baby," she wept hysterically. "Oh, my only child! Oh, my son! My son!"

Trumbull sat in the dark room, holding the ravaged hand. His face was stone.

Chapter Twenty-Two

The return to San Francisco was always an exciting business for Fanny. She loved the clear air, the bright sun, the busy and energetic people who made up the city's life. Ordinarily after recovery from the travel weariness, she would call on friends, pick up gossip, and recapture the city. On this occasion she had come for a short visit before she returned to London to finish her Greek novel, but all that was now put aside. She moved her steamer trunks into the old Occidental Hotel at Sutter and Montgomery.

The lobby was buzzing with the news from Oakland. Had she heard the latest? the clerk asked, sparkling with zest.

"Have my trunks brought up if you don't mind," Fanny said coldly. "And the newspapers."

Once upstairs she threw aside her coat and turned to the headlines.

Trumbull's bitter words at the Alameda County Jail—described as a shameless challenge to a venerable jurist by a desperate ruffian, a ruffian whose notorieties were recalled in detail, were uniformly denounced. The city, it was reported, was seething with rumors and resentment, delegations were forming to protest the threat to law and decency. A clash between the parties was predicted.

"What damned nonsense!" she exclaimed.

She unpacked her manuscripts and dresses, bathed, sent a note, and left to dine at Schoenberg's.

"My dear girl." Smith kissed her and called for champagne. They slipped easily into their old affectionate mood. He was thinner than she remembered, but still erect and handsome as ever.

"You look worried," he said.

"It's all this nonsense I've been reading," she said, then forced a smile. "Let's not spoil this, Gramps. I've had a marvelous time, but I'm glad I'm back—this crab is marvelous. . . ."

The talk was kept to family matters and the London literary scene and only after coffee and brandy came to the story in the headlines.

Everyone had expected the courtroom proceedings to pass off without incident. The first inkling of trouble was Trumbull's verbal attack on the federal judges—total nonsense, Smith thought, since the decision was inevitable and the show of displeasure an exercise in futility.

"Then why did he castigate the Court?"

"Bravado and blind obstinacy. He had committed everything to the lawsuit—reputation, position, himself, without reserve. He was talking beyond the bench to a wider public—trying to make a mark on history. What makes him an impossible man is the passionate notion that nothing, not a speck, not a scintilla of doubt may be allowed to stain his integrity. Nonsense, of course; the corruption and hypocrisies of our society are its saving graces. Without 'em, life would be intolerable. But he had to face up to a final absurdity."

"Absurdity?"

"Oh, my dear girl. A sensible lawyer'd send a lost case to the closed files. Why marry a woman like that? Does she make any kind of sense to you?"

"Well, there is the physical side," Fanny said.

"But he's had that!" Smith said with surprising brutality. "No, the marriage was something more than that. It was a gesture, you see? It was meant to announce that he'd never admit the forgery, never give up the cause. When Sickels gave the *coup de grace,* what else was left but defiance? To admit that the lawsuit was a lie would be to admit his life a lie and the marriage sheer folly—and that would be intolerable for a man who's proud, sensitive, and essentially weak."

She raised her brows. "Trumbull weak?"

"D'ye think this behavior shows strength?" Smith retorted. "It's cost him his liberty and respect. There's not a lawyer in the city who doesn't think he's a fool. Unfortunate, too, because so unnecessary. In the early days, when they sat together on the bench, Sickels admired him inordinately. Might still, if Trumbull'd let him."

"Admired? I never heard Sickels say that."

"Oh, yes!" Smith said with a thin smile. "Trumbull was robust, good-humored, popular among men, adored by women, and brave—qualities then more highly valued than now. Sickels longed to emulate him, but convinced no one. Trumbull respected his scholarship, but little else. Polite reticence was used to mask contempt."

"Contempt? What about?"

"Can't say. Something happened while they were on the bench in Sacramento. Trumbull never explained that coolness, but over the years always attacked Sickels for corruption, for giving decisions to rich men and moneyed corporations. Sickels took it to heart, and—well, you see how it worked out. Real folly, when you consider a judge's power over litigants and lawyers."

Fanny stared at the long face, the thin mouth, the flat presbyterian cheeks. "Are you saying that the Trumbulls were put in jail for personal reasons?"

"I'm saying nothing, except that Trumbull has himself to thank. I daresay he never expected his wife's outburst, but that shows his decay as a lawyer—that he let her dominate the case and address the court, knowing her temperament. Had to lead to this. Fritz? Two more brandies."

"What about all this talk, Gramps? Is there anything in that piece in the *Examiner*?" she asked uneasily. Tom Wickwire had raised the specter of a physical encounter in an article that was being widely discussed. Wickwire had written that if Trumbull was forced to serve out his six months sentence, it would be wise for Sickels to let another judge attend to his Pacific Coast business, for Trumbull would surely assault him on the first occasion, and one or the other would surely be killed. It seemed shocking to say that of such parties, but it was not, in his opinion, the case of an ordinary litigant and an ordinary judge. It was a case of two deadly old political enemies getting into a final death struggle, growing from an unreasonable belief—an *idée fixe,* amounting to monomania—by the one that the other had used his judicial powers unfairly, from which obsession there was no swerving the man.

The article had concluded with a flourish:

> . . . One must always remember that Trumbull is known in California for his past. He is relentless, a man who has killed his man, who has lived by the bloody Code, who stops at nothing. He is a man with the heart of an Indian, the strength of a bear, and intelligence of the highest order. He is a cunning and bad foe to have. Such is the impression after a long and revealing talk at the county jail, where the animosity was frankly disclosed.

"The Code!" Fanny exclaimed, shaking her head. "I felt sick to read it. It's this sort of thing that makes moderation impossible. It sounds like such a—a throwback. Why do they write such nonsense?"

"Lack of imagination," Smith said dryly. "Those stories have always circulated about Trumbull. Part of the legend. They wouldn't know what to write without the old files. Of course," he added carefully, "it has a basis in fact and that's really what's disturbing here. Trumbull knows all this only too well. He's never before in his life put another man's personal character in question. But now he's going too far with Sickels. He's attacking not only the judge—which is permissible, even expected—but the man. He's being too reckless entirely. I'm worried about Trumbull. Something's gone wrong with his judgment. One doesn't drive a man like Sickels into a corner, certainly not when he's got you behind bars."

Fanny toyed with her glass. It was late now, the restaurant almost deserted, and the travel weariness throbbed at her temples. "Gramps. All this old-fashioned talk of threats and challenges. It's nonsense, isn't it?"

"*Is* it?" Smith teased.

"Well, it must be," she replied in alarm.

Smith relented. "Oh, yes," he said. "The Code's dead and gone, and a good thing, too. But it is ironic, really. Trumbull never wanted to fight Gore. He wanted a ceremonial exchange of shots in the air, but Zack Yates told him that Gore and his friends had come to see him killed. Trumbull had to stand. He succumbed like everyone to fear of ostracism and disgrace. He was a moral man in an immoral situation—but aren't we all? You can only say that he was brave.

"That's something, of course," he concluded and finished the brandy. "And now fellers like Wickwire who never knew or understood are rehashing those times, and Trumbull's paying for it all over again in so many, many ways. I do hope you're done with this man. I hate to see you unhappy." He studied the downcast face. "But there! I don't mean to meddle."

"I'm the meddler, not you," she said, embarrassed. "I've a strong impulse to help. What can be done?"

"Oh, don't ask me," Smith said, displeased. "I wish you'd think twice. I doubt anything can be done for the man. He should submit gracefully to the court and retreat to the wilderness to live out his life. He's set in motion larger forces than you can imagine."

Fanny spent the next day talking to friends; she read the crescendo of incitation in the newspapers, attended a painful, uneasy open meeting at the Bohemian Club, and the following morning showed up at the offices of Kearny Street. After a short wait, she was ushered into the large sunny office where Green was signing the morning's correspondence.

Green was professional, grave, humorless, and friendly. After picking up the threads, he called his stenographer and handed over the letters. "Now, Mrs. Woodruff. You say you want to help? How?"

"I'm not clear," Fanny confessed. "I'm no laywer, but I imagine the first thing is to get our friends out of jail. Is it true that Jessie had a misadventure?" she asked abruptly. Green nodded. "Dreadful," she said. "The newspapers are appalling. Did you read Tom Wickwire's piece?"

Green shrugged. "Actually, it's all a continuing attack on the California divorce and it hasn't helped. Public opinion is everything."

She frowned. "I couldn't care less about the divorce. I'm worried about Judge Trumbull. And Jessica, of course."

"Can you separate the matters?" Green asked mildly.

"Trumbull is still insistent on the divorce. Sickels is determined that he'll not get it—and now he's got a perfect excuse to keep Trumbull in jail. But you're quite right. The first task is to get them out—but I cannot say whether Trumbull will take advice. I know he won't take mine."

"What is your advice?"

Green waited. "It's not simple. There are just a few ways to go," he said thoughtfully. "The best move is a petition to Sickels to revoke the order of commitment. Judge Sinzheimer has offered to try to patch things up, but I doubt Sickels will yield. Our client was entirely too free with her insults. Trumbull'd not be in this mess but for her."

Fanny sighed. "Well, tell me what to do. I know Justice Sickels quite well. He's fond of me in a way—for that matter, so is Mrs. Sickels—but, of course, he must be quite incensed."

"He sure must be," Green said grimly, and considered the proposal. "I'm not sure anything can be done," he said slowly. "Trumbull's in serious difficulties, more than he knows. However, I have an appointment to visit him. If you'll give me a few moments to get rid of a witness, you're welcome to come along."

An hour later they were facing the refreshing breeze of the bay.

Trumbull stepped forward with pleasure and surprise. "Fanny Woodruff!" he said, clasping her hands. "I cannot tell you what this means to us. Hey, my dear," he said hoarsely.

"Oh, yes," Jessica said wanly. "We're so pleased to see friends here. True friends. You're good to come, Fanny."

"Not a bit," Fanny said. They embraced. "You look fine, Jessie, simply fine!" she said.

There was an awkward moment.

"Well!" Trumbull said uncertainly. "Can we be seated?" He brought a straightbacked chair to Jessica. "Would you like a pillow, my dear?" he asked gently.

Jessica gathered a shawl about her shoulders. "Don't fuss me," she said weakly. "I'm just concerned to deal with this dreadful situation. Fanny, dear, I hope you'll tell the world about this. Our hope—and reward—is the support and sympathy of the people. They understand."

Trumbull cleared his throat. "Natty, be so kind with that cane chair? If we can just sit about where I can consult my papers?" Chairs were grouped about a flat desk; he placed a briefcase at his feet and glanced doubtfully at Fanny. "I'll want to hear all about London and Greece," he said tentatively, "but later. First things first."

"Of course," Fanny said, taken aback. She'd been prepared for Jessica's frailty—the pallor, the stiff gait, the haunted eyes of pain, but Trumbull was a shock. What had she expected? Surely not the slow step, the stooped carriage, the rasping tired voice—or even the gray that streaked his beard and the thinning hair. And his anxiety and hovering solicitude for his wife. . . . It was strange, she thought, to sit now as strangers with this man in a strange room.

Trumbull thought that time had dealt better with Fanny than himself. She was more handsome than ever, assured and reassuring, and for that he was grateful. He suppressed an impulse to say something personal. "Can we begin?" he coughed, lowering his eyes, and began to fumble for papers.

"Well, it's just too shocking," Jessica said querulously, drawing the shawl about her shoulders. "I don't matter two cents, but the people should be outraged to see Trumbull treated like a criminal. It's entirely out of order and high-handed. A punishment for contempt is not supposed to be corporal. It's not a crime and there's no need for such punishment. Sickels is a coward. He's trying to keep Trumbull in jail to defeat my case and because he fears to meet up with him before he goes back to Washington. That is the true reason for this outrage. But I shall keep my divorce and enforce all my rights to the Hagerman estate if it takes forever. All my rights," she repeated emphatically, "and to the last penny."

"Hush, my dear. Not now," Trumbull said uncomfortably. "We have other things to talk about."

"Very well," Jessica said, "but I'm only repeating what you've said yourself—that Sickels has lied. Isn't that so?"

"Possibly," Trumbull replied, vexed, "but under provocation and not for publication. Your newspaper friends have not let up on us," he went on bitterly, turning to Fanny. "You've read Wickwire?" he demanded. "I've got those blamed clippings somewheres. Now where'd I put it?" he muttered, searching the briefcase with exasperation.

"I've read it," Fanny said.

Trumbull straightened up. "Oh, well, I said nothing like that, of course. I thought I knew Wickwire—good Southern

442

stock. Honest, too, for all his wishy-washy pseudoliberal pacifistic fence-sitting poses. That's why I asked him to come for an interview. I wanted the truth brought to the public—but somehow it's come out like that!" He stood restlessly and began to stride the room. "You see why they're doing this, I expect. They're making it impossible for Sickels to change his position, even should he wish to—which he don't. But as always, I bear the blame. It's an old story. . . .

"Now who's got the incentive for this mood of hate? Me, behind these bars? Or Galindez and Company?" He resumed his stalking. "Strength of a bear! Heart of an Indian! Damned nonsense! It's all a diversion!"

"Trumbull gave no basis for such statements," Jessica said argumentatively. "He merely told Wickwire the truth about the courtroom—that it was all a trap, that Sickels had got a crowd of men, fighters, detectives, deputy marshals, ready to assault us on any provocation. They were trying to make a record with the marshal, to say they'd done something to Trumbull—and that's why I was hustled out. It was clearly done to provoke him to defend me. I blame myself, of course. I was a fool to let him fall into the trap. I expected to be fined, or even sent to jail, but I had no idea the marshal'd put his dirty hands on me. It was inconceivable that a lady could be treated so in an American court! They had absolutely no reason to expect trouble. I trust you believe that," she exclaimed, seeing a frown.

Fanny said slowly, "Well, there was that business with Judge Goff on the train."

Jessica burst into laughter. "Oh, that," she scoffed. "That was nothing. I wooled the old man, that's all. Wooled him good, I'm glad to say. What of it?"

"It hardly showed good judgment," Fanny said.

"I don't see why not," Jessica replied, frowning. "It was an impulse, like scratching my nose. A gentleman'd not make such a fuss. What's it got to do with the case?" She shook her head at the world's inability to understand simple things.

Fanny said nothing. It was odd behavior, she thought, and just as odd that neither Jessica nor Trumbull seemed to see it so.

"Wickwire has it wrong. I did not threaten to assault Sickels," Trumbull said firmly. "I merely repeated that Sickels had put a lie in the record about me—that I drew a weapon in his presence. I kept coming back to that lie because it's the

443

sole basis for this outrage, for keeping me here without a fair hearing. Then Wickwire asked if I didn't think that remark dangerous. I said, 'How so?' He said that Sickels wasn't a man to let anyone put a deadly insult like that upon him, that he'd be sure to slap my face if we met. I said I hoped not, but if so I'd slap his, or pull his nose, or some such thing, and await his pleasure—and that's the sole basis for all that talk about a so-called threat."

What blasted idiocy, Fanny thought.

Trumbull stood ruminating. "But it was all poppycock," he went on, rousing himself. "Sickels'd never fight when young, I said, and wouldn't now. Wickwire then said that most men who'd live under the Code would fight, given the occasion, and recollected some instances about Sickels facing a mob in Marysville and cowing bullies, and such. Moonshine, of course, and I know the source—those biographical mendacities printed to help his presidential ambition. All lies, invented by literary prostitutes."

"Was that wise, Judge?" Green said. "Sickels may be all you say, but he does have friends."

"Has he now?" Trumbull said with contempt. "Of course his friends mean less than nothing. Wickwire tried to suggest that as he is not my physical equal, he'd want to use a weapon on me. Lordy, I take no notice."

A bell clanged in the cell block, marking an exercise period.

"Well, I'm not interested in Mr. Sickels," Trumbull said finally, "or his tiresome personality, but I must reckon with him as a raw fact."

He sat at the table, brooding. "Natty? What's the feeling?" He listened attentively, clucking with displeasure as Green discussed his options in the matter.

"I don't like this," Jessica complained.

"Hush, dear," Trumbull said patiently. "I have concluded that I must do something. I cannot fight for your legal rights from this place, and I must get you out where you can get rest and peace of mind. Natty? What's Sinzheimer ready to do?"

Green said, "Sinzheimer agrees that a petition to the Court is your only chance to get out. He's ready to see Sickels and sound his disposition. Then, if it seems advisable, he'll present your petition, but—"

Jessica exclaimed with pain. "My dear, I beg you not to

humiliate yourself. You're doing this for me, I know, but the world won't understand. I don't trust the man. He wants to humble you, but he'll never let you out. Oh, don't do this to yourself!"

Trumbull took the shaking hands in his own. "Don't," he said gently. "Sickels is a judge, and I must assume he'll act like one. I've got to exhaust our remedies. Now, hush, and let me handle this." He turned. "Natty?"

"Yes, Judge?"

"I sure don't want to serve six months for an act I did not do. You can tell Sinzheimer that I'm weary of this business. He can formally assure Sickels that if released I'll seek no personal satisfaction for what is past. Is that satisfactory?"

"Sounds all right," Green said dubiously.

Trumbull turned to Fanny. "If Sickels wants to do what's right, he'll revoke Mrs. Trumbull's sentence. Thirty days is entirely too harsh for the offense, considering his own behavior. Will you tell him that?" he demanded. He was breathing hard.

"I'll think of it," Fanny agreed.

"Well, I've got it all here." Trumbull handed over a formal petition addressed to the court. Green scanned the paper. There was no mistaking the deliberate and forceful style, nor the spare reiteration of the position that disrespect was not intended, nor contempt committed in the court's presence. The disclaimers were in unyielding language.

"Well, is there something else?"

"Um. Well . . ." Green handed the petition to Fanny and sat back, scratching his jaw, almost bored with the obsessive reiterations and denials he knew to surfeit. There was, he thought uneasily, a growing monotony of mind. "Sinzheimer feels it needs an apology," he said uncomfortably.

"There! You see!" Jessica exclaimed.

"Be quiet," Trumbull said. "An apology?" he asked dangerously. "That'd affirm the honesty of the decision. Is that what's being asked? In effect, to admit the wrongness of the case?"

"Not precisely . . ."

"Yes, precisely!" Trumbull smote the desk. "And you're bringing that message? Is that it? Tell me!"

"Sinzheimer thinks it's essential," Green said unhappily, "but what practical difference does it make? If Sickels accepts

445

the apology, at least you'll be released. You admit nothing about the merits, for whatever that's worth."

"For whatever that's worth?" Trumbull repeated. "Fanny, d'ye go along with this?"

She nodded. "The main thing is to get you out."

"*Et tu!*" Trumbull said heavily. "Natty, are you trying to shake me?" he asked resentfully. "What's your game?"

"No game," Green said uncomfortably.

Trumbull stood and walked to the window, deeply disturbed. The window looked on a courtyard used for exercise. It faced other barred windows from which various noises floated—clashing irons, a rattle of pots in the kitchen, a shouting demented prisoner waiting trasportation to the Melrose State Asylum. His knuckles, clutching a bar, were white and painful. "So that's it? Trumbull. Mark Trumbull who has always stood for something. Eat dirt to get out of this hole? Go on his belly back to the Pima? Is that what they expect? Ain't the petition enough apology?"

The deep voice was trembling with feeling. He wrote and handed over a letter.

"Well, there it is, Natty. It's as far as I'll go. Sinzheimer has my assurances of good behavior and conditions. I think, Mrs. Woodruff, that your visit has served its purpose. Thank you and good day."

"My dear, my dear," Jessica said miserably. "It's my doing. All my doing."

Fanny stood and found her gloves. Green assembled his papers and prepared to leave. It had been a strange meeting, Fanny thought. The fanaticism and the anger were unyielding, but covering an underlying uncertainty of purpose. "Tell me, Mark," she said finally, "can't we hope for a favorable answer from Justice Sickels?"

Trumbull looked up. "No!"

"Why not?"

"Sickels wishes to pay me for my refusal to aid his political aspirations four years ago. I believe he blames me for his humiliations at Chicago when I refused to support his drive to get the presidential nomination. And that's what makes this proposal that Sinzheimer intervene on my behalf so utterly vain. Comical, too, Because Sickels never had a chance to get the nomination."

When the door closed, Trumbull was comforting his wife.

Chapter Twenty-Three

Sickels put the petition in his pocket and showed Sinzheimer, Fanny, and Green out with an ambiguous promise to give the matter the consideration it deserved. He snarled for the marshal. Patterson entered, and stood at attention as the distinguished jurist outlined the limitations put by Section 725 of the Revised Statutes on the powers of the courts of the United States to punish in matters of contempt. The marshal was not wholly clear on the drift but grasped a vital point—the prisoner, denying the Court's version, asserted the right to confront witnesses and other due processes of law.

"You've got all that clear in mind?" Sickels demanded after making certain requirements clear.

"Sure have, Judge."

"We cannot see ourselves bandying recollections, you see," Sickels said with a penetrating stare. "Now! Do you think you can get up a good set of affidavits from your men?"

"Reckon so."

"Good. Don't try to enhance anything. It's not necessary and we intend to be fair. But also leave nothing out—threats, insults, behavior. Just get the truth and leave the rest to the Court, hey?"

After a week marked by intense activity in taking sworn statements of deputy marshals, city police, and others, Sickels mounted the bench, flanked by Goff and Abernathy, to hand down the decision of the court. Requests by Green to examine witnesses and produce evidence were peremptorily denied. After denouncing forcible resistance to an officer of the United States as an invitation to anarchy, Sickels recalled the disgraceful violence which had moved from courtroom to hall, noted that the prisoner offered no apology for himself or his wife, expressed no regrets, withdrew none of the indecent charges against the court, above all—Sickels wet his mouth for emphasis—made no reference to his violent and

447

threatening language against the judges while under arrest, all set out in affidavits of the peace officers, now filed with the clerk.

The implacable glance turned to Green, then back to the stenographer.

"Petition denied!" he said, and adjourned the court.

A week later the private railroad car departed Oakland attached to the Eastern Flyer. Sickels spent the afternoon staring at the landscape, thinking of the letter which had appeared in that morning's *Chronicle*. The call to dinner interupted. He sat to poached eggs, looking forward to the new court term in Washington, relieved to be done with San Francisco.

"Something wrong?" Minerva asked.

"No, nothing." He tried to put the matter from his mind, but after dinner he again picked up the *Chronicle*.

IN JAIL AT OAKLAND, SEPTEMBER 18TH

Editor, The San Francisco *Chronicle*

Sir: The spectacle of a lawyer thrust in a common jail under an unjust sentence has distressed my friends from the outset. It is now said that I threw myself upon the mercy of the Circuit Court, confessing wrong, and begging for my release on abject grounds. None of this is true.

The fact is that I entrusted to my friends a petition for a court hearing, but made clear that it not be filed unless favorable action were assured. Mr. Sickels highhandedly turned the building upside down and got a score of affidavits from deputy marshals, policemen, and dependent lawyers to contradict me in every particular. Then, with no motion by my attorney, and contrary to my wishes, filed my petition himself and without a hearing denied relief against all canons of fairness.

I append a part of a letter to Judge Sinzheimer which shows the truth.

Yours, etc.

M. A. Trumbull

The letter to Sinzheimer followed:

Dear Sinzheimer.

. . . I do not expect any favorable action from the Court, and reluctantly consent that an application be made but only if success be prior assured.

I have told Green that if released I would seek no personal satisfaction for what is past. You may say, as emphatically as you wish, that I will commit no breach of the peace; that so far as seeking I will avoid meeting any of the parties concerned; but I will not promise that I will refrain from denouncing the decision to revive the earlier judgment and its author. I believe that the decision was bought with coin of the Hagerman estate, and I will stay here ten years before I say what I do not believe.

If Sickels wishes to do what is right he should release my wife. I grant she was in contempt of court, but the attempt made by going entirely out of the record to besmirch her ought to go in mitigation of the sentence.

You may tell Sickels that no matter what the outcome, I propose to stay here until my wife is discharged.

Yours, truly,

M. A. Trumbull

The trip seemed interminable. Sickels reached Washington, glad to plunge into the familiar routine, but his powers of concentration seemed to have weakened. His thoughts kept returning to the man in the Alameda County Jail. A month later he found on his desk a copy of a letter to Zacharias Yates at the Department of Justice, where Yates was an Assistant Attorney General. The envelope was postmarked San Francisco. The date line was Oakland, September 18.

"Daniel?" he called.

An attendant entered. "Yes, Judge?"

"How in thunder did this get here?"

"Through the mail, Judge. Why?"

"No reason," Sickels muttered. He brought the letter to the light, frowning.

Dear Zack:

As you know, the Court's right to impose sentence without trial rests on its baseless finding that I assaulted the marshal with a weapon in its presence. Of course no such thing took place. I drew my knife in the hall, not to assault anyone, but to pass through the crowd to get to my wife—as I had every right and duty to do. I had no other motive. I could have killed any number without trouble, had I wanted to. When the marshal put a pistol to my head, he asked if I'd give up the knife if he'd let me in. I peacefully gave it up and that was all.

So much for the newspaper claptrap that I struggled like a demon and gave up the knife, foaming with insane rage, only when wrenched from my hand.

Now, Zack, I could endure jail, but I am worried about my wife. She is brave, labors without complaint, but her health is affected, and the strain has begun to tell. I must get her out—but how? Sickels's version of the disorder is false, but, since the record imports verity, I cannot show this. There is no way out except to appeal to the President. If you can help me, you will do me the greatest possible favor.

I request you see the President, tell him all you know of me, and what degree of credit to give a statement made on oath of my own direct knowledge. I trust my petition will satisfy him that the court's order is false.

I cannot fathom Sickels. I have always shown him outward formal courtesy and hoped for reciprocity when he got me to abase myself. But it is evident that he is paying me off for old scores—especially, I am sure, my refusal four years ago to support him for the Presidency. It goes back to the night I made that McCabe Memorial Address at the Hibernian Hall. I was then asked by Ike Sinzheimer to see Joe Pike at the Purdue Hotel for a confidential talk in *re* the Hagerman case, which I had not yet entered. After the usual bluff and bluster, Pike mentioned that Sickels was confident that —provided he got the vote of California—he could be nominated for President and elected, as, with his family's influence, he would certainly carry New York, and believed that I could give him California.

I gave this no answer. Pike then said that Sickels understood that I might want official honors, as, because of my duel years ago, I was still under a cloud, that I might especially welcome reappointment to the bench; that if I would aid him, I could write my own ticket.

I said I had given up those ambitions. Pike then said that, as the Hagerman case involved millions, I'd be a fool, if I aimed to enter that matter, not to reckon on the advantage to the client of getting on the friendly side of the Court, and offered his own good offices to work something out with Hagerman, who'd be influenced only by himself and Sickels, and more of the same. There was only one answer, and that I gave at once. I stated emphatically that I had no such influence as supposed, but in any case knew too much about Sickels to inflict him on the nation. I left for the Hibernian Hall where I made my views precisely clear. Next day I entered the Hagerman case and gave Sickels my best efforts in his own court. People have wondered why I did so. I can now tell you that I acted in response to that gross attempt at bribery.

I cannot take the credit, but the results at Chicago, you'll recall, were humiliating and apparently not forgotten to this day.

Whether to give all this to the President, I leave to your good judgment.

Yours, gratefully, etc.

Mark

Sickels pocketed the letter with shaking hands and left in haste for the White House for a session with its occupant, whom in truth he cordially detested. As he reached the entrance, Zacharias Yates, a ruddy, strong-faced man with a vaulting acquiline nose, was leaving. They bowed and passed in silence.

Soon after, a marked copy of the Pima *Democrat* reached Washington. The plain envelope was postmarked San Francisco.

In Jail at Oakland, October 1st

Editor, The Pima *Democrat*

Sir: Mr. Sickels has caused his friends to publish a pamphlet called *The Trumbull Contempt,* which collects various contrived affidavits and documents to justify his shameful behavior to a member of the bar.

When I swore that the record had been corrupted,

Sickels read an opinion replete with sarcasms and innu-endos, repeating that the misbehavior was in the court-room, or the hall, and it mattered not which.

I say that the record is false. Indeed, not one affidavit supports the assertion of courtroom misbehavior but at most says that I there viole:tly thrust my hand toward my bosom. Deputy Marshal Finerty admits that I was pinioned before any such motion could be made.

Yours

M. A. Trumbull

In the months following, other items reached Washington from time to time.

Oakland, November 25th

Editor, The San Francisco *Observer*

Sir: *The Personal Reminiscences of Early Days in Cali-fornia* by Mr. Sickels seems written for political aims to show its author as a fire-eater and desperado in his youth. It proves his title to rank as an historian with Baron Munchausen.

I refer to his boastful accounts of carrying revolvers in his pocket, practicing the quick draw, sharpshooting from his pocket, and his quarrels with various persons where he says he got the nickname "Fearless Jack." As to the claim that he got his sobriquet by coolly taking a pistol from a gentleman named John Lee, I refer you to the Sacramento *Bee* of April 2, 1859, which bears his abject retraction of insults to avoid meeting Lee on the field.

In his book, Sickels claims that he defined a cocked re-volver put to his head by Judge Muldoon of Yuba County saying, "You infernal scoundrel, you cowardly assassin, you haven't the courage! Shoot and be damned!" and more to this effect, whereupon he says Muldoon fled. Brave words, but as Muldoon had been dead some years, they are safe to say now. In fact, no revolver was present. Muldoon applied his boot to the rear where it would do the most good, whereupon Sick-els fled and locked his door, and this ended the quarrel.

Thereafter "Fearless Jack" was met in every saloon with roars of laughter.

And on scores of such mendacities—which yet will be revealed—sat ambitions for the Presidency of this nation.

Yours,

M. A. Trumbull

"Damnation! Damnation," Sickels said hoarsely. He had completely forgotten the old newspaper files. The torn bits of envelope and letter went into the fire.

Oakland, February 9th

Editor, The San Francisco *Pilot*

Sir: In 1862 or 1863, a pamphlet entitled *The Gold Court* made public the corrupt decisions of the Supreme Court of California—of which Justice Sickels was then Chief Justice. That pamphlet charged that Sickels while a member of the legislature had received $6,000 in 1851 to vote the City Lots bill.

Shortly after, Senator Pike, ex-Governor Douglas, Sickels and others were in the Mint Restaurant eating oysters. Sickels bitterly denounced the pamphlet and desired to know the author to visit on him condign punishment. Douglas said quietly, "I am the author." Sickels then said he would not eat in such company and stood to leave, when Douglas said in a distinct tone: "Sit down, you——, and finish your oysters." Sickels then proved his boasted desperate courage by instantly sitting and, like his antitype, ancient Pistol, by eating his oysters "in earnest of revenge."

That pamphlet also charged that Sickels got $25,000 for the decision in the Miranda Estate Case, and in the Miracle City Case, got $50,000 worth of city lots, net after the Supreme Court go-between brokers kept the rest.

I say those were true charges, never denied.

Yours,

M. A. Trumbull

Oakland, February 20th

Editor, The Pima *Democrat*

Sir: The *Republican* deplores attacks upon "one of the purest and ablest judges that ever graced the ermine." The writer knows nothing of the man's record.

When Sickels was first elected to the Supreme Court of California, he got $6,000 a year salary and spent it all. For ten years his salary in Washington was $8,000, then went to $10,000, and his style of living was always more. Yet he has saved over $800,000.

How?

In future, further facts will be developed to show the true character of this judge. Perhaps then in a land of freedom and chivalry the cry of a woman, persecuted and maligned, against injustice will prevail. She is without money, almost without friends. But we will yet see whether any power on earth will prevail over right and conscience and truth.

Yours,

M. A. Trumbull

After a month of silence, a short item appeared in the Washington *Clarion*:

San Francisco, April 3rd

The notorious Mrs. Jessica Trumbull and Judge Mark Trumbull were finally arraigned today in the United States Circuit Court on felony indictments charging aggravated assault with a deadly weapon. Marshal Patterson put his full staff in the courtroom, augmented by the Secret Service, and the morning passed without incident. A friend, Mrs. Malvinia Lawes, well-known business woman here, produced a real property deed as surety for bail. The trial is set for August 20th.

Upon leaving the court, Judge Trumbull stated that he had but one ambition left in life—to force Justice Sickels to the witness stand under oath and finally vindicate the justice of his wife's case. He further said: "I do not intend to injure Sickels bodily, but if the opportunity presents itself, while I shall not seek it, I will certainly slap his face or horsewhip him, and let him show his

454

mettle. I have made up my mind on that, and my determination will not alter."

Mrs. Trumbull appeared in a velvet dress and matching toque hat with garnets. She appeared fatigued but composed and cheerful throughout.

Sickels felt the blood drain in the unreal moment. He drew a breath, choking and staring at the item. A white face was a mask of hatred and despair.

Chapter Twenty-Four

The night was dark, shrouded over as they rocked through the darkness. The train lurched as the air brakes clamped and the wheels screamed to a halt. There was conversation outside, then the train picked up and soon was rolling through the dark valley. Jessica tapped at the berth overhead.

Trumbull looked down through the green baize curtains. "Yes?"

"What was that stop?"

"Kingman, I reckon. Supposed to be a demonstration in our favor. This is where the McCabes staged their first protest robbery." He started to close the curtains. "Mark!" He came back. The dim berth was musky with her smell—perfumes, body odors, lozenges. A net hammock held disorderly garments. "Yes, dear?"

"Can't you join me here?"

"Honey, it's too cramped," he protested. "And we've got so many miles ahead. Try to sleep."

The compartment went quiet. Trumbull faced the ceiling, listening to the ventilator whistle with the sweet night smells of a valley, knowing sleep would not come. He was bursting, suffocated. A last conversation with Malvinia at Las Flores, where they had gone from the Federal Court for a day of rest, was gnawing.

Jessica had gone to her old darkened room for a nap while he and Malvinia had gone strolling through a pasture to discuss the case. Malvinia had put it bluntly that he ought to leave the country with Jessica and forfeit the bail. Suddenly he felt the warmth, the drowsy meadow sounds were preternaturally clear. "Forfeit the bail? What in hell are you driving at?" he demanded.

Malvinia, scratching her elbows like the old woman she now seemed, confided her fears for Jessica's mind. "I'm thinking of the strain," she said. "I'd say she's had all the courtroom she can take in one lifetime. Even if she don't do five years, she'll wind up in Melrose for sure."

Trumbull halted. "Melrose. I don't believe it," he said uncertainly.

Malvinia spat. "I know it's hard to believe. She's got this gorgeous white body, but the Rouxs has always had this wild crazy streak, and if you wrote to Cape Badeau you might get some records. Losing that baby was no help. Now, Judge, I've been her good friend all these years. I've testified, and done this and that and I'd do it again—but I've seen the signs."

Trumbull's heart dropped. "Seen what signs?"

"Oh, that famous two-week spell she had with Nellie Driscoll," Malvinia said. "And the time she was supposedly at San Jose with her brother. Actually, she was here in Las Flores with two of my strong women taking care of her. It wasn't brain fever at all."

"How d'ye know it wasn't?"

"Because I felt her and there wasn't a sign of temperature," Malvinia replied dryly. "Now, Judge, a good lawyer should know when to stop. Can she stand these ordeals and not lose her mind? That's what I'm asking. What if she turns out just another Crazy Hattie walking around the city talking to herself? Then what? Who'd believe anything?"

"You're joking me," he said.

"Joking? With this nice little house in Van Ness Avenue up for surety? Lands, I wouldn't think so. I've seen it coming, Judge, and so've you, but you're too bound and distracted to admit it."

He had a habit now of pausing to catch his breath. "That ain't so," he muttered.

Malvinia resumed walking. A meadow lark ran off, simulating a broken wing, pathetic and undeceiving. "Look 'ee, Judge, the next five years won't be that cozy county jail in Oakland. It'll be the penitentiary. Without somebody's support, could she keep her sanity? Why keep this up? What's the point?"

"Point? Why, it's still there—her place in decent society, her rightful claims."

"Rightful claims? Oh, Jesus." A thin shoulder rose and fell.

Trumbull stared at the unwinking eyes which penetrated his own. "I can't believe this," he said slowly. "You testified that Hagerman admitted to the marriage! You were the anchor! Are you now saying it wasn't so?"

"Are you sure I said that? Lands, I doubt it."

"But you swore . . ." He halted, appalled.

She squinted realistically. "Swore? To what? If you study it close, according to my evidence, Hagerman didn't really admit a thing outside that statement about signing the paper, which really meant nothing—just looked owlish, guaranteed bills, ranted, things like that. And he's dead. So what's the blamed point to it all?"

"Nellie said—" he began.

"That little rag?" Malvinia shrugged. "They're getting real tired of you, Judge," she said flatly. "I hear you are both in danger since you got all that stuff about Sickels off your chest."

"Who says that?"

"Never mind," she replied. "You can't win. You're up against too much."

"We're up against shit," he said obstinately, staring at the ground. A sigh, unexpected, unbidden, shook his body. "Lordy!" he said in despair, "if I can't believe in the woman, what in hell's this case been all about?"

Malvinia shrugged and spat.

Was he wrong? Or in her queer stare had he seen contempt?

He lay in the rocking berth, conscious of the woman in the berth below. Every fiber ached for her. So much oddness was suddenly significant—impulsive acts, bubbling aimless laughter, garrulity, Nellie . . .

What was that really all about? How far had the business gone? The thick hot blood collected at his throat. He swung out on the brace and peered into the lower berth. The white delicate neck arched and defenseless, the breasts swelling at her nightgown, could be dimly seen. Her fragility made him ache.

457

She looked directly up. "Mark," she said starkly. "Come here with me! Please?"

"Just a minute," he whispered, reluctantly. The passageway was deserted. No one was about. He left for the lavatory. A snoring porter opened a bloodshot eye, stared, lapsed asleep, drooping. He returned, tormented and undecided, then shook his head and, panting, climbed back to his own berth.

Two hours later the curtains rustled. "McAllen, Judge," the conductor whispered. "Twenty minutes."

The wind was cold on the dark and almost deserted station. A familiar figure, wrapped in sheepskins, was waiting.

"Wa'al," Cudahey drawled, "Judge. Ma'am. You all've had your fun. Now can we just settle down and practice law?"

He walked slowly, ponderously, with great deliberation, oblivious to the world. The massive shoulders stooped forward as he stared at the cold ruts at his feet.

"Mornin', Judge," someone said.

He walked on. His old shingle, freshly painted, gilt on white, was spotless and gleaming. The precious library was cleaned, smelling of neatsfoot oil and furniture polish. His hands were trembling as he sank into the comfort of the old leather chair and lit a cigar. Cudahey tilted his eyeshade and summed up the position.

Everything was standing still. The Sickels injunction was in effect, freezing the judgment of marriage and divorce in the State Court. And five months off in the Federal Circuit Court on the August calendar for trial, there loomed the indictments for criminal assault.

"Oh, Jesus!" Trumbull stood and began to pace the familiar room. "Sickels! Sickels!" he grated. "I hold him responsible. The man pollutes the air. Joe, I swore I'd tear down that edifice of injustice, brick by brick! And now I feel so unsure. I've got so many hostages to my purpose . . ." He halted. "Jail's done something to us. I don't know where I'm going, what I'm doing. For the first time in my life, I feel shaken by the prospect. I've had a suggestion to jump bail. . . ."

He described his talk with Malvinia at Las Flores.

Cudahey wet his mouth, dismayed by the haggard mask of desperation. "Hell, Judge, this ain't like you. You can't run from the law. Not you! You made the law in these parts. So what's your choice, except to go in and fight?"

Trumbull touched his mouth uncertainly and looked off. "How in hell did it ever come to happen to me at my age?"

An uneasy silence passed.

"Well, let's get to work," Trumbull said despondently, rolling up his sleeves and starting a list of witnesses grown cold indeed. The dust was choking.

The practice was slow to pick up. The Pima admired and respected his defiance of the hated federal judges, but he suffered from the antagonism of the courts and the unwillingness of litigants to share his handicap. He attended the courts, saw some clients, but it was noticed that he was not the same man. He disputed bills, denied small debts, and missed calendar calls. It was the belief that he was laboring under strong mental pressure, pressure, it was surmised, that stemmed not only from the conflict of the Hagerman matter, but from social isolation. The Pima had not lost confidence in the honorable man who best knew his wife's claims to chastity, but her notoriety was more than it was ready to accept.

A hired girl quit. Others came and left complaining of demanding orders for impossible cleanliness. A sole dinner party attended only by men saw Jessica gay beyond words, but the guests stayed sober and were glad to leave early.

In June, Tom Wickwire took the morning train and arrived at McAllen about noon. It was a hot day with a brazen sky. The station, except for a watchful deputy sheriff, was empty. He walked about the dusty city, dropped in on the *Democrat*, chatted with its editor, learned that the Trumbulls were being dogged by detectives, and sounded opinion in a local saloon. Finally he asked directions, hired a rig, and drove to the edge of town. He found Trumbull and Jessica cutting flowers in their front garden. As he lifted the latch to pass the gate, he heard (and would later so testify) Trumbull say hoarsely, "Not a word," and Jessica reply, "Agreed. Not a single word."

Jessica was in a simple cotton frock and wore gloves. She was still a striking woman. Wickwire, who was an observer of details, noticed the thickened waist and a subtle masculinity of what were now handsome, rather than beautiful, features. Trumbull was a shock. He had aged badly since the interview at the Alameda County Jail and has lost perhaps forty pounds. He rolled down his sleeves and invited the reporter to the porch.

They rocked and talked weather, crops, politics, and a pig ranch Jessica had in mind to buy. Jessica loved pigs, she proclaimed; they were cute when little, and much maligned. "Sho!" she laughed, running on. "Judge Trumbull hates pigs, but I don't see why. They're not half so hateful as people! Especially with hickory smoke—"

"Dear," Trumbull said.

Jessica stopped instantly. "Sorry. Say, Tom, what about some buttermilk to cool you off? You don't mind if I call you Tom?"

"Not a bit, ma'am," Wickwire said. Jessica left. Trumbull was silent, sunk in his own thoughts. "Oh, here we are," she said buoyantly, returning with a crock of buttermilk. She served and started on her case, denouncing all her enemies, but omitting Hagerman from the list. Wickwire raised his brows.

"Lands, that's not surprising," she said pensively, catching her breath. "The Sen had real good qualities, but he was badly influenced. I think of him fondly, and if I didn't, well, *de mortuis*, as he used to say. He was wise in many ways. I only wish the children had been more kindly to us in his lifetime. When I give my lecture, I mean to be fair to his memory." She kept talking, mixing past, present, and future. Trumbull was gentle and quiet.

"Now, dear," he said finally.

"Yes." She sat to attention, hands folded, wearing a sweet and submissive expression. "How's the buttermilk? Lumpy?"

"No, no, fine," Wickwire said. He was there to interview Trumbull on his relations with Sickels.

Trumbull shrugged. "Don't you fellers ever get tired of the reiteration? Now what's the special occasion?"

Wickwire rocked, not enjoying the view of the fields shimmering in the heat. Across the railroad tracks he had a view of a watering tank and a clump of ragged eucalyptus. The house, surrounded by a white picket fence, sat alone on a dusty road and faced a sign marked *Ciudad Jardín*. The house itself, from what he saw through the curtains, seemed pleasant enough. Except for the sense of discomfort, the Trumbulls, he thought, were like any of the easygoing friendly ranchers of the Pima. He said, "Well, Sickels returns to California tomorrow and all the papers are full of the probability of your meeting up. They're saying that Sickels is a man who always held his own; that he had enough experience as a young man to know how to defend himself; that if you meet up, you'll make an attack and there'll be trouble. That's the tenor, and I'm here to get your views."

Trumbull stared into the distance. "What papers are saying that?"

"All the papers, more or less," Wickwire replied. "My paper, the *Call*, the *Chronicle*. Also the *Hornet*."

"Appears as though they want the trouble," Trumbull muttered. "Why d'you fellers always want to pin me down? I don't want to be interviewed about these things. What if he's a brave man? What of it? What's it to do with me?"

"You have said intolerable things."

"Did I? What I had to say, I put in print, and there's been no response and I expect none. Evidently I've got business with the Court, not with Mr. Sickels."

Wickwire made a note. "Then there won't be trouble? Can I say that?"

The burning eyes turned. "I'll repeat this for the last time. I carry no weapon. I do not intend to injure Mr. Sickels bodily, but I have given my written word, that if we meet—which I will not seek—I will slap his face, and let him decide the course. Nothing"—a fist smote the chair—"nothing can change my mind except one thing—justice in his court. If so, the trouble will pass. If not. . . ."

Wickwire scribbled a note. He looked up. "What are you looking for?"

"A jury verdict of acquittal," Trumbull replied.

Wickwire glanced at Jessica. "You admitted that Mrs. Trumbull was in contempt. Isn't she then also guilty of assault?"

"No!"

"Oh? Why not?"

"She was intolerably provoked," Trumbull said. "I admit the duty of judges to judge and lawyers to obey, but you must see her situation. The Supreme Court of California at Sacramento had upheld her marriage on appeal. That was presumably final. In the face of that judgment for anyone, even a federal judge protected by his office, not only to deny her chastity, but gratuitously to impute other indecencies was an outrage. No California jury of men will fail to vindicate the woman, nor rebuke the cowardly judge."

Jessica smiled in friendly fashion. "But, Judge," Wickwire

461

said, "the federal judges don't recognize the California judgment."

"What's that to us?" Trumbull retorted. "The Hebrews don't recognize the Pope, but he's still the Pope!" Harsh laughter burst out. "Read my last brief on their appeal to Sacramento, sir! I show the history of our legal institutions . . ." He paused. "Never mind! It's a gross usurpation, but perhaps their last. It only takes the Congress to clip their wings. What the people have granted they can take away. If you'll recollect, in the Cadwallader case they so aroused the people's fury that the Congress cut off a large area of their appellate pretensions. And might well do so again. The next spark may well enkindle such a blaze of war in this land as will never go out!"

Wickwire pulled at his ear. "War? Come, Judge! Isn't that extreme?"

Trumbull laughed, not pleasantly. "We've just finished a war. What was the pretext but a test case. So who can say? Nothing, not death, not love, is stronger than the cry for justice in the land. And if not? Then not, but I'll have made my statement. But I'd rather not discuss it further," he concluded restlessly.

The interview went on but without further value. Wickwire found Trumbull evasive and uncommunicative. "Almost furtive, strange," appeared in his notes. Jessica interjected irrelevancies; among other things, she talked of a proposed California cookbook for brides, but was it four cups of cooked rice she wanted for her *arroz con pollo,* or two cups of rice, cooked? Wickwire promised to consult his wife, smiled, and left.

"Tom! Oh, Tom!" Jessica impulsively followed to the gate. She handed over a bag of gingersnaps and lowered her voice. "D'ye ever see Theo Hagerman?" she whispered. "Is he well? He wanted to marry me too, you know? And would have, if the Senator wasn't so overpowering."

Wickwire paused. "I believe he's living in New York."

"I hear he's married. Is his wife nice?"

"I have no idea."

"I'll bet she's rich," Jessica decided. "Well, too bad! It's just so unfortunate these aren't the times when the Code prevailed, otherwise that scut Sickels might have a chance to try his shot against mine. It's all in my lecture." She patted his hand and went back to the porch.

Wickwire touched his hat and drove off. The gingersnaps were like rocks, weeks old, and he threw them away.

"Christ! How does he stand it?" he thought.

A week later, disaster struck.

In a crushing moment, a newly elected bench of the Supreme Court of California, acting on an old motion by Galindez to rehear his appeal, reversed all prior decisions, and obliterated Jessica's marriage, on a point of law novel to the case—that the marriage, being secret, would not be recognized in California.

"Salted!" Trumbull cried in disbelief. "It's infamous! What can one do in the face of millions?" The judgment of the state, the rock of his position, was gone. The secrecy! That was it! He had smelled it that day—eons ago, when the case had come into his office. If only he had heeded instinct! If he had not rushed in like a fool! If! If! If!

That night, working till dawn, he drafted a last motion for reargument based on the clear doctrine that the Supreme Court of California, having once determined the matter, could not reverse its prior judgment of the case. It was unassailable law, but he had not the least sense of conviction in his brief.

Ahead lay the interminable summer and a trial at the bar of criminal justice.

Chapter Twenty-Five

The Collins Saloon at California and Montgomery was doing a fair business. The man leaning against the building was facing the sun. The world through closed lids was warm and crimson. The sour smells from the Saloon were pleasant. He was doing nothing, thinking nothing.

The traffic through the swinging doors went on. He mashed a fly against his forehead and waited. The crimson world was filled with pleasant visions of hope and purpose and future things. He had been waiting for weeks for a message.

The following morning a blue typewritten slip was delivered to his home. He dressed in a striped blue business suit, selected a dark string tie, donned a broad-brimmed hat, and studied the mirror. It was a face exactly to his taste.

He picked up a small cardboard box and rattled it. He threw the contents—a half dozen flat shiny badges—on the bed. With a satisfied nod, he slipped the newest, a gold star-shaped badge, into a trousers pocket. He examined a wallet and frowned. Rent! He was living with a married sister, she would wait but he liked things tidy.

A sound of shouting children brought him to a yard. An oldish young woman was hanging out wash.

"Going again?" she said without tone.

"Let's see. That was ten months at three dollars a month makes it thirty dollars." He blinked at the children, told his sister to take care of a doctor's bill for him, and left.

He counted the telephone wires, walked along Market Street, and then along Montgomery. Finally, wiping a sweatband, he entered the United States Assayers' Building. He walked up to the third floor and entered the Marshal's Office.

"Send him in," Patterson called out.

Sickels followed the porter to the sleeping car. The earlier passengers had already got into shirt sleeves, loosened shoelaces and belts, and were preparing for the long run south.

A cough attracted his attention. The quiet man in the opposite section looked up from a book, then returned to the vestibule.

Sickels shivered.

It was six thirty by his watch. That would mean Los Angeles by about sunup. He folded his coat fastidiously, affixed his spectacles, and settled to the evening newspapers. He was longing for his berth, but it was daylight, and it seemed too early. He dismissed all this and looked across the aisle.

Now, with his spectacles, he could make out the gaudy cover: *Exciting Times in Cochise County,* by U.S. Marshal Elmer Utt. Sickels watched the man for a bit. A coarse impassive face, sharp in profile with a lipless mouth told him nothing. The cold eyes rose and met his own.

"Looks interesting," Sickels said.

"Well, I knew the man." The response was utmost contempt.

464

A half hour later the train was racing south, rocking sickeningly on the badly graded road bed.

"First call! First call!"

The quiet man yawned, rose, and left. A few minutes later, Sickels put down his papers and went to the dining car. The quiet man was seated at a table for two, back to the galley. The seat opposite was vacant. "Kiser," he said, indicating the empty place. "Jim Kiser. I'm real pleased."

"How d'ye do," Sickels said glumly and sat. He disliked riding backward but felt disinclined to argue the point.

"I'm working on pork chops and gravy. What's your'n?"

"Just coffee."

"We're all right for now," Kiser said, "so you might as well eat up. What about these blue points on the shell? They're real delicious, I'm told."

Kiser was attentive to his food. Occasionally, as some passing object attracted attention, he punctuated the silence. "Angus," he remarked, jerked a thumb at a cluster of staring cattle. "Chino Lake," was another observation. Sickels was silent and fretful. Precisely what did Kiser understand his orders to be? he finally asked.

"My orders are to carry this out in a quiet way, to accompany you everywhere, but not to make my presence known."

"You're not wearing the badge?"

"I'm known for a peace officer, but not here," Kiser said evenly. "How would it look if they could force a federal judge to take a bodyguard while carrying out his judicial duties? Don't worry about the badge."

"I assume those orders are in writing? Where are they now?"

"In the marshal's safe," Kiser said.

"Of course, I don't believe in violence," Sickels said slowly.

"Then why give in to it?" Kiser replied. "That's my main criticism of these half-wits. They won't see that the only way to deal with violence is to stamp it out. But no! They'll twitter, every time, while the other side has got their balls. However, you can take it easy. Once we have got through the Pima, they won't move. We know that."

"Know that? How so?"

"Never mind, we just know. Why not let us handle this situation, Judge? We understand the mentality. You don't."

Sickels sighed. "Very well, do your duty. I cannot as a judge say otherwise."

Kiser nodded. "I expected that," he said coolly. "Could you stand more coffee? Or would you like to go back and rest?"

When they returned, the berths were made up. Sickels went to bed at once. Every stop along the route—Franklin, Chico, Petersville, McAllen, Ashkelon, Locust, Bitter Springs —he examined his watch nervously. He had an impression that Kiser was dead to the world.

"Los Angeles. Los Angeles."

Kiser got out stiffly and looked about keenly, but the gesture was unnecessary. The lazy little city was still overcast. He summoned a carriage and drove off with Sickels to the Westminster Hotel, not far from the federal courts. They hired adjacent rooms and settled to a regime. Sickels read opinions in the Circuit Court on an important land case that had been hanging fire for a year, heard applications for a writ of habeas corpus, and for an injunction in a complicated water case in San Diego County. Kiser attended all court sessions and, since the endless droning was Greek to him, passed the time in reading the saga of the famous U.S. Marshal Elmer Utt. All shit! he thought with contempt. Shit and dime novels!

Time dragged, but the hotel was comfortable, the food was good, and he was meeting real nice people who refused to let him spend a dime. He had no complaints.

It was mid-August. The Pima was yellow and baked in the long hot months of unending sun. The heated air shimmered under the blaze from the Coastal Range to the Sierras. The interminable weeks of endless preparation for the trial went on.

Trumbull rose late and made his own breakfast. He left Jessica sleeping and walked to his office through a hot deserted city. His shoulders were bowed.

He stopped at the depot and paid for two coach seats the next Tuesday to Oakland. The Flyer would leave McAllen at two fifty-five in the morning and reach the terminus by eight.

"Thank 'ee, Mr. Ford," he said, counting change. "Can we manage to reserve those seats?"

"We don't reserve coach seats," the agent replied.

"I know, but perhaps informally?"

"I don't see how."

"Oh, you can manage," Trumbull said, "when you telegraph in your report on me."

"Report? What report?" The agent seemed disturbed.

"Well, perhaps I'm mistaken," Trumbull's voice was rasping. "Someone's been filing reports. But never mind. I'll take our chances on finding seats," he said, and went on. The heat was intolerable.

The office was full of echoes. He took off his tie and collar and fell into the old leather chair. It was unfamiliar and—strangely—so was the barren chamber. Cudahey brought the mail.

"Later," Trumbull said in a whisper. "I ain't slept a wink in weeks, Joe. Not a blessed wink. I'm troubled about my wife. Real troubled. Sometimes . . ." He broke off with a gray smile. "I could plead guilty," he said hopefully. "Mebbe Sickels'd let Mrs. Trumbull get off?"

"D'ye think it likely?" Cudahey said.

Trumbull shrugged. "It's me he's after," he said slowly, "but I cannot put Mrs. Trumbull through any further humiliation. She's proud, Joe. Real proud, and smart! Smartest woman I've ever met. Most uncommon grasp of law. But she ain't well. I ain't sure I'd be justified to go on."

Oh, Lordy! Cudahey thought. He said, "Would Mrs. Trumbull agree?"

Trumbull looked aside. "She'll hear nothing but to go on with the fight. She's got the spirit and means to win. How can I blame her?" he said with simple wonder. "Her life—both our lives—and honor are at stake. And where's that found? On the moon? I never yet gave up a just cause till I've won—or pressed to the limit. Anything less would accept dishonor and I don't know how! I simply don't! Do I make any kind of sense?"

Cudahey said gravely, "You make sense, Judge."

"I wish I felt so. I'm feeling some changes. Getting forgetful. Sometimes, I . . . well! I dunno, Joe, I just dunno." His gaze turned inward. "But we still can win!" Trumbull exclaimed violently, striking the desk. "I'm convinced on it! We'll blow this criminal prosecution sky-high and come back! One scrap of new evidence! One morsel of fresh proof and we'll come back for a new trial. We'll never let this rest!"

"Then you don't mean to beg out?" Cudahey said patiently. "Judge, what's got into you lately? Why d'you keep saying things you can't mean?"

Trumbull sighed. "Just to hear myself talk, I reckon. I never pulled a knife or assaulted the marshall. Sickels lied, Joe. Lied on the record, and I've no way to show it. It's more than I can live with." He forced a taut smile. "Have you got some of that whiskey left?"

Cudahey brought a bottle. "Better read your mail," he said.

Trumbull swallowed a whiskey, then another. It had no effect. He turned to the envelope on the silver salver. He read slowly, almost without comprehension, and then lost color. The letter from Archbishop Tosefa gave a last touch of despair.

My dear Judge Trumbull,

I regret to report failure of any intelligence of your Pedro Ramirez. If he exists, he is not known in California or Mexico. Or even Spain or South America, to our knowledge. It is strange that no one of his striking appearance has come to our attention in these years of earnest inquiries. Does he exist or is he a chimera?

I have this to add. If the description fitted your forger, Maldonado, it cannot now affect your case. I have word that Maldonado died in Mazatlán fifteen years ago. Perhaps (I hesitate to suggest this) Mrs. Trumbull got her description from Mr. Hagerman or even from Mr. Dabney when she visited the Spanish Archives. I regret nothing is resolved.

I grieve for your predicament and wish I could help. Go with God, my dear friend, and my best wishes.

With deepest respect, I am,
Juan Tosefa ✠ Abp

Trumbull handed over the letter. "Well, it makes no difference now," he said, touching a trembling hand to his mouth. "It's come too late, even if it were favorable. File it, hey?"

Cudahey put the letter aside. "Anything else?"

Trumbull sat in desolation. "No. Nothing," he said painfully. "Not for the moment. I reckon we ought to tidy things up. Close files. Make a new Will, mebbe. Something. I really cannot think." He sat wordless. What in hell was meant by "deepest respect"?

"Ramirez!" Trumbull said softly, mockingly. "Peed-ro Ramir-ez! Lordy!" After a time, he gave up and left for home.

Trumbull turned to the rising moon. He was thinking of the criminal trial ahead, struggling to reconstruct the prepared outline for the defense. He could not think, and that was frightening. He ignored the stirring at his side.

"Mark, you've got to kill those mice," Jessica said with desperation. "They're stinking up the bathroom. They're filthy. They bring diseases and things. The toilet paper's glowing. I couldn't use it because of them and you just lie there!"

That again! he thought with despair. "Sugar," he said, touching her hair, "there's nothing wrong with the toilet paper. I changed it, just before you went in."

"Then why do I have this feeling?"

"You're nervous, and it's natural to imagine things. Now don't give it a thought. We've got to hang on till we're through this trial and then I'll take you away, Jess. Go to Europe, maybe. We'll put all this behind us. Would you like that?"

Her answer was a kiss, thrusting into his mouth. He turned his head. "Please, please," she said, kissing desperately. "Let me make you happy, Mark! Oh, it may be the last time! Please? Please?" She covered his eyes, probed his ears, gnawed his beard, and went lower. Gasping, she sank under the bedclothes and reached under the nightgown.

"Oh, sugar, stop trying," he said.

"No!" She rose on her knees and pulled off her nightgown. "Am I still lovely? Am I? Am I?" she demanded in an odd strained voice. He nodded. "Then why don't you take me? Don't you love me anymore?"

In the dim light, she was indeed still lovely, he thought, large breasts outthrust, belly rounded and bold, the thick graying hair, falling in tresses to the swelling hips. Her eyes were tragic. "I love you," he said.

"Then do something!" She placed his hand between her thighs and squatted against her heels. From this position she smiled invitingly and leaned forward. Her breasts grazed his chest. "Hurt me," she whispered fiercely. "Hurt me hard. Do it! Do it, Mark! Do it!"

"Jess," he said reproachfully.

"Then I'll hurt *you!*" She threw back the covers, angered,

469

and clutched the humid tangle. "I can, you know!" she said threateningly. Pain stabbed—cold, sickening—then he felt a wet, hot mouth upon him. She probed desperately, licking, frantic. A bitch's hind quarters were at his face. "Mark, what's gone wrong?" she moaned. "What's happened?"

"It's nothing," he said despondently. The matter of the Archbishop's letter was on his tongue. "Truly nothing. I'll tell you at breakfast."

"Oh, that damned trial!" she cried and threw herself aside in a fury. "Never mind explaining!" she smoldered. "Men! What in hell do I need with men? You don't even try anymore! Oh, hell!"

"I don't like that language," he said, offended.

"What a stick you are!" she burst out, and fell back on the pillow. He waited for the paroxysm to end. "What is it? Tell me," he said gently, touching her.

"I think my lump has come back!" she said starkly. "Does that satisfy you? You'll be shed of me quick enough! Go! I'll face the Court alone! I don't need you! I'll be dead soon enough."

"There's no lump and you know it," he sighed.

A bird was singing in the lemon tree. Hard agate eyes searched his, gleamed with fear. "Mark, I love you so very much! Why won't anyone ever love me back?" She threw back her head and wept without restraint. The exposed slender throat was convulsive and bare.

"Mark, sweetie?" she gasped finally, wiping her eyes. "Take me to the bathroom? I'm afraid to go alone."

The chamber smelled of rough plaster and paint. The tiles were cool to his naked feet. "Dearest, you're not ashamed of me?" she whispered apologetically, clutching his hand to her cheek. "No, of course not," he replied. She was silent. "I want to but I cannot," she said. "You must try," he said with pain, stroking her hair, "and then you'll sleep."

"Oh, Mark," she said, returning to bed, "without you I'd die."

"Good night, dear," he said and left for the parlor. He lay on the sofa and covered his eyes.

"Oh, Alex!" he muttered childishly. "What'll I do? Tell me."

At dawn he drove into town and roused the Western Union office. A telegram went off begging Malvinia to come without delay.

It was dusk when the rapper struck. Jessica answered. "Oh, it's you," she exclaimed excitedly. "What in hell brings you here? I didn't send for you."

Malvinia said nothing.

"Well, come in if you must," Jessica said resentfully, "But I don't need you. I'm as clear as a bell."

The business in Los Angeles concluded, but Sickels, contrary to custom, lingered in the dusty little city. He moped, read the newspapers, and remained in his suite, writing letters. He was only too aware of the man across the hall.

"When in hell do we leave?" he snarled.

"I'll let you know, Judge," Kiser replied.

A week later, Kiser knocked and entered with a telegram from San Francisco. Two sections were reserved for Monday, August 12, on the Flyer. Sickels looked up from breakfast with a worried frown.

"Well, I would prefer to leave sooner," he said, drawing a breath, "but since I have put myself in your hands entirely, I'll do as you bid."

"We leave Monday," Kiser repeated. "I'll ask you to be packed and ready by eleven. It leaves the depot at one thirty o'clock, but I'll ask you to board at Loma Avenue. I wouldn't want your movements advertised."

"As you say, Marshal," Sickels said grimly. "Although, I must say, I find this skulking most disagreeable. Loma Avenue it is."

Number 18, the northbound Oakland passenger train, was laboring through the pass leading north through the San Gabriel Range. The orange groves and real estate subdivisions of Los Angeles were left far behind. They were entering the vast hot, desiccated valley. The passengers were in shirt sleeves, collars removed, shoes loose, hot and apathetic. The sun, enormous and crimson, settled behind the coastal ranges to the west. Suddenly it was night.

"Your berth's ready, Judge," the porter said deferentially. The wind was cold, and Sickels was more than glad to turn in early. "What about you?" he asked.

"Not likely to sleep tonight," Kiser replied. "Sleep tight, Judge. I'll be on hand." He left for the men's lounge, where he settled down for the run.

"Whoo-hee!" the porter said, collapsing. "Sure is hard work, I tell you!"

471

"Each to his own," Kiser said reflectively, swaying with the train. "Actually, it's a question of education. If a man's got it, he can go anyplace in the world. If not, what's he add up to? Nothing!"

"That's so true," the porter said agreeably.

Kiser took out a notebook. "What actual stops do we make before McAllen?"

"You'd have to ask the conductor."

"I'm asking you."

The porter frowned dubiously. It could vary, he thought, depending on orders from the station agents, but the scheduled stops—roughly at half-hourly intervals for a stretch, then hourly intervals—would include Wilmot and Slade. After Independence came Bitter Spring, Locust, Solitaire, Poretz, Ashkelon, McAllen. And then? Well, Petersville, Chico, Pima, Pima Junction, Franklin, Hog Junction, and Oakland.

Kiser drew a circle around McAllen. "George?"

"Sir?"

"What time do we get to McAllen?"

"Two thirty, more or less."

Kiser made a note and glanced at his watch. "Four hours from now. Can you wake me up before we reach the station? Can you do that?"

"Yes, sir. I can do that."

Kiser handed over a silver dollar and returned to his berth. His boots went into the clothes hammock. A heavy Navy Colt revolver went to the shelf above his head. He lay, fully dressed, outstretched, fingering his badge of office. The landscape fled past in darkness. The night was soft and luminous with a crescent moon rising in the east. The soft pounding in his ear was his pulse. He might have dozed, or perhaps not. In any case, he awoke with a sense that time had passed. The curtain was rustling. It was the porter.

"Mr. Kiser, sir! It's McAllen."

Kiser was instantly alert. He pulled on his shoes, stuck the Colt revolver in his belt, and got out. He hit the platform as the train came to a halt. He swung off immediately and studied the crowd. Several scores of passengers were boarding the coaches ahead—drummers, ranchers, businessmen intent on reaching San Francisco before noon. Mail pouches and freight were being exchanged at the baggage cars. And then in the line of passengers could be seen the gaunt bowed figure of Trumbull and his wife, accompanied by a tall black woman in a shovel hat. Kiser drew back in the shadows.

"Board! Bo-oard!"

Sickels turned from the window, listening to the sounds of the car. Voices murmured, went silent, the familiar footsteps of the conductor disappeared. "Sst! Marshal?" he called. The curtains parted and Kiser looked in. "What's up?" Sickels said.

Kiser said in an undertone. "They have got on the train, I think."

"They? Who's they?"

"I think Judge Trumbull and his wife."

"What's that mean, think?"

"I couldn't be sure," Kiser said evenly. "It was dark and only an impression. I'll have to make sure by asking around."

Sickels was silent. "Well, I hope they sleep well," he said and turned on his side.

The engine bell was tolling.

Jessica leaned forward. "Something wrong, my dear? You're not worried?"

Ttrumbull shook his head. "No."

"Then say something. You look so glum," she whispered.

Trumbull forced a strained smile. "Nothing to say. I'm just thinking ahead."

"You're not angry, then?"

"No."

"Well, I can't wait to get this over," she said with conviction. "It'll be a vindication, Mark! I'll be letter-perfect; you'll see!"

The great driving wheels slipped, spun, gripped, and turned slowly at first, then faster.

Jessica said sharply, "Don't rub your eyes, Mark."

"Yes, dear," he said.

"You must be hungry. What time is it?"

"Three fifteen."

"It seems later."

"No. My watch is right."

"I can't believe it. Sir! Mister!" Jessica leaned across the aisle. She awoke a grumpy grain merchant with a shake and verified the time. "I could have sworn!" she muttered. "Just seems endless." She leaned forward. "Vinnie? I'm starved. Did you pack the chicken sandwiches?"

Malvinia opened her eyes. "You said not to bother."

"I never!"

"Then you never," Malvinia said tiredly. "Try to get some rest, Jess. You've been driving real frantic. There's no sandwiches."

"This beats everything. Well, we'll have breakfast at Pima Junction," Jessica said disconsolately." She was silent. "Sickels! I could scratch his eyes out," she said viciously. "I just cannot wait to have him face you, Mark! To have you rip aside his corrupt mask! It's all too disgraceful!"

"Dearest, please!" Trumbull murmured.

"Well, I don't care who hears!"

They rode on through the darkness, swaying in unison.

Kiser studied his watch. Two hours to Petersville. He lay in his berth and continued awake until the clanging signal announced Petersville. He arose quietly and left the car. Milk cans were being loaded ahead. The conductor, a bluff red-faced man, was on the platform flailing his arms against the cold. Kiser took the conductor aside and showed his badge. "Can we talk?"

The conductor nodded. "Shoot."

Kiser rubbed his chin. "I'll have to ask you to remember everything clearly in case we run into trouble. Can you confirm if Judge Trumbull and Mrs. Trumbull got on this train at McAllen?"

"Yes, sir, they did," the conductor said.

"Any special reason why they might take this particular train?"

"No-o," the conductor replied. "Except that it gets 'em to Oakland for the early ferry. This is the one they usually take."

"Do they know Justice Sickels is aboard?"

"I've got no idea."

"But it's possible?" Kiser persisted.

"Everything is possible," the conductor replied.

"I see. Now, is there any officer who might meet this train at Pima Junction?"

"Yes, a constable is always supposed to be there when the trains come in," the conductor said uneasily. The banging of milk cans came to an end. A signal was made from the freight car for the "all clear." Kiser said, "I'll ask you to telegraph ahead to have that constable there. Tell him that Justice Sickels is here on board, also the Trumbulls, and to prepare to arrest them at once if they make trouble. Tell him I'll give any help I can. Can you do that?"

"I will do so," the conductor replied.

Kiser took the blue lapel firmly. "Be sure you do," he said distinctly, "because I mean to make a report on this. Where are the Trumbulls now?"

The conductor studied the clutching hand. "In the second coach past the sleeper. The smoker is between."

Kiser dropped the lapel. "Well, I'll be in the smoker. We are doing our best to avoid any kind of encounter whatsoever. So I do not want the Trumbulls to know the location of Sickels. Is that clear?"

"Clear enough," the conductor replied. "Now I've got to move this string along. Board! Board!" he shouted, making the high sign.

The train rolled along.

Kiser returned to the smoker and examined his watch. Two hours to Pima Junction. He sat quietly, smoking, keeping his eye on the coach ahead. At Chico, he arose and went back to the vestibule of the sleeper. The conductor was ticking off his cash and tickets and introduced him to Mr. Ephraim Robbins, president of the Chico Savings and Loan Society.

The conductor explained that Kiser was fearful of trouble ahead with Trumbull.

Robbins remarked that trouble was unlikely. He had resided in the Pima for over thirty years and had known Trumbull as attorney and adviser for and against in lawsuits and business ventures. He did not think Trumbull was quarrelsome at all.

Kiser said, "Well, mister, if Judge Trumbull were to make a threat, would he carry out his intention, in your opinion?

Robbins shrugged. "I'd take his word," he said. "But I have not heard of any bodily threat, merely that he would affront Sickels by pulling his nose, or slapping his face. Judge Trumbull is a precise man. He will do exactly what he said."

Kiser said, "He counts on Justice Sickels to resent the affront and will then reply with a deadly assault. Let's hope he proves wise enough not to try." He returned to the smoker. He struck up a conversation with Mr. Abraham Humperdink, proprietor of the hotel and railway eatinghouse at Pima Junction, and again expressed his fears that the Trumbulls would make trouble and inquired about the security of patrons of that dining place. Humperdink changed his seat with a marked air of dislike. Kiser seemed unaffected. He sat facing the coach ahead, smoking cigar after cigar.

"What are you thinking, Mark?"

"Nothing. Nothing."

"Something's happened. You've had bad news."

"I tell 'ee, nothing's happened."

"I wish I could believe that."

"Stop picking at scabs, then," Trumbull said irritably.

Jessica bit her lip. "Well, I'd like to change my seat. I feel the rattling."

"You have changed twice," Trumbull said.

"I'll change again if I like. Will you ask those people to move?"

"I cannot ask them to change."

"If you don't, I will," Jessica replied with an edge.

"I dislike this," Trumbull said.

The Pintsch lamps, with their ghastly light, were turned off. There were snores in the darkness and a stale smell of humanity. Trumbull stumbled forward, spoke patiently in an undertone with a family group, explained his wife's idiosyncrasy, and arranged to change seats.

"Is this satisfactory?" he said finally.

"Not really," Jessica replied, twisting about. She plumped her handbag against the side of the car. "But at least this way I've got an eye on 'em."

"Eye? What does that mean?"

"I am ready for 'em," Jessica said significantly. "If you won't take precautions, I will. I've got my pistol."

Trumbull froze. "Pistol? Lordy, where'd you get it?"

"Never you mind. If you're blind to danger, I'm not. I've not traveled without my gun for the past six months."

Trumbull stared. "I wouldn't want another sentence for contempt," he said in a strained voice. "It'd just play into their hands."

"Would it?" she said with indifference. "I reckon it'll be cheap at the price. I'd just as soon be charged with a homicide, if it comes to that!"

Trumbull glanced down the aisle. Malvinia was dozing. He turned back to Jessica. "Give me that gun," he whispered.

"No," she said.

"You must give it to me."

"I shall not. I will not give up my protection!"

He leaned forward. "If we are in danger, this'd be precisely the justification. You'll be rid of that before we reach the city? I want your promise."

The entire exchange was furtive and in low tones. She laughed and patted his wrist. "You're such a ninny, Mark! Pooh! I only said it for effect. Oh, say! Did you remember to pay the butcher? Lands! For the putrid meat he sells, it's a wonder he stays in business! Can't we *not* pay? Claim unfitness or something? He's a real robber."

"Dear!" he broke in.

"Yes?"

"There is a trial ahead," he said. "Can you not be calm? You must, you know."

"Very well, provided you tell what's on your mind. You tend to eat your craw, but what's the good? What is it? Is it only the trial? Tell me!"

"My dear . . ." he said miserably and broke off. "You told me the truth, did you not? That man, Ramirez, was in Hagerman's office that day?"

"Of course," she said tranquilly.

"You actually saw such a man? You could not have said that for effect too?"

"Certainly not! I'm not that crazy to invent such things. Ramirez was as real as your nose. Lands! Next you'll ask if I forged the Senator's hand? Is that it?" An intense peculiar smile formed. "Well, I didn't, but if I did—which I still deny —be sure it was only to get the Senator to do the right thing. I sure never thought it would ever come to court. I'd be fully justified. You said yourself no man in California would blame me. Oh, my dear," she said indulgently, touching his cheek, "don't have doubts. Don't ever have doubts! Oh, look!" she said. Broad rays of dawn were dispersing in the east. "Isn't that a new water tank? If that new irrigation comes through, this acreage should go sky-high . . ." She rattled on with rising vehemence, then broke off.

"Anything wrong, my dear?" she asked anxiously. "You look so gray." He shook his head, wordless. The train was fleeing north to a point to which he had been driving, it would seem, all his life. "Good! I am sure of you, Mark," she said with satisfaction, "and you'll win my case for me, I've no doubt!" He had a sudden impression of a man's face cold with calculation looking at him through hers. It was a fleeting impression, obscene and shocking beyond words. She smoothed her hair gracefully and turned back to the window, and it was gone. A chasm had opened at his feet.

Dear God! he thought in despair. What's happened to me? What's become of Mark Trumbull?

Daylight flooded the great valley of the Pima.

"Mark, dear?" Jessica said, shaking him. "We're here. Let's have some food. We'll feel better."

Trumbull looked numb. "Is it hot?"

"Hot, no. It's a real chilly morning."

"Funny. I thought it was hot. Very well."

"Go ahead, I'm half asleep," Malvinia said.

Trumbull rose, feeling flushed. There was a surge of people. "Easy, Judge," a voice said as he stumbled in a world gone unreal.

The dining room was large and noisy and seemed unusually full. A partition hid the kitchen door. Opposite, a door led to the barroom and the depot. Large windows of frosted glass were bright. A score of plain square tables covered with cloths filled the room. Cutlery sprouted from glasses on each table. Cheerful waitresses in Elsie collars were rushing trays to worn travelers. Trumbull led Jessica to a far corner, oblivious to greetings. Some were to testify that his manner was downhearted indeed.

"Morning, Judge. Ma'am," a waitress sang out.

Jessica threw back her coat and looked about with serenity. "My dear, would you like me to order something?" she said.

"Hey? Oh, I'll take anything. Please yourself."

"Is there something wrong?"

"No. Just seems there's lots of flies," Trumbull replied, staring at the strands of dangling flypaper. "Wonder where they're from?"

"From the stables, most likely."

"Yes, but how do they get here?"

Jessica frowned. "Why, they fly here, I reckon." She gave the waitress precise directions for her husband's breakfast— hot cereal, poached eggs just so, and toast. She stopped dead. "Mark, excuse me!" Her voice was strangled. She stood, pale. "Don't move till I get back. Not a move!"

"Where are you off to?"

"To the Ladies Room," she said tensely, and hurried off. Trumbull finished the order in a low, almost inaudible voice. He had to repeat himself twice.

Sickels had seen their entrance. "Mr. Kiser, there are Judge Trumbull and that woman," he said in a low voice.

"I see them," Kiser said and continued to eat.

Humperdink was at the door when Jessica came past. "Ma'am, where are you going?" he asked, seizing her arm.

"What's it your business?" she exclaimed. She twisted free and hurried out to the train. Humperdink went to the rear table. "Judge Trumbull," he said firmly, "I hope Mrs. Trumbull won't be so indiscreet as to make a disturbance in my premises?"

Trumbull looked up uncertainly. "Why, sir? Why should she do that?"

"Justice Sickels is at breakfast," Humperdink said, "and I trust there will be no trouble. . . ."

"Sickels? Where?" Trumbull said, looking about the room. Space was suddenly askew. He stared across that space, saw the moment in all its reality down to the dust on the floor. There was a dark tunnel and at the end of the tunnel Sickels was bringing a fork to his mouth. Sickels was eating nearsightedly, spectacles up, forehead beaded with sweat. He looked up and met Trumbull's glance and resumed eating.

And besides Sickels the remembered man. Jutting cheekbones, scarlet-patched. Eyes unwinking, cold like that remembered day. The buzzing was intolerable.

"D'ye hear me, Judge?" Humperdink repeated.

"Hey?"

". . . through the kitchen?" Humperdink said. "Go out the back?"

Trumbull blinked. "There will be no trouble, sir. I will leave," he said courteously, strained. He placed a tip and stood. He longed for the coffee.

He knew the man—Kiser.

Two aisles led to the door. He walked down the far aisle and counted each table in that moment as he passed. His legs were trembling.

His mind was clear. He strode down the aisle and passed Sickels. Twenty strides more and the door was ahead.

A force was upon him.

He paused. Something childish came to him. He was praying. Oh, God! Strengthen me this once and only this once that I may . . .

He turned and saw himself stride back with firm purpose and stand behind the old judge.

A waitress would recall a strange, detached expression. Instantly Kiser leaped up and fired. "Stop, stop! I'm an officer! Stop!" he said, firing. The shots roared in succession. Once, and again. Sickels looked about, dazed and frightened.

Trumbull fell back and staggered and lay quivering in the sawdust of the eating room.

The smell of gunpowder filled the room. The clatter, the hum stopped. Kiser backed away from the crowd, holding his hand gun at shoulder level. Although cool in manner, his voice was high-pitched. He announced that he was a deputy United States marshal, that he had acted to defend the life of Justice Sickels, an associate justice of the United States Supreme Court, and wanted no trouble.

At that moment, Jessica appeared at the entrance holding a revolver. She stood incredulous. Malvinia was at her elbow. Behind them steam gushed and the Westinghouse panted. The sun threw a blazing light on the scene, but none of this counted. Jessica's expression caught everyone. Even Sickels felt the tragedy of overwhelming disbelief and horror. Trumbull was arched in agony. One leg lay askew; the other jerked in paroxysms; his massive arms were thrown back by the blast. He lay supine, blinking with the shock and pain. With a moan of grief, Jessica came forward and took the bloody head to her breast.

In the silence, a high-pitched voice was distinct. "Jesus Christ," the voice squealed, "they got Trumbull at last!"

The crowd waited, sighing as one, and gave way as Malvinia came through and took the revolver. Jessica turned with a piteous gesture. "If I hadn't left him, Vinnie. . . . If I'd stayed by his side!"

Malvinia said, "It'd not have helped. It was a thing determined on. Look at the man." A look of hate stabbed at the old judge.

"He was unarmed! Everyone can see: He was unarmed!" Jessica cried, frantically opening Trumbull's coat. "Look, everyone. They shot an unarmed man!"

Trumbull was breathing stertorously. Bright arterial blood drained from an implacable mouth into the thick beard. The face was a mask of determination and courage. "Oh, my love, my love, I have brought you to your death." She rocked in grief, cradling his head.

The train whistle broke the silence. Trumbull's eyes went wide. "My darling wife," he said distinctly, and died. He seemed to have addressed not his wife, but the frightened venomous old man behind her. It seemed not an endearment, but a legal point, one of last defiance, spoken to the distant Court.

Jessica raised a piercing cry.

"Judge Sickels has murdered my husband!" she screamed. "Lynch him! Lynch old Sickels! Are there any Masons here? My husband was a Mason. He was a friend of the working-men! Oh, please, please! Won't someone kill that horrible old man for me!" The weird screams went on, insensate, animal-like, monotonous, mixed with appeals to the onlookers, especially Masons and Workingmen's Party men among them, to avenge the death. One judge killed by another judge—an inciting thought to the crowd of Pima travelers. A nervous movement started on the outskirts, someone talked about finding a rope. Without leadership it was desultory and unconvincing. And then the town constable came to assert the rule of law.

"Let's cut out, Judge," Kiser said in a low aside. Half pushing, half stumbling, he got Sickels out through the kitchen and back to the safety of the Pullman sleeper.

An hour later the train pulled out. The demented woman, breaking out of restraint, stumbled after it. She tore her dress, exposed her breasts, crying blindly for vengeance. Tears of misery and hate ran down her cheeks.

The Men's Lounge was set aside for privacy. Some miles out of Pima Junction, Kiser found the sunbaked wheatfields without interest. "Well, Judge, what happens next?" he asked.

"Nothing happens next," Sickels said savagely. "You had your orders. The state has no authority over you in the matter."

"I know that, Judge," Kiser said, sipping warm whiskey. "I don't know much, but I sure know that." He was puzzled, then alarmed, then outraged when the train was stopped at Sweetwater where the sheriff, backed by an angry posse, arrested him for the murder of Mark Trumbull.

Sickels went on alone to San Francisco. Next morning, by appointment, surrounded by friends, including judges, lawyers, and marshals, he received the sheriff, who held a warrant for his arrest, at chambers. "I recognize your authority,"

481

he said with icy courtesy, "and will submit. A judge's first duty is to obey the law. Proceed, sir." He was instantly taken into custody as an accomplice in murder at Pima Junction.

And almost as instantly discharged.

Part Three

Chapter Twenty-Six

Sickels threw aside a steel pen and went to the grate. It was April in Washington. All his life he had appeared at his desk at dawn to polish off a day's work before the Court could assemble, but on this day the usual pile of foolscap, neatly inscribed, ready for clerk and typist, disposing of his share of the Court's business, was missing. This inability to work was becoming frightening.

He considered his last assignment given by Chief Justice Amos Tucker with growing anger. It concerned a patent for an animal glue substitute and the case was beneath contempt —amateur chemistry and worse patent law. He felt enraged at its triviality. A discreet tap at the door was repeated.

"Come in!" he said testily.

His attendant entered. "Mr. Justice Brewster asks: Can he call before Court assembles?"

"Did he say what he wants this time, Daniel?"

"No, sir!"

"Very well, I'll see him." Sickels wandered to the fireplace and faced a reproduction of the familiar painting of Chief Justice John Marshall. Marshall stood at ease, hand on hip, alert and firm, facing the viewer with that same good-humored courtesy he had displayed throughout his long life. Sickels stared yearningly for some meaning the painting might throw on his own life. He turned away with a sigh of dissatisfaction.

A lump of coal hissed in the grate. Outside it was raw, gusty, with fog and rain swirling around a sodden Capitol. San Francisco weather, he thought wistfully, and at the thought of that distant city with its rich homes sitting on high hills, the cable cars rattling through the streets, its cosmopolitan and stylish population, the despondent scowl deepened. Would he ever again return to California? That damn case on the day's calendar. This should be his moment of triumph and vindication, and he felt—what? Confused and old and incredibly empty. He went to a side table and picked up a record on appeal.

Paul Cliburn, Sheriff of Pima County, State of California, Appellant, vs. James Kiser.

Sickels turned the pages and stopped at a paragraph he had underscored the day of its arrival:

. . . The issue is whether a deputy United States marshal, as such, is justified in killing a man who, within the state of California, makes a murderous assault upon a justice of the Supreme Court of the United States while in the discharge of his duties. . . .

A grimace twisted the bloodless mouth. He still felt the shock of gunfire over his shoulder. Still heard the voice monotonously exclaim at Trumbull's death. Still recalled every phase of the day's events. Kiser had submitted almost with relief to arrest. Once in the lockup, he ate calmly and fell asleep. Then, shortly after midnight, a special train returned to Pima. Minutes later, a force of federal marshals, led by Patterson, appeared with the writ of habeas corpus commanding the sheriff to produce Kiser forthwith before the Federal Circuit Court in San Francisco to determine the lawfulness of the arrest.

Three days later Kiser was discharged from custody by Judge Goff with praise for his courage and fidelity in a moment of peril to the man whose safety and life had been entrusted to his care.

And now all that was up for final review in the Supreme Court at Washington. His own court! Sickels thought with satisfaction. He looked up with a start as the door opened. "Oh, Wesley! Come in," he said sourly. "Glad it's you."

Mr. Justice Wesley Brewster, a portly man with a habitual expression of bland surprise, shook hands with Sickels. Brewster was struck by the frailty of the other's grip.

"Sit down, Wesley," Sickels said. "I was just thinking where all this started. I do believe it goes back to that first Chinese decision I handed down in the Circuit Court in San Francisco. D'ye know I cannot recall the name of that case? It simply eludes me."

486

"Ah Luk Fow?" Brewster said.

"Yes, yes! Something like that," Sickels said quickly and emphatically. "Things might've worked out differently if I'd gone along with the mob, but that decision was right, absolutely right." He sat musing, "Well, I was warned. All the popularity went the other way. What's on your mind, Wesley?"

Brewster went silent. It was really the matter of Trumbull he had come to discuss; in his opinion Ah Luk Fow was a typical Sickels diversion. He had come to the discussion with some dread. A few days earlier, following the weekly conference of the justices, at which Sickels' irate inattentiveness had been marked by all, he had been invited to meet Chief Justice Tucker in the latter's office. The Chief Justice had offered brandy and cigars and like a good lawyer had begun with a general discourse on the Supreme Court. A most difficult problem, he observed, was the reluctance of old judges to make way for the young. While the Congress could not compel a judge of the Supreme Court to retire because of age, it could provide for decent retirement at full pay at age seventy and after ten years of service. Yet to press a judge to retire was always disagreeable. It was with this in mind that he had invited Brewster to discuss the case of Sickels, who certainly was undergoing a serious change of personality.

The Chief Justice paused. "Well, there's the question of this scandal. That episode in California last August did him no good, Brewster. Horrible sight, even for an old Western hand."

"I daresay," Brewster said. "I'd never have expected the old man to take it so much to heart. Of course, as he testified at Kiser's hearing in San Francisco, it was terribly distressing to see a man in the fullness of his life destroyed before his eyes—no matter what the circumstances. Especially a man he had known for almost forty years. And all that clamor by Trumbull's friends of his complicity with the marshal naturally preys on his mind. It's most unpleasant. Shocking and too dreadful that he ever got arrested himself."

Amos Tucker smiled through the drifting cigar smoke. The arrest of Sickels had aroused the instant anger of the nation. It was of course an unspeakable outrage which brought instant condemnation, matched only by sympathy and support for its victim. A press campaign which pictured Trumbull as a mad frontier ruffian who deserved death had had only praise for the venerable judge's behavior. The White House spoke for all in expressing admiration for Sickels' coolness and bravery under fire. Nevertheless it was clear, the Chief Justice said, that the event had had its effect and that Sickels had tarried too long on the bench. As he had written to an old friend, the Lord Chancellor of England, Sickels had physically weakened since his return from California. The decline had been indeed precipitous, and the old man who carried living memories back to Taney and Lincoln and Chase and Waite finally showed the ravages of age. He would be missed if induced to depart peacefully, Tucker observed, something easier said than done, especially since the appeal taken by the State of California on behalf of the sheriff had heightened his irascibility past all reason.

Brewster considered the matter. "Is it absolutely necessary to raise the issue at this time? I don't believe he's that far over the line. He might well pick up. Once the Court passes on this California case, he'll feel better. He hasn't slept since he got back. I've tried to reassure him that the Court is bound to vindicate him, but he's felt depressed and unhappy about the whole business. He won't take my word that the Court will be unanimous."

The Chief Justice grunted noncommittally.

"Oh, sir! You don't imagine the Court would split where the issues are so clear? Especially where one of us is so directly involved? There's bound to be that much loyalty."

"Loyalty?"

"But you are satisfied with the record on appeal!"

"Oh, yes, yes. Remarkable record from first to last," the Chief Justice said in neutral tones. "Sums it up quite fully. Violent behavior of the Trumbulls and all that. Quite atmospheric. What concerns me is the public understanding. I could wish that the United States Attorney had not appointed that swarm of railroad lawyers to conduct the hearing on behalf of Kiser. Most awkward position. There is such a thing as finesse, although not, I feel sad to observe, in the Ninth Circuit."

"Oh, but why? The Circuit Court made a clear finding that Kiser acted pursuant to a law of the United States. If so, he was surely immune to prosecution and they were right to discharge the man. And we're bound to sustain them, I should think."

"Ah, but was it so? The argument is that Kiser went on a frolic and detour of his own and committed a murder. We've

488

got no federal law which allows murder, and that's the charge that California makes, isn't it?"

"Oh, that's nonsense!"

"Yes, I'm sure it is," the Chief Justice agreed, "but my worry is that we cannot close the mouth of doubt where so much evidence was excluded. Whether Kiser took proper action or not depended on what Trumbull did that moment, did it not? And how can we know that without benefit, as we see, of cross-examination?"

"Well, we're not called on to weigh that point," Brewster said slowly, scandalized by the bizarre turn of the argument. "The question is immunity. When the Attorney General heard of the real danger from the Trumbulls, he wrote to ask the marshal to ensure Sickels' safety, so the mandate's clear."

The Chief Justice was a patient, courteous man. No show of feeling appeared. "The marshal's duties are limited. No federal law gives him any special right or duty to defend a justice when in his private capacity. In fact, the Attorney General's letter simply authorized the marshal to hire some extra deputies to deal with court disorders and to pay the per diem costs from his appropriation. His letter gave no authority to act away from the Court, or as a secret agent, although Kiser, I observe, testified that he had orders not to disclose his identity. To hold that this marshal, though given no statutory authority, acted pursuant to a law of the nation, based merely on an executive letter, would be the broadest interpretation we've yet given the implied powers of the government under the Constitution. I have faith that there are no limits to how far we can and will stretch the Constitution, but it's got to be done in small inoculations. My own taste runs to caution and guile."

Brewster let a moment pass. "Sir, Sickels has been a Justice of the Court for over thirty years. What possible judgment can we reach after his dreadful experience, to which he personally testified? We've got to see him through this ordeal, don't you think?"

The Chief Justice smiled thinly and shrugged. "Very well, Brewster," he said and went on to make his wishes clear.

And now Brewster was on a mission, less than drastic in scope, but still uncomfortable. It was the Chief Justice's hope, he said gravely, that Sickels would not appear in court that day to hear the argument on the appeal of *Cliburn v. Kiser.*

Sickels scowled. "Why not? I want to look down the throats of those lawyers and hear what they've got to say against me. What's his name again? The one that's leading off for the sheriff?"

"Zack Yates. Assistant Attorney General. He's on leave."

"Trumbull's friend, eh? Does the Attorney General agree to this?"

"Oh, yes. The California people asked for him. The Attorney General just had to give permission under that pressure. But that shouldn't matter too much. I doubt Yates will get far with his argument."

Sickels considered this information suspiciously. "Of course I've disqualified myself. But if Yates is arguing this appeal, it's exactly why I ought to sit out there while he gets chewed up by the government. . . ."

A clock struck and Brewster stood. It was time to assemble in the robing room. Sickels drove on with intensity. "This is personal, Wesley," he said, panting with the effort of ordering his thoughts. "I've got an interest in this appeal. That deputy marshal saved my life. If we let this case slip out of our hands, he'll have to stand trial for murder in the state court in Pima County. A court packed with Trumbull's friends. I can't abandon him now, can I?" Sickels looked up strangely. "That marshal and I were together when it happened, Wesley. That meant something in the West. A man sticks. Something you fellers never seem to understand."

"That's strange language, Judge. I've read this record, and the facts are clear. Trumbull attacked you. The marshal was justified to fire in your defense. Can you doubt the outcome of this appeal?"

Sickels flopped into a leather chair. "You really think I shouldn't sit during the argument?"

"It would make a bad impression, Judge. And it's not necessary. We're all with you and Mrs. Sickels."

"You're sure?"

"Oh, Judge!" Brewster protested.

"Well, well!" Sickels continued. "All that talk about hating Trumbull for not supporting me as Presidential candidate are lies. Rotten lies. Actually, I made that attempt only to please my friends. I was relieved when it failed. Absolutely relieved. Fact is, Wesley, I don't know what in hell I'm doing," he muttered, suddenly tremulous and clutching the younger judge's hand in appeal. "I'll sit in the robing room, if you'll take me there. I want the rest to know I'm listening. I want a unanimous court. After all these years, I'm entitled to that much. I can assure you that when I saw that great form of Trumbull's with that right arm raised and that fist clinched to strike a terrific blow in a curved way at my temple, I saw my own corpse lying on the floor. I am still convinced that two seconds later we'd both have been Trumbull's victims. There was no occasion to arrest the marshal, who was only preventing a felony on us both. Anything less than unanimity, even one dissenting vote of doubt, would be disgraceful. I'd feel personally censured."

Brewster paused. "But as I recall, Kiser swore that Trumbull was reaching inside his vest when he fired the shots."

"Exactly," Sickels said emphatically. "That's precisely why we were both endangered." He paused. "Don't know what possessed Trumbull in those last months. Truly I don't. I always thought we had the most pleasant relationship until that contempt, but I'd have jailed my brother for that behavior. The man changed unaccountably. Softening of the brain, or some other mysterious process must've set in. Still, in a funny way, I regret what's happened." With a sigh, he followed the younger judge to the robing room, where the rest of the court was already gathered.

As the clock struck the hour, the procession of judges in black robes quietly entered and took their seats. One seat remained vacant directly right of Chief Justice Amos Tucker. Tucker noted in a low, pleasant twang that Mr. Justice Sickels would not sit that day.

Sickels sat staring at the walls of the robing room, straining to hear the sounds of the courtroom. It was strange not to occupy his accustomed chair of seniority beside the Chief Justice.

"Paul Cliburn, Sheriff of Pima County, State of California, Appellant, versus James Kiser."

Sickels nodded with satisfaction. He could visualize the lawyers advancing to place in the quiet, mellow chamber of the high court. A murmur of voices could be heard through the open door. The Attorney General was advising the Court that his office would be represented by the Honorable Bart Hodges of New York. A sardonic grin twisted Sickels' pale mouth. Hodges, the most eminent lawyer in the nation and dear family friend, had taken the brief as his own special entreaty.

And then the passionate, familiar, and strangely distinct voice of Zacharias Yates, high-pitched and Texan, filled the stillness.

Sickels felt his heart beat strongly.

Yates began: "May the Court please! On the fourteenth day of August of last year, while Mr. John Haddam Sickels, a justice of this honorable court, was sitting at breakfast in a railroad restaurant at Pima Junction, Pima County, State of California, the Honorable Marcus Aurelius Trumbull, once chief justice of the Supreme Court of that state, approached Mr. Justice Sickels and with his open hand slapped him twice about the face, whereupon James Kiser, who was seated near Mr. Sickels, sprang to his feet and called out, "Stop, stop! I am an officer! Stop!" And instantly shot Judge Trumbull twice through the breast, killing him on the spot.

"This is the substance of the ex parte testimony on behalf of Kiser taken in San Francisco by a commissioner of the Federal Circuit Court so far as the same is without material conflict. For this homicide, Kiser was arrested by the sheriff of Pima County upon sworn complaint and warrant charging him with murder. The sheriff later arrested Justice Sickels upon the same sworn complaint. This is the sole instance where a justice of this court was ever arrested for murder. Since Justice Sickels was at once released upon intervention of the Governor of California, I will pass over that matter."

There was insolence and hard humor in the nasal drawl of east Texas. Brewster's voice broke the silence. "Who swore to the complaint?"

Yates replied, "The widow."

"She was not an eyewitness to the homicide?"

"She appeared instantly the shot was fired. She saw Kiser with a gun in hand, still smoking."

"As I understand the record, she too had a gun in hand?"

"It may be surmised that she feared the attack of Marshal Kiser on her husband."

"That is not in the record?"

"Very little is in the record."

"But are we bound by the record?"

"Such are the rules."

"I simply wanted that clear. Proceed, sir, Proceed."

Sickels chuckled.

Yates returned to a higher pitch to describe the events which followed, ending in the appeal which brought the case to the Supreme Court in Washington. "We have here an immense record of six hundred pages," the passionate voice went on, "the bulk of which consists of evidence—or what purports to be evidence—intended to prove that this slaying was justifiable. Our position however is that the question here on appeal is solely jurisdictional. We hold that the Circuit Court was wrong to pass on the question at all. The question of murder was solely for the California State Court to try and determine.

"Indeed, the Circuit Court says quite candidly at page 88, folio 163: 'The homicide in question, if wrongful, is an offense only under the laws of California and only the state can deal with it as such.' It is not claimed to be an offense under the laws of the United States. A federal marshal has no greater right than anyone else to commit a homicide. If his shot was malicious, wanton, or reckless, without reasonable need to protect Justice Sickels, then it was done outside his duty as a federal officer, outside the umbrella of United States law, and clearly he is not entitled to its protection."

The thin accents of Texas filled the chamber and the robing room beyond. "Now I am not here to justify the unfortunate victim of this homicide. If Judge Trumbull made an assault to kill or seriously wound Justice Sickels, then the killing by Kiser was doubtless justifiable. But if, on the other hand, there was no assault but merely a ceremonial insult to demonstrate Justice Sickels' lack of courage, then the killing was a crime against the state of California—the crime of murder. And her courts alone have jurisdiction to try the case.

"But which is the case? I must ask the Court to bear in mind that the introduction and examination of witnesses was a strictly ex parte proceeding, in which nobody took any part except Kiser and his attorneys. There was nobody interested to bring out the dark side of the picture, but everybody interested to conceal it. The district attorney, the marshal, the deputy marshals, the Circuit Court judges, and everyone brought to testify showed a peculiar venom and hatred for Judge Trumbull and his wife. Indeed, Judge Goff introduced a statement of an old grievance when his hair was twitched by Mrs. Trumbull—although the relevance of that episode

493

escapes my understanding. Just how far it went to convince Judge Goff that Judge Trumbull deserved to be slain, and that the Court had legal jurisdiction to exonerate his slayer, I cannot say. It must have been a delicate duty to weigh in the scales of justice his own personal grievances and determine exactly how far they ought to justify the killing of the man by whom he was aggrieved.

"I come to something more direct—the undeniable fact that no witness could say that Judge Trumbull had about his person a weapon of any kind when slain. True, the record before us carries a picture of a formidable bowie knife at three places, but that knife was not on him the day he was killed, nor for a long time before. What business they have in this record I cannot imagine, unless as a sort of scarecrow to keep this Court from the real kernel of this case.

"Or perhaps that knife, taken from Trumbull a year before, was to support another claim—Kiser's assertion that Trumbull put his hand to his breast, as if to draw a weapon, and that he, Kiser, feared in another two seconds to be hacked to pieces and have his head cut off. He says that Trumbull struck him as an infuriated giant who bore a look of intense hate and passion, the most malignant that he had ever seen in life, that he had seen many men in such situations, that such a look meant life or death for one or the other—and more of such prose befitting the cheapest literature of our age.

"All fascinating but contradicted by the other witnesses who say that Trumbull was calm and serene in death. These witnesses also testified that Trumbull had his hand aloft at all times, at most brushing Justice Sickels' cheek as though to attract attention. Even Mr. Sickels testifies that, as he turned after a first surprise blow, Trumbull's fist was clinched aloft as though to strike again. I do not, of course, dispute the Honorable Justice's veracity. I would not dream of it. I do say, however, that he was subject to the natural distortions of his excited state. He testified that he felt two blows so close together that they seemed like one assault. He says that he heard Kiser cry, 'Stop, stop!' and turned in a daze to see Trumbull with his arm still aloft while the shots were still firing. He describes his horror while waiting for Trumbull to fall and his shock at seeing that particular movement of the eyes that indicates the presence of death. As he testified, it was impossible to see a man in the full vigor of life expire without being affected and so, I trust, he was—although reasonably cool in stating to a bystander Kiser's legal qualifications for the deed. If his recollection is accurate, then Kiser's is not. I assume that Kiser's is not. It is Kiser's case which sits before you.

"I believe, if the Court please, that Judge Trumbull never would attempt to draw a knife unless he had a knife to draw. No knife was found on him, and the witnesses contradict the claim. So which was it? The original story was that Kiser had to protect Justice Sickels from an uplifted, empty clinched fist. Then—presto, change! That was a mistake. It really was to protect himself against a supposed knife. But if Trumbull had no knife, what then? The Circuit Court sayeth not. Is it not more likely that Kiser himself, realizing that an empty fist would not justify a homicide, has embroidered the tale?

"What was Trumbull's motive? Mr. Sickels in his testimony tells us how Trumbull years before resigned as chief justice of California to fight a duel with Senator Gore, to which resignation Mr. Sickels, as he tells us, owed his own elevation to that post and thus his subsequent appointment to this court. If dueling is a sin against the moral law—which I believe—it is one into which, alas! the noblest men and brightest intellects have fallen. It was the sin of Senator Gore, who fell in a duel fairly fought by mutual agreement. It was the sin of Hamilton, of Randolph, of Jackson, and of Clay. I am no expert in the dueling code, but its laws and rules, as we all know—and however quaint it now seems—call for an insult, by slap or otherwise, to provoke a challenge or prove the cowardice of the person slapped. It surely forbids a murderous assault with a deadly weapon upon an unsuspecting victim.

"And was the 'victim' unsuspecting? Mr. Kiser testifies—perhaps unguardedly—that Mr. Sickels espied Judge Trumbull and continued to eat his breakfast in the railway dining room. Sausages, as it turned out, of peculiar fatality. It does look strange that a man in fear of death should invite assault, but I verily believe that there are many who, much as they fear death, prefer a thousand times to face it than be publicly confronted with the truth. And this, I take it, was the matter then between the men.

"What then was the truth as it must have stood between them? Judge Trumbull had many grievances arising from his wife's lawsuits from whence all this sprang. Major injustices, as he saw and proclaimed, but all within the rough and ready rules of the Western courts where he spent his lifetime. In all his life, he took defeats with utmost good humor. But one grievance rankled, and when earlier he was imprisoned for assaulting a marshal with a knife, he publicly denounced the record made by Justice Sickels as a lie which he could not prove in any legal way. Having drawn no response, he wrongfully, as I think, resolved to publicly insult Mr. Sickels and if possible draw him into a duel. He fell back, I well believe, to an early mode to redress a just grievance."

Brewster leaned forward. "Now, sir, that is sheer effrontery. Can you show any evidence of untruth by Justice Sickels in the record of that contempt?"

Yates paused at the danger sign from the bench. "I do not say Judge Trumbull was right. However false he believed the record, however improper he thought Justice Sickels' motives, it was grievously wrong to take the law into his own hands and most grievously has he answered for it. But consider the years of toil and agony on his wife's behalf that went up in smoke when he was thrust in jail and we can see how humiliation gnawed his mind and guided his perhaps unwilling feet. I agreed that Mr. Sickels stood in danger of a slap but not of his life. If Trumbull had a deadly purpose, we may be sure he would not have attacked with only his bare hand.

"What then was the purpose to send in disguise a bodyguard armed with a deadly revolver; one required to travel in citizen's dress, to wear no badge of office, to show no sign of authority, but ordered on any affront to then proclaim his office and instantly shoot down its author? I believe that Marshal Kiser was acting under advice and direction of another. But I do not of course believe that the other was the Attorney General or the government of the United States."

Yates had reached the climax of a violent and relentless moment. He sensed rather than heard the stir that ran through the chamber. Sickels came through the curtain and slid into his chair. He wiped his skull and fixed a malevolent glare at the lectern. It was a painful and embarrassing moment.

Chief Justice Tucker said quietly, "Go on, sir. You have an hour."

Yates wiped his mouth slowly, eyeing the old man with contempt, and went on. "May the Court please, we have often read of masked batteries used in time of war between deadly foes. But who ever heard of a general that masked his batteries when he desired to keep the enemy afar and preserve the peace? Who of this generation does not know that to mask a battery is to invite and not to prevent attack—and more, to so ambush the adversary as to cut off all escape? If Kiser honestly meant to prevent a breach of the peace, would he hide until the peace was broken? He cannot plead surprise. His sole business during a journey of seven hundred miles was to watch Trumbull—and so he did, sitting quietly, his eye upon Trumbull every step until the last moment and even then proclaimed himself only as the shots were firing. Yes, he feared a challenge to a duel and surely dueling is a criminal mode to avenge an insult. But is this not ten thousand times more criminal?

"And is this our new fangled federal police? Clothed with secret authority, armed with concealed weapons, with which this great government will keep the peace between its officers and its citizens? From such and their dark and hidden methods may the ever-living God and the Honorable Court protect us.

"What a commentary have we here upon the writ of habeas corpus! No man in the state of California bore a higher reputation for truth and veracity, strict integrity and simple honor. Judge Trumbull had his faults, but were they so bad, desperate, and dangerous that it was necessary, according to the government, to kill him to keep the peace? If this writ is sustained, Kiser will never stand trial to answer for this violent deed, so that an impartial jury may say if this really was a justified homicide or one of the most deeply planned, cunningly devised, and cold-blooded assassinations that ever darkened the annals of crime—all the more diabolical for being done under the cloak, real or pretended, of official authority. This tribunal of last resort, from which there is no appeal except to the sword, alone now weighs the truth of this man's life."

The shrill voice went on in the embarrassed hush to the greater questions before the Court—the nature of the Republic, the rights reserved to the several states, the power of the Court to preserve or destroy constitutional liberty and indeed the power to preserve or destroy the Union itself. Every eye was on the old judge to whom the words were addressed, but he was no longer attending. The moment in the eating place was vivid before him, the smell of gunpowder, the buzz of bluebottles. He was really listening to nothing but a voice of his own.

Chapter Twenty-Seven

Two years later Fanny was lunching with Archbishop Tosefa under the pepper tree in his pleasant garden, at the archiepiscopal residence. A chill was in the air, but the pavement stones under the clear straw-colored sunlight were warm. She wore a fur cape over her broad shoulders. The Archbishop sat close to the table, eating austerely, glancing at his guest with pleasure. Fanny had grown more assured, more handsome in her years abroad, and her crisp speech had the vehemence of the successful woman of letters. He was entertained by her description of the literary scene in Europe, fascinated by a streak of gray and by vigorous English table manners—the roast lamb had been polished off with hungry dispatch—and interested in her description of Washington, a city from which she had recently returned. He was a good listener, content to let the point come in its own good time. She was talking on the Kiser matter.

"I saw the chief justice, you know," Fanny said abruptly, mopping gravy. "Quite pleasant, considering that he dislikes clever women. He thinks I'm clever because I write. I'm not. I'm merely direct and intelligent. I found him alone in his favorite restaurant and simply sat down and tackled him. Poor man! He was helpless to deal with an aggressive woman."

"Aggressive? Oh, how?" the Archbishop asked.

"I told him I was not happy with the decision," Fanny said. "Frightful cheek, I admit, but I saw no reason to hold back. Quite exhilarating, in fact, to tell off the chief justice about his Court. How many ever do? I'm not sure why he let me talk. Curiosity, perhaps. Or perhaps, since he'd written the dissenting opinion, he wanted to know my grief with the majority opinion. I said I'd leave the legal side to the lawyers —but I was distressed by what they did to Trumbull. Ruddy outrage! I felt the Court ought to correct itself. Did you ever read the decision?"

"No-o," the Archbishop said cautiously. "Only the newspaper summaries. But really! How could you hope to accomplish that? The Court's decision that the matter end is final."

"Final?" Fanny shrugged. She was memorizing the garden. It was most peaceful, with a quality of sky and air like nowhere else on earth. The last blob of gravy—a good cook had done the lamb rare—was blotted up. "One cannot let things rest because officially pronounced. It wasn't Kiser, nor even Sickels, who was on trial. The truth is that they'd held an inquest on Mark Trumbull's life and nothing in their power could make that final. At least not for me. I told the chief justice—charming man, by the way, lovely white Vandyke and such benign interested eyes—that I'd read the decision with complete dissatisfaction. I couldn't care less for their beastly technicalities, I said, but the thought of future generations accepting their horrid version of the facts as gospel kept me sleepless. I felt a terrible injustice had been done." She wiped her mouth carefully. The Archbishop looked scandalized or amused, one could not say which. "Your Excellency," she said suddenly, "you knew Trumbull. Do you believe that he meant to murder Justice Sickels?"

The Most Reverend Juan Tosefa blushed. "No, no, surely not," he said uneasily, "I knew him too well. Great friend, kindly. Most helpful in the recovery of our Mexican benefactions. I thought, the soul of honor. But he had suffered disappointments and miseries in that wretched Hagerman business and faced more. He was not the same man. He had an unfortunate temper and momentarily lost control. We must accept the Court's findings that he had no just grievance against Justice Sickels."

"Why must we?" she asked.

"Why? Well, because we must," he replied. He waited for fruit and cheese to be served, discomfited by the polite smile. No one ever really argued back, he thought with vexation. "Surely the Supreme Court knows the facts."

She shook her head. "They are supremely competent as lawyers, but as to human insights, I wouldn't let 'em write book reviews. No! Character is the touchstone. If it was not in character, it could not happen. I agree that the Court's version carries great weight. Like everyone, I took the decision with numb acceptance. I too thought that Trumbull must have changed or gone mad. I could scarcely doubt the Court. But when I got back from abroad, I read the record. I felt something wrong in the narrative. It was too villainous to portray the man I had known. I was aware too that the coroner's inquest in Pima County had heard another set of witnesses who testified that Trumbull never struck Sickels at all."

The Archbishop stared. "But I distinctly recall that Sickels testified he was struck twice."

"Yes, I know, and of course no one, least of all his colleagues, would doubt his word. I say only that the record of Pima County says otherwise. I don't presume to choose. I simply pointed out that fact."

"What was his response?"

"That the coroner was entitled to hold any inquest he pleased," Fanny said with a cold formal smile. "I asked if the veil of silence was absolute, or whether the Court might reverse itself if it knew something more about Kiser—if they knew that he had a precedent for what he did."

"Precedent?"

Fanny smiled grimly. "He was a deputy sheriff in Arizona when the United States marshal, a man named Utt, was arrested with his brother and charged with murder at a place called Jericho Creek. They produced their badges and claimed justification and were released. Now Kiser, who saw those men swagger from the courtroom, turned up at Pima Junction. I did think his version called for the grain of salt which it didn't get in San Francisco. As between live Kiser and dead Trumbull, I will always believe the man I knew. He came to that last moment of his life trapped in Sickels' conscience as a man. Trumbull was there to make a point. Each had purpose. Kiser was armed. He was not. But he could not turn back. He was there to show that Sickels would not offer to defend a lie. He took the only action open to him. Tragic! Ultimately tragic! Because the proof was there. Too bad he never knew where it lay."

"Proof? Of what?" the Archbishop frowned.

Her eyes were not pleasant. "The truth. It's in the record, but not visible. No one, as I told the chief justice, ever thought to go behind the record. I had."

"Not visible, you said?"

Her eyes were glittering. "Yes. The record is printed, you see? The printer smooths out wrinkles, makes corrections.

Sickels' order, which put Turnbull in jail, as it appears in print says that Trumbull drew his knife in the court. That was the lie that they brushed aside.

"In the *court*," she emphasized. "At first I too had accepted the authority of type. But I have strong library instincts and I felt uneasy at Trumbull's bitter insistence that Sickels had changed the record. I went to the Clerk's Office, where I found the typewritten order. What I saw was not nice. Originally the order recited that Trumbull drew his knife in the *hall*. The typist, at someone's direction, had changed the place from "hall" to "courtroom." It was quite visible. A small change, but it served to keep Trumbull in jail without a trial. Bitterness? Ruddy hell! I should think so!

"Poor Sickels," she said derisively. "Who can tell what rage and mortification trapped him into that trifling lapse of a lifetime. Too angry at first to admit it. In the end too fearful of discovery to live with it. What an unbearable, heartbreaking farce! But d'ye think it made a difference? I told Chief Justice Tucker that I had a few other items to mention. Ugly things I'd learned about Kiser, all sorts of suspicious circumstances. I wanted only to bring out the truth. There was one point I did not raise—the statement by the Attorney General that Sickels had requested a bodyguard although he'd sworn otherwise—that he'd wanted no protection."

"What did the chief justice reply?" the Archbishop said after a pause.

"He was quite unmoved. All that should have been raised in the lower court, he said, where the record was made. Oh, he quite understood my frustration—people often feel helpless anger in the court of last appeal. He had expressed his own views in the dissenting opinion that Kiser should have stood trial, but the majority had ruled otherwise. There it had to end, he said. The law was settled and the matter closed.

"I'm afraid I was rude. I said, 'To hell with his blasted law!' I could not believe that the Court could not find a way to do simple human justice to this man if they wished. All I got was a gentle smile of skepticism. He simply couldn't wait to get rid of me. Incredible!"

The Archbishop's flat pouchy eyes were less than happy, but detached. "But what brought you here, my dear? I cannot possibly intercede, if that's your hope. You were in the wrong place. I agree with the chief justice. Justice is for the lower courts. Law for the higher. What matters is finality.

501

This passion for textual revisionism is the curse of Germany. Nothing good can come of it."

The sound of shouting boys from the day school attached to the Cathedral could be faintly heard.

"But you do see it?" she demanded miserably. "I feel appalled that this man, of all men, will be read in history in this false version.

"Such a rotten business," she muttered. "That blasted marriage paper! Was it forged? Only two people ever knew. Hagerman's dead. And Jessie's insane. And there it stands. I wonder if Trumbull knew."

The Archbishop slipped a silver ring over his napkin and rose. "Ah, as to that, we should first have to know what Trumbull himself saw when he invited death. Now, my dear, if you'll excuse me?"

"Yes, of course." She began to button her gloves with a wry smile, having gotten nothing from the interview. She was brooding over the toil of months. The news of Trumbull's death—which had reached her in England—had not truly surprised her. A premonition of disaster had haunted her since the departure from San Francisco. Her grandfather's letter had seemed an expected thing. Distance and isolation had muted grief. The news of death seemed like a stranger's. That night, she had gone to a dinner party given by the American Ambassador, feeling nothing at all, and had chattered like mad. Months later, buying flowers from a barrow, a shudder had convulsed her. She had wept like a child, cleansed of grief.

The sense of Trumbull, his animality and strength, the coarse broad features and thick mouth, with its indolence and hint of feminine weakness, were vivid in this garden. And what did it all mean? His case would become a leading case, frequently cited, a landmark in the constitutional law of the nation, and forever misunderstood.

She was shown to a side entrance leading to California Street. There were errands ahead—notes to put in order, a diary to write up, a visit to the talkative woman with wild eyes at Melrose—then perhaps the pain would leave.

She lingered at the gate. "Strange, isn't it? To end in ambiguity?"

The Archbishop smiled. "Does it disturb you?"

Fanny considered the point. "Not too much," she confessed. "I prefer ambiguity. But I'd be happier not to know

502

that Sickels gave that man Kiser an inscribed gold watch lauding his courage under peril."

The Archbishop laughed. "But why be so unhappy? You are not bound by any Court's decision. It's you who are the last and ultimate court of appeal, are you not? Go with God," he said in Spanish and stepped aside.

With a most thoughtful look, Fanny left.

A cable car was rattling toward the stop outside the Archbishop's residence. She climbed on and braced herself for the lurch, considering the last remark. As the materials began to take shape, a vision of a hushed chamber in Washington, a long bench with its robed judges began to form in her mind. Her eyes narrowed to slits. She could scarcely wait to get to her desk.

"This book should make plain...that Miss Renault is one of the major novelists of our time."
—NEW YORK HERALD TRIBUNE

THE CHARIOTEER

A contemporary novel by

MARY RENAULT

75181/75¢

author of THE MASK OF APOLLO and THE BULL FROM THE SEA

PUBLISHED BY POCKET BOOKS